EDITH WHARTON

THREE COMPLETE NOVELS

EDITH WHARTON

THREE COMPLETE NOVELS

The House of Mirth

Ethan Frome

The Custom of the Country

GRAMERCY BOOKS
New York • Avenel

Introduction and compilation copyright © 1994 by
Random House Value Publishing, Inc.
All rights reserved.

This 1994 edition is published by Gramercy Books,
distributed by Random House Value Publishing, Inc.,
40 Engelhard Avenue, Avenel, New Jersey 07001.

Random House
New York · Toronto · London · Sydney · Auckland

Printed and bound in the United States of America

Library of Congress Cataloging-in-Publication Data
Wharton, Edith, 1862–1937.
[Novels. Selections]
Edith Wharton: three complete novels.
p. cm.
Contents: Ethan Frome—The house of mirth—
The custom of the country.
ISBN 0-517-11828-9
I. Title.
PS3545.H16A15   1994
813'.52—dc20   94-14792
                                                      CIP

8   7   6   5   4   3   2

Contents

INTRODUCTION

E DITH WHARTON, one of America's greatest women of letters, was born into a patrician New York family on January 24, 1862, and christened Edith Newbold Jones. In Edith Wharton's world, not only was a career forbidden to women, but most men did not work either, except the few who dabbled in law and banking. Her father, George Frederic Jones, was a "gentleman." Society ladies dressed beautifully and spoke quietly of household and social events. The greatest sin was any expression of emotion.

From her earliest years Edith Jones was frustrated and isolated, with apparently no way to take control of her own life. Although she received no formal education, she read widely and prodigiously, ransacking her father's library. During annual trips abroad with her parents, she learned several foreign languages. Her mind simply could not be reined in. At the age of fifteen she secretly wrote a thirty-thousand-word novel that she called *Fast and Loose*, coolly satirizing the society in which she lived. She also tried her hand at poetry. Edith's mother, Lucretia, always seemed coldly disapproving, apparently appalled by Edith's powerful intelligence. Her father was kinder but more remote, and he died when she was nineteen.

At the age of twenty-three, Edith agreed to marry Edward Wharton, an idle sportsman and man-about-Society. Edith and Teddy Wharton accommodated her mother by setting up housekeeping within sight of Lucretia's houses in Newport and New York. Teddy Wharton did not share his wife's intellectual and literary tastes, nor apparetnly, were husband and wife sexually compatible. For the next few years, Edith gave up writing to play the role of a young Society matron. She and her husband lived largely on her income from various inheritances, spending their time in Newport, New York, and Europe. Edith dressed well, decorated a series of houses, and entertained lavishly. But the harder she tried to conform to the expectations of her mother and Society, the weaker she became. She was frequently ill, and suffered from asthma. Gradually Edith began to distance herself from her mother. Eventually, she left Newport and built a great mansion in Lenox, Massachusetts, which she called The Mount.

In 1889, when she was twenty-seven, she began to write again. She made her literary debut two years later with "Mrs. Manstey's View," a short story that appeared in *Scribner's Magazine*. Over the next few years she continued to write short stories. She was often ill with asthma, and in 1894 she suffered a nervous breakdown. Then, in the spring of 1898, she wrote a half-dozen new stories—some of the finest work she would ever do. Yet she seemed to have little confidence, and whenever a story was rejected by a publisher, she became severely depressed. In the autumn of 1898 she suffered a second, more serious, breakdown and withdrew for four months to a hotel in Philadelphia, isolated from her friends and her husband. Here her talent and intelligence eventually won out against her need to conform. She emerged in 1899 determined to be a writer.

That year Scribner's published her first collection of short stories, The Greater Inclination. In her autobiography, A Backward Glance, Wharton called this the event that "broke the chains that had held me so long in a kind of torpor. For nearly twelve years I had tried to adjust myself to the life I had led since my marriage; but now I was overmastered by the longing to meet people who shared my interests." From this time on, and for the rest of her life, she enjoyed good health.

She began to gather around her other artists and intellectuals. During her annual travels in Europe, she created a network of friends, and in their company she gained self-confidence and the conviction that she was entitled to write. The publication of The Greater Inclination attracted international attention, and she was soon labeled "the female Henry James," a misnomer that would follow her the rest of her life. It was in Europe where she first met James, who was to have a profound influence on her.

Wharton's first full-length book, a collaboration with Ogden Codman called The Decoration of Houses, was published in 1897. She also produced more collections of stories, including The Touchstone and Crucial Instances. In 1902 her first novel, The Valley of Decision, was published, soon followed by Sanctuary and The Descent of Man and Other Stories. There is a remarkable consistency in these early stories, but few clues as to how she worked her way toward writing her brilliant and melancholy masterpiece, The House of Mirth. The novel was first serialized in Scribner's, and then became an immediate best-seller when it was published in book form on October 14, 1905. The House of Mirth sold thirty thousand copies in the first ten days.

The novel's heroine, like most of Wharton's women, is in a precarious situation. Brought up to be a beautiful and accommodating ornament for a man wealthy enough to afford her, Lily Bart appears weak, but she is very appealing, and at heart, noble. She continually ruins her chances for a marriage despite her increasingly desperate need for one. At twenty-nine years of age, Lily is poor, and if she is to survive in Society she must marry well. To this purpose, she continuously turns away from Lawrence Selden, a man of only moderate means, but someone she could really love. But even as she seems to head into a "proper" marriage, an inner force pulls her away. She inevitably loses her footing and falls from favor with New York Society. At the novel's conclusion, the reader can feel Lily Bart in the room, her dilemma so palpitating that the words seem to melt off the pages into the heart. Despite some unfavorable commentary, many reviewers acknowledged that with *The House of Mirth* Edith Wharton had become one of the most important and accomplished novelists of her time.

In 1907 Edith Wharton moved to Paris, where artists and writers were recognized and welcomed. She furnished a beautiful house, and with her inheritance and the royalties pouring in from her stories and novels, she lived grandly, entertaining lavishly and receiving scores of interesting guests. She had prodigious energy, and was able to combine a life of travel and entertaining with the strict discipline of a writer's life.

The higher her star rose, however, the more erratic and depressed her husband's behavior became. Teddy returned to America for long periods while Edith remained in Paris. During one of these separations, Edith fell in love for the first time and began at last to come to terms with her own passionate sexual nature. Her affair with expatriate American journalist Morton Fullerton ended after two years. She later learned that even before her own affair had begun, Teddy had embezzled money from her trust fund and had set himself up with a mistress in Boston. Eventually he told his family, and Edith removed him from any control of her finances. She continued to look after him, however, sending him wherever he needed to go for rest and treatment.

Through all of this grief and turmoil, she continued to write. In 1911, with the publication of *Ethan Frome*, she turned her bitter view of love and marriage toward culturally and economically deprived farm folk and convincingly projected her dark vision onto people and customs far removed from her own life.

Ethan Frome is a story of frustrated love between Ethan and his wife Zeena's young and destitute cousin, Mattie. It is a chilling portrait of poverty and wintry rural isolation in the hard-pressed village she called Starkfield. With powerful strokes Wharton describes the poverty and claustrophobia of village life and the numbing, feeble exchanges between Ethan and his tyrannical wife. *Ethan Frome* is a forceful treatment of one of Wharton's favorite themes: illicit love and suppressed emotion. She is pitiless in drawing her characters, with the exception of Ethan himself, whom she imbues with sensitivity.

Ethan Frome was quickly recognized as possibly Edith Wharton's finest achievement. Despite the critical praise, the novel was not at first a commercial success. Finally, in the 1930s, the book suddenly took off and a long-running dramatic version was produced on Broadway. Since then *Ethan Frome* has been translated into many languages, and it is to this day a standard classroom text.

In her own home, Edith Wharton could do nothing to help her husband. In 1913, their marriage finally ended in divorce. During the months that followed, Wharton traveled constantly and compulsively, but nevertheless managed to complete her most substantial novel, *The Custom of the Country*, which she had begun four years earlier.

In *The Custom of the Country*, Undine Spragg, a beautiful young woman, propels herself by sheer drive from the small town in which her father made his fortune into the highest circles of Society. Raised in a cultural desert, Undine has nothing to do. Without a place in the world, Undine uses her only weapon, sex, to achieve her desires. Undine is cold-hearted and unpolished, but her physical beauty blinds Ralph Marvell, the son of an aristocratic old New York family. After they marry, Undine quickly becomes bored by Ralph and his relatives. For Undine, when one idea doesn't work out, she moves on to the next, determined to find a satisfying place for herself. The reader may be appalled by her behavior but can somehow admire, by the book's conclusion, Undine's stubborn refusal to be defeated.

The Custom of the Country was published in October 1913, to generally excellent reviews. There was universal praise for its lack of sentiment, although one reviewer complained that Undine Spragg was the most disagreeable girl in American fiction.

Almost simultaneous with her enormous achievements, the European society that she had adopted began to fall apart. When the world war began in 1914, Wharton remained in France, founding hostels for thousands of Belgian refugees and work-relief organizations to help French women. She delivered supplies to the front and rescued sick children and orphans. She wrote articles, arranged fund-raising benefits, and donated her own money, seriously depleting her fortune.

After the war, she tried to return to her own life, creating two homes for herself, one north of Paris, one in the south of France. She began to look back with a new appreciation on the quiet, settled New York of her childhood, which by now had totally disappeared. She confessed in her memoirs: "When I was young it used to seem to me that the group in which I grew up was like an empty vessel into which no new wine would ever again be poured. Now I see that one of its uses lay in preserving a few drops of an old vintage too rare to be savored by a youthful palate."

In this mood of nostalgia she wrote *The Age of Innocence*, for which she received the Pulitzer Prize, the first woman ever so honored. In 1924 she was the first woman and only the second novelist to receive the gold medal from the National Institute of Arts and Letters.

In the forty-six years between 1895 and 1937 Edith Wharton produced more than forty books, including several books of poetry, a treatise on Italian villas and their gardens, travel books, an autobiography, and a volume of literary criticism. Wharton's greatest writing years were between 1905 and 1920, bracketing the major novels *The House of Mirth, Ethan Frome, The Reef, The Custom of the Country*, and *The Age of Innocence*. Of the eighty-six short stories published throughout her career, nearly a third were ghost stories. Whatever sorrow she felt, she also knew that she had accomplished much. Her final ghost story was published in 1937; later that year Edith Wharton died of a stroke in France. She was seventy-five years old.

CHRISTINE MESSINA

New York, 1994

THE HOUSE
OF MIRTH

Book One

Book One

1

SELDEN paused in surprise. In the afternoon rush of the Grand Central Station his eyes had been refreshed by the sight of Miss Lily Bart.

It was a Monday in early September, and he was returning to his work from a hurried dip into the country; but what was Miss Bart doing in town at that season? If she had appeared to be catching a train, he might have inferred that he had come on her in the act of transition between one and another of the country houses which disputed her presence after the close of the Newport season; but her desultory air perplexed him. She stood apart from the crowd, letting it drift by her to the platform or the street, and wearing an air of irresolution which might, as he surmised, be the mask of a very definite purpose. It struck him at once that she was waiting for someone, but he hardly knew why the idea arrested him. There was nothing new about Lily Bart, yet he could never see her without a faint movement of interest: it was characteristic of her that she always roused speculation, that her simplest acts seemed the result of far-reaching intentions.

An impulse of curiosity made him turn out of his direct line to the door and stroll past her. He knew that if she did not wish to be seen she would contrive to elude him, and it amused him to think of putting her skill to the test.

"Mr. Selden—what good luck!"

She came forward smiling, eager almost, in her resolve to intercept him. One or two persons, in brushing past them, lingered to look; for Miss Bart was a figure to arrest even the suburban traveler rushing to his last train.

Selden had never seen her more radiant. Her vivid head, relieved against the dull tints of the crowd, made her more conspicuous than in a ballroom, and under her dark hat and veil she regained the girlish smoothness, the purity of tint, that she was beginning to lose after eleven years of late hours and indefatigable dancing. Was it really eleven years, Selden found himself wondering, and had she indeed reached the nine-and-twentieth birthday with which her rivals credited her?

"What luck!" she repeated. "How nice of you to come to my rescue!"

He responded joyfully that to do so was his mission in life and asked what form the rescue was to take.

"Oh, almost any—even to sitting on a bench and talking to me. One sits out a cotillion—why not sit out a train? It isn't a bit hotter here than in Mrs. Van Osburgh's conservatory—and some of the women are not a bit uglier."

She broke off, laughing, to explain that she had come up to town from Tuxedo, on her way to the Gus Trenors' at Bellomont, and had missed the three-fifteen train to Rhinebeck.

"And there isn't another till half-past five." She consulted the little jeweled watch among her laces. "Just two hours to wait. And I don't know what to do with myself. My maid came up this morning to do some shopping for me, and was to go on to Bellomont at one o'clock, and my aunt's house is closed, and I don't know a soul in town." She glanced plaintively about the station. "It *is* hotter than Mrs. Van Osburgh's, after all. If you can spare the time, do take me somewhere for a breath of air."

He declared himself entirely at her disposal: the adventure struck him as diverting. As a spectator, he had always enjoyed Lily Bart; and his course lay so far out of her orbit that it amused him to be drawn for a moment into the sudden intimacy which her proposal implied.

"Shall we go over to Sherry's for a cup of tea?"

She smiled assentingly, and then made a slight grimace.

"So many people come up to town on a Monday—one is sure to meet a lot of bores. I'm as old as the hills, of course, and it ought not to make any difference; but if *I'm* old enough, you're not," she objected gaily. "I'm dying for tea—but isn't there a quieter place?"

He answered her smile, which rested on him vividly. Her discretions interested him almost as much as her imprudences: he was so sure that both were part of the same carefully elaborated plan. In judging Miss Bart, he had always made use of the "argument from design."

"The resources of New York are rather meager," he said, "but I'll find a hansom first, and then we'll invent something."

He led her through the throng of returning holiday-makers, past sallow-faced girls in preposterous hats, and flat-chested women struggling with paper bundles and palm-leaf fans. Was it possible that she belonged to the same race? The dinginess, the crudity of this average section of womanhood made him feel how highly specialized she was.

A rapid shower had cooled the air, and clouds still hung refreshingly over the moist street.

"How delicious! Let us walk a little," she said as they emerged from the station.

They turned into Madison Avenue and began to stroll northward. As she moved beside him, with her long light step, Selden was conscious of taking a luxurious pleasure in her nearness: in the modeling of her little ear, the crisp upward wave of her hair—was it ever so slightly brightened by art? —and the thick planting of her straight black lashes. Everything about her was at once vigorous and exquisite, at once strong and fine. He had a confused sense that she must have cost a great deal to make, that a great many dull and ugly people must, in some mysterious way, have been sacrificed to produce her. He was aware that the qualities distinguishing her from the herd of her sex were chiefly external: as though a fine glaze of beauty and fastidiousness had been applied to vulgar clay. Yet the analogy left him unsatisfied, for a coarse texture will not take a high finish; and was it not possible that the material was fine, but that circumstance had fashioned it into a futile shape?

As he reached this point in his speculations the sun came out, and her lifted parasol cut off his enjoyment. A moment or two later she paused with a sigh.

"Oh, dear, I'm so hot and thirsty—and what a hideous place New York is!" She looked despairingly up and down the dreary thoroughfare. "Other cities put on their best clothes in summer, but New York seems to sit in its shirt-sleeves." Her eyes wandered down one of the side-streets. "Someone has had the humanity to plant a few trees over there. Let us go into the shade."

"I am glad my street meets with your approval," said Selden as they turned the corner.

"Your street? Do you live here?"

She glanced with interest along the new brick and limestone housefronts, fantastically varied in obedience to the American craving for novelty, but fresh and inviting with their awnings and flower-boxes.

"Ah, yes—to be sure: The Benedick. What a nice-looking building! I don't think I've ever seen it before." She looked across at the flat-house with its marble porch and pseudo-Georgian façade. "Which are your windows? Those with the awnings down?"

"On the top floor—yes."

"And that nice little balcony is yours? How cool it looks up there!"

He paused a moment. "Come up and see," he suggested. "I can give you a cup of tea in no time—and you won't meet any bores."

Her color deepened—she still had the art of blushing at the right time— but she took the suggestion as lightly as it was made.

"Why not? It's too tempting—I'll take the risk," she declared.

"Oh, I'm not dangerous," he said in the same key. In truth, he had never liked her as well as at that moment. He knew she had accepted without afterthought: he could never be a factor in her calculations, and there was a surprise, a refreshment almost, in the spontaneity of her consent.

On the threshold he paused a moment, feeling for his latch-key.

"There's no one here; but I have a servant who is supposed to come in the mornings, and it's just possible he may have put out the tea things and provided some cake."

He ushered her into a slip of a hall hung with old prints. She noticed the letters and notes heaped on the table among his gloves and sticks; then she found herself in a small library, dark but cheerful, with its walls of books, a pleasantly faded Turkey rug, a littered desk, and, as he had foretold, a tea-tray on a low table near the window. A breeze had sprung up, swaying inward the muslin curtains, and bringing a fresh scent of mignonette and petunias from the flower-box on the balcony.

Lily sank with a sigh into one of the shabby leather chairs.

"How delicious to have a place like this all to one's self! What a miserable thing it is to be a woman." She leaned back in a luxury of discontent.

Selden was rummaging in a cupboard for the cake.

"Even women," he said, "have been known to enjoy the privileges of a flat."

"Oh, governesses—or widows. But not girls—not poor, miserable, marriageable girls!"

"I even know a girl who lives in a flat."

She sat up in surprise. "You do?"

"I do," he assured her, emerging from the cupboard with the sought-for cake.

"Oh, I know—you mean Gerty Farish." She smiled a little unkindly. "But I said *marriageable*—and besides, she has a horrid little place, and no maid, and such queer things to eat. Her cook does the washing and the food tastes of soap. I should hate that, you know."

"You shouldn't dine with her on wash-days," said Selden, cutting the cake.

They both laughed, and he knelt by the table to light the lamp under the kettle, while she measured out the tea into a little teapot of green glaze. As he watched her hand, polished as a bit of old ivory, with its slender pink nails, and the sapphire bracelet slipping over her wrist, he was struck with the irony of suggesting to her such a life as his cousin Gertrude Farish had chosen. She was so evidently the victim of the civilization which had produced her, that the links of her bracelet seemed like manacles chaining her to her fate.

She seemed to read his thought. "It was horrid of me to say that of Gerty," she said with charming compunction. "I forgot she was your cousin. But we're so different, you know: she likes being good, and I like being happy. And besides, she is free and I am not. If I were, I daresay I could manage to be happy even in her flat. It must be pure bliss to arrange the furniture just as one likes, and give all the horrors to the ash-man. If I could only do over my aunt's drawing-room I know I should be a better woman."

"Is it so very bad?" he asked sympathetically.

She smiled at him across the teapot which she was holding up to be filled.

"That shows how seldom you come there. Why don't you come oftener?"

"When I do come, it's not to look at Mrs. Peniston's furniture."

"Nonsense," she said. "You don't come at all—and yet we get on so well when we meet."

"Perhaps that's the reason," he answered promptly. "I'm afraid I haven't any cream, you know—shall you mind a slice of lemon instead?"

"I shall like it better." She waited while he cut the lemon and dropped a thin disk into her cup. "But that is not the reason," she insisted.

"The reason for what?"

"For your never coming." She leaned forward with a shade of perplexity in her charming eyes. "I wish I knew—I wish I could make you out. Of course I know there are men who don't like me—one can tell that at a glance. And there are others who are afraid of me: they think I want to marry them." She smiled up at him frankly. "But I don't think you dislike me—and you can't possibly think I want to marry you."

"No—I absolve you of that," he agreed.

"Well, then —?"

He had carried his cup to the fireplace, and stood leaning against the chimney-piece and looking down on her with an air of indolent amusement. The provocation in her eyes increased his amusement—he had not supposed she would waste her powder on such small game; but perhaps she was only keeping her hand in; or perhaps a girl of her type had no conversation but of the personal kind. At any rate, she was amazingly pretty, and he had asked her to tea and must live up to his obligations.

"Well, then," he said with a plunge, "perhaps *that's* the reason."

"What?"

"The fact that you don't want to marry me. Perhaps I don't regard it as such a strong inducement to go and see you." He felt a slight shiver down his spine as he ventured this, but her laugh reassured him.

"Dear Mr. Selden, that wasn't worthy of you. It's stupid of you to make love to me, and it isn't like you to be stupid." She leaned back, sipping her tea with an air so enchantingly judicial that, if they had been in her aunt's drawing-room, he might almost have tried to disprove her deduction.

"Don't you see," she continued, "that there are men enough to say pleasant things to me, and that what I want is a friend who won't be afraid to say disagreeable ones when I need them? Sometimes I have fancied you might be that friend—I don't know why, except that you are neither a prig nor a bounder, and that I shouldn't have to pretend with you or be on my guard against you." Her voice had dropped to a note of seriousness, and she sat gazing up at him with the troubled gravity of a child.

"You don't know how much I need such a friend," she said. "My aunt is full of copy-book axioms, but they were all meant to apply to conduct in the early fifties. I always feel that to live up to them would include wearing book-muslin with gigot sleeves. And the other women—my best friends— well, they use me or abuse me; but they don't care a straw what happens to me. I've been about too long—people are getting tired of me; they are beginning to say I ought to marry."

There was a moment's pause, during which Selden meditated one or two replies calculated to add a momentary zest to the situation, but he rejected them in favor of the simple question: "Well, why don't you?"

She colored and laughed. "Ah, I see you *are* a friend after all, and that is one of the disagreeable things I was asking for."

"It wasn't meant to be disagreeable," he returned amicably. "Isn't marriage your vocation? Isn't it what you're all brought up for?"

She sighed. "I suppose so. What else is there?"

"Exactly. And so why not take the plunge and have it over?"

She shrugged her shoulders. "You speak as if I ought to marry the first man who came along."

"I didn't mean to imply that you are as hard put to it as that. But there must be someone with the requisite qualifications."

She shook her head wearily. "I threw away one or two good chances when I first came out—I suppose every girl does; and you know I am horribly poor—and very expensive. I must have a great deal of money."

Selden had turned to reach for a cigarette-box on the mantelpiece.

"What's become of Dillworth?" he asked.

"Oh, his mother was frightened—she was afraid I should have all the family jewels reset. And she wanted me to promise that I wouldn't do over the drawing-room."

"The very thing you are marrying for!"

"Exactly. So she packed him off to India."

"Hard luck—but you can do better than Dillworth."

He offered the box, and she took out three or four cigarettes, putting one between her lips and slipping the others into a little gold case attached to her long pearl chain.

"Have I time? Just a whiff, then." She leaned forward, holding the tip of her cigarette to his. As she did so, he noted, with a purely impersonal enjoyment, how evenly the black lashes were set in her smooth white lids, and how the purplish shade beneath them melted into the pure pallor of the cheek.

She began to saunter about the room, examining the bookshelves between the puffs of her cigarette smoke. Some of the volumes had the ripe tints of good tooling and old morocco, and her eyes lingered on them caressingly, not with the appreciation of the expert, but with the pleasure in agreeable tones and textures that was one of her inmost susceptibilities. Suddenly her expression changed from desultory enjoyment to active conjecture, and she turned to Selden with a question.

"You collect, don't you—you know about first editions and things?"

"As much as a man may who has no money to spend. Now and then I pick up something in the rubbish heap; and I go and look on at the big sales."

She had again addressed herself to the shelves, but her eyes now swept them inattentively, and he saw that she was preoccupied with a new idea.

"And Americana—do you collect Americana?"

Selden stared and laughed.

"No, that's rather out of my line. I'm not really a collector, you see; I simply like to have good editions of the books I am fond of."

She made a slight grimace. "And Americana are horribly dull, I suppose?"

"I should fancy so—except to the historian. But your real collector values a thing for its rarity. I don't suppose the buyers of Americana sit up reading them all night—old Jefferson Gryce certainly didn't."

She was listening with keen attention. "And yet they fetch fabulous prices, don't they? It seems so odd to want to pay a lot for an ugly badly printed book that one is never going to read! And I suppose most of the owners of Americana are not historians either?"

"No, very few of the historians can afford to buy them. They have to use those in the public libraries or in private collections. It seems to be the mere rarity that attracts the average collector."

He had seated himself on an arm of the chair near which she was standing, and she continued to question him, asking which were the rarest volumes, whether the Jefferson Gryce collection was really considered the finest in the world, and what was the largest price ever fetched by a single volume.

It was so pleasant to sit there looking up at her, as she lifted now one book and then another from the shelves, fluttering the pages between her fingers, while her drooping profile was outlined against the warm background of old bindings, that he talked on without pausing to wonder at her sudden interest in so unsuggestive a subject. But he could never be long with her without trying to find a reason for what she was doing, and as she replaced his first edition of La Bruyère and turned away from the bookcases, he began to ask himself what she had been driving at. Her next question was not of a nature to enlighten him. She paused before him with a smile which seemed at once designed to admit him to her familiarity, and to remind him of the restrictions it imposed.

"Don't you ever mind," she asked suddenly, "not being rich enough to buy all the books you want?"

He followed her glance about the room, with its worn furniture and shabby walls.

"Don't I just? Do you take me for a saint on a pillar?"

"And having to work—do you mind that?"

"Oh, the work itself is not so bad—I'm rather fond of the law."

"No, but the being tied down, the routine—don't you ever want to get away, to see new places and people?"

"Horribly—especially when I see all my friends rushing to the steamer."

She drew a sympathetic breath. "But do you mind enough—to marry to get out of it?"

Selden broke into a laugh. "God forbid!" he declared.

She rose with a sigh, tossing her cigarette into the grate.

"Ah, there's the difference—a girl must, a man may if he chooses." She surveyed him critically. "Your coat's a little shabby—but who cares? It doesn't keep people from asking you to dine. If I were shabby no one would have me: a woman is asked out as much for her clothes as for herself. The clothes are the background, the frame, if you like: they don't make success, but they are a part of it. Who wants a dingy woman? We are expected to be pretty and well-dressed till we drop—and if we can't keep it up alone, we have to go into partnership."

Selden glanced at her with amusement. It was impossible, even with her lovely eyes imploring him, to take a sentimental view of her case.

"Ah, well, there must be plenty of capital on the lookout for such an investment. Perhaps you'll meet your fate tonight at the Trenors'."

She returned his look interrogatively.

"I thought you might be going there—oh, not in that capacity! But there are to be a lot of your set—Gwen Van Osburgh, the Wetheralls, Lady Cressida Raith—and the George Dorsets."

She paused a moment before the last name, and shot a query through her lashes; but he remained imperturbable.

"Mrs. Trenor asked me, but I can't get away till the end of the week, and those big parties bore me."

"Ah, so they do me," she exclaimed.

"Then why go?"

"It's part of the business—you forget! And besides, if I didn't, I should be playing bézique with my aunt at Richfield Springs."

"That's almost as bad as marrying Dillworth," he agreed, and they both laughed for pure pleasure in their sudden intimacy.

She glanced at the clock.

"Dear me! I must be off. It's after five."

She paused before the mantelpiece, studying herself in the mirror while she adjusted her veil. The attitude revealed the long slope of her slender sides, which gave a kind of wild-wood grace to her outline—as though she were a captured dryad subdued to the conventions of the drawing-room; and Selden reflected that it was the same streak of sylvan freedom in her nature that lent such savor to her artificiality.

He followed her across the room to the entrance-hall; but on the threshold she held out her hand with a gesture of leave-taking.

"It's been delightful; and now you will have to return my visit."

"But don't you want me to see you to the station?"

"No; goodbye here, please."

She let her hand lie in his a moment, smiling up at him adorably.

"Goodbye, then—and good luck at Bellomont!" he said, opening the door for her.

On the landing she paused to look about her. There were a thousand chances to one against her meeting anybody, but one could never tell, and she always paid for her rare indiscretions by a violent reaction of prudence. There was no one in sight, however, but a charwoman who was scrubbing the stairs. Her own stout person and its surrounding implements took up so much room that Lily, to pass her, had to gather up her skirts and brush against the wall. As she did so, the woman paused in her work and looked up curiously, resting her clenched red fists on the wet cloth she had just drawn from her pail. She had a broad sallow face, slightly pitted with smallpox, and thin straw-colored hair through which her scalp shone unpleasantly.

"I beg your pardon," said Lily, intending by her politeness to convey a criticism of the other's manner.

The woman, without answering, pushed her pail aside, and continued to stare as Miss Bart swept by with a murmur of silken linings. Lily felt herself flushing under the look. What did the creature suppose? Could one never do the simplest, the most harmless thing, without subjecting one's self to some odious conjecture? Half way down the next flight, she smiled to think that a charwoman's stare should so perturb her. The poor thing was probably dazzled by such an unwonted apparition. But *were* such apparitions unwonted on Selden's stairs? Miss Bart was not familiar with the moral code of bachelors' flat-houses, and her color rose again as it occurred to her that the woman's persistent gaze implied a groping among past associations. But she put aside the thought with a smile at her own fears, and hastened downward, wondering if she should find a cab short of Fifth Avenue.

Under the Georgian porch she paused again, scanning the street for a hansom. None was in sight, but as she reached the sidewalk she ran against a small glossy-looking man with a gardenia in his coat, who raised his hat with a surprised exclamation.

"Miss Bart? Well—of all people! This *is* luck," he declared, and she caught a twinkle of amused curiosity between his screwed-up lids.

"Oh, Mr. Rosedale—how are you?" she said, perceiving that the irrepressible annoyance on her face was reflected in the sudden intimacy of his smile.

Mr. Rosedale stood scanning her with interest and approval. He was a plump rosy man of the blond Jewish type, with smart London clothes fitting him like upholstery, and small sidelong eyes which gave him the air of appraising people as if they were bric-a-brac. He glanced up interrogatively at the porch of the Benedick.

"Been up to town for a little shopping, I suppose?" he said, in a tone which had the familiarity of a touch.

Miss Bart shrank from it slightly, and then flung herself into precipitate explanations.

"Yes—I came up to see my dressmaker. I am just on my way to catch the train to the Trenors'."

"Ah—your dressmaker; just so," he said blandly. "I didn't know there were any dressmakers in the Benedick."

"The Benedick?" She looked gently puzzled. "Is that the name of this building?"

"Yes, that's the name. I believe it's an old word for bachelor, isn't it? I happen to own the building—that's the way I know." His smile deepened as he added with increasing assurance: "But you must let me take you to the station. The Trenors are at Bellomont, of course? You've barely time to catch the five-forty. The dressmaker kept you waiting, I suppose."

Lily stiffened under the pleasantry.

"Oh, thanks," she stammered; and at that moment her eye caught a hansom drifting down Madison Avenue, and she hailed it with a desperate gesture.

"You're very kind, but I couldn't think of troubling you," she said, extending her hand to Mr. Rosedale; and heedless of his protestations, she sprang into the rescuing vehicle, and called out a breathless order to the driver.

2

I N the hansom she leaned back with a sigh.

Why must a girl pay so dearly for her least escape from routine? Why could one never do a natural thing without having to screen it behind a structure of artifice? She had yielded to a passing impulse in going to Lawrence Selden's rooms, and it was so seldom that she could allow herself the luxury of an impulse! This one, at any rate, was going to cost her rather more than she could afford. She was vexed to see that, in spite of so many years of vigilance, she had blundered twice within five minutes. That stupid story about her dressmaker was bad enough—it would have been so simple to tell Rosedale that she had been taking tea with Selden! The mere statement of the fact would have rendered it innocuous. But, after having let herself be surprised in a falsehood, it was doubly stupid to snub the witness of her discomfiture. If she had had the presence of mind to let Rosedale drive her to the station, the concession might have purchased his silence. He had his race's accuracy in the appraisal of values, and to be seen walking down the platform at the crowded afternoon hour in the company of Miss Lily Bart would have been money in his pocket, as he might himself have phrased it. He knew, of course, that there would be a large house-party at Bellomont, and the possibility of being taken for one of Mrs. Trenor's guests was doubtless included in his calculations. Mr. Rosedale was still at a stage in his social ascent when it was of importance to produce such impressions.

The provoking part was that Lily knew all this—knew how easy it would have been to silence him on the spot, and how difficult it might be to do so afterward. Mr. Simon Rosedale was a man who made it his business to know everything about everyone, whose idea of showing himself to be at home in society was to display an inconvenient familiarity with the habits of those with whom he wished to be thought intimate. Lily was sure that within twenty-four hours the story of her visiting her dressmaker at the Benedick would be in active circulation among Mr. Rosedale's acquaintances. The worst of it was that she had always snubbed and ignored him. On his first appearance—when her improvident cousin, Jack Stepney, had obtained for him (in return for favors too easily guessed) a card to one of the vast impersonal Van Osburgh "crushes"—Rosedale, with that mixture of artistic sensibility and business astuteness which characterizes his race, had instantly gravitated toward Miss Bart. She understood his motives, for her own course was guided by as nice calculations. Training and experience had taught her to be hospitable to newcomers, since the most unpromising might be useful later on, and there were plenty of available *oubliettes* to swallow them if they were not. But some intuitive repugnance, getting the better of years of social discipline, had made her push Mr. Rosedale into his *oubliette* without a trial. He had left behind only the ripple of amusement which his speedy dispatch had caused among her friends; and though later (to shift the metaphor) he reappeared lower down the stream, it was only in fleeting glimpses, with long submergences between.

Hitherto Lily had been undisturbed by scruples. In her little set Mr. Rosedale had been pronounced "impossible," and Jack Stepney roundly snubbed for his attempt to pay his debts in dinner invitations. Even Mrs. Trenor, whose taste for variety had led her into some hazardous experiments, resisted Jack's attempts to disguise Mr. Rosedale as a novelty, and declared that he was the same little Jew who had been served up and rejected at the social board a dozen times within her memory; and while Judy Trenor was obdurate there was small chance of Mr. Rosedale's penetrating beyond the outer limbo of the Van Osburgh crushes. Jack gave up the contest with a laughing "You'll see," and, sticking manfully to his guns, showed himself with Rosedale at the fashionable restaurants, in company with the personally vivid if socially obscure ladies who are available for such purposes. But the attempt had hitherto been vain, and as Rosedale undoubt-edly paid for the dinners, the laugh remained with his debtor.

Mr. Rosedale, it will be seen, was thus far not a factor to be feared—unless one put one's self in his power. And this was precisely what Miss Bart had done. Her clumsy fib had let him see that she had something to con-ceal; and she was sure he had a score to settle with her. Something in his smile told her he had not forgotten. She turned from the thought with a little shiver, but it hung on her all the way to the station, and dogged her down the platform with the persistency of Mr. Rosedale himself.

She had just time to take her seat before the train started; but having arranged herself in her corner with the instinctive feeling for effect which never forsook her, she glanced about in the hope of seeing some other member of the Trenors' party. She wanted to get away from herself, and conversation was the only means of escape that she knew.

Her search was rewarded by the discovery of a very blond young man with a soft reddish beard, who, at the other end of the carriage, appeared to be dissembling himself behind an unfolded newspaper. Lily's eye brightened, and a faint smile relaxed the drawn lines of her mouth. She had known that Mr. Percy Gryce was to be at Bellomont, but she had not counted on the luck of having him to herself in the train; and the fact banished all per-turbing thoughts of Mr. Rosedale. Perhaps, after all, the day was to end more favorably than it had begun.

She began to cut the pages of a novel, tranquilly studying her prey through downcast lashes while she organized a method of attack. Something in his attitude of conscious absorption told her that he was aware of her presence: no one had ever been quite so engrossed in an evening paper! She guessed that he was too shy to come up to her, and that she would have to devise some means of approach which should not appear to be an advance on her part. It amused her to think that anyone as rich as Mr. Percy Gryce should be shy; but she was gifted with treasures of indulgence for such idiosyncrasies, and besides, his timidity might serve her purpose better than too much assurance. She had the art of giving self-confidence to the embar-rassed, but she was not equally sure of being able to embarrass the self-confident.

She waited till the train had emerged from the tunnel and was racing between the ragged edges of the northern suburbs. Then, as it lowered its speed near Yonkers, she rose from her seat and drifted slowly down the carriage. As she passed Mr. Gryce, the train gave a lurch, and he was aware of a slender hand gripping the back of his chair. He rose with a start, his ingenuous face looking as though it had been dipped in crimson: even the reddish tint in his beard seemed to deepen.

The train swayed again, almost flinging Miss Bart into his arms. She steadied herself with a laugh and drew back; but he was enveloped in the scent of her dress, and his shoulder had felt her fugitive touch.

"Oh, Mr. Gryce, is it you? I'm so sorry—I was trying to find the porter and get some tea."

She held out her hand as the train resumed its level rush, and they stood exchanging a few words in the aisle. Yes—he was going to Bellomont. He had heard she was to be of the party—he blushed again as he admitted it. And was he to be there for a whole week? How delightful!

But at this point one or two belated passengers from the last station forced their way into the carriage, and Lily had to retreat to her seat.

"The chair next to mine is empty—do take it," she said over her shoulder; and Mr. Gryce, with considerable embarrassment, succeeded in effecting an exchange which enabled him to transport himself and his bags to her side.

"Ah—and here is the porter, and perhaps we can have some tea."

She signalled to that official, and in a moment, with the ease that seemed to attend the fulfillment of all her wishes, a little table had been set up between the seats, and she had helped Mr. Gryce to bestow his encumbering properties beneath it.

When the tea came he watched her in silent fascination while her hands flitted above the tray, looking miraculously fine and slender in contrast to the coarse china and lumpy bread. It seemed wonderful to him that anyone should perform with such careless ease the difficult task of making tea in public in a lurching train. He would never have dared to order it for himself lest he should attract the notice of his fellow passengers; but, secure in the shelter of her conspicuousness, he sipped the inky draught with a delicious sense of exhilaration.

Lily, with the flavor of Selden's caravan tea on her lips, had no great fancy to drown it in the railway brew which seemed such nectar to her companion; but, rightly judging that one of the charms of tea is the fact of drinking it together, she proceeded to give the last touch to Mr. Gryce's enjoyment by smiling at him across her lifted cup.

"Is it quite right—I haven't made it too strong?" she asked solicitously; and he replied with conviction that he had never tasted better tea.

"I daresay it is true," she reflected; and her imagination was fired by the thought that Mr. Gryce, who might have sounded the depths of the most complex self-indulgence, was perhaps actually taking his first journey alone with a pretty woman.

It struck her as providential that she should be the instrument of his initiation. Some girls would not have known how to manage him. They would have over-emphasized the novelty of the adventure, trying to make him feel in it the zest of an escapade. But Lily's methods were more delicate. She remembered that her cousin Jack Stepney had once defined Mr. Gryce as the young man who had promised his mother never to go out in the rain without his overshoes; and acting on this hint, she resolved to impart a gently domestic air to the scene, in the hope that her companion, instead of feeling that he was doing something reckless or unusual, would merely be led to dwell on the advantage of always having a companion to make one's tea in the train.

But in spite of her efforts, conversation flagged after the tray had been removed, and she was driven to take a fresh measurement of Mr. Gryce's limitations. It was not, after all, opportunity but imagination that he lacked: he had a mental palate which would never learn to distinguish between railway tea and nectar. There was, however, one topic she could rely on: one spring that she had only to touch to set his simple machinery in motion. She had refrained from touching it because it was a last resource, and she had relied on other arts to stimulate other sensations; but as a settled look of dullness began to creep over his candid features, she saw that extreme measures were necessary.

"And how," she said, leaning forward, "are you getting on with your Americana?"

His eye became a degree less opaque: it was as though an incipient film had been removed from it, and she felt the pride of a skillful operator.

"I've got a few new things," he said, suffused with pleasure, but lowering his voice as though he feared his fellow passengers might be in league to despoil him.

She returned a sympathetic inquiry, and gradually he was drawn on to talk of his latest purchases. It was the one subject which enabled him to forget himself, or allowed him, rather, to remember himself without constraint, because he was at home in it, and could assert a superiority that there were few to dispute. Hardly any of his acquaintances cared for Americana, or knew anything about them; and the consciousness of this ignorance threw Mr. Gryce's knowledge into agreeable relief. The only difficulty was to introduce the topic and to keep it to the front; most people showed no desire to have their ignorance dispelled, and Mr. Gryce was like a merchant whose warehouses are crammed with an unmarketable commodity.

But Miss Bart, it appeared, really did want to know about Americana; and moreover, she was already sufficiently informed to make the task of farther instruction as easy as it was agreeable. She questioned him intelligently, she heard him submissively; and, prepared for the look of lassitude which usually crept over his listeners' faces, he grew eloquent under her receptive gaze. The "points" she had had the presence of mind to glean from Selden, in anticipation of this very contingency, were serving her to such good purpose that she began to think her visit to him had been the luckiest incident of the day. She had once more shown her talent for profiting by the unexpected, and dangerous theories as to the advisability of yielding to impulse were germinating under the surface of smiling attention which she continued to present to her companion.

Mr. Gryce's sensations, if less definite, were equally agreeable. He felt the confused titillation with which the lower organisms welcome the gratification of their needs, and all his senses floundered in a vague well-being, through which Miss Bart's personality was dimly but pleasantly perceptible.

Mr. Gryce's interest in Americana had not originated with himself: it was impossible to think of him as evolving any taste of his own. An uncle had left him a collection already noted among bibliophiles; the existence of the collection was the only fact that had ever shed glory on the name of Gryce, and the nephew took as much pride in his inheritance as though it had been his own work. Indeed, he gradually came to regard it as such, and to feel a sense of personal complacency when he chanced on any reference to the Gryce Americana. Anxious as he was to avoid personal notice, he took, in the printed mention of his name, a pleasure so exquisite and excessive that it seemed a compensation for his shrinking from publicity.

To enjoy the sensation as often as possible, he subscribed to all the reviews dealing with book-collecting in general, and American history in particular, and as allusions to his library abounded in the pages of these journals, which formed his only reading, he came to regard himself as figuring prominently in the public eye, and to enjoy the thought of the interest which would be excited if the persons he met in the street, or sat among in traveling, were suddenly to be told that he was the possessor of the Gryce Americana.

Most timidities have such secret compensations, and Miss Bart was discerning enough to know that the inner vanity is generally in proportion to the outer self-depreciation. With a more confident person she would not have dared to dwell so long on one topic, or to show such exaggerated interest in it; but she had rightly guessed that Mr. Gryce's egoism was a thirsty soil, requiring constant nurture from without. Miss Bart had the gift of following an undercurrent of thought while she appeared to be sailing on the surface of conversation; and in this case her mental excursion took the form of a rapid survey of Mr. Percy Gryce's future as combined with her own. The Gryces were from Albany, and but lately introduced to the metropolis, where the mother and son had come, after old Jefferson Gryce's death, to take possession of his house in Madison Avenue—an appalling house, all brown stone without and black walnut within, with the Gryce library in a fire-proof annex that looked like a mausoleum. Lily, however, knew all about them: young Mr. Gryce's arrival had fluttered the maternal breasts of New York, and when a girl has no mother to palpitate for her she must needs be on the alert for herself. Lily, therefore, had not only contrived to put herself in the young man's way, but had made the acquaintance of Mrs. Gryce, a monumental woman with the voice of a pulpit orator and a mind preoccupied with the iniquities of her servants, who came sometimes to sit with Mrs. Peniston and learn from that lady how she managed to prevent the kitchenmaid's smuggling groceries out of the house. Mrs. Gryce had a kind of impersonal benevolence: cases of individual need she regarded with suspicion, but she subscribed to institutions when their annual reports showed an impressive surplus. Her domestic duties were manifold, for they extended from furtive inspections of the servants' bed-rooms to unannounced descents to the cellar; but she had never allowed herself many pleasures. Once, however, she had had a special edition of the Sarum Rule printed in rubric and presented to every clergyman in the diocese; and the gilt album in which their letters of thanks were pasted formed the chief ornament of her drawing-room table.

Percy had been brought up in the principles which so excellent a woman was sure to inculcate. Every form of prudence and suspicion had been grafted on a nature originally reluctant and cautious, with the result that it would have seemed hardly needful for Mrs. Gryce to extract his promise about the overshoes, so little likely was he to hazard himself abroad in the rain. After attaining his majority, and coming into the fortune which the late Mr. Gryce had made out of a patent device for excluding fresh air from hotels, the young man continued to live with his mother in Albany; but on Jefferson Gryce's death, when another large property passed into her son's hands, Mrs. Gryce thought that what she called his "interests" de-manded his presence in New York. She accordingly installed herself in the Madison Avenue house, and Percy, whose sense of duty was not inferior to his mother's, spent all his week days in the handsome Broad Street office where a batch of pale men on small salaries had grown gray in the manage-ment of the Gryce estate, and where he was initiated with becoming rever-ence into every detail of the art of accumulation.

As far as Lily could learn, this had hitherto been Mr. Gryce's only occupation, and she might have been pardoned for thinking it not too hard a task to interest a young man who had been kept on such low diet. At any rate, she felt herself so completely in command of the situation that she yielded to a sense of security in which all fear of Mr. Rosedale, and of the difficulties on which that fear was contingent, vanished beyond the edge of thought.

The stopping of the train at Garrisons would not have distracted her from these thoughts, had she not caught a sudden look of distress in her companion's eye. His seat faced toward the door, and she guessed that he had been perturbed by the approach of an acquaintance; a fact confirmed by the turning of heads and general sense of commotion which her own en-trance into a railway-carriage was apt to produce.

She knew the symptoms at once, and was not surprised to be hailed by the high notes of a pretty woman, who entered the train accompanied by a maid, a bull-terrier, and a footman staggering under a load of bags and dressing-cases.

"Oh, Lily—are you going to Bellomont? Then you can't let me have your seat, I suppose? But I *must* have a seat in this carriage—porter, you must find me a place at once. Can't someone be put somewhere else? I want to be with my friends. Oh, how do you do, Mr. Gryce? Do please make him understand that I must have a seat next to you and Lily."

Mrs. George Dorset, regardless of the mild efforts of a traveler with a carpetbag, who was doing his best to make room for her by getting out of the train, stood in the middle of the aisle, diffusing about her that general sense of exasperation which a pretty woman on her travels not infrequently creates.

She was smaller and thinner than Lily Bart, with a restless pliability of pose, as if she could have been crumpled up and run through a ring, like the sinuous draperies she affected. Her small pale face seemed the mere setting of a pair of dark exaggerated eyes, of which the visionary gaze contrasted curiously with her self-assertive tone and gestures; so that, as one of her friends observed, she was like a disembodied spirit who took up a great deal of room.

Having finally discovered that the seat adjoining Miss Bart's was at her disposal, she possessed herself of it with a farther displacement of her surroundings, explaining meanwhile that she had come across from Mount Kisco in her motorcar that morning, and had been kicking her heels for an hour at Garrisons, without even the alleviation of a cigarette, her brute of a husband having neglected to replenish her case before they parted that morning.

"And at this hour of the day I don't suppose you've a single one left, have you, Lily?" she plaintively concluded.

Miss Bart caught the startled glance of Mr. Percy Gryce, whose own lips were never defiled by tobacco.

"What an absurd question, Bertha!" she exclaimed, blushing at the thought of the store she had laid in at Lawrence Selden's.

"Why, don't you smoke? Since when have you given it up? What—you never. And you don't either, Mr. Gryce? Ah, of course—how stupid of me —I understand."

And Mrs. Dorset leaned back against her traveling cushions with a smile which made Lily wish there had been no vacant seat beside her own.

3

BRIDGE at Bellomont usually lasted till the small hours; and when Lily went to bed that night she had played too long for her own good.

Feeling no desire for the self-communion which awaited her in her room, she lingered on the broad stairway, looking down into the hall below, where the last cardplayers were grouped about the tray of tall glasses and silver-collared decanters which the butler had just placed on a low table near the fire.

The hall was arcaded, with a gallery supported on columns of pale yellow marble. Tall clumps of flowering plants were grouped against a background of dark foliage in the angles of the walls. On the crimson carpet a deerhound and two or three spaniels dozed luxuriously before the fire, and the light from the great central lantern overhead shed a brightness on the women's hair and struck sparks from their jewels as they moved.

There were moments when such scenes delighted Lily, when they gratified her sense of beauty and her craving for the external finish of life; there were others when they gave a sharper edge to the meagerness of her own opportunities. This was one of the moments when the sense of contrast was uppermost, and she turned away impatiently as Mrs. George Dorset, glittering in serpentine spangles, drew Percy Gryce in her wake to a confidential nook beneath the gallery.

It was not that Miss Bart was afraid of losing her newly acquired hold over Mr. Gryce. Mrs. Dorset might startle or dazzle him, but she had neither the skill nor the patience to effect his capture. She was too self-engrossed to penetrate the recesses of his shyness, and besides, why should she care to give herself the trouble? At most it might amuse her to make sport of his simplicity for an evening—after that he would be merely a burden to her, and knowing this, she was far too experienced to encourage him. But the mere thought of that other woman, who could take a man up and toss him aside as she willed, without having to regard him as a possible factor in her plans, filled Lily Bart with envy. She had been bored all the afternoon by Percy Gryce—the mere thought seemed to waken an echo of his droning voice—but she could not ignore him on the morrow, she must follow up her success, must submit to more boredom, must be ready with fresh compliances and adaptabilities, and all on the bare chance that he might ultimately decide to do her the honor of boring her for life.

It was a hateful fate—but how escape from it? What choice had she? To be herself or a Gerty Farish. As she entered her bedroom, with its softly shaded lights, her lace dressing-gown lying across the silken bedspread, her little embroidered slippers before the fire, a vase of carnations filling the air with perfume, and the last novels and magazines lying uncut on a table beside the reading-lamp, she had a vision of Miss Farish's cramped flat, with its cheap conveniences and hideous wallpapers. No; she was not made for mean and shabby surroundings, for the squalid compromises of poverty. Her whole being dilated in an atmosphere of luxury; it was the background she required, the only climate she could breathe in. But the luxury of others was not what she wanted. A few years ago it had sufficed her: she had taken her daily meed of pleasure without caring who provided it. Now she was beginning to chafe at the obligations it imposed, to feel herself a mere pensioner on the splendor which had once seemed to belong to her. There were even moments when she was conscious of having to pay her way.

For a long time she had refused to play bridge. She knew she could not afford it, and she was afraid of acquiring so expensive a taste. She had seen the danger exemplified in more than one of her associates—in young Ned Silverton, for instance, the charming fair boy now seated in abject rapture at the elbow of Mrs. Fisher, a striking divorcée with eyes and gowns as emphatic as the headlines of her "case." Lily could remember when young Silverton had stumbled into their circle, with the air of a strayed Arcadian who has published charming sonnets in his college journal. Since then he had developed a taste for Mrs. Fisher and bridge, and the latter at least had involved him in expenses from which he had been more than once rescued by harassed maiden sisters, who treasured the sonnets, and went without sugar in their tea to keep their darling afloat. Ned's case was familiar to Lily: she had seen his charming eyes—which had a good deal more poetry in them than the sonnets—change from surprise to amusement, and from amusement to anxiety, as he passed under the spell of the terrible god of chance; and she was afraid of discovering the same symptoms in her own case.

For in the last year she had found that her hostesses expected her to take a place at the card-table. It was one of the taxes she had to pay for their prolonged hospitality, and for the dresses and trinkets which occasionally replenished her insufficient wardrobe. And since she had played regularly the passion had grown on her. Once or twice of late she had won a large sum, and instead of keeping it against future losses, had spent it in dress or jewelry; and the desire to atone for this imprudence, combined with the increasing exhilaration of the game, drove her to risk higher stakes at each fresh venture. She tried to excuse herself on the plea that, in the Trenor set, if one played at all one must either play high or be set down as priggish or stingy; but she knew that the gambling passion was upon her, and that in her present surroundings there was small hope of resisting it.

Tonight the luck had been persistently bad, and the little gold purse which hung among her trinkets was almost empty when she returned to her room. She unlocked the wardrobe, and taking out her jewel-case, looked under the tray for the roll of bills from which she had replenished the purse before going down to dinner. Only twenty dollars were left: the discovery was so startling that for a moment she fancied she must have been robbed. Then she took paper and pencil, and seating herself at the writing-table, tried to reckon up what she had spent during the day. Her head was throbbing with fatigue, and she had to go over the figures again and again; but at last it became clear to her that she had lost three hundred dollars at cards. She took out her checkbook to see if her balance was larger than she remembered, but found she had erred in the other direction. Then she returned to her calculations; but figure as she would, she could not conjure back the vanished three hundred dollars. It was the sum she had set aside to pacify her dressmaker—unless she should decide to use it as a sop to the jeweler. At any rate, she had so many uses for it that its very insufficiency had caused her to play high in the hope of doubling it. But of course she had lost—she who needed every penny, while Bertha Dorset, whose husband showered money on her, must have pocketed at least five hundred, and Judy Trenor, who could have afforded to lose a thousand a night, had left the table clutching such a heap of bills that she had been unable to shake hands with her guests when they bade her good night.

A world in which such things could be seemed a miserable place to Lily Bart; but then she had never able to understand the laws of a universe which was so ready to leave her out of its calculations.

She began to undress without ringing for her maid, whom she had sent to bed. She had been long enough in bondage to other people's pleasure to be considerate of those who depended on hers, and in her bitter moods it sometimes struck her that she and her maid were in the same position, except that the latter received her wages more regularly.

As she sat before the mirror brushing her hair, her face looked hollow and pale, and she was frightened by two little lines near her mouth, faint flaws in the smooth curve of the cheek.

"Oh, I must stop worrying!" she exclaimed. "Unless it's the electric light —" she reflected, springing up from her seat and lighting the candles on the dressing-table.

She turned out the wall-lights, and peered at herself between the candle-flames. The white oval of her face swam out waveringly from a background of shadows, the uncertain light blurring it like a haze; but the two lines about the mouth remained.

Lily rose and undressed in haste.

"It is only because I am tired and have such odious things to think about," she kept repeating; and it seemed an added injustice that petty cares should leave a trace on the beauty which was her only defense against them.

But the odious things were there, and remained with her. She returned wearily to the thought of Percy Gryce, as a wayfarer picks up a heavy load and toils on after a brief rest. She was almost sure she had "landed" him: a few days' work and she would win her reward. But the reward itself seemed unpalatable just then: she could get no zest from the thought of victory. It would be a rest from worry, no more—and how little that would have seemed to her a few years earlier! Her ambitions had shrunk gradually in the desiccating air of failure. But why had she failed? Was it her own fault or that of destiny?

She remembered how her mother, after they had lost their money, used to say to her with a kind of fierce vindictiveness, "But you'll get it all back —you'll get it all back, with your face." The remembrance roused a whole train of association, and she lay in the darkness reconstructing the past out of which her present had grown.

A house in which no one ever dined at home unless there was "company"; a doorbell perpetually ringing; a hall-table showered with square envelopes which were opened in haste, and oblong envelopes which were allowed to gather dust in the depths of a bronze jar; a series of French and English maids giving warning amid a chaos of hurriedly ransacked wardrobes and dress-closets; an equally changing dynasty of nurses and footmen; quarrels in the pantry, the kitchen and the drawing-room; precipitate trips to Europe, and returns with gorged trunks and days of interminable unpacking; semiannual discussions as to where the summer should be spent, gray interludes of economy and brilliant reactions of expense—such was the setting of Lily Bart's first memories.

Ruling the turbulent element called home was the vigorous and determined figure of a mother still young enough to dance her ball-dresses to rags, while the hazy outline of a neutral-tinted father filled an intermediate space between the butler and the man who came to wind the clocks. Even to the eyes of infancy, Mrs. Hudson Bart had appeared young; but Lily could not recall the time when her father had not been bald and slightly stooping, with streaks of gray in his hair, and a tired walk. It was a shock to her to learn afterward that he was but two years older than her mother.

Lily seldom saw her father by daylight. All day he was "downtown"; and in winter it was long after nightfall when she heard his fagged step on the stairs and his hand on the schoolroom door. He would kiss her in silence, and ask one or two questions of the nurse or the governess; then Mrs. Bart's maid would come to remind him that he was dining out, and he would hurry away with a nod to Lily. In summer, when he joined them for a Sunday at Newport or Southampton, he was even more effaced and silent than in winter. It seemed to tire him to rest, and he would sit for hours staring at the sea-line from a quiet corner of the verandah, while the clatter of his wife's existence went on unheeded a few feet off. Generally, however, Mrs. Bart and Lily went to Europe for the summer, and before the steamer was half way over Mr. Bart had dipped below the horizon. Sometimes his daughter heard him denounced for having neglected to forward Mrs. Bart's remittances; but for the most part he was never mentioned or thought of till his patient stooping figure presented itself on the New York dock as a buffer between the magnitude of his wife's luggage and the restrictions of the American custom-house.

In this desultory yet agitated fashion life went on through Lily's teens: a zig-zag broken course down which the family craft glided on a rapid current of amusement, tugged at by the underflow of a perpetual need—the need of more money. Lily could not recall the time when there had been money enough, and in some vague way her father seemed always to blame for the deficiency. It could certainly not be the fault of Mrs. Bart, who was spoken of by her friends as a "wonderful manager." Mrs. Bart was famous for the unlimited effect she produced on limited means; and to the lady and her acquaintances there was something heroic in living as though one were much richer than one's bank-book denoted.

Lily was naturally proud of her mother's aptitude in this line: she had been brought up in the faith that, whatever it cost, one must have a good cook, and be what Mrs. Bart called "decently dressed." Mrs. Bart's worst reproach to her husband was to ask him if he expected her to "live like a pig"; and his replying in the negative was always regarded as a justification for cabling to Paris for an extra dress or two, and telephoning to the jeweler that he might, after all, send home the turquoise bracelet which Mrs. Bart had looked at that morning.

Lily knew people who "lived like pigs," and their appearance and surroundings justified her mother's repugnance to that form of existence. They were mostly cousins, who inhabited dingy houses with engravings from Cole's Voyage of Life on the drawing-room walls, and slatternly parlor maids who said "I'll go and see" to visitors calling at an hour when all right-minded persons are conventionally if not actually out. The disgusting part of it was that many of these cousins were rich, so that Lily imbibed the idea that if people lived like pigs it was from choice, and through the lack of any proper standard of conduct. This gave her a sense of reflected superiority, and she did not need Mrs. Bart's comments on the family frumps and misers to foster her naturally lively taste for splendor.

Lily was nineteen when circumstances caused her to revise her view of the universe.

The previous year she had made a dazzling debut fringed by a heavy thunder-cloud of bills. The light of the debut still lingered on the horizon, but the cloud had thickened; and suddenly it broke. The suddenness added to the horror; and there were still times when Lily relived with painful vividness every detail of the day on which the blow fell. She and her mother had been seated at the luncheon-table, over the *chaufroix* and cold salmon of the previous night's dinner: it was one of Mrs. Bart's few economies to consume in private the expensive remnants of her hospitality. Lily was feeling the pleasant languor which is youth's penalty for dancing till dawn; but her mother, in spite of a few lines about the mouth, and under the yellow waves on her temples, was as alert, determined and high in color as if she had risen from an untroubled sleep.

In the center of the table, between the melting *marrons glacés* and candied cherries, a pyramid of American Beauties lifted their vigorous stems; they held their heads as high as Mrs. Bart, but their rose-color had turned to a dissipated purple, and Lily's sense of fitness was disturbed by their reappearance on the luncheon-table.

"I really think, Mother," she said reproachfully, "we might afford a few fresh flowers for luncheon. Just some jonquils or lilies-of-the-valley —"

Mrs. Bart stared. Her own fastidiousness had its eye fixed on the world, and she did not care how the luncheon-table looked when there was no one present at it but the family. But she smiled at her daughter's innocence.

"Lilies-of-the-valley," she said calmly, "cost two dollars a dozen at this season."

Lily was not impressed. She knew very little of the value of money.

"It would not take more than six dozen to fill that bowl," she argued.

"Six dozen what?" asked her father's voice in the doorway.

The two women looked up in surprise; though it was a Saturday, the sight of Mr. Bart at luncheon was an unwonted one. But neither his wife nor his daughter was sufficiently interested to ask an explanation.

Mr. Bart dropped into a chair, and sat gazing absently at the fragment of jellied salmon which the butler had placed before him.

"I was only saying," Lily began, "that I hate to see faded flowers at luncheon; and Mother says a bunch of lilies-of-the-valley would not cost more than twelve dollars. Mayn't I tell the florist to send a few every day?"

She leaned confidently toward her father: he seldom refused her any-thing, and Mrs. Bart had taught her to plead with him when her own entreaties failed.

Mr. Bart sat motionless, his gaze still fixed on the salmon, and his lower jaw dropped; he looked even paler than usual, and his thin hair lay in untidy streaks on his forehead. Suddenly he looked at his daughter and laughed. The laugh was so strange that Lily colored under it: she disliked being ridiculed, and her father seemed to see something ridiculous in the request. Perhaps he thought it foolish that she should trouble him about such a trifle.

"Twelve dollars—twelve dollars a day for flowers? Oh, certainly, my dear —give him an order for twelve hundred." He continued to laugh.

Mrs. Bart gave him a quick glance.

"You needn't wait, Poleworth—I will ring for you," she said to the butler.

The butler withdrew with an air of silent disapproval, leaving the re-mains of the *chaufroix* on the sideboard.

"What is the matter, Hudson? Are you ill?" said Mrs. Bart severely.

She had no tolerance for scenes which were not of her own making, and it was odious to her that her husband should make a show of himself before the servants.

"Are you ill?" she repeated.

"Ill?—No, I'm ruined," he said.

Lily made a frightened sound, and Mrs. Bart rose to her feet.

"Ruined—?" she cried; but controlling herself instantly, she turned a calm face to Lily.

"Shut the pantry door," she said.

Lily obeyed, and when she turned back into the room her father was sitting with both elbows on the table, the plate of salmon between them and his head bowed on his hands.

Mrs. Bart stood over him with a white face which made her hair unnaturally yellow. She looked at Lily as the latter approached: her look was terrible, but her voice was modulated to a ghastly cheerfullness.

"Your father is not well—he doesn't know what he is saying. It is nothing—but you had better go upstairs; and don't talk to the servants," she added.

Lily obeyed; she always obeyed when her mother spoke in that voice. She had not been deceived by Mrs. Bart's words: she knew at once that they were ruined. In the dark hours which followed, that awful fact overshadowed even her father's slow and difficult dying. To his wife he no longer counted: he had become extinct when he ceased to fulfill his purpose, and she sat at his side with the provisional air of a traveler who waits for a belated train to start. Lily's feelings were softer: she pitied him in a frightened ineffectual way. But the fact that he was for the most part unconscious, and that his attention, when she stole into the room, drifted away from her after a moment, made him even more of a stranger than in the nursery days when he had never come home till after dark. She seemed always to have seen him through a blur—first of sleepiness, then of distance and indifference—and now the fog had thickened till he was almost indistinguishable. If she could have performed any little services for him, or have exchanged with him a few of those affecting words which an extensive perusal of fiction had led her to connect with such occasions, the filial instinct might have stirred in her; but her pity, finding no active expression, remained in a state of spectatorship overshadowed by her mother's grim unflagging resentment. Every look and act of Mrs. Bart's seemed to say: "You are sorry for him now—but you will feel differently when you see what he has done to us."

It was a relief to Lily when her father died.

Then a long winter set in. There was a little money left, but to Mrs. Bart it seemed worse than nothing—the mere mockery of what she was entitled to. What was the use of living if one had to live like a pig? She sank into a kind of furious apathy, a state of inert anger against fate. Her faculty for "managing" deserted her, or she no longer took sufficient pride in it to exert it. It was well enough to "manage" when by so doing one could keep one's own carriage; but when one's best contrivance did not conceal the fact that one had to go on foot, the effort was no longer worth making.

Lily and her mother wandered from place to place, now paying long visits to relations whose housekeeping Mrs. Bart criticized, and who deplored the fact that she let Lily breakfast in bed when the girl had no prospects before her, and now vegetating in cheap continental refuges, where Mrs. Bart held herself fiercely aloof from the frugal tea-tables of her companions in misfortune. She was especially careful to avoid her old friends and the scenes of her former successes. To be poor seemed to her such a confession of failure that it amounted to disgrace; and she detected a note of condescension in the friendliest advances.

Only one thought consoled her, and that was the contemplation of Lily's beauty. She studied it with a kind of passion, as though it were some weapon she had slowly fashioned for her vengeance. It was the last asset in their fortunes, the nucleus around which their life was to be rebuilt. She watched it jealously, as though it were her own property and Lily its mere custodian; and she tried to instill into the latter a sense of the responsibility that such a charge involved. She followed in imagination the career of other beauties, pointing out to her daughter what might be achieved through such a gift, and dwelling on the awful warning of those who, in spite of it, had failed to get what they wanted: to Mrs. Bart, only stupidity could explain the lamentable denouement of some of her examples. She was not above the inconsistency of charging fate, rather than herself, with her own misfortunes; but she inveighed so acrimoniously against love-matches that Lily would have fancied her own marriage had been of that nature, had not Mrs. Bart frequently assured her that she had been "talked into it"—by whom, she never made clear.

Lily was duly impressed by the magnitude of her opportunities. The dinginess of her present life threw into enchanting relief the existence to which she felt herself entitled. To a less illuminated intelligence Mrs. Bart's counsels might have been dangerous; but Lily understood that beauty is only the raw material of conquest, and that to convert it into success other arts are required. She knew that to betray any sense of superiority was a subtler form of the stupidity her mother denounced, and it did not take her long to learn that a beauty needs more tact than the possessor of an average set of features.

Her ambitions were not as crude as Mrs. Bart's. It had been among that lady's grievances that her husband—in the early days, before he was too tired—had wasted his evenings in what she vaguely described as "reading poetry"; and among the effects packed off to auction after his death were a score or two of dingy volumes which had struggled for existence among the boots and medicine bottles of his dressing-room shelves. There was in Lily a vein of sentiment, perhaps transmitted from this source, which gave an idealizing touch to her most prosaic purposes. She liked to think of her beauty as a power for good, as giving her the opportunity to attain a position where she should make her influence felt in the vague diffusion of refinement and good taste. She was fond of pictures and flowers, and of sentimental fiction, and she could not help thinking that the possession of such tastes ennobled her desire for worldly advantages. She would not indeed have cared to marry a man who was merely rich: she was secretly ashamed of her mother's crude passion for money. Lily's preference would have been for an English nobleman with political ambitions and vast estates; or, for second choice, an Italian prince with a castle in the Apennines and an hereditary office in the Vatican. Lost causes had a romantic charm for her, and she liked to picture herself as standing aloof from the vulgar press of the Quirinal, and sacrificing her pleasure to the claims of an immemorial tradition. . . .

How long ago and how far off it all seemed! Those ambitions were hardly more futile and childish than the earlier ones which had centered about the possession of a French jointed doll with real hair. Was it only ten years since she had wavered in imagination between the English earl and the Italian prince? Relentlessly her mind traveled on over the dreary interval. . . .

After two years of hungry roaming Mrs. Bart had died—died of a deep disgust. She had hated dinginess, and it was her fate to be dingy. Her visions of a brilliant marriage for Lily had faded after the first year.

"People can't marry you if they don't see you—and how can they see you in these holes where we're stuck?" That was the burden of her lament; and her last adjuration to her daughter was to escape from dinginess if she could.

"Don't let it creep up on you and drag you down. Fight your way out of it somehow—you're young and can do it," she insisted.

She had died during one of their brief visits to New York, and there Lily at once became the center of a family council composed of the wealthy relatives whom she had been taught to despise for living like pigs. It may be that they had an inkling of the sentiments in which she had been brought up, for none of them manifested a very lively desire for her company; indeed, the question threatened to remain unsolved till Mrs. Peniston with a sigh announced: "I'll try her for a year."

Every one was surprised, but one and all concealed their surprise, lest Mrs. Peniston should be alarmed by it into reconsidering her decision.

Mrs. Peniston was Mr. Bart's widowed sister, and if she was by no means the richest of the family group, its other members nevertheless abounded in reasons why she was clearly destined by Providence to assume the charge of Lily. In the first place she was alone, and it would be charming for her to have a young companion. Then she sometimes traveled, and Lily's familiarity with foreign customs—deplored as a misfortune by her more conservative relatives—would at least enable her to act as a kind of courier. But as a matter of fact Mrs. Peniston had not been affected by these considerations. She had taken the girl simply because no one else would have her, and because she had the kind of moral *mauvaise honte* which makes the public display of selfishness difficult, though it does not interfere with its private indulgence. It would have been impossible for Mrs. Peniston to be heroic on a desert island, but with the eyes of her little world upon her she took a certain pleasure in her act.

She reaped the reward to which disinterestedness is entitled, and found an agreeable companion in her niece. She had expected to find Lily head-strong, critical and "foreign"—for even Mrs. Peniston, though she occasion-ally went abroad, had the family dread of foreignness—but the girl showed a pliancy which, to a more penetrating mind than her aunt's, might have been less reassuring than the open selfishness of youth. Misfortune had made Lily supple instead of hardening her, and a pliable substance is less easy to break than a stiff one.

Mrs. Peniston, however, did not suffer from her niece's adaptability. Lily had no intention of taking advantage of her aunt's good nature. She was in truth grateful for the refuge offered her: Mrs. Peniston's opulent interior was at least not externally dingy. But dinginess is a quality which assumes all manner of disguises; and Lily soon found that it was as latent in the expen-sive routine of her aunt's life as in the makeshift existence of a continental pension.

Mrs. Peniston was one of the episodical persons who form the padding of life. It was impossible to believe that she had herself ever been a focus of activities. The most vivid thing about her was the fact that her grand-mother had been a Van Alstyne. This connection with the well-fed and industrious stock of early New York revealed itself in the glacial neatness of Mrs. Peniston's drawing-room and in the excellence of her cuisine. She belonged to the class of old New Yorkers who have always lived well, dressed expensively, and done little else; and to these inherited obligations Mrs. Peniston faithfully conformed. She had always been a looker-on at life, and her mind resembled one of those little mirrors which her Dutch ances-tors were accustomed to affix to their upper windows, so that from the depths of an impenetrable domesticity they might see what was happening in the street.

Mrs. Peniston was the owner of a country-place in New Jersey, but she had never lived there since her husband's death—a remote event, which appeared to dwell in her memory chiefly as a dividing point in the personal reminiscences that formed the staple of her conversation. She was a woman who remembered dates with intensity, and could tell at a moment's notice whether the drawing-room curtains had been renewed before or after Mr. Peniston's last illness.

Mrs. Peniston thought the country lonely and trees damp, and cherished a vague fear of meeting a bull. To guard against such contingencies she frequented the more populous watering-places, where she installed herself impersonally in a hired house and looked on at life through the matting screen of her verandah. In the care of such a guardian, it soon became clear to Lily that she was to enjoy only the material advantages of good food and expensive clothing; and, though far from underrating these, she would gladly have exchanged them for what Mrs. Bart had taught her to regard as opportunities. She sighed to think what her mother's fierce energies would have accomplished, had they been coupled with Mrs. Peniston's resources.

Lily had abundant energy of her own, but it was restricted by the necessity of adapting herself to her aunt's habits. She saw that at all costs she must keep Mrs. Peniston's favor till, as Mrs. Bart would have phrased it, she could stand on her own legs. Lily had no mind for the vagabond life of the poor relation, and to adapt herself to Mrs. Peniston she had, to some degree, to assume that lady's passive attitude. She had fancied at first that it would be easy to draw her aunt into the whirl of her own activities, but there was a static force in Mrs. Peniston against which her niece's efforts spent themselves in vain. To attempt to bring her into active relation with life was like tugging at a piece of furniture which has been screwed to the floor. She did not, indeed, expect Lily to remain equally immovable: she had all the American guardian's indulgence for the volatility of youth. She had indulgence also for certain other habits of her niece's. It seemed to her natural that Lily should spend all her money on dress, and she supplemented the girl's scanty income by occasional "handsome presents" meant to be applied to the same purpose. Lily, who was intensely practical, would have preferred a fixed allowance; but Mrs. Peniston liked the periodical recurrence of gratitude evoked by unexpected checks, and was perhaps shrewd enough to perceive that such a method of giving kept alive in her niece a salutary sense of dependence.

Beyond this, Mrs. Peniston had not felt called upon to do anything for her charge: she had simply stood aside and let her take the field. Lily had taken it, at first with the confidence of assured possessorship, then with gradually narrowing demands, till now she found herself actually struggling for a foothold on the broad space which had once seemed her own for the asking. How it happened she did not yet know. Sometimes she thought it was because Mrs. Peniston had been too passive, and again she feared it was because she herself had not been passive enough. Had she shown an undue eagerness for victory? Had she lacked patience, pliancy and dissimulation? Whether she charged herself with these faults or absolved herself from them, made no difference in the sum-total of her failure. Younger and plainer girls had been married off by dozens, and she was nine-and-twenty, and still Miss Bart.

She was beginning to have fits of angry rebellion against fate, when she longed to drop out of the race and make an independent life for herself. But what manner of life would it be? She had barely enough money to pay her dressmakers' bills and her gambling debts; and none of the desultory interests which she dignified with the name of tastes was pronounced enough to enable her to live contentedly in obscurity. Ah, no—she was too intelligent not to be honest with herself. She knew that she hated dinginess as much as her mother had hated it, and to her last breath she meant to fight against it, dragging herself up again and again above its flood till she gained the bright pinnacles of success which presented such a slippery surface to her clutch.

4

THE next morning, on her breakfast tray, Miss Bart found a note from her hostess.

"Dearest Lily," it ran, "if it is not too much of a bore to be down by ten, will you come to my sitting-room to help me with some tiresome things?"

Lily tossed aside the note and subsided on her pillows with a sigh. It *was* a bore to be down by ten—an hour regarded at Bellomont as vaguely synchronous with sunrise—and she knew too well the nature of the tiresome things in question. Miss Pragg, the secretary, had been called away, and there would be notes and dinner-cards to write, lost addresses to hunt up, and other social drudgery to perform. It was understood that Miss Bart should fill the gap in such emergencies, and she usually recognized the obligation without a murmur.

Today, however, it renewed the sense of servitude which the previous night's review of her checkbook had produced. Everything in her surroundings ministered to feelings of ease and amenity. The windows stood open to the sparkling freshness of the September morning, and between the yellow boughs she caught a perspective of hedges and parterres leading by degrees of lessening formality to the free undulations of the park. Her maid had kindled a little fire on the hearth, and it contended cheerfully with the sunlight which slanted across the moss-green carpet and caressed the curved sides of an old marquetry desk. Near the bed stood a table holding her breakfast tray, with its harmonious porcelain and silver, a handful of violets in a slender glass, and the morning paper folded beneath her letters. There was nothing new to Lily in these tokens of a studied luxury; but, though they formed a part of her atmosphere, she never lost her sensitiveness to their charm. Mere display left her with a sense of superior distinction; but she felt an affinity to all the subtler manifestations of wealth.

Mrs. Trenor's summons, however, suddenly recalled her state of dependence, and she rose and dressed in a mood of irritability that she was usually too prudent to indulge. She knew that such emotions leave lines on the face as well as in the character, and she had meant to take warning by the little creases which her midnight survey had revealed.

The matter-of-course tone of Mrs. Trenor's greeting deepened her irritation. If one did drag one's self out of bed at such an hour, and come down fresh and radiant to the monotony of note-writing, some special recognition of the sacrifice seemed fitting. But Mrs. Trenor's tone showed no consciousness of the fact.

"Oh, Lily, that's nice of you," she merely sighed across the chaos of letters, bills and other domestic documents which gave an incongruously commercial touch to the slender elegance of her writing-table.

"There are such lots of horrors this morning," she added, clearing a space in the center of the confusion and rising to yield her seat to Miss Bart.

Mrs. Trenor was a tall fair woman, whose height just saved her from redundancy. Her rosy blondness had survived some forty years of futile activity without showing much trace of ill-usage except in a diminished play of feature. It was difficult to define her beyond saying that she seemed to exist only as a hostess, not so much from any exaggerated instinct of hospitality as because she could not sustain life except in a crowd. The collective nature of her interests exempted her from the ordinary rivalries of her sex, and she knew no more personal emotion than that of hatred for the woman who presumed to give bigger dinners or have more amusing house-parties than herself. As her social talents, backed by Mr. Trenor's bank account, almost always assured her ultimate triumph in such competitions, success had developed in her an unscrupulous good nature toward the rest of her sex, and in Miss Bart's utilitarian classification of her friends. Mrs. Trenor ranked as the woman who was least likely to "go back" on her.

"It was simply inhuman of Pragg to go off now," Mrs. Trenor declared, as her friend seated herself at the desk. "She says her sister is going to have a baby—as if that were anything to having a house-party! I'm sure I shall get most horribly mixed up and there will be some awful rows. When I was down at Tuxedo I asked a lot of people for next week, and I've mislaid the list and can't remember who is coming. And this week is going to be a horrid failure too—and Gwen Van Osburgh will go back and tell her mother how bored people were. I didn't mean to ask the Wetheralls—that was a blunder of Gus's. They disapprove of Carry Fisher, you know. As if one could help having Carry Fisher! It *was* foolish of her to get that second divorce—Carry always overdoes things—but she said the only way to get a penny out of Fisher was to divorce him and make him pay alimony. And poor Carry has to consider every dollar. It's really absurd of Alice Wetherall to make such a fuss about meeting her, when one thinks of what society is coming to. Someone said the other day that there was a divorce and a case of appendicitis in every family one knows. Besides, Carry is the only person who can keep Gus in a good humor when we have bores in the house. Have you noticed that *all* the husbands like her? All, I mean, except her own. It's rather clever of her to have made a specialty of devoting herself to dull people—the field is such a large one, and she has it practically to herself. She finds compensations, no doubt—I know she borrows money of Gus—but then I'd *pay* her to keep him in a good humor, so I can't complain, after all."

Mrs. Trenor paused to enjoy the spectacle of Miss Bart's efforts to un-ravel her tangled correspondence.

"But it isn't only the Wetheralls and Carry," she resumed, with a fresh note of lament. "The truth is, I'm awfully disappointed in Lady Cressida Raith."

"Disappointed? Hadn't you known her before?"

"Mercy, no—never saw her till yesterday. Lady Skiddaw sent her over with letters to the Van Osburghs, and I heard that Maria Van Osburgh was asking a big party to meet her this week, so I thought it would be fun to get her away, and Jack Stepney, who knew her in India, managed it for me. Maria was furious, and actually had the impudence to make Gwen invite herself here, so that they shouldn't be *quite* out of it—if I'd known what Lady Cressida was like, they could have had her and welcome! But I thought any friend of the Skiddaws' was sure to be amusing. You remember what fun Lady Skiddaw was? There were times when I simply had to send the girls out of the room. Besides, Lady Cressida is the duchess of Beltshire's sister, and I naturally supposed she was the same sort; but you never can tell in those English families. They are so big that there's room for all kinds, and it turns out that Lady Cressida is the moral one—married a clergyman and does missionary work in the East End. Think of my taking such a lot of trouble about a clergyman's wife, who wears Indian jewelry and botanizes! She made Gus take her all through the glass-houses yesterday, and bothered him to death by asking him the names of the plants. Fancy treating Gus as if he were the gardener!"

Mrs. Trenor brought this out in a crescendo of indignation.

"Oh, well, perhaps Lady Cressida will reconcile the Wetheralls to meet-ing Carry Fisher," said Miss Bart pacifically.

"I'm sure I hope so! But she is boring all the men horribly, and if she takes to distributing tracts, as I hear she does, it will be too depressing. The worst of it is that she would have been so useful at the right time. You know we have to have the bishop once a year, and she would have given just the right tone to things. I always have horrid luck about the bishop's visits," added Mrs. Trenor, whose present misery was being fed by a rapidly rising tide of reminiscence. "Last year, when he came, Gus forgot all about his being here, and brought home the Ned Wintons and the Farleys—five di-vorces and six sets of children between them!"

"When is Lady Cressida going?" Lily inquired.

Mrs. Trenor cast up her eyes in despair. "My dear, if one only knew! I was in such a hurry to get her away from Maria that I actually forgot to name a date, and Gus says she told someone she meant to stop here all winter."

"To stop here? In this house?"

"Don't be silly—in America. But if no one else asks her—you know they *never* go to hotels."

"Perhaps Gus only said it to frighten you."

"No—I heard her tell Bertha Dorset that she had six months to put in while her husband was taking the cure in the Engadine. You should have seen Bertha look vacant! But it's no joke, you know—if she stays here all the autumn she'll spoil everything, and Maria Van Osburgh will simply exult."

At this affecting vision Mrs. Trenor's voice trembled with self-pity.

"Oh, Judy—as if anyone were ever bored at Bellomont!" Miss Bart tactfully protested. "You know perfectly well that, if Mrs. Van Osburgh were to get all the right people and leave you with all the wrong ones, you'd manage to make things go off, and she wouldn't."

Such an assurance would usually have restored Mrs. Trenor's complacency; but on this occasion it did not chase the cloud from her brow.

"It isn't only Lady Cressida," she lamented. "Everything has gone wrong this week. I can see that Bertha Dorset is furious with me."

"Furious with you? Why?"

"Because I told her that Lawrence Selden was coming; but he wouldn't, after all, and she's quite unreasonable enough to think it's my fault."

Miss Bart put down her pen and sat absently gazing at the note she had begun.

"I thought that was all over," she said.

"So it is, on his side. And of course Bertha hasn't been idle since. But I fancy she's out of a job just at present—and someone gave me a hint that I had better ask Lawrence. Well, I *did* ask him—but I couldn't make him come; and now I suppose she'll take it out of me by being perfectly nasty to everyone else."

"Oh, she may take it out of *him* by being perfectly charming—to someone else."

Mrs. Trenor shook her head dolefully. "She knows he wouldn't mind. And who else is there? Alice Wetherall won't let Lucius out of her sight. Ned Silverton can't take his eyes off Carry Fisher—poor boy! Gus is bored by Bertha, Jack Stepney knows her too well—and—well, to be sure, there's Percy Gryce!"

She sat up smiling at the thought.

Miss Bart's countenance did not reflect the smile.

"Oh, she and Mr. Gryce would not be likely to hit it off."

"You mean that she'd shock him and he'd bore her? Well, that's not such a bad beginning, you know. But I hope she won't take it into her head to be nice to him, for I asked him here on purpose for you."

Lily laughed. "*Merci du compliment!* I should certainly have no show against Bertha."

"Do you think I am uncomplimentary? I'm not really, you know. Everyone knows you're a thousand times handsomer and cleverer than Bertha;

but then you're not nasty. And for always getting what she wants in the long run, commend me to a nasty woman."

Miss Bart stared in affected reproval. "I thought you were so fond of Bertha."

"Oh, I am—it's much safer to be fond of dangerous people. But she *is* dangerous—and if I ever saw her up to mischief it's now. I can tell by poor George's manner. That man is a perfect barometer—he always knows when Bertha is going to —"

"To fall?" Miss Bart suggested.

"Don't be shocking! You know he believes in her still. And, of course, I don't say there's any real harm in Bertha. Only she delights in making people miserable, and especially poor George."

"Well, he seems cut out for the part—I don't wonder she likes more cheerful companionship."

"Oh, George is not as dismal as you think. If Bertha didn't worry him he would be quite different. Or if she'd leave him alone, and let him arrange his life as he pleases. But she doesn't dare lose her hold of him on account of the money, and so when *he* isn't jealous she pretends to be."

Miss Bart went on writing in silence, and her hostess sat following her train of thought with frowning intensity.

"Do you know," she exclaimed after a long pause, "I believe I'll call up Lawrence on the telephone and tell him he simply *must* come?"

"Oh, don't," said Lily, with a quick suffusion of color. The blush surprised her almost as much as it did her hostess, who, though not commonly observant of facial changes, sat staring at her with puzzled eyes.

"Good gracious, Lily, how handsome you are! Why? Do you dislike him so much?"

"Not at all; I like him. But if you are actuated by the benevolent intention of protecting me from Bertha—I don't think I need your protection."

Mrs. Trenor sat up with an exclamation. "Lily!—*Percy?* Do you mean to say you've actually done it?"

Miss Bart smiled. "I only mean to say that Mr. Gryce and I are getting to be very good friends."

"H'm—I see." Mrs. Trenor fixed a rapt eye upon her. "You know, they say he has eight hundred thousand a year—and spends nothing, except on some rubbishy old books. And his mother has heart disease and will leave him a lot more. *Oh, Lily, do go slowly,*" her friend adjured her.

Miss Bart continued to smile without annoyance. "I shouldn't, for instance," she remarked, "be in any haste to tell him that he had a lot of rubbishy old books."

"No, of course not; I know you're wonderful about getting up people's subjects. But he's horribly shy, and easily shocked, and—and —"

"Why don't you say it, Judy? I have the reputation of being on the hunt for a rich husband?"

"Oh, I don't mean that; he wouldn't believe it of you—at first," said Mrs. Trenor, with candid shrewdness. "But you know things are rather lively here at times—I must give Jack and Gus a hint—and if he thought you were what his mother would call fast—oh, well, you know what I mean. Don't wear your scarlet crepe de Chine for dinner, and don't smoke if you can help it, Lily, dear!"

Lily pushed aside her finished work with a dry smile. "You're very kind, Judy. I'll lock up my cigarettes and wear that last year's dress you sent me this morning. And if you are really interested in my career, perhaps you'll be kind enough not to ask me to play bridge again this evening."

"Bridge? Does he mind bridge, too? Oh, Lily, what an awful life you'll lead! But, of course, I won't—why didn't you give me a hint last night? There's nothing I wouldn't do, you poor duck, to see you happy!"

And Mrs. Trenor, glowing with her sex's eagerness to smooth the course of true love, enveloped Lily in a long embrace.

"You're quite sure," she added solicitously, as the latter extricated herself, "that you wouldn't like me to telephone for Lawrence Selden?"

"Quite sure," said Lily.

The next three days demonstrated to her own complete satisfaction Miss Bart's ability to manage her affairs without extraneous aid.

As she sat, on the Saturday afternoon, on the terrace at Bellomont, she smiled at Mrs. Trenor's fear that she might go too fast. If such a warning had ever been needful, the years had taught her a salutary lesson, and she flattered herself that she now knew how to adapt her pace to the object of pursuit. In the case of Mr. Gryce she had found it well to flutter ahead, losing herself elusively and luring him on from depth to depth of unconscious intimacy. The surrounding atmosphere was propitious to this scheme of courtship. Mrs. Trenor, true to her word, had shown no signs of expecting Lily at the bridge-table, and had even hinted to the other cardplayers that they were to betray no surprise at her unwonted defection. In consequence of this hint, Lily found herself the center of that feminine solicitude which envelops a young woman in the mating season. A solitude was tacitly created for her in the crowded existence of Bellomont, and her friends could not have shown a greater readiness for self-effacement had her wooing been adorned with all the attributes of romance. In Lily's set this conduct implied a sympathetic comprehension of her motives, and Mr. Gryce rose in her esteem as she saw the consideration he inspired.

The terrace at Bellomont on a September afternoon was a spot propitious to sentimental musings, and as Miss Bart stood leaning against the balustrade above the sunken garden, at a little distance from the animated group about the tea-table, she might have been lost in the mazes of an inarticulate happiness. In reality, her thoughts were finding definite utterance in the tranquil recapitulation of the blessings in store for her. From where she stood she could see them embodied in the form of Mr. Gryce, who, in a light overcoat and muffler, sat somewhat nervously on the edge of his chair, while Carry Fisher, with all the energy of eye and gesture with which nature and art had combined to endow her, pressed on him the duty of taking part in the task of municipal reform.

Mrs. Fisher's latest hobby was municipal reform. It had been preceded by an equal zeal for socialism, which had in turn replaced an energetic advocacy of Christian Science. Mrs. Fisher was small, fiery and dramatic; and her hands and eyes were admirable instruments in the service of whatever cause she happened to espouse. She had, however, the fault common to enthusiasts of ignoring any slackness of response on the part of her hearers, and Lily was amused by her unconsciousness of the resistance displayed in every angle of Mr. Gryce's attitude. Lily herself knew that his mind was divided between the dread of catching cold if he remained out of doors too long at that hour, and the fear that, if he retreated to the house, Mrs. Fisher might follow him up with a paper to be signed. Mr. Gryce had a constitutional dislike to what he called "committing himself," and tenderly as he cherished his health, he evidently concluded that it was safer to stay out of reach of pen and ink till chance released him from Mrs. Fisher's toils. Meanwhile he cast agonized glances in the direction of Miss Bart, whose only response was to sink into an attitude of more graceful abstraction. She had learned the value of contrast in throwing her charms into relief, and was fully aware of the extent to which Mrs. Fisher's volubility was enhancing her own repose.

She was roused from her musings by the approach of her cousin Jack Stepney who, at Gwen Van Osburgh's side, was returning across the garden from the tennis court.

The couple in question were engaged in the same kind of romance in which Lily figured, and the latter felt a certain annoyance in contemplating what seemed to her a caricature of her own situation. Miss Van Osburgh was a large girl with flat surfaces and no highlights: Jack Stepney had once said of her that she was as reliable as roast mutton. His own taste was in the line of less solid and more highly seasoned diet; but hunger makes any fare palatable, and there had been times when Mr. Stepney had been reduced to a crust.

Lily considered with interest the expression of their faces: the girl's turned toward her companion's like an empty plate held up to be filled, while the man lounging at her side already betrayed the encroaching boredom which would presently crack the thin veneer of his smile.

"How impatient men are!" Lily reflected. "All Jack has to do to get everything he wants is to keep quiet and let that girl marry him; whereas I have to calculate and contrive, and retreat and advance, as if I were going through an intricate dance, where one misstep would throw me hopelessly out of time."

As they drew nearer she was whimsically struck by a kind of family likeness between Miss Van Osburgh and Percy Gryce. There was no resemblance of feature. Gryce was handsome in a didactic way—he looked like a clever pupil's drawing from a plaster-cast—while Gwen's countenance had no more modeling than a face painted on a toy balloon. But the deeper affinity was unmistakable: the two had the same prejudices and ideals, and the same quality of making other standards nonexistent by ignoring them. This attribute was common to most of Lily's set: they had a force of negation which eliminated everything beyond their own range of perception. Gryce and Miss Van Osburgh were, in short, made for each other by every law of moral and physical correspondence. "Yet they wouldn't look at each other," Lily mused, "they never do. Each of them wants a creature of a different race, of Jack's race and mine, with all sorts of intuitions, sensations and perceptions that they don't even guess the existence of. And they always get what they want."

She stood talking with her cousin and Miss Van Osburgh, till a slight cloud on the latter's brow advised her that even cousinly amenities were subject to suspicion, and Miss Bart, mindful of the necessity of not exciting enmities at this crucial point of her career, dropped aside while the happy couple proceeded toward the tea-table.

Seating herself on the upper step of the terrace, Lily leaned her head against the honeysuckles wreathing the balustrade. The fragrance of the late blossoms seemed an emanation of the tranquil scene, a landscape tutored to the last degree of rural elegance. In the foreground glowed the warm tints of the gardens. Beyond the lawn, with its pyramidal pale-gold maples and velvety firs, sloped pastures dotted with cattle; and through a long glade the river widened like a lake under the silver light of September. Lily did not want to join the circle about the tea-table. They represented the future she had chosen, and she was content with it, but in no haste to anticipate its joys. The certainty that she could marry Percy Gryce when she pleased had lifted a heavy load from her mind, and her money troubles were too recent for their removal not to leave a sense of relief which a less discerning intelligence might have taken for happiness. Her vulgar cares were at an end. She would be able to arrange her life as she pleased, to soar into that empyrean of security where creditors cannot penetrate. She would have smarter gowns than Judy Trenor, and far, far more jewels than Bertha Dorset. She would be free forever from the shifts, the expedients, the humiliations of the relatively poor. Instead of having to flatter, she would be flattered; instead of being grateful, she would receive thanks. There were old scores she could pay off as well as old benefits she could return. And she had no doubts as to the extent of her power. She knew that Mr. Gryce was of the small chary type most inaccessible to impulses and emotions. He had the kind of character in which prudence is a vice, and good advice the most dangerous nourishment. But Lily had known the species before: she was aware that such a guarded nature must find one huge outlet of egoism, and she determined to be to him what his Americana had hitherto been: the one possession in which he took sufficient pride to spend money on it. She knew that this generosity to self is one of the forms of meanness, and she resolved so to identify herself with her husband's vanity that to gratify her wishes would be to him the most exquisite form of self-indulgence. The system might at first necessitate a resort to some of the very shifts and expedients from which she intended it should free her; but she felt sure that in a short time she would be able to play the game in her own way. How should she have distrusted her powers? Her beauty itself was not the mere ephemeral possession it might have been in the hands of inexperience: her skill in enhancing it, the care she took of it, the use she made of it, seemed to give it a kind of permanence. She felt she could trust it to carry her through to the end.

And the end, on the whole, was worthwhile. Life was not the mockery she had thought it three days ago. There was room for her, after all, in this crowded selfish world of pleasure whence, so short a time since, her poverty had seemed to exclude her. These people whom she had ridiculed and yet envied were glad to make a place for her in the charmed circle about which all her desires revolved. They were not as brutal and self-engrossed as she had fancied—or rather, since it would no longer be necessary to flatter and humor them, that side of their nature became less conspicuous. Society is a revolving body which is apt to be judged according to its place in each man's heaven; and at present it was turning its illuminated face to Lily.

In the rosy glow it diffused her companions seemed full of amiable qualities. She liked their elegance, their lightness, their lack of emphasis: even the self-assurance which at times was so like obtuseness now seemed the natural sin of social ascendency. They were lords of the only world she cared for, and they were ready to admit her to their ranks and let her lord it with them. Already she felt within her a stealing allegiance to their standards, an acceptance of their limitations, a disbelief in the things they did not believe in, a contemptuous pity for the people who were not able to live as they lived.

The early sunset was slanting far across the park. Through the boughs of the long avenue beyond the gardens she caught the flash of wheels, and divined that more visitors were approaching. There was a movement behind her, a scattering of steps and voices: it was evident that the party about the tea-table was breaking up. Presently she heard a tread behind her on the terrace. She supposed that Mr. Gryce had at last found means to escape from his predicament, and she smiled at the significance of his coming to join her instead of beating an instant retreat to the fireside.

She turned to give him the welcome which such gallantry deserved; but her greeting wavered into a blush of wonder, for the man who had approached her was Lawrence Selden.

"You see, I came after all," he said; but before she had time to answer, Mrs. Dorset, breaking away from a lifeless colloquy with her host, had stepped between them with a little gesture of appropriation.

5

THE observance of Sunday at Bellomont was chiefly marked by the punctual appearance of the smart omnibus destined to convey the household to the little church at the gates. Whether anyone got into the omnibus or not was a matter of secondary importance, since by standing there it not only bore witness to the orthodox intentions of the family, but made Mrs. Trenor feel, when she finally heard it drive away, that she had somehow vicariously made use of it.

It was Mrs. Trenor's theory that her daughters actually did go to church every Sunday; but their French governess's convictions calling her to the rival fane, and the fatigues of the week keeping their mother in her room till luncheon, there was seldom anyone present to verify the fact. Now and then, in a spasmodic burst of virtue—when the house had been too uproarious overnight—Gus Trenor forced his genial bulk into a tight frock-coat and routed his daughters from their slumbers; but habitually, as Lily explained to Mr. Gryce, this parental duty was forgotten till the church bells were ringing across the park, and the omnibus had driven away empty.

Lily had hinted to Mr. Gryce that this neglect of religious observances was repugnant to her early traditions, and that during her visits to Bellomont she regularly accompanied Muriel and Hilda to church. This tallied with the assurance, also confidentially imparted, that, never having played bridge before, she had been "dragged into it" on the night of her arrival, and had lost an appalling amount of money in consequence of her ignorance of the game and of the rules of betting. Mr. Gryce was undoubtedly enjoying Bellomont. He liked the ease and glitter of the life, and the luster conferred on him by being a member of this group of rich and conspicuous people. But he thought it a very materialistic society; there were times when he was frightened by the talk of the men and the looks of the ladies, and he was glad to find that Miss Bart, for all her ease and self-possession, was not at home in so ambiguous an atmosphere. For this reason he had been especially pleased to learn that she would, as usual, attend the young Trenors to church on Sunday morning; and as he paced the gravel sweep before the door, his light overcoat on his arm and his prayer-book in one carefully gloved hand, he reflected agreeably on the strength of character which kept her true to her early training in surroundings so subversive to religious principles.

For a long time Mr. Gryce and the omnibus had the gravel sweep to themselves; but, far from regretting this deplorable indifference on the part of the other guests, he found himself nourishing the hope that Miss Bart might be unaccompanied. The precious minutes were flying, however; the big chestnuts pawed the ground and flecked their impatient sides with foam; the coachman seemed to be slowly petrifying on the box, and the groom on the doorstep; and still the lady did not come. Suddenly, however, there was a sound of voices and a rustle of skirts in the doorway, and Mr. Gryce, restoring his watch to his pocket, turned with a nervous start; but it was only to find himself handing Mrs. Wetherall into the carriage.

The Wetheralls always went to church. They belonged to the vast group of human automata who go through life without neglecting to perform a single one of the gestures executed by the surrounding puppets. It is true that the Bellomont puppets did not go to church; but others equally important did—and Mr. and Mrs. Wetherall's circle was so large that God was included in their visiting list. They appeared, therefore, punctual and re-signed, with the air of people bound for a dull "At Home," and after them Hilda and Muriel straggled, yawning and pinning each other's veils and ribbons as they came. They had promised Lily to go to church with her, they declared, and Lily was such a dear old duck that they didn't mind doing it to please her, though they couldn't fancy what had put the idea in her head, and though for their own part they would much rather have played lawn tennis with Jack and Gwen, if she hadn't told them she was coming. The Misses Trenor were followed by Lady Cressida Raith, a weather-beaten person in Liberty silk and ethnological trinkets, who, on seeing the omnibus, expressed her surprise that they were not to walk across the park; but at Mrs. Wetherall's horrified protest that the church was a mile away, her ladyship, after a glance at the height of the other's heels, acquiesced in the necessity of driving, and poor Mr. Gryce found himself rolling off between four ladies for whose spiritual welfare he felt not the least concern.

It might have afforded him some consolation could he have known that Miss Bart had really meant to go to church. She had even risen earlier than usual in the execution of her purpose. She had an idea that the sight of her in a gray gown of devotional cut, with her famous lashes drooped above a prayer-book, would put the finishing touch to Mr. Gryce's subjugation, and render inevitable a certain incident which she had resolved should form a part of the walk they were to take together after luncheon. Her intentions, in short, had never been more definite; but poor Lily, for all the hard glaze of her exterior, was inwardly as malleable as wax. Her faculty for adapting herself, for entering into other people's feelings, if it served her now and then in small contingencies, hampered her in the decisive moments of life.

She was like a water-plant in the flux of the tides, and today the whole current of her mood was carrying her toward Lawrence Selden. Why had he come? Was it to see herself or Bertha Dorset? It was the last question which, at that moment, should have engaged her. She might better have contented herself with thinking that he had simply responded to the despairing summons of his hostess, anxious to interpose him between herself and the ill-humor of Mrs. Dorset. But Lily had not rested till she learned from Mrs. Trenor that Selden had come of his own accord.

"He didn't even wire me—he just happened to find the trap at the station. Perhaps it's not over with Bertha after all," Mrs. Trenor musingly concluded; and went away to arrange her dinner-cards accordingly.

Perhaps it was not, Lily reflected; but it should be soon, unless she had lost her cunning. If Selden had come at Mrs. Dorset's call, it was at her own that he would stay. So much the previous evening had told her. Mrs. Trenor, true to her simple principle of making her married friends happy, had placed Selden and Mrs. Dorset next to each other at dinner; but, in obedience to the time-honored traditions of the matchmaker, she had separated Lily and Mr. Gryce, sending in the former with George Dorset, while Mr. Gryce was coupled with Gwen Van Osburgh.

George Dorset's talk did not interfere with the range of his neighbor's thoughts. He was a mournful dyspeptic, intent on finding out the deleterious ingredients of every dish and diverted from this care only by the sound of his wife's voice. On this occasion, however, Mrs. Dorset took no part in the general conversation. She sat talking in low murmurs with Selden, and turning a contemptuous and denuded shoulder toward her host, who, far from resenting his exclusion, plunged into the excesses of the menu with the joyous irresponsibility of a free man. To Mr. Dorset, however, his wife's attitude was a subject of such evident concern that, when he was not scraping the sauce from his fish, or scooping the moist breadcrumbs from the interior of his roll, he sat straining his thin neck for a glimpse of her between the lights.

Mrs. Trenor, as it chanced, had placed the husband and wife on opposite sides of the table, and Lily was therefore able to observe Mrs. Dorset also, and by carrying her glance a few feet farther, to set up a rapid comparison between Lawrence Selden and Mr. Gryce. It was that comparison which was her undoing. Why else had she suddenly grown interested in Selden? She had known him for eight years or more: ever since her return to America he had formed a part of her background. She had always been glad to sit next to him at dinner, had found him more agreeable than most men, and had vaguely wished that he possessed the other qualities needful to fix her attention; but till now she had been too busy with her own affairs to regard him as more than one of the pleasant accessories of life. Miss Bart was a keen reader of her own heart, and she saw that her sudden preoccupation with Selden was due to the fact that his presence shed a new light on her surroundings. Not that he was notably brilliant or exceptional; in his own profession he was surpassed by more than one man who had bored Lily through many a weary dinner. It was rather that he had preserved a certain social detachment, a happy air of viewing the show objectively, of having points of contact outside the great gilt cage in which they were all huddled for the mob to gape at. How alluring the world outside the cage appeared to Lily, as she heard its door clang on her! In reality, as she knew, the door never clanged: it stood always open; but most of the captives were like flies in a bottle, and having once flown in, could never regain their freedom. It was Selden's distinction that he had never forgotten the way out.

That was the secret of his way of readjusting her vision. Lily, turning her eyes from him, found herself scanning her little world through his retina: it was as though the pink lamps had been shut off and the dusty daylight let in. She looked down the long table, studying its occupants one by one, from Gus Trenor, with his heavy carnivorous head sunk between his shoulders, as he preyed on a jellied plover, to his wife, at the opposite end of the long bank of orchids, suggestive, with her glaring good looks, of a jeweler's window lit by electricity. And between the two, what a long stretch of vacuity! How dreary and trivial these people were! Lily reviewed them with a scornful impatience: Carry Fisher, with her shoulders, her eyes, her divorces, her general air of embodying a "spicy paragraph"; young Silverton, who had meant to live on proofreading and write an epic, and who now lived on his friends and had become critical of truffles; Alice Wetherall, an animated visiting list, whose most fervid convictions turned on the wording of invitations and the engraving of dinner-cards; Wetherall, with his perpetual nervous nod of acquiescence, his air of agreeing with people before he knew what they were saying; Jack Stepney, with his confident smile and anxious eyes, half way between the sheriff and an heiress; Gwen Van Osburgh, with all the guileless confidence of a young girl who has always been told that there is no one richer than her father.

Lily smiled at her classification of her friends. How different they had seemed to her a few hours ago! Then they had symbolized what she was gaining, now they stood for what she was giving up. That very afternoon they had seemed full of brilliant qualities; now she saw that they were merely dull in a loud way. Under the glitter of their opportunities she saw the poverty of their achievement. It was not that she wanted them to be more disinterested; but she would have liked them to be more picturesque. And she had a shamed recollection of the way in which, a few hours since, she had felt the centripetal force of their standards. She closed her eyes an instant, and the vacuous routine of the life she had chosen stretched before her like a long white road without dip or turning: it was true she was to roll over it in a carriage instead of trudging it on foot, but sometimes the pedestrian enjoys the diversion of a short cut which is denied to those on wheels.

She was roused by a chuckle which Mr. Dorset seemed to eject from the depths of his lean throat.

"I say, do look at her," he exclaimed, turning to Miss Bart with lugubrious merriment—"I beg your pardon, but do just look at my wife making a fool of that poor devil over there! One would really suppose she was gone on him—and it's all the other way round, I assure you."

Thus adjured, Lily turned her eyes on the spectacle which was affording Mr. Dorset such legitimate mirth. It certainly appeared, as he said, that Mrs. Dorset was the more active participant in the scene: her neighbor seemed to receive her advances with a temperate zest which did not distract him from his dinner. The sight restored Lily's good humor, and knowing the peculiar disguise which Mr. Dorset's marital fears assumed, she asked gaily: "Aren't you horribly jealous of her?"

Dorset greeted the sally with delight. "Oh, abominably—you've just hit it—keeps me awake at night. The doctors tell me that's what has knocked my digestion out—being so infernally jealous of her. I can't eat a mouthful of this stuff, you know," he added suddenly, pushing back his plate with a clouded countenance; and Lily, unfailingly adaptable, accorded her radiant attention to his prolonged denunciation of other people's cooks, with a supplementary tirade on the toxic qualities of melted butter.

It was not often that he found so ready an ear; and, being a man as well as a dyspeptic, it may be that as he poured his grievances into it he was not insensible to its rosy symmetry. At any rate he engaged Lily so long that the sweets were being handed when she caught a phrase on her other side, where Miss Corby, the comic woman of the company, was bantering Jack Stepney on his approaching engagement. Miss Corby's role was jocularity: she always entered the conversation with a handspring.

"And, of course, you'll have Sim Rosedale as best man!" Lily heard her fling out as the climax of her prognostications; and Stepney responded, as if struck: "Jove, that's an idea. What a thumping present I'd get out of him!"

Sim Rosedale! The name, made more odious by its diminutive, obtruded itself on Lily's thoughts like a leer. It stood for one of the many hated possibilities hovering on the edge of life. If she did not marry Percy Gryce, the day might come when she would have to be civil to such men as Rosedale. *If she did not marry him?* But she meant to marry him—she was sure of him and sure of herself. She drew back with a shiver from the pleasant paths in which her thoughts had been straying, and set her feet once more in the middle of the long white road. . . . When she went upstairs that night she found that the late post had brought her a fresh batch of bills. Mrs. Peniston, who was a conscientious woman, had forwarded them all to Bellomont.

Miss Bart, accordingly, rose the next morning with the most earnest conviction that it was her duty to go to church. She tore herself betimes from the lingering enjoyment of her breakfast-tray, rang to have her gray gown laid out, and dispatched her maid to borrow a prayer-book from Mrs. Trenor.

But her course was too purely reasonable not to contain the germs of rebellion. No sooner were her preparations made than they roused a smothered sense of resistance. A small spark was enough to kindle Lily's imagination, and the sight of the gray dress and the borrowed prayer-book flashed a long light down the years. She would have to go to church with Percy Gryce every Sunday. They would have a front pew in the most expensive church in New York, and his name would figure handsomely in the list of parish charities. In a few years, when he grew stouter, he would be made a warden. Once in the winter the rector would come to dine, and her husband would beg her to go over the list and see that no divorcées were included, except those who had showed signs of penitence by being remarried to the very wealthy. There was nothing especially arduous in this round of religious obligations; but it stood for a fraction of that great bulk of boredom which loomed across her path. And who could consent to be bored on such a morning? Lily had slept well, and her bath had filled her with a pleasant glow, which was becomingly reflected in the clear curve of her cheek. No lines were visible this morning, or else the glass was at a happier angle.

And the day was the accomplice of her mood: it was a day for impulse and truancy. The light air seemed full of powdered gold; below the dewy bloom of the lawns the woodlands blushed and smoldered, and the hills across the river swam in molten blue. Every drop of blood in Lily's veins invited her to happiness.

The sound of wheels roused her from these musings, and leaning behind her shutters she saw the omnibus take up its freight. She was too late, then —but the fact did not alarm her. A glimpse of Mr. Gryce's crestfallen face even suggested that she had done wisely in absenting herself, since the disappointment he so candidly betrayed would surely whet his appetite for the afternoon walk. That walk she did not mean to miss; one glance at the bills on her writing-table was enough to recall its necessity. But meanwhile she had the morning to herself, and could muse pleasantly on the disposal of its hours. She was familiar enough with the habits of Bellomont to know that she was likely to have a free field till luncheon. She had seen the Wetheralls, the Trenor girls and Lady Cressida packed safely into the omnibus; Judy Trenor was sure to be having her hair shampooed; Carry Fisher had doubtless carried off her host for a drive; Ned Silverton was probably smoking the cigarette of young despair in his bedroom; and Kate Corby was certain to be playing tennis with Jack Stepney and Miss Van Osburgh. Of the ladies, this left only Mrs. Dorset unaccounted for, and Mrs. Dorset never came down till luncheon: her doctors, she averred, had forbidden her to expose herself to the crude air of the morning.

To the remaining members of the party Lily gave no special thought;

wherever they were, they were not likely to interfere with her plans. These, for the moment, took the shape of assuming a dress somewhat more rustic and summerlike in style than the garment she had first selected, and rustling downstairs, sunshade in hand, with the disengaged air of a lady in quest of exercise. The great hall was empty but for the knot of dogs by the fire, who, taking in at a glance the outdoor aspect of Miss Bart, were upon her at once with lavish offers of companionship. She put aside the ramping paws which conveyed these offers, and assuring the joyous volunteers that she might presently have a use for their company, sauntered on through the empty drawing-room to the library at the end of the house. The library was almost the only surviving portion of the old manor-house of Bellomont: a long spacious room, revealing the traditions of the mother-country in its classi- cally cased doors, the Dutch tiles of the chimney, and the elaborate hob- grate with its shining brass urns. A few family portraits of lantern-jawed gentlemen in tie-wigs, and ladies with large headdresses and small bodies, hung between the shelves lined with pleasantly shabby books: books mostly contemporaneous with the ancestors in question, and to which the subse- quent Trenors had made no perceptible additions. The library at Bellomont was in fact never used for reading, though it had a certain popularity as a smoking-room or a quiet retreat for flirtation. It had occurred to Lily, how- ever, that it might on this occasion have been resorted to by the only member of the party in the least likely to put it to its original use. She advanced noiselessly over the dense old rug scattered with easy-chairs, and before she reached the middle of the room she saw that she had not been mistaken. Lawrence Selden was in fact seated at its farther end; but though a book lay on his knee, his attention was not engaged with it, but directed to a lady whose lace-clad figure, as she leaned back in an adjoining chair, detached itself with exaggerated slimness against the dusky leather of the upholstery.

Lily paused as she caught sight of the group; for a moment she seemed about to withdraw, but thinking better of this, she announced her approach by a slight shake of her skirts which made the couple raise their heads. Mrs. Dorset with a look of frank displeasure, and Selden with his usual quiet smile. The sight of his composure had a disturbing effect on Lily; but to be disturbed was in her case to make a more brilliant effort at self-possession.

"Dear me, am I late?" she asked, putting a hand in his as he advanced to greet her.

"Late for what?" inquired Mrs. Dorset tartly. "Not for luncheon, cer- tainly—but perhaps you had an earlier engagement?"

"Yes, I had," said Lily confidingly.

"Really? Perhaps I am in the way, then? But Mr. Selden is entirely at your disposal." Mrs. Dorset was pale with temper, and her antagonist felt a certain pleasure in prolonging her distress.

"Oh, dear, no—do stay," she said good-humoredly. "I don't in the least want to drive you away."

"You're awfully good, dear, but I never interfere with Mr. Selden's engagements."

The remark was uttered with a little air of proprietorship not lost on its object, who concealed a faint blush of annoyance by stooping to pick up the book he had dropped at Lily's approach. The latter's eyes widened charmingly and she broke into a light laugh.

"But I have no engagement with Mr. Selden! My engagement was to go to church; and I'm afraid the omnibus has started without me. *Has* it started, do you know?"

She turned to Selden, who replied that he had heard it drive away some time since.

"Ah, then I shall have to walk; I promised Hilda and Muriel to go to church with them. It's too late to walk there, you say? Well, I shall have the credit of trying, at any rate—and the advantage of escaping part of the service. I'm not so sorry for myself, after all!"

And with a bright nod to the couple on whom she had intruded, Miss Bart strolled through the glass doors and carried her rustling grace down the long perspective of the garden walk.

She was taking her way churchward, but at no very quick pace; a fact not lost on one of her observers, who stood in the doorway looking after her with an air of puzzled amusement. The truth is that she was conscious of a somewhat keen shock of disappointment. All her plans for the day had been built on the assumption that it was to see her that Selden had come to Bellomont. She had expected, when she came downstairs, to find him on the watch for her, and she had found him, instead, in a situation which might well denote that he had been on the watch for another lady. Was it possible, after all, that he had come for Bertha Dorset? The latter had acted on the assumption to the extent of appearing at an hour when she never showed herself to ordinary mortals, and Lily, for the moment, saw no way of putting her in the wrong. It did not occur to her that Selden might have been actuated merely by the desire to spend a Sunday out of town: women never learn to dispense with the sentimental motive in their judgments of men. But Lily was not easily disconcerted; competition put her on her mettle, and she reflected that Selden's coming, if it did not declare him to be still in Mrs. Dorset's toils, showed him to be so completely free from them that he was not afraid of her proximity.

These thoughts so engaged her that she fell into a gait hardly likely to carry her to church before the sermon, and at length, having passed from the gardens to the wood-path beyond, so far forgot her intention as to sink into a rustic seat at a bend of the walk. The spot was charming, and Lily was not insensible to the charm, or to the fact that her presence enhanced it; but she was not accustomed to taste the joys of solitude except in company, and the combination of a handsome girl and a romantic scene struck her as too good to be wasted. No one, however, appeared to profit by the opportunity; and after a half hour of fruitless waiting she rose and wandered on. She felt a stealing sense of fatigue as she walked; the sparkle had died out of her, and the taste of life was stale on her lips. She hardly knew what she had been seeking, or why the failure to find it had so blotted the light from her sky: she was only aware of a vague sense of failure, of an inner isolation deeper than the loneliness about her.

Her footsteps flagged, and she stood gazing listlessly ahead, digging the ferny edge of the path with the tip of her sun-shade. As she did so a step sounded behind her, and she saw Selden at her side.

"How fast you walk!" he remarked. "I thought I should never catch up with you."

She answered gaily: "You must be quite breathless! I've been sitting under that tree for an hour."

"Waiting for me, I hope?" he rejoined; and she said with a vague laugh:

"Well—waiting to see if you would come."

"I seize the distinction, but I don't mind it, since doing the one involved doing the other. But weren't you sure that I should come?"

"If I waited long enough—but you see I had only a limited time to give to the experiment."

"Why limited? Limited by luncheon?"

"No, by my other engagement."

"Your engagement to go to church with Muriel and Hilda?"

"No; but to come home from church with another person."

"Ah, I see; I might have known you were fully provided with alternatives. And is the other person coming home this way?"

Lily laughed again. "That's just what I don't know; and to find out, it is my business to get to church before the service is over."

"Exactly; and it is my business to prevent your doing so; in which case the other person, piqued by your absence, will form the desperate resolve of driving back in the omnibus."

Lily received this with fresh appreciation; his nonsense was like the bubbling of her inner mood. "Is that what you would do in such an emergency?" she inquired.

Selden looked at her with solemnity. "I am here to prove to you," he cried, "what I am capable of doing in an emergency!"

"Walking a mile in an hour—you must own that the omnibus would be quicker!"

"Ah—but will he find you in the end? That's the only test of success."

They looked at each other with the same luxury of enjoyment that they had felt in exchanging absurdities over his tea-table; but suddenly Lily's face changed, and she said: "Well, if it is, he has succeeded."

Selden, following her glance, perceived a party of people advancing toward them from the farther bend of the path. Lady Cressida had evidently insisted on walking home, and the rest of the church-goers had thought it their duty to accompany her. Lily's companion looked rapidly from one to the other of the two men of the party; Wetherall walking respectfully at Lady Cressida's side with his little sidelong look of nervous attention, and Percy Gryce bringing up the rear with Mrs. Wetherall and the Trenors.

"Ah—now I see why you were getting up your Americana!" Selden exclaimed with a note of the freest admiration; but the blush in which the sally was received checked whatever amplification he had meant to give it.

That Lily Bart should object to being bantered about her suitors, or even about her means of attracting them, was so new to Selden that he had a momentary flash of surprise, which lit up a number of possibilities; but she rose gallantly to the defense of her confusion, by saying, as its object approached: "That was why I was waiting for you—to thank you for having given me so many points!"

"Ah, you can hardly do justice to the subject in such a short time," said Selden, as the Trenor girls caught sight of Miss Bart; and while she signalled a response to their boisterous greeting, he added quickly: "Won't you devote your afternoon to it? You know I must be off tomorrow morning. We'll take a walk, and you can thank me at your leisure."

6

THE afternoon was perfect. A deeper stillness possessed the air, and the glitter of the American autumn was tempered by a haze which diffused the brightness without dulling it.

In the woody hollows of the park there was already a faint chill; but as the ground rose the air grew lighter, and ascending the long slopes beyond the highroad, Lily and her companion reached a zone of lingering summer. The path wound across a meadow with scattered trees; then it dipped into a lane plumed with asters and purpling sprays of bramble, whence, through the light quiver of ash-leaves, the country unrolled itself in pastoral distances.

Higher up, the lane showed thickening tufts of fern and of the creeping glossy verdure of shaded slopes; trees began to overhang it, and the shade deepened to the checkered dusk of a beech-grove. The boles of the trees stood well apart, with only a light feathering of undergrowth; the path wound along the edge of the wood, now and then looking out on a sunlit pasture or on an orchard spangled with fruit.

Lily had no real intimacy with nature, but she had a passion for the appropriate and could be keenly sensitive to a scene which was the fitting background of her own sensations. The landscape outspread below her seemed an enlargement of her present mood, and she found something of herself in its calmness, its breadth, its long free reaches. On the nearer slopes the sugar-maples wavered like pyres of light; lower down was a massing of gray orchards, and here and there the lingering green of an oak grove. Two or three red farmhouses dozed under the apple trees, and the white wooden spire of a village church showed beyond the shoulder of the hill; while far below, in a haze of dust, the highroad ran between the fields.

"Let us sit here," Selden suggested, as they reached an open ledge of rock above which the beeches rose steeply between mossy boulders.

Lily dropped down on the rock, glowing with her long climb. She sat quiet, her lips parted by the stress of the ascent, her eyes wandering peacefully over the broken ranges of the landscape. Selden stretched himself on the grass at her feet, tilting his hat against the level sun-rays, and clasping his hands behind his head, which rested against the side of the rock. He had no wish to make her talk; her quick-breathing silence seemed a part of the general hush and harmony of things. In his own mind there was only a lazy sense of pleasure, veiling the sharp edges of sensation as the September haze veiled the scene at their feet. But Lily, though her attitude was as calm as his, was throbbing inwardly with a rush of thoughts. There were in her at the moment two beings, one drawing deep breaths of freedom and exhilaration, the other gasping for air in a little black prison-house of fears. But gradually the captive's gasps grew fainter, or the other paid less heed to them: the horizon expanded, the air grew stronger, and the free spirit quivered for flight.

She could not herself have explained the sense of buoyancy which seemed to lift and swing her above the sun-suffused world at her feet. Was it love, she wondered, or a mere fortuitous combination of happy thoughts and sensations? How much of it was owing to the spell of the perfect afternoon, the scent of the fading woods, the thought of the dullness she had fled from? Lily had no definite experience by which to test the quality of her feelings. She had several times been in love with fortunes or careers, but only once with a man. That was years ago, when she first came out, and had been smitten with a romantic passion for a young gentleman named Herbert Melson, who had blue eyes and a little wave in his hair. Mr. Melson, who was possessed of no other negotiable securities, had hastened to employ these in capturing the eldest Miss Van Osburgh: since then he had grown stout and wheezy, and was given to telling anecdotes about his children. If Lily recalled this early emotion it was not to compare it with that which now possessed her; the only point of comparison was the sense of lightness, of emancipation, which she remembered feeling, in the whirl of a waltz or the seclusion of a conservatory, during the brief course of her youthful romance. She had not known again till today that lightness, that glow of freedom; but now it was something more than a blind groping of the blood. The peculiar charm of her feeling for Selden was that she understood it; she could put her finger on every link of the chain that was drawing them together. Though his popularity was of the quiet kind, felt rather than actively expressed among his friends, she had never mistaken his inconspic- uousness for obscurity. His reputed cultivation was generally regarded as a slight obstacle to easy intercourse, but Lily, who prided herself on her broad- minded recognition of literature, and always carried an Omar Khayam in her traveling-bag, was attracted by this attribute, which she felt would have had its distinction in an older society. It was, moreover, one of his gifts to look his part; to have a height which lifted his head above the crowd, and the keenly modeled dark features which, in a land of amorphous types, gave him the air of belonging to a more specialized race, of carrying the impress of a concentrated past. Expansive persons found him a little dry, and very young girls thought him sarcastic; but this air of friendly aloofness, as far removed as possible from any assertion of personal advantage, was the qual- ity which piqued Lily's interest. Everything about him accorded with the fastidious element in her taste, even to the light irony with which he sur- veyed what seemed to be most sacred. She admired him most of all, perhaps, for being able to convey as distinct a sense of superiority as the richest man she had ever met.

It was the unconscious prolongation of this thought which led her to say presently, with a laugh: "I have broken two engagements for you today. How many have you broken for me?"

"None," said Selden calmly. "My only engagement at Bellomont was with you."

She glanced down at him, faintly smiling.

"Did you really come to Bellomont to see me?"

"Of course I did."

Her look deepened meditatively. "Why?" she murmured, with an accent which took all tinge of coquetry from the question.

"Because you're such a wonderful spectacle: I always like to see what you are doing."

"How do you know what I should be doing if you were not here?"

Selden smiled. "I don't flatter myself that my coming has deflected your course of action by a hair's breadth."

"That's absurd—since, if you were not here, I could obviously not be taking a walk with you."

"No; but your taking a walk with me is only another way of making use of your material. You are an artist and I happen to be the bit of color you are using today. It's a part of your cleverness to be able to produce premeditated effects extemporaneously."

Lily smiled also: his words were too acute not to strike her sense of humor. It was true that she meant to use the accident of his presence as part of a very definite effect; or that, at least, was the secret pretext she had found for breaking her promise to walk with Mr. Gryce. She had sometimes been accused of being too eager—even Judy Trenor had warned her to go slowly. Well, she would not be too eager in this case; she would give her suitor a longer taste of suspense. Where duty and inclination jumped together, it was not in Lily's nature to hold them asunder. She had excused herself from the walk on the plea of a headache: the horrid headache which, in the morning, had prevented her venturing to church. Her appearance at luncheon justified the excuse. She looked languid, full of a suffering sweetness; she carried a scent-bottle in her hand. Mr. Gryce was new to such manifestations; he wondered rather nervously if she were delicate, having far-reaching fears about the future of his progeny. But sympathy won the day, and he besought her not to expose herself: he always connected the outer air with ideas of exposure.

Lily had received his sympathy with languid gratitude, urging him, since she should be such poor company, to join the rest of the party who, after luncheon, were starting in automobiles on a visit to the Van Osburghs at Peekskill. Mr. Gryce was touched by her disinterestedness, and, to escape from the threatened vacuity of the afternoon, had taken her advice and departed mournfully, in a dust-hood and goggles: as the motorcar lunged down the avenue she smiled at his resemblance to a baffled beetle.

Selden had watched her maneuvers with lazy amusement. She had made no reply to his suggestion that they should spend the afternoon together, but as her plan unfolded itself he felt fairly confident of being included in it. The house was empty when at length he heard her step on the stair and strolled out of the billiard-room to join her. She had on a hat and walking-dress, and the dogs were bounding at her feet.

"I thought, after all, the air might do me good," she explained; and he agreed that so simple a remedy was worth trying.

The excursionists would be gone at least four hours; Lily and Selden had the whole afternoon before them, and the sense of leisure and safety gave the last touch of lightness to her spirit. With so much time to talk, and no definite object to be led up to, she could taste the rare joys of mental vagrancy.

She felt so free from ulterior motives that she took up his charge with a touch of resentment.

"I don't know," she said, "why you are always accusing me of premeditation."

"I thought you confessed to it: you told me the other day that you had to follow a certain line—and if one does a thing at all it is a merit to do it thoroughly."

"If you mean that a girl who has no one to think for her is obliged to think for herself, I am quite willing to accept the imputation. But you must find me a dismal kind of person if you suppose that I never yield to an impulse."

"Ah, but I don't suppose that: haven't I told you that your genius lies in converting impulses into intentions?"

"My genius?" she echoed with a sudden note of weariness. "Is there any final test of genius but success? And I certainly haven't succeeded."

Selden pushed his hat back and took a side-glance at her. "Success— what is success? I shall be interested to have your definition."

"Success?" She hesitated. "Why, to get as much as one can out of life, I suppose. It's a relative quality, after all. Isn't that your idea of it?"

"My idea of it? God forbid!" He sat up with sudden energy, resting his elbows on his knees and staring out upon the mellow fields. "My idea of success," he said, "is personal freedom."

"Freedom? Freedom from worries?"

"From everything—from money, from poverty, from ease and anxiety, from all the material accidents. To keep a kind of republic of the spirit— that's what I call success."

She leaned forward with a responsive flash. "I know—I know—it's strange; but that's just what I've been feeling today."

He met her eyes with the latent sweetness of his. "Is the feeling so rare with you?" he said.

She blushed a little under his gaze. "You think me horribly sordid, don't you? But perhaps it's rather that I never had any choice. There was no one, I mean, to tell me about the republic of the spirit."

"There never is—it's a country one has to find the way to one's self."

"But I should never have found my way there if you hadn't told me."

"Ah, there are signposts—but one has to know how to read them."

"Well, I have known, I have known!" she cried with a glow of eagerness. "Whenever I see you, I find myself spelling out a letter of the sign—and yesterday—last evening at dinner—I suddenly saw a little way into your republic."

Selden was still looking at her, but with a changed eye. Hitherto he had found, in her presence and her talk, the aesthetic amusement which a reflective man is apt to seek in desultory intercourse with pretty women. His attitude had been one of admiring spectatorship and he would have been almost sorry to detect in her any emotional weakness which should interfere with the fulfilllment of her aims. But now the hint of this weakness had become the most interesting thing about her. He had come on her that morning in a moment of disarray; her face had been pale and altered, and the diminution of her beauty had lent her a poignant charm. *That is how she looks when she is alone!* had been his first thought; and the second was to note in her the change which his coming produced. It was the danger-point of their intercourse that he could not doubt the spontaneity of her liking. From whatever angle he viewed their dawning intimacy, he could not see it as part of her scheme of life; and to be the unforeseen element in a career so accurately planned was stimulating even to a man who had renounced sentimental experiments.

"Well," he said, "did it make you want to see more? Are you going to become one of us?"

He had drawn out his cigarettes as he spoke, and she reached her hand toward the case.

"Oh, do give me one—I haven't smoked for days!"

"Why such unnatural abstinence? Everybody smokes at Bellomont."

"Yes—but it is not considered becoming in a *jeune fille à marier*; and at the present moment I am a *jeune fille à marier*."

"Ah, then I'm afraid we can't let you into the republic."

"Why not? Is it a celibate order?"

"Not in the least, though I'm bound to say there are not many married people in it. But you will marry someone very rich, and it's as hard for rich people to get into as the kingdom of heaven."

"That's unjust, I think, because, as I understand it, one of the conditions of citizenship is not to think too much about money, and the only way not to think about money is to have a great deal of it."

"You might as well say that the only way not to think about air is to have enough to breathe. That is true enough in a sense; but your lungs are thinking about the air, if you are not. And so it is with your rich people—they may not be thinking of money, but they're breathing it all the while; take them into another element and see how they squirm and gasp!"

Lily sat gazing absently through the blue rings of her cigarette-smoke.

"It seems to me," she said at length, "that you spend a good deal of your time in the element you disapprove of."

Selden received this thrust without discomposure. "Yes, but I have tried to remain amphibious: it's all right as long as one's lungs can work in another air. The real alchemy consists in being able to turn gold back again into something else; and that's the secret that most of your friends have lost."

Lily mused. "Don't you think," she rejoined after a moment, "that the people who find fault with society are too apt to regard it as an end and not a means, just as the people who despise money speak as if its only use were to be kept in bags and gloated over? Isn't it fairer to look at them both as opportunities, which may be used either stupidly or intelligently, according to the capacity of the user?"

"That is certainly the sane view; but the queer thing about society is that the people who regard it as an end are those who are in it, and not the critics on the fence. It's just the other way with most shows—the audience may be under the illusion, but the actors know that real life is on the other side of the footlights. The people who take society as an escape from work are putting it to its proper use; but when it becomes the thing worked for it distorts all the relations of life." Selden raised himself on his elbow. "Good heavens!" he went on, "I don't underrate the decorative side of life. It seems to me the sense of splendor has justified itself by what it has produced. The worst of it is that so much human nature is used up in the process. If we're all the raw stuff of the cosmic effects, one would rather be the fire that tempers a sword than the fish that dyes a purple cloak. And a society like ours wastes such good material in producing its little patch of purple! Look at a boy like Ned Silverton—he's really too good to be used to refurbish anybody's social shabbiness. There's a lad just setting out to discover the universe; isn't it a pity he should end by finding it in Mrs. Fisher's drawing-room?"

"Ned is a dear boy, and I hope he will keep his illusions long enough to write some nice poetry about them; but do you think it is only in society that he is likely to lose them?"

Selden answered her with a shrug. "Why do we call all our generous ideas illusions, and the mean ones truths? Isn't it a sufficient condemnation of society to find one's self accepting such phraseology? I very nearly acquired the jargon at Silverton's age, and I know how names can alter the color of beliefs."

She had never heard him speak with such energy of affirmation. His habitual touch was that of the eclectic, who lightly turns over and compares; and she was moved by this sudden glimpse into the laboratory where his faiths were formed.

"Ah, you are as bad as the other sectarians," she exclaimed. "Why do you call your republic a republic? It is a close corporation, and you create arbitrary objections in order to keep people out."

"It is not *my* republic; if it were, I should have a *coup d'état* and seat you on the throne."

"Whereas, in reality, you think I can never even get my foot across the threshold? Oh, I understand what you mean. You despise my ambitions—you think them unworthy of me!"

Selden smiled, but not ironically. "Well, isn't that a tribute? I think them quite worthy of most of the people who live by them."

She had turned to gaze on him gravely. "But isn't it possible that, if I had the opportunities of these people, I might make a better use of them? Money stands for all kinds of things—its purchasing quality isn't limited to diamonds and motorcars."

"Not in the least: you might expiate your enjoyment of them by founding a hospital."

"But if you think they are what I should really enjoy, you must think my ambitions are good enough for me."

Selden met this appeal with a laugh. "Ah, my dear Miss Bart, I am not divine Providence, to guarantee your enjoying the things you are trying to get!"

"Then the best you can say for me is that after struggling to get them I probably shan't like them?" She drew a deep breath. "What a miserable future you foresee for me!"

"Well—have you never foreseen it for yourself?"

The slow color rose to her cheek, not a blush of excitement but drawn from the deep wells of feeling; it was as if the effort of her spirit had produced it.

"Often and often," she said. "But it looks so much darker when you show it to me!"

He made no answer to this exclamation, and for a while they sat silent, while something throbbed between them in the wide quiet of the air. But suddenly she turned on him with a kind of vehemence.

"Why do you do this to me?" she cried. "Why do you make the things I have chosen seem hateful to me, if you have nothing to give me instead?"

The words roused Selden from the musing fit into which he had fallen. He himself did not know why he had led their talk along such lines; it was the last use he would have imagined himself making of an afternoon's solitude with Miss Bart. But it was one of those moments when neither seemed to speak deliberately, when an indwelling voice in each called to the other across unsounded depths of feeling.

"No, I have nothing to give you instead," he said, sitting up and turning so that he faced her. "If I had, it should be yours, you know."

She received this abrupt declaration in a way even stranger than the manner of its making: she dropped her face on her hands and he saw that for a moment she wept.

It was for a moment only, however; for when he leaned nearer and drew down her hands with a gesture less passionate than grave, she turned on him a face softened but not disfigured by emotion, and he said to himself, somewhat cruelly, that even her weeping was an art.

The reflection steadied his voice as he asked, between pity and irony: "Isn't it natural that I should try to belittle all the things I can't offer you?"

Her face brightened at this, but she drew her hand away, not with a gesture of coquetry, but as though renouncing something to which she had no claim.

"But you belittle *me*, don't you," she returned gently, "in being so sure they are the only things I care for?"

Selden felt an inner start; but it was only the last quiver of his egoism. Almost at once he answered quite simply: "But you do care for them, don't you? And no wishing of mine can alter that."

He had so completely ceased to consider how far this might carry him that he had a distinct sense of disappointment when she turned on him a face sparkling with derision.

"Ah," she cried, "for all your fine phrases you're really as great a coward as I am, for you wouldn't have made one of them if you hadn't been so sure of my answer."

The shock of this retort had the effect of crystallizing Selden's wavering intentions.

"I am not so sure of your answer," he said quietly. "And I do you the justice to believe that you are not either."

It was her turn to look at him with surprise; and after a moment—"Do you want to marry me?" she asked.

He broke into a laugh. "No, I don't want to—but perhaps I should if you did!"

"That's what I told you—you're so sure of me that you can amuse yourself with experiments." She drew back the hand he had regained, and sat looking down on him sadly.

"I am not making experiments," he returned. "Or if I am, it is not on you but on myself. I don't know what effect they are going to have on me—but if marrying you is one of them, I will take the risk."

She smiled faintly. "It would be a great risk, certainly—I have never concealed from you how great."

"Ah, it's you who are the coward!" he exclaimed.

She had risen, and he stood facing her with his eyes on hers. The soft isolation of the falling day enveloped them: they seemed lifted into a finer air. All the exquisite influences of the hour trembled in their veins, and drew them to each other as the loosened leaves were drawn to the earth.

"It's you who are the coward," he repeated, catching her hands in his.

She leaned on him for a moment, as if with a drop of tired wings: he felt as though her heart were beating rather with the stress of a long flight than the thrill of new distances. Then, drawing back with a little smile of warning—"I shall look hideous in dowdy clothes; but I can trim my own hats," she declared.

They stood silent for a while after this, smiling at each other like adventurous children who have climbed to a forbidden height from which they discover a new world. The actual world at their feet was veiling itself in dimness, and across the valley a clear moon rose in the denser blue.

Suddenly they heard a remote sound, like the hum of a giant insect, and following the highroad, which wound whiter through the surrounding twilight, a black object rushed across their vision.

Lily started from her attitude of absorption; her smile faded and she began to move toward the lane.

"I had no idea it was so late! We shall not be back till after dark," she said, almost impatiently.

Selden was looking at her with surprise: it took him a moment to regain his usual view of her; then he said, with an uncontrollable note of dryness: "That was not one of our party; the motor was going the other way."

"I know—I know—" She paused, and he saw her redden through the twilight. "But I told them I was not well—that I should not go out. Let us go down!" she murmured.

Selden continued to look at her; then he drew his cigarette case from his pocket and slowly lit a cigarette. It seemed to him necessary, at this moment, to proclaim, by some habitual gesture of this sort, his recovered hold on the actual: he had an almost puerile wish to let his companion see that, their flight over, he had landed on his feet.

She waited while the spark flickered under his curved palm; then he held out the cigarettes to her.

She took one with an unsteady hand, and putting it to her lips, leaned forward to draw her light from his. In the indistinctness the little red gleam lit up the lower part of her face, and he saw her mouth tremble into a smile.

"Were you serious?" she asked, with an odd thrill of gaiety which she might have caught up, in haste, from a heap of stock inflections, without having time to select the just note.

Selden's voice was under better control. "Why not?" he returned. "You see I took no risks in being so." And as she continued to stand before him, a little pale under the retort, he added quickly: "Let us go down."

7

IT spoke much for the depth of Mrs. Trenor's friendship that her voice, in admonishing Miss Bart, took the same note of personal despair as if she had been lamenting the collapse of a house-party.

"All I can say is, Lily, that I can't make you out!" She leaned back, sighing, in the morning abandon of lace and muslin, turning an indifferent shoulder to the heaped-up importunities of her desk, while she considered, with the eye of a physician who has given up the case, the erect exterior of the patient confronting her.

"If you hadn't told me you were going in for him seriously—but I'm sure you made that plain enough from the beginning! Why else did you ask me to let you off bridge, and to keep away Carry and Kate Corby? I don't suppose you did it because he amused you; we could none of us imagine your putting up with him for a moment unless you meant to marry him. And I'm sure everybody played fair! They all wanted to help it along. Even Bertha kept her hands off—I will say that—till Lawrence came down and you dragged him away from her. After that she had a right to retaliate—why on earth did you interfere with her? You've known Lawrence Selden for years— why did you behave as if you had just discovered him? If you had a grudge against Bertha it was a stupid time to show it—you could have paid her back just as well after you were married! I told you Bertha was dangerous. She was in an odious mood when she came here, but Lawrence's turning up put her in a good humor, and if you'd only let her think he came for *her* it would have never occurred to her to play you this trick. Oh, Lily, you'll never do anything if you're not serious!"

Miss Bart accepted this exhortation in a spirit of the purest impartiality. Why should she have been angry? It was the voice of her own conscience which spoke to her through Mrs. Trenor's reproachful accents. But even to her own conscience she must trump up a semblance of defense.

"I only took a day off—I thought he meant to stay on all this week, and I knew Mr. Selden was leaving this morning."

Mrs. Trenor brushed aside the plea with a gesture which laid bare its weakness.

"He did mean to stay—that's the worst of it. It shows that he's run away from you; that Bertha's done her work and poisoned him thoroughly."

Lily gave a slight laugh. "Oh, if he's running I'll overtake him!"

Her friend threw out an arresting hand. "Whatever you do, Lily, do nothing!"

Miss Bart received the warning with a smile. "I don't mean, literally, to take the next train. There are ways —" But she did not go on to specify them.

Mrs. Trenor sharply corrected the tense. "There *were* ways—plenty of them! I didn't suppose you needed to have them pointed out. But don't deceive yourself—he's thoroughly frightened. He has run straight home to his mother, and she'll protect him!"

"Oh, to the death," Lily agreed, dimpling at the vision.

"How you can *laugh* —" her friend rebuked her; and she dropped back to a soberer perception of things with the question: "What was it Bertha really told him?"

"Don't ask me—horrors! She seemed to have raked up everything. Oh, you know what I mean—of course there isn't anything, *really*; but I suppose she brought in Prince Varigliano—and Lord Hubert—and there was some story of your having borrowed money of old Ned Van Alstyne: did you ever?"

"He is my father's cousin," Miss Bart interposed.

"Well, of course she left *that* out. It seems Ned told Carry Fisher; and she told Bertha, naturally. They're all alike, you know: they hold their tongues for years, and you think you're safe, but when their opportunity comes they remember everything."

Lily had grown pale: her voice had a harsh note in it. "It was some money I lost at bridge at the Van Osburghs'. I repaid it, of course."

"Ah, well, they wouldn't remember that; besides, it was the idea of the gambling debt that frightened Percy. Oh, Bertha knew her man—she knew just what to tell him!"

In this strain Mrs. Trenor continued for nearly an hour to admonish her friend. Miss Bart listened with admirable equanimity. Her naturally good temper had been disciplined by years of enforced compliance, since she had almost always had to attain her ends by the circuitous path of other people's; and, being naturally inclined to face unpleasant facts as soon as they presented themselves, she was not sorry to hear an impartial statement of what her folly was likely to cost, the more so as her own thoughts were still insisting on the other side of the case. Presented in the light of Mrs. Trenor's vigorous comments, the reckoning was certainly a formidable one, and Lily, as she listened, found herself gradually reverting to her friend's view of the situation. Mrs. Trenor's words were moreover emphasized for her hearer by anxieties which she herself could scarcely guess. Affluence, unless stimulated by a keen imagination, forms but the vaguest notion of the practical strain of poverty. Judy knew it must be "horrid" for poor Lily to have to stop to consider whether she could afford real lace on her petticoats, and not to have a motorcar and a steam-yacht at her orders; but the daily friction of unpaid bills, the daily nibble of small temptations to expenditure, were trials as far out of her experience as the domestic problems of the charwoman. Mrs. Trenor's unconsciousness of the real stress of the situation had the effect of making it more galling to Lily. While her friend reproached her for missing the opportunity to eclipse her rivals, she was once more battling in imagination with the mounting tide of indebtedness from which she had so nearly escaped. What wind of folly had driven her out again on those dark seas?

If anything was needed to put the last touch to her self-abasement it was the sense of the way her old life was opening its ruts again to receive her. Yesterday her fancy had fluttered free pinions above a choice of occupations; now she had to drop to the level of the familiar routine, in which moments of seeming brilliancy and freedom alternated with long hours of subjection.

She laid a deprecating hand on her friend's. "Dear Judy! I'm sorry to have been such a bore, and you are very good to me. But you must have some letters for me to answer—let me at least be useful."

She settled herself at the desk, and Mrs. Trenor accepted her resumption of the morning's task with a sigh, which implied that, after all, she had proved herself unfit for higher uses.

The luncheon table showed a depleted circle. All the men but Jack Stepney and Dorset had returned to town (it seemed to Lily a last touch of irony that Selden and Percy Gryce should have gone in the same train), and Lady Cressida and the attendant Wetheralls had been dispatched by motor to lunch at a distant country house. At such moments of diminished interest it was usual for Mrs. Dorset to keep her room till the afternoon; but on this occasion she drifted in when luncheon was half over, hollowed-eyed and drooping, but with an edge of malice under her indifference.

She raised her eyebrows as she looked about the table. "How few of us are left! I do so enjoy the quiet—don't you, Lily? I wish the men would always stop away—it's really much nicer without them. Oh, you don't count, George: one doesn't have to talk to one's husband. But I thought Mr. Gryce was to stay for the rest of the week?" she added inquiringly. "Didn't he intend to, Judy? He's such a nice boy—I wonder what drove him away? He is rather shy, and I'm afraid we may have shocked him: he has been brought up in such an old-fashioned way. Do you know, Lily, he told me he had never seen a girl play cards for money till he saw you doing it the other night? And he lives on the interest of his income, and always has a lot left over to invest!"

Mrs. Fisher leaned forward eagerly. "I do believe it is someone's duty to educate that young man. It is shocking that he has never been made to realize his duties as a citizen. Every wealthy man should be compelled to study the laws of his country."

Mrs. Dorset glanced at her quietly. "I think he *has* studied the divorce laws. He told me he had promised the Bishop to sign some kind of a petition against divorce."

Mrs. Fisher reddened under her powder, and Stepney said with a laughing glance at Miss Bart: "I suppose he is thinking of marriage, and wants to tinker up the old ship before he goes aboard."

His betrothed looked shocked at the metaphor, and George Dorset exclaimed with a sardonic growl: "Poor devil! It isn't the ship that will do for him, it's the crew."

"Or the stowaways," said Miss Corby brightly. "If I contemplated a voyage with him I should try to start with a friend in the hold."

Miss Van Osburgh's vague feeling of pique was struggling for appropriate expression. "I'm sure I don't see why you laugh at him; I think he's very nice," she exclaimed; "and, at any rate, a girl who married him would always have enough to be comfortable."

She looked puzzled at the redoubled laughter which hailed her words, but it might have consoled her to know how deeply they had sunk into the breast of one of her hearers.

Comfortable! At that moment the word was more eloquent to Lily Bart than any other in the language. She could not even pause to smile over the heiress's view of a colossal fortune as a mere shelter against want: her mind was filled with the vision of what that shelter might have been to her. Mrs. Dorset's pinpricks did not smart, for her own irony cut deeper: no one could hurt her as much as she was hurting herself, for no one else—not even Judy Trenor—knew the full magnitude of her folly.

She was roused from these unprofitable considerations by a whispered request from her hostess, who drew her apart as they left the luncheon-table.

"Lily, dear, if you've nothing special to do, may I tell Carry Fisher that you intend to drive to the station and fetch Gus? He will be back at four, and I know she has it in her mind to meet him. Of course I'm very glad to have him amused, but I happen to know that she has bled him rather severely since she's been here, and she is so keen about going to fetch him that I fancy she must have got a lot more bills this morning. It seems to me," Mrs. Trenor feelingly concluded, "that most of her alimony is paid by other women's husbands!"

Miss Bart, on her way to the station, had leisure to muse over her friend's words, and their peculiar application to herself. Why should she have to suffer for having once, for a few hours, borrowed money of an elderly cousin, when a woman like Carry Fisher could make a living un-rebuked from the good-nature of her men friends and the tolerance of their wives? It all turned on the tiresome distinction between what a married woman might, and a girl might not, do. Of course it was shocking for a married woman to borrow money—and Lily was expertly aware of the im-plication involved—but still, it was the mere *malum prohibitum* which the world decries but condones, and which, though it may be punished by private vengeance, does not provoke the collective disapprobation of soci-ety. To Miss Bart, in short, no such opportunities were possible. She could, of course, borrow from her women friends—a hundred here or there, at the utmost—but they were more ready to give a gown or a trinket, and looked a little askance when she hinted her preference for a check. Women are not generous lenders, and those among whom her lot was cast were either in the same case as herself, or else too far removed from it to understand its necessities. The result of her meditations was the decision to join her aunt at Richfield. She could not remain at Bellomont without playing bridge, and being involved in other expenses; and to continue her usual series of autumn visits would merely prolong the same difficulties. She had reached a point where abrupt retrenchment was necessary, and the only cheap life was a dull life. She would start the next morning for Richfield.

At the station she thought Gus Trenor seemed surprised, and not wholly unrelieved, to see her. She yielded up the reins of the light runabout in which she had driven over, and as he climbed heavily to her side, crushing her into a scant third of the seat, he said: "Halloo! It isn't often you honor me. You must have been uncommonly hard up for something to do."

The afternoon was warm, and propinquity made her more than usually conscious that he was red and massive, and that beads of moisture had caused the dust of the train to adhere unpleasantly to the broad expanse of cheek and neck which he turned to her; but she was aware also, from the look in his small dull eyes, that the contact with her freshness and slender-ness was as agreeable to him as the sight of a cooling beverage.

The perception of this fact helped her to answer gaily: "It's not often I have the chance. There are too many ladies to dispute the privilege with me."

"The privilege of driving me home? Well, I'm glad you won the race, anyhow. But I know what really happened—my wife sent you. Now didn't she?"

He had the dull man's unexpected flashes of astuteness, and Lily could not help joining in the laugh with which he had pounced on the truth.

"You see, Judy thinks I'm the safest person for you to be with; and she's quite right," she rejoined.

"Oh, is she, though? If she is, it's because you wouldn't waste your time on an old hulk like me. We married men have to put up with what we can get: all the prizes are for the clever chaps who've kept a free foot. Let me light a cigar, will you? I've had a beastly day of it."

He drew up in the shade of the village street, and passed the reins to her while he held a match to his cigar. The little flame under his hand cast a deeper crimson on his puffing face, and Lily averted her eyes with a momentary feeling of repugnance. And yet some women thought him handsome!

As she handed back the reins, she said sympathetically: "Did you have such a lot of tiresome things to do?"

"I should say so—rather!" Trenor, who was seldom listened to, either by his wife or her friends, settled down into the rare enjoyment of a confidential talk. "You don't know how a fellow has to hustle to keep this kind of thing going." He waved his whip in the direction of the Bellomont acres, which lay outspread before them in opulent undulations. "Judy has no idea of what she spends—not that there isn't plenty to keep the thing going," he interrupted himself, "but a man has got to keep his eyes open and pick up all the tips he can. My father and mother used to live like fighting-cocks on their income, and put by a good bit of it too—luckily for me—but at the pace we go now, I don't know where I should be if it weren't for taking a flyer now and then. The women all think—I mean Judy thinks—I've nothing to do but to go downtown once a month and cut off coupons, but the truth is it takes a devilish lot of hard work to keep the machinery running. Not that I ought to complain today, though," he went on after a moment, "for I did a very neat stroke of business, thanks to Stepney's friend Rosedale: by the way, Miss Lily, I wish you'd try to persuade Judy to be decently civil to that chap. He's going to be rich enough to buy us all out one of these days, and if she'd only ask him to dine now and then I could get almost anything out of him. The man is mad to know the people who don't want to know him, and when a fellow's in that state there is nothing he won't do for the first woman who takes him up."

Lily hesitated a moment. The first part of her companion's discourse had started an interesting train of thought, which was rudely interrupted by the mention of Mr. Rosedale's name. She uttered a faint protest.

"But you know Jack did try to take him about, and he was impossible."

"Oh, hang it—because he's fat and shiny, and has a shoppy manner! Well, all I can say is that the people who are clever enough to be civil to him now will make a mighty good thing of it. A few years from now he'll be in it whether we want him or not, and then he won't be giving away a half-a-million tip for a dinner."

Lily's mind had reverted from the intrusive personality of Mr. Rosedale to the train of thought set in motion by Trenor's first words. This vast mysterious Wall Street world of "tips" and "deals"—might she not find in it the means of escape from her dreary predicament? She had often heard of women making money in this way through their friends: she had no more notion than most of her sex of the exact nature of the transaction, and its vagueness seemed to diminish its indelicacy. She could not, indeed, imagine herself, in any extremity, stooping to extract a "tip" from Mr. Rosedale; but at her side was a man in possession of that precious commodity, and who, as the husband of her dearest friend, stood to her in a relation of almost fraternal intimacy.

In her inmost heart Lily knew it was not by appealing to the fraternal instinct that she was likely to move Gus Trenor, but this way of explaining the situation helped to drape its crudity, and she was always scrupulous about keeping up appearances to herself. Her personal fastidiousness had a moral equivalent, and when she made a tour of inspection in her own mind there were certain closed doors she did not open.

As they reached the gates of Bellomont she turned to Trenor with a smile.

"The afternoon is so perfect—don't you want to drive me a little farther? I've been rather out of spirits all day, and it's so restful to be away from people, with someone who won't mind if I'm a little dull."

She looked so plaintively lovely as she proffered the request, so trustfully sure of his sympathy and understanding, that Trenor felt himself wishing that his wife could see how other women treated him—not battered wire-pullers like Mrs. Fisher, but a girl that most men would have given their boots to get such a look from.

"Out of spirits? Why on earth should you ever be out of spirits? Is your last box of Doucet dresses a failure, or did Judy rook you out of everything at bridge last night?"

Lily shook her head with a sigh. "I have had to give up Doucet; and bridge too—I can't afford it. In fact I can't afford any of the things my friends do, and I am afraid Judy often thinks me a bore because I don't play cards any longer, and because I am not as smartly dressed as the other women. But you will think me a bore too if I talk to you about my worries, and I only mention them because I want you to do me a favor—the very greatest of favors."

Her eyes sought his once more, and she smiled inwardly at the tinge of apprehension that she read in them.

"Why, of course—if it's anything I can manage —" He broke off, and she guessed that his enjoyment was disturbed by the remembrance of Mrs. Fisher's methods.

"The greatest of favors," she rejoined gently. "The fact is, Judy is angry with me, and I want you to make my peace."

"Angry with you? Oh, come, nonsense —" his relief broke through in a laugh. "Why, you know she's devoted to you."

"She is the best friend I have, and that is why I mind having to vex her. But I daresay you know what she has wanted me to do. She has set her heart —poor dear—on my marrying—marrying a great deal of money."

She paused with a slight falter of embarrassment, Trenor, turning abruptly, fixed on her a look of growing intelligence.

"A great deal of money? Oh, by Jove—you don't mean Gryce? What— you do? Oh, no, of course I won't mention it—you can trust me to keep my mouth shut—but Gryce—good Lord, *Gryce!* Did Judy really think you could bring yourself to marry that portentous little ass? But you couldn't, eh? And so you gave him the sack, and that's the reason why he lit out by the first train this morning?" He leaned back, spreading himself farther across the seat, as if dilated by the joyful sense of his own discernment. "How on earth could Judy think you would do such a thing? *I* could have told her you'd never put up with such a little milksop!"

Lily sighed more deeply. "I sometimes think," she murmured, "that men understand a woman's motives better than other women do."

"Some men—I'm certain of it! I could have *told* Judy," he repeated, exulting in the implied superiority over his wife.

"I thought you would understand; that's why I wanted to speak to you," Miss Bart rejoined. "I *can't* make that kind of marriage; it's impossible. But neither can I go on living as all the women in my set do. I am almost entirely dependent on my aunt, and though she is very kind to me she makes me no regular allowance, and lately I've lost money at cards, and I don't dare tell her about it. I have paid my card debts, of course, but there is hardly anything left for my other expenses, and if I go on with my present life I shall be in horrible difficulties. I have a tiny income of my own, but I'm afraid it's badly invested, for it seems to bring in less every year, and I am so ignorant of money matters that I don't know if my aunt's agent, who looks after it, is a good adviser." She paused a moment, and added in a lighter tone: "I didn't mean to bore you with all this, but I want your help in making Judy understand that I can't, at present, go on living as one must live among you all. I am going away tomorrow to join my aunt at Richfield, and I shall stay there for the rest of the autumn, and dismiss my maid and learn how to mend my own clothes."

At this picture of loveliness in distress, the pathos of which was heightened by the light touch with which it was drawn, a murmur of indignant sympathy broke from Trenor. Twenty-four hours earlier, if his wife had consulted him on the subject of Miss Bart's future, he would have said that a girl with extravagant tastes and no money had better marry the first rich man she could get; but with the subject of discussion at his side, turning to him for sympathy, making him feel that he understood her better than her dearest friends, and confirming the assurance by the appeal of her exquisite nearness, he was ready to swear that such a marriage was a desecration, and that, as a man of honor, he was bound to do all he could to protect her from the results of her disinterestedness. This impulse was reinforced by the reflection that if she had married Gryce she would have been surrounded by flattery and approval, whereas, having refused to sacrifice herself to expediency, she was left to bear the whole cost of her resistance. Hang it, if he could find a way out of such difficulties for a professional sponge like Carry Fisher, who was simply a mental habit corresponding to the physical titillations of the cigarette or the cocktail, he could surely do as much for a girl who appealed to his highest sympathies, and who brought her troubles to him with the trustfullness of a child.

Trenor and Miss Bart prolonged their drive till long after sunset; and before it was over he had tried, with some show of success, to prove to her that, if she would only trust him, he could make a handsome sum of money for her without endangering the small amount she possessed. She was too genuinely ignorant of the manipulations of the stock-market to understand his technical explanations, or even perhaps to perceive that certain points in them were slurred; the haziness enveloping the transaction served as a veil for her embarrassment, and through the general blur her hopes dilated like lamps in a fog. She understood only that her modest investments were to be mysteriously multiplied without risk to herself; and the assurance that this miracle would take place within a short time, that there would be no tedious interval for suspense and reaction, relieved her of her lingering scruples.

Again she felt the lightening of her load, and with it the release of repressed activities. Her immediate worries conjured, it was easy to resolve that she would never again find herself in such straits, and as the need of economy and self-denial receded from her foreground she felt herself ready to meet any other demand which life might make. Even the immediate one of letting Trenor, as they drove homeward, lean a little nearer and rest his hand reassuringly on hers, cost her only a momentary shiver of reluctance. It was part of the game to make him feel that her appeal had been an uncalculated impulse, provoked by the liking he inspired; and the renewed sense of power in handling men, while it consoled her wounded vanity, helped also to obscure the thought of the claim at which his manner hinted. He was a coarse dull man who, under all his show of authority, was a mere supernumerary in the costly show for which his money paid: surely, to a clever girl, it would be easy to hold him by his vanity, and so keep the obligation on his side.

8

THE first thousand dollar check which Lily received with a blotted scrawl from Gus Trenor strengthened her self-confidence in the exact degree to which it effaced her debts.

The transaction had justified itself by its results: she saw now how absurd it would have been to let any primitive scruple deprive her of this easy means of appeasing her creditors. Lily felt really virtuous as she dispensed the sum in sops to her tradesmen, and the fact that a fresh order accompanied each payment did not lessen her sense of disinterestedness. How many women, in her place, would have given the orders without making the payment!

She had found it reassuringly easy to keep Trenor in a good humor. To listen to his stories, to receive his confidence and laugh at his jokes, seemed for the moment all that was required of her, and the complacency with which her hostess regarded these attentions freed them of the least hint of ambiguity. Mrs. Trenor evidently assumed that Lily's growing intimacy with her husband was simply an indirect way of returning her own kindness.

"I'm so glad you and Gus have become such good friends," she said approvingly. "It's too delightful of you to be so nice to him, and put up with all his tiresome stories. I know what they are, because I had to listen to them when we were engaged—I'm sure he is telling the same ones still. And now I shan't always have to be asking Carry Fisher here to keep him in a good humor. She's a perfect vulture, you know; and she hasn't the least moral sense. She is always getting Gus to speculate for her, and I'm sure she never pays when she loses."

Miss Bart could shudder at this state of things without the embarrassment of a personal application. Her own position was surely quite different. There could be no question of her not paying when she lost, since Trenor had assured her that she was certain not to lose. In sending her the check he had explained that he had made five thousand for her out of Rosedale's "tip," and had put four thousand back in the same venture, as there was the promise of another "big rise"; she understood therefore that he was now speculating with her own money, and that she consequently owed him no more than the gratitude which such a trifling service demanded. She

vaguely supposed that, to raise the first sum, he had borrowed on her securities; but this was a point over which her curiosity did not linger. It was
concentrated, for the moment, on the probable date of the next "big rise."

The news of this event was received by her some weeks later, on the
occasion of Jack Stepney's marriage to Miss Van Osburgh. As a cousin of
the bridegroom, Miss Bart had been asked to act as bridesmaid; but she had
declined on the plea that, since she was much taller than the other attendant virgins, her presence might mar the symmetry of the group. The truth
was, she had attended too many brides to the altar: when next seen there
she meant to be the chief figure in the ceremony. She knew the pleasantries
made at the expense of young girls who have been too long before the
public, and she was resolved to avoid such assumptions of youthfullness as
might lead people to think her older than she really was.

The Van Osburgh marriage was celebrated in the village church near
the paternal estate on the Hudson. It was the "simple country wedding" to
which guests are convoyed in special trains, and from which the hordes of
the uninvited have to be fended off by the intervention of the police. While
these sylvan rites were taking place, in a church packed with fashion and
festooned with orchids, the representatives of the press were threading their
way, notebook in hand, through the labyrinth of wedding presents, and the
agent of a cinematograph syndicate was setting up his apparatus at the
church door. It was the kind of scene in which Lily had often pictured
herself as taking the principal part, and on this occasion the fact that she
was once more merely a casual spectator, instead of the mystically veiled
figure occupying the center of attention, strengthened her resolve to assume
the latter part before the year was over. The fact that her immediate anxieties were relieved did not blind her to a possibility of their recurrence; it
merely gave her enough buoyancy to rise once more above her doubts and
feel a renewed faith in her beauty, her power, and her general fitness to
attract a brilliant destiny. It could not be that one conscious of such apti-
tudes for mastery and enjoyment was doomed to a perpetuity of failure;
and her mistakes looked easily reparable in the light of her restored self-
confidence.

A special appositeness was given to these reflections by the discovery, in
a neighboring pew, of the serious profile and neatly trimmed beard of Mr.
Percy Gryce. There was something almost bridal in his own aspect: his large
white gardenia had a symbolic air that struck Lily as a good omen. After all,
seen in an assemblage of his kind he was not ridiculous-looking: a friendly
critic might have called his heaviness weighty, and he was at his best in the
attitude of vacant passivity which brings out the oddities of the restless. She
fancied he was the kind of man whose sentimental associations would be
stirred by the conventional imagery of a wedding, and she pictured herself,
in the seclusion of the Van Osburgh conservatories, playing skillfully upon
sensibilities thus prepared for her touch. In fact, when she looked at the

other women about her, and recalled the image she had brought away from her own glass, it did not seem as though any special skill would be needed to repair her blunder and bring him once more to her feet.

The sight of Selden's dark head, in a pew almost facing her, disturbed for a moment the balance of her complacency. The rise of her blood as their eyes met was succeeded by a contrary motion, a wave of resistance and withdrawal. She did not wish to see him again, not because she feared his influence, but because his presence always had the effect of cheapening her aspirations, of throwing her whole world out of focus. Besides, he was a living reminder of the worst mistake in her career, and the fact that he had been its cause did not soften her feelings toward him. She could still imagine an ideal state of existence in which, all else being superadded, intercourse with Selden might be the last touch of luxury; but in the world as it was, such a privilege was likely to cost more than it was worth.

"Lily, dear, I never saw you look so lovely! You look as if something delightful had just happened to you!"

The young lady who thus formulated her admiration of her brilliant friend did not, in her own person, suggest such happy possibilities. Miss Gertrude Farish, in fact, typified the mediocre and the ineffectual. If there were compensating qualities in her wide frank glance and the freshness of her smile, these were qualities which only the sympathetic observer would perceive before noticing that her eyes were of a workaday gray and her lips without haunting curves. Lily's own view of her wavered between pity for her limitations and impatience at her cheerful acceptance of them. To Miss Bart, as to her mother, acquiescence in dinginess was evidence of stupidity; and there were moments when, in the consciousness of her own power to look and to be so exactly what the occasion required, she almost felt that other girls were plain and inferior from choice. Certainly no one need have confessed such acquiescence in her lot as was revealed in the "useful" color of Gerty Farish's gown and the subdued lines of her hat: it is almost as stupid to let your clothes betray that you know you are ugly as to have them proclaim that you think you are beautiful.

Of course, being fatally poor and dingy, it was wise of Gerty to have taken up philanthropy and symphony concerts; but there was something irritating in her assumption that existence yielded no higher pleasures, and that one might get as much interest and excitement out of life in a cramped flat as in the splendors of the Van Osburgh establishment. Today, however, her chirping enthusiasms did not irritate Lily. They seemed only to throw her own exceptionalness into becoming relief, and give a soaring vastness to her scheme of life.

"Do let us go and take a peep at the presents before everyone else leaves the dining-room!" suggested Miss Farish, linking her arm in her friend's. It was characteristic of her to take a sentimental and unenvious interest in all the details of a wedding: she was the kind of person who always kept her handkerchief out during the service, and departed clutching a box of wedding cake.

"Isn't everything beautifully done?" she pursued, as they entered the distant drawing-room assigned to the display of Miss Van Osburgh's bridal spoils. "I always say no one does things better than cousin Grace! Did you ever taste anything more delicious than that mousse of lobster with champagne sauce? I made up my mind weeks ago that I wouldn't miss this wedding, and just fancy how delightfully it all came about. When Lawrence Selden heard I was coming, he insisted on fetching me himself and driving me to the station, and when we go back this evening I am to dine with him at Sherry's. I really feel as excited as if I were getting married myself!"

Lily smiled: she knew that Selden had always been kind to his dull cousin, and she had sometimes wondered why he wasted so much time in such an unremunerative manner; but now the thought gave her a vague pleasure.

"Do you see him often?" she asked.

"Yes, he is very good about dropping in on Sundays. And now and then we do a play together; but lately I haven't seen much of him. He doesn't look well, and he seems nervous and unsettled. The dear fellow! I do wish he would marry some nice girl. I told him so today, but he said he didn't care for the really nice ones, and the other kind didn't care for him—but that was just his joke, of course. He could never marry a girl who *wasn't* nice. Oh, my dear, did you ever see such pearls?"

They had paused before the table on which the bride's jewels were displayed, and Lily's heart gave an envious throb as she caught the refraction of light from their surfaces—the milky gleam of perfectly matched pearls, the flash of rubies relieved against contrasting velvet, the intense blue rays of sapphires kindled into light by surrounding diamonds: all these precious tints enhanced and deepened by the varied art of their setting. The glow of the stones warmed Lily's veins like wine. More completely than any other expression of wealth they symbolized the life she longed to lead, the life of fastidious aloofness and refinement in which every detail should have the finish of a jewel, and the whole form a harmonious setting to her own jewellike rareness.

"Oh, Lily, do look at this diamond pendant—it's as big as a dinnerplate! Who can have given it?" Miss Farish bent short-sightedly over the accompanying card. "*Mr. Simon Rosedale.* What, that horrid man? Oh, yes —I remember he's a friend of Jack's, and I suppose cousin Grace had to ask him here today; but she must rather hate having to let Gwen accept such a present from him."

Lily smiled. She doubted Mrs. Van Osburgh's reluctance, but was aware of Miss Farish's habit of ascribing her own delicacies of feeling to the persons least likely to be encumbered by them.

"Well, if Gwen doesn't care to be seen wearing it she can always exchange it for something else," she remarked.

"Ah, here is something so much prettier," Miss Farish continued. "Do look at this exquisite white sapphire. I'm sure the person who chose it must have taken particular pains. What is the name? Percy Gryce? Ah, then I'm not surprised!" She smiled significantly as she replaced the card. "Of course you've heard that he's perfectly devoted to Evie Van Osburgh? Cousin Grace is so pleased about it—it's quite a romance! He met her first at the George Dorsets', only about six weeks ago, and it's just the nicest possible marriage for dear Evie. Oh, I don't mean the money—of course she has plenty of her own—but she's such a quiet stay-at-home kind of girl, and it seems he has just the same tastes; so they are exactly suited to each other."

Lily stood staring vacantly at the white sapphire on its velvet bed. Evie Van Osburgh and Percy Gryce? The names rang derisively through her brain. *Evie Van Osburgh?* The youngest, dumpiest, dullest of the four dull and dumpy daughters whom Mrs. Van Osburgh, with unsurpassed astuteness, had "placed" one by one in enviable niches of existence! Ah, lucky girls who grow up in the shelter of a mother's love—a mother who knows how to contrive opportunities without conceding favors, how to take advantage of propinquity without allowing appetite to be dulled by habit! The cleverest girl may miscalculate where her own interests are concerned, may yield too much at one moment and withdraw too far at the next: it takes a mother's unerring vigilance and foresight to land her daughters safely in the arms of wealth and suitability.

Lily's passing light-heartedness sank beneath a renewed sense of failure. Life was too stupid, too blundering! Why should Percy Gryce's millions be joined to another great fortune, why should this clumsy girl be put in possession of powers she would never know how to use?

She was roused from these speculations by a familiar touch on her arm, and turning saw Gus Trenor beside her. She felt a thrill of vexation: what right had he to touch her? Luckily Gerty Farish had wandered off to the next table, and they were alone.

Trenor, looking stouter than ever in his tight frock-coat, and unbecomingly flushed by the bridal libations, gazed at her with undisguised approval.

"By Jove, Lily, you do look a stunner!" He had slipped insensibly into the use of her Christian name, and she had never found the right moment to correct him. Besides, in her set all the men and women called each other by their Christian names; it was only on Trenor's lips that the familiar address had an unpleasant significance.

"Well," he continued, still jovially impervious to her annoyance, "have you made up your mind which of these little trinkets you mean to duplicate at Tiffany's tomorrow? I've got a check for you in my pocket that will go a long way in that line!"

Lily gave him a startled look: his voice was louder than usual, and the room was beginning to fill with people. But as her glance assured her that they were still beyond earshot a sense of pleasure replaced her apprehension.

"Another dividend?" she asked, smiling and drawing near him in the desire not to be overheard.

"Well, not exactly: I sold out on the rise and I've pulled off four thou' for you. Not so bad for a beginner, eh? I suppose you'll begin to think you're a pretty knowing speculator. And perhaps you won't think poor old Gus such an awful ass as some people do."

"I think you the kindest of friends; but I can't thank you properly now."

She let her eyes shine into his with a look that made up for the hand-clasp he would have claimed if they had been alone—and how glad she was that they were not! The news filled her with the glow produced by a sudden cessation of physical pain. The world was not so stupid and blundering after all: now and then a stroke of luck came to the unluckiest. At the thought her spirits began to rise: it was characteristic of her that one trifling piece of good fortune should give wings to all her hopes. Instantly came the reflection that Percy Gryce was not irretrievably lost; and she smiled to think of the excitement of recapturing him from Evie Van Osburgh. What chance could such a simpleton have against her if she chose to exert herself? She glanced about, hoping to catch a glimpse of Gryce; but her eyes lit instead on the glossy countenance of Mr. Rosedale, who was slipping through the crowd with an air half obsequious, half obtrusive, as though, the moment his presence was recognized, it would swell to the dimensions of the room.

Not wishing to be the means of effecting this enlargement, Lily quickly transferred her glance to Trenor, to whom the expression of her gratitude seemed not to have brought the complete gratification she had meant it to give.

"Hang thanking me—I don't want to be thanked, but I should like the chance to say two words to you now and then," he grumbled. "I thought you were going to spend the whole autumn with us, and I've hardly laid eyes on you for the last month. Why can't you come back to Bellomont this evening? We're all alone, and Judy is as cross as two sticks. Do come and cheer a fellow up. If you say yes I'll run you over in the motor, and you can telephone your maid to bring your traps from town by the next train."

Lily shook her head with a charming semblance of regret. "I wish I could —but it's quite impossible. My aunt has come back to town, and I must be with her for the next few days."

"Well, I've seen a good deal less of you since we've got to be such pals than I used to when you were Judy's friend," he continued with unconscious penetration.

"When I was Judy's friend? Am I not her friend still? Really, you say the most absurd things! If I were always at Bellomont you would tire of me much sooner than Judy—but come and see me at my aunt's the next afternoon you are in town; then we can have a nice quiet talk, and you can tell me how I had better invest my fortune."

It was true that, during the last three or four weeks, she had absented herself from Bellomont on the pretext of having other visits to pay; but she now began to feel that the reckoning she had thus contrived to evade had rolled up interest in the interval.

The prospect of the nice quiet talk did not appear as all-sufficing to Trenor as she had hoped, and his brows continued to lower as he said: "Oh, I don't know that I can promise you a fresh tip every day. But there's one thing you might do for me; and that is, just to be a little civil to Rosedale. Judy has promised to ask him to dine when we get to town, but I can't induce her to have him at Bellomont, and if you would let me bring him up now it would make a lot of difference. I don't believe two women have spoken to him this afternoon, and I can tell you he's a chap it pays to be decent to."

Miss Bart made an impatient movement, but suppressed the words which seemed about to accompany it. After all, this was an unexpectedly easy way of acquitting her debt; and had she not reasons of her own for wishing to be civil to Mr. Rosedale?

"Oh, bring him by all means," she said smiling; "perhaps I can get a tip out of him on my own account."

Trenor paused abruptly, and his eyes fixed themselves on hers with a look which made her change color.

"I say, you know—you'll please remember he's a blooming bounder," he said; and with a slight laugh she turned toward the open window near which they had been standing.

The throng in the room had increased, and she felt a desire for space and fresh air. Both of these she found on the terrace, where only a few men were lingering over cigarettes and liqueur, while scattered couples strolled across the lawn to the autumn-tinted borders of the flower-garden.

As she emerged, a man moved toward her from the knot of smokers, and she found herself face to face with Selden. The stir of the pulses which his nearness always caused was increased by a slight sense of constraint. They had not met since their Sunday afternoon walk at Bellomont, and that episode was still so vivid to her that she could hardly believe him to be less conscious of it. But his greeting expressed no more than the satisfaction which every pretty woman expects to see reflected in masculine eyes; and the discovery, if distasteful to her vanity, was reassuring to her nerves. Between the relief of her escape from Trenor, and the vague apprehension of her meeting with Rosedale, it was pleasant to rest a moment on the sense of complete understanding which Lawrence Selden's manner always conveyed.

"This is luck," he said smiling. "I was wondering if I should be able to have a word with you before the special snatches us away. I came with

Gerty Farish, and promised not to let her miss the train, but I am sure she is still extracting sentimental solace from the wedding presents. She appears to regard their number and value as evidence of the disinterested affection of the contracting parties."

There was not the least trace of embarrassment in his voice, and as he spoke, leaning slightly against the jamb of the window, and letting his eyes rest on her in the frank enjoyment of her grace, she felt with a faint chill of regret that he had gone back without an effort to the footing on which they had stood before their last talk together. Her vanity was stung by the sight of his unscathed smile. She longed to be to him something more than a piece of sentient prettiness, a passing diversion to his eye and brain; and the longing betrayed itself in her reply.

"Ah," she said, "I envy Gerty that power she has of dressing up with romance all our ugly and prosaic arrangements! I have never recovered my self-respect since you showed me how poor and unimportant my ambitions were."

The words were hardly spoken when she realized their infelicity. It seemed to be her fate to appear at her worst to Selden.

"I thought, on the contrary," he returned lightly, "that I had been the means of proving they were more important to you than anything else."

It was as if the eager current of her being had been checked by a sudden obstacle which drove it back upon itself. She looked at him helplessly, like a hurt or frightened child: this real self of hers, which he had the faculty of drawing out of the depths, was so little accustomed to go alone!

The appeal of her helplessness touched in him, as it always did, a latent chord of inclination. It would have meant nothing to him to discover that his nearness made her more brilliant, but this glimpse of a twilight mood to which he alone had the clue seemed once more to set him in a world apart with her.

"At least you can't think worse things of me than you say!" she exclaimed with a trembling laugh; but before he could answer, the flow of comprehension between them was abruptly stayed by the reappearance of Gus Trenor, who advanced with Mr. Rosedale in his wake.

"Hang it, Lily, I thought you'd given me the slip: Rosedale and I have been hunting all over for you!"

His voice had a note of conjugal familiarity: Miss Bart fancied she detected in Rosedale's eye a twinkling perception of the fact, and the idea turned her dislike of him to repugnance.

She returned his profound bow with a slight nod, made more disdainful by the sense of Selden's surprise that she should number Rosedale among her acquaintances. Trenor had turned away, and his companion continued to stand before Miss Bart, alert and expectant, his lips parted in a smile at whatever she might be about to say, and his very back conscious of the privilege of being seen with her.

It was the moment for tact; for the quick bridging over of gaps; but Selden still leaned against the window, a detached observer of the scene, and under the spell of his observation Lily felt herself powerless to exert her usual arts. The dread of Selden's suspecting that there was any need for her to propitiate such a man as Rosedale checked the trivial phrases of politeness. Rosedale still stood before her in an expectant attitude, and she continued to face him in silence, her glance just level with his polished baldness. The look put the finishing touch to what her silence implied.

He reddened slowly, shifting from one foot to the other, fingered the plump black pearl in his tie, and gave a nervous twist to his moustache; then, running his eye over her, he drew back, and said, with a side-glance at Selden: "Upon my soul, I never saw a more ripping get-up. Is that the last creation of the dressmaker you go to see at the Benedick? If so, I wonder all the other women don't go to her too!"

The words were projected sharply against Lily's silence, and she saw in a flash that her own act had given them their emphasis. In ordinary talk they might have passed unheeded; but following on her prolonged pause they acquired a special meaning. She felt, without looking, that Selden had immediately seized it, and would inevitably connect the allusion with her visit to himself. The consciousness increased her irritation against Rosedale, but also her feeling that now, if ever, was the moment to propitiate him, hateful as it was to do so in Selden's presence.

"How do you know the other women don't go to my dressmaker?" she returned. "You see I'm not afraid to give her address to my friends!"

Her glance and accent so plainly included Rosedale in this privileged circle that his small eyes puckered with gratification, and a knowing smile drew up his moustache.

"By Jove, you needn't be!" he declared. "You could give 'em the whole outfit and win at a canter!"

"Ah, that's nice of you; and it would be nicer still if you would carry me off to a quiet corner, and get me a glass of lemonade or some innocent drink before we all have to rush for the train."

She turned away as she spoke, letting him strut at her side through the gathering groups on the terrace, while every nerve in her throbbed with the consciousness of what Selden must have thought of the scene.

But under her angry sense of the perverseness of things, and the light surface of her talk with Rosedale, a third idea persisted: she did not mean to leave without an attempt to discover the truth about Percy Gryce. Chance, or perhaps his own resolve, had kept them apart since his hasty withdrawal from Bellomont; but Miss Bart was an expert in making the most of the unexpected, and the distasteful incidents of the last few minutes—the revelation to Selden of precisely that part of her life which she most wished him to ignore—increased her longing for shelter, for escape from such humiliating contingencies. Any definite situation would be more tolerable than this buffeting of chances, which kept her in an attitude of uneasy alertness toward every possibility of life.

Indoors there was a general sense of dispersal in the air, as of an audience gathering itself up for departure after the principal actors had left the stage; but among the remaining groups, Lily could discover neither Gryce nor the youngest Miss Van Osburgh. That both should be missing struck her with foreboding; and she charmed Mr. Rosedale by proposing that they should make their way to the conservatories at the farther end of the house. There were just enough people left in the long suite of rooms to make their progress conspicuous, and Lily was aware of being followed by looks of amusement and interrogation, which glanced off as harmlessly from her indifference as from her companion's self-satisfaction. She cared very little at that moment about being seen with Rosedale: all her thoughts were centered on the object of her search. The latter, however, was not discoverable in the conservatories, and Lily, oppressed by a sudden conviction of failure, was casting about for a way to rid herself of her now superfluous companion, when they came upon Mrs. Van Osburgh, flushed and exhausted, but beaming with the consciousness of duty performed.

She glanced at them a moment with the benign but vacant eye of the tired hostess, to whom her guests have become mere whirling spots in a kaleidoscope of fatigue; then her attention became suddenly fixed, and she seized on Miss Bart with a confidential gesture.

"My dear Lily, I haven't had time for a word with you, and now I suppose you are just off. Have you seen Evie? She's been looking everywhere for you: she wanted to tell you her little secret; but I daresay you have guessed it already. The engagement is not to be announced till next week— but you are such a friend of Mr. Gryce's that they both wished you to be the first to know of their happiness."

9

I N Mrs. Peniston's youth, fashion had returned to town in October; therefore on the tenth day of the month the blinds of her Fifth Avenue residence were drawn up, and the eyes of the Dying Gladiator in bronze who occupied the drawing-room window resumed their survey of that deserted thoroughfare.

The first two weeks after her return represented to Mrs. Peniston the domestic equivalent of a religious retreat. She "went through" the linen and blankets in the precise spirit of the penitent exploring the inner folds of

conscience; she sought for moths as the stricken soul seeks for lurking infir-
mities. The topmost shelf of every closet was made to yield up its secret,
cellar and coal-bin were probed to their darkest depths and, as a final stage
in the lustral rites, the entire house was swathed in penitential white and
deluged with expiatory soapsuds.

It was on this phase of the proceedings that Miss Bart entered on the
afternoon of her return from the Van Osburgh wedding. The journey back
to town had not been calculated to soothe her nerves. Though Evie Van
Osburgh's engagement was still officially a secret, it was one of which the
innumerable intimate friends of the family were already possessed; and the
trainful of returning guests buzzed with allusions and anticipations. Lily was
acutely aware of her own part in this drama of innuendo: she knew the
exact quality of the amusement the situation evoked. The crude forms in
which her friends took their pleasure included a loud enjoyment of such
complications: the zest of surprising destiny in the act of playing a practical
joke. Lily knew well enough how to bear herself in difficult situations. She
had, to a shade, the exact manner between victory and defeat: every insinuation was shed without an effort by the bright indifference of her manner.
But she was beginning to feel the strain of the attitude; the reaction was
more rapid, and she lapsed to a deeper self-disgust.

As was always the case with her, this moral repulsion found a physical
outlet in a quickened distaste for her surroundings. She revolted from the
complacent ugliness of Mrs. Peniston's black walnut, from the slippery gloss
of the vestibule tiles, and the mingled odor of sapolio and furniture polish
that met her at the door.

The stairs were still carpetless, and on the way up to her room she was
arrested on the landing by an encroaching tide of soapsuds. Gathering up
her skirts, she drew aside with an impatient gesture; and as she did so she
had the odd sensation of having already found herself in the same situation
but in different surroundings. It seemed to her that she was again descending the staircase from Selden's rooms; and looking down to remonstrate
with the dispenser of the soapy flood, she found herself met by a lifted stare
which had once before confronted her under similar circumstances. It was
the charwoman of the Benedick who, resting on crimson elbows, examined
her with the same unflinching curiosity, the same apparent reluctance to let
her pass. On this occasion, however, Miss Bart was on her own ground.

"Don't you see that I wish to go by? Please move your pail," she said
sharply.

The woman at first seemed not to hear; then, without a word of excuse,
she pushed back her pail and dragged a wet floor-cloth across the landing,
keeping her eyes fixed on Lily while the latter swept by. It was insufferable
that Mrs. Peniston should have such creatures about the house; and Lily
entered her room resolved that the woman should be dismissed that
evening.

Mrs. Peniston, however, was at the moment inaccessible to remonstrance: since early morning she had been shut up with her maid, going over her furs, a process which formed the culminating episode in the drama of household renovation. In the evening also Lily found herself alone, for her aunt, who rarely dined out, had responded to the summons of a Van Alstyne cousin who was passing through town. The house, in its state of unnatural immaculateness and order, was as dreary as a tomb, and as Lily, turning from her brief repast between shrouded sideboards, wandered into the newly uncovered glare of the drawing-room she felt as though she were buried alive in the stifling limits of Mrs. Peniston's existence.

She usually contrived to avoid being at home during the season of domestic renewal. On the present occasion, however, a variety of reasons had combined to bring her to town; and foremost among them was the fact that she had fewer invitations than usual for the autumn. She had so long been accustomed to pass from one country house to another, till the close of the holidays brought her friends to town, that the unfilled gaps of time confronting her produced a sharp sense of waning popularity. It was as she had said to Selden—people were tired of her. They would welcome her in a new character, but as Miss Bart they knew her by heart. She knew herself by heart, too, and was sick of the old story. There were moments when she longed blindly for anything different, anything strange, remote and untried; but the utmost reach of her imagination did not go beyond picturing her usual life in a new setting. She could not figure herself as anywhere but in a drawing-room, diffusing elegance as a flower sheds perfume.

Meanwhile, as October advanced she had to face the alternative of returning to the Trenors or joining her aunt in town. Even the desolating dullness of New York in October, and the soapy discomforts of Mrs. Peniston's interior, seemed preferable to what might await her at Bellomont; and with an air of heroic devotion she announced her intention of remaining with her aunt till the holidays.

Sacrifices of this nature are sometimes received with feelings as mixed as those which actuate them; and Mrs. Peniston remarked to her confidential maid that, if any of the family were to be with her at such a crisis (though for forty years she had been thought competent to see to the hanging of her own curtains), she would certainly have preferred Miss Grace to Miss Lily. Grace Stepney was an obscure cousin, of adaptable manners and vicarious interests, who "ran in" to sit with Mrs. Peniston when Lily dined out too continuously; who played bézique, picked up dropped stitches, read out the deaths from the Times, and sincerely admired the purple satin drawing-room curtains, the Dying Gladiator in the window, and the seven-by-five painting of Niagara which represented the one artistic excess of Mr. Peniston's temperate career.

Mrs. Peniston, under ordinary circumstances, was as much bored by her excellent cousin as the recipient of such services usually is by the person who performs them. She greatly preferred the brilliant and unreliable Lily, who did not know one end of a crochet-needle from the other, and had frequently wounded her susceptibilities by suggesting that the drawing-room should be "done over." But when it came to hunting for missing napkins, or helping to decide whether the backstairs needed recarpeting, Grace's judgment was certainly sounder than Lily's: not to mention the fact that the latter resented the smell of beeswax and brown soap, and behaved as though she thought a house ought to keep clean of itself, without extraneous assistance.

Seated under the cheerless blaze of the drawing-room chandelier—Mrs. Peniston never lit the lamps unless there was "company"—Lily seemed to watch her own figure retreating down vistas of neutral-tinted dullness to a middle age like Grace Stepney's. When she ceased to amuse Judy Trenor and her friends she would have to fall back on amusing Mrs. Peniston; whichever way she looked she saw only a future of servitude to the whims of others, never the possibility of asserting her own eager individuality.

A ring at the doorbell, sounding emphatically through the empty house, roused her suddenly to the extent of her boredom. It was as though all the weariness of the past months had culminated in the vacuity of that interminable evening. If only the ring meant a summons from the outer world—a token that she was still remembered and wanted!

After some delay a parlor maid presented herself with the announcement that there was a person outside who was asking to see Miss Bart; and on Lily's pressing for a more specific description, she added:

"It's Mrs. Haffen, Miss; she won't say what she wants."

Lily, to whom the name conveyed nothing, opened the door upon a woman in a battered bonnet, who stood firmly planted under the hall light. The glare of the unshaded gas shone familiarly on her pock-marked face and the reddish baldness visible through thin strands of straw-colored hair. Lily looked at the charwoman in surprise.

"Do you wish to see me?" she asked.

"I should like to say a word to you, Miss." The tone was neither aggressive nor conciliatory: it revealed nothing of the speaker's errand. Nevertheless, some precautionary instinct warned Lily to withdraw beyond earshot of the hovering parlor maid.

She signed to Mrs. Haffen to follow her into the drawing-room, and closed the door when they had entered.

"What is it that you wish?" she inquired.

The charwoman, after the manner of her kind, stood with her arms folded in her shawl. Unwinding the latter, she produced a small parcel wrapped in dirty newspaper.

"I have something here that you might like to see, Miss Bart." She spoke the name with an unpleasant emphasis, as though her knowing it made a part of her reason for being there. To Lily the intonation sounded like a threat.

"You have found something belonging to me?" she asked, extending her hand.

Mrs. Haffen drew back. "Well, if it comes to that, I guess it's mine as much as anybody's," she returned.

Lily looked at her perplexedly. She was sure, now, that her visitor's manner conveyed a threat; but, expert as she was in certain directions, there was nothing in her experience to prepare her for the exact significance of the present scene. She felt, however, that it must be ended as promptly as possible.

"I don't understand; if this parcel is not mine, why have you asked for me?"

The woman was unabashed by the question. She was evidently prepared to answer it, but like all her class she had to go a long way back to make a beginning, and it was only after a pause that she replied: "My husband was janitor to the Benedick till the first of the month; since then he can't get nothing to do."

Lily remained silent and she continued: "It wasn't no fault of our own, neither: the agent had another man he wanted the place for, and we was put out, bag and baggage, just to suit his fancy. I had a long sickness last winter, and an operation that ate up all we'd put by; and it's hard for me and the children, Haffen being so long out of a job."

After all, then, she had come only to ask Miss Bart to find a place for her husband; or, more probably, to seek the young lady's intervention with Mrs. Peniston. Lily had such an air of always getting what she wanted that she was used to being appealed to as an intermediary, and, relieved of her vague apprehension, she took refuge in the conventional formula.

"I am sorry you have been in trouble," she said.

"Oh, that we have, Miss, and it's on'y just beginning. If on'y we'd 'a got another situation—but the agent, he's dead against us. It ain't no fault of ours, neither, but —"

At this point Lily's impatience overcame her. "If you have anything to say to me —" she interposed.

The woman's resentment of the rebuff seemed to spur her lagging ideas.

"Yes, Miss; I'm coming to that," she said. She paused again, with her eyes on Lily, and then continued, in a tone of diffuse narrative: "When we was at the Benedick I had charge of some of the gentlemen's rooms; least-ways, I swep' 'em out on Saturdays. Some of the gentlemen got the greatest sight of letters: I never saw the like of it. Their wastepaper baskets'd be fairly brimming, and papers falling over on the floor. Maybe havin' so many is how they get so careless. Some of 'em is worse than others. Mr. Selden, Mr. Lawrence Selden, he was always one of the carefullest: burnt his letters in winter, and tore 'em in little bits in summer. But sometimes he'd have so many he'd just bunch 'em together, the way the others did, and tear the lot through once—like this."

While she spoke she had loosened the string from the parcel in her hand, and now she drew forth a letter which she laid on the table between Miss Bart and herself. As she had said, the letter was torn in two; but with a rapid gesture she laid the torn edges together and smoothed out the page.

A wave of indignation swept over Lily. She felt herself in the presence of something vile, as yet but dimly conjectured—the kind of vileness of which people whispered, but which she had never thought of as touching her own life. She drew back with a motion of disgust, but her withdrawal was checked by a sudden discovery: under the glare of Mrs. Peniston's chandelier she had recognized the handwriting of the letter. It was a large disjointed hand, with a flourish of masculinity which but slightly disguised its rambling weakness, and the words, scrawled in heavy ink on pale-tinted notepaper, smote on Lily's ear as though she had heard them spoken.

At first she did not grasp the full import of the situation. She understood only that before her lay a letter written by Bertha Dorset, and addressed, presumably, to Lawrence Selden. There was no date, but the blackness of the ink proved the writing to be comparatively recent. The packet in Mrs. Haffen's hand doubtless contained more letters of the same kind—a dozen, Lily conjectured from its thickness. The letter before her was short, but its few words, which had leapt into her brain before she was conscious of reading them, told a long history—a history over which, for the last four years, the friends of the writer had smiled and shrugged, viewing it merely as one among the countless "good situations" of the mundane comedy. Now the other side presented itself to Lily, the volcanic nether side of the surface over which conjecture and innuendo glide so lightly till the first fissure turns their whisper to a shriek. Lily knew that there is nothing society resents so much as having given its protection to those who have not known how to profit by it: it is for having betrayed its connivance that the body social punishes the offender who is found out. And in this case there was no doubt of the issue. The code of Lily's world decreed that a woman's husband should be the only judge of her conduct: she was technically above suspicion while she had the shelter of his approval, or even of his indifference. But with a man of George Dorset's temper there could be no thought of condonation—the possessor of his wife's letters could overthrow with a touch the whole structure of her existence. And into what hands Bertha Dorset's secret had been delivered! For a moment the irony of the coincidence tinged Lily's disgust with a confused sense of triumph. But the disgust prevailed—all her instinctive resistances, of taste, of training, of blind inherited scruples, rose against the other feeling. Her strongest sense was one of personal contamination.

She moved away, as though to put as much distance as possible between

herself and her visitor. "I know nothing of these letters," she said; "I have
no idea why you have brought them here."

Mrs. Haffen faced her steadily. "I'll tell you why, Miss. I brought 'em to
you to sell, because I ain't got no other way of raising money, and if we
don't pay our rent by tomorrow night we'll be put out. I never done anythin'
of the kind before, and if you'd speak to Mr. Selden or to Mr. Rosedale
about getting Haffen taken on again at the Benedick—I seen you talking to
Mr. Rosedale at the steps that day you come out of Mr. Selden's rooms —"

The blood rushed to Lily's forehead. She understood now—Mrs. Haffen
supposed her to be the writer of the letters. In the first leap of her anger she
was about to ring and order the woman out; but an obscure impulse restrained her. The mention of Selden's name had started a new train of
thought. Bertha Dorset's letters were nothing to her—they might go where
the current of chance carried them! But Selden was inextricably involved in
their fate. Men do not, at worst, suffer much from such exposure; and in this
instance the flash of divination which had carried the meaning of the letters
to Lily's brain had revealed also that they were appeals—repeated and
therefore probably unanswered—for the renewal of a tie which time had
evidently relaxed. Nevertheless, the fact that the correspondence had been
allowed to fall into strange hands would convict Selden of negligence in a
matter where the world holds it least pardonable; and there were graver
risks to consider where a man of Dorset's ticklish balance was concerned.

If she weighed all these things it was unconsciously: she was aware only
of feeling that Selden would wish the letters rescued, and that therefore she
must obtain possession of them. Beyond that her mind did not travel. She
had, indeed, a quick vision of returning the packet to Bertha Dorset, and of
the opportunities the restitution offered; but this thought lit up abysses from
which she shrank back ashamed.

Meanwhile Mrs. Haffen, prompt to perceive her hesitation, had already
opened the packet and ranged its contents on the table. All the letters had
been pieced together with strips of thin paper. Some were in small fragments, the others merely torn in half. Though there were not many, thus
spread out they nearly covered the table. Lily's glance fell on a word here
and there—then she said in a low voice: "What do you wish me to pay
you?"

Mrs. Haffen's face reddened with satisfaction. It was clear that the
young lady was badly frightened, and Mrs. Haffen was the woman to make
the most of such fears. Anticipating an easier victory than she had foreseen,
she named an exorbitant sum.

But Miss Bart showed herself a less ready prey than might have been
expected from her imprudent opening. She refused to pay the price named,
and after a moment's hesitation, met it by a counter-offer of half the
amount.

Mrs. Haffen immediately stiffened. Her hand traveled toward the outspread letters, and folding them slowly, she made as though to restore them to their wrapping.

"I guess they're worth more to you than to me, Miss, but the poor has got to live as well as the rich," she observed sententiously.

Lily was throbbing with fear, but the insinuation fortified her resistance.

"You are mistaken," she said indifferently. "I have offered all I am willing to give for the letters; but there may be other ways of getting them."

Mrs. Haffen raised a suspicious glance: she was too experienced not to know that the traffic she was engaged in had perils as great as its rewards, and she had a vision of the elaborate machinery of revenge which a word of this commanding young lady's might set in motion.

She applied the corner of her shawl to her eyes, and murmured through it that no good came of bearing too hard on the poor, but that for her part she had never been mixed up in such a business before, and that on her honor as a Christian all she and Haffen had thought of was that the letters mustn't go any farther.

Lily stood motionless, keeping between herself and the charwoman the greatest distance compatible with the need of speaking in low tones. The idea of bargaining for the letters was intolerable to her, but she knew that, if she appeared to weaken, Mrs. Haffen would at once increase her original demand.

She could never afterward recall how long the duel lasted, or what was the decisive stroke which finally, after a lapse of time recorded in minutes by the clock, in hours by the precipitate beat of her pulses, put her in possession of the letters; she knew only that the door had finally closed, and that she stood alone with the packet in her hand.

She had no idea of reading the letters; even to unfold Mrs. Haffen's dirty newspaper would have seemed degrading. But what did she intend to do with its contents? The recipient of the letters had meant to destroy them, and it was her duty to carry out his intention. She had no right to keep them—to do so was to lessen whatever merit lay in having secured their possession. But how destroy them so effectually that there should be no second risk of their falling in such hands? Mrs. Peniston's icy drawing-room grate shone with a forbidding luster: the fire, like the lamps, was never lit except when there was company.

Miss Bart was turning to carry the letters upstairs when she heard the opening of the outer door, and her aunt entered the drawing-room. Mrs. Peniston was a small plump woman, with a colorless skin lined with trivial wrinkles. Her gray hair was arranged with precision, and her clothes looked excessively new and yet slightly old-fashioned. They were always black and tightly fitting, with an expensive glitter: she was the kind of woman who wore jet at breakfast. Lily had never seen her when she was not cuirassed in shining black, with small tight boots, and an air of being packed and ready to start; yet she never started.

She looked about the drawing-room with an expression of minute scrutiny. "I saw a streak of light under one of the blinds as I drove up: it's extraordinary that I can never teach that woman to draw them down evenly."

Having corrected the irregularity, she seated herself on one of the glossy purple armchairs; Mrs. Peniston always sat on a chair, never in it. Then she turned her glance to Miss Bart.

"My dear, you look tired; I suppose it's the excitement of the wedding. Cornelia Van Alstyne was full of it: Molly was there, and Gerty Farish ran in for a minute to tell us about it. I think it was odd, their serving melons before the consommé: a wedding breakfast should always begin with consommé. Molly didn't care for the bridesmaids' dresses. She had it straight from Julia Melson that they cost three hundred dollars apiece at Céleste's, but she says they didn't look it. I'm glad you decided not to be a bridesmaid; that shade of salmon-pink wouldn't have suited you."

Mrs. Peniston delighted in discussing the minutest details of festivities in which she had not taken part. Nothing would have induced her to undergo the exertion and fatigue of attending the Van Osburgh wedding, but so great was her interest in the event that, having heard two versions of it, she now prepared to extract a third from her niece. Lily, however, had been deplorably careless in noting the particulars of the entertainment. She had failed to observe the color of Mrs. Van Osburgh's gown, and could not even say whether the old Van Osburgh Sévres had been used at the bride's table: Mrs. Peniston, in short, found that she was of more service as a listener than as a narrator.

"Really, Lily, I don't see why you took the trouble to go to the wedding, if you don't remember what happened or whom you saw there. When I was a girl I used to keep the menu of every dinner I went to, and write the names of the people on the back; and I never threw away my cotillion favors till after your uncle's death, when it seemed unsuitable to have so many colored things about the house. I had a whole closetful, I remember; and I can tell to this day what balls I got them at. Molly Van Alstyne reminds me of what I was at that age; it's wonderful how she notices. She was able to tell her mother exactly how the wedding-dress was cut, and we knew at once, from the fold in the back, that it must have come from Paquin."

Mrs. Peniston rose abruptly, and, advancing to the ormulu clock surmounted by a helmeted Minerva, which throned on the chimney-piece between two malachite vases, passed her lace handkerchief between the helmet and its visor.

"I knew it—the parlor maid never dusts there!" she exclaimed, triumphantly displaying a minute spot on the handkerchief; then, reseating herself, she went on: "Molly thought Mrs. Dorset the best-dressed woman at the wedding. I've no doubt her dress *did* cost more than anyone else's, but I can't quite like the idea—a combination of sable and point de Milan. It seems she goes to a new man in Paris, who won't take an order till his client has spent a day with him at his villa at Neuilly. He says he must study his subject's home life—a most peculiar arrangement, I should say! But Mrs. Dorset told Molly about it herself: she said the villa was full of the most exquisite things and she was really sorry to leave. Molly said she never saw her looking better; she was in tremendous spirits, and said she had made a match between Evie Van Osburgh and Percy Gryce. She really seems to have a very good influence on young men. I hear she is interesting herself now in that silly Silverton boy, who has had his head turned by Carry Fisher, and has been gambling so dreadfully. Well, as I was saying, Evie is really engaged: Mrs. Dorset had her to stay with Percy Gryce, and managed it all, and Grace Van Osburgh is in the seventh heaven—she had almost despaired of marrying Evie."

Mrs. Peniston again paused, but this time her scrutiny addressed itself not to the furniture, but to her niece.

"Cornelia Van Alstyne was so surprised: she had heard that you were to marry young Gryce. She saw the Wetheralls just after they had stopped with you at Bellomont, and Alice Wetherall was quite sure there was an engagement. She said that when Mr. Gryce left unexpectedly one morning, they all thought he had rushed to town for the ring."

Lily rose and moved toward the door.

"I believe I *am* tired: I think I will go to bed," she said; and Mrs. Peniston, suddenly distracted by the discovery that the easel sustaining the late Mr. Peniston's crayon-portrait was not exactly in line with the sofa in front of it, presented an absent-minded brow to her kiss.

In her own room Lily turned up the gas jet and glanced toward the grate. It was as brilliantly polished as the one below, but here at least she could burn a few papers with less risk of incurring her aunt's disapproval. She made no immediate motion to do so, however, but dropping into a chair looked wearily about her. Her room was large and comfortably furnished—it was the envy and admiration of poor Grace Stepney, who boarded; but, contrasted with the light tints and luxurious appointments of the guest-rooms where so many weeks of Lily's existence were spent, it seemed as dreary as a prison. The monumental wardrobe and bedstead of black walnut had migrated from Mr. Peniston's bedroom, and the magenta "flock" wallpaper, of a pattern dear to the early 'sixties, was hung with large steel engravings of an anecdotic character. Lily had tried to mitigate this charmless background by a few frivolous touches, in the shape of a lace-decked toilet table and a little painted desk surmounted by photographs; but the futility of the attempt struck her as she looked about the room. What a contrast to the subtle elegance of the setting she had pictured for herself—an apartment which should surpass the complicated luxury of her friends' surroundings by the whole extent of that artistic sensibility which made her feel herself their superior; in which every tint and line should combine to enhance her beauty and give distinction to her leisure! Once more the haunting sense of physical ugliness was intensified by her mental depression, so that each piece of the offending furniture seemed to thrust forth its most aggressive angle.

Her aunt's words had told her nothing new; but they had revived the vision of Bertha Dorset, smiling, flattered, victorious, holding her up to ridicule by insinuations intelligible to every member of their little group. The thought of the ridicule struck deeper than any other sensation: Lily knew every turn of the allusive jargon which could flay its victims without the shedding of blood. Her cheek burned at the recollection, and she rose and caught up the letters. She no longer meant to destroy them: that intention had been effaced by the quick corrosion of Mrs. Peniston's words.

Instead, she approached her desk, and lighting a taper, tied and sealed the packet; then she opened the wardrobe, drew out a dispatch-box, and deposited the letters within it. As she did so, it struck her with a flash of irony that she was indebted to Gus Trenor for the means of buying them.

10

THE autumn dragged on monotonously. Miss Bart had received one or two notes from Judy Trenor, reproaching her for not returning to Bellomont; but she replied evasively, alleging the obligation to remain with her aunt. In truth, however, she was fast wearying of her solitary existence with Mrs. Peniston, and only the excitement of spending her newly acquired money lightened the dullness of the days.

All her life Lily had seen money go out as quickly as it came in, and whatever theories she cultivated as to the prudence of setting aside a part of her gains, she had unhappily no saving vision of the risks of the opposite course. It was a keen satisfaction to feel that, for a few months at least, she would be independent of her friends' bounty, that she could show herself abroad without wondering whether some penetrating eye would detect in her dress the traces of Judy Trenor's refurbished splendor. The fact that the money freed her temporarily from all minor obligations obscured her sense of the greater one it represented, and having never before known what it was to command so large a sum, she lingered delectably over the amusement of spending it.

It was on one of these occasions that, leaving a shop where she had spent an hour of deliberation over a dressing-case of the most complicated elegance, she ran across Miss Farish, who had entered the same establishment with the modest object of having her watch repaired. Lily was feeling unusually virtuous. She had decided to defer the purchase of the dressing-case till she should receive the bill for her new opera-cloak, and the resolve made her feel much richer than when she had entered the shop. In this mood of self-approval she had a sympathetic eye for others, and she was struck by her friend's air of dejection.

Miss Farish, it appeared, had just left the committee meeting of a struggling charity in which she was interested. The object of the association was to provide comfortable lodgings, with a reading-room and other modest distractions, where young women of the class employed in downtown offices might find a home when out of work, or in need of rest, and the first year's financial report showed so deplorably small a balance that Miss Farish, who was convinced of the urgency of the work, felt proportionately discouraged by the small amount of interest it aroused. The other-regarding sentiments had not been cultivated in Lily, and she was often bored by the relation of her friend's philanthropic efforts, but today her quick dramatizing fancy seized on the contrast between her own situation and that represented by some of Gerty's "cases." These were young girls, like herself; some perhaps pretty, some not without a trace of her finer sensibilities. She pictured herself leading such a life as theirs—a life in which achievement seemed as squalid as failure—and the vision made her shudder sympathetically. The price of the dressing-case was still in her pocket; and drawing out her little gold purse she slipped a liberal fraction of the amount into Miss Farish's hand.

The satisfaction derived from this act was all that the most ardent moralist could have desired. Lily felt a new interest in herself as a person of charitable instincts; she had never before thought of doing good with the wealth she had so often dreamed of possessing, but now her horizon was enlarged by the vision of a prodigal philanthropy. Moreover, by some obscure process of logic, she felt that her momentary burst of generosity had justified all previous extravagances, and excused any in which she might subsequently indulge. Miss Farish's surprise and gratitude confirmed this feeling, and Lily parted from her with a sense of self-esteem which she naturally mistook for the fruits of altruism.

About this time she was further cheered by an invitation to spend the Thanksgiving week at a camp in the Adirondacks. The invitation was one which, a year earlier, would have provoked a less ready response, for the party, though organized by Mrs. Fisher, was ostensibly given by a lady of obscure origin and indomitable social ambitions, whose acquaintance Lily had hitherto avoided. Now, however, she was disposed to coincide with Mrs. Fisher's view, that it didn't matter who gave the party, as long as things were well done; and doing things well (under competent direction) was Mrs. Wellington Bry's strong point. The lady (whose consort was known as

"Welly" Bry on the Stock Exchange and in sporting circles) had already sacrificed one husband, and sundry minor considerations, to her determination to get on; and, having obtained a hold on Carry Fisher, she was astute enough to perceive the wisdom of committing herself entirely to that lady's guidance. Everything, accordingly, was well done, for there was no limit to Mrs. Fisher's prodigality when she was not spending her own money, and as she remarked to her pupil, a good cook was the best introduction to society. If the company was not as select as the cuisine, the Welly Brys at least had the satisfaction of figuring for the first time in the society columns in company with one or two noticeable names; and foremost among these was of course Miss Bart's. The young lady was treated by her hosts with corresponding deference; and she was in the mood when such attentions are acceptable, whatever their source. Mrs. Bry's admiration was a mirror in which Lily's self-complacency recovered its lost outline. No insect hangs its nest on threads as frail as those which will sustain the weight of human vanity; and the sense of being of importance among the insignificant was enough to restore to Miss Bart the gratifying consciousness of power. If these people paid court to her it proved that she was still conspicuous in the world to which they aspired; and she was not above a certain enjoyment in dazzling them by her fineness, in developing their puzzled perception of her superiorities.

Perhaps, however, her enjoyment proceeded more than she was aware from the physical stimulus of the excursion, the challenge of crisp cold and hard exercise, the responsive thrill of her body to the influences of the winter woods. She returned to town in a glow of rejuvenation, conscious of a clearer color in her cheeks, a fresh elasticity in her muscles. The future seemed full of a vague promise, and all her apprehensions were swept out of sight on the buoyant current of her mood.

A few days after her return to town she had the unpleasant surprise of a visit from Mr. Rosedale. He came late, at the confidential hour when the tea-table still lingers by the fire in friendly expectancy; and his manner showed a readiness to adapt itself to the intimacy of the occasion.

Lily, who had a vague sense of his being somehow connected with her lucky speculations, tried to give him the welcome he expected; but there was something in the quality of his geniality which chilled her own, and she was conscious of marking each step in their acquaintance by a fresh blunder.

Mr. Rosedale—making himself promptly at home in an adjoining easy-chair, and sipping his tea critically, with the comment: "You ought to go to my man for something really good"—appeared totally unconscious of the repugnance which kept her in frozen erectness behind the urn. It was perhaps her very manner of holding herself aloof that appealed to his collector's passion for the rare and unattainable. He gave, at any rate, no sign of resenting it and seemed prepared to supply in his own manner all the ease that was lacking in hers.

His object in calling was to ask her to go to the opera in his box on the opening night, and seeing her hesitate he said persuasively: "Mrs. Fisher is coming, and I've secured a tremendous admirer of yours, who'll never forgive me if you don't accept."

As Lily's silence left him with this allusion on his hands, he added with a confidential smile: "Gus Trenor has promised to come to town on purpose. I fancy he'd go a good deal farther for the pleasure of seeing you."

Miss Bart felt an inward motion of annoyance: it was distasteful enough to hear her name coupled with Trenor's, and on Rosedale's lips the allusion was peculiarly unpleasant.

"The Trenors are my best friends—I think we should all go a long way to see each other," she said, absorbing herself in the preparation of fresh tea.

Her visitor's smile grew increasingly intimate. "Well, I wasn't thinking of Mrs. Trenor at the moment—they say Gus doesn't always, you know." Then, dimly conscious that he had not struck the right note, he added, with a well-meant effort at diversion: "How's your luck been going in Wall Street, by the way? I hear Gus pulled off a nice little pile for you last month."

Lily put down the tea-caddy with an abrupt gesture. She felt that her hands were trembling, and clasped them on her knee to steady them; but her lip trembled too, and for a moment she was afraid the tremor might communicate itself to her voice. When she spoke, however, it was in a tone of perfect lightness.

"Ah, yes—I had a little bit of money to invest, and Mr. Trenor, who helps me about such matters, advised my putting it in stocks instead of a mortgage, as my aunt's agent wanted me to do; and as it happened, I made a lucky 'turn'—is that what you call it? For you make a great many yourself, I believe."

She was smiling back at him now, relaxing the tension of her attitude, and admitting him, by imperceptible gradations of glance and manner, a step farther toward intimacy. The protective instinct always nerved her to successful dissimulation, and it was not the first time she had used her beauty to divert attention from an inconvenient topic.

When Mr. Rosedale took leave, he carried with him, not only her acceptance of his invitation, but a general sense of having comported himself in a way calculated to advance his cause. He had always believed he had a light touch and a knowing way with women, and the prompt manner in which Miss Bart (as he would have phrased it) had "come into line" confirmed his confidence in his powers of handling the skittish sex. Her way of glossing over the transaction with Trenor he regarded at once as a tribute to his own acuteness, and a confirmation of his suspicions. The girl was evidently nervous, and Mr. Rosedale, if he saw no other means of advancing his acquaintance with her, was not above taking advantage of her nervousness.

He left Lily to a passion of disgust and fear. It seemed incredible that Gus Trenor should have spoken of her to Rosedale. With all his faults, Trenor had the safeguard of his traditions, and was the less likely to overstep them because they were so purely instinctive. But Lily recalled with a pang that there were convivial moments when, as Judy had confided to her, Gus "talked foolishly": in one of these, no doubt, the fatal word had slipped from him. As for Rosedale, she did not, after the first shock, greatly care what conclusions he had drawn. Though usually adroit enough where her own interests were concerned, she made the mistake, not uncommon to persons in whom the social habits are instinctive, of supposing that the inability to acquire them quickly implies a general dullness. Because a bluebottle bangs irrationally against a windowpane, the drawing-room naturalist may forget that under less artificial conditions it is capable of measuring distances and drawing conclusions with all the accuracy needful to its welfare; and the fact that Mr. Rosedale's drawing-room manner lacked perspective made Lily class him with Trenor and the other dull men she knew, and assume that a little flattery, and the occasional acceptance of his hospitality, would suffice to render him innocuous. However, there could be no doubt of the expediency of showing herself in his box on the opening night of the opera; and after all, since Judy Trenor had promised to take him up that winter, it was as well to reap the advantage of being first in the field.

For a day or two after Rosedale's visit, Lily's thoughts were dogged by the consciousness of Trenor's shadowy claim, and she wished she had a clearer notion of the exact nature of the transaction which seemed to have put her in his power; but her mind shrank from any unusual application, and she was always helplessly puzzled by figures. Moreover she had not seen Trenor since the day of the Van Osburgh wedding, and in his continued absence the trace of Rosedale's words was soon effaced by other impressions.

When the opening night of the opera came, her apprehensions had so completely vanished that the sight of Trenor's ruddy countenance in the back of Mr. Rosedale's box filled her with a sense of pleasant reassurance. Lily had not quite reconciled herself to the necessity of appearing as Rosedale's guest on so conspicuous an occasion, and it was a relief to find herself supported by anyone of her own set—for Mrs. Fisher's social habits were too promiscuous for her presence to justify Miss Bart's.

To Lily, always inspirited by the prospect of showing her beauty in public, and conscious tonight of all the added enhancements of dress, the insistency of Trenor's gaze merged itself in the general stream of admiring looks of which she felt herself the center. Ah, it was good to be young, to be radiant, to glow with the sense of slenderness, strength and elasticity, of well-poised lines and happy tints, to feel one's self lifted to a height apart by that incommunicable grace which is the bodily counterpart of genius!

All means seemed justifiable to attain such an end, or rather, by a happy shifting of lights with which practice had familiarized Miss Bart, the cause shrank to a pinpoint in the general brightness of the effect. But brilliant young ladies, a little blinded by their own effulgence, are apt to forget that the modest satellite drowned in their light is still performing its own revolutions and generating heat at its own rate. If Lily's poetic enjoyment of the moment was undisturbed by the base thought that her gown and opera cloak had been indirectly paid for by Gus Trenor, the latter had not sufficient poetry in his composition to lose sight of these prosaic facts. He knew only that he had never seen Lily look smarter in her life, that there wasn't a woman in the house who showed off good clothes as she did, and that hitherto he, to whom she owed the opportunity of making this display, had reaped no return beyond that of gazing at her in company with several hundred other pairs of eyes.

It came to Lily therefore as a disagreeable surprise when, in the back of the box, where they found themselves alone between two acts, Trenor said, without preamble, and in a tone of sulky authority: "Look here, Lily, how is a fellow ever to see anything of you? I'm in town three or four days in the week, and you know a line to the club will always find me, but you don't seem to remember my existence nowadays unless you want to get a tip out of me."

The fact that the remark was in distinctly bad taste did not make it any easier to answer, for Lily was vividly aware that it was not the moment for that drawing up of her slim figure and surprised lifting of the brows by which she usually quelled incipient signs of familiarity.

"I'm very much flattered by your wanting to see me," she returned, essaying lightness instead, "but, unless you have mislaid my address, it would have been easy to find me any afternoon at my aunt's—in fact, I rather expected you to look me up there."

If she hoped to mollify him by this last concession the attempt was a failure, for he only replied, with the familiar lowering of the brows that made him look his dullest when he was angry: "Hang going to your aunt's, and wasting the afternoon listening to a lot of other chaps talking to you! You know I'm not the kind to sit in a crowd and jaw—I'd always rather clear out when that sort of circus is going on. But why can't we go off somewhere on a little lark together—a nice quiet little expedition like that drive at Bellomont, the day you met me at the station?"

He leaned unpleasantly close in order to convey this suggestion, and she fancied she caught a significant aroma which explained the dark flush on his face and the glistening dampness of his forehead.

The idea that any rash answer might provoke an unpleasant outburst tempered her disgust with caution, and she answered with a laugh: "I don't see how one can very well take country drives in town, but I am not always surrounded by an admiring throng, and if you will let me know what afternoon you are coming I will arrange things so that we can have a nice quiet talk."

"Hang talking! That's what you always say," returned Trenor, whose expletives lacked variety. "You put me off with that at the Van Osburgh wedding—but the plain English of it is that, now you've got what you wanted out of me, you'd rather have any other fellow about."

His voice had risen sharply with the last words, and Lily flushed with annoyance, but she kept command of the situation and laid a persuasive hand on his arm.

"Don't be foolish, Gus; I can't let you talk to me in that ridiculous way. If you really want to see me, why shouldn't we take a walk in the Park some afternoon? I agree with you that it's amusing to be rustic in town, and if you like I'll meet you there, and we'll go and feed the squirrels, and you shall take me out on the lake in the steam-gondola."

She smiled as she spoke, letting her eyes rest on his in a way that took the edge from her banter and made him suddenly malleable to her will.

"All right, then: that's a go. Will you come tomorrow? Tomorrow at three o'clock, at the end of the Mall? I'll be there sharp, remember; you won't go back on me, Lily?"

But to Miss Bart's relief the repetition of her promise was cut short by the opening of the box door to admit George Dorset.

Trenor sulkily yielded his place, and Lily turned a brilliant smile on the newcomer. She had not talked with Dorset since their visit at Bellomont, but something in his look and manner told her that he recalled the friendly footing on which they had last met. He was not a man to whom the expression of admiration came easily: his long sallow face and distrustful eyes seemed always barricaded against the expansive emotions. But, where her own influence was concerned, Lily's intuitions sent out threadlike feelers, and as she made room for him on the narrow sofa she was sure he found a dumb pleasure in being near her. Few women took the trouble to make themselves agreeable to Dorset, and Lily had been kind to him at Bellomont, and was now smiling on him with a divine renewal of kindness.

"Well, here we are, in for another six months of caterwauling," he began complainingly. "Not a shade of difference between this year and last, except that the women have got new clothes and the singers haven't got new voices. My wife's musical, you know—puts me through a course of this every winter. It isn't so bad on Italian nights—then she comes late, and there's time to digest. But when they give Wagner we have to rush dinner, and I pay up for it. And the draughts are damnable—asphyxia in front and pleurisy in the back. There's Trenor leaving the box without drawing the curtain! With a hide like that draughts don't make any difference. Did you ever watch Trenor eat? If you did, you'd wonder why he's alive; I suppose he's leather inside too. But I came to say that my wife wants you to come down to our place next Sunday. Do for heaven's sake say yes. She's got a lot of bores coming—intellectual ones, I mean; that's her new line, you know, and I'm not sure it ain't worse than the music. Some of 'em have long hair, and they start an argument with the soup, and don't notice when things are handed to them. The consequence is the dinner gets cold, and I have dyspepsia. That silly ass Silverton brings them to the house—he writes poetry, you know, and Bertha and he are getting tremendously thick. She could write better than any of 'em if she chose, and I don't blame her for wanting clever fellows about; all I say is: 'Don't let me see 'em eat!' " The gist of this strange communication gave Lily a distinct thrill of pleasure. Under ordinary circumstances, there would have been nothing surprising in an invitation from Bertha Dorset; but since the Bellomont episode an unavowed hostility had kept the two women apart. Now, with a start of inner wonder, Lily felt that her thirst for retaliation had died out. *If you would forgive your enemy*, says the Malay proverb, *first inflict a hurt on him*; and Lily was experiencing the truth of the apothegm. If she had destroyed Mrs. Dorset's letters, she might have continued to hate her; but the fact that they remained in her possession had fed her resentment to satiety.

She uttered a smiling acceptance, hailing in the renewal of the tie an escape from Trenor's importunities.

11

MEANWHILE the holidays had gone by and the season was beginning. Fifth Avenue had become a nightly torrent of carriages surging upward to the fashionable quarters about the Park, where illuminated windows and outspread awnings betokened the usual routine of hospitality. Other tributary currents crossed the main stream, bearing their freight to the theaters, restaurants or opera; and Mrs. Peniston, from the secluded watchtower of her upper window, could tell to a nicety just when the chronic volume of sound was increased by the sudden influx setting toward a Van Osburgh ball, or when the multiplication of wheels meant merely that the opera was over, or that there was a big supper at Sherry's.

Mrs. Peniston followed the rise and culmination of the season as keenly as the most active sharer in its gaieties; and, as a looker-on, she enjoyed opportunities of comparison and generalization such as those who take part must proverbially forego. No one could have kept a more accurate record of social fluctuations, or have put a more unerring finger on the distinguishing features of each season: its dullness, its extravagance, its lack of balls or excess of divorces. She had a special memory for the vicissitudes of the "new people" who rose to the surface with each recurring tide, and were either submerged beneath its rush or landed triumphantly beyond the reach of envious breakers; and she was apt to display a remarkable retrospective insight into their ultimate fate, so that, when they had fulfilled their destiny, she was almost always able to say to Grace Stepney—the recipient of her prophecies—that she had known exactly what would happen. This particular season Mrs. Peniston would have characterized as that in which everybody "felt poor" except the Welly Brys and Mr. Simon Rosedale. It had been a bad autumn in Wall Street, where prices fell in accordance with that peculiar law which proves railway stocks and bales of cotton to be more sensitive to the allotment of executive power than many estimable citizens trained to all the advantages of self-government. Even fortunes supposed to be independent of the market either betrayed a secret dependence on it, or suffered from a sympathetic affection: fashion sulked in its country houses, or came to town incognito, general entertainments were discountenanced, and informality and short dinners became the fashion.

But society, amused for a while at playing Cinderella, soon wearied of the hearthside role, and welcomed the fairy godmother in the shape of any magician powerful enough to turn the shrunken pumpkin back again into the golden coach. The mere fact of growing richer at a time when most people's investments are shrinking is calculated to attract envious attention; and according to Wall Street rumors, Welly Bry and Rosedale had found the secret of performing this miracle.

Rosedale, in particular, was said to have doubled his fortune, and there was talk of his buying the newly finished house of one of the victims of the crash, who, in the space of twelve short months, had made the same number of millions, built a house in Fifth Avenue, filled a picture gallery with old masters, entertained all New York in it, and been smuggled out of the country between a trained nurse and a doctor, while his creditors mounted guard over the old masters, and his guests explained to each other that they had dined with him only because they wanted to see the pictures. Mr. Rosedale meant to have a less meteoric career. He knew he should have to go slowly, and the instincts of his race fitted him to suffer rebuffs and put up with delays. But he was prompt to perceive that the general dullness of the season afforded him an unusual opportunity to shine, and he set about with patient industry to form a background for his growing glory. Mrs. Fisher was of immense service to him at this period. She had set off so many newcomers on the social stage that she was like one of those pieces of stock scenery which tell the experienced spectator exactly what is going to take place. But Mr. Rosedale wanted, in the long run, a more individual environment. He was sensitive to shades of difference which Miss Bart would never have credited him with perceiving, because he had no corresponding variations of manner; and it was becoming more and more clear to him that Miss Bart herself possessed precisely the complementary qualities needed to round off his social personality.

Such details did not fall within the range of Mrs. Peniston's vision. Like many minds of panoramic sweep, hers was apt to overlook the minutiae of the foreground, and she was much more likely to know where Carry Fisher had found the Welly Brys' chef for them, than what was happening to her own niece. She was not, however, without purveyors of information ready to supplement her deficiencies. Grace Stepney's mind was like a kind of moral flypaper, to which the buzzing items of gossip were drawn by a fatal attraction, and where they hung fast in the toils of an inexorable memory. Lily would have been surprised to know how many trivial facts concerning herself were lodged in Miss Stepney's head. She was quite aware that she was of interest to dingy people, but she assumed that there is only one form of dinginess, and that admiration for brilliancy is the natural expression of its inferior state. She knew that Gerty Farish admired her blindly, and therefore supposed that she inspired the same sentiments in Grace Stepney, whom she classified as a Gerty Farish without the saving traits of youth and enthusiasm.

In reality, the two differed from each other as much as they differed from the object of their mutual contemplation. Miss Farish's heart was a fountain of tender illusions, Miss Stepney's a precise register of facts as manifested in their relation to herself. She had sensibilities which, to Lily, would have seemed comic in a person with a freckled nose and red eyelids, who lived in a boardinghouse and admired Mrs. Peniston's drawing-room; but poor Grace's limitations gave them a more concentrated inner life, as poor soil starves certain plants into intenser efflorescence. She had in truth no abstract propensity to malice: she did not dislike Lily because the latter was brilliant and predominant, but because she thought that Lily disliked her. It is less mortifying to believe one's self unpopular than insignificant, and vanity prefers to assume that indifference is a latent form of unfriendliness. Even such scant civilities as Lily accorded to Mr. Rosedale would have made Miss Stepney her friend for life; but how could she foresee that such a friend was worth cultivating? How, moreover, can a young woman who has never been ignored measure the pang which this injury inflicts? And, lastly, how could Lily, accustomed to choose between a pressure of engagements, guess that she had mortally offended Miss Stepney by causing her to be excluded from one of Mrs. Peniston's infrequent dinner parties?

Mrs. Peniston disliked giving dinners, but she had a high sense of family obligation, and on the Jack Stepneys' return from their honeymoon she felt it incumbent upon her to light the drawing-room lamps and extract her best silver from the safe deposit vaults. Mrs. Peniston's rare entertainments were preceded by days of heart-rending vacillation as to every detail of the feast, from the seating of the guests to the pattern of the tablecloth, and in the course of one of these preliminary discussions she had imprudently suggested to her cousin Grace that, as the dinner was a family affair, she might be included in it. For a week the prospect had lighted up Miss Stepney's color-less existence; then she had been given to understand that it would be more convenient to have her another day. Miss Stepney knew exactly what had happened. Lily, to whom family reunions were occasions of unalloyed dullness, had persuaded her aunt that a dinner of "smart" people would be much more to the taste of the young couple, and Mrs. Peniston, who leaned helplessly on her niece in social matters, had been prevailed upon to pronounce Grace's exile. After all, Grace could come any other day; why should she mind being put off?

It was precisely because Miss Stepney could come any other day—and because she knew her relations were in the secret of her unoccupied evenings—that this incident loomed gigantically on her horizon. She was aware that she had Lily to thank for it; and dull resentment was turned to active animosity.

Mrs. Peniston, on whom she had looked in a day or two after the dinner, laid down her crochet-work and turned abruptly from her oblique survey of Fifth Avenue.

"Gus Trenor?—Lily and Gus Trenor?" she said, growing so suddenly pale that her visitor was almost alarmed.

"Oh, Cousin Julia . . . of course I don't mean . . ."

"I don't know what you *do* mean," said Mrs. Peniston, with a frightened quiver in her small fretful voice. "Such things were never heard of in my day. And my own niece! I'm not sure I understand you. Do people say he's in love with her?"

Mrs. Peniston's horror was genuine. Though she boasted an unequalled familiarity with the secret chronicles of society, she had the innocence of the schoolgirl who regards wickedness as a part of "history," and to whom it never occurs that the scandals she reads of in lesson-hours may be repeating themselves in the next street. Mrs. Peniston had kept her imagination shrouded, like the drawing-room furniture. She knew, of course, that society was "very much changed," and that many women her mother would have thought "peculiar" were now in a position to be critical about their visiting lists; she had discussed the perils of divorce with her rector, and had felt thankful at times that Lily was still unmarried; but the idea that any scandal could attach to a young girl's name, above all that it could be lightly coupled with that of a married man, was so new to her that she was as much aghast as if she had been accused of leaving her carpets down all summer, or of violating any of the other cardinal laws of housekeeping.

Miss Stepney, when her first fright had subsided, began to feel the superiority that greater breadth of mind confers. It was really pitiable to be as ignorant of the world as Mrs. Peniston!

She smiled at the latter's question. "People always say unpleasant things —and certainly they're a great deal together. A friend of mine met them the other afternoon in the Park—quite late, after the lamps were lit. It's a pity Lily makes herself so conspicuous."

"*Conspicuous!*" gasped Mrs. Peniston. She bent forward, lowering her voice to mitigate the horror. "What sort of things do they say? That he means to get a divorce and marry her?"

Grace Stepney laughed outright. "Dear me, no! He would hardly do that. It—it's a flirtation—nothing more."

"A flirtation? Between my niece and a married man? Do you mean to tell me that, with Lily's looks and advantages, she could find no better use for her time than to waste it on a fat stupid man almost old enough to be her father?" This argument had such a convincing ring that it gave Mrs. Peniston sufficient reassurance to pick up her work, while she waited for Grace Stepney to rally her scattered forces.

But Miss Stepney was on the spot in an instant. "That's the worst of it —people say she isn't wasting her time! Everyone knows, as you say, that Lily is too handsome and—and charming—to devote herself to a man like Gus Trenor unless —"

"Unless?" echoed Mrs. Peniston.

Her visitor drew breath nervously. It was agreeable to shock Mrs. Peniston, but not to shock her to the verge of anger. Miss Stepney was not sufficiently familiar with the classic drama to have recalled in advance how bearers of bad tidings are proverbially received, but she now had a rapid vision of forfeited dinners and a reduced wardrobe as the possible consequence of her disinterestedness. To the honor of her sex, however, hatred of Lily prevailed over more personal considerations. Mrs. Peniston had chosen the wrong moment to boast of her niece's charms.

"Unless," said Grace, leaning forward to speak with low-toned emphasis, "unless there are material advantages to be gained by making herself agreeable to him."

She felt that the moment was tremendous, and remembered suddenly that Mrs. Peniston's black brocade, with the cut jet fringe, would have been hers at the end of the season.

Mrs. Peniston put down her work again. Another aspect of the same idea had presented itself to her, and she felt that it was beneath her dignity to have her nerves racked by a dependent relative who wore her old clothes.

"If you take pleasure in annoying me by mysterious insinuations," she said coldly, "you might at least have chosen a more suitable time than just as I am recovering from the strain of giving a large dinner."

The mention of the dinner dispelled Miss Stepney's last scruples. "I don't know why I should be accused of taking pleasure in telling you about Lily. I was sure I shouldn't get any thanks for it," she returned with a flare of temper. "But I have some family feeling left, and as you are the only person who has any authority over Lily, I thought you ought to know what is being said of her."

"Well," said Mrs. Peniston, "what I complain of is that you haven't told me yet what is being said."

"I didn't suppose I should have to put it so plainly. People say that Gus Trenor pays her bills."

"Pays her bills—her bills?" Mrs. Peniston broke into a laugh. "I can't imagine where you can have picked up such rubbish. Lily has her own income—and I provide for her very handsomely —"

"Oh, we all know that," interposed Miss Stepney drily. "But Lily wears a great many smart gowns —"

"I like her to be well-dressed—it's only suitable!"

"Certainly; but then there are her gambling debts besides."

Miss Stepney, in the beginning, had not meant to bring up this point; but Mrs. Peniston had only her own incredulity to blame. She was like the stiff-necked unbelievers of Scripture, who must be annihilated to be convinced.

"Gambling debts? Lily?" Mrs. Peniston's voice shook with anger and bewilderment. She wondered whether Grace Stepney had gone out of her mind. "What do you mean by her gambling debts?"

"Simply that if one plays bridge for money in Lily's set one is liable to lose a great deal—and I don't suppose Lily always wins."

"Who told you that my niece played cards for money?"

"Mercy, Cousin Julia, don't look at me as if I were trying to turn you against Lily! Everybody knows she is crazy about bridge. Mrs. Gryce told me herself that it was her gambling that frightened Percy Gryce—it seems he was really taken with her at first. But, of course, among Lily's friends it's quite the custom for girls to play for money. In fact, people are inclined to excuse her on that account—"

"To excuse her for what?"

"For being hard up—and accepting attentions from men like Gus Trenor —and George Dorset —"

Mrs. Peniston gave another cry. "George Dorset? Is there anyone else? I should like to know the worst, if you please."

"Don't put it in that way, cousin Julia. Lately Lily has been a good deal with the Dorsets, and he seems to admire her—but of course that's only natural. And I'm sure there is no truth in the horrid things people say; but she *has* been spending a great deal of money this winter. Evie Van Osburgh was at Céleste's ordering her trousseau the other day—yes, the marriage takes place next month—and she told me that Céleste showed her the most exquisite things she was just sending home to Lily. And people say that Judy Trenor has quarrelled with her on account of Gus; but I'm sure I'm sorry I spoke, though I only meant it as a kindness."

Mrs. Peniston's genuine incredulity enabled her to dismiss Miss Stepney with a disdain which boded ill for that lady's prospect of succeeding to the black brocade; but minds impenetrable to reason have generally some crack through which suspicion filters, and her visitor's insinuations did not glide off as easily as she had expected. Mrs. Peniston disliked scenes, and her determination to avoid them had always led her to hold herself aloof from the details of Lily's life. In her youth, girls had not been supposed to require close supervision. They were generally assumed to be taken up with the legitimate business of courtship and marriage, and interference in such affairs on the part of their natural guardians was considered as unwarrantable as a spectator's suddenly joining in a game. There had of course been "fast" girls even in Mrs. Peniston's early experience; but their fastness, at worst, was understood to be a mere excess of animal spirits, against which there could be no graver charge than that of being "unladylike." The modern fastness appeared synonymous with immorality, and the mere idea of immorality was as offensive to Mrs. Peniston as a smell of cooking in the drawing-room: it was one of the conceptions her mind refused to admit.

She had no immediate intention of repeating to Lily what she had heard, or even of trying to ascertain its truth by means of discreet interrogation. To do so might be to provoke a scene; and a scene, in the shaken state of Mrs. Peniston's nerves, with the effects of her dinner not worn off, and her mind still tremulous with new impressions, was a risk she deemed it her duty to avoid. But there remained in her thoughts a settled deposit of resentment against her niece, all the denser because it was not to be cleared by explanation or discussion. It was horrible of a young girl to let herself be talked about; however unfounded the charges against her, she must be to blame for their having been made. Mrs. Peniston felt as if there had been a contagious illness in the house, and she was doomed to sit shivering among her contaminated furniture.

12

Miss Bart had in fact been treading a devious way, and none of her critics could have been more alive to the fact than herself; but she had a fatalistic sense of being drawn from one wrong turning to another, without ever perceiving the right road till it was too late to take it.

Lily, who considered herself above narrow prejudices, had not imagined that the fact of letting Gus Trenor make a little money for her would ever disturb her self-complacency. And the fact in itself still seemed harmless enough; only it was a fertile source of harmful complications. As she exhausted the amusement of spending the money these complications became more pressing, and Lily, whose mind could be severely logical in tracing the causes of her ill-luck to others, justified herself by the thought that she owed all her troubles to the enmity of Bertha Dorset. This enmity, however, had apparently expired in a renewal of friendliness between the two women. Lily's visit to the Dorsets had resulted, for both, in the discovery that they could be of use to each other; and the civilized instinct finds a subtler pleasure in making use of its antagonist than in confounding him. Mrs. Dorset was, in fact, engaged in a new sentimental experiment, of which Mrs. Fisher's late property, Ned Silverton, was the rosy victim; and at such moments, as Judy Trenor had once remarked, she felt a peculiar need of distracting her husband's attention. Dorset was as difficult to amuse as a savage; but even his self-engrossment was not proof against Lily's arts, or rather these were especially adapted to soothe an uneasy egoism. Her experience with Percy Gryce stood her in good stead in ministering to Dorset's humors, and if the incentive to please was less urgent, the difficulties of her situation were teaching her to make much of minor opportunities.

Intimacy with the Dorsets was not likely to lessen such difficulties on the material side. Mrs. Dorset had none of Judy Trenor's lavish impulses, and Dorset's admiration was not likely to express itself in financial "tips" even had Lily cared to renew her experiences in that line. What she required, for the moment, of the Dorsets' friendship, was simply its social sanction. She knew that people were beginning to talk of her; but this fact did not alarm her as it had alarmed Mrs. Peniston. In her set such gossip was not unusual, and a handsome girl who flirted with a married man was merely assumed to be pressing to the limit of her opportunities. It was Trenor himself who frightened her. Their walk in the Park had not been a success. Trenor had married young, and since his marriage his intercourse with women had not taken the form of the sentimental small-talk which doubles upon itself like the paths in a maze. He was first puzzled and then irritated to find himself always led back to the same starting-point, and Lily felt that she was gradually losing control of the situation. Trenor was in truth in an unmanageable mood. In spite of his understanding with Rosedale he had been somewhat heavily "touched" by the fall in stocks; his household expenses weighed on him, and he seemed to be meeting, on all sides, a sullen opposition to his wishes, instead of the easy good luck he had hitherto encountered.

Mrs. Trenor was still at Bellomont, keeping the townhouse open, and descending on it now and then for a taste of the world, but preferring the recurrent excitement of weekend parties to the restrictions of a dull season. Since the holidays she had not urged Lily to return to Bellomont, and the first time they met in town Lily fancied there was a shade of coldness in her manner. Was it merely the expression of her displeasure at Miss Bart's neglect, or had disquieting rumors reached her? The latter contingency seemed improbable, yet Lily was not without a sense of uneasiness. If her roaming sympathies had struck root anywhere, it was in her friendship with Judy Trenor. She believed in the sincerity of her friend's affection, though it sometimes showed itself in self-interested ways, and she shrank with peculiar reluctance from any risk of estranging it. But, aside from this, she was keenly conscious of the way in which such an estrangement would react on herself. The fact that Gus Trenor was Judy's husband was at times Lily's strongest reason for disliking him, and for resenting the obligation under which he had placed her.

To set her doubts at rest, Miss Bart, soon after the New Year, "proposed" herself for a weekend at Bellomont. She had learned in advance that the presence of a large party would protect her from too great assiduity on Trenor's part, and his wife's telegraphic "come by all means" seemed to assure her of her usual welcome.

Judy received her amicably. The cares of a large party always prevailed over personal feelings, and Lily saw no change in her hostess's manner. Nevertheless, she was soon aware that the experiment of coming to Bellomont was destined not to be successful. The party was made up of what Mrs. Trenor called "poky people"—her generic name for persons who did not play bridge—and, it being her habit to group all such obstructionists in one class, she usually invited them together, regardless of their other characteristics. The result was apt to be an irreducible combination of persons having no other quality in common than their abstinence from bridge, and the antagonisms developed in a group lacking the one taste which might have amalgamated them, were in this case aggravated by bad weather, and by the ill-concealed boredom of their host and hostess. In such emergencies, Judy would usually have turned to Lily to fuse the discordant elements; and Miss Bart, assuming that such a service was expected of her, threw herself into it with her accustomed zeal. But at the outset she perceived a subtle resistance to her efforts. If Mrs. Trenor's manner toward her was unchanged, there was certainly a faint coldness in that of the other ladies. An occasional caustic allusion to "your friends the Wellington Brys," or to "the little Jew who has bought the Greiner house—someone told us you knew him, Miss Bart,"—showed Lily that she was in disfavor with that portion of society which, while contributing least to its amusement, has assumed the right to decide what forms that amusement shall take. The indication was a slight one, and a year ago Lily would have smiled at it, trusting to the charm of her personality to dispel any prejudice against her. But now she had grown more sensitive to criticism and less confident in her power of disarming it. She knew, moreover, that if the ladies at Bellomont permitted themselves to criticize her friends openly, it was a proof that they were not afraid of subjecting her to the same treatment behind her back. The nervous dread lest anything in Trenor's manner should seem to justify their disapproval made her seek every pretext for avoiding him, and she left Bellomont conscious of having failed in every purpose which had taken her there.

In town she returned to preoccupations which, for the moment, had the happy effect of banishing troublesome thoughts. The Welly Brys, after much debate, and anxious counsel with their newly acquired friends, had decided on the bold move of giving a general entertainment. To attack society collectively, when one's means of approach are limited to a few acquaintances, is like advancing into a strange country with an insufficient number of scouts; but such rash tactics have sometimes led to brilliant victories, and the Brys had determined to put their fate to the touch. Mrs. Fisher, to whom they had entrusted the conduct of the affair, had decided that tableaux vivants and expensive music were the two baits most likely to attract the desired prey, and after prolonged negotiations, and the kind of wire-pulling in which she was known to excel, she had induced a dozen fashionable women to exhibit themselves in a series of pictures which, by a further miracle of persuasion, the distinguished portrait painter, Paul Morpeth, had been prevailed upon to organize.

Lily was in her element on such occasions. Under Morpeth's guidance her vivid plastic sense, hitherto nurtured on no higher food than dress-making and upholstery, found eager expression in the disposal of draperies, the study of attitudes, the shifting of lights and shadows. Her dramatic instinct was roused by the choice of subjects, and the gorgeous reproductions of historic dress stirred an imagination which only visual impressions could reach. But keenest of all was the exhilaration of displaying her own beauty under a new aspect: of showing that her loveliness was no mere fixed quality, but an element shaping all emotions to fresh forms of grace.

Mrs. Fisher's measures had been well-taken, and society, surprised in a dull moment, succumbed to the temptation of Mrs. Bry's hospitality. The protesting minority were forgotten in the throng which abjured and came; and the audience was almost as brilliant as the show.

Lawrence Selden was among those who had yielded to the proffered inducements. If he did not often act on the accepted social axiom that a man may go where he pleases, it was because he had long since learned that his pleasures were mainly to be found in a small group of the like-minded. But he enjoyed spectacular effects, and was not insensible to the part money plays in their production: all he asked was that the very rich should live up to their calling as stage-managers, and not spend their money in a dull way. This the Brys could certainly not be charged with doing. Their recently built house, whatever it might lack as a frame for domesticity, was almost as well-designed for the display of a festal assemblage as one of those airy pleasure-halls which the Italian architects improvised to set off the hospitality of princes. The air of improvisation was in fact strikingly present: so recent, so rapidly evoked was the whole mise en scène that one had to touch the marble columns to learn they were not of cardboard, to seat one's self in one of the damask-and-gold armchairs to be sure it was not painted against the wall.

Selden, who had put one of these seats to the test, found himself, from an angle of the ballroom, surveying the scene with frank enjoyment. The company, in obedience to the decorative instinct which calls for fine clothes in fine surroundings, had dressed rather with an eye to Mrs. Bry's background than to herself. The seated throng, filling the immense room without undue crowding, presented a surface of rich tissues and jeweled shoulders in harmony with the festooned and gilded walls, and the flushed splendors of the Venetian ceiling. At the farther end of the room a stage had been constructed behind a proscenium arch curtained with folds of old damask; but in the pause before the parting of the folds there was little thought of what they might reveal, for every woman who had accepted Miss Bry's invitation was engaged in trying to find out how many of her friends had done the same.

Gerty Farish, seated next to Selden, was lost in that indiscriminate and uncritical enjoyment so irritating to Miss Bart's finer perceptions. It may be that Selden's nearness had something to do with the quality of his cousin's pleasure; but Miss Farish was so little accustomed to refer her enjoyment of such scenes to her own share in them, that she was merely conscious of a deeper sense of contentment.

"Wasn't it dear of Lily to get me an invitation? Of course it would never have occurred to Carry Fisher to put me on the list, and I should have been so sorry to miss seeing it all—and especially Lily herself. Someone told me the ceiling was by Veronese—you would know, of course, Lawrence. I suppose it's very beautiful, but his women are so dreadfully fat. Goddesses? Well, I can only say that if they'd been mortals and had to wear corsets, it would have been better for them. I think our women are much handsomer. And this room is wonderfully becoming—everyone looks so well! Did you ever see such jewels? Do look at Mrs. George Dorset's pearls—I suppose the smallest of them would pay the rent of our Girls' Club for a year. Not that I ought to complain about the club; everyone has been so wonderfully kind. Did I tell you that Lily had given us three hundred dollars? Wasn't it splendid of her? And then she collected a lot of money from her friends— Mrs. Bry gave us five hundred, and Mr. Rosedale a thousand. I wish Lily were not so nice to Mr. Rosedale, but she says it's no use being rude to him, because he doesn't see the difference. She really can't bear to hurt people's feelings—it makes me so angry when I hear her called cold and conceited! The girls at the club don't call her that. Do you know she has been there with me twice?—yes, Lily! And you should have seen their eyes! One of them said it was as good as a day in the country just to look at her. And she sat there, and laughed and talked with them—not a bit as if she were being *charitable*, you know, but as if she liked it as much as they did. They've been asking ever since when she's coming back; and she's promised me—oh!"

Miss Farish's confidences were cut short by the parting of the curtain on the first tableau—a group of nymphs dancing across flower-strewn sward in the rhythmic postures of Botticelli's *Spring*. Tableaux vivants depend for their effect not only on the happy disposal of lights and the delusive interposition of layers of gauze, but on a corresponding adjustment of the mental vision. To unfurnished minds they remain, in spite of every enhancement of art, only a superior kind of wax-works; but to the responsive fancy they may give magic glimpses of the boundary world between fact and imagination. Selden's mind was of this order: he could yield to vision-making influences as completely as a child to the spell of a fairytale. Mrs. Bry's tableaux wanted none of the qualities which go to the producing of such illusions, and under Morpeth's organizing hand the pictures succeeded each other with the rhythmic march of some splendid frieze, in which the fugitive curves of living flesh and the wandering light of young eyes have been subdued to plastic harmony without losing the charm of life.

The scenes were taken from old pictures, and the participators had been cleverly fitted with characters suited to their types. No one, for instance, could have made a more typical Goya than Carry Fisher, with her short dark-skinned face, the exaggerated glow of her eyes, the provocation of her frankly painted smile. A brilliant Miss Smedden from Brooklyn showed to perfection the sumptuous curves of Titian's Daughter, lifting her gold salver laden with grapes above the harmonizing gold of rippled hair and rich brocade, and a young Mrs. Van Alstyne, who showed the frailer Dutch type, with high blue-veined forehead and pale eyes and lashes, made a characteristic Vandyck, in black satin, against a curtained archway. Then there were Kauffmann nymphs garlanding the altar of Love; a Veronese supper, all sheeny textures, pearl-woven heads and marble architecture; and a Watteau group of lute-playing comedians, lounging by a fountain in a sunlit glade.

Each evanescent picture touched the vision-building faculty in Selden, leading him so far down the vistas of fancy that even Gerty Farish's running commentary—"Oh, how lovely Lulu Melson looks!" or: "That must be Kate Corby, to the right there, in purple"—did not break the spell of the illusion. Indeed, so skillfully had the personality of the actors been subdued to the scenes they figured in that even the least imaginative of the audience must have felt a thrill of contrast when the curtain suddenly parted on a picture which was simply and undisguisedly the portrait of Miss Bart.

Here there could be no mistaking the predominance of personality—the unanimous "Oh!" of the spectators was a tribute, not to the brush-work of Reynolds's "Mrs. Lloyd" but to the flesh and blood loveliness of Lily Bart. She had shown her artistic intelligence in selecting a type so like her own that she could embody the person represented without ceasing to be herself. It was as though she had stepped, not out of, but into, Reynolds's canvas, banishing the phantom of his dead beauty by the beams of her living grace. The impulse to show herself in a splendid setting—she had thought for a moment of representing Tiepolo's Cleopatra—had yielded to the truer instinct of trusting to her unassisted beauty, and she had purposely chosen a picture without distracting accessories of dress or surroundings. Her pale draperies, and the background of foliage against which she stood, served only to relieve the long dryadlike curves that swept upward from her poised foot to her lifted arm. The noble buoyancy of her attitude, its suggestion of soaring grace, revealed the touch of poetry in her beauty that Selden always felt in her presence, yet lost the sense of when he was not with her. Its expression was now so vivid that for the first time he seemed to see before him the real Lily Bart, divested of the trivialities of her little world, and catching for a moment a note of that eternal harmony of which her beauty was a part.

"Deuced bold thing to show herself in that get-up but, gad, there isn't a break in the lines anywhere, and I suppose she wanted us to know it!"

These words, uttered by that experienced connoisseur, Mr. Ned Van Alstyne, whose scented white moustache had brushed Selden's shoulder whenever the parting of the curtains presented any exceptional opportunity for the study of the female outline, affected their hearer in an unexpected way. It was not the first time that Selden had heard Lily's beauty lightly remarked on, and hitherto the tone of the comments had imperceptibly colored his view of her. But now it woke only a motion of indignant contempt. This was the world she lived in, these were the standards by which she was fated to be measured! Does one go to Caliban for a judgment on Miranda?

In the long moment before the curtain fell, he had time to feel the whole tragedy of her life. It was as though her beauty, thus detached from all that cheapened and vulgarized it, had held out suppliant hands to him from the world in which he and she had once met for a moment, and where he felt an overmastering longing to be with her again.

He was roused by the pressure of ecstatic fingers. "Wasn't she too beautiful, Lawrence? Don't you like her best in that simple dress? It makes her look like the real Lily—the Lily I know."

He met Gerty Farish's brimming gaze. "The Lily *we* know," he corrected; and his cousin, beaming at the implied understanding, exclaimed joyfully: "I'll tell her that! She always says you dislike her."

The performance over, Selden's first impulse was to seek Miss Bart. During the interlude of music which succeeded the tableaux, the actors had seated themselves here and there in the audience, diversifying its conventional appearance by the varied picturesqueness of their dress. Lily, however, was not among them, and her absence served to protract the effect she had produced on Selden: it would have broken the spell to see her too soon in the surroundings from which accident had so happily detached her. They had not met since the day of the Van Osburgh wedding, and on his side the avoidance had been intentional. Tonight, however, he knew that, sooner or later, he should find himself at her side; and though he let the dispersing crowd drift him whither it would, without making an immediate effort to reach her, his procrastination was not due to any lingering resistance, but to the desire to luxuriate a moment in the sense of complete surrender.

Lily had not an instant's doubt as to the meaning of the murmur greeting her appearance. No other tableau had been received with that precise
note of approval: it had obviously been called forth by herself, and not by
the picture she impersonated. She had feared at the last moment that she
was risking too much in dispensing with the advantages of a more sumptuous setting, and the completeness of her triumph gave her an intoxicating
sense of recovered power. Not caring to diminish the impression she had
produced, she held herself aloof from the audience till the movement of
dispersal before supper, and thus had a second opportunity of showing herself to advantage, as the throng poured slowly into the empty drawing-room
where she was standing.

She was soon the center of a group which increased and renewed itself
as the circulation became general, and the individual comments on her
success were a delightful prolongation of the collective applause. At such
moments she lost something of her natural fastidiousness, and cared less for
the quality of the admiration received than for its quantity. Differences of
personality were merged in a warm atmosphere of praise, in which her
beauty expanded like a flower in sunlight; and if Selden had approached a
moment or two sooner he would have seen her turning on Ned Van Alstyne
and George Dorset the look he had dreamed of capturing for himself.

Fortune willed, however, that the hurried approach of Mrs. Fisher, as
whose aide-de-camp Van Alstyne was acting, should break up the group
before Selden reached the threshold of the room. One or two of the men
wandered off in search of their partners for supper, and the others, noticing
Selden's approach, gave way to him in accordance with the tacit free-
masonry of the ballroom. Lily was therefore standing alone when he reached
her; and finding the expected look in her eye, he had the satisfaction of
supposing he had kindled it. The look did indeed deepen as it rested on
him, for even in that moment of self-intoxication Lily felt the quicker beat
of life that his nearness always produced. She read, too, in his answering
gaze the delicious confirmation of her triumph, and for the moment it
seemed to her that it was for him only she cared to be beautiful.

Selden had given her his arm without speaking. She took it in silence,
and they moved away, not toward the supper-room, but against the tide
which was setting thither. The faces about her flowed by like the streaming
images of sleep: she hardly noticed where Selden was leading her, till they
passed through a glass doorway at the end of the long suite of rooms and
stood suddenly in the fragrant hush of a garden. Gravel grated beneath their
feet, and about them was the transparent dimness of a midsummer night.
Hanging lights made emerald caverns in the depths of foliage, and whitened
the spray of a fountain falling among lilies. The magic place was deserted:
there was no sound but the plash of the water on the lily-pads, and a distant
drift of music that might have been blown across a sleeping lake.

Selden and Lily stood still, accepting the unreality of the scene as a part

of their own dreamlike sensations. It would not have surprised them to feel
a summer breeze on their faces, or to see the lights among the boughs
reduplicated in the arch of a starry sky. The strange solitude about them was
no stranger than the sweetness of being alone in it together.

At length Lily withdrew her hand, and moved away a step, so that her
white-robed slimness was outlined against the dusk of the branches. Selden
followed her, and still without speaking they seated themselves on a bench
beside the fountain.

Suddenly she raised her eyes with the beseeching earnestness of a child.
"You never speak to me—you think hard things of me," she murmured.

"I think of you at any rate, God knows!" he said.

"Then why do we never see each other? Why can't we be friends? You
promised once to help me," she continued in the same tone, as though the
words were drawn from her unwillingly.

"The only way I can help you is by loving you," Selden said in a low
voice.

She made no reply, but her face turned to him with the soft motion of a
flower. His own met it slowly, and their lips touched.

She drew back and rose from her seat. Selden rose too, and they stood
facing each other. Suddenly she caught his hand and pressed it a moment
against her cheek.

"Ah, love me, love me—but don't tell me so!" she sighed with her eyes
in his; and before he could speak she had turned and slipped through the
arch of boughs, disappearing in the brightness of the room beyond.

Selden stood where she had left him. He knew too well the transiency of
exquisite moments to attempt to follow her; but presently he reentered the
house and made his way through the deserted rooms to the door. A few
sumptuously cloaked ladies were already gathered in the marble vestibule,
and in the coat-room he found Van Alstyne and Gus Trenor.

The former, at Selden's approach, paused in the careful selection of a
cigar from one of the silver boxes invitingly set out near the door.

"Hallo, Selden, going, too? You're an Epicurean like myself, I see: you
don't want to see all those goddesses gobbling terrapin. Gad, what a show of
good-looking women; but not one of them could touch that little cousin of
mine. Talk of jewels—what's a woman want with jewels when she's got
herself to show? The trouble is that all these fal-bals they wear cover up
their figures when they've got 'em. I never knew till tonight what an outline
Lily has."

"It's not her fault if everybody don't know it now," growled Trenor,
flushed with the struggle of getting into his fur-lined coat. "Damned bad
taste, I call it—no, no cigar for me. You can't tell what you're smoking in
one of these new houses—likely as not the chef buys the cigars. Stay for
supper? Not if I know it! When people crowd their rooms so that you can't

get near anyone you want to speak to, I'd as soon sup in the elevated at the rush hour. My wife was dead right to stay away: she says life's too short to spend it in breaking in new people."

13

L ILY woke from happy dreams to find two notes at her bedside.
        One was from Mrs. Trenor, who announced that she was coming to town that afternoon for a flying visit, and hoped Miss Bart would be able to dine with her.

The other was from Selden. He wrote briefly that an important case called him to Albany, whence he would be unable to return till the evening, and asked Lily to let him know at what hour on the following day she would see him.

Lily, leaning back among her pillows, gazed musingly at his letter. The scene in the Brys' conservatory had been like a part of her dreams; she had not expected to wake to such evidence of its reality. Her first movement was one of annoyance: this unforeseen act of Selden's added another complication to life. It was so unlike him to yield to such an irrational impulse! Did he really mean to ask her to marry him? She had once shown him the impossibility of such a hope, and his subsequent behavior seemed to prove that he had accepted the situation with a reasonableness somewhat mortifying to her vanity. It was all the more agreeable to find that this reasonableness was maintained only at the cost of not seeing her; but, though nothing in life was as sweet as the sense of her power over him, she saw the danger of allowing the episode of the previous night to have a sequel. Since she could not marry him, it would be kinder to him, as well as easier for herself, to write a line amicably evading his request to see her: he was not the man to mistake such a hint, and when next they met it would be on their usual friendly footing.

Lily sprang out of bed, and went straight to her desk. She wanted to write at once, while she could trust to the strength of her resolve. She was still languid from her brief sleep and the exhilaration of the evening, and the sight of Selden's writing brought back the culminating moment of her triumph: the moment when she had read in his eyes that no philosophy was proof against her power. It would be pleasant to have that sensation again . . . no one else could give it to her in its fullness; and she could not bear to mar her mood of luxurious retrospection by an act of definite refusal. She took up her pen and wrote hastily: *"Tomorrow at four"*—murmuring to herself, as she slipped the sheet into its envelope: "I can easily put him off when tomorrow comes."

Judy Trenor's summons was very welcome to Lily. It was the first time she had received a direct communication from Bellomont since the close of her last visit there, and she was still visited by the dread of having incurred Judy's displeasure. But this characteristic command seemed to reestablish their former relations; and Lily smiled at the thought that her friend had probably summoned her in order to hear about the Brys' entertainment. Mrs. Trenor had absented herself from the feast, perhaps for the reason so frankly enunciated by her husband, perhaps because, as Mrs. Fisher somewhat differently put it, she "couldn't bear new people when she hadn't discovered them herself." At any rate, though she remained haughtily at Bellomont, Lily suspected in her a devouring eagerness to hear of what she had missed, and to learn exactly in what measure Mrs. Wellington Bry had surpassed all previous competitors for social recognition. Lily was quite ready to gratify this curiosity, but it happened that she was dining out. She determined, however, to see Mrs. Trenor for a few moments, and ringing for her maid she dispatched a telegram to say that she would be with her friend that evening at ten.

She was dining with Mrs. Fisher, who had gathered at an informal feast a few of the performers of the previous evening. There was to be plantation music in the studio after dinner—for Mrs. Fisher, despairing of the republic, had taken up modeling, and annexed to her small crowded house a spacious apartment, which, whatever its uses in her hours of plastic inspiration, served at other times for the exercise of an indefatigable hospitality. Lily was reluctant to leave, for the dinner was amusing, and she would have liked to lounge over a cigarette and hear a few songs; but she could not break her engagement with Judy, and shortly after ten she asked her hostess to ring for a hansom, and drove up Fifth Avenue to the Trenors'.

She waited long enough on the doorstep to wonder that Judy's presence in town was not signalized by a greater promptness in admitting her; and her surprise was increased when, instead of the expected footman, pushing his shoulders into a tardy coat, a shabby caretaking person in calico let her into the shrouded hall. Trenor, however, appeared at once on the threshold of the drawing-room, welcoming her with unusual volubility while he relieved her of her cloak and drew her into the room.

"Come along to the den; it's the only comfortable place in the house. Doesn't this room look as if it was waiting for the body to be brought down? Can't see why Judy keeps the house wrapped up in this awful slippery white stuff—it's enough to give a fellow pneumonia to walk through these rooms on a cold day. You look a little pinched yourself, by the way: it's rather a sharp night out. I noticed it walking up from the club. Come along, and I'll give you a nip of brandy, and you can toast yourself over the fire and try some of my new Egyptians—that little turkish chap at the embassy put me on to a brand that I want you to try, and if you like 'em I'll get out a lot for you: they don't have 'em here yet, but I'll cable."

He led her through the house to the large room at the back, where Mrs. Trenor usually sat, and where, even in her absence, there was an air of occupancy. Here, as usual, were flowers, newspapers, a littered writing-table, and a general aspect of lamp-lit familiarity, so that it was a surprise not to see Judy's energetic figure start up from the armchair near the fire.

It was apparently Trenor himself who had been occupying the seat in question, for it was overhung by a cloud of cigar smoke, and near it stood one of those intricate folding tables which British ingenuity has devised to facilitate the circulation of tobacco and spirits. The sight of such appliances in a drawing-room was not unusual in Lily's set, where smoking and drinking were unrestricted by considerations of time and place, and her first movement was to help herself to one of the cigarettes recommended by Trenor, while she checked his loquacity by asking, with a surprised glance: "Where's Judy?"

Trenor, a little heated by his unusual flow of words, and perhaps by prolonged propinquity with the decanters, was bending over the latter to decipher their silver labels.

"Here, now, Lily, just a drop of cognac in a little fizzy water—you do look pinched, you know: I swear the end of your nose is red. I'll take another glass to keep you company—Judy?—Why, you see, Judy's got a devil of a headache—quite knocked out with it, poor thing—she asked me to explain—make it all right, you know—Do come up to the fire, though; you look dead-beat, really. Now do let me make you comfortable, there's a good girl."

He had taken her hand, half-banteringly, and was drawing her toward a low seat by the hearth; but she stopped and freed herself quietly.

"Do you mean to say that Judy's not well enough to see me? Doesn't she want me to go upstairs?"

Trenor drained the glass he had filled for himself, and paused to set it down before he answered.

"Why, no—the fact is, she's not up to seeing anybody. It came on suddenly, you know, and she asked me to tell you how awfully sorry she was —if she'd known where you were dining she'd have sent you word."

"She did know where I was dining; I mentioned it in my telegram. But it doesn't matter, of course. I suppose if she's so poorly she won't go back to Bellomont in the morning, and I can come and see her then."

"Yes: exactly—that's capital. I'll tell her you'll pop in tomorrow morning. And now do sit down a minute, there's a dear, and let's have a nice quiet jaw together. You won't take a drop, just for sociability? Tell me what you think of that cigarette. Why, don't you like it? What are you chucking it away for?"

"I am chucking it away because I must go, if you'll have the goodness to call a cab for me," Lily returned with a smile.

She did not like Trenor's unusual excitability, with its too evident explanation, and the thought of being alone with him, with her friend out of reach upstairs, at the other end of the great empty house, did not conduce to a desire to prolong their tête-à-tête.

But Trenor, with a promptness which did not escape her, had moved between herself and the door.

"Why must you go, I should like to know? If Judy'd been here you'd have sat gossiping till all hours—and you can't even give me five minutes! It's always the same story. Last night I couldn't get near you—I went to that damned vulgar party just to see you, and there was everybody talking about you, and asking me if I'd ever seen anything so stunning, and when I tried to come up and say a word, you never took any notice, but just went on laughing and joking with a lot of asses who only wanted to be able to swagger about afterward, and look knowing when you were mentioned."

He paused, flushed by his diatribe, and fixing on her a look in which resentment was the ingredient she least disliked. But she had regained her presence of mind, and stood composedly in the middle of the room, while her slight smile seemed to put an ever increasing distance between herself and Trenor.

Across it she said: "Don't be absurd, Gus. It's past eleven, and I must really ask you to ring for a cab."

He remained immovable, with the lowering forehead she had grown to detest.

"And supposing I won't ring for one—what'll you do then?"

"I shall go upstairs to Judy if you force me to disturb her."

Trenor drew a step nearer and laid his hand on her arm. "Look here, Lily, won't you give me five minutes of your own accord?"

"Not tonight, Gus: you —"

"Very good, then, I'll take 'em. And as many more as I want." He had squared himself on the threshold, his hands thrust deep in his pockets. He nodded toward the chair on the hearth.

"Go and sit down there, please: I've got a word to say to you."

Lily's quick temper was getting the better of her fears. She drew herself up and moved toward the door.

"If you have anything to say to me, you must say it another time. I shall go up to Judy unless you call a cab for me at once."

He burst into a laugh. "Go upstairs and welcome, my dear; but you won't find Judy. She ain't there."

Lily cast a startled look upon him. "Do you mean that Judy is not in the house—not in town?" she exclaimed.

"That's just what I do mean," returned Trenor, his bluster sinking to sullenness under her look.

"Nonsense—I don't believe you. I am going upstairs," she said impatiently.

He drew unexpectedly aside, letting her reach the threshold unimpeded.

"Go up and welcome; but my wife is at Bellomont."

But Lily had a flash of reassurance. "If she hadn't come she would have sent me word —"

"She did; she telephoned me this afternoon to let you know."

"I received no message."

"I didn't send any."

The two measured each other for a moment, but Lily still saw her opponent through a blur of scorn that made all other considerations indistinct.

"I can't imagine your object in playing such a stupid trick on me; but if you have fully gratified your peculiar sense of humor I must again ask you to send for a cab."

It was the wrong note, and she knew it as she spoke. To be stung by irony it is not necessary to understand it, and the angry streaks on Trenor's face might have been raised by an actual lash.

"Look here, Lily, don't take that high and mighty tone with me." He had again moved toward the door, and in her instinctive shrinking from him she let him regain command of the threshold. "I did play a trick on you; I own up to it; but if you think I'm ashamed you're mistaken. Lord knows I've been patient enough—I've hung round and looked like an ass. And all the while you were letting a lot of other fellows make up to you . . . letting 'em make fun of me, I daresay . . . I'm not sharp, and can't dress my friends up to look funny, as you do . . . but I can tell when it's being done to me . . . I can tell fast enough when I'm made a fool of. . . ."

"Ah, I shouldn't have thought that!" flashed from Lily, but her laugh dropped to silence under his look.

"No, you wouldn't have thought it; but you'll know better now. That's what you're here for tonight. I've been waiting for a quiet time to talk things over, and now I've got it I mean to make you hear me out."

His first rush of inarticulate resentment had been followed by a steadiness and concentration of tone more disconcerting to Lily than the excitement preceding it. For a moment her presence of mind forsook her. She had more than once been in situations where a quick swordplay of wit had been needful to cover her retreat; but her frightened heart-throbs told her that here such skill would not avail.

To gain time she repeated: "I don't understand what you want."

Trenor had pushed a chair between herself and the door. He threw himself in it, and leaned back, looking up at her.

"I'll tell you what I want: I want to know just where you and I stand.

Hang it, the man who pays for the dinner is generally allowed to have a seat at table."

She flamed with anger and abasement, and the sickening need of having to conciliate where she longed to humble.

"I don't know what you mean—but you must see, Gus, that I can't stay here talking to you at this hour —"

"Gad, you go to men's houses fast enough in broad daylight—strikes me you're not always so deuced careful of appearances."

The brutality of the thrust gave her the sense of dizziness that follows on a physical blow. Rosedale had spoken then—this was the way men talked of her—She felt suddenly weak and defenseless: there was a throb of self-pity in her throat. But all the while another self was sharpening her to vigilance, whispering the terrified warning that every word and gesture must be measured.

"If you have brought me here to say insulting things —" she began.

Trenor laughed. "Don't talk stage-rot. I don't want to insult you. But a man's got his feelings—and you've played with mine too long. I didn't begin this business—kept out of the way, and left the track clear for the other chaps, till you rummaged me out and set to work to make an ass of me—and an easy job you had of it, too. That's the trouble—it was too easy for you— you got reckless—thought you could turn me inside out, and chuck me in the gutter like an empty purse. But, by gad, that ain't playing fair: that's dodging the rules of the game. Of course, I know now what you wanted—it wasn't my beautiful eyes you were after—but I tell you what, Miss Lily, you've got to pay up for making me think so —"

He rose, squaring his shoulders aggressively, and stepped toward her with a reddening brow; but she held her footing, though every nerve tore at her to retreat as he advanced.

"Pay up?" she faltered. "Do you mean that I owe you money?"

He laughed again. "Oh, I'm not asking for payment in kind. But there's such a thing as fair play—and interest on one's money—and hang me if I've had as much as a look from you —"

"Your money? What have I to do with your money? You advised me how to invest mine . . . you must have seen I knew nothing of business . . . you told me it was all right —"

"It *was* all right—it is, Lily: you're welcome to all of it, and ten times more. I'm only asking for a word of thanks from you." He was closer still, with a hand that grew formidable; and the frightened self in her was dragging the other down.

"I *have* thanked you; I've shown I was grateful. What more have you done than any friend might do, or anyone accept from a friend?"

Trenor caught her up with a sneer. "I don't doubt you've accepted as much before—and chucked the other chaps as you'd like to chuck me. I don't care how you settled your score with them—if you fooled 'em I'm that much to the good. Don't stare at me like that—I know I'm not talking the way a man is supposed to talk to a girl—but, hang it, if you don't like it you can stop me quick enough—you know I'm mad about you—damn the money, there's plenty more of it—if *that* bothers you. . . . I was a brute, Lily—Lily!—just look at me —"

Over and over her the sea of humiliation broke—wave crashing on wave so close that the moral shame was one with the physical dread. It seemed to her that self-esteem would have made her invulnerable—that it was her own dishonor which put a fearful solitude about her.

His touch was a shock to her drowning consciousness. She drew back from him with a desperate assumption of scorn.

"I've told you I don't understand—but if I owe you money you shall be paid —"

Trenor's face darkened to rage: her recoil of abhorrence had called out the primitive man.

"Ah—you'll borrow from Selden or Rosedale—and take your chances of fooling them as you've fooled me. Unless—unless you've settled your other scores already—and I'm the only one left out in the cold!"

She stood silent, frozen to her place. The words—the words were worse than the touch! Her heart was beating all over her body—in her throat, her limbs, her helpless useless hands. Her eyes traveled despairingly about the room—they lit on the bell, and she remembered that help was in call. Yes, but scandal with it—a hideous mustering of tongues. No, she must fight her way out alone. It was enough that the servants knew her to be in the house with Trenor—there must be nothing to excite conjecture in her way of leaving it.

She raised her head, and achieved a last clear look at him.

"I am here alone with you," she said. "What more have you to say?"

To her surprise, Trenor answered the look with a speechless stare. With his last gust of words the flame had died out, leaving him chill and humbled. It was as though a cold air had dispersed the fumes of his libations, and the situation loomed before him black and naked as the ruins of a fire. Old habits, old restraints, the hand of inherited order, plucked back the bewildered mind which passion had jolted from its ruts. Trenor's eye had the haggard look of the sleepwalker waked on a deathly ledge.

"Go home! Go away from here" —he stammered, and turning his back on her walked toward the hearth.

The sharp release from her fears restored Lily to immediate lucidity. The collapse of Trenor's will left her in control, and she heard herself, in a voice that was her own yet outside herself bidding him ring for the servant, bidding him give the order for a hansom, directing him to put her in it when it came. Whence the strength came to her she knew not; but an insistent voice warned her that she must leave the house openly, and nerved her, in the hall before the hovering caretaker, to exchange light words with Trenor, and charge him with the usual messages for Judy, while all the while she shook with inward loathing. On the doorstep, with the street before her, she felt a mad throb of liberation, intoxicating as the prisoner's first draught of free air; but the clearness of brain continued, and she noted the mute aspect of Fifth Avenue, guessed at the lateness of the hour, and even observed a man's figure—was there something half-familiar in its outline?—which, as she entered the hansom, turned from the opposite corner and vanished in the obscurity of the side street.

But with the turn of the wheels reaction came, and shuddering darkness closed on her. "I can't think—I can't think," she moaned, and leaned her head against the rattling side of the cab. She seemed a stranger to herself, or rather there were two selves in her, the one she had always known, and a new abhorrent being to which it found itself chained. She had once picked up, in a house where she was staying, a translation of the *Eumenides*, and her imagination had been seized by the high terror of the scene where Orestes, in the cave of the oracle, finds his implacable huntresses asleep, and snatches an hour's repose. Yes, the Furies might sometimes sleep, but they were there, always there in the dark corners, and now they were awake and the iron clang of their wings was in her brain. . . . She opened her eyes and saw the streets passing—the familiar alien streets. All she looked on was the same and yet changed. There was a great gulf fixed between today and yesterday. Everything in the past seemed simple, natural, full of daylight—and she was alone in a place of darkness and pollution. Alone! It was the loneliness that frightened her. Her eyes fell on an illuminated clock at a street corner, and she saw that the hands marked the half hour after eleven. Only half-past eleven—there were hours and hours left of the night! And she must spend them alone, shuddering sleepless on her bed. Her soft nature recoiled from this ordeal, which had none of the stimulus of conflict to goad her through it. Oh, the slow cold drip of the minutes on her head! She had a vision of herself lying on the black walnut bed—and the darkness would frighten her, and if she left the light burning the dreary details of the room would brand themselves forever on her brain. She had always hated her room at Mrs. Peniston's—its ugliness, its impersonality, the fact that nothing in it was really hers. To a torn heart uncomforted by human nearness a room may open almost human arms, and the being to whom no four walls mean more than any others, is, at such hours, expatriate everywhere.

Lily had no heart to lean on. Her relation with her aunt was as superficial as that of chance lodgers who pass on the stairs. But even had the two been in closer contact, it was impossible to think of Mrs. Peniston's mind as offering shelter or comprehension to such misery as Lily's. As the pain that can be told is but half a pain, so the pity that questions has little healing in its touch. What Lily craved was the darkness made by enfolding arms, the silence which is not solitude, but compassion holding its breath.

She started up and looked forth on the passing streets. Gerty!—they were nearing Gerty's corner. If only she could reach there before this laboring anguish burst from her breast to her lips—if only she could feel the hold of Gerty's arms while she shook in the ague-fit of fear that was coming upon her! She pushed up the door in the roof and called the address to the driver. It was not so late—Gerty might still be waking. And even if she were not, the sound of the bell would penetrate every recess of her tiny apartment, and rouse her to answer her friend's call.

14

GERTY Farish, the morning after the Wellington Brys' entertainment, woke from dreams as happy as Lily's. If they were less vivid in hue, more subdued to the half-tints of her personality and her experience, they were for that very reason better suited to her mental vision. Such flashes of joy as Lily moved in would have blinded Miss Farish, who was accustomed, in the way of happiness, to such scant light as shone through the cracks of other people's lives.

Now she was the center of a little illumination of her own: a mild but unmistakable beam, compounded of Lawrence Selden's growing kindness to herself and the discovery that he extended his liking to Lily Bart. If these two factors seem incompatible to the student of feminine psychology, it must be remembered that Gerty had always been a parasite in the moral order, living on the crumbs of other tables, and content to look through the window at the banquet spread for her friends. Now that she was enjoying a little private feast of her own, it would have seemed incredibly selfish not to lay a plate for a friend; and there was no one with whom she would rather have shared her enjoyment than Miss Bart.

As to the nature of Selden's growing kindness, Gerty would no more have dared to define it than she would have tried to learn a butterfly's color by knocking the dust from its wings. To seize on the wonder would be to brush off its bloom, and perhaps see it fade and stiffen in her hand: better the sense of beauty palpitating out of reach, while she held her breath and watched where it would alight. Yet Selden's manner at the Brys' had brought the flutter of wings so close that they seemed to be beating in her own heart. She had never seen him so alert, so responsive, so attentive to what she had to say. His habitual manner had an absent-minded kindliness which she accepted, and was grateful for, as the liveliest sentiment her presence was likely to inspire; but she was quick to feel in him a change implying that for once she could give pleasure as well as receive it.

And it was so delightful that this higher degree of sympathy should be reached through their interest in Lily Bart! Gerty's affection for her friend —a sentiment that had learned to keep itself alive on the scantiest diet— had grown to active adoration since Lily's restless curiosity had drawn her into the circle of Miss Farish's work. Lily's taste of beneficence had wakened in her a momentary appetite for well-doing. Her visit to the Girls' Club had first brought her in contact with the dramatic contrasts of life. She had always accepted with philosophic calm the fact that such existences as hers were pedestalled on foundations of obscure humanity. The dreary limbo of dinginess lay all around and beneath that little illuminated circle in which life reached its finest efflorescence, as the mud and sleet of a winter night enclose a hothouse filled with tropical flowers. All this was in the natural order of things, and the orchid basking in its artificially created atmosphere could round the delicate curves of its petals undisturbed by the ice on the panes.

But it is one thing to live comfortably with the abstract conception of poverty, another to be brought in contact with its human embodiments. Lily had never conceived of these victims of fate otherwise than in the mass. That the mass was composed of individual lives, innumerable separate centers of sensation, with her own eager reachings for pleasure, her own fierce revulsions from pain—that some of these bundles of feeling were clothed in shapes not so unlike her own, with eyes meant to look on glad-ness, and young lips shaped for love—this discovery gave Lily one of those sudden shocks of pity that sometimes decentralize a life. Lily's nature was incapable of such renewal: she could feel other demands only through her own, and no pain was long vivid which did not press on an answering nerve. But for the moment she was drawn out of herself by the interest of her direct relation with a world so unlike her own. She had supplemented her first gift by personal assistance to one or two of Miss Farish's most appealing subjects, and the admiration and interest her presence excited among the tired workers at the club ministered in a new form to her insatiable desire to please.

Gerty Farish was not a close enough reader of character to disentangle the mixed threads of which Lily's philanthropy was woven. She supposed her beautiful friend to be actuated by the same motive as herself—that sharpening of the moral vision which makes all human suffering so near and insistent that the other aspects of life fade into remoteness. Gerty lived by such simple formulas that she did not hesitate to class her friend's state with the emotional "change of heart" to which her dealings with the poor had accustomed her; and she rejoiced in the thought that she had been the humble instrument of this renewal. Now she had an answer to all criticisms of Lily's conduct: as she had said, she knew "the real Lily," and the discov-ery that Selden shared her knowledge raised her placid acceptance of life to a dazzled sense of its possibilities—a sense farther enlarged, in the course of the afternoon, by the receipt of a telegram from Selden asking if he might dine with her that evening.

While Gerty was lost in the happy bustle which this announcement produced in her small household, Selden was at one with her in thinking with intensity of Lily Bart. The case which had called him to Albany was not complicated enough to absorb all his attention, and he had the professional faculty of keeping a part of his mind free when its services were not needed. This part—which at the moment seemed dangerously like the whole—was filled to the brim with the sensations of the previous evening. Selden understood the symptoms: he recognized the fact that he was paying up, as there had always been a chance of his having to pay up, for the voluntary exclusions of his past. He had meant to keep free from permanent ties, not from any poverty of feeling, but because, in a different way, he was, as much as Lily, the victim of his environment. There had been a germ of truth in his declaration to Gerty Farish that he had never wanted to marry a "nice" girl: the adjective connoting, in his cousin's vocabulary, certain utilitarian qualities which are apt to preclude the luxury of charm. Now it had been Selden's fate to have a charming mother: her graceful portrait, all smiles and cashmere, still emitted a faded scent of the undefinable quality. His father was the kind of man who delights in a charming woman: who quotes her, stimulates her, and keeps her perennially charming. Neither one of the couple cared for money, but their disdain of it took the form of always spending a little more than was prudent. If their house was shabby, it was exquisitely kept; if there were good books on the shelves there were also good dishes on the table. Selden senior had an eye for a picture, his wife an understanding of old lace; and both were so conscious of restraint and discrimination in buying that they never quite knew how it was that the bills mounted up.

Though many of Selden's friends would have called his parents poor, he had grown up in an atmosphere where restricted means were felt only as a check on aimless profusion: where the few possessions were so good that their rarity gave them a merited relief and abstinence was combined with elegance in a way exemplified by Mrs. Selden's knack of wearing her old velvet as if it were new. A man has the advantage of being delivered early from the home point of view, and before Selden left college he had learned that there are as many different ways of going without money as of spending it. Unfortunately, he found no way as agreeable as that practiced at home; and his views of womankind in especial were tinged by the remembrance of the one woman who had given him his sense of "values." It was from her that he inherited his detachment from the sumptuary side of life: the stoic's carelessness of material things, combined with the Epicurean's pleasure in them. Life shorn of either feeling appeared to him a diminished thing; and nowhere was the blending of the two ingredients so essential as in the character of a pretty woman.

It had always seemed to Selden that experience offered a great deal besides the sentimental adventure, yet he could vividly conceive of a love which should broaden and deepen till it became the central fact of life. What he could not accept, in his own case, was the makeshift alternative of a relation that should be less than this: that should leave some portions of his nature unsatisfied, while it put an undue strain on others. He would not, in other words, yield to the growth of an affection which might appeal to pity yet leave the understanding untouched: sympathy should no more delude him than a trick of the eyes, the grace of helplessness than a curve of the cheek.

But now—that little *but* passed like a sponge over all his vows. His reasoned-out resistances seemed for the moment so much less important than the question as to when Lily would receive his note! He yielded himself to the charm of trivial preoccupations, wondering at what hour her reply would be sent, with what words it would begin. As to its import he had no doubt—he was as sure of her surrender as of his own. And so he had leisure to muse on all its exquisite details, as a hard worker, on a holiday morning, might lie still and watch the beam of light travel gradually across his room. But if the new light dazzled, it did not blind him. He could still discern the outline of facts, though his own relation to them had changed. He was no less conscious than before of what was said of Lily Bart, but he could separate the woman he knew from the vulgar estimate of her. His mind turned to Gerty Farish's words, and the wisdom of the world seemed a groping thing beside the insight of innocence. *Blessed are the pure in heart, for they shall see God*—even the hidden god in their neighbor's breast! Selden was in the state of impassioned self-absorption that the first surrender to love produces. His craving was for the companionship of one whose point of view should justify his own, who should confirm, by deliberate observation, the truth to which his intuitions had leaped. He could not wait for the midday recess, but seized a moment's leisure in court to scribble his telegram to Gerty Farish.

Reaching town, he was driven direct to his club, where he hoped a note from Miss Bart might await him. But his box contained only a line of rapturous assent from Gerty, and he was turning away disappointed when he was hailed by a voice from the smoking room.

"Hallo, Lawrence! Dining here? Take a bite with me—I've ordered a canvas-back."

He discovered Trenor, in his day clothes, sitting, with a tall glass at his elbow, behind the folds of a sporting journal.

Selden thanked him, but pleaded an engagement.

"Hang it, I believe every man in town has an engagement tonight. I shall have the club to myself. You know how I'm living this winter, rattling round in that empty house. My wife meant to come to town today, but she's put it off again, and how is a fellow to dine alone in a room with the looking glasses covered, and nothing but a bottle of Harvey sauce on the sideboard? I say, Lawrence, chuck your engagement and take pity on me—it gives me the blue devils to dine alone, and there's nobody but that canting ass Wetherall in the club."

"Sorry, Gus—I can't do it."

As Selden turned away, he noticed the dark flush on Trenor's face, the unpleasant moisture of his intensely white forehead, the way his jeweled rings were wedged in the creases of his fat red fingers. Certainly the beast was predominating—the beast at the bottom of the glass. And he had heard this man's name coupled with Lily's! Bah—the thought sickened him; all the way back to his rooms he was haunted by the sight of Trenor's fat creased hands —

On his table lay the note: Lily had sent it to his rooms. He knew what was in it before he broke the seal—a gray seal with *Beyond!* beneath a flying ship. Ah, he would take her beyond—beyond the ugliness, the pettiness, the attrition and corrosion of the soul—

Gerty's little sitting-room sparkled with welcome when Selden entered it. Its modest "effects," compact of enamel paint and ingenuity, spoke to him in the language just then sweetest to his ear. It is surprising how little narrow walls and a low ceiling matter, when the roof of the soul has suddenly been raised. Gerty sparkled too; or at least shone with a tempered radiance. He had never before noticed that she had "points"—really, some good fellow might do worse . . . Over the little dinner (and here, again, the effects were wonderful) he told her she ought to marry—he was in a mood to pair off the whole world. She had made the caramel custard with her own hands? It was sinful to keep such gifts to herself. He reflected with a throb of pride that Lily could trim her own hats—she had told him so the day of their walk at Bellomont.

He did not speak of Lily till after dinner. During the little repast he kept the talk on his hostess, who, flattered at being the center of observation, shone as rosy as the candle-shades she had manufactured for the occasion. Selden evinced an extraordinary interest in her household arrangements: complimented her on the ingenuity with which she had utilized every inch of her small quarters, asked how her servant managed about afternoons out, learned that one may improvise delicious dinners in a chafing-dish, and uttered thoughtful generalizations on the burden of a large establishment.

When they were in the sitting-room again, where they fitted as snugly as bits in a puzzle, and she had brewed the coffee, and poured it into her grandmother's egg-shell cups, his eye, as he leaned back, basking in the warm fragrance, lighted on a recent photograph of Miss Bart, and the desired transition was effected without an effort. The photograph was well enough—but to catch her as she had looked last night! Gerty agreed with him—never had she been so radiant. But could photography capture that light? There had been a new look in her face—something different; yes, Selden agreed, there had been something different. The coffee was so exqui-site that he asked for a second cup: such a contrast to the watery stuff at the club! Ah, your poor bachelor with his impersonal club fare, alternating with the equally impersonal cuisine of the dinner-party! A man who lived in lodgings missed the best part of life—he pictured the flavorless solitude of Trenor's repast, and felt a moment's compassion for the man. . . . But to return to Lily—and again and again he returned, questioning, conjecturing, leading Gerty on, draining her inmost thoughts of their stored tenderness for her friend.

At first she poured herself out unstintingly, happy in this perfect com-munion of their sympathies. His understanding of Lily helped to confirm her own belief in her friend. They dwelt together on the fact that Lily had had no chance. Gerty instanced her generous impulses—her restlessness and discontent. The fact that her life had never satisfied her proved that she was made for better things. She might have married more than once—the con-ventional rich marriage which she had been taught to consider the sole end of existence—but when the opportunity came she had always shrunk from it. Percy Gryce, for instance, had been in love with her—everyone at Bel-lomont had supposed them to be engaged, and her dismissal of him was thought inexplicable. This view of the Gryce incident chimed too well with Selden's mood not to be instantly adopted by him, with a flash of retrospec-tive contempt for what had once seemed the obvious solution. If rejection there had been—and he wondered now that he had ever doubted it!—then he held the key to the secret, and the hillsides of Bellomont were lit up, not with sunset, but with dawn. It was he who had wavered and disowned the face of opportunity—and the joy now warming his breast might have been a familiar inmate if he had captured it in its first flight.

It was at this point, perhaps, that a joy just trying its wings in Gerty's heart dropped to earth and lay still. She sat facing Selden, repeating mechanically: "No, she has never been understood —" and all the while she herself seemed to be sitting in the center of a great glare of comprehension. The little confidential room, where a moment ago their thoughts had touched elbows like their chairs, grew to unfriendly vastness, separating her from Selden by all the length of her new vision of the future—and that future stretched out interminably, with her lonely figure toiling down it, a mere speck on the solitude.

"She is herself with a few people only; and you are one of them," she heard Selden saying. And again: "Be good to her, Gerty, won't you?" and: "She has it in her to become whatever she is believed to be—you'll help her by believing the best of her?"

The words beat on Gerty's brain like the sound of a language which has seemed familiar at a distance, but on approaching is found to be unintel-ligible. He had come to talk to her of Lily—that was all! There had been a third at the feast she had spread for him, and that third had taken her own place. She tried to follow what he was saying, to cling to her own part in the talk—but it was all as meaningless as the boom of waves in a drowning head, and she felt, as the drowning may feel, that to sink would be nothing beside the pain of struggling to keep up.

Selden rose, and she drew a deep breath, feeling that soon she could yield to the blessed waves.

"Mrs. Fisher's? You say she was dining there? There's music afterward; I believe I had a card from her." He glanced at the foolish pink-faced clock that was drumming out this hideous hour. "A quarter past ten? I might look in there now; the Fisher evenings are amusing. I haven't kept you up too late, Gerty? You look tired—I've rambled on and bored you." And in the unwonted overflow of his feelings, he left a cousinly kiss upon her cheek.

At Mrs. Fisher's, through the cigar-smoke of the studio, a dozen voices greeted Selden. A song was pending as he entered, and he dropped into a seat near his hostess, his eyes roaming in search of Miss Bart. But she was not there, and the discovery gave him a pang out of all proportion to its seriousness; since the note in his breast-pocket assured him that at four the next day they would meet. To his impatience it seemed immeasurably long to wait, and half-ashamed of the impulse, he leaned to Mrs. Fisher to ask, as the music ceased, if Miss Bart had not dined with her.

"Lily? She's just gone. She had to run off, I forget where. Wasn't she wonderful last night?"

"Who's that? Lily?" asked Jack Stepney, from the depths of a neighboring armchair. "Really, you know, I'm no child, but when it comes to a girl standing there as if she was up at auction—I thought seriously of speaking to cousin Julia."

"You didn't know Jack had become our social censor?" Mrs. Fisher said to Selden with a laugh; and Stepney spluttered, amid the general derision: "But she's a cousin, hang it, and when a man's married—*Town Talk* was full of her this morning."

"Yes: lively reading that was," said Mr. Ned Van Alstyne, stroking his moustache to hide the smile behind it. "Buy the dirty sheet? No, of course not; some fellow showed it to me—but I'd heard the stories before. When a girl's as good-looking as that she'd better marry; then no questions are asked. In our imperfectly organized society there is no provision as yet for the young woman who claims the privileges of marriage without assuming its obligations."

"Well, I understand Lily is about to assume them in the shape of Mr. Rosedale," Mrs. Fisher said with a laugh.

"Rosedale—good heavens!" exclaimed Van Alstyne, dropping his eyeglass. "Stepney, that's your fault for foisting the brute on us."

"Oh, confound it, you know, we don't *marry* Rosedale in our family,"

Stepney languidly protested; but his wife, who sat in oppressive bridal finery at the other side of the room, quelled him with the judicial reflection: "In Lily's circumstances it's a mistake to have too high a standard."

"I hear even Rosedale has been scared by the talk lately," Mrs. Fisher rejoined; "but the sight of her last night sent him off his head. What do you think he said to me after her tableau? 'My God, Mrs. Fisher, if I could get Paul Morpeth to paint her like that, the picture'd appreciate a hundred percent in ten years.' "

"By Jove—but isn't she about somewhere?" exclaimed Van Alstyne, restoring his glass with an uneasy glance.

"No; she ran off while you were all mixing the punch downstairs. Where was she going, by the way? What's on tonight? I hadn't heard of anything."

"Oh, not a party, I think," said an inexperienced young Farish who had arrived late. "I put her in her cab as I was coming in, and she gave the driver the Trenors' address."

"The Trenors'?" exclaimed Mrs. Jack Stepney. "Why, the house is closed —Judy telephoned me from Bellomont this evening."

"Did she? That's queer. I'm sure I'm not mistaken. Well, come now, Trenor's there, anyhow—I—oh, well, the fact is, I've no head for numbers," he broke off, admonished by the nudge of an adjoining foot, and the smile that circled the room.

In its unpleasant light Selden had risen and was shaking hands with his hostess. The air of the place stifled him, and he wondered why he had stayed in it so long.

On the doorstep he stood still, remembering a phrase of Lily's: "It seems to me you spend a good deal of time in the element you disapprove of."

Well—what had brought him there but the quest of her? It was her element, not his. But he would lift her out of it, take her beyond! That *Beyond!* on her letter was like a cry for rescue. He knew that Perseus's task is not done when he has loosed Andromeda's chains, for her limbs are numb with bondage, and she cannot rise and walk, but clings to him with dragging arms as he beats back to land with his burden. Well, he had strength for both—it was her weakness which had put the strength in him. It was not, alas, a clean rush of waves they had to win through, but a clogging morass of old associations and habits, and for the moment its vapors were in his throat. But he would see clearer, breathe freer in her presence: she was at once the dead weight at his breast and the spar which should float them to safety. He smiled at the whirl of metaphor with which he was trying to build up a defense against the influences of the last hour. It was pitiable that he, who knew the mixed motives on which social judgments depend, should still feel himself so swayed by them. How could he lift Lily to a freer vision of life, if his own view of her was to be colored by any mind in which he saw her reflected?

The moral oppression had produced a physical craving for air, and he strode on, opening his lungs to the reverberating coldness of the night. At the corner of Fifth Avenue Van Alstyne hailed him with an offer of company.

"Walking? A good thing to blow the smoke out of one's head. Now that women have taken to tobacco we live in a bath of nicotine. It would be a curious thing to study the effect of cigarettes on the relation of the sexes. Smoke is almost as great a solvent as divorce: both tend to obscure the moral issue."

Nothing could have been less consonant with Selden's mood than Van Alstyne's after-dinner aphorisms, but as long as the latter confined himself to generalities his listener's nerves were in control. Happily Van Alstyne prided himself on his summing up of social aspects, and with Selden for audience was eager to show the sureness of his touch. Mrs. Fisher lived in an East Side street near the Park, and as the two men walked down Fifth Avenue the new architectural developments of that versatile thoroughfare invited Van Alstyne's comment.

"That Greiner house, now—a typical rung in the social ladder! The man who built it came from a milieu where all the dishes are put on the table at once. His façade is a complete architectural meal; if he had omitted a style his friends might have thought the money had given out. Not a bad purchase for Rosedale, though: attracts attention, and awes the Western sight-seer. By and by he'll get out of that phase, and want something that the crowd will pass and the few pause before. Especially if he marries my clever cousin —"

Selden dashed in with the query: "And the Wellington Brys'? Rather clever of its kind, don't you think?"

They were just beneath the wide white facade, with its rich restraint of line, which suggested the clever corseting of a redundant figure.

"That's the next stage: the desire to imply that one has been to Europe, and has a standard. I'm sure Mrs. Bry thinks her house a copy of the *Trianon*; in America every marble house with gilt furniture is thought to be a copy of the *Trianon*. What a clever chap that architect is, though—how he takes his client's measure! He has put the whole of Mrs. Bry in his use of the composite order. Now for the Trenors, you remember, he chose the Corinthian: exuberant, but based on the best precedent. The Trenor house is one of his best things—doesn't look like a banqueting-hall turned inside out. I hear Mrs. Trenor wants to build out a new ballroom, and that divergence from Gus on that point keeps her at Bellomont. The dimensions of the Brys' ballroom must rankle: you may be sure she knows 'em as well as if she'd been there last night with a yard-measure. Who said she was in town, by the way? That Farish boy? She isn't, I know; Mrs. Stepney was right; the house is dark, you see: I suppose Gus lives in the back."

He had halted opposite the Trenors' corner, and Selden perforce stayed his steps also. The house loomed obscure and uninhabited; only an oblong gleam above the door spoke of provisional occupancy.

"They've bought the house at the back: it gives them a hundred and fifty feet in the side street. There's where the ballroom's to be, with a gallery connecting it: billiard-room and so on above. I suggested changing the entrance, and carrying the drawing-room across the whole Fifth Avenue front: you see the front door corresponds with the windows —"

The walking-stick which Van Alstyne swung in demonstration dropped to a startled "Hallo!" as the door opened and two figures were seen silhouetted against the hall-light. At the same moment a hansom halted at the curbstone, and one of the figures floated down to it in a haze of evening draperies; while the other, black and bulky, remained persistently projected against the light.

For an immeasurable second the two spectators of the incident were silent; then the house-door closed, the hansom rolled off, and the whole scene slipped by as if with the turn of a stereopticon.

Van Alstyne dropped his eyeglass with a low whistle.

"A—hem—nothing of this, eh, Selden? As one of the family, I know I may count on you—appearances are deceptive—and Fifth Avenue is so imperfectly lighted —"

"Good night," said Selden, turning sharply down the side street without seeing the other's extended hand.

Alone with her cousin's kiss, Gerty stared upon her thoughts. He had kissed her before—but not with another woman on his lips. If he had spared her that she could have drowned quietly, welcoming the dark flood as it submerged her. But now the flood was shot through with glory, and it was harder to drown at sunrise than in darkness. Gerty hid her face from the light, but it pierced to the crannies of her soul. She had been so contented, life had seemed so simple and sufficient—why had he come to trouble her with new hopes? And Lily—Lily, her best friend! Womanlike, she accused the woman. Perhaps, had it not been for Lily, her fond imagining might have become truth. Selden had always liked her—had understood and sympathized with the modest independence of her life. He, who had the reputation of weighing all things in the nice balance of fastidious perceptions, had been uncritical and simple in his view of her: his cleverness had never overawed her because she had felt at home in his heart. And now she was thrust out, and the door barred against her by Lily's hand! Lily, for whose admission there she herself had pleaded! The situation was lighted up by a dreary flash of irony. She knew Selden—she saw how the force of her faith in Lily must have helped to dispel his hesitations. She remembered, too, how Lily had talked of him—she saw herself bringing the two together, making them known to each other. On Selden's part, no doubt, the wound inflicted was inconscient; he had never guessed her foolish secret; but Lily—

Lily must have known! When, in such matters, are a woman's perceptions at fault? And if she knew, then she had deliberately despoiled her friend, and in mere wantonness of power, since, even to Gerty's suddenly flaming jealousy, it seemed incredible that Lily should wish to be Selden's wife. Lily might be incapable of marrying for money, but she was equally incapable of living without it, and Selden's eager investigations into the small economies of housekeeping made him appear to Gerty as tragically duped as herself.

She remained long in her sitting-room, where the embers were crumbling to cold gray, and the lamp paled under its gay shade. Just beneath it stood the photograph of Lily Bart, looking out imperially on the cheap gimcracks, the cramped furniture of the little room. Could Selden picture her in such an interior? Gerty felt the poverty, the insignificance of her surroundings: she beheld her life as it must appear to Lily. And the cruelty of Lily's judgments smote upon her memory. She saw that she had dressed her idol with the attributes of her own making. When had Lily ever really felt, or pitied, or understood? All she wanted was the taste of new experiences: she seemed like some cruel creature experimenting in a laboratory.

The pink-faced clock drummed out another hour, and Gerty rose with a start. She had an appointment early the next morning with a district visitor on the East Side. She put out her lamp, covered the fire, and went into her bedroom to undress. In the little glass above her dressing-table she saw her face reflected against the shadows of the room, and tears blotted the reflection. What right had she to dream the dreams of loveliness? A dull face invited a dull fate. She cried quietly as she undressed, laying aside her clothes with her habitual precision, setting everything in order for the next day, when the old life must be taken up as though there had been no break in its routine. Her servant did not come till eight o'clock, and she prepared her own tea-tray and placed it beside the bed. Then she locked the door of the flat, extinguished her light and lay down. But on her bed sleep would not come, and she lay face to face with the fact that she hated Lily Bart. It closed with her in the darkness like some formless evil to be blindly grappled with. Reason, judgment, renunciation, all the sane daylight forces, were beaten back in the sharp struggle for self-preservation. She wanted happiness—wanted it as fiercely and unscrupulously as Lily did, but without Lily's power of obtaining it. And in her conscious impotence she lay shivering, and hated her friend —

A ring at the doorbell caught her to her feet. She struck a light and stood startled, listening. For a moment her heart beat incoherently, then she felt the sobering touch of fact, and remembered that such calls were not unknown in her charitable work. She flung on her dressing-gown to answer the summons, and unlocking her door, confronted the shining vision of Lily Bart.

Gerty's first movement was one of revulsion. She shrank back as though

Lily's presence flashed too sudden a light upon her misery. Then she heard her name in a cry, had a glimpse of her friend's face, and felt herself caught and clung to.

"Lily—what is it?" she exclaimed.

Miss Bart released her, and stood breathing brokenly, like one who has gained shelter after a long flight.

"I was so cold—I couldn't go home. Have you a fire?"

Gerty's compassionate instincts, responding to the swift call of habit, swept aside all her reluctances. Lily was simply someone who needed help, for what reason, there was no time to pause and conjecture: disciplined sympathy checked the wonder on Gerty's lips, and made her draw her friend silently into the sitting-room and seat her by the darkened hearth.

"There is kindling wood here: the fire will burn in a minute."

She knelt down, and the flame leapt under her rapid hands. It flashed strangely through the tears which still blurred her eyes, and smote on the white ruin of Lily's face. The girls looked at each other in silence; then Lily repeated: "I couldn't go home."

"No—no—you came here, dear! You're cold and tired—sit quiet, and I'll make you some tea."

Gerty had unconsciously adopted the soothing note of her trade: all personal feeling was merged in the sense of ministry, and experience had taught her that the bleeding must be stayed before the wound is probed.

Lily sat quiet, leaning to the fire: the clatter of cups behind her soothed her as familiar noises hush a child whom silence has kept wakeful. But when Gerty stood at her side with the tea she pushed it away, and turned an estranged eye on the familiar room.

"I came here because I couldn't bear to be alone," she said.

Gerty set down the cup and knelt beside her.

"Lily! Something has happened—can't you tell me?"

"I couldn't bear to lie awake in my room till morning. I hate my room at Aunt Julia's—so I came here —"

She stirred suddenly, broke from her apathy, and clung to Gerty in a fresh burst of fear.

"Oh, Gerty, the furies . . . you know the noise of their wings—alone, at night, in the dark? But you don't know—there is nothing to make the dark dreadful to you—"

The words, flashing back on Gerty's last hours, struck from her a faint derisive murmur; but Lily, in the blaze of her own misery, was blinded to everything outside it.

"You'll let me stay? I shan't mind when daylight comes—Is it late? Is the night nearly over? It must be awful to be sleepless—everything stands by the bed and stares —"

Miss Farish caught her straying hands. "Lily, look at me! Something has happened—an accident? You have been frightened—what has frightened you? Tell me if you can—a word or two—so that I can help you."

Lily shook her head.

"I am not frightened: that's not the word. Can you imagine looking into your glass some morning and seeing a disfigurement—some hideous change that has come to you while you slept? Well, I seem to myself like that—I can't bear to see myself in my own thoughts—I hate ugliness, you know—I've always turned from it—but I can't explain to you—you wouldn't understand."

She lifted her head and her eyes fell on the clock.

"How long the night is! And I know I shan't sleep tomorrow. Someone told me my father used to lie sleepless and think of horrors. And he was not wicked, only unfortunate—and I see now how he must have suffered, lying alone with his thoughts! But I am bad—a bad girl—all my thoughts are bad —I have always had bad people about me. Is that any excuse? I thought I could manage my own life—I was proud—proud! but now I'm on their level —"

Sobs shook her, and she bowed to them like a tree in a dry storm.

Gerty knelt beside her, waiting, with the patience born of experience, till this gust of misery should loosen fresh speech. She had first imagined some physical shock, some peril of the crowded streets, since Lily was presumably on her way home from Carry Fisher's; but she now saw that other nerve-centers were smitten, and her mind trembled back from conjecture.

Lily's sobs ceased, and she lifted her head.

"There are bad girls in your slums. Tell me—do they ever pick themselves up? Ever forget, and feel as they did before?"

"Lily! you mustn't speak so—you're dreaming."

"Don't they always go from bad to worse? There's no turning back—your old self rejects you, and shuts you out."

She rose, stretching her arms as if in utter physical weariness. "Go to bed, dear! You work hard and get up early. I'll watch here by the fire, and you'll leave the light, and your door open. All I want is to feel that you are near me." She laid both hands on Gerty's shoulders, with a smile that was like sunrise on a sea strewn with wreckage.

"I can't leave you, Lily. Come and lie on my bed. Your hands are frozen —you must undress and be made warm." Gerty paused with sudden compunction. "But Mrs. Peniston—it's past midnight! What will she think?"

"She goes to bed. I have a latch-key. It doesn't matter—I can't go back there."

"There's no need to: you shall stay here. But you must tell me where you have been. Listen, Lily—it will help you to speak!" She regained Miss Bart's hands, and pressed them against her. "Try to tell me—it will clear your poor head. Listen—you were dining at Carry Fisher's." Gerty paused and added with a flash of heroism: "Lawrence Selden went from here to find you."

At the word, Lily's face melted from locked anguish to the open misery of a child. Her lips trembled and her gaze widened with tears.

"He went to find me? And I missed him! Oh, Gerty, he tried to help me. He told me—he warned me long ago—he foresaw that I should grow hateful to myself!"

The name, as Gerty saw with a clutch at the heart, had loosened the springs of self-pity in her friend's dry breast, and tear by tear Lily poured out the measure of her anguish. She had dropped sideways in Gerty's big arm-chair, her head buried where lately Selden's had leaned, in a beauty of abandonment that drove home to Gerty's aching senses the inevitableness of her own defeat. Ah, it needed no deliberate purpose on Lily's part to rob her of her dream! To look on that prone loveliness was to see in it a natural force, to recognize that love and power belong to such as Lily, as renunciation and service are the lot of those they despoil. But if Selden's infatuation seemed a fatal necessity, the effect that his name produced shook Gerty's steadfastness with a last pang. Men pass through such superhuman loves and outlive them, they are the probation subduing the heart to human joys. How gladly Gerty would have welcomed the ministry of healing: how willingly have soothed the sufferer back to tolerance of life! But Lily's self-betrayal took this last hope from her. The mortal maid on the shore is helpless against the siren who loves her prey: such victims are floated back dead from their adventure.

Lily sprang up and caught her with strong hands. "Gerty, you know him—you understand him—tell me; if I went to him, if I told him everything—if I said: 'I am bad through and through—I want admiration, I want excitement, I want money—' Yes, *money!* That's my shame, Gerty—and it's known, it's said of me—it's what men think of me—If I said it all to him—told him the whole story—said plainly: 'I've sunk lower than the lowest, for I've taken what they take, and not paid as they pay'—oh, Gerty, you know him, you can speak for him: if I told him everything would he loathe me? Or would he pity me, and understand me, and save me from loathing myself?"

Gerty stood cold and passive. She knew the hour of her probation had come, and her poor heart beat wildly against its destiny. As a dark river sweeps by under a lightning flash, she saw her chance of happiness surge past under a flash of temptation. What prevented her from saying: "He is like other men"? She was not so sure of him, after all. But to do so would have been like blaspheming her love. She could not put him before herself in any light but the noblest: she must trust him to the height of her own passion. "Yes, I know him; he will help you," she said; and in a moment Lily's passion was weeping itself out against her breast.

There was but one bed in the little flat, and the two girls lay down on it side by side, when Gerty had unlaced Lily's dress and persuaded her to put her lips to the warm tea. The light extinguished, they lay still in the darkness, Gerty shrinking to the outer edge of the narrow couch to avoid contact with her bedfellow. Knowing that Lily disliked to be caressed, she had long ago learned to check her demonstrative impulses toward her friend. But tonight every fiber in her body shrank from Lily's nearness: it was torture to listen to her breathing, and feel the sheet stir with it. As Lily turned, and settled to completer rest, a strand of her hair swept Gerty's cheek with its fragrance. Everything about her was warm and soft and scented: even the stains of her grief became her as raindrops do the beaten rose. But as Gerty lay with arms drawn down her side, in the motionless narrowness of an effigy, she felt a stir of sobs from the breathing warmth beside her, and Lily flung out her hand, groped for her friend's, and held it fast.

"Hold me, Gerty, hold me, or I shall think of things," she moaned; and Gerty silently slipped an arm under her, pillowing her head in its hollow as a mother makes a nest for a tossing child. In the warm hollow Lily lay still and her breathing grew low and regular. Her hand still clung to Gerty's as if to ward off evil dreams, but the hold of her fingers relaxed, her head sank deeper into its shelter, and Gerty felt that she slept.

15

WHEN Lily woke she had the bed to herself, and the winter light was in the room.

She sat up, bewildered by the strangeness of her surroundings; then memory returned, and she looked about her with a shiver. In the cold slant of light reflected from the back wall of a neighboring building, she saw her evening dress and opera cloak lying in a tawdry heap on a chair. Finery laid off is as unappetizing as the remains of a feast, and it occurred to Lily that, at home, her maid's vigilance had always spared her the sight of such incongruities. Her body ached with fatigue, and with the constriction of her attitude in Gerty's bed. All through her troubled sleep she had been conscious of having no space to toss in, and the long effort to remain motionless made her feel as if she had spent her night in a train.

This sense of physical discomfort was the first to assert itself; then she perceived, beneath it, a corresponding mental prostration, a languor of horror more insufferable than the first rush of her disgust. The thought of having to wake every morning with this weight on her breast roused her tired mind to fresh effort. She must find some way out of the slough into which she had stumbled: it was not so much compunction as the dread of her morning thoughts that pressed on her the need of action. But she was

unutterably tired; it was weariness to think connectedly. She lay back, looking about the poor slit of a room with a renewal of physical distaste. The
outer air, penned between high buildings, brought no freshness through the
window; steam-heat was beginning to sing in a coil of dingy pipes, and a
smell of cooking penetrated the crack of the door.

The door opened, and Gerty, dressed and hatted, entered with a cup of
tea. Her face looked sallow and swollen in the dreary light, and her dull hair
shaded imperceptibly into the tones of her skin.

She glanced shyly at Lily, asking in an embarrassed tone how she felt;
Lily answered with the same constraint, and raised herself up to drink the
tea.

"I must have been over-tired last night; I think I had a nervous attack in
the carriage," she said, as the drink brought clearness to her sluggish
thoughts.

"You were not well; I am so glad you came here," Gerty returned.

"But how am I to get home? And Aunt Julia—?"

"She knows; I telephoned early, and your maid has brought your things.
But won't you eat something? I scrambled the eggs myself."

Lily could not eat; but the tea strengthened her to rise and dress under
her maid's searching gaze. It was a relief to her that Gerty was obliged to
hasten away: the two kissed silently, but without a trace of the previous
night's emotion.

Lily found Mrs. Peniston in a state of agitation. She had sent for Grace
Stepney and was taking digitalis. Lily breasted the storm of inquiries as best
she could, explaining that she had had an attack of faintness on her way
back from Carry Fisher's; that, fearing she would not have strength to reach
home, she had gone to Miss Farish's instead; but that a quiet night had
restored her, and that she had no need of a doctor.

This was a relief to Mrs. Peniston, who could give herself up to her own
symptoms, and Lily was advised to go and lie down, her aunt's panacea for
all physical and moral disorders. In the solitude of her own room she was
brought back to a sharp contemplation of facts. Her daylight view of them
necessarily differed from the cloudy vision of the night. The winged furies
were now prowling gossips who dropped in on each other for tea. But her
fears seemed the uglier, thus shorn of their vagueness; and besides, she had
to act, not rave. For the first time she forced herself to reckon up the exact
amount of her debt to Trenor; and the result of this hateful computation was
the discovery that she had, in all, received nine thousand dollars from him.
The flimsy pretext on which it had been given and received shrivelled up in
the blaze of her shame: she knew that not a penny of it was her own, and
that to restore her self-respect she must at once repay the whole amount.
The inability thus to solace her outraged feelings gave her a paralyzing sense
of insignificance. She was realizing for the first time that a woman's dignity
may cost more to keep up than her carriage; and that the maintenance of a

moral attribute should be dependent on dollars and cents made the world appear a more sordid place than she had conceived it.

After luncheon, when Grace Stepney's prying eyes had been removed, Lily asked for a word with her aunt. The two ladies went upstairs to the sitting-room, where Mrs. Peniston seated herself in her black satin armchair tufted with yellow buttons, beside a bead-work table bearing a bronze box with a miniature of Beatrice Cenci in the lid. Lily felt for these objects the same distaste which the prisoner may entertain for the fittings of the court-room. It was here that her aunt received her rare confidences, and the pink-eyed smirk of the turbaned Beatrice was associated in her mind with the gradual fading of the smile from Mrs. Peniston lips. That lady's dread of a scene gave her an inexorableness which the greatest strength of character could not have produced, since it was independent of all considerations of right or wrong; and knowing this, Lily seldom ventured to assail it. She had never felt less like making the attempt than on the present occasion; but she had sought in vain for any other means of escape from an intolerable situation.

Mrs. Peniston examined her critically. "You're a bad color, Lily: this incessant rushing about is beginning to tell on you," she said.

Miss Bart saw an opening. "I don't think it's that, Aunt Julia; I've had worries," she replied.

"Ah," said Mrs. Peniston, shutting her lips with the snap of a purse closing against a beggar.

"I'm sorry to bother you with them," Lily continued, "but I really believe my faintness last night was brought on partly by anxious thoughts —"

"I should have said Carry Fisher's cook was enough to account for it. She has a woman who was with Maria Melson in 1891—the spring of the year we went to Aix—and I remember dining there two days before we sailed, and feeling *sure* the coppers hadn't been scoured."

"I don't think I ate much; I can't eat or sleep." Lily paused, and then said abruptly: "The fact is, Aunt Julia, I owe some money."

Mrs. Peniston's face clouded perceptibly, but did not express the astonishment her niece had expected. She was silent, and Lily was forced to continue: "I have been foolish —"

"No doubt you have: extremely foolish," Mrs. Peniston interposed. "I fail to see how anyone with your income, and no expenses—not to mention the handsome presents I've always given you —"

"Oh, you've been most generous, Aunt Julia; I shall never forget your kindness. But perhaps you don't quite realize the expense a girl is put to nowadays —"

"I don't realize that *you* are put to any expense except for your clothes and your railway fares. I expect you to be handsomely dressed; but I paid Céleste's bill for you last October."

Lily hesitated: her aunt's implacable memory had never been more inconvenient. "You were as kind as possible; but I have had to get a few things since —"

"What kind of things? Clothes? How much have you spent? Let me see the bill—I daresay the woman is swindling you."

"Oh, no, I think not: clothes have grown so frightfully expensive; and one needs so many different kinds, with country visits, and golf and skating, and Aiken and Tuxedo —"

"Let me see the bill," Mrs. Peniston repeated.

Lily hesitated again. In the first place, Mme. Céleste had not yet sent in her account, and secondly, the amount it represented was only a fraction of the sum that Lily needed.

"She hasn't sent in the bill for my winter things, but I *know* it's large; and there are one or two other things. I've been careless and imprudent— I'm frightened to think of what I owe —"

She raised the troubled loveliness of her face to Mrs. Peniston, vainly hoping that a sight so moving to the other sex might not be without effect upon her own. But the effect produced was that of making Mrs. Peniston shrink back apprehensively.

"Really, Lily, you are old enough to manage your own affairs, and after frightening me to death by your performance of last night you might at least choose a better time to worry me with such matters." Mrs. Peniston glanced at the clock, and swallowed a tablet of digitalis. "If you owe Céleste another thousand, she may send me her account," she added, as though to end the discussion at any cost.

"I am very sorry, Aunt Julia; I hate to trouble you at such a time, but I have really no choice—I ought to have spoken sooner—I owe a great deal more than a thousand dollars."

"A great deal more? Do you owe two? She must have robbed you!"

"I told you it was not only Céleste. I—there are other bills—more pressing—that must be settled."

"What on earth have you been buying? Jewelry? You must have gone off your head," said Mrs. Peniston with asperity. "But if you have run into debt, you must suffer the consequences, and put aside your monthly income till your bills are paid. If you stay quietly here until next spring, instead of racing about all over the country, you will have no expenses at all, and surely in four or five months you can settle the rest of your bills if I pay the dressmaker now."

Lily was again silent. She knew she could not hope to extract even a thousand dollars from Mrs. Peniston on the mere plea of paying Céleste's bill: Mrs. Peniston would expect to go over the dressmaker's account, and would make out the check to her and not to Lily. And yet the money must be obtained before the day was over!

"The debts I speak of are—different—not like tradesmen's bills," she began confusedly; but Mrs. Peniston's look made her almost afraid to con-

tinue. Could it be that her aunt suspected anything? The idea precipitated
Lily's avowal.

"The fact is, I've played cards a good deal—bridge; the women all do it;
girls, too—it's expected. Sometimes I've won—won a good deal—but lately
I've been unlucky—and of course such debts can't be paid off gradually —"

She paused: Mrs. Peniston's face seemed to be petrifying as she listened.

"Cards—you've played cards for money? It's true, then: when I was told
so I wouldn't believe it. I won't ask if the other horrors I was told were true,
too; I've heard enough for the state of my nerves. When I think of the
example you've had in this house! But I suppose it's your foreign bringing-
up—no one knew where your mother picked up her friends. And her Sundays were a scandal—that I know." Mrs. Peniston wheeled round suddenly.
"You play cards on Sunday?"

Lily flushed with the recollection of certain rainy Sundays at Bellomont
and with the Dorsets.

"You're hard on me, Aunt Julia: I have never really cared for cards, but a
girl hates to be thought priggish and superior, and one drifts into doing what
the others do. I've had a dreadful lesson, and if you'll help me out this time I
promise you —"

Mrs. Peniston raised her hand warningly. "You needn't make any promises: it's unnecessary. When I offered you a home I didn't undertake to pay
your gambling debts."

"Aunt Julia! You don't mean that you won't help me?"

"I shall certainly not do anything to give the impression that I countenance your behavior. If you really owe your dressmaker, I will settle with her
—beyond that I recognize no obligation to assume your debts."

Lily had risen, and stood pale and quivering before her aunt. Pride
stormed in her, but humiliation forced the cry from her lips: "Aunt Julia, I
shall be disgraced—I —" But she could go no farther. If her aunt turned
such a stony ear to the fiction of the gambling debts, in what spirit would
she receive the terrible avowal of the truth?

"I consider that you *are* disgraced, Lily; disgraced by your conduct far
more than by its results. You say your friends have persuaded you to play
cards with them; well, they may as well learn a lesson, too. They can
probably afford to lose a little money—and at any rate, I am not going to
waste any of mine in paying them. And now I must ask you to leave me—
this scene has been extremely painful, and I have my own health to consider. Draw down the blinds, please; and tell Jennings I will see no one this
afternoon but Grace Stepney."

Lily went up to her own room and bolted the door. She was trembling
with fear and anger—the rush of the furies' wings was in her ears. She
walked up and down the room with blind irregular steps. The last door of
escape was closed—she felt herself shut in with her dishonor —

Suddenly her wild pacing brought her before the clock on the chimney-piece. Its hands stood at half-past three, and she remembered that Selden was to come to her at four. She had meant to put him off with a word—but now her heart leaped at the thought of seeing him. Was there not a promise of rescue in his love? As she had lain at Gerty's side the night before, she had thought of his coming, and of the sweetness of weeping out her pain upon his breast. Of course, she had meant to clear herself of its consequences before she met him—she had never really doubted that Mrs. Peniston would come to her aid. And she had felt, even in the full storm of her misery, that Selden's love could not be her ultimate refuge; only it would be so sweet to take a moment's shelter there, while she gathered fresh strength to go on.

But now his love was her only hope, and as she sat alone with her wretchedness the thought of confiding in him became as seductive as the river's flow to the suicide. The first plunge would be terrible—but afterward, what blessedness might come! She remembered Gerty's words: "I know him —he will help you"; and her mind clung to them as a sick person might cling to a healing relic. Oh, if he really understood—if he would help her to gather up her broken life, and put it together in some new semblance in which no trace of the past should remain! He had always made her feel that she was worthy of better things, and she had never been in greater need of such solace. Once and again she shrank at the thought of imperiling his love by her confession: for love was what she needed—it would take the glow of passion to weld together the shattered fragments of her self-esteem. But she recurred to Gerty's words and held fast to them. She was sure that Gerty knew Selden's feeling for her, and it had never dawned upon her blindness that Gerty's own judgment of him was colored by emotions far more ardent than her own.

Four o'clock found her in the drawing-room: she was sure that Selden would be punctual. But the hour came and passed—it moved on feverishly, measured by her impatient heartbeats. She had time to take a fresh survey of her wretchedness, and to fluctuate anew between the impulse to confide in Selden and the dread of destroying his illusions. But as the minutes passed the need of throwing herself on his comprehension became more urgent: she could not bear the weight of her misery alone. There would be a perilous moment, perhaps: but could she not trust to her beauty to bridge it over, to land her safe in the shelter of his devotion?

But the hour sped on and Selden did not come. Doubtless he had been detained, or had misread her hurriedly scrawled note, taking the four for a five. The ringing of the doorbell a few minutes after five confirmed this supposition, and made Lily hastily resolve to write more legibly in future. The sound of steps in the hall, and of the butler's voice preceding them, poured fresh energy into her veins. She felt herself once more the alert and competent molder of emergencies, and the remembrance of her power over

Selden flushed her with sudden confidence. But when the drawing-room door opened it was Rosedale who came in.

The reaction caused her a sharp pang, but after a passing movement of irritation at the clumsiness of fate, and at her own carelessness in not denying the door to all but Selden, she controlled herself and greeted Rosedale amicably. It was annoying that Selden, when he came, should find that particular visitor in possession, but Lily was mistress of the art of ridding herself of superfluous company, and to her present mood Rosedale seemed distinctly negligible.

His own view of the situation forced itself upon her after a few moments' conversation. She had caught at the Brys' entertainment as an easy impersonal subject, likely to tide them over the interval till Selden appeared, but Mr. Rosedale, tenaciously planted beside the tea-table, his hands in his pockets, his legs a little too freely extended, at once gave the topic a personal turn.

"Pretty well done—well, yes, I suppose it was: Welly Bry's got his back up and don't mean to let go till he's got the hang of the thing. Of course, there were things here and there—things Mrs. Fisher couldn't be expected to see to—the champagne wasn't cold, and the coats got mixed in the coatroom. I would have spent more money on the music. But that's my character: if I want a thing I'm willing to pay: I don't go up to the counter, and then wonder if the article's worth the price. I wouldn't be satisfied to entertain like the Welly Brys; I'd want something that would look more easy and natural, more as if I took it in my stride. And it takes just two things to do that, Miss Bart: money, and the right woman to spend it."

He paused, and examined her attentively while she affected to rearrange the teacups.

"I've got the money," he continued, clearing his throat, "and what I want is the woman—and I mean to have her, too."

He leaned forward a little, resting his hands on the head of his walking-stick. He had seen men of Ned Van Alstyne's type bring their hats and sticks into a drawing-room, and he thought it added a touch of elegant familiarity to their appearance.

Lily was silent, smiling faintly, with her eyes absently resting on his face. She was in reality reflecting that a declaration would take some time to make, and that Selden must surely appear before the moment of refusal had been reached. Her brooding look, as of a mind withdrawn yet not averted, seemed to Mr. Rosedale full of a subtle encouragement. He would not have liked any evidence of eagerness.

"I mean to have her, too," he repeated, with a laugh intended to strengthen his self-assurance. "I generally *have* got what I wanted in life, Miss Bart. I wanted money, and I've got more than I know how to invest; and now the money doesn't seem to be of any account unless I can spend it on the right woman. That's what I want to do with it: I want my wife to make all the other women feel small. I'd never grudge a dollar that was spent on that. But it isn't every woman can do it, no matter how much you spend on her. There was a girl in some history book who wanted gold shields, or something, and the fellows threw 'em at her, and she was crushed under 'em: they killed her. Well, that's true enough; some women looked buried under their jewelry. What I want is a woman who'll hold her head higher the more diamonds I put on it. And when I looked at you the other night at the Brys, in that plain white dress, looking as if you had a crown on, I said to myself: 'By gad, if she had one she'd wear it as if it grew on her.' "

Still Lily did not speak, and he continued, warming with his theme: "Tell you what it is, though; that kind of woman costs more than all the rest of 'em put together. If a woman's going to ignore her pearls, they want to be better than anybody else's—and so it is with everything else. You know what I mean—you know it's only the showy things that are cheap. Well, I should want my wife to be able to take the earth for granted if she wanted to. I know there's one thing vulgar about money, and that's the thinking about it; and my wife would never have to demean herself in that way." He paused, and then added, with an unfortunate lapse to an earlier manner: "I guess you know the lady I've got in view, Miss Bart."

Lily raised her head, brightening a little under the challenge. Even through the dark tumult of her thoughts, the clink of Mr. Rosedale's millions had a faintly seductive note. Oh, for enough of them to cancel her one miserable debt! But the man behind them grew increasingly repugnant in the light of Selden's expected coming. The contrast was too grotesque: she could scarcely suppress the smile it provoked. She decided that directness would be best.

"If you mean me, Mr. Rosedale, I am very grateful—very much flattered; but I don't know what I have ever done to make you think —"

"Oh, if you mean you're not dead in love with me, I've got sense enough left to see that. And I ain't talking to you as if you were—I presume I know the kind of talk that's expected under those circumstances. I'm confoundedly gone on you—that's about the size of it—and I'm just giving you a plain business statement of the consequences. You're not very fond of me—yet—but you're fond of luxury, and style, and amusement, and of not having to worry about cash. You like to have a good time, and not to have to settle for it; and what I propose to do is to provide for the good time and do the settling."

He paused, and she returned with a chilling smile: "You are mistaken in one point, Mr. Rosedale: whatever I enjoy I am prepared to settle for."

She spoke with the intention of making him see that, if his words implied a tentative allusion to her private affairs, she was prepared to meet and repudiate it. But if he recognized her meaning it failed to abash him and he went on in the same tone: "I didn't mean to give offense; excuse me if

I've spoken too plainly. But why ain't you straight with me—why do you put up that kind of bluff? You know there've been times when you were bothered—damned bothered—and as a girl gets older, and things keep moving along, why, before she knows it, the things she wants are liable to move past her and not come back. I don't say it's anywhere near that with you yet; but you've had a taste of bothers that a girl like yourself ought never to have known about, and what I'm offering you is the chance to turn your back on them once for all."

The color burned in Lily's face as he ended; there was no mistaking the point he meant to make, and to permit it to pass unheeded was a fatal confession of weakness, while to resent it too openly was to risk offending him at a perilous moment. Indignation quivered on her lip; but it was quelled by the secret voice which warned her that she must not quarrel with him. He knew too much about her, and even at the moment when it was essential that he should show himself at his best, he did not scruple to let her see how much he knew. How then would he use his power when her expression of contempt had dispelled his one motive for restraint? Her whole future might hinge on her way of answering him: she had to stop and consider that, in the stress of her other anxieties, as a breathless fugitive may have to pause at the crossroads and try to decide coolly which turn to take.

"You are quite right, Mr. Rosedale. I *have* had bothers; and I am grateful to you for wanting to relieve me of them. It is not always easy to be quite independent and self-respecting when one is poor and lives among rich people; I have been careless about money, and have worried about my bills. But I should be selfish and ungrateful if I made that a reason for accepting all you offer, with no better return to make than the desire to be free from my anxieties. You must give me time—time to think of your kindness—and of what I could give you in return for it —"

She held out her hand with a charming gesture in which dismissal was shorn of its rigor. Its hint of future leniency made Rosedale rise in obedience to it, a little flushed with his unhoped-for success, and disciplined by the tradition of his blood to accept what was conceded, without undue haste to press for more. Something in his prompt acquiescence frightened her; she felt behind it the stored force of a patience that might subdue the strongest will. But at least they had parted amicably, and he was out of the house without meeting Selden—Selden, whose continued absence now smote her with a new alarm. Rosedale had remained over an hour, and she understood that it was now too late to hope for Selden. He would write explaining his absence, of course; there would be a note from him by the late post. But her confession would have to be postponed; and the chill of the delay settled heavily on her fagged spirit.

It lay heavier when the postman's last ring brought no note for her, and she had to go upstairs to a lonely night—a night as grim and sleepless as her tortured fancy had pictured it to Gerty. She had never learned to live with her own thoughts, and to be confronted with them through such hours of lucid misery made the confused wretchedness of her previous vigil seem easily bearable.

Daylight disbanded the phantom crew, and made it clear to her that she would hear from Selden before noon; but the day passed without his writing or coming. Lily remained at home, lunching and dining alone with her aunt, who complained of flutterings of the heart, and talked icily on general topics. Mrs. Peniston went to bed early, and when she had gone Lily sat down and wrote a note to Selden. She was about to ring for a messenger to dispatch it when her eye fell on a paragraph in the evening paper which lay at her elbow: "Mr. Lawrence Selden was among the passengers sailing this afternoon for Havana and the West Indies on the Windward Liner Antilles."

She laid down the paper and sat motionless, staring at her note. She understood now that he was never coming—that he had gone away because he was afraid that he might come. She rose, and walking across the floor stood gazing at herself for a long time in the brightly-lit mirror above the mantelpiece. The lines in her face came out terribly—she looked old; and when a girl looks old to herself, how does she look to other people? She moved away, and began to wander aimlessly about the room, fitting her steps with mechanical precision between the monstrous roses of Mrs. Peniston's Axminster. Suddenly she noticed that the pen with which she had written to Selden still rested against the uncovered ink-stand. She seated herself again, and taking out an envelope, addressed it rapidly to Rosedale. Then she laid out a sheet of paper, and sat over it with suspended pen. It had been easy enough to write the date, and "Dear Mr. Rosedale"—but after that her inspiration flagged. She meant to tell him to come to her, but the words refused to shape themselves. At length she began: "I have been thinking—" then she laid the pen down, and sat with her elbows on the table and her face hidden in her hands.

Suddenly she started up at the sound of the doorbell. It was not late—barely ten o'clock—and there might still be a note from Selden, or a message—or he might be there himself, on the other side of the door! The announcement of his sailing might have been a mistake—it might be another Lawrence Selden who had gone to Havana—all these possibilities had time to flash through her mind, and build up the conviction that she was after all to see or hear from him, before the drawing-room door opened to admit a servant carrying a telegram.

Lily tore it open with shaking hands, and read Bertha Dorset's name below the message: "Sailing unexpectedly tomorrow. Will you join us on a cruise in Mediterranean?"

Book Two

16

I T came vividly to Selden on the Casino steps that Monte Carlo had, more than any other place he knew, the gift of accommodating itself to each man's humor.

His own, at the moment, lent it a festive readiness of welcome that might well, in a disenchanted eye, have turned to paint and facility. So frank an appeal for participation—so outspoken a recognition of the holiday vein in human nature—struck refreshingly on a mind jaded by prolonged hard work in surroundings made for the discipline of the senses. As he surveyed the white square set in an exotic coquetry of architecture, the studied tropicality of the gardens, the groups loitering in the foreground against mauve mountains which suggested a sublime stage-setting forgotten in a hurried shifting of scenes—as he took in the whole outspread effect of light and leisure, he felt a movement of revulsion from the last few months of his life.

The New York winter had presented an interminable perspective of snow-burdened days, reaching toward a spring of raw sunshine and furious air, when the ugliness of things rasped the eye as the gritty wind ground into the skin. Selden, immersed in his work, had told himself that external conditions did not matter to a man in his state, and that cold and ugliness were a good tonic for relaxed sensibilities. When an urgent case summoned him abroad to confer with a client in Paris, he broke reluctantly with the routine of the office; and it was only now that, having dispatched his business, and slipped away for a week in the south, he began to feel the renewed zest of spectatorship that is the solace of those who take an objective interest in life.

The multiplicity of its appeals—the perpetual surprise of its contrasts and resemblances! All these tricks and turns of the show were upon him with a spring as he descended the Casino steps and paused on the pavement at its doors. He had not been abroad for seven years—and what changes the renewed contact produced! If the central depths were untouched, hardly a pin-point of surface remained the same. And this was the very place to bring out the completeness of the renewal. The sublimities, the perpetuities, might have left him as he was: but this tent pitched for a day's revelry spread a roof of oblivion between himself and his fixed sky.

It was mid-April, and one felt that the revelry had reached its climax and that the desultory groups in the square and gardens would soon dissolve and reform in other scenes. Meanwhile, the last moments of the perfor-mance seemed to gain an added brightness from the hovering threat of the curtain. The quality of the air, the exuberance of the flowers, the blue intensity of sea and sky, produced the effect of a closing tableau, when all the lights are turned on at once. This impression was presently heightened by the way in which a consciously conspicuous group of people advanced to the middle front and stood before Selden with the air of the chief perform-ers gathered together by the exigencies of the final effect. Their appearance confirmed the impression that the show had been staged regardless of ex-pense, and emphasized its resemblance to one of those "costume-plays" in which the protagonists walk through the passions without displacing a drap-ery. The ladies stood in unrelated attitudes calculated to isolate their effects, and the men hung about them as irrelevantly as stage heroes whose tailors are named in the program. It was Selden himself who unwittingly fused the group by arresting the attention of one of its members.

"Why, Mr. Selden!" Mrs. Fisher exclaimed in surprise; and with a ges-ture toward Mrs. Jack Stepney and Mrs. Wellington Bry, she added plain-tively: "We're starving to death because we can't decide where to lunch."

Welcomed into their group, and made the confidant of their difficulty, Selden learned with amusement that there were several places where one might miss something by not lunching, or forfeit something by lunching; so that eating actually became a minor consideration on the very spot con-secrated to its rites.

"Of course, one gets the best things at the Terrasse—but that looks as if one hadn't any other reason for being there: the Americans who don't know anyone always rush for the best food. And the duchess of Beltshire has taken up Bécassin's lately," Mrs. Bry earnestly summed up.

Mrs. Bry, to Mrs. Fisher's despair, had not progressed beyond the point of weighing her social alternatives in public. She could not acquire the air of doing things because she wanted to, and making her choice the final seal of their fitness.

Mr. Bry, a short pale man, with a business face and leisure clothes, met the dilemma hilariously.

"I guess the duchess goes where it's cheapest, unless she can get her meal paid for. If you offered to blow her off at the Terrasse she'd turn up fast enough."

But Mrs. Jack Stepney interposed. "The grand dukes go to that little place at the Condamine. Lord Hubert says it's the only restaurant in Europe where they can cook peas."

Lord Hubert Dacey, a slender shabby-looking man, with a charming worn smile, and the air of having spent his best years in piloting the wealthy to the right restaurant, assented with gentle emphasis: "It's quite that."

"*Peas?*" said Mr. Bry contemptuously. "Can they cook terrapin? It just shows," he continued, "what these European markets are, when a fellow can make a reputation cooking peas!"

Jack Stepney intervened with authority. "I don't know that I quite agree with Dacey: there's a little hole in Paris, off the Quai Voltaire—but in any case, I can't advise the Condamine gargote; at least not with ladies."

Stepney, since his marriage, had thickened and grown prudish, as the Van Osburgh husbands were apt to do, but his wife, to his surprise and discomfiture, had developed an earth-shaking fastness of gait which left him trailing breathlessly in her wake.

"That's where we'll go then!" she declared, with a heavy toss of her plumage. "I'm so tired of the Terrasse: it's as dull as one of mother's dinners. And Lord Hubert has promised to tell us who all the awful people are at the other place—hasn't he, Carry? Now, Jack, don't look so solemn!"

"Well," said Mrs. Bry, "all I want to know is who their dressmakers are."

"No doubt Dacey can tell you that, too," remarked Stepney, with an ironic intention which the other received with the light murmur, "I can at least *find out,* my dear fellow"; and Mrs. Bry having declared that she couldn't walk another step, the party hailed two or three of the light phaetons which hover attentively on the confines of the gardens, and rattled off in procession toward the Condamine.

Their destination was one of the little restaurants overhanging the boulevard which dips steeply down from Monte Carlo to the low intermediate quarter along the quay. From the window in which they presently found themselves installed, they overlooked the intense blue curve of the harbor, set between the verdure of twin promontories: to the right, the cliff of Monaco, topped by the medieval silhouette of its church and castle, to the left the terraces and pinnacles of the gambling house. Between the two, the waters of the bay were furrowed by a light coming and going of pleasure-craft, through which, just at the culminating moment of luncheon, the majestic advance of a great steam-yacht drew the company's attention from the peas.

"By Jove, I believe that's the Dorsets back!" Stepney exclaimed; and Lord Hubert, dropping his single eyeglass, corroborated: "It's the *Sabrina*—yes."

"So soon? They were to spend a month in Sicily," Mrs. Fisher observed.

"I guess they feel as if they had: there's only one up-to-date hotel in the whole place," said Mr. Bry disparagingly.

"It was Ned Silverton's idea—but poor Dorset and Lily Bart must have been horribly bored." Mrs. Fisher added in an undertone to Selden: "I do hope there hasn't been a row."

"It's most awfully jolly having Miss Bart back," said Lord Hubert, in his mild deliberate voice; and Mrs. Bry added ingenuously: "I daresay the duchess will dine with us, now that Lily's here."

"The duchess admires her immensely: I'm sure she'd be charmed to have it arranged," Lord Hubert agreed, with the professional promptness of the man accustomed to draw his profit from facilitating social contacts: Selden was struck by the businesslike change in his manner.

"Lily has been a tremendous success here," Mrs. Fisher continued, still addressing herself confidentially to Selden. "She looks ten years younger—I never saw her so handsome. Lady Skiddaw took her everywhere in Cannes, and the crown princess of Macedonia had her to stop for a week at Cimiez. People say that was one reason why Bertha whisked the yacht off to Sicily: the crown princess didn't take much notice of her, and she couldn't bear to look on at Lily's triumph."

Selden made no reply. He was vaguely aware that Miss Bart was cruising in the Mediterranean with the Dorsets, but it had not occurred to him that there was any chance of running across her on the Riviera, where the season was virtually at an end. As he leaned back, silently contemplating his filigree cup of Turkish coffee, he was trying to put some order in his thoughts, to tell himself how the news of her nearness was really affecting him. He had a personal detachment enabling him, even in moments of emotional high-pressure, to get a fairly clear view of his feelings, and he was sincerely surprised by the disturbance which the sight of the *Sabrina* had produced in him. He had reason to think that his three months of engrossing professional work, following on the sharp shock of his disillusionment, had cleared his mind of its sentimental vapors. The feeling he had nourished and given prominence to was one of thankfullness for his escape: he was like a traveler so grateful for rescue from a dangerous accident that at first he is hardly conscious of his bruises. Now he suddenly felt the latent ache, and realized that after all he had not come off unhurt.

An hour later, at Mrs. Fisher's side in the Casino gardens, he was trying to find fresh reasons for forgetting the injury received in the contemplation of the peril avoided. The party had dispersed with the loitering indecision characteristic of social movements at Monte Carlo, where the whole place, and the long gilded hours of the day, seem to offer an infinity of ways of being idle. Lord Hubert Dacey had finally gone off in quest of the duchess of Beltshire, charged by Mrs. Bry with the delicate negotiation of securing that lady's presence at dinner, the Stepneys had left for Nice in their motorcar, and Mr. Bry had departed to take his place in the pigeon-shooting match which was at the moment engaging his highest faculties.

Mrs. Bry, who had a tendency to grow red and stertorous after luncheon, had been judiciously prevailed upon by Carry Fisher to withdraw to her hotel for an hour's repose; and Selden and his companion were thus left to a stroll propitious to confidences. The stroll soon resolved itself into a tranquil session on a bench overhung with laurel and Banksian roses, from which they caught a dazzle of blue sea between marble balusters, and the fiery shafts of cactus-blossoms shooting meteorlike from the rock. The soft shade of their niche, and the adjacent glitter of the air, were conducive to an easy lounging mood, and to the smoking of many cigarettes; and Selden, yielding to these influences, suffered Mrs. Fisher to unfold to him the history of her recent experiences. She had come abroad with the Welly Brys at the moment when fashion flees the inclemency of the New York spring. The Brys, intoxicated by their first success, already thirsted for new kingdoms, and Mrs. Fisher, viewing the Riviera as an easy introduction to London society, had guided their course thither. She had affiliations of her own in every capital, and a facility for picking them up again after long absences; and the carefully disseminated rumor of the Brys' wealth had at once gathered about them a group of cosmopolitan pleasure-seekers.

"But things are not going as well as I expected," Mrs. Fisher frankly admitted. "It's all very well to say that everybody with money can get into society; but it would be truer to say that *nearly* everybody can. And the London market is so glutted with new Americans that, to succeed there now, they must be either very clever or awfully queer. The Brys are neither. *He* would get on well enough if she'd let him alone; they like his slang and his brag and his blunders. But Louisa spoils it all by trying to repress him and put herself forward. If she'd be natural herself—fat and vulgar and bouncing—it would be all right; but as soon as she meets anybody smart she tries to be slender and queenly. She tried it with the Duchess of Beltshire and Lady Skiddaw, and they fled. I've done my best to make her see her mistake—I've said to her again and again: 'Just let yourself go, Louisa'; but she keeps up the humbug even with me—I believe she keeps on being queenly in her own room, with the door shut.

"The worst of it is," Mrs. Fisher went on, "that she thinks it's all *my* fault. When the Dorsets turned up here six weeks ago, and everybody began to make a fuss about Lily Bart, I could see Louisa thought that if she'd had Lily in tow instead of me she would have been hobnobbing with all the royalties by this time. She doesn't realize that it's Lily's beauty that does it: Lord Hubert tells me Lily is thought even handsomer than when he knew her at Aix ten years ago. It seems she was tremendously admired there. An Italian prince, rich and the real thing, wanted to marry her; but just at the critical moment a good-looking stepson turned up, and Lily was silly enough to flirt with him while her marriage settlements with the stepfather were being drawn up. Some people said the young man did it on purpose. You can fancy the scandal: there was an awful row between the men, and people began to look at Lily so queerly that Mrs. Peniston had to pack up and finish her cure elsewhere. Not that *she* ever understood: to this day she thinks that Aix didn't suit her, and mentions her having been sent there as proof of the incompetence of French doctors. That's Lily all over, you know: she works like a slave preparing the ground and sowing her seed; but the day she ought to be reaping the harvest she oversleeps herself or goes off on a picnic."

Mrs. Fisher paused and looked reflectively at the deep shimmer of sea between the cactus-flowers. "Sometimes," she added, "I think it's just flight-iness—and sometimes I think it's because, at heart, she despises the things she's trying for. And it's the difficulty of deciding that makes her such an interesting study." She glanced tentatively at Selden's motionless profile, and resumed with a slight sigh: "Well, all I can say is, I wish she'd give me some of her discarded opportunities. I wish we could change places now, for instance. She could make a very good thing out of the Brys if she managed them properly, and I should know just how to look after George Dorset while Bertha is reading Verlaine with Neddy Silverton."

She met Selden's sound of protest with a sharp derisive glance. "Well, what's the use of mincing matters? We all know that's what Bertha brought her abroad for. When Bertha wants to have a good time she has to provide occupation for George. At first I thought Lily was going to play her cards well *this* time, but there are rumors that Bertha is jealous of her success here and at Cannes, and I shouldn't be surprised if there were a break any day. Lily's only safeguard is that Bertha needs her badly—oh, very badly. The Silverton affair is in the acute stage: it's necessary that George's attention should be pretty continuously distracted. And I'm bound to say Lily *does* distract it: I believe he'd marry her tomorrow if he found out there was anything wrong with Bertha. But you know him—he's as blind as he's jealous; and of course Lily's present business is to keep him blind. A clever woman might know just the right moment to tear off the bandage: but Lily isn't clever in that way, and when George does open his eyes she'll probably contrive not to be in his line of vision."

Selden tossed away his cigarette. "By Jove—it's time for my train," he exclaimed, with a glance at his watch; adding, in reply to Mrs. Fisher's surprised comment—"Why, I thought of course you were at Monte!"—a murmured word to the effect that he was making Nice his headquarters.

"The worst of it is, she snubs the Brys now," he heard irrelevantly flung after him.

Ten minutes later, in the high-perched bedroom of an hotel overlooking the Casino, he was tossing his effects into a couple of gaping portmanteaux, while the porter waited outside to transport them to the cab at the door. It took but a brief plunge down the steep white road to the station to land him safely in the afternoon express for Nice; and not till he was installed in the corner of an empty carriage, did he exclaim to himself, with a reaction of self-contempt: "What the deuce am I running away from?"

The pertinence of the question checked Selden's fugitive impulse before the train had started. It was ridiculous to be flying like an emotional coward from an infatuation his reason had conquered. He had instructed his bank-ers to forward some important business letters to Nice, and at Nice he would quietly await them. He was already annoyed with himself for having left Monte Carlo, where he had intended to pass the week which remained to him before sailing; but it would now be difficult to return on his steps without an appearance of inconsistency from which his pride recoiled. In his inmost heart he was not sorry to put himself beyond the probability of meeting Miss Bart. Completely as he had detached himself from her, he could not yet regard her merely as a social instance; and viewed in a more personal way she was not likely to be a reassuring object of study. Chance encounters, or even the repeated mention of her name, would send his thoughts back into grooves from which he had resolutely detached them; whereas, if she could be entirely excluded from his life, the pressure of new and varied impressions, with which no thought of her was connected, would soon complete the work of separation. Mrs. Fisher's conversation had, indeed, operated to that end; but the treatment was too painful to be voluntarily chosen while milder remedies were untried; and Selden thought he could trust himself to return gradually to a reasonable view of Miss Bart, if only he did not see her.

Having reached the station early, he had arrived at this point in his reflections before the increasing throng on the platform warned him that he could not hope to preserve his privacy; the next moment there was a hand on the door, and he turned to confront the very face he was fleeing.

Miss Bart, glowing with the haste of a precipitate descent upon the train, headed a group composed of the Dorsets, young Silverton and Lord Hubert Dacey, who had barely time to spring into the carriage, and envelop Selden in ejaculations of surprise and welcome, before the whistle of departure sounded. The party, it appeared, were hastening to Nice in response to a sudden summons to dine with the duchess of Beltshire and to see the water-fête in the bay; a plan evidently improvised—in spite of Lord Hubert's protesting "Oh, I say, you know"—for the express purpose of defeating Mrs. Bry's endeavor to capture the duchess.

During the laughing relation of this maneuver, Selden had time for a rapid impression of Miss Bart, who had seated herself opposite to him in the golden afternoon light. Scarcely three months had elapsed since he had parted from her on the threshold of the Brys' conservatory; but a subtle change had passed over the quality of her beauty. Then it had had a transparency through which the fluctuations of the spirit were sometimes tragically visible; now its impenetrable surface suggested a process of crystallization which had fused her whole being into one hard brilliant substance. The change had struck Mrs. Fisher as a rejuvenation: to Selden it seemed like that moment of pause and arrest when the warm fluidity of youth is chilled into its final shape.

He felt it in the way she smiled on him, and in the readiness and competence with which, flung unexpectedly into his presence, she took up the thread of their intercourse as though that thread had not been snapped with a violence from which he still reeled. Such facility sickened him—but he told himself that it was with the pang which precedes recovery. Now he would really get well—would eject the last drop of poison from his blood.

Already he felt himself calmer in her presence than he had learned to be in the thought of her. Her assumptions and elisions, her shortcuts and long detours, the skill with which she contrived to meet him at a point from which no inconvenient glimpses of the past were visible, suggested what opportunities she had had for practicing such arts since their last meeting. He felt that she had at last arrived at an understanding with herself: had made a pact with her rebellious impulses, and achieved a uniform system of self-government, under which all vagrant tendencies were either held captive or forced into the service of the state.

And he saw other things too in her manner: saw how it had adjusted itself to the hidden intricacies of a situation in which, even after Mrs. Fisher's elucidating flashes, he still felt himself agrope. Surely Mrs. Fisher could no longer charge Miss Bart with neglecting her opportunities! To Selden's exasperated observation she was only too completely alive to them. She was "perfect" to everyone: subservient to Bertha's anxious predominance, good-naturedly watchful of Dorset's moods, brightly companionable to Silverton and Dacey, the latter of whom met her on an evident footing of old admiration, while young Silverton, portentously self-absorbed, seemed conscious of her only as of something vaguely obstructive. And suddenly, as Selden noted the fine shades of manner by which she harmonized herself with her surroundings, it flashed on him that, to need such adroit handling, the situation must indeed be desperate. She was on the edge of something— that was the impression left with him. He seemed to see her poised on the brink of a chasm, with one graceful foot advanced to assert her unconsciousness that the ground was failing her.

On the Promenade des Anglais, where Ned Silverton hung on him for the half hour before dinner, he received a deeper impression of the general insecurity. Silverton was in a mood of titanic pessimism. How anyone could come to such a damned hole as the Riviera—anyone with a grain of imagination—with the whole Mediterranean to choose from: but then, if one's estimate of a place depended on the way they broiled a spring chicken! Gad! what a study might be made of the tyranny of the stomach—the way a sluggish liver or insufficient gastric juices might affect the whole course of the universe, overshadow everything in reach—chronic dyspepsia ought to be among the "statutory causes;" a woman's life might be ruined by a man's inability to digest fresh bread. Grotesque? Yes—and tragic—like most absurdities. There's nothing grimmer than the tragedy that wears a comic mask. . . . Where was he? Oh—the reason they chucked Sicily and rushed back? Well—partly, no doubt, Miss Bart's desire to get back to bridge and smartness. Dead as a stone to art and poetry—the light never *was* on sea or land for her! And, of course, she persuaded Dorset that the Italian food was bad for him. Oh, she could make him believe anything—*anything!* Mrs. Dorset was aware of it—oh, perfectly: nothing *she* didn't see! But she could hold her tongue—she'd had to, often enough. Miss Bart was an intimate friend—

she wouldn't hear a word against her. Only it hurts a woman's pride—there are some things one doesn't get used to. . . . All this in confidence, of course? Ah—and there were the ladies signaling from the balcony of the hotel. . . . He plunged across the Promenade, leaving Selden to a meditative cigar.

The conclusions it led him to were fortified, later in the evening, by some of those faint corroborative hints that generate a light of their own in the dusk of a doubting mind. Selden, stumbling on a chance acquaintance, had dined with him, and adjourned, still in his company, to the brightly lit Promenade, where a line of crowded stands commanded the glittering darkness of the waters. The night was soft and persuasive. Overhead hung a summer sky furrowed with the rush of rockets; and from the east a late moon, pushing up beyond the lofty bend of the coast, sent across the bay a shaft of brightness which paled to ashes in the red glitter of the illuminated boats. Down the lantern-hung Promenade, snatches of band music floated above the hum of the crowd and the soft tossing of boughs in dusky gardens; and between these gardens and the backs of the stands there flowed a stream of people in whom the vociferous carnival mood seemed tempered by the growing languor of the season.

Selden and his companion, unable to get seats on one of the stands facing the bay, had wandered for a while with the throng, and then found a point of vantage on a high garden-parapet above the Promenade. Thence they caught but a triangular glimpse of the water, and of the flashing play of boats across its surface; but the crowd in the street was under their immediate view, and seemed to Selden, on the whole, of more interest than the show itself. After a while, however, he wearied of his perch and, dropping alone to the pavement, pushed his way to the first corner and turned into the moonlit silence of a side street. Long garden-walls overhung by trees made a dark boundary to the pavement; an empty cab trailed along the deserted thoroughfare, and presently Selden saw two persons emerge from the opposite shadows, signal to the cab, and drive off in it toward the center of the town. The moonlight touched them as they paused to enter the carriage, and he recognized Mrs. Dorset and young Silverton.

Beneath the nearest lamppost he glanced at his watch and saw that the time was close on eleven. He took another cross street, and without breasting the throng on the Promenade, made his way to the fashionable club which overlooks that thoroughfare. Here, amid the blaze of crowded baccarat tables, he caught sight of Lord Hubert Dacey, seated with his habitual worn smile behind a rapidly dwindling heap of gold. The heap being in due course wiped out, Lord Hubert rose with a shrug, and joining Selden, adjourned with him to the deserted terrace of the club. It was now past midnight, and the throng on the stands was dispersing, while the long trails of red-lit boats scattered and faded beneath a sky repossessed by the tranquil splendor of the moon.

Lord Hubert looked at his watch. "By Jove, I promised to join the duchess for supper at the London House; but it's past twelve, and I suppose they've all scattered. The fact is, I lost them in the crowd soon after dinner, and took refuge here, for my sins. They had seats on one of the stands, but of course they couldn't stop quiet: the duchess never can. She and Miss Bart went off in quest of what they call adventures—gad, it ain't their fault if they don't have some queer ones!" He added tentatively, after pausing to grope for a cigarette: "Miss Bart's an old friend of yours, I believe? So she told me. Ah, thanks—I don't seem to have one left." He lit Selden's proffered cigarette, and continued, in his high-pitched drawling tone: "None of my business, of course, but I didn't introduce her to the duchess. Charming woman, the duchess, you understand; and a very good friend of mine; but *rather* a liberal education."

Selden received this in silence, and after a few puffs Lord Hubert broke out again: "Sort of thing one can't communicate to the young lady—though young ladies nowadays are so competent to judge for themselves; but in this case—I'm an old friend, too, you know . . . and there seemed no one else to speak to. The whole situation's a little mixed, as I see it—but there used to be an aunt somewhere, a diffuse and innocent person, who was great at bridging over chasms she didn't see. . . . Ah, in New York, is she? Pity New York's such a long way off!"

17

M ISS Bart, emerging late the next morning from her cabin, found herself alone on the deck of the Sabrina.

The cushioned chairs, disposed expectantly under the wide awning, showed no signs of recent occupancy, and she presently learned from a steward that Mrs. Dorset had not yet appeared, and that the gentlemen— separately—had gone ashore as soon as they had breakfasted. Supplied with these facts, Lily leaned awhile over the side, giving herself up to a leisurely enjoyment of the spectacle before her. Unclouded sunlight enveloped sea and shore in a bath of purest radiancy. The purpling waters drew a sharp white line of foam at the base of the shore; against its irregular eminences, hotels and villas flashed from the grayish verdure of olive and eucalyptus; and the background of bare and finely pencilled mountains quivered in a pale intensity of light.

How beautiful it was—and how she loved beauty! She had always felt that her sensibility in this direction made up for certain obtusenesses of feeling of which she was less proud; and during the last three months she had indulged it passionately. The Dorsets' invitation to go abroad with them had come as an almost miraculous release from crushing difficulties; and her faculty for renewing herself in new scenes, and casting off problems of conduct as easily as the surroundings in which they had arisen, made the mere change from one place to another seem not merely a postponement, but a solution of her troubles. Moral complications existed for her only in the environment that had produced them; she did not mean to slight or ignore them, but they lost their reality when they changed their background. She could not have remained in New York without repaying the money she owed to Trenor; to acquit herself of that odious debt she might even have faced a marriage with Rosedale; but the accident of placing the Atlantic between herself and her obligations made them dwindle out of sight as if they had been milestones and she had traveled past them.

Her two months on the *Sabrina* had been especially calculated to aid this illusion of distance. She had been plunged into new scenes, and had found in them a renewal of old hopes and ambitions. The cruise itself charmed her as a romantic adventure. She was vaguely touched by the names and scenes amid which she moved, and had listened to Ned Silverton reading Theocritus by moonlight, as the yacht rounded the Sicilian promontories, with a thrill of the nerves that confirmed her belief in her intellectual superiority. But the weeks at Cannes and Nice had really given her more pleasure. The gratification of being welcomed in high company, and of making her own ascendency felt there, so that she found herself figuring once more as the "beautiful Miss Bart" in the interesting journal devoted to recording the least movements of her cosmopolitan companions —all these experiences tended to throw into the extreme background of memory the prosaic and sordid difficulties from which she had escaped.

If she was faintly aware of fresh difficulties ahead, she was sure of her ability to meet them: it was characteristic of her to feel that the only problems she could not solve were those with which she was familiar. Meanwhile she could honestly be proud of the skill with which she had adapted herself to somewhat delicate conditions. She had reason to think that she had made herself equally necessary to her host and hostess; and if only she had seen any perfectly irreproachable means of drawing a financial profit from the situation, there would have been no cloud on her horizon. The truth was that her funds, as usual, were inconveniently low; and to neither Dorset nor his wife could this vulgar embarrassment be safely hinted. Still, the need was not a pressing one; she could worry along, as she had so often done before, with the hope of some happy change of fortune to sustain her; and meanwhile life was gay and beautiful and easy, and she was conscious of figuring not unworthily in such a setting.

She was engaged to breakfast that morning with the Duchess of Beltshire, and at twelve o'clock she asked to be set ashore in the gig. Before this she had sent her maid to inquire if she might see Mrs. Dorset; but the reply came back that the latter was tired, and trying to sleep. Lily thought she understood the reason of the rebuff. Her hostess had not been included in the duchess's invitation, though she herself had made the most loyal efforts in that direction. But her grace was impervious to hints, and invited or omitted as she chose. It was not Lily's fault if Mrs. Dorset's complicated attitudes did not fall in with the duchess's easy gait. The duchess, who seldom explained herself, had not formulated her objection beyond saying: "She's rather a bore, you know. The only one of your friends I like is that little Mr. Bry—*he's* funny—" but Lily knew enough not to press the point, and was not altogether sorry to be thus distinguished at her friend's expense. Bertha certainly *had* grown tiresome since she had taken to poetry and Ned Silverton.

On the whole, it was a relief to break away now and then from the *Sabrina*; and the duchess's little breakfast, organized by Lord Hubert with all his usual virtuosity, was the pleasanter to Lily for not including her traveling-companions. Dorset, of late, had grown more than usually morose and incalculable, and Ned Silverton went about with an air that seemed to challenge the universe. The freedom and lightness of the ducal intercourse made an agreeable change from these complications, and Lily was tempted, after luncheon, to adjourn in the wake of her companions to the hectic atmosphere of the Casino. She did not mean to play; her diminished pocket-money offered small scope for the adventure; but it amused her to sit on a divan, under the doubtful protection of the duchess's back, while the latter hung above her stakes at a neighboring table.

The rooms were packed with the gazing throng which, in the afternoon hours, trickles heavily between the tables, like the Sunday crowd in a lion-house. In the stagnant flow of the mass, identities were hardly distinguishable; but Lily presently saw Mrs. Bry cleaving her determined way through the doors, and, in the broad wake she left, the light figure of Mrs. Fisher bobbing after her like a rowboat at the stern of a tug. Mrs. Bry pressed on, evidently animated by the resolve to reach a certain point in the rooms; but Mrs. Fisher, as she passed Lily, broke from her towing-line, and let herself float to the girl's side.

"Lose her?" she echoed the latter's query, with an indifferent glance at Mrs. Bry's retreating back. "I daresay—it doesn't matter: I *have* lost her already." And, as Lily exclaimed, she added: "We had an awful row this morning. You know, of course, that the duchess chucked her at dinner last night, and she thinks it was my fault—my want of management. The worst of it is, the message—just a mere word by telephone—came so late that the dinner had to be paid for; and Bécassin *had* run it up—it had been so drummed into him that the duchess was coming!" Mrs. Fisher indulged in a faint laugh at the remembrance. "Paying for what she doesn't get rankles so dreadfully with Louisa: I can't make her see that it's one of the preliminary steps to getting what you haven't paid for—and as I was the nearest thing to smash, she smashed me to atoms, poor dear!"

Lily murmured her commiseration. Impulses of sympathy came naturally to her, and it was instinctive to proffer her help to Mrs. Fisher.

"If there's anything I can do—if it's only a question of meeting the duchess! I heard her say she thought Mr. Bry amusing —"

But Mrs. Fisher interposed with a decisive gesture. "My dear, I have my pride: the pride of my trade. *I* couldn't manage the duchess, and I can't palm off your arts on Louisa Bry as mine. I've taken the final step: I go to Paris tonight with the Sam Gormers. *They're* still in the elementary stage; an Italian prince is a great deal more than a prince to them, and they're always on the brink of taking a courier for one. To save them from that is my present mission." She laughed again at the picture. "But before I go I want to make my last will and testament—I want to leave you the Brys."

"Me?" Miss Bart joined in her amusement. "It's charming of you to remember me, dear; but really—"

"You're already so well provided for?" Mrs. Fisher flashed a sharp glance at her. "*Are* you, though, Lily—to the point of rejecting my offer?"

Miss Bart colored slowly. "What I really meant was, that the Brys wouldn't in the least care to be so disposed of."

Mrs. Fisher continued to probe her embarrassment with an unflinching eye. "What you really meant was that you've snubbed the Brys horribly; and you know that they know it—"

"Carry!"

"Oh, on certain sides Louisa bristles with perceptions. If you'd even managed to have them asked once on the Sabrina—especially when royalties were coming! But it's not too late," she ended earnestly, "it's not too late for either of you."

Lily smiled. "Stay over, and I'll get the duchess to dine with them."

"I shan't stay over—the Gormers have paid for my salon-lit," said Mrs. Fisher with simplicity. "But get the duchess to dine with them all the same."

Lily's smile again flowed into a slight laugh: her friend's importunity was beginning to strike her as irrelevant. "I'm sorry I have been negligent about the Brys —" she began.

"Oh, as to the Brys—it's you I'm thinking of," said Mrs. Fisher abruptly. She paused, and then, bending forward, with a lowered voice: "You know we all went on to Nice last night when the duchess chucked us. It was Louisa's idea—I told her what I thought of it."

Miss Bart assented. "Yes—I caught sight of you on the way back, at the station."

"Well, the man who was in the carriage with you and George Dorset— that horrid little Dabham who does 'Society Notes from the Riviera'—had been dining with us at Nice. And he's telling everybody that you and Dorset came back alone after midnight."

"Alone—? When he was with us?" Lily laughed, but her laugh faded into gravity under the prolonged implication of Mrs. Fisher's look. "We *did* come back alone—if that's so very dreadful! But whose fault was it? The duchess was spending the night at Cimiez with the crown princess; Bertha got bored with the show, and went off early, promising to meet us at the station. We turned up on time, but she didn't—she didn't turn up at all!"

Miss Bart made this announcement in the tone of one who presents, with careless assurance, a complete vindication; but Mrs. Fisher received it in a manner almost inconsequent. She seemed to have lost sight of her friend's part in the incident; her inward vision had taken another slant.

"Bertha never turned up at all? Then how on earth did she get back?"

"Oh, by the next train, I suppose; there were two extra ones for the fete. At any rate, I know she's safe on the yacht, though I haven't yet seen her; but you see it was not my fault," Lily summed up.

"Not your fault that Bertha didn't turn up? My poor child, if only you don't have to pay for it!" Mrs. Fisher rose—she had seen Mrs. Bry surging back in her direction. "There's Louisa, and I must be off—oh, we're on the best of terms externally; we're lunching together; but at heart it's *me* she's lunching on," she explained. And with a last handclasp and a last look, she added: "Remember, I leave her to you; she's hovering now, ready to take you in."

Lily carried the impression of Mrs. Fisher's leave-taking away with her from the Casino doors. She had accomplished, before leaving, the first step toward her reinstatement in Mrs. Bry's good graces. An affable advance—a vague murmur that they must see more of each other—an allusive glance to a near future that was felt to include the duchess as well as the *Sabrina*—how easily it was all done, if one possessed the knack of doing it! She wondered at herself, as she had so often wondered, that, possessing the knack, she did not more consistently exercise it. But sometimes she was forgetful—and sometimes, could it be that she was proud? Today, at any rate, she had been vaguely conscious of a reason for sinking her pride, had in fact even sunk it to the point of suggesting to Lord Hubert Dacey, whom she ran across on the Casino steps, that he might really get the duchess to dine with the Brys, if *she* undertook to have them asked on the *Sabrina*. Lord Hubert had promised his help, with the readiness on which she could always count: it was his only way of ever reminding her that he had once been ready to do so much more for her. Her path, in short, seemed to smooth itself before her as she advanced; yet the faint stir of uneasiness persisted. Had it been produced, she wondered, by her chance meeting with Selden? She thought not—time and change seemed so completely to have relegated him to his proper distance. The sudden and exquisite reaction from her anxieties had had the effect of throwing the recent past so far back that even Selden, as part of it, retained a certain air of unreality. And he had made it so clear that they were not to meet again; that he had merely dropped down to Nice for a day or two, and had almost his foot on the next steamer. No—that part of the past had merely surged up for a moment on the fleeing surface of events; and now that it was submerged again, the uncertainty, the apprehension persisted.

They grew to sudden acuteness as she caught sight of George Dorset descending the steps of the Hôtel de Paris and making for her across the square. She had meant to drive down to the quay and regain the yacht; but she now had the immediate impression that something more was to happen first.

"Which way are you going? Shall we walk a bit?" he began, putting the second question before the first was answered, and not waiting for a reply to either before he directed her silently toward the comparative seclusion of the lower gardens.

She detected in him at once all the signs of extreme nervous tension. The skin was puffed out under his sunken eyes, and its sallowness had paled to a leaden white against which his irregular eyebrows and long reddish moustache were relieved with a saturnine effect. His appearance, in short, presented an odd mixture of the bedraggled and the ferocious.

He walked beside her in silence, with quick precipitate steps, till they reached the embowered slopes to the east of the Casino; then, pulling up abruptly, he said: "Have you seen Bertha?"

"No—when I left the yacht she was not yet up."

He received this with a laugh like the whirring sound in a disabled clock. "Not yet up? Had she gone to bed? Do you know at what time she came on board? This morning at seven!" he exclaimed.

"At seven?" Lily started. "What happened—an accident to the train?"

He laughed again. "They missed the train—all the trains—they had to drive back."

"Well —?" She hesitated, feeling at once how little even this necessity accounted for the fatal lapse of hours.

"Well, they couldn't get a carriage at once—at that time of night, you know —" the explanatory note made it almost seem as though he were putting the case for his wife—"and when they finally did, it was only a one-horse cab, and the horse was lame!"

"How tiresome! I see," she affirmed, with the more earnestness because she was so nervously conscious that she did not; and after a pause she added: "I'm so sorry—but ought we to have waited?"

"Waited for the one-horse cab? It would scarcely have carried the four of us, do you think?"

She took this in what seemed the only possible way, with a laugh intended to sink the question itself in his humorous treatment of it. "Well, it would have been difficult; we should have had to walk by turns. But it would have been jolly to see the sunrise."

"Yes: the sunrise *was* jolly," he agreed.

"Was it? You saw it, then?"

"I saw it, yes; from the deck. I waited up for them."

"Naturally—I suppose you were worried. Why didn't you call on me to share your vigil?"

He stood still, dragging at his moustache with a lean weak hand. "I don't think you would have cared for its denouement," he said with sudden grimness.

Again she was disconcerted by the abrupt change in his tone, and as in one flash she saw the peril of the moment, and the need of keeping her sense of it out of her eyes.

"Denouement—isn't that too big a word for such a small incident? The worst of it, after all, is the fatigue which Bertha has probably slept off by this time."

She clung to the note bravely, though its futility was now plain to her in the glare of his miserable eyes.

"Don't—don't! —" he broke out, with the hurt cry of a child; and while she tried to merge her sympathy, and her resolve to ignore any cause for it, in one ambiguous murmur of deprecation, he dropped down on the bench near which they had paused, and poured out the wretchedness of his soul.

It was a dreadful hour—an hour from which she emerged shrinking and seared, as though her lids had been scorched by its actual glare. It was not that she had never had premonitory glimpses of such an outbreak; but rather because, here and there throughout the three months, the surface of life had shown such ominous cracks and vapors that her fears had always been on the alert for an upheaval. There had been moments when the situation had presented itself under a homelier yet more vivid image—that of a shaky vehicle, dashed by unbroken steeds over a bumping road, while she cowered within, aware that the harness wanted mending, and wondering what would give way first. Well—everything had given way now; and the wonder was that the crazy outfit had held together so long. Her sense of being involved in the crash, instead of merely witnessing it from the road, was intensified by the way in which Dorset, through his furies of denunciation and wild reactions of self-contempt, made her feel the need he had of her, the place she had taken in his life. But for her, what ear would have been open to his cries? And what hand but hers could drag him up again to a footing of sanity and self-respect? All through the stress of the struggle with him, she had been conscious of something faintly maternal in her efforts to guide and uplift him. But for the present, if he clung to her, it was not in order to be dragged up, but to feel someone floundering in the depths with him: he wanted her to suffer with him, not to help him to suffer less.

Happily for both, there was little physical strength to sustain his frenzy.

It left him, collapsed and breathing heavily, to an apathy so deep and prolonged that Lily almost feared the passers-by would think it the result of a seizure, and stop to offer their aid. But Monte Carlo is, of all places, the one where the human bond is least close, and odd sights are the least arresting. If a glance or two lingered on the couple, no intrusive sympathy disturbed them; and it was Lily herself who broke the silence by rising from her seat. With the clearing of her vision the sweep of peril had extended, and she saw that the post of danger was no longer at Dorset's side.

"If you won't go back, I must—don't make me leave you!" she urged.

But he remained mutely resistant, and she added: "What are you going to do? You really can't sit here all night."

"I can go to a hotel. I can telegraph my lawyers." He sat up, roused by a new thought. "By Jove, Selden's at Nice—I'll send for Selden!"

Lily, at this, reseated herself with a cry of alarm. "No, no, *no!*" she protested.

He swung round on her distrustfully. "Why not Selden? He's a lawyer, isn't he? One will do as well as another in a case like this."

"As badly as another, you mean. I thought you relied on *me* to help you."

"You do—by being so sweet and patient with me. If it hadn't been for you I'd have ended the thing long ago. But now it's got to end." He rose suddenly, straightening himself with an effort. "You can't want to see me ridiculous."

She looked at him kindly. "That's just it." Then, after a moment's pondering, almost to her own surprise she broke out with a flash of inspiration: "Well, go over and see Mr. Selden. You'll have time to do it before dinner."

"Oh, *dinner* —" he mocked her; but she left him with the smiling rejoinder: "Dinner on board, remember; we'll put it off till nine if you like."

It was past four already; and when a cab had dropped her at the quay, and she stood waiting for the gig to put off for her, she began to wonder what had been happening on the yacht. Of Silverton's whereabouts there had been no mention. Had he returned to the *Sabrina?* Or could Bertha—the dread alternative sprang on her suddenly—could Bertha, left to herself, have gone ashore to rejoin him? Lily's heart stood still at the thought. All her concern had hitherto been for young Silverton, not only because, in such affairs, the woman's instinct is to side with the man, but because his case made a peculiar appeal to her sympathies. He was so desperately in earnest, poor youth, and his earnestness was of so different a quality from Bertha's, though hers too was desperate enough. The difference was that Bertha was in earnest only about herself while he was in earnest about her. But now, at the actual crisis, this difference seemed to throw the weight of destitution on Bertha's side, since at least he had her to suffer for, and she had only herself.

At any rate, viewed less ideally, all the disadvantages of such a situation were for the woman; and it was to Bertha that Lily's sympathies now went out. She was not fond of Bertha Dorset, but neither was she without a sense of obligation, the heavier for having so little personal liking to sustain it. Bertha had been kind to her, they had lived together, during the last months, on terms of easy friendship, and the sense of friction of which Lily had recently become aware seemed to make it the more urgent that she should work undividedly in her friend's interest.

It was in Bertha's interest, certainly, that she had dispatched Dorset to consult with Lawrence Selden. Once the grotesqueness of the situation was accepted, she had seen at a glance that it was the safest in which Dorset could find himself. Who but Selden could thus miraculously combine the skill to save Bertha with the obligation of doing so? The consciousness that much skill would be required made Lily rest thankfully in the greatness of the obligation. Since he would *have* to pull Bertha through she could trust him to find a way; and she put the fullness of her trust in the telegram she managed to send him on her way to the quay.

Thus far, then, Lily felt that she had done well; and the conviction strengthened her for the task that remained. She and Bertha had never been on confidential terms, but at such a crisis the barriers of reserve must surely fall: Dorset's wild allusions to the scene of the morning made Lily feel that they were down already, and that any attempt to rebuild them would be beyond Bertha's strength. She pictured the poor creature shivering behind her fallen defenses and awaiting with suspense the moment when she could take refuge in the first shelter that offered. If only that shelter had not already offered itself elsewhere! As the gig traversed the short distance between the quay and the yacht, Lily grew more than ever alarmed at the possible consequences of her long absence. What if the wretched Bertha, finding in all the long hours no soul to turn to—but by this time Lily's eager foot was on the side-ladder, and her first step on the Sabrina showed the worst of her apprehensions to be unfounded; for there, in the luxurious shade of the afterdeck, the wretched Bertha, in full command of her usual attenuated elegance, sat dispensing tea to the duchess of Beltshire and Lord Hubert.

The sight filled Lily with such surprise that she felt that Bertha, at least, must read its meaning in her look, and she was proportionately disconcerted by the blankness of the look returned. But in an instant she saw that Mrs. Dorset had, of necessity, to look blank before the others, and that, to mitigate the effect of her own surprise, she must at once produce some simple reason for it. The long habit of rapid transitions made it easy for her to exclaim to the duchess: "Why, I thought you'd gone back to the princess!" and this sufficed for the lady she addressed, if it was hardly enough for Lord Hubert.

At least it opened the way to a lively explanation of how the duchess was, in fact, going back the next moment, but had first rushed out to the yacht for a word with Mrs. Dorset on the subject of tomorrow's dinner—the dinner with the Brys, to which Lord Hubert had finally insisted on dragging them.

"To save my neck, you know!" he explained, with a glance that appealed to Lily for some recognition of his promptness; and the duchess added, with her noble candor: "Mr. Bry has promised him a tip, and he says if we go he'll pass it on to us."

This led to some final pleasantries, in which, as it seemed to Lily, Mrs. Dorset bore her part with astounding bravery, and at the close of which Lord Hubert, from half way down the side-ladder, called back, with an air of numbering heads: "And, of course, we may count on Dorset too?"

"Oh, count on him," his wife assented gaily. She was keeping up well to the last—but as she turned back from waving her adieux over the side, Lily said to herself that the mask must drop and the soul of fear look out.

Mrs. Dorset turned back slowly; perhaps she wanted time to steady her muscles; at any rate, they were still under perfect control when, dropping once more into her seat behind the tea-table, she remarked to Miss Bart with a faint touch of irony: "I suppose I ought to say good morning."

If it was a cue, Lily was ready to take it, though with only the vaguest sense of what was expected of her in return. There was something unnerving in the contemplation of Mrs. Dorset's composure, and she had to force the light tone in which she answered: "I tried to see you this morning, but you were not yet up."

"No—I got to bed late. After we missed you at the station I thought we ought to wait for you till the last train." She spoke very gently, but with just the least tinge of reproach.

"You missed us? You waited for us at the station?"

Now indeed Lily was too far adrift in bewilderment to measure the other's words or keep watch on her own. "But I thought you didn't get to the station till after the last train had left!"

Mrs. Dorset, examining her between lowered lids, met this with the immediate query: "Who told you that?"

"George—I saw him just now in the gardens."

"Ah, is that George's version? Poor George—he was in no state to remember what I told him. He had one of his worst attacks this morning, and I packed him off to see the doctor. Do you know if he found him?"

Lily, still lost in conjecture, made no reply, and Mrs. Dorset settled herself indolently in her seat. "He'll wait to see him; he was horribly frightened about himself. It's very bad for him to be worried, and whenever anything upsetting happens, it always brings on an attack."

This time Lily felt sure that a cue was being pressed on her; but it was put forth with such startling suddenness, and with so incredible an air of ignoring what it led up to, that she could only falter out doubtfully: "Anything upsetting?"

"Yes—such as having you so conspicuously on his hands in the small hours. You know, my dear, you're rather a big responsibility in such a scandalous place after midnight."

At that—at the complete unexpectedness and the inconceivable audacity of it—Lily could not restrain the tribute of an astonished laugh.

"Well, really—considering it was you who burdened him with the responsibility!"

Mrs. Dorset took this with an exquisite mildness. "By not having the superhuman cleverness to discover you in that frightful rush for the train? Or the imagination to believe that you'd take it without us—you and he all alone—instead of waiting quietly in the station till we *did* manage to meet you?"

Lily's color rose: it was growing clear to her that Bertha was pursuing an object, following a line she had marked out for herself. Only, with such a doom impending, why waste time in these childish efforts to avert it? The puerility of the attempt disarmed Lily's indignation: did it not prove how horribly the poor creature was frightened?

"No, by our simply all keeping together at Nice," she returned.

"Keeping together? When it was you who seized the first opportunity to rush off with the duchess and her friends? My dear Lily, you are not a child to be led by the hand!"

"No—nor to be lectured, Bertha, really; if that's what you are doing to me now."

Mrs. Dorset smiled on her reproachfully. "Lecture you—I? Heaven forbid! I was merely trying to give you a friendly hint. But it's usually the other way round, isn't it? I'm expected to take hints, not to give them: I've positively lived on them all these last months."

"Hints—from me to you?" Lily repeated.

"Oh, negative ones merely—what not to be and to do and to see. And I think I've taken them to admiration. Only, my dear, if you'll let me say so, I didn't understand that one of my negative duties was *not* to warn you when you carried your imprudence too far."

A chill of fear passed over Miss Bart: a sense of remembered treachery that was like the gleam of a knife in the dusk. But compassion, in a moment, got the better of her instinctive recoil. What was this outpouring of senseless bitterness but the tracked creature's attempt to cloud the medium through which it was fleeing? It was on Lily's lips to exclaim: "You poor soul, don't double and turn—come straight back to me, and we'll find a way out!" But the words died under the impenetrable insolence of Bertha's smile. Lily sat silent, taking the brunt of it quietly, letting it spend itself on her to the last drop of its accumulated falseness; then, without a word, she rose and went down to her cabin.

18

Miss Bart's telegram caught Lawrence Selden at the door of his hotel, and having read it, he turned back to wait for Dorset. The message necessarily left large gaps for conjecture; but all that he had recently heard and seen made these but too easy to fill in. On the whole he was surprised; for though he had perceived that the situation contained all the elements of an explosion, he had often enough, in the range of his personal experience, seen just such combinations subside into harmlessness. Still, Dorset's spasmodic temper, and his wife's reckless disregard of appearances, gave the situation a particular insecurity; and it was less from the sense of any special relation to the case than from a purely professional zeal, that Selden resolved to guide the pair to safety. Whether, in the present instance, safety for either lay in repairing so damaged a tie, it was no business of his to consider; he had only, on general principles, to think of averting a scandal, and his desire to avert it was increased by his fear of its involving Miss Bart. There was nothing specific in this apprehension; he merely wished to spare her the embarrassment of being ever so remotely connected with the public washing of the Dorset linen.

How exhaustive and unpleasant such a process would be, he saw even more vividly after his two hours' talk with poor Dorset. If anything came out at all, it would be such a vast unpacking of accumulated moral rags as left him, after his visitor had gone, with the feeling that he must fling open the windows and have his room swept out. But nothing should come out; and happily for his side of the case, the dirty rags, however pieced together, could not, without considerable difficulty, be turned into a homogeneous grievance. The torn edges did not always fit—there were missing bits, there were disparities of size and color, all of which it was naturally Selden's business to make the most of in putting them under his client's eye. But to a man in Dorset's mood the completest demonstration could not carry conviction, and Selden saw that for the moment all he could do was to soothe and temporize, to offer sympathy and to counsel prudence. He let Dorset depart charged to the brim with the sense that, till their next meeting, he must maintain a strictly noncommittal attitude; that, in short, his share in the game consisted for the present in looking on. Selden knew, however, that he could not long keep such violences in equilibrium; and he promised to meet Dorset, the next morning, at an hotel in Monte Carlo. Meanwhile he counted not a little on the reaction of weakness and self-distrust that, in such natures, follows on every unwonted expenditure of moral force; and his telegraphic reply to Miss Bart consisted simply in the injunction: "Assume that everything is as usual."

On this assumption, in fact, the early part of the following day was lived through. Dorset, as if in obedience to Lily's imperative bidding, had actually returned in time for a late dinner on the yacht. The repast had been the most difficult moment of the day. Dorset was sunk in one of the abysmal silences which so commonly followed on what his wife called his "attacks" that it was easy, before the servants, to refer it to this cause; but Bertha herself seemed, perversely enough, little disposed to make use of this obvious means of protection. She simply left the brunt of the situation on her husband's hands, as if too absorbed in a grievance of her own to suspect that she might be the object of one herself. To Lily this attitude was the most ominous, because the most perplexing, element in the situation. As she tried to fan the weak flicker of talk, to build up, again and again, the crumbling structure of "appearances," her own attention was perpetually distracted by the question: "What on earth can she be driving at?" There was something positively exasperating in Bertha's attitude of isolated defiance. If only she would have given her friend a hint they might still have worked together successfully; but how could Lily be of use, while she was thus obstinately shut out from participation? To be of use was what she honestly wanted; and not for her own sake but for the Dorsets'. She had not thought of her own situation at all: she was simply engrossed in trying to put a little order in theirs. But the close of the short dreary evening left her with a sense of effort hopelessly wasted. She had not tried to see Dorset alone: she had positively shrunk from a renewal of his confidences. It was Bertha whose confidence she sought, and who should as eagerly have invited her own; and Bertha, as if in the infatuation of self-destruction, was actually pushing away her rescuing hand.

Lily, going to bed early, had left the couple to themselves; and it seemed part of the general mystery in which she moved that more than an hour should elapse before she heard Bertha walk down the silent passage and regain her room. The morrow, rising on an apparent continuance of the same conditions, revealed nothing of what had occurred between the confronted pair. One fact alone outwardly proclaimed the change they were all conspiring to ignore; and that was the nonappearance of Ned Silverton. No one referred to it, and this tacit avoidance of the subject kept it in the immediate foreground of consciousness. But there was another change, perceptible only to Lily; and that was that Dorset now avoided her almost as pointedly as his wife. Perhaps he was repenting his rash outpourings of the previous day; perhaps only trying, in his clumsy way, to conform to Selden's counsel to behave "as usual." Such instructions no more make for easiness of attitude than the photographer's behest to "look natural"; and in a creature as unconscious as poor Dorset of the appearance he habitually presented, the struggle to maintain a pose was sure to result in queer contortions.

It resulted, at any rate, in throwing Lily strangely on her own resources. She had learned, on leaving her room, that Mrs. Dorset was still invisible, and that Dorset had left the yacht early; and feeling too restless to remain alone, she too had herself ferried ashore. Straying toward the Casino, she attached herself to a group of acquaintances from Nice, with whom she lunched, and in whose company she was returning to the rooms when she encountered Selden crossing the square. She could not, at the moment, separate herself definitely from her party, who had hospitably assumed that she would remain with them till they took their departure; but she found time for a momentary pause of inquiry, to which he promptly returned: "I've seen him again—he's just left me."

She waited before him anxiously. "Well? what has happened? What *will* happen?"

"Nothing as yet—and nothing in the future, I think."

"It's over, then? It's settled? You're sure?"

He smiled. "Give me time. I'm not sure—but I'm a good deal surer." And with that she had to content herself, and hasten on to the expectant group on the steps.

Selden had in fact given her the utmost measure of his sureness, had even stretched it a shade to meet the anxiety in her eyes. And now, as he turned away, strolling down the hill toward the station, that anxiety remained with him as the visible justification of his own. It was not, indeed, anything specific that he feared: there had been a literal truth in his declaration that he did not think anything would happen. What troubled him was that, though Dorset's attitude had perceptibly changed, the change was not clearly to be accounted for. It had certainly not been produced by Selden's arguments, or by the action of his own soberer reason. Five minutes' talk sufficed to show that some alien influence had been at work, and that it had not so much subdued his resentment as weakened his will, so that he moved under it in a state of apathy, like a dangerous lunatic who has been drugged. Temporarily, no doubt, however exerted, it worked for the general safety: the question was how long it would last, and by what kind of reaction it was likely to be followed. On these points Selden could gain no light; for he saw that one effect of the transfomation had been to shut him off from free communion with Dorset. The latter, indeed, was still moved by the irresistible desire to discuss his wrong; but, though he revolved about it with the same forlorn tenacity, Selden was aware that something always restrained him from full expression. His state was one to produce first weariness and then impatience in his hearer; and when their talk was over, Selden began to feel that he had done his utmost, and might justifiably wash his hands of the sequel.

It was in this mind that he had been making his way back to the station when Miss Bart crossed his path; but though, after his brief word with her, he kept mechanically on his course, he was conscious of a gradual change in his purpose. The change had been produced by the look in her eyes; and in his eagerness to define the nature of that look, he dropped into a seat in the gardens, and sat brooding upon the question. It was natural enough, in all conscience, that she should appear anxious: a young woman placed, in the close intimacy of a yachting-cruise, between a couple on the verge of disaster, could hardly, aside from her concern for her friends, be insensible to the awkwardness of her own position. The worst of it was that, in interpreting Miss Bart's state of mind, so many alternative readings were possible; and one of these, in Selden's troubled mind, took the ugly form suggested by Mrs. Fisher. If the girl was afraid, was she afraid for herself or for her friends? And to what degree was her dread of a catastrophe intensified by the sense of being fatally involved in it? The burden of offense lying manifestly with Mrs. Dorset, this conjecture seemed on the face of it gratuitously unkind; but Selden knew that in the most one-sided matrimonial quarrel there are generally countercharges to be brought, and that they are brought with the greater audacity where the original grievance is so emphatic. Mrs. Fisher had not hesitated to suggest the likelihood of Dorset's marrying Miss Bart "if anything happened"; and though Mrs. Fisher's conclusions were notoriously rash, she was shrewd enough in reading the signs from which they were drawn. Dorset had apparently shown marked interest in the girl, and this interest might be used to cruel advantage in his wife's struggle for rehabilitation. Selden knew that Bertha would fight to the last round of powder: the rashness of her conduct was illogically combined with a cold determination to escape its consequences. She could be as unscrupulous in fighting for herself as she was reckless in courting danger, and whatever came to her hand at such moments was likely to be used as a defensive missile. He did not, as yet, see clearly just what course she was likely to take, but his perplexity increased his apprehension, and with it the sense that, before leaving, he must speak again with Miss Bart. Whatever her share in the situation—and he had always honestly tried to resist judging her by her surroundings—however free she might be from any personal connection with it, she would be better out of the way of a possible crash; and since she had appealed to him for help, it was clearly his business to tell her so.

This decision at last brought him to his feet, and carried him back to the gambling rooms, within whose doors he had seen her disappearing; but a prolonged exploration of the crowd failed to put him on her traces. He saw instead, to his surprise, Ned Silverton loitering somewhat ostentatiously about the tables; and the discovery that this actor in the drama was not only hovering in the wings, but actually inviting the exposure of the footlights, though it might have seemed to imply that all peril was over, served rather to deepen Selden's sense of foreboding. Charged with this impression he returned to the square, hoping to see Miss Bart move across it, as everyone

in Monte Carlo seemed inevitably to do at least a dozen times a day; but
here again he waited vainly for a glimpse of her, and the conclusion was
slowly forced on him that she had gone back to the Sabrina. It would be
difficult to follow her there, and still more difficult, should he do so, to contrive the opportunity for a private word; and he had almost decided on the
unsatisfactory alternative of writing, when the ceaseless diorama of the
square suddenly unrolled before him the figures of Lord Hubert and
Mrs. Bry.

Hailing them at once with his question, he learned from Lord Hubert
that Miss Bart had just returned to the *Sabrina* in Dorset's company; an
announcement so evidently disconcerting to him that Mrs. Bry, after a
glance from her companion, which seemed to act like the pressure on
a spring, brought forth the prompt proposal that he should come and meet
his friends at dinner that evening— "At Bécassin's—a little dinner to
the duchess," she flashed out before Lord Hubert had time to remove the
pressure.

Selden's sense of the privilege of being included in such company
brought him early in the evening to the door of the restaurant, where he
paused to scan the ranks of diners approaching down the brightly lit terrace.
There, while the Brys hovered within over the last agitating alternatives of
the menu, he kept watch for the guests from the *Sabrina*, who at length rose
on the horizon in company with the duchess, Lord and Lady Skiddaw and
the Stepneys. From this group it was easy for him to detach Miss Bart on the
pretext of a moment's glance into one of the brilliant shops along the
terrace, and to say to her, while they lingered together in the white dazzle of
a jeweler's window: "I stopped over to see you—to beg of you to leave the
yacht."

The eyes she turned on him showed a quick gleam of her former fear.
"To leave—? What do you mean? What has happened?"

"Nothing. But if anything should, why be in the way of it?"

The glare from the jeweler's window, deepening the pallor of her face,
gave to its delicate lines the sharpness of a tragic mask. "Nothing will, I am
sure; but while there's even a doubt left, how can you think I would leave
Bertha?"

The words rang out on a note of contempt—was it possibly of contempt
for himself? Well, he was willing to risk its renewal to the extent of insisting, with an undeniable throb of added interest: "You have yourself to think
of, you know—" to which, with a strange fall of sadness in her voice, she
answered, meeting his eyes: "If you knew how little difference that makes!"

"Oh, well, nothing *will* happen," he said, more for his own reassurance
than for hers; and "Nothing, nothing, of course!" she valiantly assented, as
they turned to overtake their companions.

In the thronged restaurant, taking their places about Mrs. Bry's illuminated board, their confidence seemed to gain support from the familiarity of

their surroundings. Here were Dorset and his wife once more presenting their customary faces to the world, she engrossed in establishing her relation with an intensely new gown, he shrinking with dyspeptic dread from the multiplied solicitations of the menu. The mere fact that they thus showed themselves together, with the utmost openness the place afforded, seemed to declare beyond a doubt that their differences were composed. How this end had been attained was still matter for wonder, but it was clear that for the moment Miss Bart rested confidently in the result; and Selden tried to achieve the same view by telling himself that her opportunities for observation had been ampler than his own.

Meanwhile, as the dinner advanced through a labyrinth of courses, in which it became clear that Mrs. Bry had occasionally broken away from Lord Hubert's restraining hand, Selden's general watchfullness began to lose itself in a particular study of Miss Bart. It was one of the days when she was so handsome that to be handsome was enough, and all the rest—her grace, her quickness, her social felicities—seemed the overflow of a bounteous nature. But what especially struck him was the way in which she detached herself by a hundred undefinable shades, from the persons who most abounded in her own style. It was in just such company, the fine flower and complete expression of the state she aspired to, that the differences came out with special poignancy, her grace cheapening the other women's smartness as her finely discriminated silences made their chatter dull. The strain of the last hours had restored to her face the deeper eloquence which Selden had lately missed in it, and the bravery of her words to him still fluttered in her voice and eyes. Yes, she was matchless—it was the one word for her; and he could give his admiration the freer play because so little personal feeling remained in it. His real detachment from her had taken place, not at the lurid moment of disenchantment, but now, in the sober afterlight of discrimination, where he saw her definitely divided from him by the crudeness of a choice which seemed to deny the very differences he felt in her. It was before him again in its completeness—the choice in which she was content to rest: in the stupid costliness of the food and the showy dullness of the talk, in the freedom of speech which never arrived at wit and the freedom of act which never made for romance. The strident setting of the restaurant, in which their table seemed set apart in a special glare of publicity, and the presence at it of little Dabham of the "Riviera Notes," emphasized the ideals of a world where conspicuousness passed for distinction, and the society column had become the roll of fame.

It was as the immortalizer of such occasions that little Dabham, wedged in modest watchfullness between two brilliant neighbors, suddenly became the center of Selden's scrutiny. How much did he know of what was going on, and how much, for his purpose, was still worth finding out? His little eyes were like tentacles thrown out to catch the floating intimations with which, to Selden, the air at moments seemed thick; then again it cleared to its normal emptiness, and he could see nothing in it for the journalist but leisure to note the elegance of the ladies' gowns. Mrs. Dorset's, in particular, challenged all the wealth of Mr. Dabham's vocabulary: it had surprises and subtleties worthy of what he would have called "the literary style." At first, as Selden had noticed, it had been almost too preoccupying to its wearer; but now she was in full command of it, and was even producing her effects with unwonted freedom. Was she not, indeed, too free, too fluent, for perfect naturalness? And was not Dorset, to whom his glance had passed by a natural transition, too jerkily wavering between the same extremes? Dorset indeed was always jerky; but it seemed to Selden that tonight each vibration swung him farther from his center.

The dinner, meanwhile, was moving to its triumphant close, to the evident satisfaction of Mrs. Bry, who, throned in apoplectic majesty between Lord Skiddaw and Lord Hubert, seemed in spirit to be calling on Mrs. Fisher to witness her achievement. Short of Mrs. Fisher her audience might have been called complete; for the restaurant was crowded with persons mainly gathered there for the purpose of spectatorship, and accurately posted as to the names and faces of the celebrities they had come to see. Mrs. Bry, conscious that all her feminine guests came under that heading, and that each one looked her part to admiration, shone on Lily with all the pent-up gratitude that Mrs. Fisher had failed to deserve. Selden, catching the glance, wondered what part Miss Bart had played in organizing the entertainment. She did, at least, a great deal to adorn it; and as he watched the bright security with which she bore herself, he smiled to think that he should have fancied her in need of help. Never had she appeared more serenely mistress of the situation than when, at the moment of dispersal, detaching herself a little from the group about the table, she turned with a smile and a graceful slant of the shoulders to receive her cloak from Dorset.

The dinner had been protracted over Mr. Bry's exceptional cigars and a bewildering array of liqueurs, and many of the other tables were empty; but a sufficient number of diners still lingered to give relief to the leave-taking of Mrs. Bry's distinguished guests. This ceremony was drawn out and complicated by the fact that it involved, on the part of the duchess and Lady Skiddaw, definite farewells, and pledges of speedy reunion in Paris, where they were to pause and replenish their wardrobes on the way to England. The quality of Mrs. Bry's hospitality, and of the tips her husband had presumably imparted, lent to the manner of the English ladies a general effusiveness which shed the rosiest light over their hostess's future. In its glow Mrs. Dorset and the Stepneys were also visibly included, and the whole scene had touches of intimacy worth their weight in gold to the watchful pen of Mr. Dabham.

A glance at her watch caused the duchess to exclaim to her sister that they had just time to dash for their train, and the flurry of this departure over, the Stepneys, who had their motor at the door, offered to convey the

Dorsets and Miss Bart to the quay. The offer was accepted, and Mrs. Dorset moved away with her husband in attendance. Miss Bart had lingered for a last word with Lord Hubert, and Stepney, on whom Mr. Bry was pressing a final, and still more expensive, cigar, called out: "Come on, Lily, if you're going back to the yacht."

Lily turned to obey; but as she did so, Mrs. Dorset, who had paused on her way out, moved a few steps back toward the table.

"Miss Bart is not going back to the yacht," she said in a voice of singular distinctness.

A startled look ran from eye to eye; Mrs. Bry crimsoned to the verge of congestion, Mrs. Stepney slipped nervously behind her husband, and Selden, in the general turmoil of his sensations, was mainly conscious of a longing to grip Dabham by the collar and fling him out into the street.

Dorset, meanwhile, had stepped back to his wife's side. His face was white, and he looked about him with cowed angry eyes. "Bertha!—Miss Bart . . . this is some misunderstanding . . . some mistake. . . ."

"Miss Bart remains here," his wife rejoined incisively.

"And, I think, George, we had better not detain Mrs. Stepney any longer."

Miss Bart, during this brief exchange of words, remained in admirable erectness, slightly isolated from the embarrassed group about her. She had paled a little under the shock of the insult, but the discomposure of the surrounding faces was not reflected in her own. The faint disdain of her smile seemed to lift her high above her antagonist's reach, and it was not till she had given Mrs. Dorset the full measure of the distance between them that she turned and extended her hand to her hostess.

"I am joining the duchess tomorrow," she explained, "and it seemed easier for me to remain on shore for the night."

She held firmly to Mrs. Bry's wavering eye while she gave this explanation, but when it was over Selden saw her send a tentative glance from one to another of the women's faces. She read their incredulity in their averted looks, and in the mute wretchedness of the men behind them, and for a miserable half-second he thought she quivered on the brink of failure. Then, turning to him with an easy gesture, and the pale bravery of her recovered smile— "Dear Mr. Selden," she said, "you promised to see me to my cab."

Outside, the sky was gusty and overcast, and as Lily and Selden moved toward the deserted gardens below the restaurant, spurts of warm rain blew fitfully against their faces. The fiction of the cab had been tacitly abandoned; they walked on in silence, her hand on his arm, till the deeper shade of the gardens received them, and pausing beside a bench, he said: "Sit down a moment."

She dropped to the seat without answering, but the electric lamp at the

bend of the path shed a gleam on the struggling misery of her face. Selden
sat down beside her, waiting for her to speak, fearful lest any word he chose
should touch too roughly on her wound, and kept also from free utterance
by the wretched doubt which had slowly renewed itself within him. What
had brought her to this pass? What weakness had placed her so abominably
at her enemy's mercy? And why should Bertha Dorset have turned into an
enemy at the very moment when she so obviously needed the support of her
sex? Even while his nerves raged at the subjection of husbands to their
wives, and at the cruelty of women to their kind, reason obstinately harped
on the proverbial relation between smoke and fire. The memory of Mrs.
Fisher's hints, and the corroboration of his own impressions, while they
deepened his pity also increased his constraint, since, whichever way he
sought a free outlet for sympathy, it was blocked by the fear of committing a
blunder.

Suddenly it struck him that his silence must seem almost as accusatory
as that of the men he had despised for turning from her; but before he could
find the fitting word she had cut him short with a question.

"Do you know of a quiet hotel? I can send for my maid in the morning."

"An hotel—*here*—that you can go to alone? It's not possible."

She met this with a pale gleam of her old playfullness. "What *is*, then?
It's too wet to sleep in the gardens."

"But there must be someone —"

"Someone to whom I can go? Of course—any number—but at *this* hour?
You see my change of plan was rather sudden —"

"Good God—if you'd listened to me!" he cried, venting his helplessness
in a burst of anger.

She still held him off with the gentle mockery of her smile. "But haven't
I?" she rejoined. "You advised me to leave the yacht, and I'm leaving it."

He saw then, with a pang of self-reproach, that she meant neither to
explain nor to defend herself; that by his miserable silence he had forfeited
all chance of helping her, and that the decisive hour was past.

She had risen, and stood before him in a kind of clouded majesty, like
some deposed princess moving tranquilly to exile.

"Lily!" he exclaimed, with a note of despairing appeal; but—"Oh, not
now," she gently admonished him; and then, in all the sweetness of her
recovered composure: "Since I must find shelter somewhere, and since
you're so kindly here to help me —"

He gathered himself up at the challenge. "You will do as I tell you?
There's but one thing, then; you must go straight to your cousins, the
Stepneys."

"Oh—" broke from her with a movement of instinctive resistance; but
he insisted: "Come—it's late, and you must appear to have gone there
directly."

He had drawn her hand into his arm, but she held him back with a last gesture of protest. "I can't—I can't—not that—you don't know Gwen: you mustn't ask me."

"I *must* ask you—you must obey me," he persisted, though infected at heart by her own fear.

Her voice sank to a whisper: "And if she refuses?"—but, "Oh, trust me —trust me!" he could only insist in return; and yielding to his touch, she let him lead her back in silence to the edge of the square.

In the cab they continued to remain silent through the brief drive which carried them to the illuminated portals of the Stepneys' hotel. Here he left her outside, in the darkness of the raised hood, while his name was sent up to Stepney, and he paced the showy hall, awaiting the latter's descent. Ten minutes later the two men passed out together between the gold-laced custodians of the threshold; but in the vestibule Stepney drew up with a last flare of reluctance.

"It's understood, then?" he stipulated nervously, with his hand on Selden's arm. "She leaves tomorrow by the early train—and my wife's asleep, and can't be disturbed."

19

THE blinds of Mrs. Peniston's drawing-room were drawn down against the oppressive June sun, and in the sultry twilight the faces of her assembled relatives took on a fitting shadow of bereavement.

They were all there: Van Alstynes, Stepneys and Melsons—even a stray Peniston or two, indicating, by a greater latitude in dress and manner, the fact of remoter relationship and more settled hopes. The Peniston side was, in fact, secure in the knowledge that the bulk of Mr. Peniston's property "went back"; while the direct connection hung suspended on the disposal of his widow's private fortune and on the uncertainty of its extent. Jack Stepney, in his new character as the richest nephew, tacitly took the lead, emphasizing his importance by the deeper gloss of his mourning and the subdued authority of his manner; while his wife's bored attitude and frivolous gown proclaimed the heiress's disregard of the insignificant interests at stake. Old Ned Van Alstyne, seated next to her in a coat that made affliction dapper, twirled his white moustache to conceal the eager twitch of his lips; and Grace Stepney, red-nosed and smelling of crape, whispered emotionally to Mrs. Herbert Melson: "I couldn't *bear* to see the Niagara anywhere else!"

A rustle of weeds and quick turning of heads hailed the opening of the door, and Lily Bart appeared, tall and noble in her black dress, with Gerty Farish at her side. The women's faces, as she paused interrogatively on the threshold, were a study in hesitation. One or two made faint motions of recognition, which might have been subdued either by the solemnity of the scene, or by the doubt as to how far the others meant to go; Mrs. Jack Stepney gave a careless nod, and Grace Stepney, with a sepulchral gesture, indicated a seat at her side. But Lily, ignoring the invitation, as well as Jack Stepney's official attempt to direct her, moved across the room with her smooth free gait, and seated herself in a chair which seemed to have been purposely placed apart from the others.

It was the first time that she had faced her family since her return from Europe, two weeks earlier; but if she perceived any uncertainty in their welcome, it served only to add a tinge of irony to the usual composure of her bearing. The shock of dismay with which, on the dock, she had heard from Gerty Farish of Mrs. Peniston's sudden death, had been mitigated, almost at once, by the irrepressible thought that now, at last, she would be able to pay her debts. She had looked forward with considerable uneasiness to her first encounter with her aunt. Mrs. Peniston had vehemently opposed her niece's departure with the Dorsets, and had marked her continued disapproval by not writing during Lily's absence. The certainty that she had heard of the rupture with the Dorsets made the prospect of the meeting more formidable; and how should Lily have repressed a quick sense of relief at the thought that, instead of undergoing the anticipated ordeal, she had only to enter gracefully on a long-assured inheritance? It had been, in the consecrated phrase, "always understood" that Mrs. Peniston was to provide handsomely for her niece; and in the latter's mind the understanding had long since crystallized into fact.

"She gets everything, of course—I don't see what we're here for," Mrs. Jack Stepney remarked with careless loudness to Ned Van Alstyne; and the latter's deprecating murmur—"Julia was always a just woman"—might have been interpreted as signifying either acquiescence or doubt.

"Well, it's only about four hundred thousand," Mrs. Stepney rejoined with a yawn; and Grace Stepney, in the silence produced by the lawyer's preliminary cough, was heard to sob out: "They won't find a towel missing —I went over them with her the very day —"

Lily, oppressed by the close atmosphere, and the stifling odor of fresh mourning, felt her attention straying as Mrs. Peniston's lawyer, solemnly erect behind the Buhl table at the end of the room, began to rattle through the preamble of the will.

"It's like being in church," she reflected, wondering vaguely where Gwen Stepney had got such an awful hat. Then she noticed how stout Jack had grown—he would soon be almost as plethoric as Herbert Melson, who sat a few feet off, breathing puffily as he leaned his black-gloved hands on his stick.

"I wonder why rich people always grow fat—I suppose it's because there's nothing to worry them. If I inherit, I shall have to be careful of my figure," she mused, while the lawyer droned on through a labyrinth of legacies. The servants came first, then a few charitable institutions, then several remoter Melsons and Stepneys, who stirred consciously as their names rang out, and then subsided into a state of impassiveness befitting the solemnity of the occasion. Ned Van Alstyne, Jack Stepney, and a cousin or two followed, each coupled with the mention of a few thousands: Lily wondered that Grace Stepney was not among them. Then she heard her own name— "to my niece Lily Bart ten thousand dollars—" and after that the lawyer again lost himself in a coil of unintelligible periods, from which the concluding phrase flashed out with startling distinctness: "and the residue of my estate to my dear cousin and namesake, Grace Julia Stepney."

There was a subdued gasp of surprise, a rapid turning of heads, and a surging of sable figures toward the corner in which Miss Stepney wailed out her sense of unworthiness through the crumpled ball of a black-edged handkerchief.

Lily stood apart from the general movement, feeling herself for the first time utterly alone. No one looked at her, no one seemed aware of her presence; she was probing the very depths of insignificance. And under her sense of the collective indifference came the acuter pang of hopes deceived. Disinherited—she had been disinherited—and for Grace Stepney! She met Gerty's lamentable eyes, fixed on her in a despairing effort at consolation, and the look brought her to herself. There was something to be done before she left the house: to be done with all the nobility she knew how to put into such gestures. She advanced to the group about Miss Stepney, and holding out her hand said simply: "Dear Grace, I am so glad."

The other ladies had fallen back at her approach, and a space created itself about her. It widened as she turned to go, and no one advanced to fill it up. She paused a moment, glancing about her, calmly taking the measure of her situation. She heard someone ask a question about the date of the will; she caught a fragment of the lawyer's answer—something about a sudden summons, and an "earlier instrument." Then the tide of dispersal began to drift past her; Mrs. Jack Stepney and Mrs. Herbert Melson stood on the doorstep awaiting their motor; a sympathizing group escorted Grace Stepney to the cab it was felt to be fitting she should take, though she lived but a street or two away; and Miss Bart and Gerty found themselves almost alone in the purple drawing-room, which more than ever, in its stuffy dimness, resembled a well-kept family vault, in which the last corpse had just been decently deposited.

In Gerty Farish's sitting-room, whither a hansom had carried the two friends, Lily dropped into a chair with a faint sound of laughter: it struck her as a humorous coincidence that her aunt's legacy should so nearly represent the amount of her debt to Trenor. The need of discharging that debt had reasserted itself with increased urgency since her return to America, and she spoke her first thought in saying to the anxiously hovering Gerty: "I wonder when the legacies will be paid."

But Miss Farish could not pause over the legacies; she broke into a larger indignation. "Oh, Lily, it's unjust; it's cruel—Grace Stepney must *feel* she has no right to all that money!"

"Any one who knew how to please Aunt Julia has a right to her money," Miss Bart rejoined philosophically.

"But she was devoted to you—she led everyone to think —" Gerty checked herself in evident embarrassment, and Miss Bart turned to her with a direct look. "Gerty, be honest: this will was made only six weeks ago. She had heard of my break with the Dorsets?"

"Every one heard, of course, that there had been some disagreement—some misunderstanding —"

"Did she hear that Bertha turned me off the yacht?"

"Lily!"

"That was what happened, you know. She said I was trying to marry George Dorset. She did it to make him think she was jealous. Isn't that what she told Gwen Stepney?"

"I don't know—I don't listen to such horrors."

"I *must* listen to them—I must know where I stand." She paused, and again sounded a faint note of derision. "Did you notice the women? They were afraid to snub me while they thought I was going to get the money—afterward they scuttled off as if I had the plague." Gerty remained silent, and she continued: "I stayed on to see what would happen. They took their cue from Gwen Stepney and Lulu Melson—I saw them watching to see what Gwen would do. Gerty, I must know just what is being said of me."

"I tell you I don't listen —"

"One hears such things without listening." She rose and laid her resolute hands on Miss Farish's shoulders. "Gerty, are people going to cut me?"

"Your *friends*, Lily—how can you think it?"

"Who are one's friends at such a time? Who, but you, you poor trustful darling? And heaven knows what *you* suspect me of!" She kissed Gerty with a whimsical murmur. "You'd never let it make any difference—but then you're fond of criminals, Gerty! How about the irreclaimable ones, though? For I'm absolutely impenitent, you know."

She drew herself up to the full height of her slender majesty, towering like some dark angel of defiance above the troubled Gerty, who could only falter out: "Lily, Lily—how can you laugh about such things?"

"So as not to weep, perhaps. But no—I'm not of the tearful order. I discovered early that crying makes my nose red, and the knowledge has helped me through several painful episodes." She took a restless turn about the room, and then, reseating herself, lifted the bright mockery of her eyes to Gerty's anxious countenance.

"I shouldn't have minded, you know, if I'd got the money—" and at Miss Farish's protesting "Oh!" she repeated calmly: "Not a straw, my dear; for, in the first place, they wouldn't have quite dared to ignore me; and if they had, it wouldn't have mattered, because I should have been independent of them. But now—!" The irony faded from her eyes, and she bent a clouded face upon her friend.

"How can you talk so, Lily? Of course the money ought to have been yours, but after all that makes no difference. The important thing —" Gerty paused, and then continued firmly: "The important thing is that you should clear yourself—should tell your friends the whole truth."

"The whole truth?" Miss Bart laughed. "What is truth? Where a woman is concerned, it's the story that's easiest to believe. In this case it's a great deal easier to believe Bertha Dorset's story than mine, because she has a big house and an opera-box, and it's convenient to be on good terms with her."

Miss Farish still fixed her with an anxious gaze. "But what is your story, Lily? I don't believe anyone knows it yet."

"My story?—I don't believe I know it myself. You see I never thought of preparing a version in advance as Bertha did—and if I had, I don't think I should take the trouble to use it now."

But Gerty continued with her quiet reasonableness: "I don't want a version prepared in advance—but I want you to tell me exactly what happened from the beginning."

"From the beginning?" Miss Bart gently mimicked her. "Dear Gerty, how little imagination you good people have! Why, the beginning was in my cradle, I suppose—in the way I was brought up, and the things I was taught to care for. Or no—I won't blame anybody for my faults: I'll say it was in my blood, that I got it from some wicked pleasure-loving ancestress, who reacted against the homely virtues of New Amsterdam, and wanted to be back at the court of the Charleses!" And as Miss Farish continued to press her with troubled eyes, she went on impatiently: "You asked me just now for the truth—well, the truth about any girl is that once she's talked about she's done for; and the more she explains her case the worse it looks. —My good Gerty, you don't happen to have a cigarette about you?"

In her stuffy room at the hotel to which she had gone on landing, Lily Bart that evening reviewed her situation. It was the last week in June, and none of her friends were in town. The few relatives who had stayed on, or returned, for the reading of Mrs. Peniston's will, had taken flight again that afternoon to Newport or Long Island; and not one of them had made any offer of hospitality to Lily. For the first time in her life she found herself utterly alone except for Gerty Farish. Even at the actual moment of her break with the Dorsets she had not had so keen a sense of its consequences, for the duchess of Beltshire, hearing of the catastrophe from Lord Hubert, had instantly offered her protection, and under her sheltering wing Lily had made an almost triumphant progress to London. There she had been sorely tempted to linger on in a society which asked of her only to amuse and charm it, without inquiring too curiously how she had acquired her gift for doing so; but Selden, before they parted, had pressed on her the urgent need of returning at once to her aunt, and Lord Hubert, when he presently reappeared in London, abounded in the same counsel. Lily did not need to be told that the duchess's championship was not the best road to social rehabilitation and as she was besides aware that her noble defender might at any moment drop her in favor of a new protégée, she reluctantly decided to return to America. But she had not been ten minutes on her native shore before she realized that she had delayed too long to regain it. The Dorsets, the Stepneys, the Brys—all the actors and witnesses in the miserable drama —had preceded her with their version of the case; and, even had she seen the least chance of gaining a hearing for her own, some obscure disdain and reluctance would have restrained her. She knew it was not by explanations and countercharges that she could ever hope to recover her lost standing; but even had she felt the least trust in their efficacy, she would still have been held back by the feeling which had kept her from defending herself to Gerty Farish—a feeling that was half pride and half humiliation. For though she knew she had been ruthlessly sacrificed to Bertha Dorset's determination to win back her husband, and though her own relation to Dorset had been that of the merest good-fellowship, yet she had been perfectly aware from the outset that her part in the affair was, as Carry Fisher brutally put it, to distract Dorset's attention from his wife. That was what she was "there for": it was the price she had chosen to pay for three months of luxury and freedom from care. Her habit of resolutely facing the facts, in her rare moments of introspection, did not now allow her to put any false gloss on the situation. She had suffered for the very faithfullness with which she had carried out her part of the tacit compact, but the part was not a handsome-one at best, and she saw it now in all the ugliness of failure.

She saw, too, in the same uncompromising light, the train of conse-quences resulting from that failure; and these became clearer to her with every day of her weary lingering in town. She stayed on partly for the comfort of Gerty Farish's nearness, and partly for lack of knowing where to go. She understood well enough the nature of the task before her. She must set out to regain, little by little, the position she had lost; and the first step in the tedious task was to find out, as soon as possible, on how many of her friends she could count. Her hopes were mainly centered on Mrs. Trenor, who had treasures of easygoing tolerance for those who were amusing or useful to her, and in the noisy rush of whose existence the still small voice of detraction was slow to make itself heard. But Judy, though she must have been apprised of Miss Bart's return, had not even recognized it by the formal

note of condolence which her friend's bereavement demanded. Any advance on Lily's side might have been perilous: there was nothing to do but
to trust to the happy chance of an accidental meeting, and Lily knew that,
even so late in the season, there was always a hope of running across her
friends in their frequent passages through town.

To this end she assiduously showed herself at the restaurants they frequented, where, attended by the troubled Gerty, she lunched luxuriously, as
she said, on her expectations.

"My dear Gerty, you wouldn't have me let the headwaiter see that I've
nothing to live on but Aunt Julia's legacy? Think of Grace Stepney's satisfaction if she came in and found us lunching on cold mutton and tea! What
sweet shall we have today, dear—*Coupe Jacques* or *Pêches à la Melba?*"

She dropped the menu abruptly, with a quick heightening of color, and
Gerty, following her glance, was aware of the advance, from an inner room,
of a party headed by Mrs. Trenor and Carry Fisher. It was impossible for
these ladies and their companions—among whom Lily had at once distinguished both Trenor and Rosedale—not to pass, in going out, the table at
which the two girls were seated; and Gerty's sense of the fact betrayed itself
in the helpless trepidation of her manner.

Miss Bart, on the contrary, borne forward on the wave of her buoyant
grace, and neither shrinking from her friends nor appearing to lie in wait for
them, gave to the encounter the touch of naturalness which she could
impart to the most strained situations. Such embarrassment as was shown
was on Mrs. Trenor's side, and manifested itself in the mingling of exaggerated warmth with imperceptible reservations. Her loudly affirmed pleasure
at seeing Miss Bart took the form of a nebulous generalization, which included neither inquiries as to her future nor the expression of a definite wish
to see her again.

Lily, well-versed in the language of these omissions, knew that they
were equally intelligible to the other members of the party: even Rosedale,
flushed as he was with the importance of keeping such company, at once
took the temperature of Mrs. Trenor's cordiality, and reflected it in his
offhand greeting of Miss Bart. Trenor, red and uncomfortable, had cut short
his salutations on the pretext of a word to say to the headwaiter; and the
rest of the group soon melted away in Mrs. Trenor's wake.

It was over in a moment—the waiter, menu in hand, still hung on the
result of the choice between *Coupe Jacques* and *Pêches à la Melba*—but Miss
Bart, in the interval, had taken the measure of her fate. Where Judy Trenor
led, all the world would follow; and Lily had the doomed sense of the
castaway who has signalled in vain to fleeing sails.

In a flash she remembered Mrs. Trenor's complaints of Carry Fisher's
rapacity, and saw that they denoted an unexpected acquaintance with her
husband's private affairs. In the large tumultuous disorder of the life at
Bellomont, where no one seemed to have time to observe anyone else, and

private aims and personal interests were swept along unheeded in the rush of collective activities, Lily had fancied herself sheltered from inconvenient scrutiny; but if Judy knew when Mrs. Fisher borrowed money of her husband, was she likely to ignore the same transaction on Lily's part? If she was careless of his affections she was plainly jealous of his pocket; and in that fact Lily read the explanation of her rebuff. The immediate result of these conclusions was the passionate resolve to pay back her debt to Trenor. That obligation discharged, she would have but a thousand dollars of Mrs. Peniston's legacy left, and nothing to live on but her own small income, which was considerably less than Gerty Farish's wretched pittance; but this consideration gave way to the imperative claim of her wounded pride. She must be quits with the Trenors first; after that she would take thought for the future.

In her ignorance of legal procrastinations she had supposed that her legacy would be paid over within a few days of the reading of her aunt's will; and after an interval of anxious suspense, she wrote to inquire the cause of the delay. There was another interval before Mrs. Peniston's lawyer, who was also one of the executors, replied to the effect that, some questions having arisen relative to the interpretation of the will, he and his associates might not be in a position to pay the legacies till the close of the twelve-month legally allotted for their settlement. Bewildered and indignant, Lily resolved to try the effect of a personal appeal; but she returned from her expedition with a sense of the powerlessness of beauty and charm against the unfeeling process of the law. It seemed intolerable to live on for another year under the weight of her debt; and in her extremity she decided to turn to Miss Stepney, who still lingered in town, immersed in the delectable duty of "going over" her benefactress's effects. It was bitter enough for Lily to ask a favor of Grace Stepney, but the alternative was bitterer still; and one morning she presented herself at Mrs. Peniston's, where Grace, for the facilitation of her pious task, had taken up a provisional abode.

The strangeness of entering as a suppliant the house where she had so long commanded, increased Lily's desire to shorten the ordeal; and when Miss Stepney entered the darkened drawing-room, rustling with the best quality of crape, her visitor went straight to the point: would she be willing to advance the amount of the expected legacy?

Grace, in reply, wept and wondered at the request, bemoaned the inexorableness of the law, and was astonished that Lily had not realized the exact similarity of their positions. Did she think that only the payment of the legacies had been delayed? Why, Miss Stepney herself had not received a penny of her inheritance, and was paying rent—yes, actually—for the privilege of living in a house that belonged to her. She was sure it was not what poor dear cousin Julia would have wished—she had told the executors so to their faces; but they were inaccessible to reason, and there was nothing to do but to wait. Let Lily take example by her and be patient—let them both remember how beautifully patient cousin Julia had always been.

Lily made a movement which showed her imperfect assimilation of this example. "But you will have everything, Grace—it would be easy for you to borrow ten times the amount I am asking for."

"Borrow—easy for me to borrow?" Grace Stepney rose up before her in sable wrath. "Do you imagine for a moment that I would raise money on my expectations from cousin Julia, when I know so well her unspeakable horror of every transaction of the sort? Why, Lily, if you must know the truth, it was the idea of your being in debt that brought on her illness—you remember she had a slight attack before you sailed. Oh, I don't know the particulars, of course—I don't want to know them—but there were rumors about your affairs that made her most unhappy—no one could be with her without seeing that. I can't help it if you are offended by my telling you this now—if I can do anything to make you realize the folly of your course, and how deeply she disapproved of it, I shall feel it is the truest way of making up to you for her loss."

20

IT seemed to Lily, as Mrs. Peniston's door closed on her, that she was taking a final leave of her old life. The future stretched before her dull and bare as the deserted length of Fifth Avenue, and opportunities showed as meagerly as the few cabs trailing in quest of fares that did not come. The completeness of the analogy was, however, disturbed as she reached the sidewalk by the rapid approach of a hansom which pulled up at sight of her.

From beneath its luggage-laden top, she caught the wave of a signaling hand; and the next moment Mrs. Fisher, springing to the street, had folded her in a demonstrative embrace.

"My dear, you don't mean to say you're still in town? When I saw you the other day at Sherry's I didn't have time to ask—" She broke off, and added with a burst of frankness: "The truth is I was *horrid*, Lily, and I've wanted to tell you so ever since."

"Oh—" Miss Bart protested, drawing back from her penitent clasp; but Mrs. Fisher went on with her usual directness: "Look here, Lily, don't let's beat about the bush: half the trouble in life is caused by pretending there isn't any. That's not my way, and I can only say I'm thoroughly ashamed of myself for following the other women's lead. But we'll talk of that by and by —tell me now where you're staying and what your plans are. I don't suppose you're keeping house in there with Grace Stepney, eh?—and it struck me you might be rather at loose ends."

In Lily's present mood there was no resisting the honest friendliness of this appeal, and she said with a smile: "I *am* at loose ends for the moment, but Gerty Farish is still in town, and she's good enough to let me be with her whenever she can spare the time."

Mrs. Fisher made a slight grimace. "H'm—that's a temperate joy. Oh, I know—Gerty's a trump, and worth all the rest of us put together; but *à la longue* you're used to a little higher seasoning, aren't you, dear? And besides, I suppose she'll be off herself before long—the first of August, you say? Well, look here, you can't spend your summer in town; we'll talk of that later, too. But meanwhile, what do you say to putting a few things in a trunk and coming down with me to the Sam Gormers' tonight?"

And as Lily stared at the breathless suddenness of the suggestion, she continued with her easy laugh: "You don't know them and they don't know you; but that don't make a rap of difference. They've taken the Van Alstyne place at Roslyn, and I've got carte blanche to bring my friends down there —the more the merrier. They do things awfully well, and there's to be rather a jolly party there this week—" she broke off, checked by an undefinable change in Miss Bart's expression. "Oh, I don't mean *your* particular set, you know: rather a different crowd, but very good fun. The fact is, the Gormers have struck out on a line of their own: what they want is to have a good time, and to have it in their own way. They gave the other thing a few months' trial, under my distinguished auspices, and they were really doing extremely well—getting on a good deal faster than the Brys, just because they didn't care as much—but suddenly they decided that the whole business bored them, and that what they wanted was a crowd they could really feel at home with. Rather original of them, don't you think so? Mattie Gormer *has* got aspirations still; women always have; but she's awfully easygoing, and Sam won't be bothered, and they both like to be the most important people in sight, so they've started a sort of continuous performance of their own, a kind of social Coney Island, where everybody is welcome who can make noise enough and doesn't put on airs. *I* think it's awfully good fun myself—some of the artistic set, you know, any pretty actress that's going, and so on. This week, for instance, they have Audrey Anstell, who made such a hit last spring in *The Winning of Winny;* and Paul Morpeth—he's painting Mattie Gormer—and the Dick Bellingers, and Kate Corby—well, everyone you can think of who's jolly and makes a row. Now don't stand there with your nose in the air, my dear—it will be a good deal better than a broiling Sunday in town, and you'll find clever people as well as noisy ones—Morpeth, who admires Mattie enormously, always brings one or two of his set."

Mrs. Fisher drew Lily toward the hansom with friendly authority. "Jump in now, there's a dear, and we'll drive round to your hotel and have your things packed, and then we'll have tea, and the two maids can meet us at the train."

* * *

It was a good deal better than a broiling Sunday in town—of that no doubt remained to Lily as, reclining in the shade of a leafy verandah, she looked seaward across a stretch of greensward picturesquely dotted with groups of ladies in lace raiment and men in tennis flannels. The huge Van Alstyne house and its rambling dependencies were packed to their fullest capacity with the Gormers' weekend guests, who now, in the radiance of the Sunday forenoon, were dispersing themselves over the grounds in quest of the various distractions the place afforded: distractions ranging from tennis courts to shooting-galleries, from bridge and whiskey within doors to motors and steam-launches without. Lily had the odd sense of having been caught up into the crowd as carelessly as a passenger is gathered in by an express train. The blonde and genial Mrs. Gormer might, indeed, have figured the conductor, calmly assigning seats to the rush of travelers, while Carry Fisher represented the porter pushing their bags into place, giving them their numbers for the dining-car, and warning them when their station was at hand. The train, meanwhile, had scarcely slackened speed—life whizzed on with a deafening rattle and roar, in which one traveler at least found a welcome refuge from the sound of her own thoughts.

The Gormer milieu represented a social outskirt which Lily had always fastidiously avoided; but it struck her, now that she was in it, as only a flamboyant copy of her own world, a caricature approximating the real thing as the "society play" approaches the manners of the drawing-room. The people about her were doing the same things as the Trenors, the Van Osburghs and the Dorsets: the difference lay in a hundred shades of aspect and manner, from the pattern of the men's waistcoats to the inflection of the women's voices. Everything was pitched in a higher key, and there was more of each thing: more noise, more color, more champagne, more familiarity— but also greater good-nature, less rivalry, and a fresher capacity for enjoyment.

Miss Bart's arrival had been welcomed with an uncritical friendliness that first irritated her pride and then brought her to a sharp sense of her own situation—of the place in life which, for the moment, she must accept and make the best of. These people knew her story—of that her first long talk with Carry Fisher had left no doubt: she was publicly branded as the heroine of a "queer" episode—but instead of shrinking from her as her own friends had done, they received her without question into the easy promiscuity of their lives. They swallowed her past as easily as they did Miss Anstell's, and with no apparent sense of any difference in the size of the mouthful: all they asked was that she should—in her own way, for they recognized a diversity of gifts—contribute as much to the general amusement as that graceful actress, whose talents, when off the stage, were of the most varied order. Lily felt at once that any tendency to be "stuck-up," to mark a sense of differences and distinctions, would be fatal to her continuance in the Gormer set. To be taken in on such terms—and into such a world!—was hard enough to the lingering pride in her; but she realized, with a pang of self-contempt, that to be excluded from it would, after all, be harder still. For, almost at once, she had felt the insidious charm of slipping back into a life where every material difficulty was smoothed away. The sudden escape from a stifling hotel in a dusty deserted city to the space and luxury of a great country house fanned by sea breezes, had produced a state of moral lassitude agreeable enough after the nervous tension and physical discomfort of the past weeks. For the moment she must yield to the refreshment her senses craved—after that she would reconsider her situation, and take counsel with her dignity. Her enjoyment of her surroundings was, indeed, tinged by the unpleasant consideration that she was accepting the hospitality and courting the approval of people she had disdained under other conditions. But she was growing less sensitive on such points: a hard glaze of indifference was fast forming over her delicacies and susceptibilities, and each concession to expediency hardened the surface a little more.

On the Monday, when the party disbanded with uproarious adieux, the return to town threw into stronger relief the charms of the life she was leaving. The other guests were dispersing to take up the same existence in a different setting: some at Newport, some at Bar Harbor, some in the elaborate rusticity of an Adirondack camp. Even Gerty Farish, who welcomed Lily's return with tender solicitude, would soon be preparing to join the aunt with whom she spent her summers on Lake George: only Lily herself remained without plan or purpose, stranded in a backwater of the great current of pleasure. But Carry Fisher, who had insisted on transporting her to her own house, where she herself was to perch for a day or two on the way to the Brys' camp, came to the rescue with a new suggestion.

"Look here, Lily—I'll tell you what it is: I want you to take my place with Mattie Gormer this summer. They're taking a party out to Alaska next month in their private car, and Mattie, who is the laziest woman alive, wants me to go with them, and relieve her of the bother of arranging things; but the Brys want me too—oh, yes, we've made it up: didn't I tell you?— and, to put it frankly, though I like the Gormers best, there's more profit for me in the Brys. The fact is, they want to try Newport this summer, and if I can make it a success for them they—well, they'll make it a success for *me*." Mrs. Fisher clasped her hands enthusiastically. "Do you know, Lily, the more I think of my idea the better I like it—quite as much for you as for myself. The Gormers have both taken a tremendous fancy to you, and the trip to Alaska is—well—the very thing I should want for you just at present."

Miss Bart lifted her eyes with a keen glance. "To take me out of my friends' way, you mean?" she said quietly; and Mrs. Fisher responded with a deprecating kiss: "To keep you out of their sight till they realize how much they miss you."

* * *

Miss Bart went with the Gormers to Alaska; and the expedition, if it did not produce the effect anticipated by her friend, had at least the negative advantage of removing her from the fiery center of criticism and discussion. Gerty Farish had opposed the plan with all the energy of her somewhat inarticulate nature. She had even offered to give up her visit to Lake George, and remain in town with Miss Bart, if the latter would renounce her journey; but Lily could disguise her real distaste for this plan under a sufficiently valid reason.

"You dear innocent, don't you see," she protested, "that Carry is quite right, and that I must take up my usual life, and go about among people as much as possible? If my old friends choose to believe lies about me I shall have to make new ones, that's all; and you know beggars mustn't be choosers. Not that I don't like Mattie Gormer—I *do* like her: she's kind and honest and unaffected; and don't you suppose I feel grateful to her for making me welcome at a time when, as you've yourself seen, my own family have unanimously washed their hands of me?"

Gerty shook her head, mutely unconvinced. She felt not only that Lily was cheapening herself by making use of an intimacy she would never have cultivated from choice, but that, in drifting back now to her former manner of life, she was forfeiting her last chance of ever escaping from it. Gerty had but an obscure conception of what Lily's actual experience had been: but its consequences had established a lasting hold on her pity since the memorable night when she had offered up her own secret hope to her friend's extremity. To characters like Gerty's such a sacrifice constitutes a moral claim on the part of the person in whose behalf it has been made. Having once helped Lily, she must continue to help her; and helping her, must believe in her, because faith is the mainspring of such natures. But even if Miss Bart, after her renewed taste of the amenities of life, could have returned to the barrenness of a New York August, mitigated only by poor Gerty's presence, her worldly wisdom would have counselled her against such an act of abnegation. She knew that Carry Fisher was right: that an opportune absence might be the first step toward rehabilitation, and that, at any rate, to linger on in town out of season was a fatal admission of defeat.

From the Gormers' tumultuous progress across their native continent, she returned with an altered view of her situation. The renewed habit of luxury—the daily waking to an assured absence of care and presence of material ease—gradually blunted her appreciation of these values, and left her more conscious of the void they could not fill. Mattie Gormer's undiscriminating good-nature, and the slapdash sociability of her friends, who treated Lily precisely as they treated each other—all these characteristic notes of difference began to wear upon her endurance; and the more she saw to criticize in her companions, the less justification she found for making use of them. The longing to get back to her former surroundings hardened to a fixed idea; but with the strengthening of her purpose came the inevitable perception that, to attain it, she must exact fresh concessions from her pride. These, for the moment, took the unpleasant form of continuing to cling to her hosts after their return from Alaska. Little as she was in the key of their milieu, her immense social facility, her long habit of adapting herself to others without suffering her own outline to be blurred, the skilled manipulation of all the polished implements of her craft, had won for her an important place in the Gormer group. If their resonant hilarity could never be hers, she contributed a note of easy elegance more valuable to Mattie Gormer than the louder passages of the band. Sam Gormer and his special cronies stood indeed a little in awe of her; but Mattie's following, headed by Paul Morpeth, made her feel that they prized her for the very qualities they most conspicuously lacked. If Morpeth, whose social indolence was as great as his artistic activity, had abandoned himself to the easy current of the Gormer existence, where the minor exactions of politeness were unknown or ignored, and a man could either break his engagements, or keep them in a painting-jacket and slippers, he still preserved his sense of differences, and his appreciation of graces he had no time to cultivate. During the preparations for the Brys' tableaux he had been immensely struck by Lily's plastic possibilities—"not the face: too self-controlled for expression; but the rest of her—gad, what a model she'd make!"—and though his abhorrence of the world in which he had seen her was too great for him to think of seeking her there, he was fully alive to the privilege of having her to look at and listen to while he lounged in Mattie Gormer's dishevelled drawing-room.

Lily had thus formed, in the tumult of her surroundings, a little nucleus of friendly relations which mitigated the crudeness of her course in lingering with the Gormers after their return. Nor was she without pale glimpses of her own world, especially since the breaking-up of the Newport season had set the social current once more toward Long Island. Kate Corby, whose tastes made her as promiscuous as Carry Fisher was rendered by her necessities, occasionally descended on the Gormers, where, after a first stare of surprise, she took Lily's presence almost too much as a matter of course. Mrs. Fisher, too, appearing frequently in the neighborhood, drove over to impart her experiences and give Lily what she called the latest report from the weather bureau; and the latter, who had never directly invited her confidence, could yet talk with her more freely than with Gerty Farish, in whose presence it was impossible even to admit the existence of much that Mrs. Fisher conveniently took for granted.

Mrs. Fisher, moreover, had no embarrassing curiosity. She did not wish to probe the inwardness of Lily's situation, but simply to view it from the outside, and draw her conclusions accordingly; and these conclusions, at the end of a confidential talk, she summed up to her friend in the succinct remark: "You must marry as soon as you can."

Lily uttered a faint laugh—for once Mrs. Fisher lacked originality. "Do you mean, like Gerty Farish, to recommend the unfailing panacea of 'a good man's love'?"

"No—I don't think either of my candidates would answer to that description," said Mrs. Fisher after a pause of reflection.

"Either? Are there actually two?"

"Well, perhaps I ought to say one and a half—for the moment."

Miss Bart received this with increasing amusement. "Other things being equal, I think I should prefer a half-husband: who is he?"

"Don't fly out at me till you hear my reasons—George Dorset."

"Oh—" Lily murmured reproachfully; but Mrs. Fisher pressed on unrebuffed. "Well, why not? They had a few weeks' honeymoon when they first got back from Europe, but now things are going badly with them again. Bertha has been behaving more than ever like a madwoman, and George's powers of credulity are very nearly exhausted. They're at their place here, you know, and I spent last Sunday with them. It was a ghastly party—no one else but poor Neddy Silverton, who looks like a galley-slave (they used to talk of my making that poor boy unhappy!)—and after luncheon George carried me off on a long walk, and told me the end would have to come soon."

Miss Bart made an incredulous gesture. "As far as that goes, the end will never come—Bertha will always know how to get him back when she wants him."

Mrs. Fisher continued to observe her tentatively. "Not if he has anyone else to turn to! Yes—that's just what it comes to: the poor creature can't stand alone. And I remember him such a good fellow, full of life and enthusiasm." She paused, and went on, dropping her glance from Lily's: "He wouldn't stay with her ten minutes if he *knew*—"

"Knew—?" Miss Bart repeated.

"What *you* must, for instance—with the opportunities you've had! If he had positive proof, I mean—"

Lily interrupted her with a deep blush of displeasure. "Please let us drop the subject, Carry: it's too odious to me." And to divert her companion's attention she added, with an attempt at lightness: "And your second candidate? We must not forget him."

Mrs. Fisher echoed her laugh. "I wonder if you'll cry out just as loud if I say—Sim Rosedale?"

Miss Bart did not cry out: she sat silent, gazing thoughtfully at her friend. The suggestion, in truth, gave expression to a possibility which, in the last weeks, had more than once recurred to her; but after a moment she said carelessly: "Mr. Rosedale wants a wife who can establish him in the bosom of the Van Osburghs and Trenors."

Mrs. Fisher caught her up eagerly. "And so *you* could—with his money! Don't you see how beautifully it would work out for you both?"

"I don't see any way of making him see it," Lily returned, with a laugh intended to dismiss the subject.

But in reality it lingered with her long after Mrs. Fisher had taken leave. She had seen very little of Rosedale since her annexation by the Gormers, for he was still steadily bent on penetrating to the inner Paradise from which she was now excluded; but once or twice, when nothing better offered, he had turned up for a Sunday, and on these occasions he had left her in no doubt as to his view of her situation. That he still admired her was, more than ever, offensively evident; for in the Gormer circle, where he expanded as in his native element, there were no puzzling conventions to check the full expression of his approval. But it was in the quality of his admiration that she read his shrewd estimate of her case. He enjoyed letting the Gormers see that he had known "Miss Lily"—she was "Miss Lily" to him now—before they had had the faintest social existence: enjoyed more especially impressing Paul Morpeth with the distance to which their intimacy dated back. But he let it be felt that intimacy was a mere ripple on the surface of a rushing social current, the kind of relaxation which a man of large interests and manifold preoccupations permits himself in his hours of ease.

The necessity of accepting this view of their past relation, and of meeting it in the key of pleasantry prevalent among her new friends, was deeply humiliating to Lily. But she dared less than ever to quarrel with Rosedale. She suspected that her rejection rankled among the most unforgettable of his rebuffs, and the fact that he knew something of her wretched transaction with Trenor, and was sure to put the basest construction on it, seemed to place her hopelessly in his power. Yet at Carry Fisher's suggestion a new hope had stirred in her. Much as she disliked Rosedale, she no longer absolutely despised him. For he was gradually attaining his object in life, and that, to Lily, was always less despicable than to miss it. With the slow unalterable persistency which she had always felt in him, he was making his way through the dense mass of social antagonisms. Already his wealth, and the masterly use he had made of it, were giving him an enviable prominence in the world of affairs, and placing Wall Street under obligations which only Fifth Avenue could repay. In response to these claims, his name began to figure on municipal committees and charitable boards; he appeared at banquets to distinguished strangers, and his candidacy at one of the fashionable clubs was discussed with diminishing opposition. He had figured once or twice at the Trenor dinners, and had learned to speak with just the right note of disdain of the big Van Osburgh crushes; and all he now needed was a wife whose affiliations would shorten the last tedious steps of his ascent. It was with that object that, a year earlier, he had fixed his affections on Miss Bart; but in the interval he had mounted nearer to the goal, while she had lost the power to abbreviate the remaining steps of the way. All this she saw with the clearness of vision that came to her in moments of despondency. It was success that dazzled her—she could distinguish facts plainly enough in the twilight of failure. And the twilight, as she now sought to pierce it, was gradually lighted by a faint spark of reassurance. Under the utilitarian motive of Rosedale's wooing she had felt, clearly enough, the heat of personal inclination. She would not have detested him so heartily had she not known that he dared to admire her. What, then, if the passion persisted, though the other motive had ceased to sustain it? She had never even tried to please him—he had been drawn to her in spite of her manifest disdain. What if she now chose to exert the power which, even in its passive state, he had felt so strongly? What if she made him marry her for love, now that he had no other reason for marrying her?

21

As became persons of their rising consequence, the Gormers were engaged in building a country house on Long Island; and it was a part of Miss Bart's duty to attend her hostess on frequent visits of inspection to the new estate. There, while Mrs. Gormer plunged into problems of lighting and sanitation, Lily had leisure to wander, in the bright autumn air, along the tree-fringed bay to which the land declined. Little as she was addicted to solitude, there had come to be moments when it seemed a welcome escape from the empty noises of her life. She was weary of being swept passively along a current of pleasure and business in which she had no share; weary of seeing other people pursue amusement and squander money, while she felt herself of no more account among them than an expensive toy in the hands of a spoiled child.

It was in this frame of mind that, striking back from the shore one morning into the windings of an unfamiliar lane, she came suddenly upon the figure of George Dorset. The Dorset place was in the immediate neighborhood of the Gormers' newly acquired estate, and in her motor-flights thither with Mrs. Gormer, Lily had caught one or two passing glimpses of the couple; but they moved in so different an orbit that she had not considered the possibility of a direct encounter.

Dorset, swinging along with bent head, in moody abstraction, did not see Miss Bart till he was close upon her; but the sight, instead of bringing him to a halt as she had half-expected, sent him toward her with an eagerness which found expression in his opening words.

"Miss Bart!—You'll shake hands, won't you? I've been hoping to meet you—I should have written to you if I'd dared." His face, with its tossed red hair and straggling moustache, had a driven uneasy look, as though life had become an unceasing race between himself and the thoughts at his heels.

The look drew a word of compassionate greeting from Lily, and he pressed on, as if encouraged by her tone: "I wanted to apologize—to ask you to forgive me for the miserable part I played—"

She checked him with a quick gesture. "Don't let us speak of it: I was very sorry for you," she said, with a tinge of disdain which, as she instantly perceived, was not lost on him.

He flushed to his haggard eyes, flushed so cruelly that she repented the thrust. "You might well be; you don't know—you must let me explain. I was deceived: abominably deceived—"

"I am still more sorry for you, then," she interposed, without irony; "but you must see that I am not exactly the person with whom the subject can be discussed."

He met this with a look of genuine wonder. "Why not? Isn't it to you, of all people, that I owe an explanation—"

"No explanation is necessary: the situation was perfectly clear to me."

"Ah—" he murmured, his head drooping again, and his irresolute hand switching at the underbrush along the lane. But as Lily made a movement to pass on, he broke out with fresh vehemence: "Miss Bart, for God's sake don't turn from me! We used to be good friends—you were always kind to me—and you don't know how I need a friend now."

The lamentable weakness of the words roused a motion of pity in Lily's breast. She too needed friends—she had tasted the pang of loneliness; and her resentment of Bertha Dorset's cruelty softened her heart to the poor wretch who was after all the chief of Bertha's victims.

"I still wish to be kind; I feel no ill-will toward you," she said. "But you must understand that after what has happened we can't be friends again—we can't see each other."

"Ah, you *are* kind—you're merciful—you always were!" He fixed his miserable gaze on her. "But why can't we be friends—why not, when I've repented in dust and ashes? Isn't it hard that you should condemn me to suffer for the falseness, the treachery of others? I was punished enough at the time—is there to be no respite for me?"

"I should have thought you had found complete respite in the reconciliation which was effected at my expense," Lily began, with renewed impatience; but he broke in imploringly: "Don't put it in that way—that's been the worst of my punishment. My God! what could I do—wasn't I powerless? You were singled out as a sacrifice: any word I might have said would have been turned against you—"

"I have told you I don't blame you; all I ask you to understand is that, after the use Bertha chose to make of me—after all that her behavior has since implied—it's impossible that you and I should meet."

He continued to stand before her, in his dogged weakness. "Is it—need it be? Mightn't there be circumstances—?" he checked himself, slashing at the wayside weeds in a wider radius. Then he began again: "Miss Bart, listen —give me a minute. If we're not to meet again, at least let me have a hearing now. You say we can't be friends after—after what has happened. But can't I at least appeal to your pity? Can't I move you if I ask you to think of me as a prisoner—a prisoner you alone can set free?"

Lily's inward start betrayed itself in a quick blush: was it possible that this was really the sense of Carry Fisher's adumbrations?

"I can't see how I can possibly be of any help to you," she murmured, drawing back a little from the mounting excitement of his look.

Her tone seemed to sober him, as it had so often done in his stormiest moments. The stubborn lines of his face relaxed, and he said, with an abrupt drop to docility: "You *would* see, if you'd be as merciful as you used to be: and heaven knows I've never needed it more!"

She paused a moment, moved in spite of herself by this reminder of her influence over him. Her fibers had been softened by suffering, and the sudden glimpse into his mocked and broken life disarmed her contempt for his weakness.

"I am very sorry for you—I would help you willingly; but you must have other friends, other advisers."

"I never had a friend like you," he answered simply. "And besides— can't you see?—you're the only person"—his voice dropped to a whisper— "the only person who knows."

Again she felt her color change; again her heart rose in precipitate throbs to meet what she felt was coming.

He lifted his eyes to her entreatingly. "You do see, don't you? You understand? I'm desperate—I'm at the end of my tether. I want to be free, and you can free me. I know you can. You don't want to keep me bound fast in hell, do you? You can't want to take such a vengeance as that. You were always kind—your eyes are kind now. You say you're sorry for me. Well, it rests with you to show it; and heaven knows there's nothing to keep you back. You understand, of course—there wouldn't be a hint of publicity—not a sound or a syllable to connect you with the thing. It would never come to that, you know: all I need is to be able to say definitely: 'I know this—and this—and this'—and the fight would drop, and the way be cleared, and the whole abominable business swept out of sight in a second."

He spoke pantingly, like a tired runner, with breaks of exhaustion between his words; and through the breaks she caught, as through the shifting rents of a fog, great golden vistas of peace and safety. For there was no mistaking the definite intention behind his vague appeal; she could have filled up the blanks without the help of Mrs. Fisher's insinuations. Here was a man who turned to her in the extremity of his loneliness and his humiliation: if she came to him at such a moment he would be hers with all the force of his deluded faith. And the power to make him so lay in her hand—

lay there in a completeness he could not even remotely conjecture. Revenge and rehabilitation might be hers at a stroke—there was something dazzling in the completeness of the opportunity.

She stood silent, gazing away from him down the autumnal stretch of the deserted lane. And suddenly fear possessed her—fear of herself and of the terrible force of the temptation. All her past weaknesses were like so many eager accomplices drawing her toward the path their feet had already smoothed. She turned quickly, and held out her hand to Dorset.

"Goodbye—I'm sorry; there's nothing in the world that I can do."

"Nothing? Ah, don't say that," he cried; "say what's true: that you abandon me like the others. You, the only creature who could have saved me!"

"Goodbye—goodbye," she repeated hurriedly; and as she moved away she heard him cry out on a last note of entreaty: "At least you'll let me see you once more?"

Lily, on regaining the Gormer grounds, struck rapidly across the lawn toward the unfinished house, where she fancied that her hostess might be speculating, not too resignedly, on the cause of her delay; for, like many unpunctual persons, Mrs. Gormer disliked to be kept waiting.

As Miss Bart reached the avenue, however, she saw a smart phaeton with a high-stepping pair disappear behind the shrubbery in the direction of the gate: and on the doorstep stood Mrs. Gormer, with a glow of retrospective pleasure on her open countenance. At sight of Lily the glow deepened to an embarrassed red, and she said with a slight laugh: "Did you see my visitor? Oh, I thought you came back by the avenue. It was Mrs. George Dorset—she said she'd dropped in to make a neighborly call."

Lily met the announcement with her usual composure, though her experience of Bertha's idiosyncrasies would not have led her to include the neighborly instinct among them; and Mrs. Gormer, relieved to see that she gave no sign of surprise, went on with a deprecating laugh: "Of course, what really brought her was curiosity—she made me take her all over the house. But no one could have been nicer—no airs, you know, and so good-natured: I can quite see why people think her so fascinating."

This surprising event, coinciding too completely with her meeting with Dorset to be regarded as contingent upon it, had yet immediately struck Lily with a vague sense of foreboding. It was not in Bertha's habits to be neighborly, much less to make advances to anyone outside the immediate circle of her affinities. She had always consistently ignored the world of outer aspirants, or had recognized its individual members only when prompted by motives of self-interest; and the very capriciousness of her condescensions had, as Lily was aware, given them special value in the eyes of the persons she distinguished. Lily saw this now in Mrs. Gormer's unconcealable complacency, and in the happy irrelevance with which, for the next day or two, she quoted Bertha's opinions and speculated on the origin of her gown. All the secret ambitions which Mrs. Gormer's native indolence, and the attitude of her companions, kept in habitual abeyance, were now germinating afresh in the glow of Bertha's advances; and whatever the cause of the latter, Lily saw that, if they were followed up, they were likely to have a disturbing effect upon her own future.

She had arranged to break the length of her stay with her new friends by one or two visits to other acquaintances as recent; and on her return from this somewhat depressing excursion she was immediately conscious that Mrs. Dorset's influence was still in the air. There had been another exchange of visits, a tea at a country-club, an encounter at a hunt ball; there was even a rumor of an approaching dinner, which Mattie Gormer, with an unnatural effort at discretion, tried to smuggle out of the conversation whenever Miss Bart took part in it.

The latter had already planned to return to town after a farewell Sunday with her friends; and, with Gerty Farish's aid, had discovered a small private hotel where she might establish herself for the winter. The hotel being on the edge of a fashionable neighborhood, the price of the few square feet she was to occupy was considerably in excess of her means; but she found a justification for her dislike of poorer quarters in the argument that, at this particular juncture, it was of the utmost importance to keep up a show of prosperity. In reality, it was impossible for her, while she had the means to pay her way for a week ahead, to lapse into a form of existence like Gerty Farish's. She had never been so near the brink of insolvency; but she could at least manage to meet her weekly hotel bill, and having settled the heaviest of her previous debts out of the money she had received from Trenor, she had a still fair margin of credit to go upon. The situation, however, was not agreeable enough to lull her to complete unconsciousness of its insecurity. Her rooms, with their cramped outlook down a sallow vista of brick walls and fire escapes, her lonely meals in the dark restaurant with its surcharged ceiling and haunting smell of coffee—all these material discomforts, which were yet to be accounted as so many privileges soon to be withdrawn, kept constantly before her the disadvantages of her state, and her mind reverted the more insistently to Mrs. Fisher's counsels. Beat about the question as she would, she knew the outcome of it was that she must try to marry Rosedale; and in this conviction she was fortified by an unexpected visit from George Dorset.

She found him, on the first Sunday after her return to town, pacing her narrow sitting-room to the imminent peril of the few knickknacks with which she had tried to disguise its plush exuberances; but the sight of her seemed to quiet him, and he said meekly that he hadn't come to bother her —that he asked only to be allowed to sit for half an hour and talk of anything she liked. In reality, as she knew, he had but one subject: himself and his wretchedness; and it was the need of her sympathy that had drawn him back. But he began with a pretence of questioning her about herself and as she replied, she saw that, for the first time, a faint realization of her plight penetrated the dense surface of his self-absorption. Was it possible that her old beast of an aunt had actually cut her off? That she was living alone like this because there was no one else for her to go to, and that she really hadn't more than enough to keep alive on till the wretched little legacy was paid? The fibers of sympathy were nearly atrophied in him, but he was suffering so intensely that he had a faint glimpse of what other sufferings might mean—and, as she perceived, an almost simultaneous perception of the way in which her particular misfortunes might serve him.

When at length she dismissed him, on the pretext that she must dress for dinner, he lingered entreatingly on the threshold to blurt out: "It's been such a comfort—do say you'll let me see you again—" But to this direct appeal it was impossible to give an assent; and she said with friendly decisiveness: "I'm sorry but you know why I can't."

He colored to the eyes, pushed the door shut, and stood before her embarrassed but insistent. "I know how you might, if you would—if things were different—and it lies with you to make them so. It's just a word to say, and you put me out of my misery!"

Their eyes met, and for a second she trembled again with the nearness of the temptation. "You're mistaken; I know nothing; I saw nothing," she exclaimed, striving, by sheer force of reiteration, to build a barrier between herself and her peril; and as he turned away, groaning out "You sacrifice us both," she continued to repeat, as if it were a charm: "I know nothing—absolutely nothing."

Lily had seen little of Rosedale since her illuminating talk with Mrs. Fisher, but on the two or three occasions when they had met she was conscious of having distinctly advanced in his favor. There could be no doubt that he admired her as much as ever, and she believed it rested with herself to raise his admiration to the point where it should bear down the lingering counsels of expediency. The task was not an easy one; but neither was it easy, in her long sleepless nights, to face the thought of what George Dorset was so clearly ready to offer. Baseness for baseness, she hated the other least: there were even moments when a marriage with Rosedale seemed the only honorable solution of her difficulties. She did not indeed let her imagination range beyond the day of plighting: after that everything faded into a haze of material well-being, in which the personality of her benefactor remained mercifully vague. She had learned, in her long vigils, that there were certain things not good to think of, certain midnight images that must at any cost be exorcised—and one of these was the image of herself as Rosedale's wife.

Carry Fisher, on the strength, as she frankly owned, of the Brys' Newport success, had taken for the autumn months a small house at Tuxedo; and thither Lily was bound on the Sunday after Dorset's visit. Though it was nearly dinner-time when she arrived, her hostess was still out, and the firelit quiet of the small silent house descended on her spirit with a sense of peace and familiarity. It may be doubted if such an emotion had ever before been evoked by Carry Fisher's surroundings; but, contrasted to the world in which Lily had lately lived, there was an air of repose and stability in the very placing of the furniture, and in the quiet competence of the parlor maid who led her up to her room. Mrs. Fisher's unconventionality was, after all, a merely superficial divergence from an inherited social creed, while the manners of the Gormer circle represented their first attempt to formulate such a creed for themselves.

It was the first time since her return from Europe that Lily had found herself in a congenial atmosphere, and the stirring of familiar associations had almost prepared her, as she descended the stairs before dinner, to enter upon a group of her old acquaintances. But this expectation was instantly checked by the reflection that the friends who remained loyal were precisely those who would be least willing to expose her to such encounters; and it was hardly with surprise that she found, instead, Mr. Rosedale kneeling domestically on the drawing-room hearth before his hostess's little girl.

Rosedale in the paternal role was hardly a figure to soften Lily; yet she could not but notice a quality of homely goodness in his advances to the child. They were not, at any rate, the premeditated and perfunctory endearments of the guest under his hostess's eye, for he and the little girl had the room to themselves; and something in his attitude made him seem a simple and kindly being compared to the small critical creature who endured his homage. Yes, he would be kind—Lily, from the threshold, had time to feel —kind in his gross, unscrupulous, rapacious way, the way of the predatory creature with his mate. She had but a moment in which to consider whether this glimpse of the fireside man mitigated her repugnance, or gave it, rather, a more concrete and intimate form; for at sight of her he was immediately on his feet again, the florid and dominant Rosedale of Mattie Gormer's drawing-room.

It was no surprise to Lily to find that he had been selected as her only fellow guest. Though she and her hostess had not met since the latter's tentative discussion of her future, Lily knew that the acuteness which enabled Mrs. Fisher to lay a safe and pleasant course through a world of antagonistic forces was not infrequently exercised for the benefit of her friends. It was, in fact, characteristic of Carry that, while she actively gleaned her own stores from the fields of affluence, her real sympathies were on the other side—with the unlucky, the unpopular, the unsuccessful, with all her hungry fellow toilers in the shorn stubble of success.

Mrs. Fisher's experience guarded her against the mistake of exposing Lily, for the first evening, to the unmitigated impression of Rosedale's personality. Kate Corby and two or three men dropped in to dinner, and Lily, alive to every detail of her friend's method, saw that such opportunities as had been contrived for her were to be deferred till she had, as it were, gained courage to make effectual use of them. She had a sense of acquiescing in this plan with the passiveness of a sufferer resigned to the surgeon's touch; and this feeling of almost lethargic helplessness continued when, after the departure of the guests, Mrs. Fisher followed her upstairs.

"May I come in and smoke a cigarette over your fire? If we talk in my room we shall disturb the child." Mrs. Fisher looked about her with the eye of the solicitous hostess. "I hope you've managed to make yourself comfortable, dear? Isn't it a jolly little house? It's such a blessing to have a few quiet weeks with the baby."

Carry, in her rare moments of prosperity, became so expansively maternal that Miss Bart sometimes wondered whether, if she could ever get time and money enough, she would not end by devoting them both to her daughter.

"It's a well-earned rest: I'll say that for myself," she continued, sinking down with a sigh of content on the pillowed lounge near the fire. "Louisa Bry is a stern taskmaster: I often used to wish myself back with the Gormers. Talk of love making people jealous and suspicious—it's nothing to social ambition! Louisa used to lie awake at night wondering whether the women who called on us called on *me* because I was with her, or on *her* because she was with me; and she was always laying traps to find out what I thought. Of course I had to disown my oldest friends, rather than let her suspect she owed me the chance of making a single acquaintance—when, all the while, that was what she had me there for, and what she wrote me a handsome check for when the season was over!"

Mrs. Fisher was not a woman who talked of herself without cause, and the practice of direct speech, far from precluding in her an occasional resort to circuitous methods, served rather, at crucial moments, the purpose of the juggler's chatter while he shifts the contents of his sleeves. Through the haze of her cigarette smoke she continued to gaze meditatively at Miss Bart, who, having dismissed her maid, sat before the toilet-table shaking out over her shoulders the loosened undulations of her hair.

"Your hair's wonderful, Lily. Thinner—? What does that matter, when it's so light and alive? So many women's worries seem to go straight to their hair—but yours looks as if there had never been an anxious thought under it. I never saw you look better than you did this evening. Mattie Gormer told me that Morpeth wanted to paint you—why don't you let him?"

Miss Bart's immediate answer was to address a critical glance to the reflection of the countenance under discussion. Then she said, with a slight touch of irritation: "I don't care to accept a portrait from Paul Morpeth."

Mrs. Fisher mused. "N—no. And just now, especially—well, he can do you after you're married." She waited a moment, and then went on: "By the way, I had a visit from Mattie the other day. She turned up here last Sunday —and with Bertha Dorset, of all people in the world!" She paused again to measure the effect of this announcement on her hearer, but the brush in Miss Bart's lifted hand maintained its unwavering stroke from brow to nape.

"I never was more astonished," Mrs. Fisher pursued. "I don't know two women less predestined to intimacy—from Bertha's standpoint, that is; for of course poor Mattie thinks it natural enough that she should be singled out—I've no doubt the rabbit always thinks it is fascinating the anaconda. Well, you know I've always told you that Mattie secretly longed to bore herself with the really fashionable; and now that the chance has come, I see that she's capable of sacrificing all her old friends to it."

Lily laid aside her brush and turned a penetrating glance upon her friend. "Including *me?*" she suggested.

"Ah, my dear," murmured Mrs. Fisher, rising to push back a log from the hearth.

"That's what Bertha means, isn't it?" Miss Bart went on steadily. "For of course she always means something; and before I left Long Island I saw that she was beginning to lay her toils for Mattie."

Mrs. Fisher sighed evasively. "She has her fast now, at any rate. To think of that loud independence of Mattie's being only a subtler form of snobbishness! Bertha can already make her believe anything she pleases—and I'm afraid she's begun, my poor child, by insinuating horrors about you."

Lily flushed under the shadow of her drooping hair. "The world is too vile," she murmured, averting herself from Mrs. Fisher's anxious scrutiny.

"It's not a pretty place; and the only way to keep a footing in it is to fight it on its own terms—and above all, my dear, not alone!" Mrs. Fisher gathered up her floating implications in a resolute grasp. "You've told me so little that I can only guess what has been happening; but in the rush we all live in there's no time to keep on hating anyone without a cause, and if Bertha is still nasty enough to want to injure you with other people it must be because she's still afraid of you. From her standpoint there's only one reason for being afraid of you; and my own idea is that, if you want to punish her, you hold the means in your hand. I believe you can marry George Dorset tomorrow; but if you don't care for that particular form of retaliation, the only thing to save you from Bertha is to marry somebody else."

22

THE light projected on the situation by Mrs. Fisher had the cheerless distinctness of a winter dawn. It outlined the facts with a cold precision unmodified by shade or color, and refracted, as it were, from the blank walls of the surrounding limitations: she had opened windows from which no sky was ever visible. But the idealist subdued to vulgar necessities must employ vulgar minds to draw the inferences to which he cannot stoop; and it was easier for Lily to let Mrs. Fisher formulate her case than to put it plainly to herself. Once confronted with it, however, she went the full length of its consequences; and these had never been more clearly present to her than when, the next afternoon, she set out for a walk with Rosedale.

It was one of those still November days when the air is haunted with the light of summer, and something in the lines of the landscape, and in the golden haze which bathed them, recalled to Miss Bart the September afternoon when she had climbed the slopes of Bellomont with Selden. The importunate memory was kept before her by its ironic contrast to her present situation, since her walk with Selden had represented an irresistible flight from just such a climax as the present excursion was designed to bring about. But other memories importuned her also; the recollection of similar situations, as skillfully led up to, but through some malice of fortune, or her own unsteadiness of purpose, always failing of the intended result. Well, her purpose was steady enough now. She saw that the whole weary work of rehabilitation must begin again, and against far greater odds, if Bertha Dorset should succeed in breaking up her friendship with the Gormers; and her longing for shelter and security was intensified by the passionate desire to triumph over Bertha, as only wealth and predominance could triumph over her. As the wife of Rosedale—the Rosedale she felt it in her power to create—she would at least present an invulnerable front to her enemy.

She had to draw upon this thought, as upon some fiery stimulant, to keep up her part in the scene toward which Rosedale was too frankly tending. As she walked beside him, shrinking in every nerve from the way in which his look and tone made free of her, yet telling herself that this momentary endurance of his mood was the price she must pay for her ultimate power over him, she tried to calculate the exact point at which concession must turn to resistance, and the price *he* would have to pay be made equally clear to him. But his dapper self-confidence seemed impenetrable to such hints, and she had a sense of something hard and self-contained behind the superficial warmth of his manner.

They had been seated for some time in the seclusion of a rocky glen above the lake, when she suddenly cut short the culmination of an impassioned period by turning upon him the grave loveliness of her gaze.

"I *do* believe what you say, Mr. Rosedale," she said quietly; "and I am ready to marry you whenever you wish."

Rosedale, reddening to the roots of his glossy hair, received this announcement with a recoil which carried him to his feet, where he halted before her in an attitude of almost comic discomfiture.

"For I suppose that is what you do wish," she continued, in the same quiet tone. "And, though I was unable to consent when you spoke to me in this way before, I am ready, now that I know you so much better, to trust my happiness to your hands."

She spoke with the noble directness which she could command on such occasions, and which was like a large steady light thrown across the tortuous darkness of the situation. In its inconvenient brightness Rosedale seemed to waver a moment, as though conscious that every avenue of escape was unpleasantly illuminated.

Then he gave a short laugh, and drew out a gold cigarette-case, in which, with plump jeweled fingers, he groped for a gold-tipped cigarette. Selecting one, he paused to contemplate it a moment before saying: "My dear Miss Lily, I'm sorry if there's been any little misapprehension between us—but you made me feel my suit was so hopeless that I had really no intention of renewing it."

Lily's blood tingled with the grossness of the rebuff, but she checked the first leap of her anger, and said in a tone of gentle dignity: "I have no one but myself to blame if I gave you the impression that my decision was final."

Her wordplay was always too quick for him, and this reply held him in puzzled silence while she extended her hand and added, with the faintest inflection of sadness in her voice: "Before we bid each other goodbye, I want at least to thank you for having once thought of me as you did."

The touch of her hand, the moving softness of her look, thrilled a vulnerable fiber in Rosedale. It was her exquisite inaccessibleness, the sense of distance she could convey without a hint of disdain, that made it most difficult for him to give her up.

"Why do you talk of saying goodbye? Ain't we going to be good friends all the same?" he urged, without releasing her hand.

She drew it away quietly. "What is your idea of being good friends?" she returned with a slight smile. "Making love to me without asking me to marry you?"

Rosedale laughed with a recovered sense of ease. "Well, that's about the size of it, I suppose. I can't help making love to you—I don't see how any man could; but I don't mean to ask you to marry me as long as I can keep out of it."

She continued to smile. "I like your frankness; but I am afraid our friendship can hardly continue on those terms."

She turned away, as though to mark that its final term had in fact been reached, and he followed her for a few steps with a baffled sense of her having after all kept the game in her own hands.

"Miss Lily—" he began impulsively; but she walked on without seeming to hear him.

He overtook her in a few quick strides, and laid an entreating hand on her arm. "Miss Lily—don't hurry away like that. You're beastly hard on a fellow; but if you don't mind speaking the truth I don't see why you shouldn't allow me to do the same."

She had paused a moment with raised brows, drawing away instinctively from his touch, though she made no effort to evade his words.

"I was under the impression," she rejoined, "that you had done so without waiting for my permission."

"Well—why shouldn't you hear my reasons for doing it, then? We're neither of us such new hands that a little plain speaking is going to hurt us. I'm all broken up on you: there's nothing new in that. I'm more in love with you than I was this time last year; but I've got to face the fact that the situation is changed."

She continued to confront him with the same air of ironic composure. "You mean to say that I'm not as desirable a match as you thought me?"

"Yes; that's what I do mean," he answered resolutely. "I won't go into what's happened. I don't believe the stories about you—I don't want to believe them. But they're there, and my not believing them ain't going to alter the situation."

She flushed to her temples, but the extremity of her need checked the retort on her lip and she continued to face him composedly. "If they are not true," she said, "doesn't *that* alter the situation?"

He met this with a steady gaze of his small stock-taking eyes, which made her feel herself no more than some superfine human merchandise. "I believe it does in novels; but I'm certain it don't in real life. You know that as well as I do: if we're speaking the truth, let's speak the whole truth. Last year I was wild to marry you, and you wouldn't look at me: this year—well, you appear to be willing. Now, what has changed in the interval? Your situation, that's all. Then you thought you could do better; now—"

"You think you can?" broke from her ironically.

"Why, yes, I do: in one way, that is." He stood before her, his hands in his pockets, his chest sturdily expanded under its vivid waistcoat. "It's this way, you see: I've had a pretty steady grind of it these last years, working up my social position. Think it's funny I should say that? Why should I mind saying I want to get into society? A man ain't ashamed to say he wants to own a racing stable or a picture gallery. Well, a taste for society's just another kind of hobby. Perhaps I want to get even with some of the people who cold-shouldered me last year—put it that way if it sounds better. Anyhow, I want to have the run of the best houses; and I'm getting it too, little by little. But I know the quickest way to queer yourself with the right people is to be seen with the wrong ones; and that's the reason I want to avoid mistakes."

Miss Bart continued to stand before him in a silence that might have expressed either mockery or a half-reluctant respect for his candor, and after a moment's pause he went on: "There it is, you see. I'm more in love with you than ever, but if I married you now I'd queer myself for good and all, and everything I've worked for all these years would be wasted."

She received this with a look from which all tinge of resentment had faded. After the tissue of social falsehoods in which she had so long moved it was refreshing to step into the open daylight of an avowed expediency.

"I understand you," she said. "A year ago I should have been of use to you, and now I should be all encumbrance; and I like you for telling me so quite honestly." She extended her hand with a smile.

Again the gesture had a disturbing effect upon Mr. Rosedale's self-command. "By George, you're a dead game sport, you are!" he exclaimed; and as she began once more to move away, he broke out suddenly—"Miss Lily—stop. You know I don't believe those stories—I believe they were all got up by a woman who didn't hesitate to sacrifice you to her own convenience—"

Lily drew away with a movement of quick disdain: it was easier to endure his insolence than his commiseration.

"You are very kind; but I don't think we need discuss the matter further."

But Rosedale's natural imperviousness to hints made it easy for him to brush such resistance aside. "I don't want to discuss anything; I just want to put a plain case before you," he persisted.

She paused in spite of herself, held by the note of a new purpose in his look and tone; and he went on, keeping his eyes firmly upon her: "The wonder to me is that you've waited so long to get square with that woman, when you've had the power in your hands." She continued silent under the rush of astonishment that his words produced, and he moved a step closer to ask with low-toned directness: "Why don't you use those letters of hers you bought last year?"

Lily stood speechless under the shock of the interrogation. In the words preceding it she had conjectured, at most, an allusion to her supposed influence over George Dorset; nor did the astonishing indelicacy of the reference diminish the likelihood of Rosedale's resorting to it. But now she saw how far short of the mark she had fallen; and the surprise of learning that he had discovered the secret of the letters left her, for the moment, unconscious of the special use to which he was in the act of putting his knowledge.

Her temporary loss of self-possession gave him time to press his point; and he went on quickly, as though to secure completer control of the situation: "You see I know where you stand—I know how completely she's in your power. That sounds like stage-talk, don't it?—but there's a lot of truth in some of those old gags; and I don't suppose you bought those letters simply because you're collecting autographs."

She continued to look at him with a deepening bewilderment: her only clear impression resolved itself into a scared sense of his power.

"You're wondering how I found out about 'em?" he went on, answering her look with a note of conscious pride. "Perhaps you've forgotten that I'm the owner of the Benedick—but never mind about that now. Getting on to things is a mighty useful accomplishment in business, and I've simply extended it to my private affairs. For this is partly my affair, you see—at least, it depends on you to make it so. Let's look the situation straight in the eye. Mrs. Dorset, for reasons we needn't go into, did you a beastly bad turn last spring. Everybody knows what Mrs. Dorset is, and her best friends wouldn't believe her on oath where their own interests were concerned; but as long as they're out of the row it's much easier to follow her lead than to set themselves against it, and you've simply been sacrificed to their laziness and selfishness. Isn't that a pretty fair statement of the case? Well, some people say you've got the neatest kind of an answer in your hands: that George Dorset would marry you tomorrow, if you'd tell him all you know, and give him the chance to show the lady the door. I daresay he would; but you don't seem to care for that particular form of getting even, and, taking a purely business view of the question, I think you're right. In a deal like that, nobody comes out with perfectly clean hands, and the only way for you to start fresh is to get Bertha Dorset to back you up, instead of trying to fight her."

He paused long enough to draw breath, but not to give her time for the expression of her gathering resistance; and as he pressed on, expounding and elucidating his idea with the directness of the man who has no doubts of his cause, she found the indignation gradually freezing on her lip, found herself held fast in the grasp of his argument by the mere cold strength of its presentation. There was no time now to wonder how he had heard of her obtaining the letters: all her world was dark outside the monstrous glare of his scheme for using them. And it was not, after the first moment, the horror of the idea that held her spellbound, subdued to his will; it was rather its subtle affinity to her own inmost cravings. He would marry her tomorrow if she could regain Bertha Dorset's friendship; and to induce the open resumption of that friendship, and the tacit retraction of all that had caused its withdrawal, she had only to put to the lady the latent menace contained in the packet so miraculously delivered into her hands. Lily saw in a flash the advantage of this course over that which poor Dorset had pressed upon her. The other plan depended for its success on the infliction of an open injury, while this reduced the transaction to a private understanding, of which no third person need have the remotest hint. Put by Rosedale in terms of businesslike give-and-take, this understanding took on the harmless air of a mutual accommodation, like a transfer of property or a revision of boundary lines. It certainly simplified life to view it as a perpetual adjustment, a play of party politics, in which every concession had its recognized equivalent: Lily's tired mind was fascinated by this escape from fluctuating ethical estimates into a region of concrete weights and measures.

Rosedale, as she listened, seemed to read in her silence not only a gradual acquiescence in his plan, but a dangerously far-reaching perception of the chances it offered; for as she continued to stand before him without speaking, he broke out, with a quick return upon himself: "You see how simple it is, don't you? Well, don't be carried away by the idea that it's *too* simple. It isn't exactly as if you'd started in with a clean bill of health. Now we're talking let's call things by their right names, and clear the whole business up. You know well enough that Bertha Dorset couldn't have touched you if there hadn't been—well—questions asked before—little points of interrogation, eh? Bound to happen to a good-looking girl with stingy relatives, I suppose; anyhow, they *did* happen, and she found the ground prepared for her. Do you see where I'm coming out? You don't want these little questions cropping up again. It's one thing to get Bertha Dorset into line—but what you want is to keep her there. You can frighten her fast enough—but how are you going to keep her frightened? By showing her that you're as powerful as she is. All the letters in the world won't do that for you as you are now; but with a big backing behind you, you'll keep her just where you want her to be. That's *my* share in the business—that's what I'm offering you. You can't put the thing through without me—don't run away with any idea that you can. In six months you'd be back again among your old worries, or worse ones; and here I am, ready to lift you out of 'em tomorrow if you say so. *Do* you say so, Miss Lily?" he added, moving suddenly nearer.

The words, and the movement which accompanied them, combined to startle Lily out of the state of tranced subservience into which she had insensibly slipped. Light comes in devious ways to the groping consciousness, and it came to her now through the disgusted perception that her would-be accomplice assumed, as a matter of course, the likelihood of her distrusting him and perhaps trying to cheat him of his share of the spoils. This glimpse of his inner mind seemed to present the whole transaction in a new aspect, and she saw that the essential baseness of the act lay in its freedom from risk.

She drew back with a quick gesture of rejection, saying, in a voice that was a surprise to her own ears: "You are mistaken—quite mistaken—both in the facts and in what you infer from them."

Rosedale stared a moment, puzzled by her sudden dash in a direction so different from that toward which she had appeared to be letting him guide her.

"Now what on earth does that mean? I thought we understood each other!" he exclaimed; and to her murmur of "Ah, we do *now*," he retorted with a sudden burst of violence: "I suppose it's because the letters are to *him*, then? Well, I'll be damned if I see what thanks you've got from him!"

23

THE autumn days declined to winter. Once more the leisure world was in transition between country and town, and Fifth Avenue, still deserted at the weekend, showed from Monday to Friday a broadening stream of carriages between housefronts gradually restored to consciousness.

The Horse Show, some two weeks earlier, had produced a passing semblance of reanimation, filling the theaters and restaurants with a human display of the same costly and high-stepping kind as circled daily about its ring. In Miss Bart's world the Horse Show, and the public it attracted, had ostensibly come to be classed among the spectacles disdained of the elect; but, as the feudal lord might sally forth to join in the dance on his village green, so society, unofficially and incidentally, still condescended to look in upon the scene. Mrs. Gormer, among the rest, was not above seizing such an occasion for the display of herself and her horses; and Lily was given one or two opportunities of appearing at her friend's side in the most conspicuous box the house afforded. But this lingering semblance of intimacy made her only the more conscious of a change in the relation between Mattie and herself, of a dawning discrimination, a gradually formed social standard, emerging from Mrs. Gormer's chaotic view of life. It was inevitable that Lily herself should constitute the first sacrifice to this new ideal, and she knew that, once the Gormers were established in town, the whole drift of fashionable life would facilitate Mattie's detachment from her. She had, in short, failed to make herself indispensable; or rather, her attempt to do so had been thwarted by an influence stronger than any she could exert. That influence, in its last analysis, was simply the power of money: Bertha Dorset's social credit was based on an impregnable bank account.

Lily knew that Rosedale had overstated neither the difficulty of her own position nor the completeness of the vindication he offered: once Bertha's match in material resources, her superior gifts would make it easy for her to dominate her adversary. An understanding of what such domination would mean, and of the disadvantages accruing from her rejection of it, was brought home to Lily with increasing clearness during the early weeks of the winter. Hitherto, she had kept up a semblance of movement outside the main flow of the social current; but with the return to town, and the concentrating of scattered activities, the mere fact of not slipping back naturally into her old habits of life marked her as being unmistakably excluded from them. If one were not a part of the season's fixed routine, one swung unsphered in a void of social nonexistence. Lily, for all her dissatisfied dreaming, had never really conceived the possibility of revolving about a different center: it was easy enough to despise the world, but decidedly difficult to find any other habitable region. Her sense of irony never quite deserted her, and she could still note, with self-directed derision, the abnormal value suddenly acquired by the most tiresome and insignificant details of her former life. Its very drudgeries had a charm now that she was involuntarily released from them: card-leaving, note-writing, enforced civilities to the dull and elderly, and the smiling endurance of tedious dinners—how pleasantly such obligations would have filled the emptiness of her days! She did indeed leave cards in plenty; she kept herself, with a smiling and valiant persistence, well in the eye of her world; nor did she suffer any of those gross rebuffs which sometimes produce a wholesome reaction of contempt in their victim. Society did not turn away from her, it simply drifted by, preoccupied and inattentive, letting her feel, to the full measure of her humbled pride, how completely she had been the creature of its favor.

She had rejected Rosedale's suggestion with a promptness of scorn almost surprising to herself: she had not lost her capacity for high flashes of indignation. But she could not breathe long on the heights; there had been nothing in her training to develop any continuity of moral strength: what she craved, and really felt herself entitled to, was a situation in which the noblest attitude should also be the easiest. Hitherto her intermittent impulses of resistance had sufficed to maintain her self-respect. If she slipped she recovered her footing, and it was only afterward that she was aware of having recovered it each time on a slightly lower level. She had rejected Rosedale's offer without conscious effort; her whole being had risen against it; and she did not yet perceive that, by the mere act of listening to him, she had learned to live with ideas which would once have been intolerable to her.

To Gerty Farish, keeping watch over her with a tenderer if less discerning eye than Mrs. Fisher's, the results of the struggle were already distinctly visible. She did not, indeed, know what hostages Lily had already given to expediency; but she saw her passionately and irretrievably pledged to the ruinous policy of "keeping up." Gerty could smile now at her own early dream of her friend's renovation through adversity: she understood clearly enough that Lily was not of those to whom privation teaches the unimportance of what they have lost. But this very fact, to Gerty, made her friend the more piteously in want of aid, the more exposed to the claims of a tenderness she was so little conscious of needing.

Lily, since her return to town, had not often climbed Miss Farish's stairs. There was something irritating to her in the mute interrogation of Gerty's sympathy: she felt the real difficulties of her situation to be incommunicable to anyone whose theory of values was so different from her own, and the restrictions of Gerty's life, which had once had the charm of contrast, now reminded her too painfully of the limits to which her own existence was shrinking. When at length, one afternoon, she put into execution the belated resolve to visit her friend, this sense of shrunken opportunities possessed her with unusual intensity. The walk up Fifth Avenue, unfolding before her, in the brilliance of the hard winter sunlight, an interminable procession of fastidiously equipped carriages—giving her, through the little squares of brougham-windows, peeps of familiar profiles bent above visiting-lists, of hurried hands dispensing notes and cards to attendant footmen—this glimpse of the ever-revolving wheels of the great social machine made Lily more than ever conscious of the steepness and narrowness of Gerty's stairs, and of the cramped blind-alley of life to which they led. Dull stairs destined to be mounted by dull people: how many thousands of insignificant figures were going up and down such stairs all over the world at that very moment—figures as shabby and uninteresting as that of the middle-aged lady in limp black who descended Gerty's flight as Lily climbed to it!

"That was poor Miss Jane Silverton—she came to talk things over with me: she and her sister want to do something to support themselves," Gerty explained, as Lily followed her into the sitting-room.

"To support themselves? Are they so hard up?" Miss Bart asked with a touch of irritation: she had not come to listen to the woes of other people.

"I'm afraid they have nothing left: Ned's debts have swallowed up everything. They had such hopes, you know, when he broke away from Carry Fisher; they thought Bertha Dorset would be such a good influence, because she doesn't care for cards, and—well, she talked quite beautifully to poor Miss Jane about feeling as if Ned were her younger brother, and wanting to carry him off on the yacht, so that he might have a chance to drop cards and racing, and take up his literary work again."

Miss Farish paused with a sigh which reflected the perplexity of her departing visitor. "But that isn't all; it isn't even the worst. It seems that Ned has quarrelled with the Dorsets; or at least Bertha won't allow him to see her, and he is so unhappy about it that he has taken to gambling again, and going about with all sorts of queer people. And cousin Grace Van Osburgh accuses him of having had a very bad influence on Bertie, who left Harvard last spring, and has been a great deal with Ned ever since. She sent for Miss Jane and made a dreadful scene; and Jack Stepney and Herbert Melson, who were there too, told Miss Jane that Bertie was threatening to marry some dreadful woman to whom Ned had introduced him, and that they could do nothing with him because now he's of age he has his own money. You can fancy how poor Miss Jane felt—she came to me at once, and seemed to think that if I could get her something to do she could earn enough to pay Ned's debts and send him away—I'm afraid she has no idea how long it would take her to pay for one of his evenings at bridge. And he was horribly in debt when he came back from the cruise—I can't see why he should have spent so much more money under Bertha's influence than Carry's, can you?"

Lily met this query with an impatient gesture. "My dear Gerty, I always understand how people can spend much more money—never how they can spend any less!"

She loosened her furs and settled herself in Gerty's easy-chair, while her friend busied herself with the teacups.

"But what can they do—the Miss Silvertons? How do they mean to support themselves?" she asked, conscious that the note of irritation still persisted in her voice. It was the very last topic she had meant to discuss—it really did not interest her in the least—but she was seized by a sudden perverse curiosity to know how the two colorless shrinking victims of young Silverton's sentimental experiments meant to cope with the grim necessity which lurked so close to her own threshold.

"I don't know—I am trying to find something for them. Miss Jane reads aloud very nicely—but it's so hard to find anyone who is willing to be read to. And Miss Annie paints a little—"

"Oh, I know—apple-blossoms on blotting-paper; just the kind of thing I shall be doing myself before long!" exclaimed Lily, starting up with a vehemence of movement that threatened destruction to Miss Farish's fragile tea-table.

Lily bent over to steady the cups; then she sank back into her seat. "I'd forgotten there was no room to dash about in—how beautifully one does have to behave in a small flat! Oh, Gerty, I wasn't meant to be good," she sighed out incoherently.

Gerty lifted an apprehensive look to her pale face, in which the eyes shone with a peculiar sleepless luster.

"You look horribly tired, Lily; take your tea, and let me give you this cushion to lean against."

Miss Bart accepted the cup of tea, but put back the cushion with an impatient hand.

"Don't give me that! I don't want to lean back—I shall go to sleep if I do."

"Well, why not, dear? I'll be as quiet as a mouse," Gerty urged affectionately.

"No—no; don't be quiet; talk to me—keep me awake! I don't sleep at night, and in the afternoon a dreadful drowsiness creeps over me."

"You don't sleep at night? Since when?"

"I don't know—I can't remember." She rose and put the empty cup on the tea-tray. "Another, and stronger, please; if I don't keep awake now I shall see horrors tonight—perfect horrors!"

"But they'll be worse if you drink too much tea."

"No, no—give it to me; and don't preach, please," Lily returned imperiously. Her voice had a dangerous edge, and Gerty noticed that her hand shook as she held it out to receive the second cup.

"But you look so tired: I'm sure you must be ill—"

Miss Bart set down her cup with a start. "Do I look ill? Does my face show it?" She rose and walked quickly toward the little mirror above the writing-table. "What a horrid looking-glass—it's all blotched and discolored. Any one would look ghastly in it!" She turned back, fixing her plaintive eyes on Gerty. "You stupid dear, why do you say such odious things to me? It's enough to make one ill to be told one looks so! And looking ill means looking ugly." She caught Gerty's wrists, and drew her close to the window. "After all, I'd rather know the truth. Look me straight in the face, Gerty, and tell me: am I perfectly frightful?"

"You're perfectly beautiful now, Lily: your eyes are shining, and your cheeks have grown so pink all of a sudden—"

"Ah, they *were* pale, then—ghastly pale, when I came in? Why don't you tell me frankly that I'm a wreck? My eyes are bright now because I'm so nervous—but in the mornings they look like lead. And I can see the lines coming in my face—the lines of worry and disappointment and failure! Every sleepless night leaves a new one—and how can I sleep, when I have such dreadful things to think about?"

"Dreadful things—what things?" asked Gerty, gently detaching her wrists from her friend's feverish fingers.

"What things? Well, poverty, for one—and I don't know any that's more dreadful." Lily turned away and sank with sudden weariness into the easy-chair near the tea-table. "You asked me just now if I could understand why Ned Silverton spent so much money. Of course I understand—he spends it on living with the rich. You think we live *on* the rich, rather than with them: and so we do, in a sense—but it's a privilege we have to pay for! We eat their dinners, and drink their wine, and smoke their cigarettes, and use their carriages and their opera-boxes and their private cars—yes, but there's a tax to pay on everyone of those luxuries. The man pays it by big tips to the servants, by playing cards beyond his means, by flowers and presents—and—and—lots of other things that cost; the girl pays it by tips and cards too—oh, yes, I've had to take up bridge again—and by going to the best dressmakers, and having just the right dress for every occasion, and always keeping herself fresh and exquisite and amusing!"

She leaned back for a moment, closing her eyes, and as she sat there, her pale lips slightly parted, and the lids dropped above her fagged brilliant gaze, Gerty had a startled perception of the change in her face—of the way in

which an ashen daylight seemed suddenly to extinguish its artificial brightness. She looked up, and the vision vanished.

"It doesn't sound very amusing, does it? And it isn't—I'm sick to death
of it! And yet the thought of giving it all up nearly kills me—it's what keeps
me awake at night, and makes me so crazy for your strong tea. For I can't go
on in this way much longer, you know—I'm nearly at the end of my tether.
And then what can I do—how on earth am I to keep myself alive? I see
myself reduced to the fate of that poor Silverton woman—slinking about to
employment agencies, and trying to sell painted blotting-pads to Women's
Exchanges! And there are thousands and thousands of women trying to do
the same thing already, and not one of the number who has less idea how to
earn a dollar than I have!"

She rose again with a hurried glance at the clock. "It's late, and I must
be off—I have an appointment with Carry Fisher. Don't look so worried,
you dear thing—don't think too much about the nonsense I've been talking." She was before the mirror again, adjusting her hair with a light hand,
drawing down her veil, and giving a dexterous touch to her furs. "Of course,
you know, it hasn't come to the employment agencies and the painted
blotting-pads yet; but I'm rather hard-up just for the moment, and if I could
find something to do—notes to write and visiting lists to make up, or that
kind of thing—it would tide me over till the legacy is paid. And Carry has
promised to find somebody who wants a kind of social secretary—you know
she makes a specialty of the helpless rich."

Miss Bart had not revealed to Gerty the full extent of her anxiety. She was
in fact in urgent and immediate need of money: money to meet the vulgar
weekly claims which could neither be deferred nor evaded. To give up her
apartment, and shrink to the obscurity of a boardinghouse, or the provisional hospitality of a bed in Gerty Farish's sitting-room, was an expedient
which could only postpone the problem confronting her; and it seemed
wiser as well as more agreeable to remain where she was and find some
means of earning her living. The possibility of having to do this was one
which she had never before seriously considered, and the discovery that, as
a bread-winner, she was likely to prove as helpless and ineffectual as poor
Miss Silverton, was a severe shock to her self-confidence.

Having been accustomed to take herself at the popular valuation, as a
person of energy and resource, naturally fitted to dominate any situation in
which she found herself, she vaguely imagined that such gifts would be of
value to seekers after social guidance; but there was unfortunately no specific head under which the art of saying and doing the right thing could be
offered in the market, and even Mrs. Fisher's resourcefullness failed before
the difficulty of discovering a workable vein in the vague wealth of Lily's
graces. Mrs. Fisher was full of indirect expedients for enabling her friends to
earn a living, and could conscientiously assert that she had put several

opportunities of this kind before Lily; but more legitimate methods of bread-winning were as much out of her line as they were beyond the capacity of the sufferers she was generally called upon to assist. Lily's failure to profit by the chances already afforded her might, moreover, have justified the abandonment of further effort on her behalf; but Mrs. Fisher's inexhaustible good-nature made her an adept at creating artificial demands in response to an actual supply. In the pursuance of this end she at once started on a voyage of discovery in Miss Bart's behalf; and as the result of her explorations she now summoned the latter with the announcement that she had "found something."

Left to herself, Gerty mused distressfully upon her friend's plight, and her own inability to relieve it. It was clear to her that Lily, for the present, had no wish for the kind of help she could give. Miss Farish could see no hope for her friend but in a life completely reorganized and detached from its old associations; whereas all Lily's energies were centered in the determined effort to hold fast to those associations, to keep herself visibly identified with them, as long as the illusion could be maintained. Pitiable as such an attitude seemed to Gerty, she could not judge it as harshly as Selden, for instance, might have done. She had not forgotten the night of emotion when she and Lily had lain in each other's arms, and she had seemed to feel her very heart's blood passing into her friend. The sacrifice she had made had seemed unavailing enough; no trace remained in Lily of the subduing influences of that hour; but Gerty's tenderness, disciplined by long years of contact with obscure and inarticulate suffering, could wait on its object with a silent forbearance which took no account of time. She could not, however, deny herself the solace of taking anxious counsel with Lawrence Selden, with whom, since his return from Europe, she had renewed her old relation of cousinly confidence.

Selden himself had never been aware of any change in their relation. He found Gerty as he had left her, simple, undemanding and devoted, but with a quickened intelligence of the heart which he recognized without seeking to explain it. To Gerty herself it would once have seemed impossible that she should ever again talk freely with him of Lily Bart; but what had passed in the secrecy of her own breast seemed to resolve itself, when the mist of the struggle cleared, into a breaking down of the bounds of self, a deflecting of the wasted personal emotion into the general current of human understanding.

It was not till some two weeks after her visit from Lily that Gerty had the opportunity of communicating her fears to Selden. The latter, having presented himself on a Sunday afternoon, had lingered on through the dowdy animation of his cousin's tea-hour, conscious of something in her voice and eye which solicited a word apart; and as soon as the last visitor was gone Gerty opened her case by asking how lately he had seen Miss Bart.

Selden's perceptible pause gave her time for a slight stir of surprise.

"I haven't seen her at all—I've perpetually missed seeing her since she came back."

This unexpected admission made Gerty pause too; and she was still hesitating on the brink of her subject when he relieved her by adding: "I've wanted to see her—but she seems to have been absorbed by the Gormer set since her return from Europe."

"That's all the more reason: she's been very unhappy."

"Unhappy at being with the Gormers?"

"Oh, I don't defend her intimacy with the Gormers; but that, too, is at an end now, I think. You know people have been very unkind since Bertha Dorset quarreled with her."

"Ah—" Selden exclaimed, rising abruptly to walk to the window, where he remained with his eyes on the darkening street while his cousin continued to explain: "Judy Trenor and her own family have deserted her, too—and all because Bertha Dorset has said such horrible things. And she is very poor—you know Mrs. Peniston cut her off with a small legacy, after giving her to understand that she was to have everything."

"Yes—I know," Selden assented curtly, turning back into the room, but only to stir about with restless steps in the circumscribed space between door and window. "Yes—she's been abominably treated; but it's unfortunately the precise thing that a man who wants to show his sympathy can't say to her."

His words caused Gerty a slight chill of disappointment. "There would be other ways of showing your sympathy," she suggested.

Selden, with a slight laugh, sat down beside her on the little sofa which projected from the hearth. "What are you thinking of, you incorrigible missionary?" he asked.

Gerty's color rose, and her blush was for a moment her only answer. Then she made it more explicit by saying: "I am thinking of the fact that you and she used to be great friends—that she used to care immensely for what you thought of her—and that, if she takes your staying away as a sign of what you think now, I can imagine its adding a great deal to her unhappiness."

"My dear child, don't add to it still more—at least to your conception of it—by attributing to her all sorts of susceptibilities of your own." Selden, for his life, could not keep a note of dryness out of his voice; but he met Gerty's look of perplexity by saying more mildly: "But, though you immensely exaggerate the importance of anything I could do for Miss Bart, you can't exaggerate my readiness to do it—if you ask me to." He laid his hand for a moment on hers, and there passed between them, on the current of the rare contact, one of those exchanges of meaning which fill the hidden reservoirs of affection. Gerty had the feeling that he measured the cost of her request as plainly as she read the significance of his reply; and the sense of all that was suddenly clear between them made her next words easier to find.

"I do ask you, then; I ask you because she once told me that you had been a help to her, and because she needs help now as she has never needed it before. You know how dependent she has always been on ease and luxury —how she has hated what was shabby and ugly and uncomfortable. She can't help it—she was brought up with those ideas, and has never been able to find her way out of them. But now all the things she cared for have been taken from her, and the people who taught her to care for them have abandoned her, too; and it seems to me that if someone could reach out a hand and show her the other side—show her how much is left in life and in herself—" Gerty broke off abashed at the sound of her own eloquence, and impeded by the difficulty of giving precise expression to her vague yearning for her friend's retrieval. "I can't help her myself: she's passed out of my reach," she continued. "I think she's afraid of being a burden to me. When she was last here, two weeks ago, she seemed dreadfully worried about her future: she said Carry Fisher was trying to find something for her to do. A few days later she wrote me that she had taken a position as private secretary, and that I was not to be anxious, for everything was all right, and she would come in and tell me about it when she had time; but she has never come, and I don't like to go to her, because I am afraid of forcing myself on her when I'm not wanted. Once, when we were children, and I had rushed up after a long separation, and thrown my arms about her, she said: 'Please don't kiss me unless I ask you to, Gerty'—and she *did* ask me, a minute later; but since then I've always waited to be asked."

Selden had listened in silence, with the concentrated look which his thin dark face could assume when he wished to guard it against any involuntary change of expression. When his cousin ended, he said with a slight smile: "Since you've learned the wisdom of waiting, I don't see why you urge me to rush in—" but the troubled appeal of her eyes made him add, as he rose to take leave: "Still, I'll do what you wish, and not hold you responsible for my failure."

Selden's avoidance of Miss Bart had not been as unintentional as he had allowed his cousin to think. At first, indeed, while the memory of their last hour at Monte Carlo still held the full heat of his indignation, he had anxiously watched for her return; but she had disappointed him by lingering in England, and when she finally reappeared it happened that business had called him to the West, whence he came back only to learn that she was starting for Alaska with the Gormers. The revelation of this suddenly established intimacy effectually chilled his desire to see her. If, at a moment when her whole life seemed to be breaking up, she could cheerfully commit its reconstruction to the Gormers, there was no reason why such accidents should ever strike her as irreparable. Every step she took seemed in fact to carry her farther from the region where, once or twice, he and she had met for an illumined moment; and the recognition of this fact, when its first pang had been surmounted, produced in him a sense of negative relief. It was much simpler for him to judge Miss Bart by her habitual conduct than by the rare deviations from it which had thrown her so disturbingly in his way; and every act of hers which made the recurrence of such deviations more unlikely, confirmed the sense of relief with which he returned to the conventional view of her.

But Gerty Farish's words had sufficed to make him see how little this view was really his, and how impossible it was for him to live quietly with the thought of Lily Bart. To hear that she was in need of help—even such vague help as he could offer—was to be at once repossessed by that thought; and by the time he reached the street he had sufficiently convinced himself of the urgency of his cousin's appeal to turn his steps directly toward Lily's hotel.

There his zeal met a check in the unforeseen news that Miss Bart had moved away; but, on his pressing his inquiries, the clerk remembered that she had left an address, for which he presently began to search through his books.

It was certainly strange that she should have taken this step without letting Gerty Farish know of her decision; and Selden waited with a vague sense of uneasiness while the address was sought for. The process lasted long enough for uneasiness to turn to apprehension; but when at length a slip of paper was handed him, and he read on it: "Care of Mrs. Norma Hatch, Emporium Hotel," his apprehension passed into an incredulous stare, and this into the gesture of disgust with which he tore the paper in two, and turned to walk quickly homeward.

24

WHEN Lily woke on the morning after her translation to the Emporium Hotel, her first feeling was one of purely physical satisfaction. The force of contrast gave an added keenness to the luxury of lying once more in a soft-pillowed bed, and looking across a spacious sunlit room at a breakfast-table set invitingly near the fire. Analysis and introspection might come later; but for the moment she was not even troubled by the excesses of the upholstery or the restless convolutions of the furniture. The sense of being once more lapped and folded in ease, as in some dense mild medium impenetrable to discomfort, effectually stilled the faintest note of criticism.

When, the afternoon before, she had presented herself to the lady to whom Carry Fisher had directed her, she had been conscious of entering a new world. Carry's vague presentment of Mrs. Norma Hatch (whose reversion to her Christian name was explained as the result of her latest divorce) left her under the implication of coming "from the West," with the not unusual extenuation of having brought a great deal of money with her. She was, in short, rich, helpless, unplaced: the very subject for Lily's hand. Mrs. Fisher had not specified the line her friend was to take; she owned herself unacquainted with Mrs. Hatch, whom she "knew about" through Melville Stancy, a lawyer in his leisure moments, and the Falstaff of a certain section of festive club life. Socially, Mr. Stancy might have been said to form a connecting link between the Gormer world and the more dimly lit region on which Miss Bart now found herself entering. It was, however, only figuratively that the illumination of Mrs. Hatch's world could be described as dim: in actual fact, Lily found her seated in a blaze of electric light, impartially projected from various ornamental excrescences on a vast concavity of pink damask and gilding, from which she rose like Venus from her shell. The analogy was justified by the appearance of the lady, whose large-eyed prettiness had the fixity of something impaled and shown under glass. This did not preclude the immediate discovery that she was some years younger than her visitor, and that under her showiness, her ease, the aggression of her dress and voice, there persisted that ineradicable innocence which, in ladies of her nationality, so curiously coexists with startling extremes of experience.

The environment in which Lily found herself was as strange to her as its inhabitants. She was unacquainted with the world of the fashionable New York hotel—a world overheated, overupholstered, and overfitted with mechanical appliances for the gratification of fantastic requirements, while the comforts of a civilized life were as unattainable as in a desert. Through this atmosphere of torrid splendor moved wan beings as richly upholstered as the furniture, beings without definite pursuits or permanent relations, who drifted on a languid tide of curiosity from restaurant to concert hall, from palm garden to music-room, from "art exhibit" to dressmaker's opening. High-stepping horses or elaborately equipped motors waited to carry these ladies into vague metropolitan distances, whence they returned, still more wan from the weight of their sables, to be sucked back into the stifling inertia of the hotel routine. Somewhere behind them, in the background of their lives, there was doubtless a real past, peopled by real human activities: they themselves were probably the product of strong ambitions, persistent energies, diversified contacts with the wholesome roughness of life; yet they had no more real existence than the poet's shades in limbo.

Lily had not been long in this pallid world without discovering that Mrs. Hatch was its most substantial figure. That lady, though still floating in the void, showed faint symptoms of developing an outline; and in this endeavor she was actively seconded by Mr. Melville Stancy. It was Mr. Stancy, a man of large resounding presence, suggestive of convivial occasions and of a chivalry finding expression in "first-night" boxes and thousand dollar bonbonnières, who had transplanted Mrs. Hatch from the scene of her first development to the higher stage of hotel life in the metropolis. It was he who had selected the horses with which she had taken the blue ribbon at the show, had introduced her to the photographer whose portraits of her formed the recurring ornament of Sunday supplements, and had got to-gether the group which constituted her social world. It was a small group still, with heterogeneous figures suspended in large unpeopled spaces; but Lily did not take long to learn that its regulation was no longer in Mr. Stancy's hands. As often happens, the pupil had outstripped the teacher, and Mrs. Hatch was already aware of heights of elegance as well as depths of luxury beyond the world of the Emporium. This discovery at once produced in her a craving for higher guidance, for the adroit feminine hand which should give the right turn to her correspondence, the right "look" to her hats, the right succession to the items of her menus. It was, in short, as the regulator of a germinating social life that Miss Bart's guidance was required; her ostensible duties as secretary being restricted by the fact that Mrs. Hatch, as yet, knew hardly anyone to write to.

The daily details of Mrs. Hatch's existence were as strange to Lily as its general tenor. The lady's habits were marked by an Oriental indolence and disorder peculiarly trying to her companion. Mrs. Hatch and her friends seemed to float together outside the bounds of time and space. No definite hours were kept; no fixed obligations existed: night and day flowed into one another in a blur of confused and retarded engagements, so that one had the impression of lunching at the tea-hour, while dinner was often merged in the noisy after-theater supper which prolonged Mrs. Hatch's vigil till daylight.

Through this jumble of futile activities came and went a strange throng of hangers-on—manicures, beauty doctors, hairdressers, teachers of bridge, of French, of "physical development": figures sometimes indistinguishable, by their appearance, or by Mrs. Hatch's relation to them, from the visitors constituting her recognized society. But strangest of all to Lily was the encounter, in this latter group, of several of her acquaintances. She had supposed, and not without relief, that she was passing, for the moment, completely out of her own circle; but she found that Mr. Stancy, one side of whose sprawling existence overlapped the edge of Mrs. Fisher's world, had drawn several of its brightest ornaments into the circle of the Emporium. To find Ned Silverton among the habitual frequenters of Mrs. Hatch's drawing-room was one of Lily's first astonishments; but she soon discovered that he was not Mr. Stancy's most important recruit. It was on little Freddy Van Osburgh, the small slim heir of the Van Osburgh millions, that the atten-tion of Mrs. Hatch's group was centered. Freddy, barely out of college, had risen above the horizon since Lily's eclipse, and she now saw with surprise what an effulgence he shed on the outer twilight of Mrs. Hatch's existence. This, then, was one of the things that young men "went in" for when released from the official social routine; this was the kind of "previous engagement" that so frequently caused them to disappoint the hopes of anxious hostesses. Lily had an odd sense of being behind the social tapestry, on the side where the threads were knotted and the loose ends hung. For a moment she found a certain amusement in the show, and in her own share of it: the situation had an ease and unconventionality distinctly refreshing after her experience of the irony of conventions. But these flashes of amusement were but brief reactions from the long disgust of her days. Compared with the vast gilded void of Mrs. Hatch's existence, the life of Lily's former friends seemed packed with ordered activities. Even the most irresponsible pretty woman of her acquaintance had her inherited obligations, her conventional benevolences, her share in the working of the great civic machine; and all hung together in the solidarity of these traditional functions. The performance of specific duties would have simplified Miss Bart's position; but the vague attendance on Mrs. Hatch was not without its perplexities.

It was not her employer who created these perplexities. Mrs. Hatch showed from the first an almost touching desire for Lily's approval. Far from asserting the superiority of wealth, her beautiful eyes seemed to urge the plea of inexperience: she wanted to do what was "nice," to be taught how to be "lovely." The difficulty was to find any point of contact between her ideals and Lily's.

Mrs. Hatch swam in a haze of indeterminate enthusiasms, of aspirations culled from the stage, the newspapers, the fashion journals, and a gaudy world of sport still more completely beyond her companion's ken. To separate from these confused conceptions those most likely to advance the lady on her way, was Lily's obvious duty; but its performance was hampered by rapidly growing doubts. Lily was in fact becoming more and more aware of a certain ambiguity in her situation. It was not that she had, in the conventional sense, any doubt of Mrs. Hatch's irreproachableness. The lady's offenses were always against taste rather than conduct; her divorce record seemed due to geographical rather than ethical conditions; and her worst laxities were likely to proceed from a wandering and extravagant good-nature. But if Lily did not mind her detaining her manicure for luncheon, or offering the "beauty doctor" a seat in Freddy Van Osburgh's box at the play, she was not equally at ease in regard to some less apparent lapses from convention. Ned Silverton's relation to Stancy seemed, for instance, closer and less clear than any natural affinities would warrant; and both appeared united in the effort to cultivate Freddy Van Osburgh's growing taste for Mrs. Hatch. There was as yet nothing definable in the situation, which might well resolve itself into a huge joke on the part of the other two; but Lily had a vague sense that the subject of their experiment was too young, too rich and too credulous. Her embarrassment was increased by the fact that Freddy seemed to regard her as cooperating with himself in the social development of Mrs. Hatch: a view that suggested, on his part, a permanent interest in the lady's future. There were moments when Lily found an ironic amusement in this aspect of the case. The thought of launching such a missile as Mrs. Hatch at the perfidious bosom of society was not without its charm: Miss Bart had even beguiled her leisure with visions of the fair Norma introduced for the first time to a family banquet at the Van Osburghs'. But the thought of being personally connected with the transaction was less agreeable; and her momentary flashes of amusement were followed by increasing periods of doubt.

The sense of these doubts was uppermost when, late one afternoon, she was surprised by a visit from Lawrence Selden. He found her alone in the wilderness of pink damask, for in Mrs. Hatch's world the tea-hour was not dedicated to social rites, and the lady was in the hands of her masseuse.

Selden's entrance had caused Lily an inward start of embarrassment; but his air of constraint had the effect of restoring her self-possession, and she took at once the tone of surprise and pleasure, wondering frankly that he should have traced her to so unlikely a place, and asking what had inspired him to make the search.

Selden met this with an unusual seriousness: she had never seen him so little master of the situation, so plainly at the mercy of any obstructions she might put in his way. "I wanted to see you," he said; and she could not resist observing in reply that he had kept his wishes under remarkable control. She had in truth felt his long absence as one of the chief bitternesses of the last months: his desertion had wounded sensibilities far below the surface of her pride.

Selden met the challenge with directness. "Why should I have come, unless I thought I could be of use to you? It is my only excuse for imagining you could want me."

This struck her as a clumsy evasion, and the thought gave a flash of keenness to her answer. "Then you have come now because you think you can be of use to me?"

He hesitated again. "Yes, in the modest capacity of a person to talk things over with."

For a clever man it was certainly a stupid beginning; and the idea that his awkwardness was due to the fear of her attaching a personal significance to his visit chilled her pleasure in seeing him. Even under the most adverse conditions, that pleasure always made itself felt: she might hate him, but she had never been able to wish him out of the room. She was very near hating him now; yet the sound of his voice, the way the light fell on his thin dark hair, the way he sat and moved and wore his clothes—she was conscious that even these trivial things were inwoven with her deepest life. In his presence a sudden stillness came upon her, and the turmoil of her spirit ceased; but an impulse of resistance to this stealing influence now prompted her to say: "It's very good of you to present yourself in that capacity; but what makes you think I have anything particular to talk about?"

Though she kept the even tone of light intercourse, the question was framed in a way to remind him that his good offices were unsought; and for a moment Selden was checked by it. The situation between them was one which could have been cleared up only by a sudden explosion of feeling; and their whole training and habit of mind were against the chances of such an explosion. Selden's calmness seemed rather to harden into resistance, and Miss Bart's into a surface of glittering irony, as they faced each other from the opposite corners of one of Mrs. Hatch's elephantine sofas. The sofa in question, and the apartment peopled by its monstrous mates, served at length to suggest the turn of Selden's reply.

"Gerty told me that you were acting as Mrs. Hatch's secretary; and I knew she was anxious to hear how you were getting on."

Miss Bart received this explanation without perceptible softening. "Why didn't she look me up herself, then?" she asked.

"Because, as you didn't send her your address, she was afraid of being importunate." Selden continued with a smile: "You see no such scruples restrained me; but then I haven't as much to risk if I incur your displeasure."

Lily answered his smile. "You haven't incurred it as yet; but I have an idea that you are going to."

"That rests with you, doesn't it? You see, my initiative doesn't go beyond putting myself at your disposal."

"But in what capacity? What am I to do with you?" she asked in the same light tone.

Selden again glanced about Mrs. Hatch's drawing-room; then he said, with a decision which he seemed to have gathered from this final inspection: "You are to let me take you away from here."

Lily flushed at the suddenness of the attack; then she stiffened under it and said coldly: "And may I ask where you mean me to go?"

"Back to Gerty in the first place, if you will; the essential thing is that it should be away from here."

The unusual harshness of his tone might have shown her how much the words cost him; but she was in no state to measure his feelings while her own were in a flame of revolt. To neglect her, perhaps even to avoid her, at a time when she had most need of her friends, and then suddenly and unwarrantably to break into her life with this strange assumption of authority, was to rouse in her every instinct of pride and self-defense.

"I am very much obliged to you," she said, "for taking such an interest in my plans; but I am quite contented where I am, and have no intention of leaving."

Selden had risen, and was standing before her in an attitude of uncontrollable expectancy.

"That simply means that you don't know where you are!" he exclaimed.

Lily rose also, with a quick flash of anger. "If you have come here to say disagreeable things about Mrs. Hatch—"

"It is only with your relation to Mrs. Hatch that I am concerned."

"My relation to Mrs. Hatch is one I have no reason to be ashamed of. She has helped me to earn a living when my old friends were quite resigned to seeing me starve."

"Nonsense! Starvation is not the only alternative. You know you can always find a home with Gerty till you are independent again."

"You show such an intimate acquaintance with my affairs that I suppose you mean—till my aunt's legacy is paid?"

"I do mean that; Gerty told me of it," Selden acknowledged without embarrassment. He was too much in earnest now to feel any false constraint in speaking his mind.

"But Gerty does not happen to know," Miss Bart rejoined, "that I owe every penny of that legacy."

"Good God!" Selden exclaimed, startled out of his composure by the abruptness of the statement.

"Every penny of it, and more too," Lily repeated; "and you now perhaps see why I prefer to remain with Mrs. Hatch rather than take advantage of Gerty's kindness. I have no money left, except my small income, and I must earn something more to keep myself alive."

Selden hesitated a moment; then he rejoined in a quieter tone: "But with your income and Gerty's—since you allow me to go so far into the details of the situation—you and she could surely contrive a life together which would put you beyond the need of having to support yourself. Gerty, I know, is eager to make such an arrangement, and would be quite happy in it—"

"But I should not," Miss Bart interposed. "There are many reasons why it would be neither kind to Gerty nor wise for myself." She paused a moment, and as he seemed to await a further explanation, added with a quick lift of her head: "You will perhaps excuse me from giving you these reasons."

"I have no claim to know them," Selden answered, ignoring her tone; "no claim to offer any comment or suggestion beyond the one I have already made. And my right to make that is simply the universal right of a man to enlighten a woman when he sees her unconsciously placed in a false position."

Lily smiled. "I suppose," she rejoined, "that by a false position you mean one outside of what we call society; but you must remember that I had been excluded from those sacred precincts long before I met Mrs. Hatch. As far as I can see, there is very little real difference in being inside or out, and I remember your once telling me that it was only those inside who took the difference seriously."

She had not been without intention in making this allusion to their memorable talk at Bellomont, and she waited with an odd tremor of the nerves to see what response it would bring; but the result of the experiment was disappointing. Selden did not allow the allusion to deflect him from his point; he merely said with completer fullness of emphasis: "The question of being inside or out is, as you say, a small one, and it happens to have nothing to do with the case, except in so far as Mrs. Hatch's desire to be inside may put you in the position I call false."

In spite of the moderation of his tone, each word he spoke had the effect of confirming Lily's resistance. The very apprehensions he aroused hardened her against him: she had been on the alert for the note of personal sympathy, for any sign of recovered power over him; and his attitude of sober impartiality, the absence of all response to her appeal, turned her hurt pride to blind resentment of his interference. The conviction that he had been sent by Gerty, and that, whatever straits he conceived her to be in, he would never voluntarily have come to her aid, strengthened her resolve not to admit him a hair's breadth further into her confidence. However doubtful she might feel her situation to be, she would rather persist in darkness than owe her enlightenment to Selden.

"I don't know," she said, when he had ceased to speak, "why you imagine me to be situated as you describe; but as you have always told me that the sole object of a bringing-up like mine was to teach a girl to get what she wants, why not assume that that is precisely what I am doing?"

The smile with which she summed up her case was like a clear barrier raised against further confidences: its brightness held him at such a distance that he had a sense of being almost out of hearing as he rejoined: "I am not sure that I have ever called you a successful example of that kind of bringing-up."

Her color rose a little at the implication, but she steeled herself with a light laugh.

"Ah, wait a little longer—give me a little more time before you decide!" And as he wavered before her, still watching for a break in the impenetrable front she presented: "Don't give me up; I may still do credit to my training!" she affirmed.

25

L OOK at those spangles, Miss Bart—everyone of 'em sewed on crooked."
The tall forewoman, a pinched perpendicular figure, dropped the condemned structure of wire and net on the table at Lily's side, and passed on to the next figure in the line.

There were twenty of them in the workroom, their fagged profiles, under exaggerated hair, bowed in the harsh north light above the utensils of their art; for it was something more than an industry, surely, this creation of ever-varied settings for the face of fortunate womanhood. Their own faces were sallow with the unwholesomeness of hot air and sedentary toil, rather than with any actual signs of want: they were employed in a fashionable millinery establishment, and were fairly well clothed and well paid; but the youngest among them was as dull and colorless as the middle-aged. In the whole workroom there was only one skin beneath which the blood still visibly played; and that now burned with vexation as Miss Bart, under the lash of the forewoman's comment, began to strip the hat-frame of its over-lapping spangles.

To Gerty Farish's hopeful spirit a solution appeared to have been reached when she remembered how beautifully Lily could trim hats. Instances of young lady-milliners establishing themselves under fashionable patronage, and imparting to their "creations" that indefinable touch which the professional hand can never give, had flattered Gerty's visions of the future, and convinced even Lily that her separation from Mrs. Norma Hatch need not reduce her to dependence on her friends.

The parting had occurred a few weeks after Selden's visit, and would have taken place sooner had it not been for the resistance set up in Lily by his ill-starred offer of advice. The sense of being involved in a transaction she would not have cared to examine too closely had soon afterward defined itself in the light of a hint from Mr. Stancy that, if she "saw them through," she would have no reason to be sorry. The implication that such loyalty would meet with a direct reward had hastened her flight, and flung her back, ashamed and penitent, on the broad bosom of Gerty's sympathy. She did not, however, propose to lie there prone, and Gerty's inspiration about the hats at once revived her hopes of profitable activity. Here was, after all, something that her charming listless hands could really do; she had no doubt of their capacity for knotting a ribbon or placing a flower to advantage. And of course only these finishing touches would be expected of her:

subordinate fingers, blunt, gray, needle-pricked fingers, would prepare the shapes and stitch the linings, while she presided over the charming little front shop—a shop all white panels, mirrors, and moss-green hangings—where her finished creations, hats, wreaths, aigrettes and the rest, perched on their stands like birds just poising for flight.

But at the very outset of Gerty's campaign this vision of the green-and-white shop had been dispelled. Other young ladies of fashion had been thus "set-up," selling their hats by the mere attraction of a name and the reputed knack of tying a bow; but these privileged beings could command a faith in their powers materially expressed by the readiness to pay their shop-rent and advance a handsome sum for current expenses. Where was Lily to find such support? And even could it have been found, how were the ladies on whose approval she depended to be induced to give her their patronage? Gerty learned that whatever sympathy her friend's case might have excited a few months since had been imperilled, if not lost, by her association with Mrs. Hatch. Once again, Lily had withdrawn from an ambiguous situation in time to save her self-respect, but too late for public vindication. Freddy Van Osburgh was not to marry Mrs. Hatch; he had been rescued at the eleventh hour—some said by the efforts of Gus Trenor and Rosedale—and dispatched to Europe with old Ned Van Alstyne; but the risk he had run would always be ascribed to Miss Bart's connivance, and would somehow serve as a summing-up and corroboration of the vague general distrust of her. It was a relief to those who had hung back from her to find themselves thus justified, and they were inclined to insist a little on her connection with the Hatch case in order to show that they had been right.

Gerty's quest, at any rate, brought up against a solid wall of resistance; and even when Carry Fisher, momentarily penitent for her share in the Hatch affair, joined her efforts to Miss Farish's, they met with no better success. Gerty had tried to veil her failure in tender ambiguities; but Carry, always the soul of candor, put the case squarely to her friend.

"I went straight to Judy Trenor; she has fewer prejudices than the others, and besides she's always hated Bertha Dorset. But what *have* you done to her, Lily? At the very first word about giving you a start she flamed out about some money you'd got from Gus; I never knew her so hot before. You know she'll let him do anything but spend money on his friends: the only reason she's decent to me now is that she knows I'm not hard up. He speculated for you, you say? Well, what's the harm? He had no business to lose. He *didn't* lose? Then what on earth—but I never *could* understand you, Lily!"

The end of it was that, after anxious inquiry and much deliberation, Mrs. Fisher and Gerty, for once oddly united in their effort to help their friend, decided on placing her in the workroom of Mme. Regina's renowned millinery establishment. Even this arrangement was not effected without considerable negotiation, for Mme. Regina had a strong prejudice against untrained assistance, and was induced to yield only by the fact that she owed the patronage of Mrs. Bry and Mrs. Gormer to Carry Fisher's influence. She had been willing from the first to employ Lily in the showroom: as a displayer of hats, a fashionable beauty might be a valuable asset. But to this suggestion Miss Bart opposed a negative which Gerty emphatically supported, while Mrs. Fisher, inwardly unconvinced, but resigned to this latest proof of Lily's unreason, agreed that perhaps in the end it would be more useful that she should learn the trade. To Regina's workroom Lily was therefore committed by her friends, and there Mrs. Fisher left her with a sigh of relief, while Gerty's watchfullness continued to hover over her at a distance.

Lily had taken up her work early in January: it was now two months later, and she was still being rebuked for her inability to sew spangles on a hat-frame. As she returned to her work she heard a titter pass down the tables. She knew she was an object of criticism and amusement to the other workwomen. They were, of course, aware of her history—the exact situation of every girl in the room was known and freely discussed by all the others—but the knowledge did not produce in them any awkward sense of class distinction: it merely explained why her untutored fingers were still blundering over the rudiments of the trade. Lily had no desire that they should recognize any social difference in her; but she had hoped to be received as their equal, and perhaps before long to show herself their superior by a special deftness of touch, and it was humiliating to find that, after two months of drudgery, she still betrayed her lack of early training. Remote was the day when she might aspire to exercise the talents she felt confident of possessing; only experienced workers were entrusted with the delicate art of shaping and trimming the hat, and the forewoman still held her inexorably to the routine of preparatory work.

She began to rip the spangles from the frame, listening absently to the buzz of talk which rose and fell with the coming and going of Miss Haines's active figure. The air was closer than usual, because Miss Haines, who had a cold, had not allowed a window to be opened even during the noon recess; and Lily's head was so heavy with the weight of a sleepless night that the chatter of her companions had the incoherence of a dream.

"I *told* her he'd never look at her again; and he didn't. I wouldn't have, either—I think she acted real mean to him. He took her to the Arion Ball, and had a hack for her both ways. . . . She's taken ten bottles, and her headaches don't seem no better—but she's written a testimonial to say the first bottle cured her, and she got five dollars and her picture in the paper. . . . Mrs. Trenor's hat? The one with the green Paradise? Here, Miss Haines—it'll be ready right off. . . . That was one of the Trenor girls here yesterday with Mrs. George Dorset. How'd I know? Why, Madam sent for me to alter the flower in that Virot hat—the blue tulle: she's tall and slight, with her hair fuzzed out—a good deal like Mamie Leach, on'y thinner. . . ."

On and on it flowed, a current of meaningless sound, on which, startlingly enough, a familiar name now and then floated to the surface. It was the strangest part of Lily's strange experience, the hearing of these names, the seeing the fragmentary and distorted image of the world she had lived in reflected in the mirror of the working-girls' minds. She had never before suspected the mixture of insatiable curiosity and contemptuous freedom with which she and her kind were discussed in this underworld of toilers who lived on their vanity and self-indulgence. Every girl in Mme. Regina's workroom knew to whom the headgear in her hands was destined, and had her opinion of its future wearer, and a definite knowledge of the latter's place in the social system. That Lily was a star fallen from that sky did not, after the first stir of curiosity had subsided, materially add to their interest in her. She had fallen, she had "gone under," and true to the ideal of their race, they were awed only by success—by the gross tangible image of material achievement. The consciousness of her different point of view merely kept them at a little distance from her, as though she were a foreigner with whom it was an effort to talk.

"Miss Bart, if you can't sew those spangles on more regular I guess you'd better give the hat to Miss Kilroy."

Lily looked down ruefully at her handiwork. The forewoman was right: the sewing on of the spangles was inexcusably bad. What made her so much more clumsy than usual? Was it a growing distaste for her task, or actual physical disability? She felt tired and confused: it was an effort to put her thoughts together. She rose and handed the hat to Miss Kilroy, who took it with a suppressed smile.

"I'm sorry; I'm afraid I am not well," she said to the forewoman.

Miss Haines offered no comment. From the first she had augured ill of Mme. Regina's consenting to include a fashionable apprentice among her workers. In that temple of art no raw beginners were wanted, and Miss Haines would have been more than human had she not taken a certain pleasure in seeing her forebodings confirmed.

"You'd better go back to binding edges," she said drily.

Lily slipped out last among the band of liberated workwomen. She did not care to be mingled in their noisy dispersal: once in the street, she always felt an irresistible return to her old standpoint, an instinctive shrinking from all that was unpolished and promiscuous. In the days—how distant they now seemed!—when she had visited the Girls' Club with Gerty Farish, she had felt an enlightened interest in the working-classes; but that was because she looked down on them from above, from the happy altitude of her grace and her beneficence. Now that she was on a level with them, the point of view was less interesting.

She felt a touch on her arm, and met the penitent eye of Miss Kilroy.

"Miss Bart, I guess you can sew those spangles on as well as I can when you're feeling right. Miss Haines didn't act fair to you."

Lily's color rose at the unexpected advance: it was a long time since real kindness had looked at her from any eyes but Gerty's.

"Oh, thank you: I'm not particularly well, but Miss Haines was right. I *am* clumsy."

"Well, it's mean work for anybody with a headache." Miss Kilroy paused irresolutely. "You ought to go right home and lay down. Ever try orangeine?"

"Thank you." Lily held out her hand. "It's very kind of you—I mean to go home."

She looked gratefully at Miss Kilroy, but neither knew what more to say. Lily was aware that the other was on the point of offering to go home with her, but she wanted to be alone and silent—even kindness, the sort of kindness that Miss Kilroy could give, would have jarred on her just then.

"Thank you," she repeated as she turned away.

She struck westward through the dreary March twilight, toward the street where her boardinghouse stood. She had resolutely refused Gerty's offer of hospitality. Something of her mother's fierce shrinking from observation and sympathy was beginning to develop in her, and the promiscuity of small quarters and close intimacy seemed, on the whole, less endurable than the solitude of a hall bedroom in a house where she could come and go unremarked among other workers. For a while she had been sustained by this desire for privacy and independence; but now, perhaps from increasing physical weariness, the lassitude brought about by hours of unwonted confinement, she was beginning to feel acutely the ugliness and discomfort of her surroundings. The day's task done, she dreaded to return to her narrow room, with its blotched wallpaper and shabby paint; and she hated every step of the walk thither, through the degradation of a New York street in the last stages of decline from fashion to commerce.

But what she dreaded most of all was having to pass the chemist's at the corner of Sixth Avenue. She had meant to take another street: she had usually done so of late. But today her steps were irresistibly drawn toward the flaring plate-glass corner; she tried to take the lower crossing, but a laden dray crowded her back, and she struck across the street obliquely, reaching the sidewalk just opposite the chemist's door.

Over the counter she caught the eye of the clerk who had waited on her before, and slipped the prescription into his hand. There could be no question about the prescription: it was a copy of one of Mrs. Hatch's, obligingly furnished by that lady's chemist. Lily was confident that the clerk would fill it without hesitation; yet the nervous dread of a refusal, or even of an expression of doubt, communicated itself to her restless hands as she affected to examine the bottles of perfume stacked on the glass case before her.

The clerk had read the prescription without comment; but in the act of handing out the bottle he paused.

"You don't want to increase the dose, you know," he remarked.

Lily's heart contracted. What did he mean by looking at her in that way?

"Of course not," she murmured, holding out her hand.

"That's all right: it's a queer-acting drug. A drop or two more, and off you go—the doctors don't know why."

The dread lest he should question her, or keep the bottle back, choked the murmur of acquiescence in her throat; and when at length she emerged safely from the shop she was almost dizzy with the intensity of her relief. The mere touch of the packet thrilled her tired nerves with the delicious promise of a night of sleep, and in the reaction from her momentary fear she felt as if the first fumes of drowsiness were already stealing over her.

In her confusion she stumbled against a man who was hurrying down the last steps of the elevated station. He drew back, and she heard her name uttered with surprise. It was Rosedale, fur-coated, glossy and prosperous—but why did she seem to see him so far off, and as if through a mist of splintered crystals? Before she could account for the phenomenon she found herself shaking hands with him. They had parted with scorn on her side and anger upon his; but all trace of these emotions seemed to vanish as their hands met, and she was only aware of a confused wish that she might continue to hold fast to him.

"Why, what's the matter, Miss Lily? You're not well!" he exclaimed; and she forced her lips into a pallid smile of reassurance.

"I'm a little tired—it's nothing. Stay with me a moment, please," she faltered. That she should be asking this service of Rosedale!

He glanced at the dirty and unpropitious corner on which they stood, with the shriek of the "elevated" and the tumult of trams and wagons contending hideously in their ears.

"We can't stay here; but let me take you somewhere for a cup of tea. The Longworth is only a few yards off, and there'll be no one there at this hour."

A cup of tea in quiet, somewhere out of the noise and ugliness, seemed for the moment the one solace she could bear. A few steps brought them to the ladies' door of the hotel he had named, and a moment later he was seated opposite to her, and the waiter had placed the tea-tray between them.

"Not a drop of brandy or whiskey first? You look regularly done up, Miss Lily. Well, take your tea strong, then; and, waiter, get a cushion for the lady's back."

Lily smiled faintly at the injunction to take her tea strong. It was the temptation she was always struggling to resist. Her craving for the keen stimulant was forever conflicting with that other craving for sleep—the midnight craving which only the little phial in her hand could still. But today, at any rate, the tea could hardly be too strong: she counted on it to pour warmth and resolution into her empty veins.

As she leaned back before him, her lids drooping in utter lassitude, though the first warm draught already tinged her face with returning life, Rosedale was seized afresh by the poignant surprise of her beauty. The dark pencilling of fatigue under her eyes, the morbid blue-veined pallor of the temples, brought out the brightness of her hair and lips, as though all her ebbing vitality were centered there. Against the dull chocolate-colored background of the restaurant, the purity of her head stood out as it had never done in the most brightly lit ballroom. He looked at her with a startled uncomfortable feeling, as though her beauty were a forgotten enemy that had lain in ambush and now sprang out on him unawares.

To clear the air he tried to take an easy tone with her. "Why, Miss Lily, I haven't seen you for an age. I didn't know what had become of you."

As he spoke, he was checked by an embarrassing sense of the complications to which this might lead. Though he had not seen her he had heard of her; he knew of her connection with Mrs. Hatch, and of the talk resulting from it. Mrs. Hatch's milieu was one which he had once assiduously frequented, and now as devoutly shunned.

Lily, to whom the tea had restored her usual clearness of mind, saw what was in his thoughts and said with a slight smile: "You would not be likely to know about me. I have joined the working classes."

He stared in genuine wonder. "You don't mean—? Why, what on earth are you doing?"

"Learning to be a milliner—at least *trying* to learn," she hastily qualified the statement.

Rosedale suppressed a low whistle of surprise. "Come off—you ain't serious, are you?"

"Perfectly serious. I'm obliged to work for my living."

"But I understood—I thought you were with Norma Hatch."

"You heard I had gone to her as her secretary?"

"Something of the kind, I believe." He leaned forward to refill her cup.

Lily guessed the possibilities of embarrassment which the topic held for him, and raising her eyes to his, she said suddenly: "I left her two months ago."

Rosedale continued to fumble awkwardly with the teapot, and she felt sure that he had heard what had been said of her. But what was there that Rosedale did not hear?

"Wasn't it a soft berth?" he inquired, with an attempt at lightness.

"Too soft—one might have sunk in too deep." Lily rested one arm on the edge of the table, and sat looking at him more intently than she had ever looked before. An uncontrollable impulse was urging her to put her case to this man, from whose curiosity she had always so fiercely defended herself.

"You know Mrs. Hatch, I think? Well, perhaps you can understand that she might make things too easy for one."

Rosedale looked faintly puzzled, and she remembered that allusiveness was lost on him.

"It was no place for you, anyhow," he agreed, so suffused and immersed in the light of her full gaze that he found himself being drawn into strange depths of intimacy. He who had had to subsist on mere fugitive glances, looks winged in flight and swiftly lost under covert, now found her eyes settling on him with a brooding intensity that fairly dazzled him.

"I left," Lily continued, "lest people should say I was helping Mrs. Hatch to marry Freddy Van Osburgh—who is not in the least too good for her—and as they still continue to say it, I see that I might as well have stayed where I was."

"Oh, Freddy—" Rosedale brushed aside the topic with an air of its unimportance which gave a sense of the immense perspective he had acquired. "Freddy don't count—but I knew *you* weren't mixed up in that. It ain't your style."

Lily colored slightly: she could not conceal from herself that the words gave her pleasure. She would have liked to sit there, drinking more tea, and continuing to talk of herself to Rosedale. But the old habit of observing the conventions reminded her that it was time to bring their colloquy to an end, and she made a faint motion to push back her chair.

Rosedale stopped her with a protesting gesture. "Wait a minute—don't go yet; sit quiet and rest a little longer. You look thoroughly played out. And you haven't told me—" He broke off, conscious of going farther than he had meant. She saw the struggle and understood it; understood also the nature of the spell to which he yielded as, with his eyes on her face, he began again abruptly: "What on earth did you mean by saying just now that you were learning to be a milliner?"

"Just what I said. I am an apprentice at Regina's."

"Good Lord—*you?* But what for? I knew your aunt had turned you down: Mrs. Fisher told me about it. But I understood you got a legacy from her—"

"I got ten thousand dollars; but the legacy is not to be paid till next summer."

"Well, but—look here: you could *borrow* on it any time you wanted."

She shook her head gravely. "No; for I owe it already."

"Owe it? The whole ten thousand?"

"Every penny." She paused, and then continued abruptly, with her eyes on his face: "I think Gus Trenor spoke to you once about having made some money for me in stocks."

She waited, and Rosedale, congested with embarrassment, muttered that he remembered something of the kind.

"He made about nine thousand dollars," Lily pursued, in the same tone of eager communicativeness. "At the time, I understood that he was speculating with my own money: it was incredibly stupid of me, but I knew nothing of business. Afterward I found out that he had *not* used my money —that what he said he had made for me he had really given me. It was meant in kindness, of course; but it was not the sort of obligation one could remain under. Unfortunately I had spent the money before I discovered my mistake; and so my legacy will have to go to pay it back. That is the reason why I am trying to learn a trade."

She made the statement clearly, deliberately, with pauses between the sentences, so that each should have time to sink deeply into her hearer's mind. She had a passionate desire that someone should know the truth about this transaction, and also that the rumor of her intention to repay the money should reach Judy Trenor's ears. And it had suddenly occurred to her that Rosedale, who had surprised Trenor's confidence, was the fitting person to receive and transmit her version of the facts. She had even felt a momentary exhilaration at the thought of thus relieving herself of her detested secret; but the sensation gradually faded in the telling, and as she ended her pallor was suffused with a deep blush of misery.

Rosedale continued to stare at her in wonder; but the wonder took the turn she had least expected.

"But see here—if that's the case, it cleans you out altogether?"

He put it to her as if she had not grasped the consequences of her act; as if her incorrigible ignorance of business were about to precipitate her into a fresh act of folly.

"Altogether—yes," she calmly agreed.

He sat silent, his thick hands clasped on the table, his little puzzled eyes exploring the recesses of the deserted restaurant.

"See here—that's fine," he exclaimed abruptly.

Lily rose from her seat with a deprecating laugh. "Oh, no—it's merely a bore," she asserted, gathering together the ends of her feather scarf.

Rosedale remained seated, too intent on his thoughts to notice her movement. "Miss Lily, if you want any backing—I like pluck—" broke from him disconnectedly.

"Thank you." She held out her hand. "Your tea has given me a tremendous backing. I feel equal to anything now."

Her gesture seemed to show a definite intention of dismissal, but her companion had tossed a bill to the waiter, and was slipping his short arms into his expensive overcoat.

"Wait a minute—you've got to let me walk home with you," he said.

Lily uttered no protest, and when he had paused to make sure of his change they emerged from the hotel and crossed Sixth Avenue again. As she led the way westward past a long line of areas which, through the distortion of their paintless rails, revealed with increasing candor the *disjecta membra* of bygone dinners, Lily felt that Rosedale was taking contemptuous note of the neighborhood; and before the doorstep at which she finally paused he looked up with an air of incredulous disgust.

"This isn't the place? Someone told me you were living with Miss Farish."

"No, I am boarding here. I have lived too long on my friends."

He continued to scan the blistered brownstone front, the windows draped with discolored lace, and the Pompeian decoration of the muddy vestibule; then he looked back at her face and said with a visible effort: "You'll let me come and see you someday?"

She smiled, recognizing the heroism of the offer to the point of being frankly touched by it. "Thank you—I shall be very glad," she made answer, in the first sincere words she had ever spoken to him.

That evening in her own room Miss Bart—who had fled early from the heavy fumes of the basement dinner table—sat musing upon the impulse which had led her to unbosom herself to Rosedale. Beneath it she discovered an increasing sense of loneliness—a dread of returning to the solitude of her room, while she could be anywhere else, or in any company but her own. Circumstances, of late, had combined to cut her off more and more from her few remaining friends. On Carry Fisher's part the withdrawal was perhaps not quite involuntary. Having made her final effort on Lily's behalf, and landed her safely in Mme. Regina's workroom, Mrs. Fisher seemed disposed to rest from her labors; and Lily, understanding the reason, could not condemn her. Carry had in fact come dangerously near to being involved in the episode of Mrs. Norma Hatch, and it had taken some verbal ingenuity to extricate herself. She frankly owned to having brought Lily and Mrs. Hatch together, but then she did not know Mrs. Hatch—she had expressly warned Lily that she did not know Mrs. Hatch—and besides, she was not Lily's keeper, and really the girl was old enough to take care of herself. Carry did not put her own case so brutally, but she allowed it to be thus put for her by her latest bosom friend, Mrs. Jack Stepney: Mrs. Stepney, trembling over the narrowness of her only brother's escape, but eager to vindicate Mrs. Fisher, at whose house she could count on the "jolly parties" which had become a necessity to her since marriage had emancipated her from the Van Osburgh point of view.

Lily understood the situation and could make allowances for it. Carry had been a good friend to her in difficult days, and perhaps only a friendship like Gerty's could be proof against such an increasing strain. Gerty's friendship did indeed hold fast; yet Lily was beginning to avoid her also. For she could not go to Gerty's without risk of meeting Selden; and to meet him now would be pure pain. It was pain enough even to think of him, whether she considered him in the distinctness of her waking thoughts, or felt the obsession of his presence through the blur of her tormented nights. That was one of the reasons why she had turned again to Mrs. Hatch's prescription. In the uneasy snatches of her natural dreams he came to her sometimes in the old guise of fellowship and tenderness; and she would rise from the sweet delusion mocked and emptied of her courage. But in the sleep which the phial procured she sank far below such half-waking visitations, sank into depths of dreamless annihilation from which she woke each morning with an obliterated past.

Gradually, to be sure, the stress of the old thoughts would return; but at least they did not importune her waking hour. The drug gave her a momentary illusion of complete renewal, from which she drew strength to take up her daily work. The strength was more and more needed as the perplexities of her future increased. She knew that to Gerty and Mrs. Fisher she was only passing through a temporary period of probation, since they believed that the apprenticeship she was serving at Mme. Regina's would enable her, when Mrs. Peniston's legacy was paid, to realize the vision of the green-and-white shop with the fuller competence acquired by her preliminary training. But to Lily herself, aware that the legacy could not be put to such a use, the preliminary training seemed a wasted effort. She understood clearly enough that, even if she could ever learn to compete with hands formed from childhood for their special work, the small pay she received would not be a sufficient addition to her income to compensate her for such drudgery. And the realization of this fact brought her recurringly face to face with the temptation to use the legacy in establishing her business. Once installed, and in command of her own workwomen, she believed she had sufficient tact and ability to attract a fashionable clientele; and if the business succeeded she could gradually lay aside money enough to discharge her debt to Trenor. But the task might take years to accomplish, even if she continued to stint herself to the utmost; and meanwhile her pride would be crushed under the weight of an intolerable obligation.

These were her superficial considerations; but under them lurked the secret dread that the obligation might not always remain intolerable. She knew she could not count on her continuity of purpose, and what really frightened her was the thought that she might gradually accommodate herself to remaining indefinitely in Trenor's debt, as she had accommodated herself to the part allotted her on the *Sabrina,* and as she had so nearly drifted into acquiescing with Stancy's scheme for the advancement of Mrs. Hatch. Her danger lay, as she knew, in her old incurable dread of discomfort and poverty; in the fear of that mounting tide of dinginess against which her mother had so passionately warned her. And now a new vista of peril opened before her. She understood that Rosedale was ready to lend her money; and the longing to take advantage of his offer began to haunt her insidiously. It was of course impossible to accept a loan from Rosedale; but proximate possibilities hovered temptingly before her. She was quite sure that he would come and see her again, and almost sure that, if he did, she could bring him to the point of offering to marry her on the terms she had previously rejected. Would she still reject them if they were offered? More and more, with every fresh mischance befalling her, did the pursuing furies seem to take the shape of Bertha Dorset; and close at hand, safely locked among her papers, lay the means of ending their pursuit. The temptation, which her scorn of Rosedale had once enabled her to reject, now insistently returned upon her; and how much strength was left her to oppose it?

What little there was must at any rate be husbanded to the utmost; she could not trust herself again to the perils of a sleepless night. Through the long hours of silence the dark spirit of fatigue and loneliness crouched upon her breast, leaving her so drained of bodily strength that her morning thoughts swam in a haze of weakness. The only hope of renewal lay in the little bottle at her bedside; and how much longer that hope would last she dared not conjecture.

26

L ILY, lingering for a moment on the corner, looked out on the afternoon spectacle of Fifth Avenue.

It was a day in late April, and the sweetness of spring was in the air. It mitigated the ugliness of the long crowded thoroughfare, blurred the gaunt rooflines, threw a mauve veil over the discouraging perspective of the side streets, and gave a touch of poetry to the delicate haze of green that marked the entrance to the Park.

As Lily stood there, she recognized several familiar faces in the passing carriages. The season was over, and its ruling forces had disbanded; but a few still lingered, delaying their departure for Europe, or passing through town on their return from the south. Among them was Mrs. Van Osburgh, swaying majestically in her C-spring barouche, with Mrs. Percy Gryce at her side, and the new heir to the Gryce millions enthroned before them on his nurse's knees. They were succeeded by Mrs. Hatch's electric victoria, in which that lady reclined in the lonely splendor of a spring toilet obviously designed for company; and a moment or two later came Judy Trenor, accompanied by Lady Skiddaw, who had come over for her annual tarpon fishing and a dip into "the street."

This fleeting glimpse of her past served to emphasize the sense of aimlessness with which Lily at length turned toward home. She had nothing to do for the rest of the day, nor for the days to come; for the season was over in millinery as well as in society, and a week earlier Mme. Regina had notified her that her services were no longer required. Mme. Regina always reduced her staff on the first of May, and Miss Bart's attendance had of late been so irregular—she had so often been unwell, and had done so little work when she came—that it was only as a favor that her dismissal had hitherto been deferred.

Lily did not question the justice of the decision. She was conscious of having been forgetful, awkward and slow to learn. It was bitter to acknowledge her inferiority even to herself, but the fact had been brought home to her that as a breadwinner she could never compete with professional ability. Since she had been brought up to be ornamental, she could hardly blame herself for failing to serve any practical purpose; but the discovery put an end to her consoling sense of universal efficiency.

As she turned homeward her thoughts shrank in anticipation from the fact that there would be nothing to get up for the next morning. The luxury of lying late in bed was a pleasure belonging to the life of ease; it had no part in the utilitarian existence of the boardinghouse. She liked to leave her room early, and to return to it as late as possible; and she was walking slowly now in order to postpone the detested approach to her doorstep.

But the doorstep, as she drew near it, acquired a sudden interest from the fact that it was occupied—and indeed filled—by the conspicuous figure of Mr. Rosedale, whose presence seemed to take on an added amplitude from the meanness of his surroundings.

The sight stirred Lily with an irresistible sense of triumph. Rosedale, a day or two after their chance meeting, had called to inquire if she had recovered from her indisposition; but since then she had not seen or heard from him, and his absence seemed to betoken a struggle to keep away, to let her pass once more out of his life. If this were the case, his return showed that the struggle had been unsuccessful, for Lily knew he was not the man to waste his time in an ineffectual sentimental dalliance. He was too busy, too practical, and above all too much preoccupied with his own advancement, to indulge in such unprofitable asides.

In the peacock-blue parlor, with its bunches of dried pampas grass, and discolored steel engravings of sentimental episodes, he looked about him with unconcealed disgust, laying his hat distrustfully on the dusty console adorned with a Rogers statuette.

Lily sat down on one of the plush and rosewood sofas, and he deposited himself in a rocking chair draped with a starched antimacassar which scraped unpleasantly against the pink fold of skin above his collar.

"My goodness—you can't go on living here!" he exclaimed.

Lily smiled at his tone. "I am not sure that I can; but I have gone over my expenses very carefully, and I rather think I shall be able to manage it."

"Be able to manage it? That's not what I mean—it's no place for you!"

"It's what *I* mean; for I have been out of work for the last week."

"Out of work—out of work! What a way for you to talk! The idea of your having to work—it's preposterous." He brought out his sentences in short violent jerks, as though they were forced up from a deep inner crater of indignation. "It's a farce—a crazy farce," he repeated, his eyes fixed on the long vista of the room reflected in the blotched glass between the windows.

Lily continued to meet his expostulations with a smile. "I don't know why I should regard myself as an exception—" she began.

"Because you *are*; that's why; and your being in a place like this is a damnable outrage. I can't talk of it calmly."

She had in truth never seen him so shaken out of his usual glibness; and there was something almost moving to her in his inarticulate struggle with his emotions.

He rose with a start which left the rocking chair quivering on its beam ends, and placed himself squarely before her.

"Look here, Miss Lily, I'm going to Europe next week: going over to Paris and London for a couple of months—and I can't leave you like this. I can't do it. I know it's none of my business—you've let me understand that often enough; but things are worse with you now than they have been before, and you must see that you've got to accept help from somebody. You spoke to me the other day about some debt to Trenor. I know what you mean—and I respect you for feeling as you do about it."

A blush of surprise rose to Lily's pale face, but before she could interrupt him he had continued eagerly: "Well, I'll lend you the money to pay Trenor; and I won't—I—see here, don't take me up till I've finished. What I mean is, it'll be a plain business arrangement, such as one man would make with another. Now, what have you got to say against that?"

Lily's blush deepened to a glow in which humiliation and gratitude were mingled; and both sentiments revealed themselves in the unexpected gentleness of her reply.

"Only this: that it is exactly what Gus Trenor proposed; and that I can never again be sure of understanding the plainest business arrangement." Then, realizing that this answer contained a germ of injustice, she added, even more kindly: "Not that I don't appreciate your kindness—that I'm not grateful for it. But a business arrangement between us would in any case be impossible, because I shall have no security to give when my debt to Gus Trenor has been paid."

Rosedale received this statement in silence: he seemed to feel the note of finality in her voice, yet to be unable to accept it as closing the question between them.

In the silence Lily had a clear perception of what was passing through his mind. Whatever perplexity he felt as to the inexorableness of her course —however little he penetrated its motive—she saw that it unmistakably tended to strengthen her hold over him. It was as though the sense in her of unexplained scruples and resistances had the same attraction as the delicacy of feature, the fastidiousness of manner, which gave her an external rarity, an air of being impossible to match. As he advanced in social experience this uniqueness had acquired a greater value for him, as though he were a collector who had learned to distinguish minor differences of design and quality in some long-coveted object.

Lily, perceiving all this, understood that he would marry her at once, on the sole condition of a reconciliation with Mrs. Dorset; and the temptation was the less easy to put aside because, little by little, circumstances were breaking down her dislike for Rosedale. The dislike, indeed, still subsisted; but it was penetrated here and there by the perception of mitigating qualities in him: of a certain gross kindliness, a rather helpless fidelity of sentiment, which seemed to be struggling through the hard surface of his material ambitions.

Reading his dismissal in her eyes, he held out his hand with a gesture which conveyed something of this inarticulate conflict.

"If you'd only let me, I'd set you up over them all—I'd put you where you could wipe your feet on 'em!" he declared; and it touched her oddly to see that his new passion had not altered his old standard of values.

Lily took no sleeping-drops that night. She lay awake viewing her situation in the crude light which Rosedale's visit had shed on it. In fending off the offer he was so plainly ready to renew, had she not sacrificed to one of those abstract notions of honor that might be called the conventionalities of the moral life? What debt did she owe to a social order which had condemned and banished her without trial? She had never been heard in her own defense; she was innocent of the charge on which she had been found guilty; and the irregularity of her conviction might seem to justify the use of methods as irregular in recovering her lost rights. Bertha Dorset, to save herself, had not scrupled to ruin her by an open falsehood; why should she hesitate to make private use of the facts that chance had put in her way? After all, half the opprobrium of such an act lies in the name attached to it. Call it blackmail and it becomes unthinkable; but explain that it injures no one, and that the rights regained by it were unjustly forfeited, and he must be a formalist indeed who can find no plea in its defense.

The arguments pleading for it with Lily were the old unanswerable ones of the personal situation: the sense of injury, the sense of failure, the passionate craving for a fair chance against the selfish despotism of society. She had learned by experience that she had neither the aptitude nor the moral constancy to remake her life on new lines; to become a worker among workers, and let the world of luxury and pleasure sweep by her unregarded. She could not hold herself much to blame for this ineffectiveness, and she was perhaps less to blame than she believed. Inherited tendencies had combined with early training to make her the highly specialized product she was: an organism as helpless out of its narrow range as the sea-anemone torn from the rock. She had been fashioned to adorn and delight; to what other end does nature round the rose-leaf and paint the hummingbird's breast? And was it her fault that the purely decorative mission is less easily and harmoniously fulfillled among social beings than in the world of nature? That it is apt to be hampered by material necessities or complicated by moral scruples?

These last were the two antagonistic forces which fought out their battle in her breast during the long watches of the night; and when she rose the next morning she hardly knew where the victory lay. She was exhausted by the reaction of a night without sleep, coming after many nights of rest artificially obtained; and in the distorting light of fatigue the future stretched out before her gray, interminable and desolate.

She lay late in bed, refusing the coffee and fried eggs which the friendly Irish servant thrust through her door, and hating the intimate domestic noises of the house and the cries and rumblings of the street. Her week of idleness had brought home to her with exaggerated force these small aggravations of the boardinghouse world, and she yearned for that other luxurious world, whose machinery is so carefully concealed that one scene flows into another without perceptible agency.

At length she rose and dressed. Since she had left Mme. Regina's she had spent her days in the streets, partly to escape from the uncongenial promiscuities of the boardinghouse, and partly in the hope that physical fatigue would help her to sleep. But once out of the house, she could not decide where to go; for she had avoided Gerty since her dismissal from the milliner's, and she was not sure of a welcome anywhere else.

The morning was in harsh contrast to the previous day. A cold gray sky threatened rain, and a high wind drove the dust in wild spirals up and down the streets. Lily walked up Fifth Avenue toward the Park, hoping to find a sheltered nook where she might sit; but the wind chilled her, and after an hour's wandering under the tossing boughs she yielded to her increasing weariness, and took refuge in a little restaurant in Fifty-ninth Street. She was not hungry, and had meant to go without luncheon; but she was too tired to return home, and the long perspective of white tables showed alluringly through the windows.

The room was full of women and girls, all too much engaged in the rapid absorption of tea and pie to remark her entrance. A hum of shrill voices reverberated against the low ceiling, leaving Lily shut out in a little circle of silence. She felt a sudden pang of profound loneliness. She had lost the sense of time, and it seemed to her as though she had not spoken to anyone for days. Her eyes sought the faces about her, craving a responsive glance, some sign of an intuition of her trouble. But the sallow preoccupied women, with their bags and notebooks and rolls of music, were all engrossed in their own affairs, and even those who sat by themselves were busy running over proof-sheets or devouring magazines between their hurried gulps of tea. Lily alone was stranded in a great waste of disoccupation.

She drank several cups of the tea which was served with her portion of stewed oysters, and her brain felt clearer and livelier when she emerged once more into the street. She realized now that, as she sat in the restaurant, she had unconsciously arrived at a final decision. The discovery gave her an immediate illusion of activity: It was exhilarating to think that she had actually a reason for hurrying home. To prolong her enjoyment of the sensation she decided to walk; but the distance was so great that she found herself glancing nervously at the clocks on the way. One of the surprises of her unoccupied state was the discovery that time, when it is left to itself and no definite demands are made on it, cannot be trusted to move at any recognized pace. Usually it loiters; but just when one has come to count upon its slowness, it may suddenly break into a wild irrational gallop.

She found, however, on reaching home, that the hour was still early enough for her to sit down and rest a few minutes before putting her plan into execution. The delay did not perceptibly weaken her resolve. She was frightened and yet stimulated by the reserved force of resolution which she felt within herself: she saw it was going to be easier, a great deal easier, than she had imagined.

At five o'clock she rose, unlocked her trunk, and took out a sealed packet which she slipped into the bosom of her dress. Even the contact with the packet did not shake her nerves as she had half-expected it would. She seemed encased in a strong armor of indifference, as though the vigorous exertion of her will had finally benumbed her finer sensibilities.

She dressed herself once more for the street, locked her door and went out. When she emerged on the pavement, the day was still high, but a threat of rain darkened the sky and cold gusts shook the signs projecting from the basement shops along the street. She reached Fifth Avenue and began to walk slowly northward. She was sufficiently familiar with Mrs. Dorset's habits to know that she could always be found at home after five. She might not, indeed, be accessible to visitors, especially to a visitor so unwelcome, and against whom it was quite possible that she had guarded herself by special orders; but Lily had written a note which she meant to send up with her name, and which she thought would secure her admission.

She had allowed herself time to walk to Mrs. Dorset's, thinking that the quick movement through the cold evening air would help to steady her nerves; but she really felt no need of being tranquilized. Her survey of the situation remained calm and unwavering.

As she reached Fiftieth Street the clouds broke abruptly, and a rush of cold rain slanted into her face. She had no umbrella and the moisture quickly penetrated her thin spring dress. She was still half a mile from her destination, and she decided to walk across to Madison Avenue and take the electric car. As she turned into the side street, a vague memory stirred in her. The row of budding trees, the new brick and limestone housefronts, the Georgian flat-house with flowerboxes on its balconies, were merged together into the setting of a familiar scene. It was down this street that she had walked with Selden, that September day two years ago; a few yards ahead was the doorway they had entered together. The recollection loosened a throng of benumbed sensations—longings, regrets, imaginings, the throbbing brood of the only spring her heart had ever known. It was strange to find herself passing his house on such an errand. She seemed suddenly to see her action as he would see it—and the fact of his own connection with it, the fact that, to attain her end, she must trade on his name, and profit by a secret of his past, chilled her blood with shame. What a long way she had traveled since the day of their first talk together! Even then her feet had been set in the path she was now following—even then she had resisted the hand he had held out.

All her resentment of his fancied coldness was swept away in this overwhelming rush of recollection. Twice he had been ready to help her—to help her by loving her, as he had said—and if, the third time, he had seemed to fail her, whom but herself could she accuse? . . . Well, that part of her life was over; she did not know why her thoughts still clung to it. But the sudden longing to see him remained; it grew to hunger as she paused on the pavement opposite his door. The street was dark and empty, swept by the rain. She had a vision of his quiet room, of the bookshelves, and the fire on the hearth. She looked up and saw a light in his window; then she crossed the street and entered the house.

27

THE library looked as she had pictured it. The green-shaded lamps made tranquil circles of light in the gathering dusk, a little fire flickered on the hearth, and Selden's easy-chair, which stood near it, had been pushed aside when he rose to admit her.

He had checked his first movement of surprise, and stood silent, waiting for her to speak, while she paused a moment on the threshold, assailed by a rush of memories.

The scene was unchanged. She recognized the row of shelves from which he had taken down his La Bruyère, and the worn arm of the chair he had leaned against while she examined the precious volume. But then the wide September light had filled the room, making it seem a part of the outer world: now the shaded lamps and the warm hearth, detaching it from the gathering darkness of the street, gave it a sweeter touch of intimacy.

Becoming gradually aware of the surprise under Selden's silence, Lily turned to him and said simply: "I came to tell you that I was sorry for the way we parted—for what I said to you that day at Mrs. Hatch's."

The words rose to her lips spontaneously. Even on her way up the stairs, she had not thought of preparing a pretext for her visit, but she now felt an intense longing to dispel the cloud of misunderstanding that hung between them.

Selden returned her look with a smile. "I was sorry, too, that we should have parted in that way; but I am not sure I didn't bring it on myself. Luckily I had foreseen the risk I was taking—"

"So that you really didn't care—?" broke from her with a flash of her old irony.

"So that I was prepared for the consequences," he corrected good-humoredly. "But we'll talk of all this later. Do come and sit by the fire. I can recommend that armchair, if you'll let me put a cushion behind you."

While he spoke she had moved slowly to the middle of the room, and paused near his writing-table, where the lamp, striking upward, cast exaggerated shadows on the pallor of her delicately hollowed face.

"You look tired—do sit down," he repeated gently.

She did not seem to hear the request. "I wanted you to know that I left Mrs. Hatch immediately after I saw you," she said, as though continuing her confession.

"Yes—yes; I know," he assented, with a rising tinge of embarrassment.

"And that I did so because you told me to. Before you came I had already begun to see that it would be impossible to remain with her—for the reasons you gave me; but I wouldn't admit it—I wouldn't let you see that I understood what you meant."

"Ah, I might have trusted you to find your own way out—don't overwhelm me with the sense of my officiousness!"

His light tone, in which, had her nerves been steadier, she would have recognized the mere effort to bridge over an awkward moment, jarred on her passionate desire to be understood. In her strange state of extra-lucidity, which gave her the sense of being already at the heart of the situation, it seemed incredible that anyone should think it necessary to linger in the conventional outskirts of wordplay and evasion.

"It was not that—I was not ungrateful," she insisted. But the power of expression failed her suddenly; she felt a tremor in her throat, and two tears gathered and fell slowly from her eyes.

Selden moved forward and took her hand. "You are very tired. Why won't you sit down and let me make you comfortable?"

He drew her to the armchair near the fire, and placed a cushion behind her shoulders.

"And now you must let me make you some tea: you know I always have that amount of hospitality at my command."

She shook her head, and two more tears ran over. But she did not weep easily, and the long habit of self-control reasserted itself, though she was still too tremulous to speak.

"You know I can coax the water to boil in five minutes," Selden continued, speaking as though she were a troubled child.

His words recalled the vision of that other afternoon when they had sat together over his tea-table and talked jestingly of her future. There were moments when that day seemed more remote than any other event in her life; and yet she could always relive it in its minutest detail.

She made a gesture of refusal. "No, I drink too much tea. I would rather sit quiet—I must go in a moment," she added confusedly.

Selden continued to stand near her, leaning against the mantelpiece. The tinge of constraint was beginning to be more distinctly perceptible under the friendly ease of his manner. Her self-absorption had not allowed her to perceive it at first; but now that her consciousness was once more putting forth its eager feelers, she saw that her presence was becoming an embarrassment to him. Such a situation can be saved only by an immediate outrush of feeling; and on Selden's side the determining impulse was still lacking.

The discovery did not disturb Lily as it might once have done. She had passed beyond the phase of well-bred reciprocity, in which every demonstration must be scrupulously proportioned to the emotion it elicits, and generosity of feeling is the only ostentation condemned. But the sense of loneliness returned with redoubled force as she saw herself forever shut out from Selden's inmost self. She had come to him with no definite purpose; the mere longing to see him had directed her; but the secret hope she had carried with her suddenly revealed itself in its death-pang.

"I must go," she repeated, making a motion to rise from her chair. "But I may not see you again for a long time, and I wanted to tell you that I have never forgotten the things you said to me at Bellomont, and that sometimes —sometimes when I seemed farthest from remembering them—they have helped me, and kept me from mistakes; kept me from really becoming what many people have thought me."

Strive as she would to put some order in her thoughts, the words would not come more clearly; yet she felt that she could not leave him without trying to make him understand that she had saved herself whole from the seeming ruin of her life.

A change had come over Selden's face as she spoke. Its guarded look had yielded to an expression still untinged by personal emotion, but full of a gentle understanding.

"I am glad to have you tell me that; but nothing I have said has really made the difference. The difference is in yourself—it will always be there.

And since it *is* there, it can't really matter to you what people think: you are so sure that your friends will always understand you."

"Ah, don't say that—don't say that what you have told me has made no difference. It seems to shut me out—to leave me all alone with the other people." She had risen and stood before him, once more completely mastered by the inner urgency of the moment. The consciousness of his half-divined reluctance had vanished. Whether he wished it or not, he must see her wholly for once before they parted.

Her voice had gathered strength, and she looked him gravely in the eyes as she continued. "Once—twice—you gave me the chance to escape from my life, and I refused it: refused it because I was a coward. Afterward I saw my mistake—I saw I could never be happy with what had contented me before. But it was too late: you had judged me—I understood. It was too late for happiness—but not too late to be helped by the thought of what I had missed. That is all I have lived on—don't take it from me now! Even in my worst moments it has been like a little light in the darkness. Some women are strong enough to be good by themselves, but I needed the help of your belief in me. Perhaps I might have resisted a great temptation, but the little ones would have pulled me down. And then I remembered—I remembered your saying that such a life could never satisfy me; and I was ashamed to admit to myself that it could. That is what you did for me—that is what I wanted to thank you for. I wanted to tell you that I have always remembered; and that I have tried—tried hard . . ."

She broke off suddenly. Her tears had risen again, and in drawing out her handkerchief her fingers touched the packet in the folds of her dress. A wave of color suffused her, and the words died on her lips. Then she lifted her eyes to his and went on in an altered voice.

"I have tried hard—but life is difficult, and I am a very useless person. I can hardly be said to have an independent existence. I was just a screw or a cog in the great machine I called life, and when I dropped out of it I found I was of no use anywhere else. What can one do when one finds that one only fits into one hole? One must get back to it or be thrown out into the rubbish heap—and you don't know what it's like in the rubbish heap!"

Her lips wavered into a smile—she had been distracted by the whimsical remembrance of the confidences she had made to him, two years earlier, in that very room. Then she had been planning to marry Percy Gryce—what was it she was planning now?

The blood had risen strongly under Selden's dark skin, but his emotion showed itself only in an added seriousness of manner.

"You have something to tell me—do you mean to marry?" he said abruptly.

Lily's eyes did not falter, but a look of wonder, of puzzled self-interrogation, formed itself slowly in their depths. In the light of his question, she had paused to ask herself if her decision had really been taken when she entered the room.

"You always told me I should have to come to it sooner or later!" she said with a faint smile.

"And you have come to it now?"

"I shall have to come to it—presently. But there is something else I must come to first." She paused again, trying to transmit to her voice the steadiness of her recovered smile. "There is someone I must say goodbye to. Oh, not you—we are sure to see each other again—but the Lily Bart you knew. I have kept her with me all this time, but now we are going to part, and I have brought her back to you—I am going to leave her here. When I go out presently she will not go with me. I shall like to think that she has stayed with you—and she'll be no trouble, she'll take up no room."

She went toward him, and put out her hand, still smiling. "Will you let her stay with you?" she asked.

He caught her hand, and she felt in his the vibration of feeling that had not yet risen to his lips. "Lily—can't I help you?" he exclaimed.

She looked at him gently. "Do you remember what you said to me once? That you could help me only by loving me? Well—you did love me for a moment; and it helped me. It has always helped me. But the moment is gone—it was I who let it go. And one must go on living. Goodbye."

She laid her other hand on his, and they looked at each other with a kind of solemnity, as though they stood in the presence of death. Something in truth lay dead between them—the love she had killed in him and could no longer call to life. But something lived between them also, and leaped up in her like an imperishable flame: it was the love his love had kindled, the passion of her soul for his.

In its light everything else dwindled and fell away from her. She understood now that she could not go forth and leave her old self with him: that self must indeed live on in his presence, but it must still continue to be hers.

Selden had retained her hand, and continued to scrutinize her with a strange sense of foreboding. The external aspect of the situation had vanished for him as completely as for her: he felt it only as one of those rare moments which lift the veil from their faces as they pass.

"Lily," he said in a low voice, "you mustn't speak in this way. I can't let you go without knowing what you mean to do. Things may change—but they don't pass. You can never go out of my life."

She met his eyes with an illumined look. "No," she said. "I see that now. Let us always be friends. Then I shall feel safe, whatever happens."

"Whatever happens? What do you mean? What is going to happen?"

She turned away quietly and walked toward the hearth.

"Nothing at present—except that I am very cold, and that before I go you must make up the fire for me."

She knelt on the hearthrug, stretching her hands to the embers. Puzzled by the sudden change in her tone, he mechanically gathered a handful of wood from the basket and tossed it on the fire. As he did so, he noticed how thin her hands looked against the rising light of the flames. He saw, too, under the loose lines of her dress, how the curves of her figure had shrunk to angularity; he remembered long afterward how the red play of the flame sharpened the depression of her nostrils, and intensified the blackness of the shadows which struck up from her cheekbones to her eyes. She knelt there for a few moments in silence; a silence which he dared not break. When she rose he fancied that he saw her draw something from her dress and drop it into the fire; but he hardly noticed the gesture at the time. His faculties seemed tranced, and he was still groping for the word to break the spell.

She went up to him and laid her hands on his shoulders. "Goodbye," she said, and as he bent over her she touched his forehead with her lips.

28

THE streetlamps were lit, but the rain had ceased, and there was a momentary revival of light in the upper sky.

Lily walked on unconscious of her surroundings. She was still treading the buoyant ether which emanates from the high moments of life. But gradually it shrank away from her and she felt the dull pavement beneath her feet. The sense of weariness returned with accumulated force, and for a moment she felt that she could walk no farther. She had reached the corner of Forty-first Street and Fifth Avenue, and she remembered that in Bryant Park there were seats where she might rest.

That melancholy pleasure-ground was almost deserted when she entered it, and she sank down on an empty bench in the glare of an electric streetlamp. The warmth of the fire had passed out of her veins, and she told herself that she must not sit long in the penetrating dampness which struck up from the wet asphalt. But her willpower seemed to have spent itself in a last great effort, and she was lost in the blank reaction which follows on all unwonted expenditure of energy. And besides, what was there to go home to? Nothing but the silence of her cheerless room—that silence of the night which may be more racking to tired nerves than the most discordant noises: that, and the bottle of chloral by her bed. The thought of the chloral was the only spot of light in the dark prospect: she could feel its lulling influence stealing over her already. But she was troubled by the thought that it was losing its power—she dared not go back to it too soon. Of late the sleep it had brought her had been more broken and less profound; there had been nights when she was perpetually floating up through it to consciousness. What if the effect of the drug should gradually fail, as all narcotics were said to fail? She remembered the chemist's warning against increasing the dose; and she had heard before of the capricious and incalculable action of the drug. Her dread of returning to a sleepless night was so great that she lingered on, hoping that excessive weariness would reinforce the waning power of the chloral.

Night had now closed in, and the roar of traffic in Forty-second Street was dying out. As complete darkness fell on the square the lingering occupants of the benches rose and dispersed; but now and then a stray figure, hurrying homeward, struck across the path where Lily sat, looming black for a moment in the white circle of electric light. One or two of these passersby slackened their pace to glance curiously at her lonely figure; but she was hardly conscious of their scrutiny.

Suddenly, however, she became aware that one of the passing shadows remained stationary between her line of vision and the gleaming asphalt; and raising her eyes she saw a young woman bending over her.

"Excuse me—are you sick?—Why, it's Miss Bart!" a half-familiar voice exclaimed.

Lily looked up. The speaker was a poorly dressed young woman with a bundle under her arm. Her face had the air of unwholesome refinement which ill-health and overwork may produce, but its common prettiness was redeemed by the strong and generous curve of the lips.

"You don't remember me," she continued, brightening with the pleasure of recognition, "but I'd know you anywhere, I've thought of you such a lot. I guess my folks all know your name by heart. I was one of the girls at Miss Farish's club—you helped me to go to the country that time I had lungtrouble. My name's Nettie Struther. It was Nettie Crane then—but I daresay you don't remember that either."

Yes: Lily was beginning to remember. The episode of Nettie Crane's timely rescue from disease had been one of the most satisfying incidents of her connection with Gerty's charitable work. She had furnished the girl with the means to go to a sanatorium in the mountains: it struck her now with a peculiar irony that the money she had used had been Gus Trenor's.

She tried to reply, to assure the speaker that she had not forgotten; but her voice failed in the effort, and she felt herself sinking under a great wave of physical weakness. Nettie Struther, with a startled exclamation, sat down and slipped a shabbily clad arm behind her back.

"Why, Miss Bart, you *are* sick. Just lean on me a little till you feel better."

A faint glow of returning strength seemed to pass into Lily from the pressure of the supporting arm.

"I'm only tired—it is nothing," she found voice to say in a moment; and then, as she met the timid appeal of her companion's eyes, she added involuntarily: "I have been unhappy—in great trouble."

"*You* in trouble? I've always thought of you as being so high up, where everything was just grand. Sometimes, when I felt real mean, and got to wondering why things were so queerly fixed in the world, I used to remember that *you* were having a lovely time, anyhow, and that seemed to show there was a kind of justice somewhere. But you mustn't sit here too long—it's fearfully damp. Don't you feel strong enough to walk on a little ways now?" she broke off.

"Yes—yes; I must go home," Lily murmured, rising.

Her eyes rested wonderingly on the thin shabby figure at her side. She had known Nettie Crane as one of the discouraged victims of overwork and anemic parentage: one of the superfluous fragments of life destined to be swept prematurely into that social refuse-heap of which Lily had so lately expressed her dread. But Nettie Struther's frail envelope was now alive with hope and energy: whatever fate the future reserved for her, she would not be cast into the refuse-heap without a struggle.

"I am very glad to have seen you," Lily continued, summoning a smile to her unsteady lips. "It will be my turn to think of you as happy—and the world will seem a less unjust place to me, too."

"Oh, but I can't leave you like this—you're not fit to go home alone. And I can't go with you, either!" Nettie Struther wailed with a start of recollection. "You see, it's my husband's night-shift—he's a motorman—and the friend I leave the baby with has to step upstairs to get *her* husband's supper at seven. I didn't tell you I had a baby, did I? She'll be four months old day after tomorrow, and to look at her you wouldn't think I'd ever had a sick day. I'd give anything to show you the baby, Miss Bart, and we live right down the street here—it's only three blocks off." She lifted her eyes tentatively to Lily's face, and then added with a burst of courage: "Why won't you get right into the cars and come home with me while I get baby's supper? It's real warm in our kitchen, and you can rest there, and I'll take *you* home as soon as ever she drops off to sleep."

It *was* warm in the kitchen, which, when Nettie Struther's match had made a flame leap from the gas-jet above the table, revealed itself to Lily as extraordinarily small and almost miraculously clean. A fire shone through the polished flanks of the iron stove, and near it stood a crib in which a baby was sitting upright, with incipient anxiety struggling for expression on a countenance still placid with sleep.

Having passionately celebrated her reunion with her offspring, and excused herself in cryptic language for the lateness of her return, Nettie restored the baby to the crib and shyly invited Miss Bart to the rocking chair near the stove.

"We've got a parlor, too," she explained with pardonable pride; "but I guess it's warmer in here, and I don't want to leave you alone while I'm getting baby's supper."

On receiving Lily's assurance that she much preferred the friendly proximity of the kitchen fire, Mrs. Struther proceeded to prepare a bottle of infantile food, which she tenderly applied to the baby's impatient lips; and while the ensuing degustation went on, she seated herself with a beaming countenance beside her visitor.

"You're sure you won't let me warm up a drop of coffee for you, Miss Bart? There's some of baby's fresh milk left over—well, maybe you'd rather just sit quiet and rest a little while. It's too lovely having you here. I've thought of it so often that I can't believe it's really come true. I've said to George again and again: 'I just wish Miss Bart could see me *now*—' and I used to watch for your name in the papers, and we'd talk over what you were doing, and read the descriptions of the dresses you wore. I haven't seen your name for a long time, though, and I began to be afraid you were sick, and it worried me so that George said I'd get sick myself, fretting about it." Her lips broke into a reminiscent smile. "Well, I can't afford to be sick again, that's a fact: the last spell nearly finished me. When you sent me off that time I never thought I'd come back alive, and I didn't much care if I did. You see, I didn't know about George and the baby then."

She paused to readjust the bottle to the child's bubbling mouth.

"You precious—don't you be in too much of a hurry! Was it mad with mommer for getting its supper so late? Marry Anto'nette—that's what we call her: after the French queen in that play at the Garden—I told George the actress reminded me of you, and that made me fancy the name. . . . I never thought I'd get married, you know, and I'd never have had the heart to go on working just for myself."

She broke off again, and meeting the encouragement in Lily's eyes, went on, with a flush rising under her anemic skin: "You see, I wasn't only just *sick* that time you sent me off—I was dreadfully unhappy, too. I'd known a gentleman where I was employed—I don't know as you remember I did typewriting in a big importing firm—and—well—I thought we were to be married: he'd gone steady with me six months and given me his mother's wedding ring. But I presume he was too stylish for me—he traveled for the firm, and had seen a great deal of society. Work girls aren't looked after the way you are, and they don't always know how to look after themselves. I didn't . . . and it pretty near killed me when he went away and left off writing. . . . It was then I came down sick—I thought it was the end of everything. I guess it would have been if you hadn't sent me off. But when I found I was getting well I began to take heart in spite of myself. And then, when I got back home, George came round and asked me to marry him. At first I thought I couldn't, because we'd been brought up together, and I knew he knew about me. But after a while I began to see that made it easier. I never could have told another man, and I'd never have married without telling; but if George cared for me enough to have me as I was, I didn't see why I shouldn't begin over again—and I did."

The strength of the victory shone forth from her as she lifted her irradiated face from the child on her knees.

"But, mercy, I didn't mean to go on like this about myself, with you sitting there looking so fagged out. Only it's so lovely having you here, and letting you see just how you've helped me." The baby had sunk back blissfully replete, and Mrs. Struther softly rose to lay the bottle aside. Then she paused before Miss Bart.

"I only wish I could help *you*—but I suppose there's nothing on earth I could do," she murmured wistfully.

Lily, instead of answering, rose with a smile and held out her arms; and the mother, understanding the gesture, laid her child in them.

The baby, feeling herself detached from her habitual anchorage, made an instinctive motion of resistance; but the soothing influences of digestion prevailed, and Lily felt the soft weight sink trustfully against her breast. The child's confidence in its safety thrilled her with a sense of warmth and returning life, and she bent over, wondering at the rosy blur of the little face, the empty clearness of the eyes, the vague tendrilly motions of the folding and unfolding fingers. At first the burden in her arms seemed as light as a pink cloud or a heap of down, but as she continued to hold it the weight increased, sinking deeper, and penetrating her with a strange sense of weakness, as though the child entered into her and became a part of herself.

She looked up, and saw Nettie's eyes resting on her with tenderness and exultation.

"Wouldn't it be too lovely for anything if she could grow up to be just like you? Of course, I know she never *could*—but mothers are always dreaming the craziest things for their children."

Lily clasped the child close for a moment and laid her back in her mother's arms.

"Oh, she must not do that—I should be afraid to come and see her too often!" she said with a smile; and then, resisting Mrs. Struther's anxious offer of companionship, and reiterating the promise that, of course, she would come back soon, and make George's acquaintance, and see the baby in her bath, she passed out of the kitchen and went alone down the tenement stairs.

As she reached the street she realized that she felt stronger and happier: the little episode had done her good. It was the first time she had ever come across the results of her spasmodic benevolence, and the surprised sense of human fellowship took the mortal chill from her heart.

It was not till she entered her own door that she felt the reaction of a deeper loneliness. It was long after seven o'clock, and the light and odors proceeding from the basement made it manifest that the boardinghouse dinner had begun. She hastened up to her room, lit the gas, and began to dress. She did not mean to pamper herself any longer, to go without food because her surroundings made it unpalatable. Since it was her fate to live in a boardinghouse, she must learn to fall in with the conditions of the life. Nevertheless she was glad that, when she descended to the heat and glare of the dining-room, the repast was nearly over.

In her own room again, she was seized with a sudden fever of activity. For weeks past she had been too listless and indifferent to set her possessions in order, but now she began to examine systematically the contents of her drawers and cupboard. She had a few handsome dresses left—survivals of her last phase of splendor, on the Sabrina and in London—but when she had been obliged to part with her maid she had given the woman a generous share of her cast-off apparel. The remaining dresses, though they had lost their freshness, still kept the long unerring lines, the sweep and amplitude of the great artist's stroke, and as she spread them out on the bed the scenes in which they had been worn rose vividly before her. An association lurked in every fold: each fall of lace and gleam of embroidery was like a letter in the record of her past. She was startled to find how the atmosphere of her old life enveloped her. But, after all, it was the life she had been made for: every dawning tendency in her had been carefully directed toward it, all her interests and activities had been taught to center around it. She was like some rare flower grown for exhibition, a flower from which every bud had been nipped except the crowning blossom of her beauty.

Last of all, she drew forth from the bottom of her trunk a heap of white drapery which fell shapelessly across her arm. It was the Reynolds dress she had worn in the Bry tableaux. It had been impossible for her to give it away, but she had never seen it since that night, and the long flexible folds, as she shook them out, gave forth an odor of violets which came to her like a breath from the flower-edged fountain where she had stood with Lawrence Selden and disowned her fate. She put back the dresses one by one, laying away with each some gleam of light, some note of laughter, some stray waft from the rosy shores of pleasure. She was still in a state of highly wrought impressionability, and every hint of the past sent a lingering tremor along her nerves.

She had just closed her trunk on the white folds of the Reynolds dress when she heard a tap at her door, and the red fist of the Irish maid-servant thrust in a belated letter. Carrying it to the light, Lily read with surprise the address stamped on the upper corner of the envelope. It was a business communication from the office of her aunt's executors, and she wondered what unexpected development had caused them to break silence before the appointed time.

She opened the envelope and a check fluttered to the floor. As she stooped to pick it up the blood rushed to her face. The check represented the full amount of Mrs. Peniston's legacy, and the letter accompanying it explained that the executors, having adjusted the business of the estate with less delay than they had expected, had decided to anticipate the date fixed for the payment of the bequests.

Lily sat down beside the desk at the foot of her bed, and spreading out the check, read over and over the *ten thousand dollars* written across it in a steely business hand. Ten months earlier the amount it stood for had represented the depths of penury; but her standard of values had changed in the interval, and now visions of wealth lurked in every flourish of the pen. As she continued to gaze at it, she felt the glitter of the visions mounting to her brain, and after a while she lifted the lid of the desk and slipped the magic formula out of sight. It was easier to think without those five figures dancing before her eyes; and she had a great deal of thinking to do before she slept.

She opened her checkbook, and plunged into such anxious calculations as had prolonged her vigil at Bellomont on the night when she had decided to marry Percy Gryce. Poverty simplifies bookkeeping, and her financial situation was easier to ascertain than it had been then; but she had not yet learned the control of money, and during her transient phase of luxury at the Emporium she had slipped back into habits of extravagance which still impaired her slender balance. A careful examination of her checkbook, and of the unpaid bills in her desk, showed that, when the latter had been settled, she would have barely enough to live on for the next three or four months; and even after that, if she were to continue her present way of living, without earning any additional money, all incidental expenses must be reduced to the vanishing point. She hid her eyes with a shudder, beholding herself at the entrance of that ever-narrowing perspective down which she had seen Miss Silverton's dowdy figure take its despondent way.

It was no longer, however, from the vision of material poverty that she turned with the greatest shrinking. She had a sense of deeper impoverishment—of an inner destitution compared to which outward conditions dwindled into insignificance. It was indeed miserable to be poor—to look forward to a shabby, anxious middle-age, leading by dreary degrees of economy and self-denial to gradual absorption in the dingy communal existence of the boardinghouse. But there was something more miserable still—it was the clutch of solitude at her heart, the sense of being swept like a stray uprooted growth down the heedless current of the years. That was the feeling which possessed her now—the feeling of being something rootless and ephemeral, mere spindrift of the whirling surface of existence, without anything to which the poor little tentacles of self could cling before the awful flood submerged them. And as she looked back she saw that there had never been a time when she had had any real relation to life. Her parents too had been rootless, blown hither and thither on every wind of fashion, without any personal existence to shelter them from its shifting gusts. She herself had grown up without anyone spot of earth being dearer to her than another: there was no center of early pieties, of grave endearing traditions, to which her heart could revert and from which it could draw strength for itself and tenderness for others. In whatever form a slowly accumulated past lives in the blood—whether in the concrete image of the old house stored with visual memories, or in the conception of the house not built with hands, but made up of inherited passions and loyalties—it has the same power of broadening and deepening the individual existence, of attaching it by mysterious links of kinship to all the mighty sum of human striving.

Such a vision of the solidarity of life had never before come to Lily. She had had a premonition of it in the blind motions of her mating-instinct; but they had been checked by the disintegrating influences of the life about her. All the men and women she knew were like atoms whirling away from each other in some wild centrifugal dance: her first glimpse of the continuity of life had come to her that evening in Nettie Struther's kitchen.

The poor little working-girl who had found strength to gather up the fragments of her life, and build herself a shelter with them, seemed to Lily to have reached the central truth of existence. It was a meager enough life, on the grim edge of poverty, with scant margin for possibilities of sickness or mischance, but it had the frail audacious permanence of a bird's nest built on the edge of a cliff—a mere wisp of leaves and straw, yet so put together that the lives entrusted to it may hang safely over the abyss.

Yes—but it had taken two to build the nest; the man's faith as well as the woman's courage. Lily remembered Nettie's words: *I knew he knew about me.* Her husband's faith in her had made her renewal possible—it is so easy for a woman to become what the man she loves believes her to be! Well—Selden had twice been ready to stake his faith on Lily Bart; but the third trial had been too severe for his endurance. The very quality of his love had made it the more impossible to recall to life. If it had been a simple instinct of the blood, the power of her beauty might have revived it. But the fact that it struck deeper, that it was inextricably wound up with inherited habits of thought and feeling, made it as impossible to restore to growth as a deep-rooted plant torn from its bed. Selden had given her of his best; but he was as incapable as herself of an uncritical return to former states of feeling.

There remained to her, as she had told him, the uplifting memory of his faith in her; but she had not reached the age when a woman can live on her memories. As she held Nettie Struther's child in her arms the frozen currents of youth had loosed themselves and run warm in her veins: the old life-hunger possessed her, and all her being clamored for its share of personal happiness. Yes—it was happiness she still wanted, and the glimpse she had caught of it made everything else of no account. One by one she had detached herself from the baser possibilities, and she saw that nothing now remained to her but the emptiness of renunciation.

It was growing late, and an immense weariness once more possessed her.

It was not the stealing sense of sleep, but a vivid wakeful fatigue, a wan lucidity of mind against which all the possibilities of the future were shadowed forth gigantically. She was appalled by the intense clearness of the vision; she seemed to have broken through the merciful veil which intervenes between intention and action, and to see exactly what she would do in all the long days to come. There was the check in her desk, for instance —she meant to use it in paying her debt to Trenor; but she foresaw that when the morning came she would put off doing so, would slip into gradual tolerance of the debt. The thought terrified her—she dreaded to fall from the height of her last moment with Lawrence Selden. But how could she trust herself to keep her footing? She knew the strength of the opposing impulses—she could feel the countless hands of habit dragging her back into some fresh compromise with fate. She felt an intense longing to prolong, to perpetuate, the momentary exaltation of her spirit. If only life could end now—end on this tragic yet sweet vision of lost possibilities, which gave her a sense of kinship with all the loving and foregoing in the world!

She reached out suddenly and, drawing the check from her writing-desk, enclosed it in an envelope which she addressed to her bank. She then wrote out a check for Trenor, and placing it, without an accompanying word, in an envelope inscribed with his name, laid the two letters side by side on her desk. After that she continued to sit at the table, sorting her papers and writing, till the intense silence of the house reminded her of the lateness of the hour. In the street the noise of wheels had ceased, and the rumble of the "elevated" came only at long intervals through the deep unnatural hush. In the mysterious nocturnal separation from all outward signs of life, she felt herself more strangely confronted with her fate. The sensation made her brain reel, and she tried to shut out consciousness by pressing her hands against her eyes. But the terrible silence and emptiness seemed to symbolize her future—she felt as though the house, the street, the world were all empty, and she alone left sentient in a lifeless universe.

But this was the verge of delirium . . . she had never hung so near the dizzy brink of the unreal. Sleep was what she wanted—she remembered that she had not closed her eyes for two nights. The little bottle was at her bedside, waiting to lay its spell upon her. She rose and undressed hastily, hungering now for the touch of her pillow. She felt so profoundly tired that she thought she must fall asleep at once; but as soon as she had lain down every nerve started once more into separate wakefulness. It was as though a great blaze of electric light had been turned on in her head, and her poor little anguished self shrank and cowered in it, without knowing where to take refuge.

She had not imagined that such a multiplication of wakefulness was possible: her whole past was reenacting itself at a hundred different points of consciousness. Where was the drug that could still this legion of insurgent nerves? The sense of exhaustion would have been sweet compared to this shrill beat of activities; but weariness had dropped from her as though some cruel stimulant had been forced into her veins.

She could bear it—yes, she could bear it; but what strength would be left her the next day? Perspective had disappeared—the next day pressed close upon her, and on its heels came the days that were to follow—they swarmed about her like a shrieking mob. She must shut them out for a few hours; she must take a brief bath of oblivion. She put out her hand, and measured the soothing drops into a glass; but as she did so, she knew they would be powerless against the supernatural lucidity of her brain. She had long since raised the dose to its highest limit, but tonight she felt she must increase it. She knew she took a slight risk in doing so—she remembered the chemist's warning. If sleep came at all, it might be a sleep without waking. But after all that was but one chance in a hundred: the action of the drug was incalculable, and the addition of a few drops to the regular dose would probably do no more than procure for her the rest she so desperately needed. . . .

She did not, in truth, consider the question very closely—the physical craving for sleep was her only sustained sensation. Her mind shrank from the glare of thought as instinctively as eyes contract in a blaze of light—darkness, darkness was what she must have at any cost. She raised herself in bed and swallowed the contents of the glass; then she blew out her candle and lay down.

She lay very still, waiting with a sensuous pleasure for the first effects of the soporific. She knew in advance what form they would take—the gradual cessation of the inner throb, the soft approach of passiveness, as though an invisible hand made magic passes over her in the darkness. The very slowness and hesitancy of the effect increased its fascination: it was delicious to lean over and look down into the dim abysses of unconsciousness. Tonight the drug seemed to work more slowly than usual: each passionate pulse had to be stilled in turn, and it was long before she felt them dropping into abeyance, like sentinels falling asleep at their posts. But gradually the sense of complete subjugation came over her, and she wondered languidly what had made her feel so uneasy and excited. She saw now that there was nothing to be excited about—she had returned to her normal view of life. Tomorrow would not be so difficult after all: she felt sure that she would have the strength to meet it. She did not quite remember what it was that she had been afraid to meet, but the uncertainty no longer troubled her. She had been unhappy, and now she was happy—she had felt herself alone, and now the sense of loneliness had vanished.

She stirred once, and turned on her side, and as she did so, she suddenly understood why she did not feel herself alone. It was odd—but Nettie Struther's child was lying on her arm: she felt the pressure of its little head against her shoulder. She did not know how it had come there, but she felt no great surprise at the fact, only a gentle penetrating thrill of warmth and pleasure. She settled herself into an easier position, hollowing her arm to pillow the round downy head, and holding her breath lest a sound should disturb the sleeping child.

As she lay there she said to herself that there was something she must tell Selden, some word she had found that should make life clear between them. She tried to repeat the word, which lingered vague and luminous on the far edge of thought—she was afraid of not remembering it when she woke; and if she could only remember it and say it to him, she felt that everything would be well.

Slowly the thought of the word faded, and sleep began to enfold her. She struggled faintly against it, feeling that she ought to keep awake on account of the baby; but even this feeling was gradually lost in an indistinct sense of drowsy peace, through which, of a sudden, a dark flash of loneliness and terror tore its way.

She started up again, cold and trembling with the shock: for a moment she seemed to have lost her hold of the child. But no—she was mistaken— the tender pressure of its body was still close to hers: the recovered warmth flowed through her once more, she yielded to it, sank into it, and slept.

29

THE next morning rose mild and bright, with a promise of summer in the air. The sunlight slanted joyously down Lily's street, mellowed the blistered housefront, gilded the paintless railings of the doorstep, and struck prismatic glories from the panes of her darkened window.

When such a day coincides with the inner mood there is intoxication in its breath; and Selden, hastening along the street through the squalor of its morning confidences, felt himself thrilling with a youthful sense of adventure. He had cut loose from the familiar shores of habit, and launched himself on uncharted seas of emotion; all the old tests and measures were left behind, and his course was to be shaped by new stars.

That course, for the moment, led merely to Miss Bart's boardinghouse; but its shabby doorstep had suddenly become the threshold of the untried. As he approached he looked up at the triple row of windows, wondering boyishly which one of them was hers. It was nine o'clock, and the house, being tenanted by workers, already showed an awakened front to the street. He remembered afterward having noticed that only one blind was down. He noticed too that there was a pot of pansies on one of the window sills, and at once concluded that the window must be hers: it was inevitable that he should connect her with the one touch of beauty in the dingy scene.

Nine o'clock was an early hour for a visit, but Selden had passed beyond all such conventional observances. He only knew that he must see Lily Bart at once—he had found the word he meant to say to her, and it could not wait another moment to be said. It was strange that it had not come to his lips sooner—that he had let her pass from him the evening before without being able to speak it. But what did that matter, now that a new day had come? It was not a word for twilight, but for the morning.

Selden ran eagerly up the steps and pulled the bell; and even in his state of self-absorption it came as a sharp surprise to him that the door should open so promptly. It was still more of a surprise to see, as he entered, that it had been opened by Gerty Farish—and that behind her, in an agitated blur, several other figures ominously loomed.

"Lawrence!" Gerty cried in a strange voice, "how could you get here so quickly?"—and the trembling hand she laid on him seemed instantly to close about his heart.

He noticed the other faces, vague with fear and conjecture—he saw the landlady's imposing bulk sway professionally toward him; but he shrank back, putting up his hand, while his eyes mechanically mounted the steep black walnut stairs, up which he was immediately aware that his cousin was about to lead him.

A voice in the background said that the doctor might be back at any minute—and that nothing, upstairs, was to be disturbed. Some one else exclaimed: "It was the greatest mercy—" then Selden felt that Gerty had taken him gently by the hand, and that they were to be suffered to go up alone.

In silence they mounted the three flights, and walked along the passage to a closed door. Gerty opened the door, and Selden went in after her. Though the blind was down, the irresistible sunlight poured a tempered golden flood into the room, and in its light Selden saw a narrow bed along the wall, and on the bed, with motionless hands and calm unrecognizing face, the semblance of Lily Bart.

That it was her real self, every pulse in him ardently denied. Her real self had lain warm on his heart but a few hours earlier—what had he to do with this estranged and tranquil face which, for the first time, neither paled nor brightened at his coming?

Gerty, strangely tranquil too, with the conscious self-control of one who has ministered to much pain, stood by the bed, speaking gently, as if transmitting a final message.

"The doctor found a bottle of chloral—she had been sleeping badly for a long time, and she must have taken an overdose by mistake. . . . There is no doubt of that—no doubt—there will be no question—he has been very kind. I told him that you and I would like to be left alone with her—to go over her things before anyone else comes. I know it is what she would have wished."

Selden was hardly conscious of what she said. He stood looking down on the sleeping face which seemed to lie like a delicate impalpable mask over the living lineaments he had known. He felt that the real Lily was still there, close to him, yet invisible and inaccessible; and the tenuity of the barrier between them mocked him with a sense of helplessness. There had never been more than a little impalpable barrier between them—and yet he had suffered it to keep them apart! And now, though it seemed slighter and frailer than ever, it had suddenly hardened to adamant, and he might beat his life out against it in vain.

He had dropped on his knees beside the bed, but a touch from Gerty aroused him. He stood up, and as their eyes met he was struck by the extraordinary light in his cousin's face.

"You understand what the doctor has gone for? He has promised that there shall be no trouble—but, of course, the formalities must be gone through. And I asked him to give us time to look through her things first—"

He nodded, and she glanced about the small bare room. "It won't take long," she concluded.

"No—it won't take long," he agreed.

She held his hand in hers a moment longer, and then, with a last look at the bed, moved silently toward the door. On the threshold she paused to add: "You will find me downstairs if you want me."

Selden roused himself to detain her. "But why are you going? She would have wished—"

Gerty shook her head with a smile. "No: this is what she would have wished—" and as she spoke a light broke through Selden's stony misery, and he saw deep into the hidden things of love.

The door closed on Gerty, and he stood alone with the motionless sleeper on the bed. His impulse was to return to her side, to fall on his knees, and rest his throbbing head against the peaceful cheek on the pillow. They had never been at peace together, they two; and now he felt himself drawn downward into the strange mysterious depths of her tranquility.

But he remembered Gerty's warning words—he knew that, though time had ceased in this room, its feet were hastening relentlessly toward the door. Gerty had given him this supreme half-hour, and he must use it as she willed.

He turned and looked about him, sternly compelling himself to regain his consciousness of outward things. There was very little furniture in the room. The shabby chest of drawers was spread with a lace cover, and set out with a few gold-topped boxes and bottles, a rose-colored pincushion, a glass tray strewn with tortoise-shell hairpins—he shrank from the poignant intimacy of these trifles, and from the blank surface of the toilet-mirror above them.

These were the only traces of luxury, of that clinging to the minute observance of personal seemliness, which showed what her other renunciations must have cost. There was no other token of her personality about the room, unless it showed itself in the scrupulous neatness of the scant articles of furniture: a washing-stand, two chairs, a small writing-desk, and the little table near the bed. On this table stood the empty bottle and glass, and from these also he averted his eyes.

The desk was closed, but on its slanting lid lay two letters which he took up. One bore the address of a bank, and as it was stamped and sealed, Selden, after a moment's hesitation, laid it aside. On the other letter he read Gus Trenor's name; and the flap of the envelope was still ungummed.

Temptation leapt on him like the stab of a knife. He staggered under it, steadying himself against the desk. Why had she been writing to Trenor—writing, presumably, just after their parting of the previous evening? The thought unhallowed the memory of that last hour, made a mock of the word he had come to speak, and defiled even the reconciling silence upon which it fell. He felt himself flung back on all the ugly uncertainties from which he thought he had cast loose forever. After all, what did he know of her life? Only as much as she had chosen to show him, and measured by the world's estimate, how little that was! By what right—the letter in his hand seemed to ask—by what right was it he who now passed into her confidence through the gate which death had left unbarred? His heart cried out that it was by right of their last hour together, the hour when she herself had placed the key in his hand. Yes—but what if the letter to Trenor had been written afterward?

He put it from him with sudden loathing, and setting his lips, addressed himself resolutely to what remained of his task. After all, that task would be easier to perform, now that his personal stake in it was annulled.

He raised the lid of the desk, and saw within it a checkbook and a few packets of bills and letters, arranged with the orderly precision which characterized all her personal habits. He looked through the letters first, because it was the most difficult part of the work. They proved to be few and unimportant, but among them he found, with a strange commotion of the heart, the note he had written her the day after the Brys' entertainment.

"When may I come to you?"—his words overwhelmed him with a realization of the cowardice which had driven him from her at the very moment of attainment. Yes—he had always feared his fate, and he was too honest to disown his cowardice now; for had not all his old doubts started to life again at the mere sight of Trenor's name?

He laid the note in his card-case, folding it away carefully, as something made precious by the fact that she had held it so; then, growing once more aware of the lapse of time, he continued his examination of the papers.

To his surprise, he found that all the bills were receipted; there was not an unpaid account among them. He opened the checkbook, and saw that, the very night before, a check of ten thousand dollars from Mrs. Peniston's executors had been entered in it. The legacy, then, had been paid sooner than Gerty had led him to expect. But, turning another page or two, he discovered with astonishment that, in spite of this recent accession of funds, the balance had already declined to a few dollars. A rapid glance at the stubs of the last checks, all of which bore the date of the previous day, showed that between four or five hundred dollars of the legacy had been spent in the settlement of bills, while the remaining thousands were comprehended in one check, made out, at the same time, to Charles Augustus Trenor.

Selden laid the book aside, and sank into the chair beside the desk. He leaned his elbows on it, and hid his face in his hands. The bitter waters of life surged high about him, their sterile taste was on his lips. Did the check to Trenor explain the mystery or deepen it? At first his mind refused to act —he felt only the taint of such a transaction between a man like Trenor and a girl like Lily Bart. Then, gradually, his troubled vision cleared, old hints and rumors came back to him, and out of the very insinuations he had feared to probe, he constructed an explanation of the mystery. It was true, then, that she had taken money from Trenor; but true also, as the contents of the little desk declared, that the obligation had been intolerable to her, and that at the first opportunity she had freed herself from it, though the act left her face to face with bare unmitigated poverty.

That was all he knew—all he could hope to unravel of the story. The mute lips on the pillow refused him more than this—unless indeed they had told him the rest in the kiss they had left upon his forehead. Yes, he could now read into that farewell all that his heart craved to find there; he could even draw from it courage not to accuse himself for having failed to reach the height of his opportunity.

He saw that all the conditions of life had conspired to keep them apart; since his very detachment from the external influences which swayed her had increased his spiritual fastidiousness, and made it more difficult for him to live and love uncritically. But at least he *had* loved her—had been willing to stake his future on his faith in her—and if the moment had been fated to pass from them before they could seize it, he saw now that, for both, it had been saved whole out of the ruin of their lives.

It was this moment of love, this fleeting victory over themselves, which had kept them from atrophy and extinction; which, in her, had reached out to him in every struggle against the influence of her surroundings, and in him, had kept alive the faith that now drew him penitent and reconciled to her side.

He knelt by the bed and bent over her, draining their last moment to its lees; and in the silence there passed between them the word which made all clear.

ETHAN FROME

I HAD the story, bit by bit, from various people, and, as generally happens in such cases, each time it was a different story.

If you know Starkfield, Massachusetts, you know the post office. If you know the post office you must have seen Ethan Frome drive up to it, drop the reins on his hollow-backed bay and drag himself across the brick pavement to the white colonnade; and you must have asked who he was.

It was there that, several years ago, I saw him for the first time; and the sight pulled me up sharp. Even then he was the most striking figure in Starkfield, though he was but the ruin of a man. It was not so much his great height that marked him, for the "natives" were easily singled out by their lank longitude from the stockier foreign breed: it was the careless powerful look he had, in spite of a lameness checking each step like the jerk of a chain. There was something bleak and unapproachable in his face, and he was so stiffened and grizzled that I took him for an old man and was surprised to hear that he was not more than fifty-two. I had this from Harmon Gow, who had driven the stage from Bettsbridge to Starkfield in pretrolley days and knew the chronicle of all the families on his line.

"He's looked that way ever since he had his smashup; and that's twenty-four years ago come next February," Harmon threw out between reminiscent pauses.

The "smashup" it was—I gathered from the same informant—which, besides drawing the red gash across Ethan Frome's forehead, had so shortened and warped his right side that it cost him a visible effort to take the few steps from his buggy to the post-office window. He used to drive in from his farm every day at about noon, and as that was my own hour for fetching my mail I often passed him in the porch or stood beside him while we waited on the motions of the distributing hand behind the grating. I noticed that, though he came so punctually, he seldom received anything but a copy of the *Bettsbridge Eagle*, which he put without a glance into his sagging pocket. At intervals, however, the postmaster would hand him an envelope addressed to Mrs. Zenobia—or Mrs. Zeena—Frome, and usually bearing conspicuously in the upper left-hand corner the address of some manufacturer of patent medicine and the name of his specific. These documents my neighbor would also pocket without a glance, as if too much used to them to wonder at their number and variety, and would then turn away with a silent nod to the postmaster.

Every one in Starkfield knew him and gave him a greeting tempered to his own grave mien; but his taciturnity was respected and it was only on rare occasions that one of the older men of the place detained him for a word. When this happened he would listen quietly, his blue eyes on the speaker's face, and answer in so low a tone that his words never reached me; then he would climb stiffly into his buggy, gather up the reins in his left hand and drive slowly away in the direction of his farm.

"It was a pretty bad smashup?" I questioned Harmon, looking after Frome's retreating figure, and thinking how gallantly his lean brown head, with its shock of light hair, must have sat on his strong shoulders before they were bent out of shape.

"Wust kind," my informant assented. "More'n enough to kill most men. But the Fromes are tough. Ethan'll likely touch a hundred."

"Good God!" I exclaimed. At the moment Ethan Frome, after climbing to his seat, had leaned over to assure himself of the security of a wooden box —also with a druggist's label on it—which he had placed in the back of the buggy, and I saw his face as it probably looked when he thought himself alone. "*That* man touch a hundred? He looks as if he was dead and in hell now!"

Harmon drew a slab of tobacco from his pocket, cut off a wedge and pressed it into the leather pouch of his cheek. "Guess he's been in Starkfield too many winters. Most of the smart ones get away."

"Why didn't *he?*"

"Somebody had to stay and care for the folks. There warn't ever anybody but Ethan. Fust his father—then his mother—then his wife."

"And then the smashup?"

Harmon chuckled sardonically. "That's so. He *had* to stay then."

"I see. And since then they've had to care for him?"

Harmon thoughtfully passed his tobacco to the other cheek. "Oh, as to that: I guess it's always Ethan done the caring."

Though Harmon Gow developed the tale as far as his mental and moral reach permitted there were perceptible gaps between his facts, and I had the sense that the deeper meaning of the story was in the gaps. But one phrase stuck in my memory and served as the nucleus about which I grouped my subsequent inferences: "Guess he's been in Starkfield too many winters."

Before my own time there was up I had learned to know what that meant. Yet I had come in the degenerate day of trolley, bicycle and rural delivery, when communication was easy between the scattered mountain villages, and the bigger towns in the valleys, such as Bettsbridge and Shadd's Falls, had libraries, theaters and YMCA halls to which the youth of the hills could descend for recreation. But when winter shut down on Starkfield, and the village lay under a sheet of snow perpetually renewed from the pale skies, I began to see what life there—or rather its negation—must have been in Ethan Frome's young manhood.

I had been sent up by my employers on a job connected with the big powerhouse at Corbury Junction, and a long-drawn carpenters' strike had so delayed the work that I found myself anchored at Starkfield—the nearest habitable spot—for the best part of the winter. I chafed at first, and then, under the hypnotizing effect of routine, gradually began to find a grim satisfaction in the life. During the early part of my stay I had been struck by the contrast between the vitality of the climate and the deadness of the community. Day by day, after the December snows were over, a blazing blue sky poured down torrents of light and air on the white landscape, which gave them back in an intenser glitter. One would have supposed that such an atmosphere must quicken the emotions as well as the blood; but it seemed to produce no change except that of retarding still more the sluggish pulse of Starkfield. When I had been there a little longer, and had seen this phase of crystal clearness followed by long stretches of sunless cold; when the storms of February had pitched their white tents about the devoted village and the wild cavalry of March winds had charged down to their support; I began to understand why Starkfield emerged from its six months' siege like a starved garrison capitulating without quarter. Twenty years earlier the means of resistance must have been far fewer, and the enemy in command of almost all the lines of access between the beleaguered villages; and, considering these things, I felt the sinister force of Harmon's phrase: "Most of the smart ones get away." But if that were the case, how could any combination of obstacles have hindered the flight of a man like Ethan Frome?

During my stay at Starkfield I lodged with a middle-aged widow colloquially known as Mrs. Ned Hale. Mrs. Hale's father had been the village lawyer of the previous generation, and "lawyer Varnum's house," where my landlady still lived with her mother, was the most considerable mansion in the village. It stood at one end of the main street, its classic portico and small-paned windows looking down a flagged path between Norway spruces to the slim white steeple of the Congregational church. It was clear that the Varnum fortunes were at the ebb, but the two women did what they could to preserve a decent dignity; and Mrs. Hale, in particular, had a certain wan refinement not out of keeping with her pale old-fashioned house.

In the "best parlor," with its black horse-hair and mahogany weakly illuminated by a gurgling Carcel lamp, I listened every evening to another and more delicately shaded version of the Starkfield chronicle. It was not that Mrs. Ned Hale felt, or affected, any social superiority to the people about her; it was only that the accident of a finer sensibility and a little more education had put just enough distance between herself and her neighbors to enable her to judge them with detachment. She was not unwilling to exercise this faculty, and I had great hopes of getting from her the missing facts of Ethan Frome's story, or rather such a key to his character as should coordinate the facts I knew. Her mind was a storehouse of innocuous anecdote and any question about her acquaintances brought forth a volume of detail; but on the subject of Ethan Frome I found her unexpectedly reticent. There was no hint of disapproval in her reserve; I merely felt in her an insurmountable reluctance to speak of him or his affairs, a low "Yes, I knew them both . . . it was awful. . . ." seeming to be the utmost concession that her distress could make to my curiosity.

So marked was the change in her manner, such depths of sad initiation did it imply, that, with some doubts as to my delicacy, I put the case anew to my village oracle, Harmon Gow; but got for my pains only an uncomprehending grunt.

"Ruth Varnum was always as nervous as a rat; and, come to think of it, she was the first one to see 'em after they was picked up. It happened right below lawyer Varnum's, down at the bend of the Corbury road, just round about the time that Ruth got engaged to Ned Hale. The young folks was all friends, and I guess she just can't bear to talk about it. She's had troubles enough of her own."

All the dwellers in Starkfield, as in more notable communities, had had troubles enough of their own to make them comparatively indifferent to those of their neighbors; and though all conceded that Ethan Frome's had been beyond the common measure, no one gave me an explanation of the look in his face which, as I persisted in thinking, neither poverty nor physical suffering could have put there. Nevertheless, I might have contented myself with the story pieced together from these hints had it not been for the provocation of Mrs. Hale's silence, and—a little later—for the accident of personal contact with the man.

On my arrival at Starkfield, Denis Eady, the rich Irish grocer, who was the proprietor of Starkfield's nearest approach to a livery stable, had entered into an agreement to send me over daily to Corbury Flats, where I had to pick up my train for the Junction. But about the middle of the winter Eady's horses fell ill of a local epidemic. The illness spread to the other Starkfield stables and for a day or two I was put to it to find a means of transport. Then Harmon Gow suggested that Ethan Frome's bay was still on his legs and that his owner might be glad to drive me over.

I stared at the suggestion. "Ethan Frome? But I've never even spoken to him. Why on earth should he put himself out for me?"

Harmon's answer surprised me still more. "I don't know as he would; but I know he wouldn't be sorry to earn a dollar." I had been told that Frome was poor, and that the sawmill and the arid acres of his farm yielded scarcely enough to keep his household through the winter; but I had not supposed him to be in such want as Harmon's words implied, and I expressed my wonder.

"Well, matters ain't gone any too well with him," Harmon said. "When a man's been setting round like a hulk for twenty years or more, seeing things that want doing, it eats inter him, and he loses his grit. That Frome farm was always 'bout as bare's a milkpan when the cat's been round; and you know what one of them old water-mills is wuth nowadays. When Ethan could sweat over 'em both from sunup to dark he kinder choked a living out of 'em; but his folks ate up most everything, even then, and I don't see how he makes out now. Fust his father got a kick, out haying, and went soft in the brain, and gave away money like Bible texts afore he died. Then his mother got queer and dragged along for years as weak as a baby; and his wife Zeena, she's always been the greatest hand at doctoring in the county. Sickness and trouble: that's what Ethan's had his plate full up with, ever since the very first helping."

The next morning, when I looked out, I saw the hollow-backed bay between the Varnum spruces, and Ethan Frome, throwing back his worn bearskin, made room for me in the sleigh at his side. After that, for a week, he drove me over every morning to Corbury Flats, and on my return in the afternoon met me again and carried me back through the icy night to Starkfield. The distance each way was barely three miles, but the old bay's pace was slow, and even with firm snow under the runners we were nearly an hour on the way. Ethan Frome drove in silence, the reins loosely held in his left hand, his brown seamed profile, under the helmetlike peak of the cap, relieved against the banks of snow like the bronze image of a hero. He never turned his face to mine, or answered, except in monosyllables, the questions I put, or such slight pleasantries as I ventured. He seemed a part of the mute melancholy landscape, an incarnation of its frozen woe, with all that was warm and sentient in him fast bound below the surface; but there was nothing unfriendly in his silence. I simply felt that he lived in a depth of moral isolation too remote for casual access, and I had the sense that his loneliness was not merely the result of his personal plight, tragic as I guessed that to be, but had in it, as Harmon Gow had hinted, the profound accumulated cold of many Starkfield winters.

Only once or twice was the distance between us bridged for a moment; and the glimpses thus gained confirmed my desire to know more. Once I happened to speak of an engineering job I had been on the previous year in Florida, and of the contrast between the winter landscape about us and that in which I had found myself the year before; and to my surprise Frome said suddenly: "Yes, I was down there once, and for a good while afterward I could call up the sight of it in winter. But now it's all snowed under."

He said no more, and I had to guess the rest from the inflection of his voice and his sharp relapse into silence.

Another day, on getting into my train at the Flats, I missed a volume of popular science—I think it was on some recent discoveries in biochemistry —which I had carried with me to read on the way. I thought no more about it till I got into the sleigh again that evening, and saw the book in Frome's hand.

"I found it after you were gone," he said.

I put the volume into my pocket and we dropped back into our usual silence; but as we began to crawl up the long hill from Corbury Flats to the Starkfield ridge I became aware in the dusk that he had turned his face to mine.

"There are things in that book that I didn't know the first word about," he said.

I wondered less at his words than at the queer note of resentment in his voice. He was evidently surprised and slightly aggrieved at his own ignorance.

"Does that sort of thing interest you?" I asked.

"It used to."

"There are one or two rather new things in the book: there have been some big strides lately in that particular line of research." I waited a moment for an answer that did not come; then I said: "If you'd like to look the book through I'd be glad to leave it with you."

He hesitated, and I had the impression that he felt himself about to yield to a stealing tide of inertia; then, "Thank you—I'll take it," he answered shortly.

I hoped that this incident might set up some more direct communication between us. Frome was so simple and straightforward that I was sure his curiosity about the book was based on a genuine interest in its subject. Such tastes and acquirements in a man of his condition made the contrast more poignant between his outer situation and his inner needs, and I hoped that the chance of giving expression to the latter might at least unseal his lips. But something in his past history, or in his present way of living, had apparently driven him too deeply into himself for any casual impulse to draw him back to his kind. At our next meeting he made no allusion to the book, and our intercourse seemed fated to remain as negative and one-sided as if there had been no break in his reserve.

Frome had been driving me over to the Flats for about a week when one morning I looked out of my window into a thick snowfall. The height of the white waves massed against the garden-fence and along the wall of the church showed that the storm must have been going on all night, and that the drifts were likely to be heavy in the open. I thought it probable that my train would be delayed; but I had to be at the powerhouse for an hour or two that afternoon, and I decided, if Frome turned up, to push through to the Flats and wait there till my train came in. I don't know why I put it in the conditional, however, for I never doubted that Frome would appear. He was not the kind of man to be turned from his business by any commotion of the elements; and at the appointed hour his sleigh glided up through the snow like a stage-apparition behind thickening veils of gauze.

I was getting to know him too well to express either wonder or gratitude at his keeping his appointment; but I exclaimed in surprise as I saw him turn his horse in a direction opposite to that of the Corbury road.

"The railroad's blocked by a freight-train that got stuck in a drift below the Flats," he explained, as we jogged off into the stinging whiteness.

"But look here—where are you taking me, then?"

"Straight to the Junction, by the shortest way," he answered, pointing up Schoolhouse Hill with his whip.

"To the Junction—in this storm? Why, it's a good ten miles!"

"The bay'll do it if you give him time. You said you had some business there this afternoon. I'll see you get there."

He said it so quietly that I could only answer: "You're doing me the biggest kind of a favor."

"That's all right," he rejoined.

Abreast of the schoolhouse the road forked, and we dipped down a lane to the left, between hemlock boughs bent inward to their trunks by the weight of the snow. I had often walked that way on Sundays, and knew that the solitary roof showing through bare branches near the bottom of the hill was that of Frome's sawmill. It looked exanimate enough, with its idle wheel looming above the black stream dashed with yellow-white spume, and its cluster of sheds sagging under their white load. Frome did not even turn his head as we drove by, and still in silence we began to mount the next slope. About a mile farther, on a road I had never traveled, we came to an orchard of starved apple trees writhing over a hillside among outcroppings of slate that nuzzled up through the snow like animals pushing out their noses to breathe. Beyond the orchard lay a field or two, their boundaries lost under drifts; and above the fields, huddled against the white immensities of land and sky, one of those lonely New England farmhouses that make the landscape lonelier.

"That's my place," said Frome, with a sideway jerk of his lame elbow; and in the distress and oppression of the scene I did not know what to answer. The snow had ceased, and a flash of watery sunlight exposed the house on the slope above us in all its plaintive ugliness. The black wraith of a deciduous creeper flapped from the porch, and the thin wooden walls, under their worn coat of paint, seemed to shiver in the wind that had risen with the ceasing of the snow.

"The house was bigger in my father's time: I had to take down the 'L,' a while back," Frome continued, checking with a twitch of the left rein the bay's evident intention of turning in through the broken-down gate.

I saw then that the unusually forlorn and stunted look of the house was partly due to the loss of what is known in New England as the "L": that long deep-roofed adjunct usually built at right angles to the main house, and connecting it, by way of storerooms and tool-house, with the woodshed and cow-barn. Whether because of its symbolic sense, the image it presents of a life linked with the soil, and enclosing in itself the chief sources of warmth and nourishment, or whether merely because of the consolatory thought that it enables the dwellers in that harsh climate to get to their morning's work without facing the weather, it is certain that the "L" rather than the house itself seems to be the center, the actual hearthstone, of the New England farm. Perhaps this connection of ideas, which had often occurred to me in my rambles about Starkfield, caused me to hear a wistful note in Frome's words, and to see in the diminished dwelling the image of his own shrunken body.

"We're kinder side-tracked here now," he added, "but there was considerable passing before the railroad was carried through to the Flats." He roused the lagging bay with another twitch; then, as if the mere sight of the house had let me too deeply into his confidence for any further pretence of reserve, he went on slowly: "I've always set down the worst of mother's trouble to that. When she got the rheumatism so bad she couldn't move around she used to sit up there and watch the road by the hour; and one year, when they was six months mending the Bettsbridge pike after the floods, and Harmon Gow had to bring his stage round this way, she picked up so that she used to get down to the gate most days to see him. But after the trains begun running nobody ever come by here to speak of, and mother never could get it through her head what had happened, and it preyed on her right along till she died."

As we turned into the Corbury road the snow began to fall again, cutting off our last glimpse of the house; and Frome's silence fell with it, letting down between us the old veil of reticence. This time the wind did not cease with the return of the snow. Instead, it sprang up to a gale which now and then, from a tattered sky, flung pale sweeps of sunlight over a landscape chaotically tossed. But the bay was as good as Frome's word, and we pushed on to the Junction through the wild white scene.

In the afternoon the storm held off, and the clearness in the west seemed to my inexperienced eye the pledge of a fair evening. I finished my business as quickly as possible, and we set out for Starkfield with a good chance of getting there for supper. But at sunset the clouds gathered again, bringing an earlier night, and the snow began to fall straight and steadily from a sky without wind, in a soft universal diffusion more confusing than the gusts and eddies of the morning. It seemed to be a part of the thickening darkness, to be the winter night itself descending on us layer by layer.

The small ray of Frome's lantern was soon lost in this smothering medium, in which even his sense of direction, and the bay's homing instinct, finally ceased to serve us. Two or three times some ghostly landmark sprang up to warn us that we were astray, and then was sucked back into the mist; and when we finally regained our road the old horse began to show signs of exhaustion. I felt myself to blame for having accepted Frome's offer, and after a short discussion I persuaded him to let me get out of the sleigh and walk along through the snow at the bay's side. In this way we struggled on for another mile or two, and at last reached a point where Frome, peering into what seemed to me formless night, said: "That's my gate down yonder."

The last stretch had been the hardest part of the way. The bitter cold and the heavy going had nearly knocked the wind out of me, and I could feel the horse's side ticking like a clock under my hand.

"Look here, Frome," I began, "there's no earthly use in your going any farther—" but he interrupted me: "Nor you neither. There's been about enough of this for anybody."

I understood that he was offering me a night's shelter at the farm, and without answering I turned into the gate at his side, and followed him to the barn, where I helped him to unharness and bed down the tired horse. When this was done he unhooked the lantern from the sleigh, stepped out again into the night, and called to me over his shoulder: "This way."

Far off above us a square of light trembled through the screen of snow. Staggering along in Frome's wake I floundered toward it, and in the darkness almost fell into one of the deep drifts against the front of the house. Frome scrambled up the slippery steps of the porch, digging a way through the snow with his heavily booted foot. Then he lifted his lantern, found the latch, and led the way into the house. I went after him into a low unlit passage, at the back of which a ladderlike staircase rose into obscurity. On our right a line of light marked the door of the room which had sent its ray across the night; and behind the door I heard a woman's voice droning querulously.

Frome stamped on the worn oil-cloth to shake the snow from his boots, and set down his lantern on a kitchen chair which was the only piece of furniture in the hall. Then he opened the door.

"Come in," he said; and as he spoke the droning voice grew still. . . .

It was that night that I found the clue to Ethan Frome, and began to put together this vision of his story . . . .
. . . .
. . . .

1

THE village lay under two feet of snow, with drifts at the windy corners. In a sky of iron the points of the Dipper hung like icicles and Orion flashed his cold fires. The moon had set, but the night was so transparent that the white housefronts between the elms looked gray against the snow, clumps of bushes made black stains on it, and the basement windows of the church sent shafts of yellow light far across the endless undulations.

Young Ethan Frome walked at a quick pace along the deserted street, past the bank and Michael Eady's new brick store and Lawyer Varnum's house with the two black Norway spruces at the gate. Opposite the Varnum gate, where the road fell away toward the Corbury valley, the church reared its slim white steeple and narrow peristyle. As the young man walked toward it the upper windows drew a black arcade along the side wall of the building, but from the lower openings, on the side where the ground sloped steeply down to the Corbury road, the light shot its long bars, illuminating many fresh furrows in the track leading to the basement door, and showing, under an adjoining shed, a line of sleighs with heavily blanketed horses.

The night was perfectly still, and the air so dry and pure that it gave little sensation of cold. The effect produced on Frome was rather of a complete absence of atmosphere, as though nothing less tenuous than ether intervened between the white earth under his feet and the metallic dome overhead. "It's like being in an exhausted receiver," he thought. Four or five years earlier he had taken a year's course at a technological college at Worcester, and dabbled in the laboratory with a friendly professor of physics; and the images supplied by that experience still cropped up, at unexpected moments, through the totally different associations of thought in which he had since been living. His father's death, and the misfortunes following it, had put a premature end to Ethan's studies; but though they had not gone far enough to be of much practical use they had fed his fancy and made him aware of huge cloudy meanings behind the daily face of things.

As he strode along through the snow the sense of such meanings glowed in his brain and mingled with the bodily flush produced by his sharp tramp. At the end of the village he paused before the darkened front of the church. He stood there a moment, breathing quickly, and looking up and down the street, in which not another figure moved. The pitch of the Corbury road, below lawyer Varnum's spruces, was the favorite coasting-ground of Starkfield, and on clear evenings the church corner rang till late with the shouts of the coasters; but tonight not a sled darkened the whiteness of the long declivity. The hush of midnight lay on the village, and all its waking life was gathered behind the church windows, from which strains of dance-music flowed with the broad bands of yellow light.

The young man, skirting the side of the building, went down the slope toward the basement door. To keep out of range of the revealing rays from within he made a circuit through the untrodden snow and gradually approached the farther angle of the basement wall. Thence, still hugging the shadow, he edged his way cautiously forward to the nearest window, holding

back his straight spare body and craning his neck till he got a glimpse of
the room.

Seen thus, from the pure and frosty darkness in which he stood, it
seemed to be seething in a mist of heat. The metal reflectors of the gas-jets
sent crude waves of light against the whitewashed walls, and the iron flanks
of the stove at the end of the hall looked as though they were heaving with
volcanic fires. The floor was thronged with girls and young men. Down the
side wall facing the window stood a row of kitchen chairs from which the
older women had just risen. By this time the music had stopped, and the
musicians—a fiddler, and the young lady who played the harmonium on
Sundays—were hastily refreshing themselves at one corner of the supper-
table which aligned its devastated pie dishes and ice-cream saucers on the
platform at the end of the hall. The guests were preparing to leave, and the
tide had already set toward the passage where coats and wraps were hung,
when a young man with a sprightly foot and a shock of black hair shot into
the middle of the floor and clapped his hands. The signal took instant
effect. The musicians hurried to their instruments, the dancers—some already half-muffled for departure—fell into line down each side of the room,
the older spectators slipped back to their chairs, and the lively young man,
after diving about here and there in the throng, drew forth a girl who had
already wound a cherry-colored "fascinator" about her head, and, leading
her up to the end of the floor, whirled her down its length to the bounding
tune of a Virginia reel.

Frome's heart was beating fast. He had been straining for a glimpse of
the dark head under the cherry-colored scarf and it vexed him that another
eye should have been quicker than his. The leader of the reel, who looked
as if he had Irish blood in his veins, danced well, and his partner caught his
fire. As she passed down the line, her light figure swinging from hand to
hand in circles of increasing swiftness, the scarf flew off her head and stood
out behind her shoulders, and Frome, at each turn, caught sight of her
laughing panting lips, the cloud of dark hair about her forehead, and the
dark eyes which seemed the only fixed points in a maze of flying lines.

The dancers were going faster and faster, and the musicians, to keep up
with them, belabored their instruments like jockeys lashing their mounts on
the home-stretch; yet it seemed to the young man at the window that the
reel would never end. Now and then he turned his eyes from the girl's face
to that of her partner, which, in the exhilaration of the dance, had taken on
a look of almost impudent ownership. Denis Eady was the son of Michael
Eady, the ambitious Irish grocer, whose suppleness and effrontery had given
Starkfield its first notion of "smart" business methods, and whose new brick
store testified to the success of the attempt. His son seemed likely to follow
in his steps, and was meanwhile applying the same arts to the conquest of
the Starkfield maidenhood. Hitherto Ethan Frome had been content to
think him a mean fellow; but now he positively invited a horse-whipping. It

was strange that the girl did not seem aware of it: that she could lift her rapt face to her dancer's, and drop her hands into his, without appearing to feel the offense of his look and touch.

Frome was in the habit of walking into Starkfield to fetch home his wife's cousin, Mattie Silver, on the rare evenings when some chance of amusement drew her to the village. It was his wife who had suggested, when the girl came to live with them, that such opportunities should be put in her way. Mattie Silver came from Stamford, and when she entered the Fromes' household to act as her cousin Zeena's aid it was thought best, as she came without pay, not to let her feel too sharp a contrast between the life she had left and the isolation of a Starkfield farm. But for this—as Frome sardonically reflected—it would hardly have occurred to Zeena to take any thought for the girl's amusement.

When his wife first proposed that they should give Mattie an occasional evening out he had inwardly demurred at having to do the extra two miles to the village and back after his hard day on the farm; but not long afterward he had reached the point of wishing that Starkfield might give all its nights to revelry.

Mattie Silver had lived under his roof for a year, and from early morning till they met at supper he had frequent chances of seeing her; but no moments in her company were comparable to those when, her arm in his, and her light step flying to keep time with his long stride, they walked back through the night to the farm. He had taken to the girl from the first day, when he had driven over to the Flats to meet her, and she had smiled and waved to him from the train, crying out "You must be Ethan!" as she jumped down with her bundles, while he reflected, looking over her slight person: "She don't look much on housework, but she ain't a fretter, anyhow." But it was not only that the coming to his house of a bit of hopeful young life was like the lighting of a fire on a cold hearth. The girl was more than the bright serviceable creature he had thought her. She had an eye to see and an ear to hear: he could show her things and tell her things, and taste the bliss of feeling that all he imparted left long reverberations and echoes he could wake at will.

It was during their night walks back to the farm that he felt most intensely the sweetness of this communion. He had always been more sensitive than the people about him to the appeal of natural beauty. His unfinished studies had given form to this sensibility and even in his unhappiest moments field and sky spoke to him with a deep and powerful persuasion. But hitherto the emotion had remained in him as a silent ache, veiling with sadness the beauty that evoked it. He did not even know whether anyone else in the world felt as he did, or whether he was the sole victim of this mournful privilege. Then he learned that one other spirit had trembled with the same touch of wonder: that at his side, living under his roof and eating his bread, was a creature to whom he could say: "That's Orion down yonder;

the big fellow to the right is Aldebaran, and the bunch of little ones—like bees swarming—they're the Pleiades . . ." or whom he could hold entranced before a ledge of granite thrusting up through the fern while he unrolled the huge panorama of the ice age, and the long dim stretches of succeeding time. The fact that admiration for his learning mingled with Mattie's wonder at what he taught was not the least part of his pleasure. And there were other sensations, less definable but more exquisite, which drew them together with a shock of silent joy: the cold red of sunset behind winter hills, the flight of cloud—flocks over slopes of golden stubble, or the intensely blue shadows of hemlocks on sunlit snow. When she said to him once: "It looks just as if it was painted!" it seemed to Ethan that the art of definition could go no farther, and that words had at last been found to utter his secret soul. . . .

As he stood in the darkness outside the church these memories came back with the poignancy of vanished things. Watching Mattie whirl down the floor from hand to hand he wondered how he could ever have thought that his dull talk interested her. To him, who was never gay but in her presence, her gaiety seemed plain proof of indifference. The face she lifted to her dancers was the same which, when she saw him, always looked like a window that has caught the sunset. He even noticed two or three gestures which, in his fatuity, he had thought she kept for him: a way of throwing her head back when she was amused, as if to taste her laugh before she let it out, and a trick of sinking her lids slowly when anything charmed or moved her.

The sight made him unhappy, and his unhappiness roused his latent fears. His wife had never shown any jealousy of Mattie, but of late she had grumbled increasingly over the housework and found oblique ways of attracting attention to the girl's inefficiency. Zeena had always been what Starkfield called "sickly," and Frome had to admit that, if she were as ailing as she believed, she needed the help of a stronger arm than the one which lay so lightly in his during the night walks to the farm. Mattie had no natural turn for housekeeping, and her training had done nothing to remedy the defect. She was quick to learn, but forgetful and dreamy, and not disposed to take the matter seriously. Ethan had an idea that if she were to marry a man she was fond of the dormant instinct would wake, and her pies and biscuits become the pride of the county; but domesticity in the abstract did not interest her. At first she was so awkward that he could not help laughing at her; but she laughed with him and that made them better friends. He did his best to supplement her unskilled efforts, getting up earlier than usual to light the kitchen fire, carrying in the wood overnight, and neglecting the mill for the farm that he might help her about the house during the day. He even crept down on Saturday nights to scrub the kitchen floor after the women had gone to bed; and Zeena, one day, had surprised him at the churn and had turned away silently, with one of her queer looks.

Of late there had been other signs of her disfavor, as intangible but more disquieting. One cold winter morning, as he dressed in the dark, his candle flickering in the draught of the ill-fitting window, he had heard her speak from the bed behind him.

"The doctor don't want I should be left without anybody to do for me," she said in her flat whine.

He had supposed her to be asleep, and the sound of her voice had startled him, though she was given to abrupt explosions of speech after long intervals of secretive silence.

He turned and looked at her where she lay indistinctly outlined under the dark calico quilt, her high-boned face taking a grayish tinge from the whiteness of the pillow.

"Nobody to do for you?" he repeated.

"If you say you can't afford a hired girl when Mattie goes."

Frome turned away again, and taking up his razor stooped to catch the reflection of his stretched cheek in the blotched looking-glass above the washstand.

"Why on earth should Mattie go?"

"Well, when she gets married, I mean," his wife's drawl came from behind him.

"Oh, she'd never leave us as long as you needed her," he returned, scraping hard at his chin.

"I wouldn't ever have it said that I stood in the way of a poor girl like Mattie marrying a smart fellow like Denis Eady," Zeena answered in a tone of plaintive self-effacement.

Ethan, glaring at his face in the glass, threw his head back to draw the razor from ear to chin. His hand was steady, but the attitude was an excuse for not making an immediate reply.

"And the doctor don't want I should be left without anybody," Zeena continued. "He wanted I should speak to you about a girl he's heard about, that might come—"

Ethan laid down the razor and straightened himself with a laugh.

"Denis Eady! If that's all I guess there's no such hurry to look round for a girl."

"Well, I'd like to talk to you about it," said Zeena obstinately.

He was getting into his clothes in fumbling haste.

"All right. But I haven't got the time now; I'm late as it is," he returned, holding his old silver turnip-watch to the candle.

Zeena, apparently accepting this as final, lay watching him in silence while he pulled his suspenders over his shoulders and jerked his arms into his coat; but as he went toward the door she said, suddenly and incisively: "I guess you're always late, now you shave every morning."

That thrust had frightened him more than any vague insinuations about Denis Eady. It was a fact that since Mattie Silver's coming he had taken to shaving every day; but his wife always seemed to be asleep when he left her side in the winter darkness, and he had stupidly assumed that she would not notice any change in his appearance. Once or twice in the past he had been faintly disquieted by Zenobia's way of letting things happen without seeming to remark them, and then, weeks afterward, in a casual phrase, revealing that she had all along taken her notes and drawn her inferences. Of late, however, there had been no room in his thoughts for such vague apprehensions. Zeena herself, from an oppressive reality, had faded into an insubstantial shade. All his life was lived in the sight and sound of Mattie Silver, and he could no longer conceive of its being otherwise. But now, as he stood· outside the church, and saw Mattie spinning down the floor with Denis Eady, a throng of disregarded hints and menaces wove their cloud about his brain. . . .

2

As the dancers poured out of the hall Frome, drawing back behind the projecting storm-door, watched the segregation of the grotesquely muffled groups, in which a moving lantern ray now and then lit up a face flushed with food and dancing. The villagers, being afoot, were the first to climb the slope to the main street, while the country neighbors packed themselves more slowly into the sleighs under the shed.

"Ain't you riding, Mattie?" a woman's voice called back from the throng about the shed, and Ethan's heart gave a jump. From where he stood he could not see the persons coming out of the hall till they had advanced a few steps beyond the wooden sides of the storm-door; but through its cracks he heard a clear voice answer: "Mercy no! Not on such a night."

She was there, then, close to him, only a thin board between. In another moment she would step forth into the night, and his eyes, accustomed to the obscurity, would discern her as clearly as though she stood in daylight. A wave of shyness pulled him back into the dark angle of the wall, and he stood there in silence instead of making his presence known to her. It had been one of the wonders of their intercourse that from the first, she, the quicker, finer, more expressive, instead of crushing him by the contrast, had given him something of her own ease and freedom; but now he felt as heavy and loutish as in his student days, when he had tried to "jolly" the Worcester girls at a picnic.

He hung back, and she came out alone and paused within a few yards of him. She was almost the last to leave the hall, and she stood looking uncertainly about her as if wondering why he did not show himself. Then a man's figure approached, coming so close to her that under their formless wrappings they seemed merged in one dim outline.

"Gentleman friend gone back on you? Say, Matt, that's tough! No, I wouldn't be mean enough to tell the other girls. I ain't as low-down as that." (How Frome hated his cheap banter!) "But look at here, ain't it lucky I got the old man's cutter down there waiting for us?"

Frome heard the girl's voice, gaily incredulous: "What on earth's your father's cutter doin' down there?"

"Why, waiting for me to take a ride. I got the roan colt, too. I kinder knew I'd want to take a ride tonight," Eady, in his triumph, tried to put a sentimental note into his bragging voice.

The girl seemed to waver, and Frome saw her twirl the end of her scarf irresolutely about her fingers. Not for the world would he have made a sign to her, though it seemed to him that his life hung on her next gesture.

"Hold on a minute while I unhitch the colt," Denis called to her, springing toward the shed.

She stood perfectly still, looking after him, in an attitude of tranquil expectancy torturing to the hidden watcher. Frome noticed that she no longer turned her head from side to side, as though peering through the night for another figure. She let Denis Eady lead out the horse, climb into the cutter and fling back the bearskin to make room for her at his side; then, with a swift motion of flight, she turned about and darted up the slope toward the front of the church.

"Goodbye! Hope you'll have a lovely ride!" she called back to him over her shoulder.

Denis laughed, and gave the horse a cut that brought him quickly abreast of her retreating figure.

"Come along! Get in quick! It's as slippery as thunder on this turn," he cried, leaning over to reach out a hand to her.

She laughed back at him: "Good night! I'm not getting in."

By this time they had passed beyond Frome's earshot and he could only follow the shadowy pantomime of their silhouettes as they continued to move along the crest of the slope above him. He saw Eady, after a moment, jump from the cutter and go toward the girl with the reins over one arm. The other he tried to slip through hers; but she eluded him nimbly, and Frome's heart, which had swung out over a black void, trembled back to safety. A moment later he heard the jingle of departing sleigh bells and discerned a figure advancing alone toward the empty expanse of snow before the church.

In the black shade of the Varnum spruces he caught up with her and she turned with a quick "Oh!"

"Think I'd forgotten you, Matt?" he asked with sheepish glee.

She answered seriously: "I thought maybe you couldn't come back for me."

"Couldn't? What on earth could stop me?"

"I knew Zeena wasn't feeling any too good today."

"Oh, she's in bed long ago." He paused, a question struggling in him. "Then you meant to walk home all alone?"

"Oh, I ain't afraid!" she laughed.

They stood together in the gloom of the spruces, an empty world glimmering about them wide and gray under the stars. He brought his question out.

"If you thought I hadn't come, why didn't you ride back with Denis Eady?"

"Why, where *were* you? How did you know? I never saw you!"

Her wonder and his laughter ran together like spring rills in a thaw. Ethan had the sense of having done something arch and ingenious. To prolong the effect he groped for a dazzling phrase, and brought out, in a growl of rapture: "Come along."

He slipped an arm through hers, as Eady had done, and fancied it was faintly pressed against her side; but neither of them moved. It was so dark under the spruces that he could barely see the shape of her head beside his shoulder. He longed to stoop his cheek and rub it against her scarf. He would have liked to stand there with her all night in the blackness. She moved forward a step or two and then paused again above the dip of the Corbury road. Its icy slope, scored by innumerable runners, looked like a mirror scratched by travelers at an inn.

"There was a whole lot of them coasting before the moon set," she said.

"Would you like to come in and coast with them some night?" he asked.

"Oh, *would* you, Ethan? It would be lovely!"

"We'll come tomorrow if there's a moon."

She lingered, pressing closer to his side. "Ned Hale and Ruth Varnum came just as *near* running into the big elm at the bottom. We were all sure they were killed." Her shiver ran down his arm. "Wouldn't it have been too awful? They're so happy!"

"Oh, Ned ain't much at steering. I guess I can take you down all right!" he said disdainfully.

He was aware that he was "talking big," like Denis Eady; but his reaction of joy had unsteadied him, and the inflection with which she had said of the engaged couple "They're so happy!" made the words sound as if she had been thinking of herself and him.

"The elm *is* dangerous, though. It ought to be cut down," she insisted.

"Would you be afraid of it, with me?"

"I told you I ain't the kind to be afraid," she tossed back, almost indifferently; and suddenly she began to walk on with a rapid step.

These alterations of mood were the despair and joy of Ethan Frome. The motions of her mind were as incalculable as the flit of a bird in the branches. The fact that he had no right to show his feelings and thus provoke the expression of hers, made him attach a fantastic importance to every change in her look and tone. Now he thought she understood him, and feared; now he was sure she did not, and despaired. Tonight the pressure of accumulated misgivings sent the scale drooping toward despair, and her indifference was the more chilling after the flush of joy into which she had plunged him by dismissing Denis Eady. He mounted Schoolhouse Hill at her side and walked on in silence till they reached the lane leading to the sawmill; then the need of some definite assurance grew too strong for him.

"You'd have found me right off if you hadn't gone back to have that last reel with Denis," he brought out awkwardly. He could not pronounce the name without a stiffening of the muscles of his throat.

"Why, Ethan, how could I tell you were there?"

"I suppose what folks say is true," he jerked out at her, instead of answering.

She stopped short, and he felt, in the darkness, that her face was lifted quickly to his. "Why, what do folks say?"

"It's natural enough you should be leaving us," he floundered on, following his thought.

"Is that what they say?" she mocked back at him; then, with a sudden drop of her sweet treble: "You mean that Zeena—ain't suited with me any more?" she faltered.

Their arms had slipped apart and they stood motionless, each seeking to distinguish the other's face.

"I know I ain't anything like as smart as I ought to be," she went on, while he vainly struggled for expression. "There's lots of things a hired girl could do that come awkward to me still—and I haven't got much strength in my arms. But if she'd only tell me I'd try. You know she hardly ever says anything, and sometimes I can see she ain't suited, and yet I don't know why." She turned on him with a sudden flash of indignation. "You'd ought to tell me, Ethan Frome—you'd ought to! Unless *you* want me to go, too—"

Unless he wanted her to go, too! The cry was balm to his raw wound. The iron heavens seemed to melt and rain down sweetness. Again he struggled for the all-expressive word, and again, his arm in hers, found only a deep "Come along."

They walked on in silence through the blackness of the hemlock-shaded lane, where Ethan's sawmill gloomed through the night, and out again into the comparative clearness of the fields. On the farther side of the hemlock belt the open country rolled away before them gray and lonely under the stars. Sometimes their way led them under the shade of an overhanging bank or through the thin obscurity of a clump of leafless trees. Here and there a farmhouse stood far back among the fields, mute and cold as a gravestone. The night was so still that they heard the frozen snow crackle under their feet. The crash of a loaded branch falling far off in the woods reverberated like a musket-shot, and once a fox barked, and Mattie shrank closer to Ethan, and quickened her steps.

At length they sighted the group of larches at Ethan's gate, and as they drew near it the sense that the walk was over brought back his words.

"Then you don't want to leave us, Matt?"

He had to stoop his head to catch her stifled whisper: "Where'd I go, if I did?"

The answer sent a pang through him but the tone suffused him with joy. He forgot what else he had meant to say and pressed her against him so closely that he seemed to feel her warmth in his veins.

"You ain't crying are you, Matt?"

"No, of course I'm not," she quavered.

They turned in at the gate and passed under the shaded knoll where, enclosed in a low fence, the Frome gravestones slanted at crazy angles through the snow. Ethan looked at them curiously. For years that quiet company had mocked his restlessness, his desire for change and freedom. "We never got away—how should you?" seemed to be written on every headstone; and whenever he went in or out of his gate he thought with a shiver: "I shall just go on living here till I join them." But now all desire for change had vanished, and the sight of the little enclosure gave him a warm sense of continuance and stability.

"I guess we'll never let you go, Matt," he whispered, as though even the dead, lovers once, must conspire with him to keep her; and brushing by the graves, he thought: "We'll always go on living here together, and someday she'll lie there beside me."

He let the vision possess him as they climbed the hill to the house. He was never so happy with her as when he abandoned himself to these dreams. Halfway up the slope Mattie stumbled against some unseen obstruction and clutched his sleeve to steady herself. The wave of warmth that went through him was like the prolongation of his vision. For the first time he stole his arm about her, and she did not resist. They walked on as if they were floating on a summer stream.

Zeena always went to bed as soon as she had had her supper, and the shutterless windows of the house were dark. A dead cucumber-vine dangled from the porch like the crape streamer tied to the door for a death, and the thought flashed through Ethan's brain: "If it was there for Zeena—" Then he had a distinct sight of his wife lying in their bedroom asleep, her mouth slightly open, her false teeth in a tumbler by the bed . . .

They walked around to the back of the house, between the rigid gooseberry bushes. It was Zeena's habit, when they came back late from the village, to leave the key of the kitchen door under the mat.

Ethan stood before the door, his head heavy with dreams, his arm still about Mattie. "Matt—" he began, not knowing what he meant to say.

She slipped out of his hold without speaking, and he stooped down and felt for the key.

"It's not there!" he said, straightening himself with a start.

They strained their eyes at each other through the icy darkness. Such a thing had never happened before.

"Maybe she's forgotten it," Mattie said in a tremulous whisper; but both of them knew that it was not like Zeena to forget.

"It might have fallen off into the snow," Mattie continued, after a pause during which they had stood intently listening.

"It must have been pushed off, then," he rejoined in the same tone. Another wild thought tore through him. What if tramps had been there— what if . . .

Again he listened, fancying he heard a distant sound in the house; then he felt in his pocket for a match, and kneeling down, passed its light slowly over the rough edges of snow about the doorstep.

He was still kneeling when his eyes, on a level with the lower panel of the door, caught a faint ray beneath it. Who could be stirring in that silent house? He heard a step on the stairs, and again for an instant the thought of tramps tore through him. Then the door opened and he saw his wife.

Against the dark background of the kitchen she stood up tall and angular, one hand drawing a quilted counterpane to her flat breast, while the other held a lamp. The light, on a level with her chin, drew out of the darkness her puckered throat and the projecting wrist of the hand that clutched the quilt, and deepened fantastically the hollows and prominences of her high-boned face under its ring of crimping-pins. To Ethan, still in the rosy haze of his hour with Mattie, the sight came with the intense precision of the last dream before waking. He felt as if he had never before known what his wife looked like.

She drew aside without speaking, and Mattie and Ethan passed into the kitchen, which had the deadly chill of a vault after the dry cold of the night.

"Guess you forgot about us, Zeena," Ethan joked, stamping the snow from his boots.

"No. I just felt so mean I couldn't sleep."

Mattie came forward, unwinding her wraps, the color of the cherry scarf in her fresh lips and cheeks. "I'm so sorry, Zeena! Isn't there anything I can do?"

"No, there's nothing." Zeena turned away from her. "You might 'a' shook off that snow outside," she said to her husband.

She walked out of the kitchen ahead of them and pausing in the hall raised the lamp at arm's-length, as if to light them up the stairs.

Ethan paused, also, affecting to fumble for the peg on which he hung his coat and cap. The doors of the two bedrooms faced each other across the narrow upper landing, and tonight it was peculiarly repugnant to him that Mattie should see him follow Zeena.

"I guess I won't come up yet awhile," he said, turning as if to go back to the kitchen.

Zeena stopped short and looked at him. "For the land's sake—what you going to do down here?"

"I've got the mill accounts to go over."

She continued to stare at him, the flame of the unshaded lamp bringing out with microscopic cruelty the fretful lines of her face.

"At this time o' night? You'll ketch your death. The fire's out long ago."

Without answering he moved away toward the kitchen. As he did so his glance crossed Mattie's and he fancied that a fugitive warning gleamed through her lashes. The next moment they sank to her flushed cheeks and she began to mount the stairs ahead of Zeena.

"That's so. It *is* powerful cold down here," Ethan assented; and with lowered head he went up in his wife's wake, and followed her across the threshold of their room.

3

THERE was some hauling to be done at the lower end of the wood-lot, and Ethan was out early the next day.

The winter morning was as clear as crystal. The sunrise burned red in a pure sky, the shadows on the rim of the wood-lot were darkly blue, and beyond the white and scintillating fields patches of far-off forest hung like smoke.

It was in the early morning stillness, when his muscles were swinging to their familiar task and his lungs expanding with long draughts of mountain air, that Ethan did his clearest thinking. He and Zeena had not exchanged a word after the door of their room had closed on them. She had measured out some drops from a medicine bottle on a chair by the bed and, after swallowing them, and wrapping her head in a piece of yellow flannel, had lain down with her face turned away. Ethan undressed hurriedly and blew out the light so that he should not see her when he took his place at her side. As he lay there he could hear Mattie moving about in her room, and her candle, sending its small ray across the landing, drew a scarcely perceptible line of light under his door. He kept his eyes fixed on the light till it vanished. Then the room grew perfectly black, and not a sound was audible but Zeena's asthmatic breathing. Ethan felt confusedly that there were manythings he ought to think about, but through his tingling veins and tired brain only one sensation throbbed: the warmth of Mattie's shoulder against his. Why had he not kissed her when he held her there? A few hours earlier he would not have asked himself the question. Even a few minutes earlier, when they had stood alone outside the house, he would not have dared to think of kissing her. But since he had seen her lips in the lamplight he felt that they were his.

Now, in the bright morning air, her face was still before him. It was part of the sun's red and of the pure glitter on the snow. How the girl had changed since she had come to Starkfield! He remembered what a colorless slip of a thing she had looked the day he had met her at the station. And all the first winter, how she had shivered with cold when the northerly gales shook the thin clapboards and the snow beat like hail against the loose-hung windows!

He had been afraid that she would hate the hard life, the cold and loneliness; but not a sign of discontent escaped her. Zeena took the view that Mattie was bound to make the best of Starkfield since she hadn't any other place to go to; but this did not strike Ethan as conclusive. Zeena, at any rate, did not apply the principle in her own case.

He felt all the more sorry for the girl because misfortune had, in a sense, indentured her to them. Mattie Silver was the daughter of a cousin of Zenobia Frome's, who had inflamed his clan with mingled sentiments of envy and admiration by descending from the hills to Connecticut, where he had married a Stamford girl and succeeded to her father's thriving "drug" business. Unhappily Orin Silver, a man of far-reaching aims, had died too soon to prove that the end justifies the means. His accounts revealed merely what the means had been; and these were such that it was fortunate for his wife and daughter that his books were examined only after his impressive funeral. His wife died of the disclosure, and Mattie, at twenty, was left alone to make her way on the fifty dollars obtained from the sale of her piano. For this purpose her equipment, though varied, was inadequate. She could trim a hat, make molasses candy, recite "Curfew Shall Not Ring Tonight," and play "The Lost Chord" and a potpourri from *Carmen*. When she tried to extend the field of her activities in the direction of stenography and book-keeping her health broke down, and six months on her feet behind the counter of a department store did not tend to restore it. Her nearest rela-tions had been induced to place their savings in her father's hands, and though, after his death, they ungrudgingly acquitted themselves of the Christian duty of returning good for evil by giving his daughter all the advice at their disposal, they could hardly be expected to supplement it by material aid. But when Zenobia's doctor recommended her looking about for someone to help her with the housework the clan instantly saw the chance of exacting a compensation from Mattie. Zenobia, though doubtful of the girl's efficiency, was tempted by the freedom to find fault without much risk of losing her; and so Mattie came to Starkfield.

Zenobia's fault-finding was of the silent kind, but not the less penetrating for that. During the first months Ethan alternately burned with the desire to see Mattie defy her and trembled with fear of the result. Then the situation grew less strained. The pure air, and the long summer hours in the open, gave back life and elasticity to Mattie, and Zeena, with more leisure to devote to her complex ailments, grew less watchful of the girl's omissions; so that Ethan, struggling on under the burden of his barren farm and failing sawmill, could at least imagine that peace reigned in his house.

There was really, even now, no tangible evidence to the contrary; but since the previous night a vague dread had hung on his skyline. It was formed of Zeena's obstinate silence, of Mattie's sudden look of warning, of the memory of just such fleeting imperceptible signs as those which told him, on certain stainless mornings, that before night there would be rain.

His dread was so strong that, manlike, he sought to postpone certainty. The hauling was not over till midday, and as the lumber was to be delivered to Andrew Hale, the Starkfield builder, it was really easier for Ethan to send Jotham Powell, the hired man, back to the farm on foot, and drive the load down to the village himself. He had scrambled up on the logs, and was sitting astride of them, close over his shaggy grays, when, coming between him and their steaming necks, he had a vision of the warning look that Mattie had given him the night before.

"If there's going to be any trouble I want to be there," was his vague reflection, as he threw to Jotham the unexpected order to unhitch the team and lead them back to the barn.

It was a slow trudge home through the heavy fields, and when the two men entered the kitchen Mattie was lifting the coffee from the stove and Zeena was already at the table. Her husband stopped short at sight of her. Instead of her usual calico wrapper and knitted shawl she wore her best dress of brown merino, and above her thin strands of hair, which still preserved the tight undulations of the crimping-pins, rose a hard perpendicular bonnet, as to which Ethan's clearest notion was that he had to pay five dollars for it at the Bettsbridge Emporium. On the floor beside her stood his old valise and a bandbox wrapped in newspapers.

"Why, where are you going, Zeena?" he exclaimed.

"I've got my shooting pains so bad that I'm going over to Bettsbridge to spend the night with Aunt Martha Pierce and see that new doctor," she answered in a matter-of-fact tone, as if she had said she was going into the storeroom to take a look at the preserves, or up to the attic to go over the blankets.

In spite of her sedentary habits such abrupt decisions were not without precedent in Zeena's history. Twice or thrice before she had suddenly packed Ethan's valise and started off to Bettsbridge, or even Springfield, to seek the advice of some new doctor, and her husband had grown to dread these expeditions because of their cost. Zeena always came back laden with expensive remedies, and her last visit to Springfield had been commemorated by her paying twenty dollars for an electric battery of which she had never been able to learn the use. But for the moment his sense of relief was so great as to preclude all other feelings. He had now no doubt that Zeena had spoken the truth in saying, the night before, that she had sat up because she felt "too mean" to sleep: her abrupt resolve to seek medical advice showed that, as usual, she was wholly absorbed in her health.

As if expecting a protest, she continued plaintively; "If you're too busy with the hauling I presume you can let Jotham Powell drive me over with the sorrel in time to ketch the train at the Flats."

Her husband hardly heard what she was saying. During the winter months there was no stage between Starkfield and Bettsbridge, and the trains which stopped at Corbury Flats were slow and infrequent. A rapid calculation showed Ethan that Zeena could not be back at the farm before the following evening. . . .

"If I'd supposed you'd 'a' made any objection to Jotham Powell's driving me over—" she began again, as though his silence had implied refusal. On the brink of departure she was always seized with a flux of words. "All I know is," she continued, "I can't go on the way I am much longer. The pains are clear away down to my ankles now, or I'd 'a' walked in to Starkfield on my own feet, sooner'n put you out, and asked Michael Eady to let me ride over on his wagon to the Flats, when he sends to meet the train that brings his groceries. I'd 'a' had two hours to wait in the station, but I'd sooner 'a' done it, even with this cold, than to have you say—"

"Of course Jotham'll drive you over," Ethan roused himself to answer. He became suddenly conscious that he was looking at Mattie while Zeena talked to him, and with an effort he turned his eyes to his wife. She sat opposite the window, and the pale light reflected from the banks of snow made her face look more than usually drawn and bloodless, sharpened the three parallel creases between ear and cheek, and drew querulous lines from her thin nose to the corners of her mouth. Though she was but seven years her husband's senior, and he was only twenty-eight, she was already an old woman.

Ethan tried to say something befitting the occasion, but there was only one thought in his mind: the fact that, for the first time since Mattie had come to live with them, Zeena was to be away for a night. He wondered if the girl were thinking of it too. . . .

He knew that Zeena must be wondering why he did not offer to drive her to the Flats and let Jotham Powell take the lumber to Starkfield, and at first he could not think of a pretext for not doing so; then he said: "I'd take you over myself, only I've got to collect the cash for the lumber."

As soon as the words were spoken he regretted them, not only because they were untrue—there being no prospect of his receiving cash payment from Hale—but also because he knew from experience the imprudence of letting Zeena think he was in funds on the eve of one of her therapeutic excursions. At the moment, however, his one desire was to avoid the long drive with her behind the ancient sorrel who never went out of a walk.

Zeena made no reply: she did not seem to hear what he had said. She had already pushed her plate aside, and was measuring out a draught from a large bottle at her elbow.

"It ain't done me a speck of good, but I guess I might as well use it up," she remarked; adding, as she pushed the empty bottle toward Mattie:

"If you can get the taste out it'll do for pickles."

4

As soon as his wife had driven off Ethan took his coat and cap from the peg. Mattie was washing up the dishes, humming one of the dance tunes of the night before. He said, "So long, Matt," and she answered gaily, "So long, Ethan," and that was all.

It was warm and bright in the kitchen. The sun slanted through the south window on the girl's moving figure, on the cat dozing in a chair, and on the geraniums brought in from the doorway, where Ethan had planted them in the summer to "make a garden" for Mattie. He would have liked to linger on, watching her tidy up and then settle down to her sewing; but he wanted still more to get the hauling done and be back at the farm before night.

All the way down to the village he continued to think of his return to Mattie. The kitchen was a poor place, not "spruce" and shining as his mother had kept it in his boyhood; but it was surprising what a homelike look the mere fact of Zeena's absence gave it. And he pictured what it would be like that evening, when he and Mattie were there after supper. For the first time they would be alone together indoors, and they would sit there, one on each side of the stove, like a married couple, he in his stocking feet and smoking his pipe, she laughing and talking in that funny way she had, which was always as new to him as if he had never heard her before.

The sweetness of the picture, and the relief of knowing that his fears of "trouble" with Zeena were unfounded, sent up his spirits with a rush, and he, who was usually so silent, whistled and sang aloud as he drove through the snowy fields. There was in him a slumbering spark of sociability which the long Starkfield winters had not yet extinguished. By nature grave and inarticulate, he admired recklessness and gaiety in others and was warmed to the marrow by friendly human intercourse. At Worcester, though he had the name of keeping to himself and not being much of a hand at a good time, he had secretly gloried in being clapped on the back and hailed as "Old Ethe" or "Old Stiff"; and the cessation of such familiarities had increased the chill of his return to Starkfield.

There the silence had deepened about him year by year. Left alone, after his father's accident, to carry the burden of farm and mill, he had had no time for convivial loiterings in the village; and when his mother fell ill the loneliness of the house grew more oppressive than that of the fields. His mother had been a talker in her day, but after her "trouble" the sound of her voice was seldom heard, though she had not lost the power of speech. Sometimes, in the long winter evenings, when in desperation her son asked her why she didn't "say something" she would lift a finger and answer: "Because I'm listening"; and on stormy nights, when the loud wind was about the house, she would complain, if he spoke to her: "They're talking so out there that I can't hear you."

It was only when she drew toward her last illness, and his cousin Zenobia Pierce came over from the next valley to help him nurse her, that human speech was heard again in the house. After the mortal silence of his long imprisonment Zeena's volubility was music in his ears. He felt that he might have "gone like his mother" if the sound of a new voice had not come to steady him. Zeena seemed to understand his case at a glance. She laughed at him for not knowing the simplest sickbed duties and told him to "go right along out" and leave her to see to things. The mere fact of obeying her orders, of feeling free to go about his business again and talk with other men, restored his shaken balance and magnified his sense of what he owed her. Her efficiency shamed and dazzled him. She seemed to possess by instinct all the household wisdom that his long apprenticeship had not instilled in him. When the end came it was she who had to tell him to hitch up and go for the undertaker, and she thought it "funny" that he had not settled beforehand who was to have his mother's clothes and the sewing-machine. After the funeral, when he saw her preparing to go away, he was seized with an unreasoning dread of being left alone on the farm; and before he knew what he was doing he had asked her to stay there with him. He had often thought since that it would not have happened if his mother had died in spring instead of winter. . . .

When they married it was agreed that, as soon as he could straighten out the difficulties resulting from Mrs. Frome's long illness, they would sell the farm and sawmill and try their luck in a large town. Ethan's love of nature did not take the form of a taste for agriculture. He had always wanted to be an engineer, and to live in towns, where there were lectures and big libraries and "fellows doing things." A slight engineering job in Florida, put in his way during his period of study at Worcester, increased his faith in his ability as well as his eagerness to see the world; and he felt sure that, with a "smart" wife like Zeena, it would not be long before he had made himself a place in it.

Zeena's native village was slightly larger and nearer to the railway than Starkfield, and she had let her husband see from the first that life on an isolated farm was not what she had expected when she married. But purchasers were slow in coming, and while he waited for them Ethan learned the impossibility of transplanting her. She chose to look down on Starkfield, but she could not have lived in a place which looked down on her. Even Bettsbridge or Shadd's Falls would not have been sufficiently aware of her, and in the greater cities which attracted Ethan she would have suffered a complete loss of identity. And within a year of their marriage she developed the "sickliness" which had since made her notable even in a community rich in pathological instances. When she came to take care of his mother she had seemed to Ethan like the very genius of health, but he soon saw that her skill as a nurse had been acquired by the absorbed observation of her own symptoms.

Then she, too, fell silent. Perhaps it was the inevitable effect of life on the farm, or perhaps, as she sometimes said, it was because Ethan "never listened." The charge was not wholly unfounded. When she spoke it was only to complain, and to complain of things not in his power to remedy; and to check a tendency to impatient retort he had first formed the habit of not answering her, and finally of thinking of other things while she talked. Of late, however, since he had had reasons for observing her more closely, her silence had begun to trouble him. He recalled his mother's growing taciturnity, and wondered if Zeena were also turning "queer." Women did, he knew. Zeena, who had at her fingers' ends the pathological chart of the whole region, had cited many cases of the kind while she was nursing his mother; and he himself knew of certain lonely farmhouses in the neighborhood where stricken creatures pined, and of others where sudden tragedy had come of their presence. At times, looking at Zeena's shut face, he felt the chill of such forebodings. At other times her silence seemed deliberately assumed to conceal far-reaching intentions, mysterious conclusions drawn from suspicions and resentments impossible to guess. That supposition was even more disturbing than the other; and it was the one which had come to him the night before, when he had seen her standing in the kitchen door.

Now her departure for Bettsbridge had once more eased his mind, and all his thoughts were on the prospect of his evening with Mattie. Only one thing weighed on him, and that was his having told Zeena that he was to receive cash for the lumber. He foresaw so clearly the consequences of this imprudence that with considerable reluctance he decided to ask Andrew Hale for a small advance on his load.

When Ethan drove into Hale's yard the builder was just getting out of his sleigh.

"Hello, Ethe!" he said. "This comes handy."

Andrew Hale was a ruddy man with a big gray moustache and a stubbly double-chin unconstrained by a collar; but his scrupulously clean shirt was always fastened by a small diamond stud. This display of opulence was misleading, for though he did a fairly good business it was known that his easygoing habits and the demands of his large family frequently kept him what Starkfield called "behind." He was an old friend of Ethan's family, and his house one of the few to which Zeena occasionally went, drawn there by the fact that Mrs. Hale, in her youth, had done more "doctoring" than any other woman in Starkfield, and was still a recognized authority on symptoms and treatment.

Hale went up to the grays and patted their sweating flanks.

"Well, sir," he said, "you keep them two as if they was pets."

Ethan set about unloading the logs and when he had finished his job he pushed open the glazed door of the shed which the builder used as his office. Hale sat with his feet up on the stove, his back propped against a battered desk strewn with papers: the place, like the man, was warm, genial and untidy.

"Sit right down and thaw out," he greeted Ethan.

The latter did not know how to begin, but at length he managed to bring out his request for an advance of fifty dollars. The blood rushed to his thin skin under the sting of Hale's astonishment. It was the builder's custom to pay at the end of three months, and there was no precedent between the two men for a cash settlement.

Ethan felt that if he had pleaded an urgent need Hale might have made shift to pay him; but pride, and an instinctive prudence, kept him from resorting to this argument. After his father's death it had taken time to get his head above water, and he did not want Andrew Hale, or anyone else in Starkfield, to think he was going under again. Besides, he hated lying; if he wanted the money he wanted it, and it was nobody's business to ask why. He therefore made his demand with the awkwardness of a proud man who will not admit to himself that he is stooping; and he was not much surprised at Hale's refusal.

The builder refused genially, as he did everything else: he treated the matter as something in the nature of a practical joke, and wanted to know if Ethan meditated buying a grand piano or adding a "cupolo" to his house; offering, in the latter case, to give his services free of cost.

Ethan's arts were soon exhausted, and after an embarrassed pause he wished Hale good day and opened the door of the office. As he passed out the builder suddenly called after him: "See here—you ain't in a tight place, are you?"

"Not a bit," Ethan's pride retorted before his reason had time to intervene.

"Well, that's good! Because I *am* a shade. Fact is, I was going to ask you to give me a little extra time on that payment. Business is pretty slack, to begin with, and then I'm fixing up a little house for Ned and Ruth when they're married. I'm glad to do it for 'em, but it costs." His look appealed to Ethan for sympathy. "The young people like things nice. You know how it is yourself: it's not so long ago since you fixed up your own place for Zeena."

Ethan left the grays in Hale's stable and went about some other business in the village. As he walked away the builder's last phrase lingered in his ears, and he reflected grimly that his seven years with Zeena seemed to Starkfield "not so long."

The afternoon was drawing to an end, and here and there a lighted pane spangled the cold gray dusk and made the snow look whiter. The bitter weather had driven everyone indoors and Ethan had the long rural street to himself. Suddenly he heard the brisk play of sleigh bells and a cutter passed him, drawn by a free-going horse. Ethan recognized Michael Eady's roan colt, and young Denis Eady, in a handsome new fur cap, leaned forward and waved a greeting. "Hello, Ethe!" he shouted and spun on.

The cutter was going in the direction of the Frome farm, and Ethan's heart contracted as he listened to the dwindling bells. What more likely than that Denis Eady had heard of Zeena's departure for Bettsbridge, and was profiting by the opportunity to spend an hour with Mattie? Ethan was ashamed of the storm of jealousy in his breast. It seemed unworthy of the girl that his thoughts of her should be so violent.

He walked on to the church corner and entered the shade of the Varnum spruces, where he had stood with her the night before. As he passed into their gloom he saw an indistinct outline just ahead of him. At his approach it melted for an instant into two separate shapes and then conjoined again, and he heard a kiss, and a half-laughing "Oh!" provoked by the discovery of his presence. Again the outline hastily disunited and the Varnum gate slammed on one half while the other hurried on ahead of him. Ethan smiled at the discomfiture he had caused. What did it matter to Ned Hale and Ruth Varnum if they were caught kissing each other? Everybody in Starkfield knew they were engaged. It pleased Ethan to have surprised a pair of lovers on the spot where he and Mattie had stood with such a thirst for each other in their hearts; but he felt a pang at the thought that these two need not hide their happiness.

He fetched the grays from Hale's stable and started on his long climb back to the farm. The cold was less sharp than earlier in the day and a thick fleecy sky threatened snow for the morrow. Here and there a star pricked through, showing behind it a deep well of blue. In an hour or two the moon would push up over the ridge behind the farm, burn a gold-edged rent in the clouds, and then be swallowed by them. A mournful peace hung on the fields, as though they felt the relaxing grasp of the cold and stretched themselves in their long winter sleep.

Ethan's ears were alert for the jingle of sleigh bells, but not a sound broke the silence of the lonely road. As he drew near the farm he saw, through the thin screen of larches at the gate, a light twinkling in the house above him. "She's up in her room," he said to himself, "fixing herself up for supper"; and he remembered Zeena's sarcastic stare when Mattie, on the evening of her arrival, had come down to supper with smoothed hair and a ribbon at her neck.

He passed by the graves on the knoll and turned his head to glance at one of the older headstones, which had interested him deeply as a boy because it bore his name.

SACRED TO THE MEMORY OF
ETHAN FROME AND ENDURANCE HIS WIFE,
WHO DWELLED TOGETHER IN PEACE
FOR FIFTY YEARS.

He used to think that fifty years sounded like a long time to live together; but now it seemed to him that they might pass in a flash. Then, with a sudden dart of irony, he wondered if, when their turn came, the same epitaph would be written over him and Zeena.

He opened the barn door and craned his head into the obscurity, half-fearing to discover Denis Eady's roan colt in the stall beside the sorrel. But the old horse was there alone, mumbling his crib with toothless jaws, and Ethan whistled cheerfully while he bedded down the grays and shook an extra measure of oats into their mangers. His was not a tuneful throat, but harsh melodies burst from it as he locked the barn and sprang up the hill to the house. He reached the kitchen-porch and turned the door-handle; but the door did not yield to his touch.

Startled at finding it locked he rattled the handle violently; then he reflected that Mattie was alone and that it was natural she should barricade herself at nightfall. He stood in the darkness expecting to hear her step. It did not come, and after vainly straining his ears he called out in a voice that shook with joy: "Hello, Matt!"

Silence answered; but in a minute or two he caught a sound on the stairs and saw a line of light about the door-frame, as he had seen it the night before. So strange was the precision with which the incidents of the previous evening were repeating themselves that he half expected, when he heard the key turn, to see his wife before him on the threshold; but the door opened, and Mattie faced him.

She stood just as Zeena had stood, a lifted lamp in her hand, against the black background of the kitchen. She held the light at the same level, and it drew out with the same distinctness her slim young throat and the brown wrist no bigger than a child's. Then, striking upward, it threw a lustrous fleck on her lips, edged her eyes with velvet shade, and laid a milky whiteness above the black curve of her brows.

She wore her usual dress of darkish stuff, and there was no bow at her neck; but through her hair she had run a streak of crimson ribbon. This tribute to the unusual transformed and glorified her. She seemed to Ethan taller, fuller, more womanly in shape and motion. She stood aside, smiling silently, while he entered, and then moved away from him with something soft and flowing in her gait. She set the lamp on the table, and he saw that it was carefully laid for supper, with fresh doughnuts, stewed blueberries and his favorite pickles in a dish of gay red glass. A bright fire glowed in the stove and the cat lay stretched before it, watching the table with a drowsy eye.

Ethan was suffocated with the sense of well-being. He went out into the passage to hang up his coat and pull off his wet boots. When he came back Mattie had set the teapot on the table and the cat was rubbing itself persuasively against her ankles.

"Why, Puss! I nearly tripped over you," she cried, the laughter sparkling through her lashes.

Again Ethan felt a sudden twinge of jealousy. Could it be his coming that gave her such a kindled face?

"Well, Matt, any visitors?" he threw off, stooping down carelessly to examine the fastening of the stove.

She nodded and laughed "Yes, one," and he felt a blackness settling on his brows.

"Who was that?" he questioned, raising himself up to slant a glance at her beneath his scowl.

Her eyes danced with malice. "Why, Jotham Powell. He came in after he got back, and asked for a drop of coffee before he went down home."

The blackness lifted and light flooded Ethan's brain. "That all? Well, I hope you made out to let him have it." And after a pause he felt it right to add: "I suppose he got Zeena over to the Flats all right?"

"Oh, yes; in plenty of time."

The name threw a chill between them, and they stood a moment looking sideways at each other before Mattie said with a shy laugh: "I guess it's about time for supper."

They drew their seats up to the table, and the cat, unbidden, jumped between them into Zeena's empty chair. "Oh, Puss!" said Mattie, and they laughed again.

Ethan, a moment earlier, had felt himself on the brink of eloquence; but the mention of Zeena had paralyzed him. Mattie seemed to feel the contagion of his embarrassment, and sat with downcast lids, sipping her tea, while he feigned an insatiable appetite for doughnuts and sweet pickles. At last, after casting about for an effective opening, he took a long gulp of tea, cleared his throat, and said: "Looks as if there'd be more snow."

She feigned great interest. "Is that so? Do you suppose it'll interfere with Zeena's getting back?"

She flushed red as the question escaped her, and hastily set down the cup she was lifting.

Ethan reached over for another helping of pickles.

"You never can tell, this time of year, it drifts so bad on the Flats." The name had benumbed him again, and once more he felt as if Zeena were in the room between them.

"Oh, Puss, you're too greedy!" Mattie cried. The cat, unnoticed, had crept up on muffled paws from Zeena's seat to the table, and was stealthily elongating its body in the direction of the milk-jug, which stood between Ethan and Mattie. The two leaned forward at the same moment and their hands met on the handle of the jug. Mattie's hand was underneath, and Ethan kept his clasped on it a moment longer than was necessary. The cat, profiting by this unusual demonstration, tried to effect an unnoticed retreat, and in doing so backed into the pickle-dish, which fell to the floor with a crash.

Mattie, in an instant, had sprung from her chair and was down on her knees by the fragments.

"Oh, Ethan, Ethan—it's all to pieces! What will Zeena say?"

But this time his courage was up. "Well, she'll have to say it to the cat, anyway!" he rejoined with a laugh, kneeling down at Mattie's side to scrape up the swimming pickles.

She lifted stricken eyes to him. "Yes, but, you see, she never meant it should be used, not even when there was company; and I had to get up on the stepladder to reach it down from the top shelf of the china closet, where she keeps it with all her best things, and of course she'll want to know why I did it—?"

The case was so serious that it called forth all of Ethan's latent resolution.

"She needn't know anything about it if you keep quiet. I'll get another just like it tomorrow. Where did it come from? I'll go to Shadd's Falls for it if I have to!"

"Oh, you'll never get another even there! It was a wedding present— don't you remember? It came all the way from Philadelphia, from Zeena's aunt that married the minister. That's why she wouldn't ever use it. Oh, Ethan, Ethan, what in the world shall I do?"

She began to cry, and he felt as if every one of her tears were pouring over him like burning lead. "Don't, Matt, don't—oh, *don't!*" he implored her.

She struggled to her feet, and he rose and followed her helplessly while she spread out the pieces of glass on the kitchen dresser. It seemed to him as if the shattered fragments of their evening lay there.

"Here, give them to me," he said in a voice of sudden authority.

She drew aside, instinctively obeying his tone. "Oh, Ethan, what are you going to do?"

Without replying he gathered the pieces of glass into his broad palm and walked out of the kitchen to the passage. There he lit a candle-end, opened the china closet, and, reaching his long arm up to the highest shelf, laid the pieces together with such accuracy of touch that a close inspection convinced him of the impossibility of detecting from below that the dish was broken. If he glued it together the next morning months might elapse before his wife noticed what had happened, and meanwhile he might after all be able to match the dish at Shadd's Falls or Bettsbridge. Having satisfied himself that there was no risk of immediate discovery he went back to the kitchen with a lighter step, and found Mattie disconsolately removing the last scraps of pickle from the floor.

"It's all right, Matt. Come back and finish supper," he commanded her.

Completely reassured, she shone on him through tear-hung lashes, and his soul swelled with pride as he saw how his tone subdued her. She did not even ask what he had done. Except when he was steering a big log down the mountain to his mill he had never known such a thrilling sense of mastery.

5

THEY finished supper, and while Mattie cleared the table Ethan went to look at the cows and then took a last turn about the house. The earth lay dark under a muffled sky and the air was so still that now and then he heard a lump of snow come thumping down from a tree far off on the edge of the wood-lot.

When he returned to the kitchen Mattie had pushed up his chair to the stove and seated herself near the lamp with a bit of sewing. The scene was just as he had dreamed of it that morning. He sat down, drew his pipe from his pocket and stretched his feet to the glow. His hard day's work in the keen air made him feel at once lazy and light of mood, and he had a confused sense of being in another world, where all was warmth and harmony and time could bring no change. The only drawback to his complete well-being was the fact that he could not see Mattie from where he sat; but he was too indolent to move and after a moment he said: "Come over here and sit by the stove."

Zeena's empty rocking chair stood facing him. Mattie rose obediently, and seated herself in it. As her young brown head detached itself against the patchwork cushion that habitually framed his wife's gaunt countenance, Ethan had a momentary shock. It was almost as if the other face, the face of the superseded woman, had obliterated that of the intruder. After a moment Mattie seemed to be affected by the same sense of constraint. She changed her position, leaning forward to bend her head above her work, so that he saw only the foreshortened tip of her nose and the streak of red in her hair; then she slipped to her feet, saying "I can't see to sew," and went back to her chair by the lamp.

Ethan made a pretext of getting up to replenish the stove, and when he returned to his seat he pushed it sideways that he might get a view of her profile and of the lamplight falling on her hands. The cat, who had been a puzzled observer of these unusual movements, jumped up into Zeena's chair, rolled itself into a ball, and lay watching them with narrowed eyes.

Deep quiet sank on the room. The clock ticked above the dresser, a piece of charred wood fell now and then in the stove, and the faint sharp scent of the geraniums mingled with the odor of Ethan's smoke, which began to throw a blue haze about the lamp and to hang its grayish cobwebs in the shadowy corners of the room.

All constraint had vanished between the two, and they began to talk easily and simply. They spoke of everyday things, of the prospect of snow, of the next church sociable, of the loves and quarrels of Starkfield. The commonplace nature of what they said produced in Ethan an illusion of long-established intimacy which no outburst of emotion could have given, and he set his imagination adrift on the fiction that they had always spent their evenings thus and would always go on doing so. . . .

"This is the night we were to have gone coasting, Matt," he said at length, with the rich sense, as he spoke, that they could go on any other night they chose, since they had all time before them.

She smiled back at him. "I guess you forgot!"

"No, I didn't forget; but it's as dark as Egypt outdoors. We might go tomorrow if there's a moon."

She laughed with pleasure, her head tilted back, the lamplight sparkling on her lips and teeth. "That would be lovely, Ethan!"

He kept his eyes fixed on her, marveling at the way her face changed with each turn of their talk, like a wheatfield under a summer breeze. It was intoxicating to find such magic in his clumsy words, and he longed to try new ways of using it.

"Would you be scared to go down the Corbury road with me on a night like this?" he asked.

Her cheeks burned redder. "I ain't any more scared than you are!"

"Well, I'd be scared, then; I wouldn't do it. That's an ugly corner down by the big elm. If a fellow didn't keep his eyes open he'd go plumb into it."

He luxuriated in the sense of protection and authority which his words conveyed. To prolong and intensify the feeling he added: "I guess we're well enough here."

She let her lids sink slowly, in the way he loved. "Yes, we're well enough here," she sighed.

Her tone was so sweet that he took the pipe from his mouth and drew his chair up to the table. Leaning forward, he touched the farther end of the strip of brown stuff that she was hemming. "Say, Matt," he began with a smile, "what do you think I saw under the Varnum spruces, coming along home just now? I saw a friend of yours getting kissed."

The words had been on his tongue all the evening, but now that he had spoken them they struck him as inexpressibly vulgar and out of place.

Mattie blushed to the roots of her hair and pulled her needle rapidly twice or thrice through her work, insensibly drawing the end of it away from him. "I suppose it was Ruth and Ned," she said in a low voice, as though he had suddenly touched on something grave.

Ethan had imagined that his allusion might open the way to the accepted pleasantries, and these perhaps in turn to a harmless caress, if only a mere touch on her hand. But now he felt as if her blush had set a flaming guard about her. He supposed it was his natural awkwardness that made him feel so. He knew that most young men made nothing at all of giving a pretty girl a kiss, and he remembered that the night before, when he had put his arm about Mattie, she had not resisted. But that had been out-of-doors, under the open irresponsible night. Now, in the warm lamplit room, with all its ancient implications of conformity and order, she seemed infinitely farther away from him and more unapproachable.

To ease his constraint he said: "I suppose they'll be setting a date before long."

"Yes. I shouldn't wonder if they got married some time along in the summer." She pronounced the word *married* as if her voice caressed it. It seemed a rustling covert leading to enchanted glades. A pang shot through Ethan, and he said, twisting away from her in his chair: "It'll be your turn next, I wouldn't wonder."

She laughed a little uncertainly. "Why do you keep on saying that?"

He echoed her laugh. "I guess I do it to get used to the idea."

He drew up to the table again and she sewed on in silence, with dropped lashes, while he sat in fascinated contemplation of the way in which her hands went up and down above the strip of stuff, just as he had seen a pair of birds make short perpendicular flights over a nest they were building. At length, without turning her head or lifting her lids, she said in a low tone: "It's not because you think Zeena's got anything against me, is it?"

His former dread started up full-armed at the suggestion. "Why, what do you mean?" he stammered.

She raised distressed eyes to his, her work dropping on the table be-tween them. "I don't know. I thought last night she seemed to have."

"I'd like to know what," he growled.

"Nobody can tell with Zeena." It was the first time they had ever spoken so openly of her attitude toward Mattie, and the repetition of the name seemed to carry it to the farther corners of the room and send it back to them in long repercussions of sound. Mattie waited, as if to give the echo time to drop, and then went on: "She hasn't said anything to *you*?"

He shook his head. "No, not a word."

She tossed the hair back from her forehead with a laugh. "I guess I'm just nervous, then. I'm not going to think about it any more."

"Oh, no—don't let's think about it, Matt!"

The sudden heat of his tone made her color mount again, not with a rush, but gradually, delicately, like the reflection of a thought stealing slowly across her heart. She sat silent, her hands clasped on her work, and it seemed to him that a warm current flowed toward him along the strip of stuff that still lay unrolled between them. Cautiously he slid his hand palm-downward along the table till his fingertips touched the end of the stuff. A faint vibration of her lashes seemed to show that she was aware of his gesture, and that it had sent a counter-current back to her; and she let her hands lie motionless on the other end of the strip.

As they sat thus he heard a sound behind him and turned his head. The cat had jumped from Zeena's chair to dart at a mouse in the wainscot, and as a result of the sudden movement the empty chair had set up a spectral rocking.

"She'll be rocking in it herself this time tomorrow," Ethan thought. "I've been in a dream, and this is the only evening we'll ever have to-gether." The return to reality was as painful as the return to consciousness after taking an anesthetic. His body and brain ached with indescribable weariness, and he could think of nothing to say or to do that should arrest the mad flight of the moments.

His alteration of mood seemed to have communicated itself to Mattie. She looked up at him languidly, as though her lids were weighted with sleep and it cost her an effort to raise them. Her glance fell on his hand, which now completely covered the end of her work and grasped it as if it were a part of herself. He saw a scarcely perceptible tremor cross her face, and without knowing what he did he stooped his head and kissed the bit of stuff in his hold. As his lips rested on it he felt it glide slowly from beneath them, and saw that Mattie had risen and was silently rolling up her work. She fastened it with a pin, and then, finding her thimble and scissors, put them with the roll of stuff into the box covered with fancy paper which he had once brought to her from Bettsbridge.

He stood up, also, looking vaguely about the room. The clock above the dresser struck eleven.

"Is the fire all right?" she asked in a low voice.

He opened the door of the stove and poked aimlessly at the embers. When he raised himself again he saw that she was dragging toward the stove the old soap-box lined with carpet in which the cat made its bed. Then she recrossed the floor and lifted two of the geranium pots in her arms, moving them away from the cold window. He followed her and brought the other geraniums, the hyacinth bulbs in a cracked custard bowl and the German ivy trained over an old croquet hoop.

When these nightly duties were performed there was nothing left to do but to bring in the tin candlestick from the passage, light the candle and blow out the lamp. Ethan put the candlestick in Mattie's hand and she went out of the kitchen ahead of him, the light that she carried before her making her dark hair look like a drift of mist on the moon.

"Good night, Matt," he said as she put her foot on the first step of the stairs.

She turned and looked at him a moment. "Good night, Ethan," she answered, and went up.

When the door of her room had closed on her he remembered that he had not even touched her hand.

6

THE next morning at breakfast Jotham Powell was between them, and Ethan tried to hide his joy under an air of exaggerated indifference, lounging back in his chair to throw scraps to the cat, growling at the weather, and not so much as offering to help Mattie when she rose to clear away the dishes.

He did not know why he was so irrationally happy, for nothing was changed in his life or hers. He had not even touched the tip of her fingers or looked her full in the eyes. But their evening together had given him a vision of what life at her side might be, and he was glad now that he had done nothing to trouble the sweetness of the picture. He had a fancy that she knew what had restrained him. . . .

There was a last load of lumber to be hauled to the village, and Jotham Powell—who did not work regularly for Ethan in winter—had "come round" to help with the job. But a wet snow, melting to sleet, had fallen in the night and turned the roads to glass. There was more wet in the air and it seemed likely to both men that the weather would "milden" toward afternoon and make the going safer. Ethan therefore proposed to his assistant that they should load the sledge at the wood-lot, as they had done on the previous morning, and put off the "teaming" to Starkfield till later in the day. This plan had the advantage of enabling him to send Jotham to the Flats after dinner to meet Zenobia, while he himself took the lumber down to the village.

He told Jotham to go out and harness up the grays, and for a moment he and Mattie had the kitchen to themselves. She had plunged the breakfast dishes into a tin dishpan and was bending above it with her slim arms bared to the elbow, the steam from the hot water beading her forehead and tightening her rough hair into little brown rings like the tendrils on the traveler's joy.

Ethan stood looking at her, his heart in his throat. He wanted to say: "We shall never be alone again like this." Instead, he reached down his tobacco-pouch from a shelf of the dresser, put it into his pocket and said: "I guess I can make out to be home for dinner."

She answered, "All right, Ethan," and he heard her singing over the dishes as he went.

As soon as the sledge was loaded he meant to send Jotham back to the farm and hurry on foot into the village to buy the glue for the pickle-dish. With ordinary luck he should have had time to carry out this plan; but everything went wrong from the start. On the way over to the wood-lot one of the grays slipped on a glare of ice and cut his knee, and when they got him up again Jotham had to go back to the barn for a strip of rag to bind the cut. Then, when the loading finally began, a sleety rain was coming down once more, and the tree trunks were so slippery that it took twice as long as usual to lift them and get them in place on the sledge. It was what Jotham called a sour morning for work, and the horses, shivering and stamping under their wet blankets, seemed to like it as little as the men. It was long past the dinner-hour when the job was done, and Ethan had to give up going to the village because he wanted to lead the injured horse home and wash the cut himself.

He thought that by starting out again with the lumber as soon as he had finished his dinner he might get back to the farm with the glue before Jotham and the old sorrel had had time to fetch Zenobia from the Flats; but he knew the chance was a slight one. It turned on the state of the roads and on the possible lateness of the Bettsbridge train. He remembered afterward, with a grim flash of self-derision, what importance he had attached to the weighing of these probabilities. . . .

As soon as dinner was over he set out again for the wood-lot, not daring to linger till Jotham Powell left. The hired man was still drying his wet feet at the stove, and Ethan could only give Mattie a quick look as he said beneath his breath: "I'll be back early."

He fancied that she nodded her comprehension; and with that scant solace he had to trudge off through the rain.

He had driven his load halfway to the village when Jotham Powell overtook him, urging the reluctant sorrel toward the Flats. "I'll have to hurry up to do it," Ethan mused, as the sleigh dropped down ahead of him over the dip of the schoolhouse hill. He worked like ten at the unloading, and when it was over hastened on to Michael Eady's for the glue. Eady and his assistant were both "down street," and young Denis, who seldom deigned to take their place, was lounging by the stove with a knot of the golden youth of Starkfield. They hailed Ethan with ironic compliment and offers of conviviality; but no one knew where to find the glue. Ethan, consumed with the longing for a last moment alone with Mattie, hung about impatiently while Denis made an ineffectual search in the obscurer corners of the store.

"Looks as if we were all sold out. But if you'll wait around till the old man comes along maybe he can put his hand on it."

"I'm obliged to you, but I'll try if I can get it down at Mrs. Homan's," Ethan answered, burning to be gone.

Denis's commercial instinct compelled him to aver on oath that what Eady's store could not produce would never be found at the widow Homan's; but Ethan, heedless of this boast, had already climbed to the sledge and was driving on to the rival establishment. Here, after considerable search, and sympathetic questions as to what he wanted it for, and whether ordinary flour paste wouldn't do as well if she couldn't find it, the widow Homan finally hunted down her solitary bottle of glue to its hiding-place in a medley of cough-lozenges and corset-laces.

"I hope Zeena ain't broken anything she sets store by," she called after him as he turned the grays toward home.

The fitful bursts of sleet had changed into a steady rain and the horses had heavy work even without a load behind them. Once or twice, hearing sleigh bells, Ethan turned his head, fancying that Zeena and Jotham might overtake him; but the old sorrel was not in sight, and he set his face against the rain and urged on his ponderous pair.

The barn was empty when the horses turned into it and, after giving them the most perfunctory ministrations they had ever received from him, he strode up to the house and pushed open the kitchen door.

Mattie was there alone, as he had pictured her. She was bending over a pan on the stove; but at the sound of his step she turned with a start and sprang to him.

"See, here, Matt, I've got some stuff to mend the dish with! Let me get at it quick," he cried, waving the bottle in one hand while he put her lightly aside; but she did not seem to hear him.

"Oh, Ethan—Zeena's come," she said in a whisper, clutching his sleeve.

They stood and stared at each other, pale as culprits.

"But the sorrel's not in the barn!" Ethan stammered.

"Jotham Powell brought some goods over from the Flats for his wife, and he drove right on home with them," she explained.

He gazed blankly about the kitchen, which looked cold and squalid in the rainy winter twilight.

"How is she?" he asked, dropping his voice to Mattie's whisper.

She looked away from him uncertainly. "I don't know. She went right up to her room."

"She didn't say anything?"

"No."

Ethan let out his doubts in a low whistle and thrust the bottle back into his pocket. "Don't fret; I'll come down and mend it in the night," he said. He pulled on his wet coat again and went back to the barn to feed the grays.

While he was there Jotham Powell drove up with the sleigh, and when the horses had been attended to Ethan said to him: "You might as well come back up for a bite." He was not sorry to assure himself of Jotham's neutralizing presence at the supper table, for Zeena was always "nervous" after a journey. But the hired man, though seldom loath to accept a meal not included in his wages, opened his stiff jaws to answer slowly: "I'm obliged to you, but I guess I'll go along back."

Ethan looked at him in surprise. "Better come up and dry off. Looks as if there'd be something hot for supper."

Jotham's facial muscles were unmoved by this appeal and, his vocabulary being limited, he merely repeated: "I guess I'll go along back."

To Ethan there was something vaguely ominous in this stolid rejection of free food and warmth, and he wondered what had happened on the drive to nerve Jotham to such stoicism. Perhaps Zeena had failed to see the new doctor or had not liked his counsels: Ethan knew that in such cases the first person she met was likely to be held responsible for her grievance.

When he reentered the kitchen the lamp lit up the same scene of shining comfort as on the previous evening. The table had been as carefully laid, a clear fire glowed in the stove, the cat dozed in its warmth, and Mattie came forward carrying a plate of doughnuts.

She and Ethan looked at each other in silence; then she said, as she had said the night before: "I guess it's about time for supper."

7

E THAN went out into the passage to hang up his wet garments. He listened for Zeena's step and, not hearing it, called her name up the stairs. She did not answer, and after a moment's hesitation he went up and opened her door. The room was almost dark, but in the obscurity he saw her sitting by the window, bolt upright, and knew by the rigidity of the outline projected against the pane that she had not taken off her traveling dress.

"Well, Zeena," he ventured from the threshold.

She did not move, and he continued: "Supper's about ready. Ain't you coming?"

She replied: "I don't feel as if I could touch a morsel."

It was the consecrated formula, and he expected it to be followed, as usual, by her rising and going down to supper. But she remained seated, and he could think of nothing more felicitous than: "I presume you're tired after the long ride."

Turning her head at this, she answered solemnly: "I'm a great deal sicker than you think."

Her words fell on his ear with a strange shock of wonder. He had often heard her pronounce them before—what if at last they were true?

He advanced a step or two into the dim room. "I hope that's not so, Zeena," he said.

She continued to gaze at him through the twilight with a mien of wan authority, as of one consciously singled out for a great fate. "I've got complications," she said.

Ethan knew the word for one of exceptional import. Almost everybody in the neighborhood had "troubles," frankly localized and specified; but only the chosen had "complications." To have them was in itself a distinction, though it was also, in most cases, a death warrant. People struggled on for years with "troubles," but they almost always succumbed to "complications."

Ethan's heart was jerking to and fro between two extremities of feeling, but for the moment compassion prevailed. His wife looked so hard and lonely, sitting there in the darkness with such thoughts.

"Is that what the new doctor told you?" he asked, instinctively lowering his voice.

"Yes. He says any regular doctor would want me to have an operation."

Ethan was aware that, in regard to the important question of surgical intervention, the female opinion of the neighborhood was divided, some glorying in the prestige conferred by operations while others shunned them as indelicate. Ethan, from motives of economy, had always been glad that Zeena was of the latter faction.

In the agitation caused by the gravity of her announcement he sought a consolatory short cut. "What do you know about this doctor anyway? Nobody ever told you that before."

He saw his blunder before she could take it up: she wanted sympathy, not consolation.

"I didn't need to have anybody tell me I was losing ground every day. Everybody but you could see it. And everybody in Bettsbridge knows about Dr. Buck. He has his office in Worcester, and comes over once a fortnight to Shadd's Falls and Bettsbridge for consultations. Eliza Spears was wasting away with kidney trouble before she went to him, and now she's up and around, and singing in the choir."

"Well, I'm glad of that. You must do just what he tells you," Ethan answered sympathetically.

She was still looking at him. "I mean to," she said. He was struck by a new note in her voice. It was neither whining nor reproachful, but drily resolute.

"What does he want you should do?" he asked, with a mounting vision of fresh expenses.

"He wants I should have a hired girl. He says I oughtn't to have to do a single thing around the house."

"A hired girl?" Ethan stood transfixed.

"Yes. And Aunt Martha found me one right off. Everybody said I was lucky to get a girl to come away out here, and I agreed to give her a dollar extry to make sure. She'll be over tomorrow afternoon."

Wrath and dismay contended in Ethan. He had foreseen an immediate demand for money, but not a permanent drain on his scant resources. He no longer believed what Zeena had told him of the supposed seriousness of her state: he saw in her expedition to Bettsbridge only a plot hatched between herself and her Pierce relations to foist on him the cost of a servant; and for the moment wrath predominated.

"If you meant to engage a girl you ought to have told me before you started," he said.

"How could I tell you before I started? How did I know what Dr. Buck would say?"

"Oh, Dr. Buck—" Ethan's incredulity escaped in a short laugh. "Did Dr. Buck tell you how I was to pay her wages?"

Her voice rose furiously with his. "No, he didn't. For I'd 'a' been ashamed to tell him that you grudged me the money to get back my health, when I lost it nursing your own mother!"

"*You* lost your health nursing Mother?"

"Yes; and my folks all told me at the time you couldn't do no less than marry me after—"

"Zeena!"

Through the obscurity which hid their faces their thoughts seemed to dart at each other like serpents shooting venom. Ethan was seized with horror of the scene and shame at his own share in it. It was as senseless and savage as a physical fight between two enemies in the darkness.

He turned to the shelf above the chimney, groped for matches and lit the one candle in the room. At first its weak flame made no impression on the shadows; then Zeena's face stood grimly out against the uncurtained pane, which had turned from gray to black.

It was the first scene of open anger between the couple in their sad seven years together, and Ethan felt as if he had lost an irretrievable advantage in descending to the level of recrimination. But the practical problem was there and had to be dealt with.

"You know I haven't got the money to pay for a girl, Zeena. You'll have to send her back: I can't do it."

"The doctor says it'll be my death if I go on slaving the way I've had to. He doesn't understand how I've stood it as long as I have."

"Slaving!—" He checked himself again, "You sha'n't lift a hand, if he says so. I'll do everything round the house myself—"

She broke in: "You're neglecting the farm enough already," and this being true, he found no answer, and left her time to add ironically: "Better send me over to the almshouse and done with it . . . I guess there's been Fromes there afore now."

The taunt burned into him, but he let it pass. "I haven't got the money. That settles it."

There was a moment's pause in the struggle, as though the combatants were testing their weapons. Then Zeena said in a level voice: "I thought you were to get fifty dollars from Andrew Hale for that lumber."

"Andrew Hale never pays under three months."

He had hardly spoken when he remembered the excuse he had made for not accompanying his wife to the station the day before; and the blood rose to his frowning brows.

"Why, you told me yesterday you'd fixed it up with him to pay cash down. You said that was why you couldn't drive me over to the Flats."

Ethan had no suppleness in deceiving. He had never before been convicted of a lie, and all the resources of evasion failed him. "I guess that was a misunderstanding," he stammered.

"You ain't got the money?"

"No."

"And you ain't going to get it?"

"No."

"Well, I couldn't know that when I engaged the girl, could I?"

"No." He paused to control his voice. "But you know it now. I'm sorry, but it can't be helped. You're a poor man's wife, Zeena; but I'll do the best I can for you."

For a while she sat motionless, as if reflecting, her arms stretched along the arms of her chair, her eyes fixed on vacancy. "Oh, I guess we'll make out," she said mildly.

The change in her tone reassured him. "Of course we will! There's a whole lot more I can do for you, and Mattie—"

Zeena, while he spoke, seemed to be following out some elaborate mental calculation. She emerged from it to say: "There'll be Mattie's board less, anyhow—"

Ethan, supposing the discussion to be over, had turned to go down to supper. He stopped short, not grasping what he heard. "Mattie's board less—?" he began.

Zeena laughed. It was an odd unfamiliar sound—he did not remember ever having heard her laugh before. "You didn't suppose I was going to keep two girls, did you? No wonder you were scared at the expense!"

He still had but a confused sense of what she was saying. From the beginning of the discussion he had instinctively avoided the mention of Mattie's name, fearing he hardly knew what: criticism, complaints, or vague allusions to the imminent probability of her marrying. But the thought of a definite rupture had never come to him, and even now could not lodge itself in his mind.

"I don't know what you mean," he said. "Mattie Silver's not a hired girl. She's your relation."

"She's a pauper that's hung onto us all after her father'd done his best to ruin us. I've kep' her here a whole year: it's somebody else's turn now."

As the shrill words shot out Ethan heard a tap on the door, which he had drawn shut when he turned back from the threshold.

"Ethan—Zeena!" Mattie's voice sounded gaily from the landing, "do you know what time it is? Supper's been ready half an hour."

Inside the room there was a moment's silence; then Zeena called out from her seat: "I'm not coming down to supper."

"Oh, I'm sorry! Aren't you well? Sha'n't I bring you up a bite of something?"

Ethan roused himself with an effort and opened the door. "Go along down, Matt. Zeena's just a little tired. I'm coming."

He heard her "All right!" and her quick step on the stairs; then he shut the door and turned back into the room. His wife's attitude was unchanged, her face inexorable, and he was seized with the despairing sense of his helplessness.

"You ain't going to do it, Zeena?"

"Do what?" she emitted between flattened lips.

"Send Mattie away—like this?"

"I never bargained to take her for life!"

He continued with rising vehemence: "You can't put her out of the house like a thief—a poor girl without friends or money. She's done her best for you and she's got no place to go to. You may forget she's your kin but everybody else'll remember it. If you do a thing like that what do you suppose folks'll say of you?"

Zeena waited a moment, as if giving him time to feel the full force of the contrast between his own excitement and her composure. Then she replied in the same smooth voice: "I know well enough what they say of my having kep' her here as long as I have."

Ethan's hand dropped from the doorknob, which he had held clenched since he had drawn the door shut on Mattie. His wife's retort was like a knife-cut across the sinews and he felt suddenly weak and powerless. He had meant to humble himself, to argue that Mattie's keep didn't cost much, after all, that he could make out to buy a stove and fix up a place in the attic for the hired girl—but Zeena's words revealed the peril of such pleadings.

"You mean to tell her she's got to go—at once?" he faltered out, in terror of letting his wife complete her sentence.

As if trying to make him see reason she replied impartially; "The girl will be over from Bettsbridge tomorrow, and I presume she's got to have somewheres to sleep."

Ethan looked at her with loathing. She was no longer the listless creature who had lived at his side in a state of sullen self-absorption, but a mysterious alien presence, an evil energy secreted from the long years of silent brooding. It was the sense of his helplessness that sharpened his antipathy. There had never been anything in her that one could appeal to; but as long as he could ignore and command he had remained indifferent. Now she had mastered him and he abhorred her. Mattie was her relation, not his: there were no means by which he could compel her to keep the girl under her roof. All the long misery of his baffled past, of his youth of failure, hardship and vain effort, rose up in his soul in bitterness and seemed to take shape before him in the woman who at every turn had barred his way. She had taken everything else from him; and now she meant to take the one thing that made up for all the others. For a moment such a flame of hate rose in him that it ran down his arm and clenched his fist against her. He took a wild step forward and then stopped.

"You're—you're not coming down?" he said in a bewildered voice.

"No. I guess I'll lay down on the bed a little while," she answered mildly; and he turned and walked out of the room.

In the kitchen Mattie was sitting by the stove, the cat curled up on her knees. She sprang to her feet as Ethan entered and carried the covered dish of meat pie to the table.

"I hope Zeena isn't sick?" she asked.

"No."

She shone at him across the table. "Well, sit right down then. You must be starving." She uncovered the pie and pushed it over to him. So they were to have one more evening together, her happy eyes seemed to say!

He helped himself mechanically and began to eat; then disgust took him by the throat and he laid down his fork.

Mattie's tender gaze was on him and she marked the gesture.

"Why, Ethan, what's the matter? Don't it taste right?"

"Yes—it's first-rate. Only I—" He pushed his plate away, rose from his chair, and walked around the table to her side. She started up with frightened eyes.

"Ethan, there's something wrong! I *knew* there was!"

She seemed to melt against him in her terror, and he caught her in his arms, held her fast there, felt her lashes beat his cheek like netted butterflies.

"What is it—what is it?" she stammered; but he had found her lips at last and was drinking unconsciousness of everything but the joy they gave him.

She lingered a moment, caught in the same strong current; then she slipped from him and drew back a step or two, pale and troubled. Her look smote him with compunction, and he cried out, as if he saw her drowning in a dream: "You can't go, Matt! I'll never let you!"

"Go—go?" she stammered. "Must I go?"

The words went on sounding between them as though a torch of warning flew from hand to hand through a black landscape.

Ethan was overcome with shame at his lack of self-control in flinging the news at her so brutally. His head reeled and he had to support himself against the table. All the while he felt as if he were still kissing her, and yet dying of thirst for her lips.

"Ethan what has happened? Is Zeena mad with me?"

Her cry steadied him, though it deepened his wrath and pity. "No, no," he assured her, "it's not that. But this new doctor has scared her about herself. You know she believes all they say the first time she sees them. And this one's told her she won't get well unless she lays up and don't do a thing about the house—not for months—"

He paused, his eyes wandering from her miserably. She stood silent a moment, drooping before him like a broken branch. She was so small and weak-looking that it wrung his heart; but suddenly she lifted her head and looked straight at him. "And she wants somebody handier in my place? Is that it?"

"That's what she says tonight."

"If she says it tonight she'll say it tomorrow."

Both bowed to the inexorable truth: they knew that Zeena never changed her mind, and that in her case a resolve once taken was equivalent to an act performed.

There was a long silence between them; then Mattie said in a low voice: "Don't be too sorry, Ethan."

"Oh, God—oh, God," he groaned. The glow of passion he had felt for her had melted to an aching tenderness. He saw her quick lids beating back the tears, and longed to take her in his arms and soothe her.

"You're letting your supper get cold," she admonished him with a pale gleam of gaiety.

"Oh, Matt—Matt—where'll you go to?"

Her lids sank and a tremor crossed her face. He saw that for the first time the thought of the future came to her distinctly. "I might get something to do over at Stamford," she faltered, as if knowing that he knew she had no hope.

He dropped back into his seat and hid his face in his hands. Despair seized him at the thought of her setting out alone to renew the weary quest for work. In the only place where she was known she was surrounded by indifference or animosity; and what chance had she, inexperienced and untrained, among the million breadseekers of the cities? There came back to him miserable tales he had heard at Worcester, and the faces of girls whose lives had begun as hopefully as Mattie's. . . . It was not possible to think of such things without a revolt of his whole being. He sprang up suddenly.

"You can't go, Matt! I won't let you! She's always had her way, but I mean to have mine now—"

Mattie lifted her hand with a quick gesture, and he heard his wife's step behind him.

Zeena came into the room with her dragging down-at-the-heel step, and quietly took her accustomed seat between them.

"I felt a little mite better, and Dr. Buck says I ought to eat all I can to keep my stren'th up, even if I ain't got any appetite," she said in her flat whine, reaching across Mattie for the teapot. Her "good" dress had been replaced by the black calico and brown knitted shawl which formed her daily wear, and with them she had put on her usual face and manner. She poured out her tea, added a great deal of milk to it, helped herself largely to pie and pickles, and made the familiar gesture of adjusting her false teeth before she began to eat. The cat rubbed itself ingratiatingly against her, and she said "Good Pussy," stooped to stroke it and gave it a scrap of meat from her plate.

Ethan sat speechless, not pretending to eat, but Mattie nibbled valiantly at her food and asked Zeena one or two questions about her visit to Bettsbridge. Zeena answered in her everyday tone and, warming to the theme, regaled them with several vivid descriptions of intestinal disturbances among her friends and relatives. She looked straight at Mattie as she spoke, a faint smile deepening the vertical lines between her nose and chin.

When supper was over she rose from her seat and pressed her hand to the flat surface over the region of her heart. "That pie of yours always sets a mite heavy, Matt," she said, not ill-naturedly. She seldom abbreviated the girl's name, and when she did so it was always a sign of affability.

"I've a good mind to go and hunt up those stomach powders I got last year over in Springfield," she continued. "I ain't tried them for quite a while, and maybe they'll help the heartburn."

Mattie lifted her eyes. "Can't I get them for you, Zeena?" she ventured.

"No. They're in a place you don't know about," Zeena answered darkly, with one of her secret looks.

She went out of the kitchen and Mattie, rising, began to clear the dishes from the table. As she passed Ethan's chair their eyes met and clung together desolately. The warm still kitchen looked as peaceful as the night before. The cat had sprung to Zeena's rocking chair, and the heat of the fire was beginning to draw out the faint sharp scent of the geraniums. Ethan dragged himself wearily to his feet.

"I'll go out and take a look round," he said, going toward the passage to get his lantern.

As he reached the door he met Zeena coming back into the room, her lips twitching with anger, a flush of excitement on her sallow face. The shawl had slipped from her shoulders and was dragging at her downtrodden heels, and in her hands she carried the fragments of the red glass pickle-dish.

"I'd like to know who done this," she said, looking sternly from Ethan to Mattie.

There was no answer, and she continued in a trembling voice: "I went to get those powders I'd put away in father's old spectacle-case, top of the china closet, where I keep the things I set store by, so's folks sha'n't meddle with them—" Her voice broke, and two small tears hung on her lashless lids and ran slowly down her cheeks. "It takes the stepladder to get at the top shelf, and I put Aunt Philura Maple's pickle-dish up there o' purpose when we was married, and it's never been down since, 'cept for the spring cleaning, and then I always lifted it with my own hands, so's 't it shouldn't get broke." She laid the fragments reverently on the table. "I want to know who done this," she quavered.

At the challenge Ethan turned back into the room and faced her. "I can tell you, then. The cat done it."

"The *cat?*"

"That's what I said."

She looked at him hard, and then turned her eyes to Mattie, who was carrying the dishpan to the table.

"I'd like to know how the cat got into my china closet," she said.

"Chasin' mice, I guess," Ethan rejoined. "There was a mouse round the kitchen all last evening."

Zeena continued to look from one to the other; then she emitted her small strange laugh. "I knew the cat was a smart cat," she said in a high voice, "but I didn't know he was smart enough to pick up the pieces of my pickle-dish and lay 'em edge to edge on the very shelf he knocked 'em off of."

Mattie suddenly drew her arms out of the steaming water. "It wasn't Ethan's fault, Zeena! The cat *did* break the dish; but I got it down from the china closet, and I'm the one to blame for its getting broken."

Zeena stood beside the ruin of her treasure, stiffening into a stony image of resentment. "*You* got down my pickle-dish—what for?"

A bright flush flew to Mattie's cheeks. "I wanted to make the supper-table pretty," she said.

"You wanted to make the supper-table pretty, and you waited till my back was turned, and took the thing I set most store by of anything I've got, and wouldn't never use it, not even when the minister come to dinner, or Aunt Martha Pierce come over from Bettsbridge—" Zeena paused with a gasp, as if terrified by her own evocation of the sacrilege. "You're a bad girl, Mattie Silver, and I always known it. It's the way your father begun, and I was warned of it when I took you, and I tried to keep my things where you couldn't get at 'em—and now you've took from me the one I cared for most of all—" She broke off in a short spasm of sobs that passed and left her more than ever like a shape of stone.

"If I'd 'a' listened to folks, you'd 'a' gone before now, and this wouldn't 'a' happened," she said; and gathering up the bits of broken glass she went out of the room as if she carried a dead body. . . .

8

W HEN Ethan was called back to the farm by his father's illness his mother gave him, for his own use, a small room behind the untenanted "best parlor." Here he had nailed up shelves for his books, built himself a box-sofa out of boards and a mattress, laid out his papers on a kitchen-table, hung on the rough plaster wall an engraving of Abraham Lincoln and a calendar with "Thoughts from the Poets," and tried, with these meager properties, to produce some likeness to the study of a "minister" who had been kind to him and lent him books when he was at Worcester. He still took refuge there in summer, but when Mattie came to live at the farm he had had to give her his stove, and consequently the room was uninhabitable for several months of the year.

To this retreat he descended as soon as the house was quiet, and Zeena's steady breathing from the bed had assured him that there was to be no

sequel to the scene in the kitchen. After Zeena's departure he and Mattie
had stood speechless, neither seeking to approach the other. Then the girl
had returned to her task of clearing up the kitchen for the night and he had
taken his lantern and gone on his usual round outside the house. The
kitchen was empty when he came back to it; but his tobacco-pouch and
pipe had been laid on the table, and under them was a scrap of paper torn
from the back of a seedsman's catalogue, on which three words were written: "Don't trouble, Ethan."

Going into his cold dark "study" he placed the lantern on the table and,
stooping to its light, read the message again and again. It was the first time
that Mattie had ever written to him, and the possession of the paper gave
him a strange new sense of her nearness; yet it deepened his anguish by
reminding him that henceforth they would have no other way of communicating with each other. For the life of her smile, the warmth of her voice,
only cold paper and dead words!

Confused motions of rebellion stormed in him. He was too young, too
strong, too full of the sap of living, to submit so easily to the destruction of
his hopes. Must he wear out all his years at the side of a bitter querulous
woman? Other possibilities had been in him, possibilities sacrificed, one by
one, to Zeena's narrow-mindedness and ignorance. And what good had
come of it? She was a hundred times bitterer and more discontented than
when he had married her: the one pleasure left her was to inflict pain on
him. All the healthy instincts of self-defense rose up in him against such
waste . . .

He bundled himself into his old coonskin coat and lay down on the box-
sofa to think. Under his cheek he felt a hard object with strange protuber-
ances. It was a cushion which Zeena had made for him when they were
engaged—the only piece of needlework he had ever seen her do. He flung it
across the floor and propped his head against the wall. . . .

He knew a case of a man over the mountain—a young fellow of about
his own age—who had escaped from just such a life of misery by going West
with the girl he cared for. His wife had divorced him, and he had married
the girl and prospered. Ethan had seen the couple the summer before at
Shadd's Falls, where they had come to visit relatives. They had a little girl
with fair curls, who wore a gold locket and was dressed like a princess. The
deserted wife had not done badly either. Her husband had given her the
farm and she had managed to sell it, and with that and the alimony she had
started a lunchroom at Bettsbridge and bloomed into activity and importance. Ethan was fired by the thought. Why should he not leave with
Mattie the next day, instead of letting her go alone? He would hide his
valise under the seat of the sleigh, and Zeena would suspect nothing till she
went upstairs for her afternoon nap and found a letter on the bed. . . .

His impulses were still near the surface, and he sprang up, re-lit the lantern, and sat down at the table. He rummaged in the drawer for a sheet of paper, found one, and began to write.

"Zeena, I've done all I could for you, and I don't see as it's been any use. I don't blame you, nor I don't blame myself. Maybe both of us will do better separate. I'm going to try my luck West, and you can sell the farm and mill, and keep the money—"

His pen paused on the word, which brought home to him the relentless conditions of his lot. If he gave the farm and mill to Zeena what would be left him to start his own life with? Once in the West he was sure of picking up work—he would not have feared to try his chance alone. But with Mattie depending on him the case was different. And what of Zeena's fate? Farm and mill were mortgaged to the limit of their value, and even if she found a purchaser—in itself an unlikely chance—it was doubtful if she could clear a thousand dollars on the sale. Meanwhile, how could she keep the farm going? It was only by incessant labor and personal supervision that Ethan drew a meager living from his land, and his wife, even if she were in better health than she imagined, could never carry such a burden alone.

Well, she could go back to her people, then, and see what they would do for her. It was the fate she was forcing on Mattie—why not let her try it herself? By the time she had discovered his whereabouts, and brought suit for divorce, he would probably—wherever he was—be earning enough to pay her a sufficient alimony. And the alternative was to let Mattie go forth alone, with far less hope of ultimate provision. . . .

He had scattered the contents of the table-drawer in his search for a sheet of paper, and as he took up his pen his eye fell on an old copy of the *Bettsbridge Eagle*. The advertising sheet was folded uppermost, and he read the seductive words: "Trips to the West: Reduced Rates."

He drew the lantern nearer and eagerly scanned the fares; then the paper fell from his hand and he pushed aside his unfinished letter. A moment ago he had wondered what he and Mattie were to live on when they reached the West; now he saw that he had not even the money to take her there. Borrowing was out of the question: six months before he had given his only security to raise funds for necessary repairs to the mill, and he knew that without security no one at Starkfield would lend him ten dollars. The inexorable facts closed in on him like prison-warders hand-cuffing a convict. There was no way out—none. He was a prisoner for life, and now his one ray of light was to be extinguished.

He crept back heavily to the sofa, stretching himself out with limbs so leaden that he felt as if they would never move again. Tears rose in his throat and slowly burned their way to his lids.

As he lay there, the window-pane that faced him, growing gradually lighter, inlaid upon the darkness a square of moon-suffused sky. A crooked tree-branch crossed it, a branch of the apple tree under which, on summer evenings, he had sometimes found Mattie sitting when he came up from the mill. Slowly the rim of the rainy vapors caught fire and burnt away, and a pure moon swung into the blue. Ethan, rising on his elbow, watched the landscape whiten and shape itself under the sculpture of the moon. This was the night on which he was to have taken Mattie coasting, and there hung the lamp to light them! He looked out at the slopes bathed in luster, the silver-edged darkness of the woods, the spectral purple of the hills against the sky, and it seemed as though all the beauty of the night had been poured out to mock his wretchedness. . . .

He fell asleep, and when he woke the chill of the winter dawn was in the room. He felt cold and stiff and hungry, and ashamed of being hungry. He rubbed his eyes and went to the window. A red sun stood over the gray rim of the fields, behind trees that looked black and brittle. He said to himself: "This is Matt's last day," and tried to think what the place would be without her.

As he stood there he heard a step behind him and she entered.

"Oh, Ethan—were you here all night?"

She looked so small and pinched, in her poor dress, with the red scarf wound about her, and the cold light turning her paleness sallow, that Ethan stood before her without speaking.

"You must be frozen," she went on, fixing lusterless eyes on him.

He drew a step nearer. "How did you know I was here?"

"Because I heard you go downstairs again after I went to bed, and I listened all night, and you didn't come up."

All his tenderness rushed to his lips. He looked at her and said: "I'll come right along and make up the kitchen fire."

They went back to the kitchen, and he fetched the coal and kindlings and cleared out the stove for her, while she brought in the milk and the cold remains of the meat pie. When warmth began to radiate from the stove, and the first ray of sunlight lay on the kitchen floor, Ethan's dark thoughts melted in the mellower air. The sight of Mattie going about her work as he had seen her on so many mornings made it seem impossible that she should ever cease to be a part of the scene. He said to himself that he had doubtless exaggerated the significance of Zeena's threats, and that she, too, with the return of daylight, would come to a saner mood.

He went up to Mattie as she bent above the stove, and laid his hand on her arm. "I don't want you should trouble either," he said, looking down into her eyes with a smile.

She flushed up warmly and whispered back: "No, Ethan, I ain't going to trouble."

"I guess things'll straighten out," he added.

There was no answer but a quick throb of her lids, and he went on: "She ain't said anything this morning?"

"No. I haven't seen her yet."

"Don't you take any notice when you do."

With this injunction he left her and went out to the cow-barn. He saw Jotham Powell walking up the hill through the morning mist, and the familiar sight added to his growing conviction of security.

As the two men were clearing out the stalls Jotham rested on his pitch-fork to say: "Dan'l Byrne's goin' over to the Flats today noon, an' he c'd take Mattie's trunk along, and make it easier ridin' when I take her over in the sleigh."

Ethan looked at him blankly, and he continued: "Mis' Frome said the new girl'd be at the Flats at five, and I was to take Mattie then, so's 't she could ketch the six o'clock train for Stamford."

Ethan felt the blood drumming in his temples. He had to wait a moment before he could find a voice to say: "Oh, it ain't so sure about Mattie's going—"

"That so?" said Jotham indifferently; and they went on with their work.

When they returned to the kitchen the two women were already at breakfast. Zeena had an air of unusual alertness and activity. She drank two cups of coffee and fed the cat with the scraps left in the pie dish; then she rose from her seat and, walking over to the window, snipped two or three yellow leaves from the geraniums. "Aunt Martha's ain't got a faded leaf on 'em; but they pine away when they ain't cared for," she said reflectively. Then she turned to Jotham and asked: "What time'd you say Dan'l Byrne'd be along?"

The hired man threw a hesitating glance at Ethan. "Round about noon," he said.

Zeena turned to Mattie. "That trunk of yours is too heavy for the sleigh, and Dan'l Byrne'll be round to take it over to the Flats," she said.

"I'm much obliged to you, Zeena," said Mattie.

"I'd like to go over things with you first," Zeena continued in an unper-turbed voice. "I know there's a huckabuck towel missing; and I can't make out what you done with that match-safe 't used to stand behind the stuffed owl in the parlor."

She went out, followed by Mattie, and when the men were alone Jo-tham said to his employer: "I guess I better let Dan'l come round, then."

Ethan finished his usual morning tasks about the house and barn; then he said to Jotham: "I'm going down to Starkfield. Tell them not to wait dinner."

The passion of rebellion had broken out in him again. That which had seemed incredible in the sober light of day had really come to pass, and he was to assist as a helpless spectator at Mattie's banishment. His manhood was humbled by the part he was compelled to play and by the thought of what Mattie must think of him. Confused impulses struggled in him as he strode along to the village. He had made up his mind to do something, but he did not know what it would be.

The early mist had vanished and the fields lay like a silver shield under the sun. It was one of the days when the glitter of winter shines through a pale haze of spring. Every yard of the road was alive with Mattie's presence, and there was hardly a branch against the sky or a tangle of brambles on the bank in which some bright shred of memory was not caught. Once, in the stillness, the call of a bird in a mountain ash was so like her laughter that his heart tightened and then grew large; and all these things made him see that something must be done at once.

Suddenly it occurred to him that Andrew Hale, who was a kind-hearted man, might be induced to reconsider his refusal and advance a small sum on the lumber if he were told that Zeena's ill-health made it necessary to hire a servant. Hale, after all, knew enough of Ethan's situation to make it possible for the latter to renew his appeal without too much loss of pride; and, moreover, how much did pride count in the ebullition of passions in his breast?

The more he considered his plan the more hopeful it seemed. If he could get Mrs. Hale's ear he felt certain of success, and with fifty dollars in his pocket nothing could keep him from Mattie. . . .

His first object was to reach Starkfield before Hale had started for his work; he knew the carpenter had a job down the Corbury road and was likely to leave his house early. Ethan's long strides grew more rapid with the accelerated beat of his thoughts, and as he reached the foot of School House Hill he caught sight of Hale's sleigh in the distance. He hurried forward to meet it, but as it drew nearer he saw that it was driven by the carpenter's youngest boy and that the figure at his side, looking like a large upright cocoon in spectacles, was that of Mrs. Hale. Ethan signed to them to stop, and Mrs. Hale leaned forward, her pink wrinkles twinkling with benevolence.

"Mr. Hale? Why, yes, you'll find him down home now. He ain't going to his work this forenoon. He woke up with a touch o' lumbago, and I just made him put on one of old Dr. Kidder's plasters and set right up into the fire."

Beaming maternally on Ethan, she bent over to add: "I on'y just heard from Mr. Hale 'bout Zeena's going over to Bettsbridge to see that new doctor. I'm real sorry she's feeling so bad again! I hope he thinks he can do something for her? I don't know anybody round here's had more sickness than Zeena. I always tell Mr. Hale I don't know what she'd 'a' done if she hadn't 'a' had you to look after her; and I used to say the same thing 'bout your mother. You've had an awful mean time, Ethan Frome."

She gave him a last nod of sympathy while her son chirped to the horse; and Ethan, as she drove off, stood in the middle of the road and stared after the retreating sleigh.

It was a long time since anyone had spoken to him as kindly as Mrs. Hale. Most people were either indifferent to his troubles, or disposed to think it natural that a young fellow of his age should have carried without repining the burden of three crippled lives. But Mrs. Hale had said "You've had an awful mean time, Ethan Frome," and he felt less alone with his misery. If the Hales were sorry for him they would surely respond to his appeal. . . .

He started down the road toward their house, but at the end of a few yards he pulled up sharply, the blood in his face. For the first time, in the light of the words he had just heard, he saw what he was about to do. He was planning to take advantage of the Hales' sympathy to obtain money from them on false pretences. That was a plain statement of the cloudy purpose which had driven him in headlong to Starkfield.

With the sudden perception of the point to which his madness had carried him, the madness fell and he saw his life before him as it was. He was a poor man, the husband of a sickly woman, whom his desertion would leave alone and destitute; and even if he had had the heart to desert her he could have done so only by deceiving two kindly people who had pitied him.

He turned and walked slowly back to the farm.

9

AT the kitchen door Daniel Byrne sat in his sleigh behind a big-boned gray who pawed the snow and swung his long head restlessly from side to side.

Ethan went into the kitchen and found his wife by the stove. Her head was wrapped in her shawl, and she was reading a book called *Kidney Troubles and Their Cure* on which he had had to pay extra postage only a few days before.

Zeena did not move or look up when he entered, and after a moment he asked: "Where's Mattie?"

Without lifting her eyes from the page she replied: "I presume she's getting down her trunk."

The blood rushed to his face. "Getting down her trunk—alone?"

"Jotham Powell's down in the wood-lot, and Dan'l Byrne says he darsn't leave that horse," she returned.

Her husband, without stopping to hear the end of the phrase, had left the kitchen and sprung up the stairs. The door of Mattie's room was shut, and he wavered a moment on the landing. "Matt," he said in a low voice; but there was no answer, and he put his hand on the doorknob.

He had never been in her room except once, in the early summer, when he had gone there to plaster up a leak in the eaves, but he remembered exactly how everything had looked: the red and white quilt on her narrow bed, the pretty pincushion on the chest of drawers, and over it the enlarged photograph of her mother, in an oxydized frame, with a bunch of dyed grasses at the back. Now these and all other tokens of her presence had vanished, and the room looked as bare and comfortless as when Zeena had shown her into it on the day of her arrival. In the middle of the floor stood her trunk, and on the trunk she sat in her Sunday dress, her back turned to the door and her face in her hands. She had not heard Ethan's call because she was sobbing; and she did not hear his step till he stood close behind her and laid his hands on her shoulders.

"Matt—oh, don't—oh, *Matt!*"

She started up, lifting her wet face to his. "Ethan—I thought I wasn't ever going to see you again!"

He took her in his arms, pressing her close, and with a trembling hand smoothed away the hair from her forehead.

"Not see me again? What do you mean?"

She sobbed out: "Jotham said you told him we wasn't to wait dinner for you, and I thought—"

"You thought I meant to cut it?" he finished for her grimly.

She clung to him without answering, and he laid his lips on her hair, which was soft yet springy, like certain mosses on warm slopes, and had the faint woody fragrance of fresh sawdust in the sun.

Through the door they heard Zeena's voice calling out from below: "Dan'l Byrne says you better hurry up if you want him to take that trunk."

They drew apart with stricken faces. Words of resistance rushed to Ethan's lips and died there. Mattie found her handkerchief and dried her eyes; then, bending down, she took hold of a handle of the trunk.

Ethan put her aside. "You let go, Matt," he ordered her.

She answered: "It takes two to coax it round the corner"; and submitting to this argument he grasped the other handle, and together they maneuvered the heavy trunk out to the landing.

"Now let go," he repeated; then he shouldered the trunk and carried it down the stairs and across the passage to the kitchen. Zeena, who had gone back to her seat by the stove, did not lift her head from her book as he passed. Mattie followed him out of the door and helped him to lift the trunk into the back of the sleigh. When it was in place they stood side by side on the doorstep, watching Daniel Byrne plunge off behind his fidgety horse.

It seemed to Ethan that his heart was bound with cords which an unseen hand was tightening with every tick of the clock. Twice he opened his lips to speak to Mattie and found no breath. At length, as she turned to reenter the house, he laid a detaining hand on her.

"I'm going to drive you over, Matt," he whispered.

She murmured back: "I think Zeena wants I should go with Jotham."

"I'm going to drive you over," he repeated; and she went into the kitchen without answering.

At dinner Ethan could not eat. If he lifted his eyes they rested on Zeena's pinched face, and the corners of her straight lips seemed to quiver away into a smile. She ate well, declaring that the mild weather made her feel better, and pressed a second helping of beans on Jotham Powell, whose wants she generally ignored.

Mattie, when the meal was over, went about her usual task of clearing the table and washing up the dishes. Zeena, after feeding the cat, had returned to her rocking chair by the stove, and Jotham Powell, who always lingered last, reluctantly pushed back his chair and moved toward the door.

On the threshold he turned back to say to Ethan: "What time'll I come round for Mattie?"

Ethan was standing near the window, mechanically filling his pipe while he watched Mattie move to and fro. He answered: "You needn't come round; I'm going to drive her over myself."

He saw the rise of the color in Mattie's averted cheek, and the quick lifting of Zeena's head.

"I want you should stay here this afternoon, Ethan," his wife said. "Jotham can drive Mattie over."

Mattie flung an imploring glance at him, but he repeated curtly: "I'm going to drive her over myself."

Zeena continued in the same even tone: "I wanted you should stay and fix up that stove in Mattie's room afore the girl gets here. It ain't been drawing right for nigh on a month now."

Ethan's voice rose indignantly. "If it was good enough for Mattie I guess it's good enough for a hired girl."

"That girl that's coming told me she was used to a house where they had a furnace," Zeena persisted with the same monotonous mildness.

"She'd better ha' stayed there then," he flung back at her; and turning to Mattie he added in a hard voice: "You be ready by three, Matt; I've got business at Corbury."

Jotham Powell had started for the barn, and Ethan strode down after him aflame with anger. The pulses in his temples throbbed and a fog was in his eyes. He went about his task without knowing what force directed him, or whose hands and feet were fulfilling its orders. It was not till he led out the sorrel and backed him between the shafts of the sleigh that he once more became conscious of what he was doing. As he passed the bridle over the horse's head, and wound the traces around the shafts, he remembered the day when he had made the same preparations in order to drive over and meet his wife's cousin at the Flats. It was little more than a year ago, on just such a soft afternoon, with a "feel" of spring in the air. The sorrel, turning the same big ringed eye on him, nuzzled the palm of his hand in the same way; and one by one all the days between rose up and stood before him. . . .

He flung the bearskin into the sleigh, climbed to the seat, and drove up to the house. When he entered the kitchen it was empty, but Mattie's bag and shawl lay ready by the door. He went to the foot of the stairs and listened. No sound reached him from above, but presently he thought he heard someone moving about in his deserted study, and pushing open the door he saw Mattie, in her hat and jacket, standing with her back to him near the table.

She started at his approach and turning quickly, said: "Is it time?"

"What are you doing here, Matt?" he asked her.

She looked at him timidly. "I was just taking a look round—that's all," she answered, with a wavering smile.

They went back into the kitchen without speaking, and Ethan picked up her bag and shawl.

"Where's Zeena?" he asked.

"She went upstairs right after dinner. She said she had those shooting pains again, and didn't want to be disturbed."

"Didn't she say goodbye to you?"

"No. That was all she said."

Ethan, looking slowly about the kitchen, said to himself with a shudder that in a few hours he would be returning to it alone. Then the sense of unreality overcame him once more, and he could not bring himself to believe that Mattie stood there for the last time before him.

"Come on," he said almost gaily, opening the door and putting her bag into the sleigh. He sprang to his seat and bent over to tuck the rug about her as she slipped into the place at his side. "Now then, go 'long," he said, with a shake of the reins that sent the sorrel placidly jogging down the hill.

"We got lots of time for a good ride, Matt!" he cried, seeking her hand beneath the fur and pressing it in his. His face tingled and he felt dizzy, as if he had stopped in at the Starkfield saloon on a zero day for a drink.

At the gate, instead of making for Starkfield, he turned the sorrel to the right, up the Bettsbridge road. Mattie sat silent, giving no sign of surprise; but after a moment she said: "Are you going round by Shadow Pond?"

He laughed and answered: "I knew you'd know!"

She drew closer under the bearskin, so that, looking sideways around his coat-sleeve, he could just catch the tip of her nose and a blown brown wave of hair. They drove slowly up the road between fields glistening under the pale sun, and then bent to the right down a lane edged with spruce and larch. Ahead of them, a long way off, a range of hills stained by mottlings of black forest flowed away in round white curves against the sky. The lane passed into a pine-wood with boles reddening in the afternoon sun and delicate blue shadows on the snow. As they entered it the breeze fell and a warm stillness seemed to drop from the branches with the dropping needles.

Here the snow was so pure that the tiny tracks of wood-animals had left on it intricate lace-like patterns, and the bluish cones caught in its surface stood out like ornaments of bronze.

Ethan drove on in silence till they reached a part of the wood where the pines were more widely spaced; then he drew up and helped Mattie to get out of the sleigh. They passed between the aromatic trunks, the snow breaking crisply under their feet, till they came to a small sheet of water with steep wooded sides. Across its frozen surface, from the farther bank, a single hill rising against the western sun threw the long conical shadow which gave the lake its name. It was a shy secret spot, full of the same dumb melancholy that Ethan felt in his heart.

He looked up and down the little pebbly beach till his eye lit on a fallen tree trunk half submerged in snow.

"There's where we sat at the picnic," he reminded her.

The entertainment of which he spoke was one of the few that they had taken part in together: a "church picnic" which, on a long afternoon of the preceding summer, had filled the retired place with merrymaking. Mattie had begged him to go with her but he had refused. Then, toward sunset, coming down from the mountain where he had been felling timber, he had been caught by some strayed revelers and drawn into the group by the lake, where Mattie, encircled by facetious youths, and bright as a blackberry under her spreading hat, was brewing coffee over a gypsy fire. He remembered the shyness he had felt at approaching her in his uncouth clothes, and then the lighting up of her face, and the way she had broken through the group to come to him with a cup in her hand. They had sat for a few minutes on the fallen log by the pond, and she had missed her gold locket, and set the young men searching for it; and it was Ethan who had spied it in the moss. . . . That was all; but all their intercourse had been made up of just such inarticulate flashes, when they seemed to come suddenly upon happiness as if they had surprised a butterfly in the winter woods. . . .

"It was right there I found your locket," he said, pushing his foot into a dense tuft of blueberry bushes.

"I never saw anybody with such sharp eyes!" she answered.

She sat down on the tree trunk in the sun and he sat down beside her.

"You were as pretty as a picture in that pink hat," he said.

She laughed with pleasure. "Oh, I guess it was the hat!" she rejoined.

They had never before avowed their inclination so openly, and Ethan, for a moment, had the illusion that he was a free man, wooing the girl he meant to marry. He looked at her hair and longed to touch it again, and to tell her that it smelt of the woods; but he had never learned to say such things.

Suddenly she rose to her feet and said: "We mustn't stay here any longer."

He continued to gaze at her vaguely, only half-roused from his dream. "There's plenty of time," he answered.

They stood looking at each other as if the eyes of each were straining to absorb and hold fast the other's image. There were things he had to say to her before they parted, but he could not say them in that place of summer memories, and he turned and followed her in silence to the sleigh. As they drove away the sun sank behind the hill and the pine-boles turned from red to gray.

By a devious track between the fields they wound back to the Starkfield road. Under the open sky the light was still clear, with a reflection of cold red on the eastern hills. The clumps of trees in the snow seemed to draw together in ruffled lumps, like birds with their heads under their wings; and the sky, as it paled, rose higher, leaving the earth more alone.

As they turned into the Starkfield road Ethan said: "Matt, what do you mean to do?"

She did not answer at once, but at length she said: "I'll try to get a place in a store."

"You know you can't do it. The bad air and the standing all day nearly killed you before."

"I'm a lot stronger than I was before I came to Starkfield."

"And now you're going to throw away all the good it's done you!"

There seemed to be no answer to this, and again they drove on for a while without speaking. With every yard of the way some spot where they had stood, and laughed together or been silent, clutched at Ethan and dragged him back.

"Isn't there any of your father's folks could help you?"

"There isn't any of 'em I'd ask."

He lowered his voice to say: "You know there's nothing I wouldn't do for you if I could."

"I know there isn't."

"But I can't—"

She was silent, but he felt a slight tremor in the shoulder against his.

"Oh, Matt," he broke out, "if I could ha' gone with you now I'd ha' done it—"

She turned to him, pulling a scrap of paper from her breast. "Ethan—I found this," she stammered. Even in the failing light he saw it was the letter to his wife that he had begun the night before and forgotten to destroy. Through his astonishment there ran a fierce thrill of joy. "Matt—" he cried, "if I could ha' done it, would you?"

"Oh, Ethan, Ethan—what's the use?" With a sudden movement she tore the letter in shreds and sent them fluttering off into the snow.

"Tell me, Matt! Tell me!" he adjured her.

She was silent for a moment; then she said, in such a low tone that he had to stoop his head to hear her: "I used to think of it sometimes, summer nights, when the moon was so bright I couldn't sleep."

His heart reeled with the sweetness of it. "As long ago as that?"

She answered, as if the date had long been fixed for her: "The first time was at Shadow Pond."

"Was that why you gave me my coffee before the others?"

"I don't know. Did I? I was dreadfully put out when you wouldn't go to the picnic with me; and then, when I saw you coming down the road, I thought maybe you'd gone home that way o' purpose; and that made me glad."

They were silent again. They had reached the point where the road dipped to the hollow by Ethan's mill and as they descended the darkness descended with them, dropping down like a black veil from the heavy hemlock boughs.

"I'm tied hand and foot, Matt. There isn't a thing I can do," he began again.

"You must write to me sometimes, Ethan."

"Oh, what good'll writing do? I want to put my hand out and touch you. I want to do for you and care for you. I want to be there when you're sick and when you're lonesome."

"You mustn't think but what I'll do all right."

"You won't need me, you mean? I suppose you'll marry!"

"Oh, Ethan!" she cried.

"I don't know how it is you make me feel, Matt. I'd a'most rather have you dead than that!"

"Oh, I wish I was, I wish I was!" she sobbed.

The sound of her weeping shook him out of his dark anger, and he felt ashamed.

"Don't let's talk that way," he whispered.

"Why shouldn't we, when it's true? I've been wishing it every minute of the day."

"Matt! You be quiet! Don't you say it."

"There's never anybody been good to me but you."

"Don't say that either, when I can't lift a hand for you!"

"Yes; but it's true just the same."

They had reached the top of Schoolhouse Hill and Starkfield lay below them in the twilight. A cutter, mounting the road from the village, passed them by in a joyous flutter of bells, and they straightened themselves and looked ahead with rigid faces. Along the main street lights had begun to shine from the housefronts and stray figures were turning in here and there at the gates. Ethan, with a touch of his whip, roused the sorrel to a languid trot.

As they drew near the end of the village the cries of children reached them, and they saw a knot of boys, with sleds behind them, scattering across the open space before the church.

"I guess this'll be their last coast for a day or two," Ethan said, looking up at the mild sky.

Mattie was silent, and he added: "We were to have gone down last night."

Still she did not speak and, prompted by an obscure desire to help himself and her through their miserable last hour, he went on discursively: "Ain't it funny we haven't been down together but just that once last winter?"

She answered: "It wasn't often I got down to the village."

"That's so," he said.

They had reached the crest of the Corbury road, and between the indistinct white glimmer of the church and the black curtain of the Varnum spruces the slope stretched away below them without a sled on its length. Some erratic impulse prompted Ethan to say: "How'd you like me to take you down now?"

She forced a laugh. "Why, there isn't time!"

"There's all the time we want. Come along!" His one desire now was to postpone the moment of turning the sorrel toward the Flats.

"But the girl," she faltered. "The girl'll be waiting at the station."

"Well, let her wait. You'd have to if she didn't. Come!"

The note of authority in his voice seemed to subdue her, and when he had jumped from the sleigh she let him help her out, saying only, with a vague feint of reluctance: "But there isn't a sled round anywheres."

"Yes, there is! Right over there under the spruces."

He threw the bearskin over the sorrel, who stood passively by the roadside, hanging a meditative head. Then he caught Mattie's hand and drew her after him toward the sled.

She seated herself obediently and he took his place behind her, so close that her hair brushed his face. "All right, Matt?" he called out, as if the width of the road had been between them.

She turned her head to say: "It's dreadfully dark. Are you sure you can see?"

He laughed contemptuously: "I could go down this coast with my eyes tied!" and she laughed with him, as if she liked his audacity. Nevertheless he sat still a moment, straining his eyes down the long hill, for it was the most confusing hour of the evening, the hour when the last clearness from the upper sky is merged with the rising night in a blur that disguises landmarks and falsifies distances.

"Now!" he cried.

The sled started with a bound, and they flew on through the dusk, gathering smoothness and speed as they went, with the hollow night opening out below them and the air singing by like an organ. Mattie sat perfectly still, but as they reached the bend at the foot of the hill, where the big elm thrust out a deadly elbow, he fancied that she shrank a little closer.

"Don't be scared, Matt!" he cried exultantly, as they spun safely past it and flew down the second slope; and when they reached the level ground beyond, and the speed of the sled began to slacken, he heard her give a little laugh of glee.

They sprang off and started to walk back up the hill. Ethan dragged the sled with one hand and passed the other through Mattie's arm.

"Were you scared I'd run you into the elm?" he asked with a boyish laugh.

"I told you I was never scared with you," she answered.

The strange exaltation of his mood had brought on one of his rare fits of boastfulness. "It *is* a tricky place, though. The least swerve, and we'd never ha' come up again. But I can measure distances to a hair's-breadth—always could."

She murmured: "I always say you've got the surest eye. . . ."

Deep silence had fallen with the starless dusk, and they leaned on each other without speaking; but at every step of their climb Ethan said to himself: "It's the last time we'll ever walk together."

They mounted slowly to the top of the hill. When they were abreast of the church he stooped his head to her to ask: "Are you tired?" and she answered, breathing quickly: "It was splendid!"

With a pressure of his arm he guided her toward the Norway spruces. "I guess this sled must be Ned Hale's. Anyhow I'll leave it where I found it." He drew the sled up to the Varnum gate and rested it against the fence. As he raised himself he suddenly felt Mattie close to him among the shadows.

"Is this where Ned and Ruth kissed each other?" she whispered breathlessly, and flung her arms about him. Her lips, groping for his, swept over his face, and he held her fast in a rapture of surprise.

"Goodbye—goodbye," she stammered, and kissed him again.

"Oh, Matt I can't let you go!" broke from him in the same old cry.

She freed herself from his hold and he heard her sobbing. "Oh, I can't go either!" she wailed.

"Matt! What'll we do? What'll we do?"

They clung to each other's hands like children, and her body shook with desperate sobs.

Through the stillness they heard the church clock striking five.

"Oh, Ethan, it's time!" she cried.

He drew her back to him. "Time for what? You don't suppose I'm going to leave you now?"

"If I missed my train where'd I go?"

"Where are you going if you catch it?"

She stood silent, her hands lying cold and relaxed in his.

"What's the good of either of us going anywheres without the other one now?" he said.

She remained motionless, as if she had not heard him. Then she snatched her hands from his, threw her arms about his neck, and pressed a sudden drenched cheek against his face. "Ethan! Ethan! I want you to take me down again!"

"Down where?"

"The coast. Right off," she panted. "So 't we'll never come up any more."

"Matt! What on earth do you mean?"

She put her lips close against his ear to say: "Right into the big elm. You said you could. So 't we'd never have to leave each other any more."

"Why, what are you talking of? You're crazy!"

"I'm not crazy; but I will be if I leave you."

"Oh, Matt, Matt—" he groaned.

She tightened her fierce hold about his neck. Her face lay close to his face.

"Ethan, where'll I go if I leave you? I don't know how to get along alone. You said so yourself just now. Nobody but you was ever good to me. And there'll be that strange girl in the house . . . and she'll sleep in my bed, where I used to lay nights and listen to hear you come up the stairs. . . ."

The words were like fragments torn from his heart. With them came the hated vision of the house he was going back to—of the stairs he would have to go up every night, of the woman who would wait for him there. And the sweetness of Mattie's avowal, the wild wonder of knowing at last that all that had happened to him had happened to her, too, made the other vision more abhorrent, the other life more intolerable to return to. . . .

Her pleadings still came to him between short sobs, but he no longer heard what she was saying. Her hat had slipped back and he was stroking her hair. He wanted to get the feeling of it into his hand, so that it would sleep there like a seed in winter. Once he found her mouth again, and they seemed to be by the pond together in the burning August sun. But his cheek touched hers, and it was cold and full of weeping, and he saw the road to the Flats under the night and heard the whistle of the train up the line.

The spruces swathed them in blackness and silence. They might have been in their coffins underground. He said to himself: "Perhaps it'll feel like this . . ." and then again: "After this I sha'n't feel anything. . . ."

Suddenly he heard the old sorrel whinny across the road, and thought: "He's wondering why he doesn't get his supper. . . ."

"Come," Mattie whispered, tugging at his hand.

Her somber violence constrained him: she seemed the embodied instrument of fate. He pulled the sled out, blinking like a night-bird as he passed from the shade of the spruces into the transparent dusk of the open. The slope below them was deserted. All Starkfield was at supper, and not a figure crossed the open space before the church. The sky, swollen with the clouds that announce a thaw, hung as low as before a summer storm. He strained his eyes through the dimness, and they seemed less keen, less capable than usual.

He took his seat on the sled and Mattie instantly placed herself in front of him. Her hat had fallen into the snow and his lips were in her hair. He stretched out his legs, drove his heels into the road to keep the sled from slipping forward, and bent her head back between his hands. Then suddenly he sprang up again.

"Get up," he ordered her.

It was the tone she always heeded, but she cowered down in her seat, repeating vehemently: "No, no, no!"

"Get up!"

"Why?"

"I want to sit in front."

"No, no! How can you steer in front?"

"I don't have to. We'll follow the track."

They spoke in smothered whispers, as though the night were listening.

"Get up! Get up!" he urged her; but she kept on repeating: "Why do you want to sit in front?"

"Because I—because I want to feel you holding me," he stammered, and dragged her to her feet.

The answer seemed to satisfy her, or else she yielded to the power of his voice. He bent down, feeling in the obscurity for the glassy slide worn by preceding coasters, and placed the runners carefully between its edges. She waited while he seated himself with crossed legs in the front of the sled; then she crouched quickly down at his back and clasped her arms about him. Her breath in his neck set him shuddering again, and he almost sprang from his seat. But in a flash he remembered the alternative. She was right: this was better than parting. He leaned back and drew her mouth to his. . . .

Just as they started he heard the sorrel's whinny again, and the familiar wistful call, and all the confused images it brought with it, went with him down the first reach of the road. Halfway down there was a sudden drop, then a rise, and after that another long delirious descent. As they took wing for this it seemed to him that they were flying indeed, flying far up into the cloudy night, with Starkfield immeasurably below them, falling away like a speck in space. . . . Then the big elm shot up ahead, lying in wait for them at the bend of the road, and he said between his teeth: "We can fetch it; I know we can fetch it—"

As they flew toward the tree Mattie pressed her arms tighter, and her blood seemed to be in his veins. Once or twice the sled swerved a little under them. He slanted his body to keep it headed for the elm, repeating to himself again and again: "I know we can fetch it"; and little phrases she had spoken ran through his head and danced before him on the air. The big tree loomed bigger and closer, and as they bore down on it he thought: "It's waiting for us: it seems to know." But suddenly his wife's face, with twisted monstrous lineaments, thrust itself between him and his goal, and he made an instinctive movement to brush it aside. The sled swerved in response, but he righted it again, kept it straight, and drove down on the black projecting mass. There was a last instant when the air shot past him like millions of fiery wires; and then the elm. . . .

The sky was still thick, but looking straight up he saw a single star, and tried vaguely to reckon whether it were Sirius, or—or— The effort tired him too much, and he closed his heavy lids and thought that he would sleep. . . . The stillness was so profound that he heard a little animal twittering some-where nearby under the snow. It made a small frightened cheep like a field mouse, and he wondered languidly if it were hurt. Then he understood that it must be in pain: pain so excruciating that he seemed, mysteriously, to feel it shooting through his own body. He tried in vain to roll over in the direction of the sound, and stretched his left arm out across the snow. And now it was as though he felt rather than heard the twittering; it seemed to be under his palm, which rested on something soft and springy. The thought of the animal's suffering was intolerable to him and he struggled to raise himself, and could not because a rock, or some huge mass, seemed to be lying on him. But he continued to finger about cautiously with his left hand, thinking he might get hold of the little creature and help it; and all at once he knew that the soft thing he had touched was Mattie's hair and that his hand was on her face.

He dragged himself to his knees, the monstrous load on him moving with him as he moved, and his hand went over and over her face, and he felt that the twittering came from her lips . . .

He got his face down close to hers, with his ear to her mouth, and in the darkness he saw her eyes open and heard her say his name.

"Oh, Matt, I thought we'd fetched it," he moaned; and far off, up the hill, he heard the sorrel whinny, and thought: "I ought to be getting him his feed. . . ."

. . . .
. . . .
. . . .

THE querulous drone ceased as I entered Frome's kitchen, and of the two women sitting there I could not tell which had been the speaker.

One of them, on my appearing, raised her tall bony figure from her seat, not as if to welcome me—for she threw me no more than a brief glance of surprise—but simply to set about preparing the meal which Frome's absence had delayed. A slatternly calico wrapper hung from her shoulders and the wisps of her thin gray hair were drawn away from a high forehead and fastened at the back by a broken comb. She had pale opaque eyes which revealed nothing and reflected nothing, and her narrow lips were of the same sallow color as her face.

The other woman was much smaller and slighter. She sat huddled in an armchair near the stove, and when I came in she turned her head quickly toward me, without the least corresponding movement of her body. Her hair was as gray as her companion's, her face as bloodless and shriveled, but amber-tinted, with swarthy shadows sharpening the nose and hollowing the temples. Under her shapeless dress her body kept its limp immobility, and her dark eyes had the bright witchlike stare that disease of the spine sometimes gives.

Even for that part of the country the kitchen was a poor-looking place. With the exception of the dark-eyed woman's chair, which looked like a soiled relic of luxury bought at a country auction, the furniture was of the roughest kind. Three coarse china plates and a broken-nosed milk-jug had been set on a greasy table scored with knife-cuts, and a couple of straw-bottomed chairs and a kitchen dresser of unpainted pine stood meagerly against the plaster walls.

"My, it's cold here! The fire must be 'most out," Frome said, glancing about him apologetically as he followed me in.

The tall woman, who had moved away from us toward the dresser, took no notice; but the other, from her cushioned niche, answered complainingly, in a high thin voice: "It's on'y just been made up this very minute. Zeena fell asleep and slep' ever so long, and I thought I'd be frozen stiff before I could wake her up and get her to 'tend to it."

I knew then that it was she who had been speaking when we entered.

Her companion, who was just coming back to the table with the remains of a cold mince pie in a battered pie dish, set down her unappetizing burden without appearing to hear the accusation brought against her.

Frome stood hesitatingly before her as she advanced; then he looked at me and said: "This is my wife, Mis' Frome." After another interval he added, turning toward the figure in the armchair: "And this is Miss Mattie Silver. . . ."

. . . .

Mrs. Hale, tender soul, had pictured me as lost in the Flats and buried under a snowdrift; and so lively was her satisfaction on seeing me safely restored to her the next morning that I felt my peril had caused me to advance several degrees in her favor.

Great was her amazement, and that of old Mrs. Varnum, on learning that Ethan Frome's old horse had carried me to and from Corbury Junction through the worst blizzard of the winter; greater still their surprise when they heard that his master had taken me in for the night.

Beneath their wondering exclamations I felt a secret curiosity to know what impressions I had received from my night in the Frome household, and divined that the best way of breaking down their reserve was to let them try to penetrate mine. I therefore confined myself to saying, in a matter-of-fact tone, that I had been received with great kindness, and that Frome had made a bed for me in a room on the ground-floor which seemed in happier days to have been fitted up as a kind of writing-room or study.

"Well," Mrs. Hale mused, "in such a storm I suppose he felt he couldn't do less than take you in—but I guess it went hard with Ethan. I don't believe but what you're the only stranger has set foot in that house for over twenty years. He's that proud he don't even like his oldest friends to go there; and I don't know as any do, any more, except myself and the doctor. . . ."

"You still go there, Mrs. Hale?" I ventured.

"I used to go a good deal after the accident, when I was first married; but after awhile I got to think it made 'em feel worse to see us. And then one thing and another came, and my own troubles. . . . But I generally make out to drive over there round about New Year's, and once in the summer. Only I always try to pick a day when Ethan's off somewheres. It's bad enough to see the two women sitting there—but *his* face, when he looks round that bare place, just kills me. . . . You see, I can look back and call it up in his mother's day, before their troubles."

Old Mrs. Varnum, by this time, had gone up to bed, and her daughter and I were sitting alone, after supper, in the austere seclusion of the horse-hair parlor. Mrs. Hale glanced at me tentatively, as though trying to see how much footing my conjectures gave her; and I guessed that if she had kept silence till now it was because she had been waiting, through all the years, for some one who should see what she alone had seen.

I waited to let her trust in me gather strength before I said: "Yes, it's pretty bad, seeing all three of them there together."

She drew her mild brows into a frown of pain. "It was just awful from the beginning. I was here in the house when they were carried up—they laid Mattie Silver in the room you're in. She and I were great friends, and she was to have been my bridesmaid in the spring. . . . When she came to I went up to her and stayed all night. They gave her things to quiet her, and she didn't know much till to'rd morning, and then all of a sudden she woke up just like herself, and looked straight at me out of her big eyes, and said . . . Oh, I don't know why I'm telling you all this," Mrs. Hale broke off, crying.

She took off her spectacles, wiped the moisture from them, and put them on again with an unsteady hand. "It got about the next day," she went on, "that Zeena Frome had sent Mattie off in a hurry because she had a hired girl coming, and the folks here could never rightly tell what she and Ethan were doing that night coasting, when they'd ought to have been on their way to the Flats to ketch the train. . . . I never knew myself what Zeena thought—I don't to this day. Nobody knows Zeena's thoughts. Anyhow, when she heard o' the accident she came right in and stayed with Ethan over to the minister's, where they'd carried him. And as soon as the doctors said that Mattie could be moved, Zeena sent for her and took her back to the farm."

"And there she's been ever since?"

Mrs. Hale answered simply: "There was nowhere else for her to go;" and my heart tightened at the thought of the hard compulsions of the poor.

"Yes, there she's been," Mrs. Hale continued, "and Zeena's done for her, and done for Ethan, as good as she could. It was a miracle, considering how sick she was—but she seemed to be raised right up just when the call came to her. Not as she's ever given up doctoring, and she's had sick spells right along; but she's had the strength given her to care for those two for over twenty years, and before the accident came she thought she couldn't even care for herself."

Mrs. Hale paused a moment, and I remained silent, plunged in the vision of what her words evoked. "It's horrible for them all," I murmured.

"Yes, it's pretty bad. And they ain't any of 'em easy people either. Mattie *was*, before the accident; I never knew a sweeter nature. But she's suffered too much—that's what I always say when folks tell me how she's soured. And Zeena, she was always cranky. Not but what she bears with Mattie wonderful—I've seen that myself. But sometimes the two of them get going at each other, and then Ethan's face'd break your heart. . . . When I see that, I think it's him that suffers most . . . anyhow it ain't Zeena, because she ain't got the time. . . . It's a pity, though," Mrs. Hale ended, sighing, "that they're all shut up there'n that one kitchen. In the summertime, on pleasant days, they move Mattie into the parlor, or out in the dooryard, and that makes it easier . . . but winters there's the fires to be thought of; and there ain't a dime to spare up at the Fromes'."

Mrs. Hale drew a deep breath, as though her memory were eased of its long burden, and she had no more to say; but suddenly an impulse of complete avowal seized her.

She took off her spectacles again, leaned toward me across the bead-work table-cover, and went on with lowered voice: "There was one day, about a week after the accident, when they all thought Mattie couldn't live. Well, I say it's a pity she *did*. I said it right out to our minister once, and he was shocked at me. Only he wasn't with me that morning when she first came to. . . . And I say, if she'd ha' died, Ethan might ha' lived; and the way they are now, I don't see's there's much difference between the Fromes up at the farm and the Fromes down in the graveyard; 'cept that down there they're all quiet, and the women have got to hold their tongues."

THE CUSTOM OF THE COUNTRY

Book One

1

"U NDINE Spragg—how *can* you?" her mother wailed, raising a prematurely wrinkled hand heavy with rings to defend the note which a languid "bellboy" had just brought in.

But her defense was as feeble as her protest, and she continued to smile on her visitor while Miss Spragg, with a turn of her quick young fingers, possessed herself of the missive and withdrew to the window to read it.

"I guess it's meant for me," she merely threw over her shoulder at her mother.

"Did you *ever*, Mrs. Heeny?" Mrs. Spragg murmured with deprecating pride.

Mrs. Heeny, a stout professional-looking person in a waterproof, her rusty veil thrown back, and a shabby alligator bag at her feet, followed the mother's glance with good-humored approval.

"I never met with a lovelier form," she agreed, answering the spirit rather than the letter of her hostess's inquiry.

Mrs. Spragg and her visitor were enthroned in two heavy gilt armchairs in one of the private drawing-rooms of the Hotel Stentorian. The Spragg rooms were known as one of the Looey suites, and the drawing-room walls, above their wainscoting of highly varnished mahogany, were hung with salmon-pink damask and adorned with oval portraits of Marie Antoinette and the princess de Lamballe. In the center of the florid carpet a gilt table with a top of Mexican onyx sustained a palm in a gilt basket tied with a pink bow. But for this ornament, and a copy of *The Hound of the Baskervilles* which lay beside it, the room showed no traces of human use, and Mrs. Spragg herself wore as complete an air of detachment as if she had been a wax figure in a show-window. Her attire was fashionable enough to justify such a post, and her pale soft-cheeked face, with puffy eyelids and drooping mouth, suggested a partially melted wax figure which had run to double-chin.

Mrs. Heeny, in comparison, had a reassuring look of solidity and reality. The planting of her firm black bulk in its chair, and the grasp of her broad red hands on the gilt arms, bespoke an organized and self-reliant activity, accounted for by the fact that Mrs. Heeny was a "society" manicure and masseuse. Toward Mrs. Spragg and her daughter she filled the double role of

335

manipulator and friend; and it was in the latter capacity that, her day's task ended, she had dropped in for a moment to "cheer up" the lonely ladies of the Stentorian.

The young girl whose "form" had won Mrs. Heeny's professional commendation suddenly shifted its lovely lines as she turned back from the window.

"Here—you can have it after all," she said, crumpling the note and tossing it with a contemptuous gesture into her mother's lap.

"Why—isn't it from Mr. Popple?" Mrs. Spragg exclaimed unguardedly.

"No—it isn't. What made you think I thought it was?" snapped her daughter; but the next instant she added, with an outbreak of childish disappointment: "It's only from Mr. Marvell's sister—at least she says she's his sister."

Mrs. Spragg, with a puzzled frown, groped for her eyeglass among the jet fringes of her tightly girded front.

Mrs. Heeny's small blue eyes shot out sparks of curiosity. "Marvell—what Marvell is that?"

The girl explained languidly: "A little fellow—I think Mr. Popple said his name was Ralph"; while her mother continued: "Undine met them both last night at that party downstairs. And from something Mr. Popple said to her about going to one of the new plays, she thought—"

"How on earth do you know what I thought?" Undine flashed back, her gray eyes darting warnings at her mother under their straight black brows.

"Why, you *said* you thought—" Mrs. Spragg began reproachfully; but Mrs. Heeny, heedless of their bickerings, was pursuing her own train of thought.

"What Popple? Claud Walsingham Popple—the portrait painter?"

"Yes—I suppose so. He said he'd like to paint me. Mabel Lipscomb introduced him. I don't care if I never see him again," the girl said, bathed in angry pink.

"Do you know him, Mrs. Heeny?" Mrs. Spragg inquired.

"I should say I did. I manicured him for his first society portrait—a full-length of Mrs. Harmon B. Driscoll." Mrs. Heeny smiled indulgently on her hearers. "I know everybody. If they don't know *me* they ain't in it, and Claud Walsingham Popple's in it. But he ain't nearly *as* in it," she continued judicially, "as Ralph Marvell—the little fellow, as you call him."

Undine Spragg, at the word, swept round on the speaker with one of the quick turns that revealed her youthful flexibility. She was always doubling and twisting on herself, and every movement she made seemed to start at the nape of her neck, just below the lifted roll of reddish-gold hair, and flow without a break through her whole slim length to the tips of her fingers and the points of her slender restless feet.

"Why, do you know the Marvells? Are *they* stylish?" she asked.

Mrs. Heeny gave the discouraged gesture of a pedagogue who has vainly striven to implant the rudiments of knowledge in a rebellious mind.

"Why, Undine Spragg, I've told you all about them time and again! His mother was a Dagonet. They live with old Urban Dagonet down in Washington Square."

To Mrs. Spragg this conveyed even less than to her daughter. " 'way down there? Why do they live with somebody else? Haven't they got the means to have a home of their own?"

Undine's perceptions were more rapid, and she fixed her eyes searchingly on Mrs. Heeny.

"Do you mean to say Mr. Marvell's as swell as Mr. Popple?"

"As swell? Why, Claud Walsingham Popple ain't in the same class with him!"

The girl was upon her mother with a spring, snatching and smoothing out the crumpled note.

"Laura Fairford—is that the sister's name?"

"Mrs. Henley Fairford; yes. What does she write about?"

Undine's face lit up as if a shaft of sunset had struck it through the triple-curtained windows of the Stentorian.

"She says she wants me to dine with her next Wednesday. Isn't it queer? Why does she want me? She's never seen me!" Her tone implied that she had long been accustomed to being "wanted" by those who had.

Mrs. Heeny laughed. "He saw you, didn't he?"

"Who? Ralph Marvell? Why, of course he did—Mr. Popple brought him to the party here last night."

"Well, there you are. . . . When a young man in society wants to meet a girl again, he gets his sister to ask her."

Undine stared at her incredulously. "How queer! But they haven't all got sisters, have they? It must be fearfully poky for the ones that haven't."

"They get their mothers—or their married friends," said Mrs. Heeny omnisciently.

"Married gentlemen?" inquired Mrs. Spragg, slightly shocked, but genuinely desirous of mastering her lesson.

"Mercy, no! Married ladies."

"But are there never any gentlemen present?" pursued Mrs. Spragg, feeling that if this were the case Undine would certainly be disappointed.

"Present where? At their dinners? Of course—Mrs. Fairford gives the smartest little dinners in town. There was an account of one she gave last week in this morning's Town Talk: I guess it's right here among my clippings." Mrs. Heeny, swooping down on her bag, drew from it a handful of newspaper cuttings, which she spread on her ample lap and proceeded to sort with a moistened forefinger. "Here," she said, holding one of the slips at arm's length; and throwing back her head she read, in a slow unpunctuated chant: " 'Mrs. Henley Fairford gave another of her natty little dinners last

Wednesday as usual it was smart small and exclusive and there was much gnashing of teeth among the left-outs as Madame Olga Loukowska gave some of her new steppe dances after dinner'—that's the French for new dance steps," Mrs. Heeny concluded, thrusting the documents back into her bag.

"Do you know Mrs. Fairford, too?" Undine asked eagerly; while Mrs. Spragg, impressed, but anxious for facts, pursued: "Does she reside on Fifth Avenue?"

"No, she has a little house in Thirty-eighth Street, down beyond Park Avenue."

The ladies' faces drooped again, and the masseuse went on promptly: "But they're glad enough to have her in the big houses!—Why, yes, I know her," she said, addressing herself to Undine. "I mass'd her for a sprained ankle a couple of years ago. She's got a lovely manner, but *no* conversation. Some of my patients converse exquisitely," Mrs. Heeny added with discrimination.

Undine was brooding over the note. "It *is* written to mother—Mrs. Abner E. Spragg—I never saw anything so funny! 'Will you *allow* your daughter to dine with me?' Allow! Is Mrs. Fairford peculiar?"

"No—you are," said Mrs. Heeny bluntly. "Don't you know it's the thing in the best society to pretend that girls can't do anything without their mothers' permission? You just remember that, Undine. You mustn't accept invitations from gentlemen without you say you've got to ask your mother first."

"Mercy! But how'll Mother know what to say?"

"Why, she'll say what you tell her to, of course. You'd better tell her you want to dine with Mrs. Fairford," Mrs. Heeny added humorously, as she gathered her waterproof together and stooped for her bag.

"Have I got to write the note, then?" Mrs. Spragg asked with rising agitation.

Mrs. Heeny reflected. "Why, no. I guess Undine can write it as if it was from you. Mrs. Fairford don't know your writing."

This was an evident relief to Mrs. Spragg, and as Undine swept to her room with the note her mother sank back, murmuring plaintively: "Oh, don't go yet, Mrs. Heeny. I haven't seen a human being all day, and I can't seem to find anything to say to that French maid."

Mrs. Heeny looked at her hostess with friendly compassion. She was well aware that she was the only bright spot on Mrs. Spragg's horizon. Since the Spraggs, some two years previously, had moved from Apex City to New York, they had made little progress in establishing relations with their new environment; and when, about four months earlier, Mrs. Spragg's doctor had called in Mrs. Heeny to minister professionally to his patient, he had done more for her spirit than for her body. Mrs. Heeny had had such "cases" before: she knew the rich helpless family, stranded in lonely splendor in a sumptuous West Side hotel, with a father compelled to seek a semblance of social life at the hotel bar, and a mother deprived of even this contact with her kind, and reduced to illness by boredom and inactivity. Poor Mrs. Spragg had done her own washing in her youth, but since her rising fortunes had made this occupation unsuitable she had sunk into the relative inertia which the ladies of Apex City regarded as one of the prerogatives of affluence. At Apex, however, she had belonged to a social club, and, until they moved to the Mealey House, had been kept busy by the incessant struggle with domestic cares; whereas New York seemed to offer no field for any form of ladylike activity. She therefore took her exercise vicariously, with Mrs. Heeny's help; and Mrs. Heeny knew how to manipulate her imagination as well as her muscles. It was Mrs. Heeny who peopled the solitude of the long ghostly days with lively anecdotes of the Van Degens, the Driscolls, the Chauncey Ellings and the other social potentates whose least doings Mrs. Spragg and Undine had followed from afar in the Apex papers, and who had come to seem so much more remote since only the width of the Central Park divided mother and daughter from their Olympian portals.

Mrs. Spragg had no ambition for herself—she seemed to have transferred her whole personality to her child—but she was passionately resolved that Undine should have what she wanted, and she sometimes fancied that Mrs. Heeny, who crossed those sacred thresholds so familiarly, might some day gain admission for Undine.

"Well—I'll stay a little mite longer if you want; and supposing I was to rub up your nails while we're talking? It'll be more sociable," the masseuse suggested, lifting her bag to the table and covering its shiny onyx surface with bottles and polishers.

Mrs. Spragg consentingly slipped the rings from her small mottled hands. It was soothing to feel herself in Mrs. Heeny's grasp, and though she knew the attention would cost her three dollars she was secure in the sense that Abner wouldn't mind. It had been clear to Mrs. Spragg, ever since their rather precipitate departure from Apex City, that Abner was resolved not to mind—resolved at any cost to "see through" the New York adventure. It seemed likely now that the cost would be considerable. They had lived in New York for two years without any social benefit to their daughter; and it was, of course, for that purpose that they had come. If, at the time, there had been other and more pressing reasons, they were such as Mrs. Spragg and her husband never touched on, even in the gilded privacy of their bedroom at the Stentorian; and so completely had silence closed in on the subject that to Mrs. Spragg it had become nonexistent: she really believed that, as Abner put it, they had left Apex because Undine was too big for the place.

She seemed as yet—poor child!—too small for New York: actually imperceptible to its heedless multitudes; and her mother trembled for the day when her invisibility should be borne in on her. Mrs. Spragg did not mind

the long delay for herself—she had stores of lymphatic patience. But she
had noticed lately that Undine was beginning to be nervous, and there was
nothing that Undine's parents dreaded so much as her being nervous. Mrs.
Spragg's maternal apprehensions unconsciously escaped in her next words.

"I do hope she'll quiet down now," she murmured, feeling quieter herself
as her hand sank into Mrs. Heeny's roomy palm.

"Who's that? Undine?"

"Yes. She seemed so set on that Mr. Popple's coming round. From the
way he acted last night she thought he'd be sure to come round this morning. She's so lonesome, poor child—I can't say as I blame her."

"Oh, he'll come round. Things don't happen as quick as that in New
York," said Mrs. Heeny, driving her nail-polisher cheeringly.

Mrs. Spragg sighed again. "They don't appear to. They say New Yorkers
are always in a hurry; but I can't say as they've hurried much to make our
acquaintance."

Mrs. Heeny drew back to study the effect of her work. "You wait, Mrs.
Spragg, you wait. If you go too fast you sometimes have to rip out the whole
seam."

"Oh, that's so—that's *so!*" Mrs. Spragg exclaimed, with a tragic emphasis that made the masseuse glance up at her.

"Of course it's so. And it's more so in New York than anywhere. The
wrong set's like flypaper: once you're in it you can pull and pull, but you'll
never get out of it again."

Undine's mother heaved another and more helpless sigh. "I wish *you'd*
tell Undine that, Mrs. Heeny."

"Oh, I guess Undine's all right. A girl like her can afford to wait. And if
young Marvell's really taken with her she'll have the run of the place in no
time."

This solacing thought enabled Mrs. Spragg to yield herself unreservedly
to Mrs. Heeny's ministrations, which were prolonged for a happy confidential hour; and she had just bidden the masseuse goodbye, and was restoring
the rings to her fingers, when the door opened to admit her husband.

Mr. Spragg came in silently, setting his high hat down on the center-
table, and laying his overcoat across one of the gilt chairs. He was tallish,
gray-bearded, and somewhat stooping, with the slack figure of the sedentary
man who would be stout if he were not dyspeptic; and his cautious gray eyes
with pouchlike underlids had straight black brows like his daughter's. His
thin hair was worn a little too long over his coat collar, and a Masonic
emblem dangled from the heavy gold chain which crossed his crumpled
black waistcoat.

He stood still in the middle of the room, casting a slow pioneering
glance about its gilded void; then he said gently: "Well, Mother?"

Mrs. Spragg remained seated, but her eyes dwelt on him affectionately.
"Undine's been asked out to a dinner-party; and Mrs. Heeny says it's to

one of the first families. It's the sister of one of the gentlemen that Mabel Lipscomb introduced her to last night."

There was a mild triumph in her tone, for it was owing to her insistence and Undine's that Mr. Spragg had been induced to give up the house they had bought in West End Avenue, and move with his family to the Stentorian. Undine had early decided that they could not hope to get on while they "kept house"—all the fashionable people she knew either boarded or lived in hotels. Mrs. Spragg was easily induced to take the same view, but Mr. Spragg had resisted, being at the moment unable either to sell his house or to let it as advantageously as he had hoped. After the move was made it seemed for a time as though he had been right, and the first social steps would be as difficult to make in a hotel as in one's own house; and Mrs. Spragg was therefore eager to have him know that Undine really owed her first invitation to a meeting under the roof of the Stentorian.

"You see we were right to come here, Abner," she added, and he absently rejoined: "I guess you two always manage to be right."

But his face remained unsmiling, and instead of seating himself and lighting his cigar, as he usually did before dinner, he took two or three aimless turns about the room, and then paused in front of his wife.

"What's the matter—anything wrong downtown?" she asked, her eyes reflecting his anxiety.

Mrs. Spragg's knowledge of what went on "downtown" was of the most elementary kind, but her husband's face was the barometer in which she had long been accustomed to read the leave to go on unrestrictedly, or the warning to pause and abstain till the coming storm should be weathered.

He shook his head. "N—no. Nothing worse than what I can see to, if you and Undine will go steady for a while." He paused and looked across the room at his daughter's door. "Where is she—out?"

"I guess she's in her room, going over her dresses with that French maid. I don't know as she's got anything fit to wear to that dinner," Mrs. Spragg added in a tentative murmur.

Mr. Spragg smiled at last. "Well—I guess she *will* have," he said prophetically.

He glanced again at his daughter's door, as if to make sure of its being shut; then, standing close before his wife, he lowered his voice to say: "I saw Elmer Moffatt downtown today."

"Oh, Abner!" A wave of almost physical apprehension passed over Mrs. Spragg. Her jeweled hands trembled in her black brocade lap, and the pulpy curves of her face collapsed as if it were a pricked balloon.

"Oh, Abner," she moaned again, her eyes also on her daughter's door.

Mr. Spragg's black eyebrows gathered in an angry frown, but it was evident that his anger was not against his wife.

"What's the good of Oh Abner-ing? Elmer Moffatt's nothing to us—no more'n if we never laid eyes on him."

"No—I know it; but what's he doing here? Did you speak to him?" she faltered.

He slipped his thumbs into his waistcoat pockets. "No—I guess Elmer and I are pretty well talked out."

Mrs. Spragg took up her moan. "Don't you tell her you saw him, Abner."

"I'll do as you say; but she may meet him herself."

"Oh, I guess not—not in this new set she's going with! Don't tell her *anyhow*."

He turned away, feeling for one of the cigars which he always carried loose in his pocket; and his wife, rising, stole after him, and laid her hand on his arm.

"He can't do anything to her, can he?"

"Do anything to her?" He swung about furiously. "I'd like to see him touch her—that's all!"

2

UNDINE'S white and gold bedroom, with sea-green panels and old rose carpet, looked along Seventy-second Street toward the leafless tree-tops of the Central Park.

She went to the window, and drawing back its many layers of lace gazed eastward down the long brownstone perspective. Beyond the Park lay Fifth Avenue—and Fifth Avenue was where she wanted to be!

She turned back into the room, and going to her writing-table laid Mrs. Fairford's note before her, and began to study it minutely. She had read in the "Boudoir Chat" of one of the Sunday papers that the smartest women were using the new pigeon-blood notepaper with white ink; and rather against her mother's advice she had ordered a large supply, with her monogram in silver. It was a disappointment, therefore, to find that Mrs. Fairford wrote on the old-fashioned white sheet, without even a monogram—simply her address and telephone number. It gave Undine rather a poor opinion of Mrs. Fairford's social standing, and for a moment she thought with considerable satisfaction of answering the note on her pigeon-blood paper. Then she remembered Mrs. Heeny's emphatic commendation of Mrs. Fairford, and her pen wavered. What if white paper were really newer than pigeon-blood? It might be more stylish, anyhow. Well, she didn't care if Mrs. Fairford didn't like red paper—*she* did! And she wasn't going to truckle to any woman who lived in a small house down beyond Park Avenue. . . .

Undine was fiercely independent and yet passionately imitative. She wanted to surprise everyone by her dash and originality, but she could not help modeling herself on the last person she met, and the confusion of ideals thus produced caused her much perturbation when she had to choose between two courses. She hesitated a moment longer, and then took from the drawer a plain sheet with the hotel address.

It was amusing to write the note in her mother's name—she giggled as she formed the phrase "I shall be happy to permit my daughter to take dinner with you" ("take dinner" seemed more elegant than Mrs. Fairford's "dine")—but when she came to the signature she was met by a new difficulty. Mrs. Fairford had signed herself "Laura Fairford"—just as one schoolgirl would write to another. But could this be a proper model for Mrs. Spragg? Undine could not tolerate the thought of her mother's abasing herself to a denizen of regions beyond Park Avenue, and she resolutely formed the signature: "Sincerely, Mrs. Abner E. Spragg." Then uncertainty overcame her, and she rewrote her note and copied Mrs. Fairford's formula: "Yours sincerely, Leota B. Spragg." But this struck her as an odd juxtaposition of formality and freedom, and she made a third attempt: "Yours with love, Leota B. Spragg." This, however, seemed excessive, as the ladies had never met; and after several other experiments she finally decided on a compromise, and ended the note: "Yours sincerely, Mrs. Leota B. Spragg." That might be conventional, Undine reflected, but it was certainly correct.

This point settled, she flung open her door, calling imperiously down the passage: "Céleste!" and adding, as the French maid appeared: "I want to look over all my dinner-dresses."

Considering the extent of Miss Spragg's wardrobe her dinner-dresses were not many. She had ordered a number the year before but, vexed at her lack of use for them, had tossed them over impatiently to the maid. Since then, indeed, she and Mrs. Spragg had succumbed to the abstract pleasure of buying two or three more, simply because they were too exquisite and Undine looked too lovely in them; but she had grown tired of these also—tired of seeing them hang unworn in her wardrobe, like so many derisive points of interrogation. And now, as Céleste spread them out on the bed, they seemed disgustingly commonplace, and as familiar as if she had danced them to shreds. Nevertheless, she yielded to the maid's persuasions and tried them on.

The first and second did not gain by prolonged inspection: they looked old-fashioned already. "It's something about the sleeves," Undine grumbled as she threw them aside.

The third was certainly the prettiest; but then it was the one she had worn at the hotel dance the night before, and the impossibility of wearing it again within the week was too obvious for discussion. Yet she enjoyed looking at herself in it, for it reminded her of her sparkling passages with

Claud Walsingham Popple, and her quieter but more fruitful talk with his little friend—the young man she had hardly noticed.

"You can go, Céleste—I'll take off the dress myself," she said: and when Céleste had passed out, laden with discarded finery, Undine bolted her door, dragged the tall pier-glass forward and, rummaging in a drawer for fan and gloves, swept to a seat before the mirror with the air of a lady arriving at an evening party. Céleste, before leaving, had drawn down the blinds and turned on the electric light, and the white and gold room, with its blazing wall-brackets, formed a sufficiently brilliant background to carry out the illusion. So untempered a glare would have been destructive to all half-tones and subtleties of modeling; but Undine's beauty was as vivid, and almost as crude, as the brightness suffusing it. Her black brows, her reddish-tawny hair and the pure red and white of her complexion defied the searching decomposing radiance: she might have been some fabled creature whose home was in a beam of light.

Undine, as a child, had taken but a lukewarm interest in the diversions of her playmates. Even in the early days when she had lived with her parents in a ragged outskirt of Apex, and hung on the fence with Indiana Frusk, the freckled daughter of the plumber "across the way," she had cared little for dolls or skipping-ropes, and still less for the riotous games in which the loud Indiana played Atalanta to all the boyhood of the quarter. Already Undine's chief delight was to "dress up" in her mother's Sunday skirt and "play lady" before the wardrobe mirror. The taste had outlasted childhood, and she still practiced the same secret pantomime, gliding in, settling her skirts, swaying her fan, moving her lips in soundless talk and laughter; but lately she had shrunk from everything that reminded her of her baffled social yearnings. Now, however, she could yield without afterthought to the joy of dramatizing her beauty. Within a few days she would be enacting the scene she was now mimicking; and it amused her to see in advance just what impression she would produce on Mrs. Fairford's guests.

For a while she carried on her chat with an imaginary circle of admirers, twisting this way and that, fanning, fidgeting, twitching at her draperies, as she did in real life when people were noticing her. Her incessant move-ments were not the result of shyness: she thought it the correct thing to be animated in society, and noise and restlessness were her only notion of vivacity. She, therefore, watched herself approvingly, admiring the light on her hair, the flash of teeth between her smiling lips, the pure shadows of her throat and shoulders as she passed from one attitude to another. Only one fact disturbed her: there was a hint of too much fullness in the curves of her neck and in the spring of her hips. She was tall enough to carry off a little extra weight, but excessive slimness was the fashion, and she shuddered at the thought that she might someday deviate from the perpendicular.

Presently she ceased to twist and sparkle at her image, and sinking into her chair gave herself up to retrospection. She was vexed, in looking back, to think how little notice she had taken of young Marvell, who turned out to be so much less negligible than his brilliant friend. She remembered thinking him rather shy, less accustomed to society; and though in his quiet deprecating way he had said one or two droll things he lacked Mr. Popple's masterly manner, his domineering yet caressing address. When Mr. Popple had fixed his black eyes on Undine, and murmured something "artistic" about the color of her hair, she had thrilled to the depths of her being. Even now it seemed incredible that he should not turn out to be more distinguished than young Marvell: he seemed so much more in the key of the world she read about in the Sunday papers—the dazzling auriferous world of the Van Degens, the Driscolls and their peers.

She was roused by the sound in the hall of her mother's last words to Mrs. Heeny. Undine waited till their adieux were over; then, opening her door, she seized the astonished masseuse and dragged her into the room.

Mrs. Heeny gazed in admiration at the luminous apparition in whose hold she found herself.

"Mercy, Undine—you do look stunning! Are you trying on your dress for Mrs. Fairford's?"

"Yes—no—this is only an old thing." The girl's eyes glittered under their black brows. "Mrs. Heeny, you've got to tell me the truth—*are* they as swell as you said?"

"Who? The Fairfords and Marvells? If they ain't swell enough for you, Undine Spragg, you'd better go right over to the court of England!"

Undine straightened herself. "I want the best. Are they as swell as the Driscolls and Van Degens?"

Mrs. Heeny sounded a scornful laugh. "Look at here, now, you unbelieving girl! As sure as I'm standing here before you, I've seen Mrs. Harmon B. Driscoll of Fifth Avenue laying in her pink velvet bed with Honiton lace sheets on it, and crying her eyes out because she couldn't get asked to one of Mrs. Paul Marvell's musicals. She'd never 'a dreamt of being asked to a dinner there! Not all of her money couldn't 'a bought her that—and she knows it!"

Undine stood for a moment with bright cheeks and parted lips; then she flung her soft arms about the masseuse.

"Oh, Mrs. Heeny—you're lovely to me!" she breathed, her lips on Mrs. Heeny's rusty veil; while the latter, freeing herself with a good-natured laugh, said as she turned away: "Go steady, Undine, and you'll get anywheres."

Go steady, Undine! Yes, that was the advice she needed. Sometimes, in her dark moods, she blamed her parents for not having given it to her. She was so young . . . and they had told her so little! As she looked back she shuddered at some of her escapes. Ever since they had come to New York she had been on the verge of one or two perilous adventures, and there had been a moment during their first winter when she had actually engaged herself to the handsome Austrian riding-master who accompanied her in the Park. He had carelessly shown her a card-case with a coronet, and had confided in her that he had been forced to resign from a crack cavalry regiment for fighting a duel about a countess; and as a result of these confidences she had pledged herself to him, and bestowed on him her pink pearl ring in exchange for one of twisted silver, which he said the countess had given him on her deathbed with the request that he should never take it off till he met a woman more beautiful than herself.

Soon afterward, luckily, Undine had run across Mabel Lipscomb, whom she had known at a middle western boarding school as Mabel Blitch. Miss Blitch occupied a position of distinction as the only New York girl at the school, and for a time there had been sharp rivalry for her favor between Undine and Indiana Frusk, whose parents had somehow contrived—for one term—to obtain her admission to the same establishment. In spite of Indiana's unscrupulous methods, and of a certain violent way she had of capturing attention, the victory remained with Undine, whom Mabel pronounced more refined; and the discomfited Indiana, denouncing her schoolmates as a "bunch of mushes," had disappeared forever from the scene of her defeat.

Since then Mabel had returned to New York and married a stockbroker; and Undine's first steps in social enlightenment dated from the day when she had met Mrs. Harry Lipscomb, and been again taken under her wing.

Harry Lipscomb had insisted on investigating the riding-master's record, and had found that his real name was Aaronson, and that he had left Cracow under a charge of swindling servant-girls out of their savings; in the light of which discoveries Undine noticed for the first time that his lips were too red and that his hair was pommaded. That was one of the episodes that sickened her as she looked back, and made her resolve once more to trust less to her impulses—especially in the matter of giving away rings. In the interval, however, she felt she had learned a good deal, especially since, by Mabel Lipscomb's advice, the Spraggs had moved to the Stentorian, where that lady was herself established.

There was nothing of the monopolist about Mabel, and she lost no time in making Undine free of the Stentorian group and its affiliated branches: a society addicted to "days," and linked together by membership in countless clubs, mundane, cultural or "earnest." Mabel took Undine to the days, and introduced her as a "guest" to the club meetings, where she was supported by the presence of many other guests—"my friend Miss Stager, of Phalanx, Georgia," or (if the lady were literary) simply "my friend Ora Prance Chettle of Nebraska—you know what Mrs. Chettle stands for."

Some of these reunions took place in the lofty hotels moored like a sonorously named fleet of battleships along the upper reaches of the West Side: the Olympian, the Incandescent, the Ormolu; while others, perhaps the more exclusive, were held in the equally lofty but more romantically styled apartment houses: the Parthenon, the Tintern Abbey or the Lido. Undine's preference was for the worldly parties, at which games were played, and she returned home laden with prizes in Dutch silver; but she was duly impressed by the debating clubs, where ladies of local distinction addressed the company from an improvised platform, or the members argued on subjects of such imperishable interest as: "What Is Charm?" or "The Problem-Novel"—after which pink lemonade and rainbow sandwiches were consumed amid heated discussion of the "ethical aspect" of the question.

It was all very novel and interesting, and at first Undine envied Mabel Lipscomb for having made herself a place in such circles; but in time she began to despise her for being content to remain there. For it did not take Undine long to learn that introduction to Mabel's "set" had brought her no nearer to Fifth Avenue. Even in Apex, Undine's tender imagination had been nurtured on the feats and gestures of Fifth Avenue. She knew all of New York's golden aristocracy by name, and the lineaments of its most distinguished scions had been made familiar by passionate poring over the daily press. In Mabel's world she sought in vain for the originals, and only now and then caught a tantalizing glimpse of one of their familiars: as when Claud Walsingham Popple, engaged on the portrait of a lady whom the Lipscombs described as "the wife of a steel magnet," felt it his duty to attend one of his client's teas, where it became Mabel's privilege to make his acquaintance and to name to him her friend Miss Spragg.

Unsuspected social gradations were thus revealed to the attentive Undine, but she was beginning to think that her sad proficiency had been acquired in vain when her hopes were revived by the appearance of Mr. Popple and his friend at the Stentorian dance. She thought she had learned enough to be safe from any risk of repeating the hideous Aaronson mistake; yet she now saw she had blundered again in distinguishing Claud Walsingham Popple while she almost snubbed his more retiring companion. It was all very puzzling, and her perplexity had been further increased by Mrs. Heeny's tale of the great Mrs. Harmon B. Driscoll's despair.

Hitherto, Undine had imagined that the Driscoll and Van Degen clans and their allies held undisputed suzerainty over New York society. Mabel Lipscomb thought so, too, and was given to bragging of her acquaintance with a Mrs. Spoff, who was merely a second cousin of Mrs. Harmon B. Driscoll's. Yet here was she, Undine Spragg of Apex, about to be introduced into an inner circle to which Driscolls and Van Degens had laid siege in vain! It was enough to make her feel a little dizzy with her triumph—to work her up into that state of perilous self-confidence in which all her worst follies had been committed.

She stood up and, going close to the glass, examined the reflection of her bright eyes and glowing cheeks. This time her fears were superfluous: there were to be no more mistakes and no more follies now! She was going to know the right people at last—she was going to get what she wanted!

As she stood there, smiling at her happy image, she heard her father's voice in the room beyond, and instantly began to tear off her dress, strip the long gloves from her arms and unpin the rose in her hair. Tossing the fallen finery aside, she slipped on a dressing-gown and opened the door into the drawing-room.

Mr. Spragg was standing near her mother, who sat in a drooping attitude, her head sunk on her breast, as she did when she had one of her "turns." He looked up abruptly as Undine entered.

"Father—has Mother told you? Mrs. Fairford has asked me to dine. She's Mrs. Paul Marvell's daughter—Mrs. Marvell was a Dagonet—and they're sweller than anybody; they *won't know* the Driscolls and Van Degens!"

Mr. Spragg surveyed her with humorous fondness.

"That so? What do they want to know you for, I wonder?" he jeered.

"Can't imagine—unless they think I'll introduce *you!*" she jeered back in the same key, her arms around his stooping shoulders, her shining hair against his cheek.

"Well—and are you going to? Have you accepted?" he took up her joke as she held him pinioned; while Mrs. Spragg, behind them, stirred in her seat with a little moan.

Undine threw back her head, plunging her eyes in his, and pressing so close that to his tired elderly sight her face was a mere bright blur.

"I want to awfully," she declared, "but I haven't got a single thing to wear."

Mrs. Spragg, at this, moaned more audibly. "Undine, I wouldn't ask Father to buy any more clothes right on top of those last bills."

"I ain't on top of those last bills yet—I'm way down under them," Mr. Spragg interrupted, raising his hands to imprison his daughter's slender wrists.

"Oh, well—if you want me to look like a scarecrow, and not get asked again, I've got a dress that'll do *perfectly,*" Undine threatened, in a tone between banter and vexation.

Mr. Spragg held her away at arm's length, a smile drawing up the loose wrinkles about his eyes.

"Well, that kind of dress might come in mighty handy on *some* occasions; so I guess you'd better hold on to it for future use, and go and select another for this Fairford dinner," he said; and before he could finish he was in her arms again, and she was smothering his last word in little cries and kisses.

3

THOUGH she would not for the world have owned it to her parents, Undine was disappointed in the Fairford dinner.

The house, to begin with, was small and rather shabby. There was no gilding, no lavish diffusion of light: the room they sat in after dinner, with its green-shaded lamps making faint pools of brightness, and its rows of books from floor to ceiling, reminded Undine of the old circulating library at Apex, before the new marble building was put up. Then, instead of a gas-log, or a polished grate with electric bulbs behind ruby glass, there was an old-fashioned wood-fire, like pictures of "Back to the Farm for Christmas"; and when the logs fell forward Mrs. Fairford or her brother had to jump up to push them in place, and the ashes scattered over the hearth untidily.

The dinner, too, was disappointing. Undine was too young to take note of culinary details, but she had expected to view the company through a bower of orchids and eat pretty-colored entrées in ruffled papers. Instead, there was only a low center-dish of ferns, and plain roasted and broiled meat that one could recognize—as if they'd been dyspeptics on a diet! With all the hints in the Sunday papers, she thought it dull of Mrs. Fairford not to have picked up something newer; and as the evening progressed she began to suspect that it wasn't a real "dinner party," and that they had just asked her in to share what they had when they were alone.

But a glance about the table convinced her that Mrs. Fairford could not have meant to treat her other guests so lightly. They were only eight in number, but one was no less a person than young Mrs. Peter Van Degen— the one who had been a Dagonet—and the consideration which this young lady, herself one of the choicest ornaments of the society column, displayed toward the rest of the company, convinced Undine that they must be more important than they looked. She liked Mrs. Fairford, a small incisive woman, with a big nose and good teeth revealed by frequent smiles. In her dowdy black and antiquated ornaments she was not what Undine would have called "stylish"; but she had a droll kind way which reminded the girl of her father's manner when he was not tired or worried about money. One of the other ladies, having white hair, did not long arrest Undine's atten-tion; and the fourth, a girl like herself, who was introduced as Miss Harriet Ray, she dismissed at a glance as plain and wearing a last year's "model." The men, too, were less striking than she had hoped. She had not expected much of Mr. Fairford, since married men were intrinsically uninteresting, and his baldness and gray moustache seemed naturally to relegate him to the background; but she had looked for some brilliant youths of her own age —in her inmost heart she had looked for Mr. Popple. He was not there, however, and of the other men one, whom they called Mr. Bowen, was hopelessly elderly—she supposed he was the husband of the white-haired lady—and the other two, who seemed to be friends of young Marvell's, were both lacking in Claud Walsingham's dash.

Undine sat between Mr. Bowen and young Marvell, who struck her as very "sweet" (it was her word for friendliness), but even shyer than at the hotel dance. Yet she was not sure if he were shy, or if his quietness were only a new kind of self-possession which expressed itself negatively instead of aggressively. Small, well-knit, fair, he sat stroking his slight blond moustache and looking at her with kindly, almost tender eyes; but he left it to his sister and the others to draw her out and fit her into the pattern.

Mrs. Fairford talked so well that the girl wondered why Mrs. Heeny had found her lacking in conversation. But though Undine thought silent people awkward she was not easily impressed by verbal fluency. All the ladies in Apex City were more voluble than Mrs. Fairford, and had a larger vocabulary: the difference was that with Mrs. Fairford conversation seemed to be a concert and not a solo. She kept drawing in the others, giving each a turn, beating time for them with her smile, and somehow harmonizing and linking together what they said. She took particular pains to give Undine her due part in the performance; but the girl's expansive impulses were always balanced by odd reactions of mistrust, and tonight the latter prevailed. She meant to watch and listen without letting herself go, and she sat very straight and pink, answering promptly but briefly, with the nervous laugh that punctuated all her phrases—saying "I don't care if I do" when her host asked her to try some grapes, and "I wouldn't wonder" when she thought anyone was trying to astonish her.

This state of lucidity enabled her to take note of all that was being said. The talk ran more on general questions, and less on people, than she was used to; but though the allusions to pictures and books escaped her, she caught and stored up every personal reference, and the pink in her cheeks deepened at a random mention of Mr. Popple.

"Yes—he's doing me," Mrs. Peter Van Degen was saying, in her slightly drawling voice. "He's doing everybody this year, you know—"

"As if that were a reason!" Undine heard Mrs. Fairford breathe to Mr. Bowen; who replied, at the same pitch: "It's a Van Degen reason, isn't it?"—to which Mrs. Fairford shrugged assentingly.

"That delightful Popple—he paints so exactly as he talks!" the white-haired lady took it up. "All his portraits seem to proclaim what a gentleman he is, and how he fascinates women! They're not pictures of Mrs. or Miss So-and-so, but simply of the impression Popple thinks he's made on them."

Mrs. Fairford smiled. "I've sometimes thought," she mused, "that Mr.

Popple must be the only gentleman I know; at least he's the only man who has ever told me he was a gentleman—and Mr. Popple never fails to mention it."

Undine's ear was too well attuned to the national note of irony for her not to perceive that her companions were making sport of the painter. She winced at their banter as if it had been at her own expense, yet it gave her a dizzy sense of being at last in the very stronghold of fashion. Her attention was diverted by hearing Mrs. Van Degen, under cover of the general laugh, say in a low tone to young Marvell: "I thought you liked his things, or I wouldn't have had him paint me."

Something in her tone made all Undine's perceptions bristle, and she strained her ears for the answer.

"I think he'll do you capitally—you must let me come and see some day soon." Marvell's tone was always so light, so unemphasized, that she could not be sure of its being as indifferent as it sounded. She looked down at the fruit on her plate and shot a side-glance through her lashes at Mrs. Peter Van Degen.

Mrs. Van Degen was neither beautiful nor imposing: just a dark girlish-looking creature with plaintive eyes and a fidgety frequent laugh. But she was more elaborately dressed and jeweled than the other ladies, and her elegance and her restlessness made her seem less alien to Undine. She had turned on Marvell a gaze at once pleading and possessive; but whether betokening merely an inherited intimacy (Undine had noticed that they were all more or less cousins) or a more personal feeling, her observer was unable to decide; just as the tone of the young man's reply might have expressed the open avowal of good-fellowship or the disguise of a different sentiment. All was blurred and puzzling to the girl in this world of half-lights, half-tones, eliminations and abbreviations; and she felt a violent longing to brush away the cobwebs and assert herself as the dominant figure of the scene.

Yet in the drawing-room, with the ladies, where Mrs. Fairford came and sat by her, the spirit of caution once more prevailed. She wanted to be noticed but she dreaded to be patronized, and here again her hostess's graduations of tone were confusing. Mrs. Fairford made no tactless allusions to her being a newcomer in New York—there was nothing as bitter to the girl as that—but her questions as to what pictures had interested Undine at the various exhibitions of the moment, and which of the new books she had read, were almost as open to suspicion, since they had to be answered in the negative. Undine did not even know that there were any pictures to be seen, much less that "people" went to see them; and she had read no new book but *When the Kissing Had to Stop*, of which Mrs. Fairford seemed not to have heard. On the theater they were equally at odds, for while Undine had seen *Oolaloo* fourteen times, and was "wild" about Ned Norris in *The Soda-Water Fountain*, she had not heard of the famous Berlin comedians who were performing Shakespeare at the German Theatre, and knew only by name the clever American actress who was trying to give "repertory" plays with a good stock company. The conversation was revived for a moment by her recalling that she had seen Sarah "Burnhard" in a play she called "Leglong," and another which she pronounced "Fade"; but even this did not carry them far, as she had forgotten what both plays were about and had found the actress a good deal older than she expected.

Matters were not improved by the return of the men from the smoking-room. Henley Fairford replaced his wife at Undine's side; and since it was unheard-of at Apex for a married man to force his society on a young girl, she inferred that the others didn't care to talk to her, and that her host and hostess were in league to take her off their hands. This discovery resulted in her holding her vivid head very high, and answering "I couldn't really say," or "Is that so?" to all Mr. Fairford's ventures; and as these were neither numerous nor striking it was a relief to both when the rising of the elderly lady gave the signal for departure.

In the hall, where young Marvell had managed to precede her, Undine found Mrs. Van Degen putting on her cloak. As she gathered it about her she laid her hand on Marvell's arm.

"Ralphie, dear, you'll come to the opera with me on Friday? We'll dine together first—Peter's got a club dinner." They exchanged what seemed a smile of intelligence, and Undine heard the young man accept. Then Mrs. Van Degen turned to her.

"Goodbye, Miss Spragg. I hope you'll come—"

"—to dine with me, too?" That must be what she was going to say, and Undine's heart gave a bound.

"—to see me some afternoon," Mrs. Van Degen ended, going down the steps to her motor, at the door of which a much-furred footman waited with more furs on his arm.

Undine's face burned as she turned to receive her cloak. When she had drawn it on with haughty deliberation she found Marvell at her side, in hat and overcoat, and her heart gave a higher bound. He was going to "escort" her home, of course! This brilliant youth—she felt now that he *was* brilliant —who dined alone with married women, whom the "Van Degen set" called "Ralphie, dear," had really no eyes for anyone but herself; and at the thought her lost self-complacency flowed back warm through her veins.

The street was coated with ice, and she had a delicious moment descending the steps on Marvell's arm, and holding it fast while they waited for her cab to come up; but when he had helped her in he closed the door and held his hand out over the lowered window.

"Goodbye," he said, smiling; and she could not help the break of pride in her voice, as she faltered out stupidly, from the depths of her disillusionment: "Oh—goodbye."

4

"FATHER, you've got to take a box for me at the opera next Friday."

From the tone of her voice Undine's parents knew at once that she was "nervous."

They had counted a great deal on the Fairford dinner as a means of tranquilization, and it was a blow to detect signs of the opposite result when, late the next morning, their daughter came dawdling into the sodden splendor of the Stentorian breakfast-room.

The symptoms of Undine's nervousness were unmistakable to Mr. and Mrs. Spragg. They could read the approaching storm in the darkening of her eyes from limpid gray to slate-color, and in the way her straight black brows met above them and the red curves of her lips narrowed to a parallel line below.

Mr. Spragg, having finished the last course of his heterogeneous meal, was adjusting his gold eyeglasses for a glance at the paper when Undine trailed down the sumptuous stuffy room, where coffee-fumes hung perpetually under the emblazoned ceiling and the spongy carpet might have absorbed a year's crumbs without a sweeping.

About them sat other pallid families, richly dressed, and silently eating their way through a bill-of-fare which seemed to have ransacked the globe for gastronomic incompatibilities; and in the middle of the room a knot of equally pallid waiters, engaged in languid conversation, turned their backs by common consent on the persons they were supposed to serve.

Undine, who rose too late to share the family breakfast, usually had her chocolate brought to her in bed by Céleste, after the manner described in the articles on "A Society Woman's Day" which were appearing in *Boudoir Chat*. Her mere appearance in the restaurant therefore prepared her parents for those symptoms of excessive tension which a nearer inspection confirmed, and Mr. Spragg folded his paper and hooked his glasses to his waistcoat with the air of a man who prefers to know the worst and have it over.

"An opera-box!" faltered Mrs. Spragg, pushing aside the bananas and cream with which she had been trying to tempt an appetite too languid for fried liver or crab mayonnaise.

"A parterre box," Undine corrected, ignoring the exclamation, and continuing to address herself to her father. "Friday's the stylish night, and that new tenor's going to sing again in 'Cavaleeria,'" she condescended to explain.

"That so?" Mr. Spragg thrust his hands into his waistcoat pockets, and began to tilt his chair till he remembered there was no wall to meet it. He regained his balance and said: "Wouldn't a couple of good orchestra seats do you?"

"No, they wouldn't," Undine answered with a darkening brow.

He looked at her humorously. "You invited the whole dinner-party, I suppose?"

"No—no one."

"Going all alone in a box?" She was disdainfully silent. "I don't s'pose you're thinking of taking mother and me?"

This was so obviously comic that they all laughed—even Mrs. Spragg—and Undine went on more mildly: "I want to do something for Mabel Lipscomb: make some return. She's always taking me 'round, and I've never done a thing for her—not a single thing."

This appeal to the national belief in the duty of reciprocal "treating" could not fail of its effect, and Mrs. Spragg murmured: "She never *has*, Abner,"—but Mr. Spragg's brow remained unrelenting.

"Do you know what a box costs?"

"No; but I s'pose you do," Undine returned with unconscious flippancy.

"I do. That's the trouble. *Why* won't seats do you?"

"Mabel could buy seats for herself."

"That's so," interpolated Mrs. Spragg—always the first to succumb to her daughter's arguments.

"Well, I guess I can't buy a box for her."

Undine's face gloomed more deeply. She sat silent, her chocolate thickening in the cup, while one hand, almost as much beringed as her mother's, drummed on the crumpled tablecloth.

"We might as well go straight back to Apex," she breathed at last between her teeth.

Mrs. Spragg cast a frightened glance at her husband. These struggles between two resolute wills always brought on her palpitations, and she wished she had her phial of digitalis with her.

"A parterre box costs a hundred and twenty-five dollars a night," said Mr. Spragg, transferring a toothpick to his waistcoat pocket.

"I only want it once."

He looked at her with a quizzical puckering of his crows'-feet. "You only want most things once, Undine."

It was an observation they had made in her earliest youth—Undine never wanted anything long, but she wanted it "right off." And until she got it the house was uninhabitable.

"I'd a good deal rather have a box for the season," she rejoined, and he saw the opening he had given her. She had two ways of getting things out of him against his principles; the tender wheedling way, and the harsh-lipped and cold—and he did not know which he dreaded most. As a child they had admired her assertiveness, had made Apex ring with their boasts of it; but it had long since cowed Mrs. Spragg, and it was beginning to frighten her husband.

"Fact is, Undie," he said, weakening, "I'm a little mite strapped just this month."

Her eyes grew absent-minded, as they always did when he alluded to business. *That* was man's province; and what did men go "downtown" for but to bring back the spoils to their women? She rose abruptly, leaving her parents seated, and said, more to herself than the others: "Think I'll go for a ride."

"Oh, Undine!" fluttered Mrs. Spragg. She always had palpitations when Undine rode, and since the Aaronson episode her fears were not confined to what the horse might do.

"Why don't you take your mother out shopping a little?" Mr. Spragg suggested, conscious of the limitation of his resources.

Undine made no answer, but swept down the room, and out of the door ahead of her mother, with scorn and anger in every line of her arrogant young back. Mrs. Spragg tottered meekly after her, and Mr. Spragg lounged out into the marble hall to buy a cigar before taking the subway to his office.

Undine went for a ride, not because she felt particularly disposed for the exercise, but because she wished to discipline her mother. She was almost sure she would get her opera-box, but she did not see why she should have to struggle for her rights, and she was especially annoyed with Mrs. Spragg for seconding her so half-heartedly. If she and her mother did not hold together in such crises she would have twice the work to do.

Undine hated "scenes": she was essentially peace-loving, and would have preferred to live on terms of unbroken harmony with her parents. But she could not help it if they were unreasonable. Ever since she could remember there had been "fusses" about money; yet she and her mother had always got what they wanted, apparently without lasting detriment to the family fortunes. It was therefore natural to conclude that there were ample funds to draw upon, and that Mr. Spragg's occasional resistances were merely due to an imperfect understanding of what constituted the necessities of life.

When she returned from her ride Mrs. Spragg received her as if she had come back from the dead. It was absurd, of course; but Undine was inured to the absurdity of parents.

"Has Father telephoned?" was her first brief question.

"No, he hasn't yet."

Undine's lips tightened, but she proceeded deliberately with the removal of her habit.

"You'd think I'd asked him to buy me the opera house, the way he's acting over a single box," she muttered, flinging aside her smartly fitting coat.

Mrs. Spragg received the flying garment and smoothed it out on the bed. Neither of the ladies could "bear" to have their maid about when they were at their toilet, and Mrs. Spragg had always performed these ancillary services for Undine.

"You know, Undie, Father hasn't always got the money in his pocket, and the bills have been pretty heavy lately. Father was a rich man for Apex, but that's different from being rich in New York."

She stood before her daughter, looking down on her appealingly.

Undine, who had seated herself while she detached her stock and waistcoat, raised her head with an impatient jerk. "Why on earth did we ever leave Apex, then?" she exclaimed.

Mrs. Spragg's eyes usually dropped before her daughter's inclement gaze; but on this occasion they held their own with a kind of awestruck courage, till Undine's lids sank above her flushing cheeks.

She sprang up, tugging at the waistband of her habit, while Mrs. Spragg, relapsing from temerity to meekness, hovered about her with obstructive zeal.

"If you'd only just let go of my skirt, Mother—I can unhook it twice as quick myself."

Mrs. Spragg drew back, understanding that her presence was no longer wanted. But on the threshold she paused, as if overruled by a stronger influence, and said, with a last look at her daughter: "You didn't meet anybody when you were out, did you, Undie?"

Undine's brows drew together: she was struggling with her long patent-leather boot.

"Meet anybody? Do you mean anybody I know? I don't *know* anybody—I never shall, if Father can't afford to let me go round with people!"

The boot was off with a wrench, and she flung it violently across the old-rose carpet, while Mrs. Spragg, turning away to hide a look of inexpressible relief, slipped discreetly from the room.

The day wore on. Undine had meant to go down and tell Mabel Lipscomb about the Fairford dinner, but its aftertaste was flat on her lips. What would it lead to? Nothing, as far as she could see. Ralph Marvell had not even asked when he might call; and she was ashamed to confess to Mabel that he had not driven home with her.

Suddenly she decided that she would go and see the pictures of which Mrs. Fairford had spoken. Perhaps she might meet some of the people she had seen at dinner—from their talk one might have imagined that they spent their lives in picture-galleries.

The thought reanimated her, and she put on her handsomest furs, and a hat for which she had not yet dared present the bill to her father. It was the fashionable hour in Fifth Avenue, but Undine knew none of the ladies who were bowing to each other from interlocked motors. She had to content herself with the gaze of admiration which she left in her wake along the pavement; but she was used to the homage of the streets and her vanity craved a choicer fare.

When she reached the art gallery which Mrs. Fairford had named she found it even more crowded than Fifth Avenue; and some of the ladies and gentlemen wedged before the pictures had the "look" which signified social consecration. As Undine made her way among them, she was aware of attracting almost as much notice as in the street, and she flung herself into rapt attitudes before the canvases, scribbling notes in the catalogue in imitation of a tall girl in sables, while ripples of self-consciousness played up and down her watchful back.

Presently her attention was drawn to a lady in black who was examining the pictures through a tortoiseshell eyeglass adorned with diamonds and hanging from a long pearl chain. Undine was instantly struck by the opportunities which this toy presented for graceful wrist movements and supercilious turns of the head. It seemed suddenly plebeian and promiscuous to look at the world with a naked eye, and all her floating desires were merged in the wish for a jeweled eyeglass and chain. So violent was this wish that, drawn on in the wake of the owner of the eyeglass, she found herself inadvertently bumping against a stout tight-coated young man whose impact knocked her catalogue from her hand.

As the young man picked the catalogue up and held it out to her she noticed that his bulging eyes and queer retreating face were suffused with a glow of admiration. He was so unpleasant-looking that she would have resented his homage had not his odd physiognomy called up some vaguely agreeable association of ideas. Where had she seen before this grotesque saurian head, with eyelids as thick as lips and lips as thick as earlobes? It fled before her down a perspective of innumerable newspaper portraits, all, like the original before her, tightly coated, with a huge pearl transfixing a silken tie. . . .

"Oh, thank you," she murmured, all gleams and graces, while he stood hat in hand, saying sociably: "The crowd's simply awful, isn't it?"

At the same moment the lady of the eyeglass drifted closer, and with a tap of her wand, and a careless "Peter, look at this," swept him to the other side of the gallery.

Undine's heart was beating excitedly, for as he turned away she had identified him. Peter Van Degen—who could he be but young Peter Van Degen, the son of the great banker, Thurber Van Degen, the husband of Ralph Marvell's cousin, the hero of "Sunday supplements," the captor of blue ribbons at horse shows, of gold cups at motor races, the owner of winning racehorses and "crack" sloops: the supreme exponent, in short, of those crowning arts that made all life seem stale and unprofitable outside the magic ring of the society column?

Undine smiled as she recalled the look with which his pale protruding eyes had rested on her—it almost consoled her for his wife's indifference!

When she reached home she found that she could not remember anything about the pictures she had seen. . . .

There was no message from her father, and a reaction of disgust set in. Of what good were such encounters if they were to have no sequel? She would probably never meet Peter Van Degen again—or, if she *did* run across him in the same accidental way, she knew they could not continue their conversation without being "introduced." What was the use of being beautiful and attracting attention if one were perpetually doomed to relapse again into the obscure mass of the Uninvited?

Her gloom was not lightened by finding Ralph Marvell's card on the drawing-room table. She thought it unflattering and almost impolite of him to call without making an appointment: it seemed to show that he did not wish to continue their acquaintance. But as she tossed the card aside her mother said: "He was real sorry not to see you, Undine—he sat here nearly an hour."

Undine's attention was roused. "Sat here—all alone? Didn't you tell him I was out?"

"Yes—but he came up all the same. He asked for me."

"Asked for *you?*"

The social order seemed to be falling in ruins at Undine's feet. A visitor who asked for a girl's mother!—she stared at Mrs. Spragg with cold incredulity. "What makes you think he did?"

"Why, they told me so. I telephoned down that you were out, and they said he'd asked for me." Mrs. Spragg let the fact speak for itself—it was too much out of the range of her experience to admit of even a hypothetical explanation.

Undine shrugged her shoulders. "It was a mistake, of course. Why on earth did you let him come up?"

"I thought maybe he had a message for you, Undie."

This plea struck her daughter as not without weight. "Well, did he?" she asked, drawing out her hat-pins and tossing down her hat on the onyx table.

"Why, no—he just conversed. He was lovely to me, but I couldn't make out what he was after," Mrs. Spragg was obliged to own.

Her daughter looked at her with a kind of chill commiseration. "You never *can,*" she murmured, turning away.

She stretched herself out moodily on one of the pink and gold sofas, and lay there brooding, an unread novel on her knee. Mrs. Spragg timidly slipped a cushion under her daughter's head, and then dissembled herself behind the lace window-curtains and sat watching the lights spring out down the long street and spread their glittering net across the Park. It was one of Mrs. Spragg's chief occupations to watch the nightly lighting of New York.

Undine lay silent, her hands clasped behind her head. She was plunged in one of the moods of bitter retrospection when all her past seemed like a long struggle for something she could not have, from a trip to Europe to an opera-box; and when she felt sure that, as the past had been, so the future would be. And yet, as she had often told her parents, all she sought for was improvement: she honestly wanted the best.

Her first struggle—after she had ceased to scream for candy, or sulk for a new toy—had been to get away from Apex in summer. Her summers, as she looked back on them, seemed to typify all that was dreariest and most exasperating in her life. The earliest had been spent in the yellow "frame" cottage where she had hung on the fence, kicking her toes against the broken palings and exchanging moist chewing gum and half-eaten apples with Indiana Frusk. Later on, she had returned from her boarding school to the comparative gentility of summer vacations at the Mealey House, whither her parents, forsaking their squalid suburb, had moved in the first flush of their rising fortunes. The tessellated floors, the plush parlors and organ-like radiators of the Mealey House had, aside from their intrinsic elegance, the immense advantage of lifting the Spraggs high above the Frusks, and making it possible for Undine, when she met Indiana in the street or at school, to chill her advances by a careless allusion to the splendors of hotel life. But even in such a setting, and in spite of the social superiority it implied, the long months of the middle western summer, fly-blown, torrid, exhaling stale odors, soon became as insufferable as they had been in the little yellow house.

At school Undine met other girls whose parents took them to the Great Lakes for August; some even went to California, others—oh bliss ineffable! —went "east."

Pale and listless under the stifling boredom of the Mealey House routine, Undine secretly sucked lemons, nibbled slate-pencils and drank pints of bitter coffee to aggravate her look of ill-health; and when she learned that even Indiana Frusk was to go on a month's visit to Buffalo it needed no artificial aids to emphasize the ravages of envy. Her parents, alarmed by her appearance, were at last convinced of the necessity of change, and timidly, tentatively, they transferred themselves for a month to a staring hotel on a glaring lake.

There Undine enjoyed the satisfaction of sending ironic postcards to Indiana, and discovering that she could more than hold her own against the youth and beauty of the other visitors. Then she made the acquaintance of a pretty woman from Richmond, whose husband, a mining engineer, had brought her west with him while he inspected the newly developed Eubaw mines; and the southern visitor's dismay, her repugnances, her recoil from

the faces, the food, the amusements, the general bareness and stridency of
the scene, were a terrible initiation to Undine. There was something still
better beyond, then—more luxurious, more exciting, more worthy of her!
She once said to herself, afterward, that it was always her fate to find out
just too late about the "something beyond." But in this case it was not too
late—and obstinately, inflexibly, she set herself to the task of forcing her
parents to take her "east" the next summer.

Yielding to the inevitable, they suffered themselves to be impelled to a
Virginia "resort," where Undine had her first glimpse of more romantic
possibilities—leafy moonlight rides and drives, picnics in mountain glades,
and an atmosphere of Christmas-chromo sentimentality that tempered her
hard edges a little, and gave her glimpses of a more delicate kind of pleasure.
But here again everything was spoiled by a peep through another door.
Undine, after a first mustering of the other girls in the hotel, had, as usual,
found herself easily first—till the arrival, from Washington, of Mr. and Mrs.
Wincher and their daughter. Undine was much handsomer than Miss
Wincher, but she saw at a glance that she did not know how to use her
beauty as the other used her plainness. She was exasperated, too, by the
discovery that Miss Wincher seemed not only unconscious of any possible
rivalry between them, but actually unaware of her existence. Listless, long-
faced, supercilious, the young lady from Washington sat apart reading
novels or playing solitaire with her parents, as though the huge hotel's loud
life of gossip and flirtation were invisible and inaudible to her. Undine
never even succeeded in catching her eye: she always lowered it to her book
when the Apex beauty trailed or rattled past her secluded corner. But one
day an acquaintance of the Winchers' turned up—a lady from Boston, who
had come to Virginia on a botanizing tour; and from scraps of Miss
Wincher's conversation with the newcomer, Undine, straining her ears behind a column of the long veranda, obtained a new glimpse into the
unimagined.

The Winchers, it appeared, found themselves at Potash Springs merely
because a severe illness of Mrs. Wincher's had made it impossible, at the last
moment, to move her farther from Washington. They had let their house on
the North Shore, and as soon as they could leave "this dreadful hole" were
going to Europe for the autumn. Miss Wincher simply didn't know how she
got through the days; though no doubt it was as good as a rest-cure after the
rush of the winter. Of course they would have preferred to hire a house, but
the "hole," if one could believe it, didn't offer one; so they had simply shut
themselves off as best they could from the "hotel crew"—had her friend,
Miss Wincher parenthetically asked, happened to notice the Sunday young
men? They were queerer even than the "belles" they came for—and had
escaped the promiscuity of the dinner-hour by turning one of their rooms
into a dining-room, and picnicking there—with the Persimmon House stan-

dards, one couldn't describe it in any other way! But luckily the awful place was doing mamma good, and now they had nearly served their term. . . .

Undine turned sick as she listened. Only the evening before she had gone on a "buggy-ride" with a young gentleman from Deposit—a dentist's assistant—and had let him kiss her, and given him the flower from her hair. She loathed the thought of him now: she loathed all the people about her, and most of all the disdainful Miss Wincher. It enraged her to think that the Winchers classed her with the "hotel crew"—with the "belles" who awaited their Sunday young men. The place was forever blighted for her, and the next week she dragged her amazed but thankful parents back to Apex.

But Miss Wincher's depreciatory talk had opened ampler vistas, and the pioneer blood in Undine would not let her rest. She had heard the call of the Atlantic seaboard, and the next summer found the Spraggs at Skog Harbor, Maine. Even now Undine felt a shiver of boredom as she recalled it. That summer had been the worst of all. The bare wind-beaten inn, all shingles without and blueberry pie within, was "exclusive," parochial, Bostonian; and the Spraggs wore through the interminable weeks in blank unmitigated isolation. The incomprehensible part of it was that every other woman in the hotel was plain, dowdy or elderly—and most of them all three. If there had been any competition on ordinary lines Undine would have won, as Van Degen said, "hands down." But there wasn't—the other "guests" simply formed a cold impenetrable group who walked, boated, played golf, and discussed Christian Science and the Subliminal, unaware of the tremulous organism drifting helplessly against their rock-bound circle.

It was on the day the Spraggs left Skog Harbor that Undine vowed to herself with set lips: "I'll never try anything again till I try New York." Now she had gained her point and tried New York, and so far, it seemed, with no better success. From small things to great, everything went against her. In such hours of self-searching she was ready enough to acknowledge her own mistakes, but they exasperated her less than the blunders of her parents. She was sure, for instance, that she was on what Mrs. Heeny called "the right tack" at last: yet just at the moment when her luck seemed about to turn she was to be thwarted by her father's stupid obstinacy about the opera-box. . . .

She lay brooding over these things till long after Mrs. Spragg had gone away to dress for dinner, and it was nearly eight o'clock when she heard her father's dragging tread in the hall.

She kept her eyes fixed on her book while he entered the room and moved about behind her, laying aside his hat and overcoat; then his steps came close and a small parcel dropped on the pages of her book.

"Oh, Father!" She sprang up, all alight, the novel on the floor, her fingers twitching for the tickets. But a substantial packet emerged, like nothing she had ever seen. She looked at it, hoping, fearing—she beamed blissful interrogation on her father while his sallow smile continued to tantalize her. Then she closed on him with a rush, smothering his words against her hair.

"It's for more than one night—why, it's for every other Friday! Oh, you darling, you darling!" she exulted.

Mr. Spragg, through the glittering meshes, feigned dismay. "That so? They must have given me the wrong—!" Then, convicted by her radiant eyes as she swung round on him: "I knew you only wanted it *once* for yourself, Undine; but I thought maybe, off nights, you'd like to send it to your friends."

Mrs. Spragg, who from her doorway had assisted with moist eyes at this closing pleasantry, came forward as Undine hurried away to dress.

"Abner—can you really manage it all right?"

He answered her with one of his awkward brief caresses. "Don't you fret about that, Leota. I'm bound to have her go round with these people she knows. I want her to be with them all she can."

A pause fell between them, while Mrs. Spragg looked anxiously into his fagged eyes.

"You seen Elmer again?"

"No. Once was enough," he returned, with a scowl like Undine's.

"Why—you *said* he couldn't come after her, Abner!"

"No more he can. But what if she was to get nervous and lonesome, and want to go after him?"

Mrs. Spragg shuddered away from the suggestion. "How'd he look? Just the same?" she whispered.

"No. Spruced up. That's what scared me."

It scared her, too, to the point of blanching her habitually lifeless cheek. She continued to scrutinize her husband broodingly. "You look fairly sick, Abner. You better let me get you some of those stomach drops right off," she proposed.

But he parried this with his unfailing humor. "I guess I'm too sick to risk that." He passed his hand through her arm with the conjugal gesture familiar to Apex City. "Come along down to dinner, Mother—I guess Undine won't mind if I don't rig up tonight."

5

S HE had looked down at them, enviously, from the balcony—she had looked up at them, reverentially, from the stalls; but now at last she was on a line with them, among them, she was part of the sacred semicircle whose privilege it is, between the acts, to make the mere public forget that the curtain has fallen.

As she swept to the left-hand seat of their crimson niche, waving Mabel Lipscomb to the opposite corner with a gesture learned during her apprenticeship in the stalls, Undine felt that quickening of the faculties that comes in the high moments of life. Her consciousness seemed to take in at once the whole bright curve of the auditorium, from the unbroken lines of spectators below her to the culminating blaze of the central chandelier; and she herself was the core of that vast illumination, the sentient throbbing surface which gathered all the shafts of light into a center.

It was almost a relief when, a moment later, the lights sank, the curtain rose, and the focus of illumination was shifted. The music, the scenery, and the movement on the stage, were like a rich mist tempering the radiance that shot on her from every side, and giving her time to subside, draw breath, adjust herself to this new clear medium which made her feel so oddly brittle and transparent.

When the curtain fell on the first act she began to be aware of a subtle change in the house. In all the boxes crosscurrents of movement had set in: groups were coalescing and breaking up, fans waving and heads twinkling, black coats emerging among white shoulders, late comers dropping their furs and laces in the red penumbra of the background. Undine, for the moment unconscious of herself, swept the house with her opera-glass, searching for familiar faces. Some she knew without being able to name them—fixed figureheads of the social prow—others she recognized from their portraits in the papers; but of the few from whom she could herself claim recognition not one was visible, and as she pursued her investigations the whole scene grew blank and featureless.

Almost all the boxes were full now, but one, just opposite, tantalized her by its continued emptiness. How queer to have an opera-box and not use it! What on earth could the people be doing—what rarer delight could they be tasting? Undine remembered that the numbers of the boxes and the names of their owners were given on the back of the program, and after a rapid computation she turned to consult the list. Mondays and Fridays, Mrs. Peter

Van Degen. That was it: the box was empty because Mrs. Van Degen was dining alone with Ralph Marvell! *"Peter will be at one of his club dinners."* Undine had a sharp vision of the Van Degen dining-room—she pictured it as oak-carved and sumptuous with gilding—with a small table in the center, and rosy lights and flowers, and Ralph Marvell, across the hothouse grapes and champagne, leaning to take a light from his hostess's cigarette. Undine had seen such scenes on the stage, she had come upon them in the glowing pages of fiction, and it seemed to her that every detail was before her now, from the glitter of jewels on Mrs. Van Degen's bare shoulders to the way young Marvell stroked his slight blond moustache while he smiled and listened.

Undine blushed with anger at her own simplicity in fancying that he had been "taken" by her—that she could ever really count among these happy self-absorbed people! They all had their friends, their ties, their delightful crowding obligations: why should they make room for an intruder in a circle so packed with the initiated?

As her imagination developed the details of the scene in the Van Degen dining-room it became clear to her that fashionable society was horribly immoral and that she could never really be happy in such a poisoned atmosphere. She remembered that an eminent divine was preaching a series of sermons against social corruption, and she determined to go and hear him on the following Sunday.

This train of thought was interrupted by the feeling that she was being intently observed from the neighboring box. She turned around with a feint of speaking to Mrs. Lipscomb, and met the bulging stare of Peter Van Degen. He was standing behind the lady of the eyeglass, who had replaced her tortoiseshell implement by one of closely set brilliants, which, at a word from her companion, she critically bent on Undine.

"No—I don't remember," she said; and the girl reddened, divining herself unidentified after this protracted scrutiny.

But there was no doubt as to young Van Degen's remembering her. She was even conscious that he was trying to provoke in her some reciprocal sign of recognition; and the attempt drove her to the haughty study of her program.

"Why, there's Mr. Popple over there!" exclaimed Mabel Lipscomb, making large signs across the house with fan and playbill.

Undine had already become aware that Mabel, planted, blond and brimming, too near the edge of the box, was somehow out of scale and out of drawing; and the freedom of her demonstrations increased the effect of disproportion. No one else was wagging and waving in that way: a gestureless mute telegraphy seemed to pass between the other boxes. Still, Undine could not help following Mrs. Lipscomb's glance, and there in fact was Claud Popple, taller and more dominant than ever, and bending easily over what she felt must be the back of a brilliant woman.

He replied by a discreet salute to Mrs. Lipscomb's intemperate motions, and Undine saw the brilliant woman's opera-glass turn in their direction, and said to herself that in a moment Mr. Popple would be "round." But the entr'acte wore on, and no one turned the handle of their door, or disturbed the peaceful somnolence of Harry Lipscomb, who, not being (as he put it) "onto" grand opera, had abandoned the struggle and withdrawn to the seclusion of the inner box. Undine jealously watched Mr. Popple's progress from box to box, from brilliant woman to brilliant woman; but just as it seemed about to carry him to their door he reappeared at his original post across the house.

"Undie, do look—there's Mr. Marvell!" Mabel began again, with another conspicuous outbreak of signalling; and this time Undine flushed to the nape as Mrs. Peter Van Degen appeared in the opposite box with Ralph Marvell behind her. The two seemed to be alone in the box—as they had doubtless been alone all the evening!—and Undine furtively turned to see if Mr. Van Degen shared her disapproval. But Mr. Van Degen had disappeared, and Undine, leaning forward, nervously touched Mabel's arm.

"What's the matter, Undine? Don't you see Mr. Marvell over there? Is that his sister he's with?"

"No.—I wouldn't beckon like that," Undine whispered between her teeth.

"Why not? Don't you want him to know you're here?"

"Yes—but the other people are not beckoning."

Mabel looked about unabashed. "Perhaps they've all found each other. Shall I send Harry over to tell him?" she shouted above the blare of the wind instruments.

"No!" gasped Undine as the curtain rose.

She was no longer capable of following the action on the stage. Two presences possessed her imagination: that of Ralph Marvell, small, unattainable, remote, and that of Mabel Lipscomb, nearby, immense and irrepressible.

It had become clear to Undine that Mabel Lipscomb was ridiculous. That was the reason why Popple did not come to the box. No one would care to be seen talking to her while Mabel was at her side: Mabel, monumental and molded while the fashionable were flexible and diaphanous, Mabel strident and explicit while they were subdued and allusive. At the Stentorian she was the center of her group—here she revealed herself as unknown and unknowing. Why, she didn't even know that Mrs. Peter Van Degen was not Ralph Marvell's sister! And she had a way of trumpeting out her ignorances that jarred on Undine's subtler methods. It was precisely at this point that there dawned on Undine what was to be one of the guiding principles of her career: "It's better to watch than to ask questions."

The curtain fell again, and Undine's eyes flew back to the Van Degen box. Several men were entering it together, and a moment later she saw

Ralph Marvell rise from his seat and pass out. Half-unconsciously she placed herself in such a way as to have an eye on the door of the box. But its handle remained unturned, and Harry Lipscomb, leaning back on the sofa, his head against the opera cloaks, continued to breathe stertorously through his open mouth and stretched his legs a little farther across the threshold. . . .

The entr'acte was nearly over when the door opened and two gentlemen stumbled over Mr. Lipscomb's legs. The foremost was Claud Walsingham Popple; and above his shoulder shone the batrachian countenance of Peter Van Degen. A brief murmur from Mr. Popple made his companion known to the two ladies, and Mr. Van Degen promptly seated himself behind Undine, relegating the painter to Mrs. Lipscomb's elbow.

"Queer go—I happened to see your friend there waving to old Popp across the house. So I bolted over and collared him: told him he'd got to introduce me before he was a minute older. I tried to find out who you were the other day at the motor show—no, where was it? Oh, those pictures at Goldmark's. What d'you think of 'em, by the way? You ought to be painted yourself—no, I mean it, you know—you ought to get old Popp to do you. He'd do your hair ripplingly. You must let me come and talk to you about it. . . . About the picture or your hair? Well, your hair if you don't mind. Where'd you say you were staying? Oh, you *live* here, do you? I say, that's first rate!"

Undine sat well forward, curving toward him a little, as she had seen the other women do, but holding back sufficiently to let it be visible to the house that she was conversing with no less a person than Mr. Peter Van Degen. Mr. Popple's talk was certainly more brilliant and purposeful, and she saw him cast longing glances at her from behind Mrs. Lipscomb's shoulder; but she remembered how lightly he had been treated at the Fairford dinner, and she wanted!—oh, how she wanted!—to have Ralph Marvell see her talking to Van Degen.

She poured out her heart to him, improvising an opinion on the pictures and an opinion on the music, falling in gaily with his suggestion of a jolly little dinner some night soon, at the Café Martin, and strengthening her position, as she thought, by an easy allusion to her acquaintance with Mrs. Van Degen. But at the word her companion's eye clouded, and a shade of constraint dimmed his enterprising smile.

"My wife—? Oh, *she* doesn't go to restaurants—she moves on too high a plane. But we'll get old Popp, and Mrs.———, Mrs.———, what'd you say your fat friend's name was? Just a select little crowd of four—and some kind of a cheerful show afterward. . . . Jove! There's the curtain, and I must skip."

As the door closed on him Undine's cheeks burned with resentment. If Mrs. Van Degen didn't go to restaurants, why had he supposed that *she* would? and to have to drag Mabel in her wake! The leaden sense of failure overcame her again. Here was the evening nearly over, and what had it led to? Looking up from the stalls, she had fancied that to sit in a box was to be in society—now she saw it might but emphasize one's exclusion. And she was burdened with the box for the rest of the season! It was really stupid of her father to have exceeded his instructions: why had he not done as she told him? . . . Undine felt helpless and tired . . . hateful memories of Apex crowded back on her. Was it going to be as dreary here as there?

She felt Lipscomb's loud whisper in her back: "Say, you girls, I guess I'll cut this and come back for you when the show busts up." They heard him shuffle out of the box, and Mabel settled back to undisturbed enjoyment of the stage.

When the last entr'acte began Undine stood up, resolved to stay no longer. Mabel, lost in the study of the audience, had not noticed her movement, and as she passed alone into the back of the box the door opened and Ralph Marvell came in.

Undine stood with one arm listlessly raised to detach her cloak from the wall. Her attitude showed the long slimness of her figure and the fresh curve of the throat below her bent-back head. Her face was paler and softer than usual, and the eyes she rested on Marvell's face looked deep and starry under their fixed brows.

"Oh—you're not going?" he exclaimed.

"I thought you weren't coming," she answered simply.

"I waited till now on purpose to dodge your other visitors."

She laughed with pleasure. "Oh, we hadn't so many!"

Some intuition had already told her that frankness was the tone to take with him. They sat down together on the red damask sofa, against the hanging cloaks. As Undine leaned back her hair caught in the spangles of the wrap behind her, and she had to sit motionless while the young man freed the captive mesh. Then they settled themselves again, laughing a little at the incident.

A glance had made the situation clear to Mrs. Lipscomb, and they saw her return to her rapt inspection of the boxes. In their mirror-hung recess the light was subdued to a rosy dimness and the hum of the audience came to them through half-drawn silken curtains. Undine noticed the delicacy and finish of her companion's features as his head detached itself against the red silk walls. The hand with which he stroked his small moustache was finely finished too, but sinewy and not effeminate. She had always associated finish and refinement entirely with her own sex, but she began to think they might be even more agreeable in a man. Marvell's eyes were gray, like her own, with chestnut eyebrows and darker lashes; and his skin was as clear as a woman's, but pleasantly reddish, like his hands.

As he sat talking in a low tone, questioning her about the music, asking her what she had been doing since he had last seen her, she was aware that he looked at her less than usual, and she also glanced away; but when she turned her eyes suddenly they always met his gaze.

His talk remained impersonal. She was a little disappointed that he did not compliment her on her dress or her hair—Undine was accustomed to hearing a great deal about her hair, and the episode of the spangles had opened the way to a graceful allusion—but the instinct of sex told her that, under his quiet words, he was throbbing with the sense of her proximity. And his self-restraint sobered her, made her refrain from the flashing and fidgeting which were the only way she knew of taking part in the immemorial love-dance. She talked simply and frankly of herself, of her parents, of how few people they knew in New York, and of how, at times, she was almost sorry she had persuaded them to give up Apex.

"You see, they did it entirely on my account; they're awfully lonesome here; and I don't believe I shall ever learn New York ways either," she confessed, turning on him the eyes of youth and truthfullness. "Of course, I know a few people; but they're not—not the way I expected New York people to be." She risked what seemed an involuntary glance at Mabel. "I've seen girls here tonight that I just *long* to know—they look so lovely and refined—but I don't suppose I ever shall. New York's not very friendly to strange girls, is it? I suppose you've got so many of your own already—and they're all so fascinating you don't care!" As she spoke she let her eyes rest on his, half-laughing, half-wistful, and then dropped her lashes while the pink stole slowly up to them.

When he left her he asked if he might hope to find her at home the next day.

The night was fine, and Marvell, having put his cousin into her motor, started to walk home to Washington Square. At the corner he was joined by Mr. Popple.

"Hallo, Ralph, old man—did you run across our auburn beauty of the Stentorian? Who'd have thought old Harry Lipscomb'd have put us onto anything as good as that? Peter Van Degen was fairly taken off his feet— pulled me out of Mrs. Monty Thurber's box and dragged me 'round by the collar to introduce him. Planning a dinner at Martin's already. Gad, young Peter must have what he wants *when* he wants it! I put in a word for you— told him you and I ought to be let in on the ground floor. Funny the luck some girls have about getting started. I believe this one'll take if she can manage to shake the Lipscombs. I think I'll ask to paint her; might be a good thing for the spring show. She'd show up splendidly as a pendant to my Mrs. Van Degen—blonde and brunette . . . night and morning. . . . Of course, I prefer Mrs. Van Degen's type—personally, I *must* have breeding —but as a mere bit of flesh and blood . . . hallo, ain't you coming into the club?"

Marvell was not coming into the club, and he drew a long breath of relief as his companion left him.

Was it possible that he had ever thought leniently of the egregious Popple? The tone of social omniscience which he had once found so comic was now as offensive to him as a coarse physical touch. And the worst of it was that Popple, with the slight exaggeration of a caricature, really expressed the ideals of the world he frequented. As he spoke of Miss Spragg, so others at any rate would think of her: almost everyone in Ralph's set would agree that it was luck for a girl from Apex to be started by Peter Van Degen at a Café Martin dinner. . . .

Ralph Marvell, mounting his grandfather's doorstep, looked up at the symmetrical old red housefront, with its frugal marble ornament, as he might have looked into a familiar human face.

"They're right—after all, in some ways they're right," he murmured, slipping his key into the door.

"They" were his mother and old Mr. Urban Dagonet, both, from Ralph's earliest memories, so closely identified with the old house in Washington Square that they might have passed for its inner consciousness as it might have stood for their outward form; and the question as to which the house now seemed to affirm their intrinsic rightness was that of the social disintegration expressed by widely different architectural physiognomies at the other end of Fifth Avenue.

As Ralph pushed the bolts behind him, and passed into the hall, with its dark mahogany doors and the quiet "Dutch interior" effect of its black and white marble paving, he said to himself that what Popple called society was really just like the houses it lived in: a muddle of misapplied ornament over a thin steel shell of utility. The steel shell was built up in Wall Street, the social trimmings were hastily added in Fifth Avenue; and the union between them was as monstrous and factitious, as unlike the gradual homogeneous growth which flowers into what other countries know as society, as that between the Blois gargoyles on Peter Van Degen's roof and the skeleton walls supporting them.

That was what "they" had always said; what, at least, the Dagonet attitude, the Dagonet view of life, the very lines of the furniture in the old Dagonet house expressed.

Ralph sometimes called his mother and grandfather the Aborigines, and likened them to those vanishing denizens of the American continent doomed to rapid extinction with the advance of the invading race. He was fond of describing Washington Square as the "Reservation," and of prophesying that before long its inhabitants would be exhibited at ethnological shows, pathetically engaged in the exercise of their primitive industries.

Small, cautious, middle class had been the ideals of aboriginal New York; but it suddenly struck the young man that they were singularly coherent and respectable as contrasted with the chaos of indiscriminate appetites which made up its modern tendencies. He too had wanted to be "modern," had revolted, half-humorously, against the restrictions and exclusions of the old code; and it must have been by one of the ironic reversions of heredity that, at this precise point, he began to see what there was to be said on the other side—*his* side, as he now felt it to be.

6

UPSTAIRS, in his brown firelit room, he threw himself into an armchair, and remembered . . .

Harvard first—then Oxford; then a year of wandering and rich initiation. Returning to New York, he had read law, and now had his desk in the office of the respectable firm in whose charge the Dagonet estate had moldered for several generations. But his profession was the least real thing in his life. The realities lay about him now: the books jamming his old college bookcases and overflowing on chairs and tables; sketches, too—he could do charming things, if only he had known how to finish them!—and, on the writing-table at his elbow, scattered sheets of prose and verse; charming things, also, but, like the sketches, unfinished.

Nothing in the Dagonet and Marvell tradition was opposed to this desultory dabbling with life. For four or five generations it had been the rule of both houses that a young fellow should go to Columbia or Harvard, read law, and then lapse into more or less cultivated inaction. The only essential was that he should live "like a gentleman"—that is, with a tranquil disdain for mere money-getting, a passive openness to the finer sensations, one or two fixed principles as to the quality of wine, and an archaic probity that had not yet learned to distinguish between private and "business" honor.

No equipment could more thoroughly have unfitted the modern youth for getting on: it hardly needed the scribbled pages on the desk to complete the hopelessness of Ralph Marvell's case. He had accepted the fact with a humorous fatalism. Material resources were limited on both sides of the house, but there would always be enough for his frugal wants—enough to buy books (not "editions"), and pay now and then for a holiday dash to the great centers of art and ideas. And meanwhile there was the world of wonders within him. As a boy at the seaside, Ralph, between tides, had once come on a cave—a secret inaccessible place with glaucous lights, mysterious murmurs, and a single shaft of communication with the sky. He had kept his find from the other boys, not churlishly, for he was always an outspoken lad, but because he felt there were things about the cave that the others, good fellows as they all were, couldn't be expected to understand, and that, anyhow, it would never be quite his cave again after he had let his thick-set freckled cousins play smuggler and pirate in it.

And so with his inner world. Though so colored by outer impressions, it wove a secret curtain about him, and he came and went in it with the same joy of furtive possession. One day, of course, someone would discover it and reign there with him—no, reign over it and him. Once or twice already a light foot had reached the threshold. His cousin Clare Dagonet, for instance: there had been a summer when her voice had sounded far down the windings . . . but he had run over to Spain for the autumn, and when he came back she was engaged to Peter Van Degen, and for a while it looked black in the cave. That was long ago, as time is reckoned under thirty; and for three years now he had felt for her only a half-contemptuous pity. To have stood at the mouth of his cave, and have turned from it to the Van Degen lair —!

Poor Clare repented, indeed—she wanted it clearly understood—but she repented in the Van Degen diamonds, and the Van Degen motor bore her broken heart from opera to ball. She had been subdued to what she worked in, and she could never again find her way to the enchanted cave. . . . Ralph, since then, had reached the point of deciding that he would never marry; reached it not suddenly or dramatically, but with such sober advisedness as is urged on those about to take the opposite step. What he most wanted, now that the first flutter of being was over, was to learn and to do—to know what the great people had thought, think about their thinking, and then launch his own boat: write some good verse if possible; if not, then critical prose. A dramatic poem lay among the stuff at his elbow; but the prose critic was at his elbow, too, and not to be satisfied about the poem; and poet and critic passed the nights in hot if unproductive debate. On the whole, it seemed likely that the critic would win the day, and the essay on "The Rhythmical Structures of Walt Whitman" take shape before "The Banished God." Yet if the light in the cave was less supernaturally blue, the chant of its tides less laden with unimaginable music, it was still a thronged and echoing place when Undine Spragg appeared on its threshold. . . .

His mother and sister, of course, wanted him to marry. They had the usual theory that he was "made" for conjugal bliss: women always thought that of a fellow who didn't get drunk and have low tastes. Ralph smiled at the idea as he sat crouched among his secret treasures. Marry—but whom, in the name of light and freedom? The daughters of his own race sold themselves to the invaders; the daughters of the invaders bought their husbands as they bought an opera-box. It ought all to have been transacted on the Stock Exchange. His mother, he knew, had no such ambitions for him: she would have liked him to fancy a "nice girl" like Harriet Ray. Harriet Ray was neither vulgar nor ambitious. She regarded Washington Square as the birthplace of society, knew by heart all the cousinships of early New

York, hated motorcars, could not make herself understood on the telephone, and was determined, if she married, never to receive a divorced woman. As Mrs. Marvell often said, such girls as Harriet were growing rare. Ralph was not sure about this. He was inclined to think that, certain modifications allowed for, there would always be plenty of Harriet Rays for unworldly mothers to commend to their sons; and he had no desire to diminish their number by removing one from the ranks of the marriageable. He had no desire to marry at all—that had been the whole truth of it till he met Undine Spragg. And now —? He lit a cigar, and began to recall his hour's conversation with Mrs. Spragg.

Ralph had never taken his mother's social faiths very seriously. Survey-ing the march of civilization from a loftier angle, he had early mingled with the invaders, and curiously observed their rites and customs. But most of those he had met had already been modified by contact with the indige-nous: they spoke the same language as his, though on their lips it had often so different a meaning. Ralph had never seen them actually in the making, before they had acquired the speech of the conquered race. But Mrs. Spragg still used the dialect of her people, and before the end of the visit Ralph had ceased to regret that her daughter was out. He felt obscurely that in the girl's presence—frank and simple as he thought her—he should have learned less of life in early Apex.

Mrs. Spragg, once reconciled—or at least resigned—to the mysterious necessity of having to "entertain" a friend of Undine's, had yielded to the first touch on the weak springs of her garrulity. She had not seen Mrs. Heeny for two days, and this friendly young man with the gentle manner was almost as easy to talk to as the masseuse. And then she could tell him things that Mrs. Heeny already knew, and Mrs. Spragg liked to repeat her stories. To do so gave her almost her sole sense of permanence among the shifting scenes of life. So that, after she had lengthily deplored the untoward accident of Undine's absence, and her visitor, with a smile, and echoes of *divers et ondoyant* in his brain, had repeated her daughter's name after her, saying: "It's a wonderful find—how could you tell it would be such a fit?"—it came to her quite easily to answer: "Why, we called her after a hair-waver father put on the market the week she was born —" and then to explain, as he remained struck and silent: "It's from *undoolay*, you know, the French for crimping; Father always thought the name made it take. He was quite a scholar, and had the greatest knack for finding names. I remember the time he invented his Goliath Glue he sat up all night over the Bible to get the name. . . . No, Father didn't start *in* as a druggist," she went on, ex-panding with the signs of Marvell's interest; "he was educated for an under-taker, and built up a first-class business; but he was always a beautiful speaker, and after a while he sorter drifted into the ministry. Of course, it didn't pay him anything like as well, so finally he opened a drugstore, and he did first-rate at that, too, though his heart was always in the pulpit. But after he made such a success with his hair-waver he got speculating in land out at Apex, and somehow everything went—though Mr. Spragg did all he *could* —." Mrs. Spragg, when she found herself embarked on a long sentence, always ballasted it by italicizing the last word.

Her husband, she continued, could not, at the time, do much for his father-in-law. Mr. Spragg had come to Apex as a poor boy, and their early married life had been a protracted struggle, darkened by domestic affliction. Two of their three children had died of typhoid in the epidemic which devastated Apex before the new waterworks were built; and this calamity, by causing Mr. Spragg to resolve that thereafter Apex should drink pure water, had led directly to the founding of his fortunes.

"He had taken over some of poor father's land for a bad debt, and when he got up the Pure Water Move the company voted to buy the land and build the new reservoir up there: and after that we began to be better off, and it *did* seem as if it had come out so to comfort us some about the children."

Mr. Spragg, thereafter, had begun to be a power in Apex, and fat years had followed on the lean. Ralph Marvell was too little versed in affairs to read between the lines of Mrs. Spragg's untutored narrative, and he understood no more than she the occult connection between Mr. Spragg's domestic misfortunes and his business triumph. Mr. Spragg had "helped out" his ruined father-in-law, and had vowed on his children's graves that no Apex child should ever again drink poisoned water—and out of those two disinterested impulses, by some impressive law of compensation, material prosperity had come. What Ralph understood and appreciated was Mrs. Spragg's unaffected frankness in talking of her early life. Here was no retrospective pretense of an opulent past, such as the other invaders were given to parading before the bland but undeceived subject race. The Spraggs had been "plain people" and had not yet learned to be ashamed of it. The fact drew them much closer to the Dagonet ideals than any sham elegance in the past tense. Ralph felt that his mother, who shuddered away from Mrs. Harmon B. Driscoll, would understand and esteem Mrs. Spragg.

But how long would their virgin innocence last? Popple's vulgar hands were on it already—Popple's and the unspeakable Van Degen's! Once they and theirs had begun the process of initiating Undine, there was no knowing—or rather there was too easy knowing—how it would end! It was incredible that she too should be destined to swell the ranks of the cheaply fashionable; yet were not her very freshness, her malleability, the mark of her fate? She was still at the age when the flexible soul offers itself to the first grasp. That the grasp should chance to be Van Degen's—that was what made Ralph's temples buzz, and swept away all his plans for his own future like a beaver's dam in a spring flood. To save her from Van Degen and Van Degenism: was that really to be his mission—the "call" for which his life had obscurely waited? It was not in the least what he had meant to do with

the fugitive flash of consciousness he called self; but all that he had pur-
posed for that transitory being sank into insignificance under the pressure of
Undine's claims.

Ralph Marvell's notion of women had been formed on the experiences
common to good-looking young men of his kind. Women were drawn to
him as much by his winning appealing quality, by the sense of a youthful
warmth behind his light ironic exterior, as by his charms of face and mind.
Except during Clare Dagonet's brief reign the depths in him had not been
stirred; but in taking what each sentimental episode had to give he had
preserved, through all his minor adventures, his faith in the great adventure
to come. It was this faith that made him so easy a victim when love had at
last appeared clad in the attributes of romance: the imaginative man's inde-
structible dream of a rounded passion.

The clearness with which he judged the girl and himself seemed the
surest proof that his feeling was more than a surface thrill. He was not blind
to her crudity and her limitations, but they were a part of her grace and her
persuasion. *Diverse et ondoyante*—so he had seen her from the first. But was
not that merely the sign of a quicker response to the world's manifold
appeal? There was Harriet Ray, sealed up tight in the vacuum of inherited
opinion, where not a breath of fresh sensation could get at her: there could
be no call to rescue young ladies so secured from the perils of reality!
Undine had no such traditional safeguards—Ralph guessed Mrs. Spragg's
opinions to be as fluid as her daughter's—and the girl's very sensitiveness to
new impressions, combined with her obvious lack of any sense of relative
values, would make her an easy prey to the powers of folly. He seemed to see
her—as he sat there, pressing his fists into his temples—he seemed to see
her like a lovely rock-bound Andromeda, with the devouring monster Society careering up to make a mouthful of her; and himself whirling down on
his winged horse—just Pegasus turned Rosinante for the nonce—to cut her
bonds, snatch her up, and whirl her back into the blue. . . .

7

SOME two months later than the date of young Marvell's midnight vigil,
Mrs. Heeny, seated on a low chair at Undine's knee, gave the girl's left
hand an approving pat as she laid aside her lapful of polishers.

"There! I guess you can put your ring on again," she said with a laugh of
jovial significance; and Undine, echoing the laugh in a murmur of compla-

cency, slipped on the fourth finger of her recovered hand a band of sapphires in an intricate setting.

Mrs. Heeny took up the hand again. "Them's old stones, Undine—they've got a different look," she said, examining the ring while she rubbed her cushioned palm over the girl's brilliant fingertips. "And the setting's quaint—I wouldn't wonder but what it was one of old Gran'ma Dagonet's."

Mrs. Spragg, hovering near in fond beatitude, looked up quickly.

"Why, don't you s'pose he *bought* it for her, Mrs. Heeny? It came in a Tiff'ny box."

The manicure laughed again. "Of course he's had Tiff'ny rub it up. Ain't you ever heard of ancestral jewels, Mrs. Spragg? In the Eu-ropean aristocracy they never go out and *buy* engagement rings; and Undine's marrying into our aristocracy."

Mrs. Spragg looked relieved. "Oh, I thought maybe they were trying to scrimp on the ring —"

Mrs. Heeny, shrugging away this explanation, rose from her seat and rolled back her shiny black sleeves.

"Look at here, Undine, if you really want me to do your hair it's time we got to work."

The girl swung about in her seat so that she faced the mirror on the dressing-table. Her shoulders shone through transparencies of lace and muslin which slipped back as she lifted her arms to draw the tortoiseshell pins from her hair.

"Of course you've got to do it—I want to look perfectly lovely!"

"Well—I dunno's my hand's in nowadays," said Mrs. Heeny in a tone that belied the doubt she cast on her own ability.

"Oh, you're an *artist*, Mrs. Heeny—and I just couldn't have had that French maid 'round tonight," sighed Mrs. Spragg, sinking into a chair near the dressing-table.

Undine, with a backward toss of her head, scattered her loose locks about her. As they spread and sparkled under Mrs. Heeny's touch, Mrs. Spragg leaned back, drinking in through half-closed lids her daughter's loveliness. Some new quality seemed added to Undine's beauty: it had a milder bloom, a kind of melting grace, which might have been lent to it by the moisture in her mother's eyes.

"So you're to see the old gentleman for the first time at this dinner?" Mrs. Heeny pursued, sweeping the live strands up into a loosely woven crown.

"Yes. I'm frightened to death!" Undine, laughing confidently, took up a hand-glass and scrutinized the small brown mole above the curve of her upper lip.

"I guess she'll know how to talk to him," Mrs. Spragg averred with a kind of quavering triumph.

"She'll know how to *look* at him, anyhow," said Mrs. Heeny; and Undine smiled at her own image.

"I hope he won't think I'm too awful!"

Mrs. Heeny laughed. "Did you read the description of yourself in the *Radiator* this morning? I wish't I'd 'a had time to cut it out. I guess I'll have to start a separate bag for *your* clippings soon."

Undine stretched her arms luxuriously above her head and gazed through lowered lids at the foreshortened reflection of her face.

"Mercy! Don't jerk about like that. Am I to put in this rose?—There— you *are* lovely!" Mrs. Heeny sighed, as the pink petals sank into the hair above the girl's forehead.

Undine pushed her chair back, and sat supporting her chin on her clasped hands while she studied the result of Mrs. Heeny's manipulations.

"Yes—that's the way Mrs. Peter Van Degen's flower was put in the other night; only hers was a camellia. Do you think I'd look better with a camellia?"

"I guess if Mrs. Van Degen looked like a rose she'd 'a worn a rose," Mrs. Heeny rejoined poetically. "Sit still a minute longer," she added. "Your hair's so heavy I'd feel easier if I was to put in another pin."

Undine remained motionless, and the manicure, suddenly laying both hands on the girl's shoulders, and bending over to peer at her reflection, said playfully: "Ever been engaged before, Undine?"

A blush rose to the face in the mirror, spreading from chin to brow, and running rosily over the white shoulders from which their covering had slipped down.

"My! If he could see you now!" Mrs. Heeny jested.

Mrs. Spragg, rising noiselessly, glided across the room and became lost in a minute examination of the dress laid out on the bed.

With a supple twist Undine slipped from Mrs. Heeny's hold.

"Engaged? Mercy, yes! Didn't you know? To the Prince of Wales. I broke it off because I wouldn't live in the Tower."

Mrs. Spragg, lifting the dress cautiously over her arm, advanced with a reassured smile.

"I s'pose Undie'll go to Europe now," she said to Mrs. Heeny.

"I guess Undie *will!*" the young lady herself declared. "We're going to sail right afterward. Here, Mother, do be careful of my hair!" She ducked gracefully to slip into the lacy fabric which her mother held above her head.

As she rose Venuslike above its folds there was a tap on the door, immediately followed by its tentative opening.

"Mabel!" Undine muttered, her brows lowering like her father's; and Mrs. Spragg, wheeling about to screen her daughter, addressed herself protestingly to the half-open door.

"Who's there? Oh, that *you*, Mrs. Lipscomb? Well, I don't know as you *can*—Undie isn't half dressed yet —"

"Just like her—always pushing in!" Undine murmured as she slipped her arms into their transparent sleeves.

"Oh, that don't matter—I'll help dress her!" Mrs. Lipscomb's large blond person surged across the threshold. "Seems to me I ought to lend a hand tonight, considering I was the one that introduced them!"

Undine forced a smile, but Mrs. Spragg, her soft wrinkles deepening with resentment, muttered to Mrs. Heeny, as she bent down to shake out the girl's train: "I guess my daughter's only got to show herself —"

The first meeting with old Mr. Dagonet was less formidable than Undine had expected. She had been once before to the house in Washington Square, when, with her mother, she had returned Mrs. Marvell's ceremonial visit; but on that occasion Ralph's grandfather had not been present. All the rites connected with her engagement were new and mysterious to Undine, and none more so than the unaccountable necessity of "dragging"—as she phrased it—Mrs. Spragg into the affair. It was an accepted article of the Apex creed that parental detachment should be completest at the moment when the filial fate was decided; and to find that New York reversed this rule was as puzzling to Undine as to her mother. Mrs. Spragg was so unprepared for the part she was to play that on the occasion of her visit to Mrs. Marvell her helplessness had infected Undine, and their half-hour in the sober faded drawingroom remained among the girl's most unsatisfactory memories.

She reentered it alone with more assurance. Her confidence in her beauty had hitherto carried her through every ordeal; and it was fortified now by the feeling of power that came with the sense of being loved. If they would only leave her mother out she was sure, in her own phrase, of being able to "run the thing", and Mrs. Spragg had providentially been left out of the Dagonet dinner.

It was to consist, it appeared, only of the small family group Undine had already met; and, seated at old Mr. Dagonet's right, in the high dark diningroom with mahogany doors and dim portraits of "Signers" and their females, she felt a conscious joy in her ascendancy. Old Mr. Dagonet—small, frail and softly sardonic—appeared to fall at once under her spell. If she felt, beneath his amenity, a kind of delicate dangerousness, like that of some fine surgical instrument, she ignored it as unimportant; for she had as yet no clear perception of forces that did not directly affect her.

Mrs. Marvell, low-voiced, faded, yet impressive, was less responsive to her arts, and Undine divined in her the head of the opposition to Ralph's marriage. Mrs. Heeny had reported that Mrs. Marvell had other views for her son; and this was confirmed by such echoes of the short sharp struggle as reached the throbbing listeners at the Stentorian. But the conflict over, the air had immediately cleared, showing the enemy in the act of unconditional surrender. It surprised Undine that there had been no reprisals, no return on the points conceded. That was not her idea of warfare, and she could ascribe the completeness of the victory only to the effect of her charms.

Mrs. Marvell's manner did not express entire subjugation; yet she seemed anxious to dispel any doubts of her good faith, and if she left the burden of the talk to her lively daughter it might have been because she felt more capable of showing indulgence by her silence than in her speech.

As for Mrs. Fairford, she had never seemed more brilliantly bent on fusing the various elements under her hand. Undine had already discovered that she adored her brother, and had guessed that this would make her either a strong ally or a determined enemy. The latter alternative, however, did not alarm the girl. She thought Mrs. Fairford "bright," and wanted to be liked by her; and she was in the state of dizzy self-assurance when it seemed easy to win any sympathy she chose to seek.

For the only other guests—Mrs. Fairford's husband, and the elderly Charles Bowen who seemed to be her special friend—Undine had no attention to spare: they remained on a plane with the dim pictures hanging at her back. She had expected a larger party; but she was relieved, on the whole, that it was small enough to permit of her dominating it. Not that she wished to do so by any loudness of assertion. Her quickness in noting external differences had already taught her to modulate and lower her voice, and to replace "The i-dea!" and "I wouldn't wonder" by more polished locutions; and she had not been ten minutes at table before she found that to seem very much in love, and a little confused and subdued by the newness and intensity of the sentiment, was, to the Dagonet mind, the becoming attitude for a young lady in her situation. The part was not hard to play, for she *was* in love, of course. It was pleasant, when she looked across the table, to meet Ralph's gray eyes, with that new look in them, and to feel that she had kindled it; but it was only part of her larger pleasure in the general homage to her beauty, in the sensations of interest and curiosity excited by everything about her, from the family portraits overhead to the old Dagonet silver on the table—which were to be hers, too, after all!

The talk, as at Mrs. Fairford's, confused her by its lack of the personal allusion, its tendency to turn to books, pictures and politics. "Politics," to Undine, had always been like a kind of back-kitchen to business—the place where the refuse was thrown and the doubtful messes were brewed. As a drawing-room topic, and one to provoke disinterested sentiments, it had the hollowness of Fourth of July orations, and her mind wandered in spite of the desire to appear informed and competent.

Old Mr. Dagonet, with his reedy staccato voice, that gave polish and relief to every syllable, tried to come to her aid by questioning her affably about her family and the friends she had made in New York. But the caryatid-parent, who exists simply as a filial prop, is not a fruitful theme, and Undine, called on for the first time to view her own progenitors as a subject of conversation, was struck by their lack of points. She had never paused to consider what her father and mother were "interested" in, and, challenged to specify, could have named—with sincerity—only herself. On the subject of her New York friends it was not much easier to enlarge; for so far her circle had grown less rapidly than she expected. She had fancied Ralph's wooing would at once admit her to all his social privileges; but he had shown a puzzling reluctance to introduce her to the Van Degen set, where he came and went with such familiarity; and the persons he seemed anxious to have her know—a few frumpy "clever women" of his sister's age, and one or two brisk old ladies in shabby houses with mahogany furniture and Stuart portraits—did not offer the opportunities she sought.

"Oh, I don't know many people yet—I tell Ralph he's got to hurry up and take me round," she said to Mr. Dagonet, with a side-sparkle for Ralph, whose gaze, between the flowers and lights, she was aware of perpetually drawing.

"My daughter will take you—you must know his mother's friends," the old gentleman rejoined while Mrs. Marvell smiled noncommittally.

"But you have a great friend of your own—the lady who takes you into society," Mr. Dagonet pursued; and Undine had the sense that the irrepressible Mabel was again "pushing in."

"Oh, yes—Mabel Lipscomb. We were schoolmates," she said indifferently.

"Lipscomb? Lipscomb? What is Mr. Lipscomb's occupation?"

"He's a broker," said Undine, glad to be able to place her friend's husband in so handsome a light. The subtleties of a professional classification unknown to Apex had already taught her that in New York it is more distinguished to be a broker than a dentist; and she was surprised at Mr. Dagonet's lack of enthusiasm.

"Ah? A broker?" He said it almost as Popple might have said "A *dentist?*" and Undine found herself astray in a new labyrinth of social distinctions. She felt a sudden contempt for Harry Lipscomb, who had already struck her as too loud, and irrelevantly comic. "I guess Mabel'll get a divorce pretty soon," she added, desiring, for personal reasons, to present Mrs. Lipscomb as favorably as possible.

Mr. Dagonet's handsome eyebrows drew together. "A divorce? H'm—that's bad. Has he been misbehaving himself?"

Undine looked innocently surprised. "Oh, I guess not. They like each other well enough. But he's been a disappointment to her. He isn't in the right set, and I think Mabel realizes she'll never really get anywhere till she gets rid of him."

These words, uttered in the high fluting tone that she rose to when sure of her subject, fell on a pause which prolonged and deepened itself to receive them, while every face at the table, Ralph Marvell's excepted, reflected in varying degree Mr. Dagonet's pained astonishment.

"But, my dear young lady—what would your friend's own situation be if, as you put it, she 'got rid' of her husband on so trivial a pretext?"

Undine, surprised at his dullness, tried to explain. "Oh, that wouldn't be the reason *given*, of course. Any lawyer could fix it up for them. Don't they generally call it desertion?"

There was another, more palpitating, silence, broken by a laugh from Ralph.

"*Ralph!*" his mother breathed; then, turning to Undine, she said with a constrained smile: "I believe in certain parts of the country such—unfortunate arrangements—are beginning to be tolerated. But in New York, in spite of our growing indifference, a divorced woman is still—thank heaven! —at a decided disadvantage."

Undine's eyes opened wide. Here at last was a topic that really interested her, and one that gave another amazing glimpse into the camera obscura of New York society. "Do you mean to say Mabel would be worse off, then? Couldn't she even go round as much as she does now?"

Mrs. Marvell met this gravely. "It would depend, I should say, on the kind of people she wished to see."

"Oh, the very best, of course! That would be her only object."

Ralph interposed with another laugh. "You see, Undine, you'd better think twice before you divorce me!"

"*Ralph!*" his mother again breathed; but the girl, flushed and sparkling, flung back: "Oh, it all depends on *you!* Out in Apex, if a girl marries a man who don't come up to what she expected, people consider it's to her credit to want to change. *You'd* better think twice of that!"

"If I were only sure of knowing what you expect!" he caught up her joke, tossing it back at her across the fascinated silence of their listeners.

"Why, *everything!*" she announced—and Mr. Dagonet, turning, laid an intricately veined old hand on hers, and said, with a change of tone that relaxed the tension of the listeners: "My child, if you look like that you'll get it."

8

I T was doubtless owing to Mrs. Fairford's foresight that such possibilities of tension were curtailed, after dinner, by her carrying off Ralph and his betrothed to the theater.

Mr. Dagonet, it was understood, always went to bed after an hour's whist with his daughter; and the silent Mr. Fairford gave his evenings to bridge at

his club. The party, therefore, consisted only of Undine and Ralph, with
Mrs. Fairford and her attendant friend. Undine vaguely wondered why the
grave and gray-haired Mr. Bowen formed so invariable a part of that lady's
train; but she concluded that it was the New York custom for married ladies
to have gentlemen " 'round" (as girls had in Apex), and that Mr. Bowen
was the sole survivor of Laura Fairford's earlier triumphs.

She had, however, little time to give to such conjectures, for the performance they were attending—the debut of a fashionable London actress—
had attracted a large audience in which Undine immediately recognized a
number of familiar faces. Her engagement had been announced only the day
before, and she had the delicious sense of being "in all the papers," and of
focusing countless glances of interest and curiosity as she swept through the
theater in Mrs. Fairford's wake. Their stalls were near the stage, and progress
thither was slow enough to permit of prolonged enjoyment of this sensation.
Before passing to her place she paused for Ralph to remove her cloak, and as
he lifted it from her shoulders she heard a lady say behind her: "There she is
—the one in white, with the lovely back—" and a man answer: "Gad!
Where did he find anything as good as that?"

Anonymous approval was sweet enough; but she was to taste a moment
more exquisite when, in the proscenium box across the house, she saw Clare
Van Degen seated beside the prim figure of Miss Harriet Ray. "They're here
to see me with him—they hate it, but they couldn't keep away!" She turned
and lifted a smile of possessorship to Ralph.

Mrs. Fairford seemed also struck by the presence of the two ladies, and
Undine heard her whisper to Mr. Bowen: "Do you see Clare over there—
and Harriet with her? Harriet *would come*—I call it Spartan! And so like
Clare to ask her!"

Her companion laughed. "It's one of the deepest instincts in human
nature. The murdered are as much given as the murderer to haunting the
scene of the crime."

Doubtless guessing Ralph's desire to have Undine to himself, Mrs.
Fairford had sent the girl in first; and Undine, as she seated herself, was
aware that the occupant of the next stall half turned to her, as with a vague
gesture of recognition. But just then the curtain rose, and she became absorbed in the development of the drama, especially as it tended to display
the remarkable toilets which succeeded each other on the person of its
leading lady. Undine, seated at Ralph Marvell's side, and feeling the thrill
of his proximity as a subtler element in the general interest she was exciting,
was at last repaid for the disappointment of her evening at the opera. It was
characteristic of her that she remembered her failures as keenly as her triumphs, and that the passionate desire to obliterate, to "get even" with
them, was always among the latent incentives of her conduct. Now at last
she was having what she wanted—she was in conscious possession of the
"real thing"; and through her other, more diffused, sensations Ralph's

adoration gave her such a last refinement of pleasure as might have come to some warrior queen borne in triumph by captive princes, and reading in the eyes of one the passion he dared not speak.

When the curtain fell this vague enjoyment was heightened by various acts of recognition. All the people she wanted to "go with," as they said in Apex, seemed to be about her in the stalls and boxes; and her eyes continued to revert with special satisfaction to the incongruous group formed by Mrs. Peter Van Degen and Miss Ray. The sight made it irresistible to whisper to Ralph: "You ought to go round and talk to your cousin. Have you told her we're engaged?"

"Clare? Of course. She's going to call on you tomorrow."

"Oh, she needn't put herself out—she's never been yet," said Undine loftily.

He made no rejoinder, but presently asked: "Who's that you're waving to?"

"Mr. Popple. He's coming round to see us. You know he wants to paint me." Undine fluttered and beamed as the brilliant Popple made his way across the stalls to the seat which her neighbor had momentarily left.

"First-rate chap next to you—whoever he is—to give me this chance," the artist declared. "Ha, Ralph, my boy, how did you pull it off? That's what we're all of us wondering." He leaned over to give Marvell's hand the ironic grasp of celibacy. "Well, you've left us lamenting: he has, you know, Miss Spragg. But I've got one pull over the others—I can paint you! He can't forbid that, can he? Not before marriage, anyhow!"

Undine divided her shining glances between the two. "I guess he isn't going to treat me any different afterward," she proclaimed with joyous defiance.

"Ah, well, there's no telling, you know. Hadn't we better begin at once? Seriously, I want awfully to get you into the spring show."

"Oh, really? That would be too lovely!"

"*You* would be, certainly—the way I mean to do you. But I see Ralph getting glum. Cheer up, my dear fellow; I daresay you'll be invited to some of the sittings—that's for Miss Spragg to say. Ah, here comes your neighbor back, confound him. . . . You'll let me know when we can begin?"

As Popple moved away Undine turned eagerly to Marvell. "Do you suppose there's time? I'd love to have him to do me!"

Ralph smiled. "My poor child—he *would* 'do' you, with a vengeance. Infernal cheek, his asking you to sit —"

She stared. "But why? He's painted your cousin, and all the smart women."

"Oh, if a 'smart' portrait's all you want!"

"I want what the others want," she answered, frowning and pouting a little.

She was already beginning to resent in Ralph the slightest sign of resistance to her pleasure; and her resentment took the form—a familiar one in Apex courtships—of turning on him, in the next entr'acte, a deliberately averted shoulder. The result of this was to bring her, for the first time, in more direct relation to her other neighbor. As she turned he turned too, showing her, above a shining shirt-front fastened with a large imitation pearl, a ruddy plump snub face without an angle in it, which yet looked sharper than a razor. Undine's eyes met his with a startled look, and for a long moment they remained suspended on each other's stare.

Undine at length shrank back with an unrecognizing face; but her movement made her opera-glass slip to the floor, and her neighbor bent down and picked it up.

"Well—don't you know me yet?" he said with a slight smile, as he restored the glass to her.

She had grown white to the lips, and when she tried to speak the effort produced only a faint click in her throat. She felt that the change in her appearance must be visible, and the dread of letting Marvell see it made her continue to turn her ravaged face to her other neighbor. The round black eyes set prominently in the latter's round glossy countenance had expressed at first only an impersonal and slightly ironic interest; but a look of surprise grew in them as Undine's silence continued.

"What's the matter? Don't you want me to speak to you?"

She became aware that Marvell, as if unconscious of her slight show of displeasure, had left his seat, and was making his way toward the aisle; and this assertion of independence, which a moment before she would so deeply have resented, now gave her a feeling of intense relief.

"No—don't speak to me, please. I'll tell you another time—I'll write." Her neighbor continued to gaze at her, forming his lips into a noiseless whistle under his small dark moustache.

"Well, I— That's about the stiffest," he murmured; and as she made no answer he added: "Afraid I'll ask to be introduced to your friend?"

She made a faint movement of entreaty. "I can't explain. I promise to see you; but I *ask* you not to talk to me now."

He unfolded his program, and went on speaking in a low tone while he affected to study it. "Anything to oblige, of course. That's always been my motto. But *is* it a bargain—fair and square? You'll see me?"

She receded farther from him. "I promise. I—I *want* to," she faltered.

"All right, then. Call me up in the morning at the Driscoll Building. Seven-o-nine—got it?"

She nodded, and he added in a still lower tone: "I suppose I can congratulate you, anyhow?" and then, without waiting for her reply, turned to study Mrs. Van Degen's box through his opera-glass.

Clare, as if aware of the scrutiny fixed on her from below, leaned back and threw a question over her shoulder to Ralph Marvell, who had just seated himself behind her.

"Who's the funny man with the red face talking to Miss Spragg?"

Ralph bent forward. "The man next to her? Never saw him before. But I think you're mistaken: she's not speaking to him."

"She *was*— Wasn't she, Harriet?"

Miss Ray pinched her lips together without speaking, and Mrs. Van Degen paused for the fraction of a second. "Perhaps he's an Apex friend," she then suggested.

"Very likely. Only I think she'd have introduced him if he had been."

His cousin faintly shrugged. "Shall you encourage that?"

Peter Van Degen, who had strayed into his wife's box for a moment, caught the colloquy, and lifted his opera-glass.

"The fellow next to Miss Spragg? (By George, Ralph, she's ripping to-night!) Wait a minute—I know his face. Saw him in old Harmon Driscoll's office the day of the Eubaw mine meeting. This chap's his secretary, or something. Driscoll called him in to give some facts to the directors, and he seemed a mighty wide-awake customer."

Clare Van Degen turned gaily to her cousin. "If he has anything to do with the Driscolls you'd better cultivate him! That's the kind of acquaintance the Dagonets have always needed. I married to set them an example!"

Ralph rose with a laugh. "You're right. I'll hurry back and make his acquaintance." He held out his hand to his cousin, avoiding her disappointed eyes.

Undine, on entering her bedroom late that evening, was startled by the presence of a muffled figure which revealed itself, through the dimness, as the ungirded midnight outline of Mrs. Spragg.

"*Mother?* What on earth —?" the girl exclaimed, as Mrs. Spragg pressed the electric button and flooded the room with light. The idea of a mother's sitting up for her daughter was so foreign to Apex customs that it roused only mistrust and irritation in the object of the demonstration.

Mrs. Spragg came forward deprecatingly to lift the cloak from her daughter's shoulders.

"I just *had* to, Undie—I told Father I *had* to. I wanted to hear all about it."

Undine shrugged away from her. "Mercy! At this hour? You'll be as white as a sheet tomorrow, sitting up all night like this."

She moved toward the toilet-table, and began to demolish with feverish hands the structure which Mrs. Heeny, a few hours earlier, had so lovingly raised. But the rose caught in a mesh of hair, and Mrs. Spragg, venturing timidly to release it, had a full view of her daughter's face in the glass.

"Why, Undie, *you're* as white as a sheet now! You look fairly sick. What's the matter, Daughter?"

The girl broke away from her.

"Oh, can't you leave me alone, Mother? There—do I look white *now?*"

she cried, the blood flaming into her pale cheeks; and as Mrs. Spragg shrank back, she added more mildly, in the tone of a parent rebuking a persistent child: "It's enough to *make* anybody sick to be stared at that way!"

Mrs. Spragg overflowed with compunction. "I'm so sorry, Undie. I guess it was just seeing you in this glare of light."

"Yes—the light's awful; do turn some off," ordered Undine, for whom, ordinarily, no radiance was too strong; and Mrs. Spragg, grateful to have commands laid upon her, hastened to obey.

Undine, after this, submitted in brooding silence to having her dress unlaced, and her slippers and dressing-gown brought to her. Mrs. Spragg visibly yearned to say more, but she restrained the impulse lest it should, provoke her dismissal.

"Won't you take just a sup of milk before you go to bed?" she suggested at length, as Undine sank into an armchair. "I've got some for you right here in the parlor."

Without looking up the girl answered: "No. I don't want anything. Do go to bed."

Her mother seemed to be struggling between the lifelong instinct of obedience and a swift unformulated fear. "I'm going, Undie." She wavered. "Didn't they receive you right, Daughter?" she asked with sudden resolution.

"What nonsense! How *should* they receive me? Everybody was lovely to me." Undine rose to her feet and went on with her undressing, tossing her clothes on the floor and shaking her hair over her bare shoulders.

Mrs. Spragg stooped to gather up the scattered garments as they fell, folding them with a wistful caressing touch, and laying them on the lounge, without daring to raise her eyes to her daughter. It was not till she heard Undine throw herself on the bed that she went toward her and drew the coverlet up with deprecating hands.

"Oh, do put the light out—I'm dead tired," the girl grumbled, pressing her face into the pillow.

Mrs. Spragg turned away obediently; then, gathering all her scattered impulses into a passionate act of courage, she moved back to the bedside.

"Undie—you didn't see anybody—I mean at the theater? *Anybody you didn't want to see?"*

Undine, at the question, raised her head and started upright against the tossed pillows, her white exasperated face close to her mother's twitching features. The two women examined each other a moment, fear and anger in their crossed glances; then Undine answered: "No, nobody. Good night."

9

UNDINE, late the next day, waited alone under the leafless trellising of a wisteria arbor on the west side of the Central Park. She had put on her plainest dress, and wound a closely patterned veil over her least vivid hat; but even thus toned down to the situation she was conscious of blazing out from it inconveniently.

The habit of meeting young men in sequestered spots was not unknown to her: the novelty was in feeling any embarrassment about it. Even now she was disturbed not so much by the unlikely chance of an accidental encounter with Ralph Marvell as by the remembrance of similar meetings, far from accidental, with the romantic Aaronson. Could it be that the hand now adorned with Ralph's engagement ring had once, in this very spot, surrendered itself to the riding-master's pressure? At the thought a wave of physical disgust passed over her, blotting out another memory as distasteful but more remote.

It was revived by the appearance of a ruddy middle-sized young man, his stoutish figure tightly buttoned into a square-shouldered overcoat, who presently approached along the path that led to the arbor. Silhouetted against the slope of the asphalt, the newcomer revealed an outline thick yet compact, with a round head set on a neck in which, at the first chance, prosperity would be likely to develop a red crease. His face, with its rounded surfaces, and the sanguine innocence of a complexion belied by prematurely astute black eyes, had a look of jovial cunning which Undine had formerly thought "smart" but which now struck her as merely vulgar. She felt that in the Marvell set Elmer Moffatt would have been stamped as "not a gentleman." Nevertheless something in his look seemed to promise the capacity to develop into any character he might care to assume; though it did not seem probable that, for the present, that of a gentleman would be among them. He had always had a brisk swaggering step, and the faintly impudent tilt of the head that she had once thought "dashing"; but whereas this look had formerly denoted a somewhat desperate defiance of the world and its judgments it now suggested an almost assured relation to these powers; and Undine's heart sank at the thought of what the change implied.

As he drew nearer, the young man's air of assurance was replaced by an expression of mildly humorous surprise.

"Well—this is white of you, Undine!" he said, taking her lifeless fingers into his dapperly gloved hand.

Through her veil she formed the words: "I said I'd come."

He laughed. "That's so. And you see I believed you. Though I might not have —"

"I don't see the use of beginning like this," she interrupted nervously.

"That's so too. Suppose we walk along a little ways? It's rather chilly standing round."

He turned down the path that descended toward the Ramble and the girl moved on beside him with her long flowing steps.

When they had reached the comparative shelter of the interlacing trees Moffatt paused again to say: "If we're going to talk I'd like to see you, Undine"; and after a first moment of reluctance she submissively threw back her veil.

He let his eyes rest on her in silence; then he said judicially: "You've filled out some; but you're paler." After another appreciative scrutiny he added: "There's mighty few women as well worth looking at, and I'm obliged to you for letting me have the chance again."

Undine's brows drew together, but she softened her frown to a quivering smile.

"I'm glad to see you too, Elmer—I am, *really!*"

He returned her smile while his glance continued to study her humorously. "You didn't betray the fact last night, Miss Spragg."

"I was so taken aback. I thought you were out in Alaska somewhere."

The young man shaped his lips into the mute whistle by which he habitually vented his surprise. "You *did?* Didn't Abner E. Spragg tell you he'd seen me downtown?"

Undine gave him a startled glance. "Father? Why, have you seen him? He never said a word about it!"

Her companion's whistle became audible. "He's running yet!" he said gaily. "I wish I could scare some people as easy as I can your father."

The girl hesitated. "I never felt toward you the way Father did," she hazarded at length; and he gave her another long look in return.

"Well, if they'd left you alone I don't believe you'd ever have acted mean to me," was the conclusion he drew from it.

"I didn't mean to, Elmer. . . . I give you my word—but I was so young . . . I didn't know anything. . . ."

His eyes had a twinkle of reminiscent pleasantry. "No—I don't suppose it *would* teach a girl much to be engaged two years to a stiff like Millard Binch; and that was about all that had happened to you before I came along."

Undine flushed to the forehead. "Oh, Elmer—I was only a child when I was engaged to Millard —"

"That's a fact. And you went on being one a good while afterward. *The Apex Eagle* always headlined you 'The child-bride' —"

"I can't see what's the use—now —."

"That ruled out of court too? See here, Undine—what *can* we talk about? I understood that was what we were here for."

"Of course." She made an effort at recovery. "I only meant to say—what's the use of raking up things that are over?"

"Rake up? That's the idea, is it? Was that why you tried to cut me last night?"

"I—oh, Elmer! I didn't mean to; only, you see, I'm engaged."

"Oh, I saw that fast enough. I'd have seen it even if I didn't read the papers." He gave a short laugh. "He was feeling pretty good, sitting there alongside of you, wasn't he? I don't wonder he was. I remember. But I don't see that that was a reason for cold-shouldering me. I'm a respectable member of society now—I'm one of Harmon B. Driscoll's private secretaries." He brought out the fact with mock solemnity.

But to Undine, though undoubtedly impressive, the statement did not immediately present itself as a subject for pleasantry.

"Elmer Moffatt—you *are?*"

He laughed again. "Guess you'd have remembered me last night if you'd known it."

She was following her own train of thought with a look of pale intensity. "You're *living* in New York, then—you're going to live here right along?"

"Well, it looks that way; as long as I can hang on to this job. Great men always gravitate to the metropolis. And I gravitated here just as Uncle Harmon B. was looking round for somebody who could give him an inside tip on the Eubaw mine deal—you know the Driscolls are pretty deep in Eubaw. I happened to go out there after our little unpleasantness at Apex, and it was just the time the deal went through. So in one way your folks did me a good turn when they made Apex too hot for me: funny to think of, ain't it?"

Undine, recovering herself, held out her hand impulsively.

"I'm real glad of it—I mean I'm real glad you've had such a stroke of luck!"

"Much obliged," he returned. "By the way, you might mention the fact to Abner E. Spragg next time you run across him."

"Father'll be real glad, too, Elmer." She hesitated, and then went on: "You must see now that it was natural Father and Mother should have felt the way they did —"

"Oh, the only thing that struck me as unnatural was their making you feel so, too. But I'm free to admit I wasn't a promising case in those days." His glance played over her for a moment. "Say, Undine—it was good while it lasted, though, wasn't it?"

She shrank back with a burning face and eyes of misery.

"Why, what's the matter? That ruled out, too? Oh, all right. Look at here, Undine, suppose you let me know what you *are* here to talk about, anyhow."

She cast a helpless glance down the windings of the wooded glen in which they had halted.

"Just to ask you—to beg you—not to say anything of this kind again—*ever* —"

"Anything about you and me?"

She nodded mutely.

"Why, what's wrong? Anybody been saying anything against me?"

"Oh, no. It's not that!"

"What on earth *is* it, then—except that you're ashamed of me, one way or another?" She made no answer, and he stood digging the tip of his walking-stick into a fissure of the asphalt. At length he went on in a tone that showed a first faint trace of irritation: "I don't want to break into your gilt-edged crowd, if it's that you're scared of."

His tone seemed to increase her distress. "No, no—you don't understand. All I want is that nothing shall be known."

"Yes; but *why*? It was all straight enough, if you come to that."

"It doesn't matter . . . whether it was straight . . . or . . . not. . . ." He interpolated a whistle which made her add: "What I mean is that out here in the East they don't even like it if a girl's been *engaged* before."

This last strain on his credulity wrung a laugh from Moffatt. "Gee! How'd they expect her fair young life to pass? Playing 'Holy City' on the melodeon, and knitting tidies for church fairs?"

"Girls are looked after here. It's all different. Their mothers go round with them."

This increased her companion's hilarity and he glanced about him with a pretense of compunction. "Excuse *me*! I ought to have remembered. Where's your chaperon, Miss Spragg?" He crooked his arm with mock ceremony. "Allow me to escort you to the bew-fay. You see I'm onto the New York style myself."

A sigh of discouragement escaped her. "Elmer—if you really believe I never wanted to act mean to you, don't you act mean to me now!"

"Act mean?" He grew serious again and moved nearer to her. "What is it you want, Undine? Why can't you say it right out?"

"What I told you. I don't want Ralph Marvell—or any of them—to know anything. If any of his folks found out, they'd never let him marry me —never! And he wouldn't want to: he'd be so horrified. And it would *kill* me, Elmer—it would just kill me!"

She pressed close to him, forgetful of her new reserves and repugnances, and impelled by the passionate absorbing desire to wring from him some definite pledge of safety.

"Oh, Elmer, if you ever liked me, help me now, and I'll help you if I get the chance!"

He had recovered his coolness as hers forsook her, and stood his ground

steadily, though her entreating hands, her glowing face, were near enough
to have shaken less sturdy nerves.

"That so, Puss? You just ask me to pass the sponge over Elmer Moffatt of
Apex City? Cut the gentleman when we meet? That the size of it?"

"Oh, Elmer, it's my first chance—I can't lose it!" she broke out, sobbing.

"Nonsense, child! Of course you shan't. Here, look up, Undine—why, I
never saw you cry before. Don't you be afraid of me—*I* ain't going to
interrupt the wedding march." He began to whistle a bar of *Lohengrin*. "I
only just want one little promise in return."

She threw a startled look at him and he added reassuringly: "Oh, don't
mistake me. I don't want to butt into your set—not for social purposes,
anyhow; but if ever it should come handy to know any of 'em in a business
way, would you fix it up for me—*after you're married?*"

Their eyes met, and she remained silent for a tremulous moment or two;
then she held out her hand. "Afterward—yes. I promise. And *you* promise,
Elmer?"

"Oh, to have and to hold!" he sang out, swinging about to follow her as
she hurriedly began to retrace her steps.

The March twilight had fallen, and the Stentorian facade was all aglow,
when Undine regained its monumental threshold. She slipped through the
marble vestibule and soared skyward in the mirror-lined lift, hardly conscious of the direction she was taking. What she wanted was solitude, and
the time to put some order into her thoughts; and she hoped to steal into
her room without meeting her mother. Through her thick veil the clusters
of lights in the Spragg drawing-room dilated and flowed together in a yellow
blur, from which, as she entered, a figure detached itself; and with a start of
annoyance she saw Ralph Marvell rise from the perusal of the "fiction
number" of a magazine which had replaced *The Hound of the Baskervilles* on
the onyx table.

"Yes; you told me not to come—and here I am." He lifted her hand to
his lips as his eyes tried to find hers through the veil.

She drew back with a nervous gesture. "I told you I'd be awfully late."

"I know—trying on! And you're horribly tired, and wishing with all
your might I wasn't here."

"I'm not so sure I'm not!" she rejoined, trying to hide her vexation in
a smile.

"What a tragic little voice! You really *are* done up. I couldn't help
dropping in for a minute; but of course if you say so I'll be off." She was
removing her long gloves, and he took her hands and drew her close. "Only
take off your veil, and let me see you."

A quiver of resistance ran through her: he felt it and dropped her hands.

"Please don't tease. I never could bear it," she stammered, drawing
away.

"Till tomorrow, then; that is, if the dressmakers permit."

She forced a laugh. "If I showed myself now you might not come back tomorrow. I look perfectly hideous—it was so hot and they kept me so long."

"All to make yourself more beautiful for a man who's blind with your beauty already?"

The words made her smile, and moving nearer she bent her head and stood still while he undid her veil. As he put it back their lips met, and his look of passionate tenderness was incense to her.

But the next moment his expression passed from worship to concern. "Dear! Why, what's the matter? You've been crying!"

She put both hands to her hat in the instinctive effort to hide her face. His persistence was as irritating as her mother's.

"I told you it was frightfully hot—and all my things were horrid; and it made me so cross and nervous!" She turned to the looking-glass with a feint of smoothing her hair.

Marvell laid his hand on her arm. "I can't bear to see you so done up. Why can't we be married tomorrow, and escape all these ridiculous preparations? I shall hate your fine clothes if they're going to make you so miserable."

She dropped her hands, and swept about on him, her face lit up by a new idea. He was extraordinarily handsome and appealing, and her heart began to beat faster.

"I hate it all too! I wish we *could* be married right away!"

Marvell caught her to him joyously. "Dearest—dearest! Don't, if you don't mean it! The thought's too glorious!"

Undine lingered in his arms, not with any intent of tenderness, but as if too deeply lost in a new train of thought to be conscious of his hold.

"I suppose most of the things *could* be got ready sooner—if I said they *must*," she brooded, with a fixed gaze that traveled past him. "And the rest —why shouldn't the rest be sent over to Europe after us? I want to go straight off with you, away from everything—ever so far away, where there'll be nobody but you and me alone!" She had a flash of illumination which made her turn her lips to his.

"Oh, my darling—my darling!" Marvell whispered.

10

M<small>R.</small> and Mrs. Spragg were both given to such long periods of ruminating apathy that the student of inheritance might have wondered
whence Undine derived her overflowing activity. The answer would have
been obtained by observing her father's business life. From the moment he
set foot in Wall Street Mr. Spragg became another man. Physically the
change revealed itself only by the subtlest signs. As he steered his way to his
office through the jostling crowd of William Street his relaxed muscles did
not grow more taut or his lounging gait less desultory. His shoulders were
hollowed by the usual droop, and his rusty black waistcoat showed the same
creased concavity at the waist, the same flabby prominence below. It was
only in his face that the difference was perceptible, though even here it
rather lurked behind the features than openly modified them: showing itself
now and then in the cautious glint of half-closed eyes, the forward thrust of
black brows, or a tightening of the lax lines of the mouth—as the gleam of a
night-watchman's light might flash across the darkness of a shuttered
housefront.

The shutters were more tightly barred than usual, when, on a morning
some two weeks later than the date of the incidents last recorded, Mr.
Spragg approached the steel and concrete tower in which his office occupied a lofty pigeonhole. Events had moved rapidly and somewhat surpris-
ingly in the interval, and Mr. Spragg had already accustomed himself to the
fact that his daughter was to be married within the week, instead of awaiting the traditional post-Lenten date. Conventionally the change meant
little to him; but on the practical side it presented unforeseen difficulties.
Mr. Spragg had learned within the last weeks that a New York marriage
involved material obligations unknown to Apex. Marvell, indeed, had been
loftily careless of such questions; but his grandfather, on the announcement
of the engagement, had called on Mr. Spragg and put before him, with
polished precision, the young man's financial situation.

Mr. Spragg, at the moment, had been inclined to deal with his visitor in
a spirit of indulgent irony. As he leaned back in his revolving chair, with
feet adroitly balanced against a tilted scrap-basket, his air of relaxed power
made Mr. Dagonet's venerable elegance seem as harmless as that of an ivory
jackstraw—and his first replies to his visitor were made with the mildness of
a kindly giant.

"Ralph don't make a living out of the law, you say? No, it didn't strike me he'd be likely to, from the talks I've had with him. Fact is, the law's a business that wants —" Mr. Spragg broke off, checked by a protest from Mr. Dagonet. "Oh, a *profession*, you call it? It ain't a business?" His smile grew more indulgent as this novel distinction dawned on him. "Why, I guess that's the whole trouble with Ralph. Nobody expects to make money in a *profession*; and if you've taught him to regard the law that way, he'd better go right into cooking-stoves and done with it."

Mr. Dagonet, within a narrower range, had his own play of humor; and it met Mr. Spragg's with a leap. "It's because I knew he would manage to make cooking-stoves as unremunerative as a profession that I saved him from so glaring a failure by putting him into the law."

The retort drew a grunt of amusement from Mr. Spragg; and the eyes of the two men met in unexpected understanding.

"That so? What *can* he do, then?" the future father-in-law inquired.

"He can write poetry—at least he tells me he can." Mr. Dagonet hesitated, as if aware of the inadequacy of the alternative, and then added: "And he can count on three thousand a year from me."

Mr. Spragg tilted himself farther back without disturbing his subtly calculated relation to the scrap-basket.

"Does it cost anything like that to print his poetry?"

Mr. Dagonet smiled again: he was clearly enjoying his visit. "Dear, no— he doesn't go in for 'luxe' editions. And now and then he gets ten dollars from a magazine."

Mr. Spragg mused. "Wasn't he ever *taught* to work?"

"No; I really couldn't have afforded that."

"I see. Then they've got to live on two hundred and fifty dollars a month."

Mr. Dagonet remained pleasantly unmoved. "Does it cost anything like that to buy your daughter's dresses?"

A subterranean chuckle agitated the lower folds of Mr. Spragg's waistcoat.

"I might put him in the way of something—I guess he's smart enough."

Mr. Dagonet made a gesture of friendly warning. "It will pay us both in the end to keep him out of business," he said, rising as if to show that his mission was accomplished.

The results of this friendly conference had been more serious than Mr. Spragg could have foreseen—and the victory remained with his antagonist. It had not entered into Mr. Spragg's calculations that he would have to give his daughter any fixed income on her marriage. He meant that she should have the "handsomest" wedding the New York press had ever celebrated, and her mother's fancy was already afloat on a sea of luxuries—a motor, a Fifth Avenue house, and a tiara that should out-blaze Mrs. Van Degen's; but these were movable benefits, to be conferred whenever Mr. Spragg happened to be "on the right side" of the market. It was a different matter to be called on, at such short notice, to bridge the gap between young Marvell's allowance and Undine's requirements; and her father's immediate conclusion was that the engagement had better be broken off. Such scissions were almost painless in Apex, and he had fancied it would be easy, by an appeal to the girl's pride, to make her see that she owed it to herself to do better.

"You'd better wait awhile and look round again," was the way he had put it to her at the opening of the talk of which, even now, he could not recall the close without a tremor.

Undine, when she took his meaning, had been terrible. Everything had gone down before her, as towns and villages went down before one of the tornadoes of her native state. Wait awhile? Look round? Did he suppose she was marrying for *money*? Didn't he see it was all a question, now and here, of the kind of people she wanted to "go with"? Did he want to throw her straight back into the Lipscomb set, to have her marry a dentist and live in a West Side flat? Why hadn't they stayed in Apex, if that was all he thought she was fit for? She might as well have married Millard Binch, instead of handing him over to Indiana Frusk! Couldn't her father understand that nice girls, in New York, didn't regard getting married like going on a buggy-ride? It was enough to ruin a girl's chances if she broke her engagement to a man in Ralph Marvell's set. All kinds of spiteful things would be said about her, and she would never be able to go with the right people again. They had better go back to Apex right off—it was they and not *she* who had wanted to leave Apex, anyhow—she could call her mother to witness it. She had always, when it came to that, done what her father and mother wanted, but she'd given up trying to make out what they were after, unless it was to make her miserable; and if that was it, hadn't they had enough of it by this time? She had, anyhow. But after this she meant to lead her own life; and they needn't ask her where she was going, or what she meant to do, because this time she'd die before she told them—and they'd made life so hateful to her that she only wished she was dead already.

Mr. Spragg heard her out in silence, pulling at his beard with one sallow wrinkled hand, while the other dragged down the armhole of his waistcoat. Suddenly he looked up and said: "Ain't you in love with the fellow, Undie?"

The girl glared back at him, her splendid brows beetling like an Amazon's. "Do you think I'd care a cent for all the rest of it if I wasn't?"

"Well, if you are, you and he won't mind beginning in a small way."

Her look poured contempt on his ignorance. "Do you s'pose I'd drag him down?" With a magnificent gesture she tore Marvell's ring from her finger. "I'll send this back this minute. I'll tell him I thought he was a rich man, and now I see I'm mistaken —" She burst into shattering sobs, rocking her beautiful body back and forward in all the abandonment of young grief; and her father stood over her, stroking her shoulder and saying helplessly: "I'll see what I can do, Undine —"

All his life, and at ever-diminishing intervals, Mr. Spragg had been called on by his womenkind to "see what he could do"; and the seeing had almost always resulted as they wished. Undine did not have to send back her ring, and in her state of trancelike happiness she hardly asked by what means her path had been smoothed, but merely accepted her mother's assurance that "Father had fixed everything all right."

Mr. Spragg accepted the situation, also. A son-in-law who expected to be pensioned like a Grand Army veteran was a phenomenon new to his experience; but if that was what Undine wanted she should have it. Only two days later, however, he was met by a new demand—the young people had decided to be married "right off," instead of waiting till June. This change of plan was made known to Mr. Spragg at a moment when he was peculiarly unprepared for the financial readjustment it necessitated. He had always declared himself able to cope with any crisis if Undine and her mother would "go steady"; but he now warned them of his inability to keep up with the new pace they had set.

Undine, not deigning to return to the charge, had commissioned her mother to speak for her; and Mr. Spragg was surprised to meet in his wife a firmness as inflexible as his daughter's.

"I can't do it, Loot—can't put my hand on the cash," he had protested; but Mrs. Spragg fought him inch by inch, her back to the wall—flinging out at last, as he pressed her closer: "Well, if you want to know, he's seen Elmer."

The bolt reached its mark, and her husband turned an agitated face on her.

"Elmer? What on earth—he didn't come *here?*"

"No; but he sat next to her the other night at the theater, and she's wild with us for not having warned her."

Mr. Spragg's scowl drew his projecting brows together. "Warned her of what? What's Elmer to her? Why's she afraid of Elmer Moffatt?"

"She's afraid of his talking."

"Talking? What on earth can he say that'll hurt *her?*"

"Oh, I don't know," Mrs. Spragg wailed. "She's so nervous I can hardly get a word out of her."

Mr. Spragg's whitening face showed the touch of a new fear. "Is she afraid he'll get round her again—make up to her? Is that what she means by 'talking'?"

"I don't know, I don't know. I only know she *is* afraid—she's afraid as death of him."

For a long interval they sat silently looking at each other while their heavy eyes exchanged conjectures: Then Mr. Spragg rose from his chair, saying, as he took up his hat: "Don't you fret, Leota; I'll see what I can do."

* * *

He had been "seeing" now for an arduous fortnight; and the strain on his vision had resulted in a state of tension such as he had not undergone since the epic days of the Pure Water Move at Apex. It was not his habit to impart his fears to Mrs. Spragg and Undine, and they continued the bridal preparations, secure in their invariable experience that, once "Father" had been convinced of the impossibility of evading their demands, he might be trusted to satisfy them by means with which his womenkind need not concern themselves. Mr. Spragg, as he approached his office on the morning in question, felt reasonably sure of fulfillling these expectations; but he reflected that a few more such victories would mean disaster.

He entered the vast marble vestibule of the Ararat Trust Building and walked toward the express elevator that was to carry him up to his office. At the door of the elevator a man turned to him, and he recognized Elmer Moffatt, who put out his hand with an easy gesture.

Mr. Spragg did not ignore the gesture: he did not even withhold his hand. In his code the cut, as a conscious sign of disapproval, did not exist. In the south, if you had a grudge against a man you tried to shoot him; in the west, you tried to do him in a mean turn in business; but in neither region was the cut among the social weapons of offense. Mr. Spragg, therefore, seeing Moffatt in his path, extended a lifeless hand while he faced the young man scowlingly. Moffatt met the hand and the scowl with equal coolness.

"Going up to your office? I was on my way there."

The elevator door rolled back, and Mr. Spragg, entering it, found his companion at his side. They remained silent during the ascent to Mr. Spragg's threshold; but there the latter turned to inquire ironically of Moffatt: "Anything left to say?"

Moffatt smiled. "Nothing *left*—no; I'm carrying a whole new line of goods."

Mr. Spragg pondered the reply; then he opened the door and suffered Moffatt to follow him in. Behind an inner glazed enclosure, with its one window dimmed by a sooty perspective barred with chimneys, he seated himself at a dusty littered desk, and groped instinctively for the support of the scrap basket. Moffatt, uninvited, dropped into the nearest chair, and Mr. Spragg said, after another silence: "I'm pretty busy this morning."

"I know you are: that's why I'm here," Moffatt serenely answered. He leaned back, crossing his legs, and twisting his small stiff moustache with a plump hand adorned by a cameo.

"Fact is," he went on, "this is a coals-of-fire call. You think I owe you a grudge, and I'm going to show you I'm not that kind. I'm going to put you onto a good thing—oh, not because I'm so fond of you; just because it happens to hit my sense of a joke."

While Moffatt talked Mr. Spragg took up the pile of letters on his desk and sat shuffling them like a pack of cards. He dealt them deliberately to two imaginary players; then he pushed them aside and drew out his watch.

"All right—I carry one, too," said the young man easily. "But you'll find it's time gained to hear what I've got to say."

Mr. Spragg considered the vista of chimneys without speaking, and Moffatt continued: "I don't suppose you care to hear the story of my life, so I won't refer you to the back numbers. You used to say out in Apex that I spent too much time loafing round the bar of the Mealey House; that was one of the things you had against me. Well, maybe I did—but it taught me to talk, and to listen to the other fellows, too. Just at present I'm one of Harmon B. Driscoll's private secretaries, and some of that Mealey House loafing has come in more useful than any job I ever put my hand to. The old man happened to hear I knew something about the inside of the Eubaw deal, and took me on to have the information where he could get at it. I've given him good talk for his money; but I've done some listening too. Eubaw ain't the only commodity the Driscolls deal in."

Mr. Spragg restored his watch to his pocket and shifted his drowsy gaze from the window to his visitor's face.

"Yes," said Moffatt, as if in reply to the movement, "the Driscolls are getting busy out in Apex. Now they've got all the street railroads in their pocket they want the water supply too—but you know that as well as I do. Fact is, they've got to have it; and there's where you and I come in."

Mr. Spragg thrust his hands in his waistcoat armholes and turned his eyes back to the window.

"I'm out of that long ago," he said indifferently.

"Sure," Moffatt acquiesced; "but you know what went on when you were in it."

"Well?" said Mr. Spragg, shifting one hand to the Masonic emblem on his watch-chain.

"Well, Representative James J. Rolliver, who was in it with you, ain't out of it yet. He's the man the Driscolls are up against. What d'you know about him?"

Mr. Spragg twirled the emblem thoughtfully. "Driscoll tell you to come here?"

Moffatt laughed. "No, sir—not by a good many miles."

Mr. Spragg removed his feet from the scrap-basket and straightened himself in his chair.

"Well—I didn't either; good morning, Mr. Moffatt."

The young man stared a moment, a humorous glint in his small black eyes; but he made no motion to leave his seat.

"Undine's to be married next week, isn't she?" he asked in a conversational tone.

Mr. Spragg's face blackened and he swung about in his revolving chair.

"You go to —"

Moffatt raised a deprecating hand. "Oh, you needn't warn me off. I don't want to be invited to the wedding. And I don't want to forbid the banns."

There was a derisive sound in Mr. Spragg's throat.

"But I *do* want to get out of Driscoll's office," Moffatt imperturbably continued. "There's no future there for a fellow like me. I see things big. That's the reason Apex was too tight a fit for me. It's only the little fellows that succeed in little places. New York's my size—without a single alteration. I could prove it to you tomorrow if I could put my hand on fifty thousand dollars."

Mr. Spragg did not repeat his gesture of dismissal: he was once more listening guardedly but intently. Moffatt saw it and continued.

"And I could put my hand on double that sum—yes, sir, *double*— if you'd just step round with me to old Driscoll's office before 5 P.M. See the connection, Mr. Spragg?"

The older man remained silent while his visitor hummed a bar or two of "In the Gloaming"; then he said: "You want me to tell Driscoll what I know about James J. Rolliver?"

"I want you to tell the truth—I want you to stand for political purity in your native state. A man of your prominence owes it to the community, sir," cried Moffatt.

Mr. Spragg was still tormenting his Masonic emblem.

"Rolliver and I always stood together," he said at last, with a tinge of reluctance.

"Well, how much have you made out of it? Ain't he always been ahead of the game?"

"I can't do it—I can't do it," said Mr. Spragg, bringing his clenched hand down on the desk, as if addressing an invisible throng of assailants.

Moffatt rose without any evidence of disappointment in his ruddy countenance. "Well, so long," he said, moving toward the door. Near the threshold he paused to add carelessly: "Excuse my referring to a personal matter— but I understand Miss Spragg's wedding takes place next Monday."

Mr. Spragg was silent.

"How's that?" Moffatt continued unabashed. "I saw in the papers the date was set for the end of June."

Mr. Spragg rose heavily from his seat. "I presume my daughter has her reasons," he said, moving toward the door in Moffatt's wake.

"I guess she has—same as I have for wanting you to step round with me to old Driscoll's. If Undine's reasons are as good as mine —"

"Stop right here, Elmer Moffatt!" the older man broke out with lifted hand.

Moffatt made a burlesque feint of evading a blow; then his face grew serious, and he moved close to Mr. Spragg, whose arm had fallen to his side.

"See here, I know Undine's reasons. I've had a talk with her—didn't she tell you? *She* don't beat about the bush the way you do. She told me straight out what was bothering her. She wants the Marvells to think she's right out of kindergarten. 'No goods sent out on approval from this counter.' And I see her point—I don't mean to publish my meemo'rs. Only a deal's a deal." He paused a moment, twisting his fingers about the heavy gold watch-chain that crossed his waistcoat. "Tell you what, Mr. Spragg, I don't bear malice— not against Undine, anyway—and if I could have afforded it I'd have been glad enough to oblige her and forget old times. But you didn't hesitate to kick me when I was down and it's taken me a day or two to get on my legs again after that kicking. I see my way now to get there and keep there; and there's a kinder poetic justice in your being the man to help me up. If I can get hold of fifty thousand dollars within a day or so I don't care who's got the start of me. I've got a dead sure thing in sight, and you're the only man that can get it for me. Now do you see where we're coming out?"

Mr. Spragg, during this discourse, had remained motionless, his hands in his pockets, his jaws moving mechanically, as though he mumbled a tooth- pick under his beard. His sallow cheek had turned a shade paler, and his brows hung threateningly over his half-closed eyes. But there was no threat —there was scarcely more than a note of dull curiosity—in the voice with which he said: "You mean to talk?"

Moffatt's rosy face grew as hard as a steel safe. "I mean *you* to talk—to old Driscoll." He paused, and then added: "It's a hundred thousand down, between us."

Mr. Spragg once more consulted his watch. "I'll see you again," he said with an effort.

Moffatt struck one fist against the other. "No, *sir*—you won't! You'll only hear from me—through the Marvell family. Your news ain't worth a dollar to Driscoll if he don't get it today."

He was checked by the sound of steps in the outer office, and Mr. Spragg's stenographer appeared in the doorway.

"It's Mr. Marvell," she announced; and Ralph Marvell, glowing with haste and happiness, stood between the two men, holding out his hand to Mr. Spragg.

"Am I awfully in the way, sir? Turn me out if I am—but first let me just say a word about this necklace I've ordered for Un—"

He broke off, made aware by Mr. Spragg's glance of the presence of Elmer Moffatt, who, with unwonted discretion, had dropped back into the shadow of the door.

Marvell turned on Moffatt a bright gaze full of the instinctive hospitality of youth; but Moffatt looked straight past him at Mr. Spragg.

The latter, as if in response to an imperceptible signal, mechanically pronounced his visitor's name; and the two young men moved toward each other.

"I beg your pardon most awfully—am I breaking up an important conference?" Ralph asked as he shook hands.

"Why, no—I guess we're pretty nearly through. I'll step outside and woo the blonde while you're talking," Moffatt rejoined in the same key.

"Thanks so much—I shan't take two seconds." Ralph broke off to scrutinize him. "But haven't we met before? It seems to me I've seen you—just lately —"

Moffatt seemed about to answer, but his reply was checked by an abrupt movement on the part of Mr. Spragg. There was a perceptible pause, during which Moffatt's bright black glance rested questioningly on Ralph; then he looked again at the older man, and their eyes held each other for a silent moment.

"Why, no—not as I'm aware of, Mr. Marvell," Moffatt said, addressing himself amicably to Ralph. "Better late than never, though—and I hope to have the pleasure soon again."

He divided a nod between the two men, and passed into the outer office, where they heard him addressing the stenographer in a strain of exaggerated gallantry.

Book Two

11

THE July sun enclosed in a ring of fire the ilex grove of a villa in the hills near Siena.

Below, by the roadside, the long yellow house seemed to waver and palpitate in the glare; but steep by steep, behind it, the cool ilex-dusk mounted to the ledge where Ralph Marvell, stretched on his back in the grass, lay gazing up at a black reticulation of branches between which bits of sky gleamed with the hardness and brilliancy of blue enamel.

Up there too the air was thick with heat; but compared with the white fire below it was a dim and tempered warmth, like that of the churches in which he and Undine sometimes took refuge at the height of the torrid days.

Ralph loved the heavy Italian summer, as he had loved the light spring days leading up to it: the long line of dancing days that had drawn them on and on ever since they had left their ship at Naples four months earlier. Four months of beauty, changeful, inexhaustible, weaving itself about him in shapes of softness and strength; and beside him, hand in hand with him, embodying that spirit of shifting magic, the radiant creature through whose eyes he saw it. This was what their hastened marriage had blessed them with, giving them leisure, before summer came, to penetrate to remote folds of the southern mountains, to linger in the shade of Sicilian orange groves, and finally, traveling by slow stages to the Adriatic, to reach the central hill-country where even in July they might hope for a breathable air.

To Ralph the Sienese air was not only breathable but intoxicating. The sun, treading the earth like a vintager, drew from it heady fragrances, crushed out of it new colors. All the values of the temperate landscape were reversed: the noon highlights were white, but the shadows had unimagined color. On the blackness of cork and ilex and cypress lay the green and purple lusters, the coppery iridescences, of old bronze; and night after night the skies were wine-blue and bubbling with stars. Ralph said to himself that no one who had not seen Italy thus prostrate beneath the sun knew what secret treasures she could yield.

As he lay there, fragments of past states of emotion, fugitive felicities of thought and sensation, rose and floated on the surface of his thoughts. It was one of those moments when the accumulated impressions of life

converge on heart and brain, elucidating, enlacing each other, in a mysterious confusion of beauty. He had had glimpses of such a state before, of such
mergings of the personal with the general life that one felt one's self a mere
wave on the wild stream of being, yet thrilled with a sharper sense of
individuality than can be known within the mere bounds of the actual. But
now he knew the sensation in its fullness, and with it came the releasing
power of language. Words were flashing like brilliant birds through the
boughs overhead; he had but to wave his magic wand to have them flutter
down to him. Only they were so beautiful up there, weaving their fantastic
flights against the blue, that it was pleasanter, for the moment, to watch
them and let the wand lie.

He stared up at the pattern they made till his eyes ached with excess of
light; then he changed his position and looked at his wife.

Undine, nearby, leaned against a gnarled tree with the slightly constrained air of a person unused to sylvan abandonments. Her beautiful back
could not adapt itself to the irregularities of the tree trunk, and she moved a
little now and then in the effort to find an easier position. But her expression was serene, and Ralph, looking up at her through drowsy lids, thought
her face had never been more exquisite.

"You look as cool as a wave," he said, reaching out for the hand on her
knee. She let him have it, and he drew it closer, scrutinizing it as if it had
been a bit of precious porcelain or ivory. It was small and soft, a mere
featherweight, a puff-ball of a hand—not quick and thrilling, not a speaking
hand, but one to be fondled and dressed in rings, and to leave a rosy blur in
the brain. The fingers were short and tapering, dimpled at the base, with
nails as smooth as rose leaves. Ralph lifted them one by one, like a child
playing with piano keys, but they were inelastic and did not spring back far
—only far enough to show the dimples.

He turned the hand over and traced the course of its blue veins from the
wrist to the rounding of the palm below the fingers; then he put a kiss in the
warm hollow between. The upper world had vanished: his universe had
shrunk to the palm of a hand. But there was no sense of diminution. In the
mystic depths whence his passion sprang, earthly dimensions were ignored
and the curve of beauty was boundless enough to hold whatever the imagination could pour into it. Ralph had never felt more convinced of his power
to write a great poem; but now it was Undine's hand which held the magic
wand of expression.

She stirred again uneasily, answering his last words with a faint accent
of reproach.

"I don't *feel* cool. You said there'd be a breeze up here."

He laughed.

"You poor darling! Wasn't it ever as hot as this in Apex?"

She withdrew her hand with a slight grimace.

"Yes—but I didn't marry you to go back to Apex!"

Ralph laughed again; then he lifted himself on his elbow and regained the hand. "I wonder what you *did* marry me for?"

"Mercy! It's too hot for conundrums." She spoke without impatience, but with a lassitude less joyous than his.

He roused himself. "Do you really mind the heat so much? We'll go, if you do."

She sat up eagerly. "Go to Switzerland, you mean?"

"Well, I hadn't taken quite as long a leap. I only meant we might drive back to Siena."

She relapsed listlessly against her tree trunk. "Oh, Siena's hotter than this."

"We could go and sit in the cathedral—it's always cool there at sunset."

"We've sat in the cathedral at sunset every day for a week."

"Well, what do you say to stopping at Lecceto on the way? I haven't shown you Lecceto yet; and the drive back by moonlight would be glorious."

This woke her to a slight show of interest. "It might be nice—but where could we get anything to eat?"

Ralph laughed again. "I don't believe we could. You're too practical."

"Well, somebody's got to be. And the food in the hotel is too disgusting if we're not on time."

"I admit that the best of it has usually been appropriated by the extremely good-looking cavalry officer who's so keen to know you."

Undine's face brightened. "You know he's not a count; he's a marquis. His name's Roviano; his palace in Rome is in the guidebooks, and he speaks English beautifully. Céleste found out about him from the headwaiter," she said, with the security of one who treats of recognized values.

Marvell, sitting upright, reached lazily across the grass for his hat. "Then there's all the more reason for rushing back to defend our share." He spoke in the bantering tone which had become the habitual expression of his tenderness; but his eyes softened as they absorbed in a last glance the glimmering submarine light of the ancient grove, through which Undine's figure wavered Nereidlike above him.

"You never looked your name more than you do now," he said, kneeling at her side and putting his arm about her. She smiled back a little vaguely, as if not seizing his allusion, and being content to let it drop into the store of unexplained references which had once stimulated her curiosity but now merely gave her leisure to think of other things. But her smile was no less lovely for its vagueness, and indeed, to Ralph, the loveliness was enhanced by the latent doubt. He remembered afterward that at that moment the cup of life seemed to brim over.

"Come, dear—here or there—it's all divine!"

In the carriage, however, she remained insensible to the soft spell of the evening, noticing only the heat and dust, and saying, as they passed under the wooded cliff of Lecceto, that they might as well have stopped there after all, since with such a headache as she felt coming on she didn't care if she dined or not.

Ralph looked up yearningly at the long walls overhead; but Undine's mood was hardly favorable to communion with such scenes, and he made no attempt to stop the carriage. Instead he presently said: "If you're tired of Italy, we've got the world to choose from."

She did not speak for a moment; then she said: "It's the heat I'm tired of. Don't people generally come here earlier?"

"Yes. That's why I chose the summer: so that we could have it all to ourselves."

She tried to put a note of reasonableness into her voice. "If you'd told me we were going everywhere at the wrong time, of course, I could have arranged about my clothes."

"You poor darling! Let us, by all means, go to the place where the clothes will be right: they're too beautiful to be left out of our scheme of life."

Her lips hardened. "I know you don't care how I look. But you didn't give me time to order anything before we were married, and I've got nothing but my last winter's things to wear."

Ralph smiled. Even his subjugated mind perceived the inconsistency of Undine's taxing him with having hastened their marriage; but her variations on the eternal feminine still enchanted him.

"We'll go wherever you please—you make every place the one place," he said, as if he were humoring an irresistible child.

"To Switzerland, then? Céleste says St. Moritz is too heavenly," exclaimed Undine, who gathered her ideas of Europe chiefly from the conversation of her experienced attendant.

"One can be cool short of the Engadine. Why not go south again—say to Capri?"

"Capri? Is that the island we saw from Naples, where the artists go?" She drew her brows together. "It would be simply awful getting there in this heat."

"Well, then, I know a little place in Switzerland where one can still get away from the crowd, and we can sit and look at a green waterfall while I lie in wait for adjectives."

Mr. Spragg's astonishment on learning that his son-in-law contemplated maintaining a household on the earnings of his Muse was still matter for pleasantry between the pair; and one of the humors of their first weeks together had consisted in picturing themselves as a primeval couple setting forth across a virgin continent and subsisting on the adjectives which Ralph was to trap for his epic. On this occasion, however, his wife did not take up the joke, and he remained silent while their carriage climbed the long dusty hill to the Fontebranda gate. He had seen her face droop as he suggested the possibility of an escape from the crowds in Switzerland, and it came to him, with the sharpness of a knife-thrust, that a crowd was what she wanted—that she was sick to death of being alone with him.

He sat motionless, staring ahead at the red-brown walls and towers on the steep above them. After all there was nothing sudden in his discovery. For weeks it had hung on the edge of consciousness, but he had turned from it with the heart's instinctive clinging to the unrealities by which it lives. Even now a hundred qualifying reasons rushed to his aid. They told him it was not of himself that Undine had wearied, but only of their present way of life. He had said a moment before, without conscious exaggeration, that her presence made any place the one place; yet how willingly would he have consented to share in such a life as she was leading before their marriage? And he had to acknowledge their months of desultory wandering from one remote Italian hilltop to another must have seemed as purposeless to her as balls and dinners would have been to him. An imagination like his, peopled with such varied images and associations, fed by so many currents from the long stream of human experience, could hardly picture the bareness of the small half-lit place in which his wife's spirit fluttered. Her mind was as destitute of beauty and mystery as the prairie schoolhouse in which she had been educated; and her ideals seemed to Ralph as pathetic as the ornaments made of corks and cigar-bands with which her infant hands had been taught to adorn it. He was beginning to understand this, and learning to adapt himself to the narrow compass of her experience. The task of opening new windows in her mind was inspiring enough to give him infinite patience; and he would not yet own to himself that her pliancy and variety were imitative rather than spontaneous.

Meanwhile he had no desire to sacrifice her wishes to his, and it distressed him that he dared not confess his real reason for avoiding the Engadine. The truth was that their funds were shrinking faster than he had expected. Mr. Spragg, after bluntly opposing their hastened marriage on the ground that he was not prepared, at such short notice, to make the necessary provision for his daughter, had shortly afterward (probably, as Undine observed to Ralph, in consequence of a lucky "turn" in the Street) met their wishes with all possible liberality, bestowing on them a wedding in conformity with Mrs. Spragg's ideals and up to the highest standard of Mrs. Heeny's clippings, and pledging himself to provide Undine with an income adequate to so brilliant a beginning. It was understood that Ralph, on their return, should renounce the law for some more paying business; but this seemed the smallest of sacrifices to make for the privilege of calling Undine his wife; and besides, he still secretly hoped that, in the interval, his real vocation might declare itself in some work which would justify his adopting the life of letters.

He had assumed that Undine's allowance, with the addition of his own small income, would be enough to satisfy their needs. His own were few, and had always been within his means; but his wife's daily requirements, combined with her intermittent outbreaks of extravagance, had thrown out all his calculations, and they were already seriously exceeding their income.

If anyone had prophesied before his marriage that he would find it difficult to tell this to Undine he would have smiled at the suggestion; and during their first days together it had seemed as though pecuniary questions were the last likely to be raised between them. But his marital education had since made strides, and he now knew that a disregard for money may imply not the willingness to get on without it but merely a blind confidence that it will somehow be provided. If Undine, like the lilies of the field, took no care, it was not because her wants were as few but because she assumed that care would be taken for her by those whose privilege it was to enable her to unite floral insouciance with Sheban elegance.

She had met Ralph's first note of warning with the assurance that she "didn't mean to worry"; and her tone implied that it was his business to do so for her. He certainly wanted to guard her from this as from all other cares; he wanted also, and still more passionately after the topic had once or twice recurred between them, to guard himself from the risk of judging where he still adored. These restraints to frankness kept him silent during the remainder of the drive, and when, after dinner, Undine again complained of her headache, he let her go up to her room and wandered out into the dimly lit streets to renewed communion with his problems.

They hung on him insistently as darkness fell, and Siena grew vocal with that shrill diversity of sounds that breaks, on summer nights, from every cleft of the masonry in old Italian towns. Then the moon rose, unfolding depth by depth the lines of the antique land; and Ralph, leaning against an old brick parapet, and watching each silver-blue remoteness disclose itself between the dark masses of the middle distance, felt his spirit enlarged and pacified. For the first time, as his senses thrilled to the deep touch of beauty, he asked himself if out of these floating and fugitive vibrations he might not build something concrete and stable, if even such dull common cares as now oppressed him might not become the motive power of creation. If he could only, on the spot, do something with all the accumulated spoils of the last months—something that should both put money into his pocket and harmony into the rich confusion of his spirit! "I'll write—I'll write: that must be what the whole thing means," he said to himself, with a vague clutch at some solution which should keep him a little longer hanging halfway down the steep of disenchantment.

He would have stayed on, heedless of time, to trace the ramifications of his idea in the complex beauty of the scene, but for the longing to share his mood with Undine. For the last few months every thought and sensation had been instantly transmuted into such emotional impulses and, though the currents of communication between himself and Undine were neither deep nor numerous, each fresh rush of feeling seemed strong enough to clear a way to her heart. He hurried back, almost breathlessly, to the inn; but even as he knocked at her door the subtle emanation of other influences seemed to arrest and chill him.

She had put out the lamp, and sat by the window in the moonlight, her head propped on a listless hand. As Marvell entered she turned; then, without speaking, she looked away again.

He was used to this mute reception, and had learned that it had no personal motive, but was the result of an extremely simplified social code. Mr. and Mrs. Spragg seldom spoke to each other when they met, and words of greeting seemed almost unknown to their domestic vocabulary. Marvell, at first, had fancied that his own warmth would call forth a response from his wife, who had been so quick to learn the forms of worldly intercourse; but he soon saw that she regarded intimacy as a pretext for escaping from such forms into a total absence of expression.

Tonight, however, he felt another meaning in her silence, and perceived that she intended him to feel it. He met it by silence, but of a different kind; letting his nearness speak for him as he knelt beside her and laid his cheek against hers. She seemed hardly aware of the gesture; but to that he was also used. She had never shown any repugnance to his tenderness, but such response as it evoked was remote and Ariel-like, suggesting, from the first, not so much of the recoil of ignorance as the coolness of the element from which she took her name.

As he pressed her to him she seemed to grow less impassive and he felt her resign herself like a tired child. He held his breath, not daring to break the spell.

At length he whispered: "I've just seen such a wonderful thing—I wish you'd been with me!"

"What sort of a thing?" She turned her head with a faint show of interest.

"A—I don't know—a vision. . . . It came to me out there just now with the moonrise."

"A vision?" Her interest flagged. "I never cared much about spirits. Mother used to try to drag me to séances—but they always made me sleepy."

Ralph laughed. "I don't mean a dead spirit but a living one! I saw the vision of a book I mean to do. It came to me suddenly, magnificently, swooped down on me as that big white moon swooped down on the black landscape, tore at me like a great white eagle—like the bird of Jove! After all, imagination *was* the eagle that devoured Prometheus!"

She drew away abruptly, and the bright moonlight showed him the apprehension in her face. "You're not going to write a book *here?*"

He stood up and wandered away a step or two; then he turned and came back. "Of course not here. Wherever you want. The main point is that it's come to me—no, that it's come *back* to me! For it's all these months together, it's all our happiness—it's the meaning of life that I've found, and it's you, dearest, you who've given it to me!"

He dropped down beside her again; but she disengaged herself and he heard a little sob in her throat.

"Undine—what's the matter?"

"Nothing . . . I don't know . . . I suppose I'm homesick. . . ."

"Homesick? You poor darling! You're tired of traveling? What is it?"

"I don't know . . . I don't like Europe . . . it's not what I expected, and I think it's all too dreadfully dreary!" The words broke from her in a long wail of rebellion.

Marvell gazed at her perplexedly. It seemed strange that such unguessed thoughts should have been stirring in the heart pressed to his. "It's less interesting than you expected—or less amusing? Is that it?"

"It's dirty and ugly—all the towns we've been to are disgustingly dirty. I loathe the smells and the beggars. I'm sick and tired of the stuffy rooms in the hotels. I thought it would all be so splendid—but New York's ever so much nicer!"

"Not New York in July?"

"I don't care—there are the roof-gardens, anyway; and there are always people round. All these places seem as if they were dead. It's all like some awful cemetery."

A sense of compunction checked Marvell's laughter. "Don't cry, dear— don't! I see, I understand. You're lonely and the heat has tired you out. It *is* dull here; awfully dull; I've been stupid not to feel it. But we'll start at once —we'll get out of it."

She brightened instantly. "We'll go up to Switzerland?"

"We'll go up to Switzerland." He had a fleeting glimpse of the quiet place with the green waterfall, where he might have made tryst with his vision; then he turned his mind from it and said: "We'll go just where you want. How soon can you be ready to start?"

"Oh, tomorrow—the first thing tomorrow! I'll make Céleste get out of bed now and pack. Can we go right through to St. Moritz? I'd rather sleep in the train than in another of these awful places."

She was on her feet in a flash, her face alight, her hair waving and floating about her as though it rose on her happy heartbeats.

"Oh, Ralph, it's *sweet* of you, and I love you!" she cried out, letting him take her to his breast.

12

I N the quiet place with the green waterfall Ralph's vision might have kept faith with him; but how could he hope to surprise it in the midsummer crowds of St. Moritz?

Undine, at any rate, had found there what she wanted; and when he was at her side, and her radiant smile included him, every other question was in abeyance. But there were hours of solitary striding over bare grassy slopes, face to face with the ironic interrogation of sky and mountains, when his anxieties came back, more persistent and importunate. Sometimes they took the form of merely material difficulties. How, for instance, was he to meet the cost of their ruinous suite at the Engadine Palace while he awaited Mr. Spragg's next remittance? And once the hotel bills were paid, what would be left for the journey back to Paris, the looming expenses there, the price of the passage to America? These questions would fling him back on the thought of his projected book, which was, after all, to be what the masterpieces of literature had mostly been—a potboiler. Well! Why not? Did not the worshipper always heap the rarest essences on the altar of his divinity? Ralph still rejoiced in the thought of giving back to Undine something of the beauty of their first months together. But even on his solitary walks the vision eluded him; and he could spare so few hours to its pursuit!

Undine's days were crowded, and it was still a matter of course that where she went he should follow. He had risen visibly in her opinion since they had been absorbed into the life of the big hotels, and she had seen that his command of foreign tongues put him at an advantage even in circles where English was generally spoken if not understood. Undine herself, hampered by her lack of languages, was soon drawn into the group of compatriots who struck the social pitch of their hotel. Their types were familiar enough to Ralph, who had taken their measure in former wanderings, and come across their duplicates in every scene of continental idleness. Foremost among them was Mrs. Harvey Shallum, a showy Parisianized figure, with a small wax-featured husband whose ultrafashionable clothes seemed a tribute to his wife's importance rather than the mark of his personal taste. Mr. Shallum, in fact, could not be said to have any personal bent. Though he conversed with a colorless fluency in the principal European tongues, he seldom exercised his gift except in intercourse with hotel managers and headwaiters; and his long silences were broken only by resigned allusions to the enormities he had suffered at the hands of this gifted but unscrupulous class.

Mrs. Shallum, though in command of but a few verbs, all of which, on her lips, became irregular, managed to express a polyglot personality as vivid as her husband's was effaced. Her only idea of intercourse with her kind was to organize it into bands and subject it to frequent displacements; and society smiled at her for these exertions like an infant vigorously rocked. She saw at once Undine's value as a factor in her scheme, and the two formed an alliance on which Ralph refrained from shedding the cold light of depreciation. It was a point of honor with him not to seem to disdain any of Undine's amusements: the noisy interminable picnics, the hot promiscuous balls, the concerts, bridge-parties and theatricals which helped to disguise the difference between the high Alps and Paris or New York. He told himself that there is always a Narcissus-element in youth, and that what Undine really enjoyed was the image of her own charm mirrored in the general admiration. With her quick perceptions and adaptabilities she would soon learn to care more about the quality of the reflecting surface; and meanwhile no criticism of his should mar her pleasure.

The appearance at their hotel of the cavalry officer from Siena was a not wholly agreeable surprise; but even after the handsome marquis had been introduced to Undine, and had whirled her through an evening's dances, Ralph was not seriously disturbed. Husband and wife had grown closer to each other since they had come to St. Moritz, and in the brief moments she could give him Undine was now always gay and approachable. Her fitful humors had vanished, and she showed qualities of comradeship that seemed the promise of a deeper understanding. But this very hope made him more subject to her moods, more fearful of disturbing the harmony between them. Least of all could he broach the subject of money: he had too keen a memory of the way her lips could narrow, and her eyes turn from him as if he were a stranger.

It was a different matter that one day brought the look he feared to her face. She had announced her intention of going on an excursion with Mrs. Shallum and three or four of the young men who formed the nucleus of their shifting circle, and for the first time she did not ask Ralph if he were coming; but he felt no resentment at being left out. He was tired of these noisy assaults on the high solitudes, and the prospect of a quiet afternoon turned his thoughts to his book. Now if ever there seemed a chance of recapturing the moonlight vision. . . .

From his balcony he looked down on the assembling party. Mrs. Shallum was already screaming bilingually at various windows in the long facade; and Undine presently came out of the hotel with the Marchese Roviano and two young English diplomatists. Slim and tall in her trim mountain garb, she made the ornate Mrs. Shallum look like a piece of ambulant upholstery. The high air brightened her cheeks and struck new lights from her hair, and Ralph had never seen her so touched with morning freshness. The party was not yet complete, and he felt a movement of annoyance when he recognized, in the last person to join it, a Russian lady of cosmopolitan notoriety whom he had run across in his unmarried days, and as to whom he had already warned Undine. Knowing what strange specimens from the depths slip through the wide meshes of the watering-place world, he had foreseen that a meeting with the Baroness Adelschein was inevitable; but he had not expected her to become one of his wife's intimate circle.

When the excursionists had started he turned back to his writing-table and tried to take up his work; but he could not fix his thoughts: they were far away, in pursuit of Undine. He had been but five months married, and it seemed, after all, rather soon for him to be dropped out of such excursions as unquestioningly as poor Harvey Shallum. He smiled away this first twinge of jealousy, but the irritation it left found a pretext in his displeasure at Undine's choice of companions. Mrs. Shallum grated on his taste, but she was as open to inspection as a shop-window, and he was sure that time would teach his wife the cheapness of what she had to show. Roviano and the Englishmen were well enough too: frankly bent on amusement, but pleasant and well-bred. But they would naturally take their tone from the women they were with; and Madame Adelschein's tone was notorious. He knew also that Undine's faculty of self-defense was weakened by the instinct of adapting herself to whatever company she was in, of copying "the others" in speech and gesture as closely as she reflected them in dress; and he was disturbed by the thought of what her ignorance might expose her to.

She came back late, flushed with her long walk, her face all sparkle and mystery, as he had seen it in the first days of their courtship; and the look somehow revived his irritated sense of having been intentionally left out of the party.

"You've been gone forever. Was it the Adelschein who made you go such lengths?" he asked her, trying to keep to his usual joking tone.

Undine, as she dropped down on the sofa and unpinned her hat, shed on him the light of her guileless gaze.

"I don't know: everybody was amusing. The marquis is awfully bright."

"I'd no idea you or Bertha Shallum knew Madame Adelschein well enough to take her off with you in that way."

Undine sat absently smoothing the tuft of glossy cock's-feathers in her hat.

"I don't see that you've got to know people particularly well to go for a walk with them. The baroness is awfully bright, too."

She always gave her acquaintances their titles, seeming not, in this respect, to have noticed that a simpler form prevailed.

"I don't dispute the interest of what she says; but I've told you what decent people think of what she does," Ralph retorted, exasperated by what seemed a willful pretense of ignorance.

She continued to scrutinize him with her clear eyes, in which there was no shadow of offense.

"You mean they don't want to go round with her? You're mistaken: it's not true. She goes round with everybody. She dined last night with the grand duchess; Roviano told me so."

This was not calculated to make Ralph take a more tolerant view of the question.

"Does he also tell you what's said of her?"

"What's said of her?" Undine's limpid glance rebuked him. "Do you mean that disgusting scandal you told me about? Do you suppose I'd let him talk to me about such things? I meant you're mistaken about her social position. He says she goes everywhere."

Ralph laughed impatiently. "No doubt Roviano's an authority; but it doesn't happen to be his business to choose your friends for you."

Undine echoed his laugh. "Well, I guess I don't need anybody to do that: I can do it myself," she said, with the good-humored curtness that was the habitual note of intercourse with the Spraggs.

Ralph sat down beside her and laid a caressing touch on her shoulder. "No, you can't, you foolish child. You know nothing of this society you're in; of its antecedents, its rules, its conventions; and it's my affair to look after you, and warn you when you're on the wrong track."

"Mercy, what a solemn speech!" She shrugged away his hand without ill-temper. "I don't believe an American woman needs to know such a lot about their old rules. They can see I mean to follow my own, and if they don't like it they needn't go with me."

"Oh, they'll go with you fast enough, as you call it. They'll be too charmed to. The question is how far they'll make you go with *them,* and where they'll finally land you."

She tossed her head back with the movement she had learned in "speaking" school pieces about freedom and the British tyrant.

"No one's ever yet gone any farther with me than I wanted!" she declared. She was really exquisitely simple.

"I'm not sure Roviano hasn't, in vouching for Madame Adelschein. But he probably thinks you know about her. To him this isn't 'society' any more than the people in an omnibus are. Society, to everybody here, means the sanction of their own special group and of the corresponding groups elsewhere. The Adelschein goes about in a place like this because it's nobody's business to stop her; but the women who tolerate her here would drop her like a shot if she set foot on their own ground."

The thoughtful air with which Undine heard him out made him fancy this argument had carried; and as he ended she threw him a bright look.

"Well, that's easy enough: I can drop her if she comes to New York."

Ralph sat silent for a moment—then he turned away and began to gather up his scattered pages.

Undine, in the ensuing days, was no less often with Madame Adelschein, and Ralph suspected a challenge in her open frequentation of the lady. But if challenge there were, he let it lie. Whether his wife saw more or less of Madame Adelschein seemed no longer of much consequence: she had so amply shown him her ability to protect herself. The pang lay in the completeness of the proof—in the perfect functioning of her instinct of self-preservation. For the first time he was face to face with his hovering dread: he was judging where he still adored.

Before long more pressing cares absorbed him. He had already begun to watch the post for his father-in-law's monthly remittance, without precisely knowing how, even with its aid, he was to bridge the gulf of expense between St. Moritz and New York. The nonarrival of Mr. Spragg's check was productive of graver fears, and these were abruptly confirmed when, coming in one afternoon, he found Undine crying over a letter from her mother.

Her distress made him fear that Mr. Spragg was ill, and he drew her to him soothingly; but she broke away with an impatient movement.

"Oh, they're all well enough—but Father's lost a lot of money. He's been speculating, and he can't send us anything for at least three months."

Ralph murmured reassuringly: "As long as there's no one ill!"—but in reality he was following her despairing gaze down the long perspective of their barren quarter.

"Three months! Three months!"

Undine dried her eyes, and sat with set lips and tapping foot while he read her mother's letter.

"Your poor father! It's a hard knock for him. I'm sorry," he said as he handed it back.

For a moment she did not seem to hear; then she said between her teeth: "It's hard for *us*. I suppose now we'll have to go straight home."

He looked at her with wonder. "If that were all! In any case I should have to be back in a few weeks."

"But we needn't have left here in August! It's the first place in Europe that I've liked, and it's just my luck to be dragged away from it!"

"I'm so awfully sorry, dearest. It's my fault for persuading you to marry a pauper."

"It's Father's fault. Why on earth did he go and speculate? There's no use his saying he's sorry now!" She sat brooding for a moment and then suddenly took Ralph's hand. "Couldn't your people do something—help us out just this once, I mean?"

He flushed to the forehead: it seemed inconceivable that she should make such a suggestion.

"I couldn't ask them—it's not possible. My grandfather does as much as he can for me, and my mother has nothing but what he gives her."

Undine seemed unconscious of his embarrassment. "He doesn't give us nearly as much as Father does," she said; and, as Ralph remained silent, she went on: "Couldn't you ask your sister, then? I must have some clothes to go home in."

His heart contracted as he looked at her. What sinister change came over her when her will was crossed? She seemed to grow inaccessible, implacable—her eyes were like the eyes of an enemy.

"I don't know—I'll see," he said, rising and moving away from her. At that moment the touch of her hand was repugnant. Yes—he might ask Laura, no doubt: and whatever she had would be his. But the necessity was bitter to him, and Undine's unconsciousness of the fact hurt him more than her indifference to her father's misfortune.

What hurt him most was the curious fact that, for all her light irresponsibility, it was always she who made the practical suggestion, hit the nail of expediency on the head. No sentimental scruple made the blow waver or deflected her resolute aim. She had thought at once of Laura, and Laura was his only, his inevitable, resource. His anxious mind pictured his sister's wonder, and made him wince under the sting of Henley Fairford's irony: Fairford, who at the time of the marriage had sat silent and pulled his moustache while every one else argued and objected, yet under whose silence Ralph had felt a deeper protest than under all the reasoning of the others. It was no comfort to reflect that Fairford would probably continue to say nothing! But necessity made light of these twinges, and Ralph set his teeth and cabled.

Undine's chief surprise seemed to be that Laura's response, though immediate and generous, did not enable them to stay on at St. Moritz. But she apparently read in her husband's look the uselessness of such a hope, for, with one of the sudden changes of mood that still disarmed him, she accepted the need of departure, and took leave philosophically of the Shallums and their band. After all, Paris was ahead, and in September one would have a chance to see the new models and surprise the secret councils of the dressmakers.

Ralph was astonished at the tenacity with which she held to her purpose. He tried, when they reached Paris, to make her feel the necessity of starting at once for home; but she complained of fatigue and of feeling vaguely unwell, and he had to yield to her desire for rest. The word, however, was to strike him as strangely misapplied, for from the day of their arrival she was in a state of perpetual activity. She seemed to have mastered her Paris by divination, and between the bounds of the boulevards and the Place Vendôme she moved at once with supernatural ease.

"Of course," she explained to him, "I understand how little we've got to spend; but I left New York without a rag, and it was you who made me countermand my trousseau, instead of having it sent after us. I wish now I hadn't listened to you—Father'd have had to pay for *that* before he lost his money. As it is, it will be cheaper in the end for me to pick up a few things here. The advantage of going to the French dressmakers is that they'll wait twice as long for their money as the people at home. And they're all crazy to dress me—Bertha Shallum will tell you so: she says no one ever had such a chance! That's why I was willing to come to this stuffy little hotel—I wanted to save every scrap I could to get a few decent things. And over here they're accustomed to being bargained with—you ought to see how I've beaten them down! Have you any idea what a dinner-dress costs in New York . . . ?"

So it went on, obtusely and persistently, whenever he tried to sound the note of prudence. But on other themes she was more than usually responsive. Paris enchanted her, and they had delightful hours at the theaters— the "little" ones—amusing dinners at fashionable restaurants, and reckless evenings in haunts where she thrilled with simple glee at the thought of what she must so obviously be "taken for." All these familiar diversions regained, for Ralph, a fresh zest in her company. Her innocence, her high spirits, her astounding comments and credulities, renovated the old Parisian adventure and flung a veil of romance over its hackneyed scenes. Beheld through such a medium the future looked less near and implacable, and Ralph, when he had received a reassuring letter from his sister, let his conscience sleep and slipped forth on the high tide of pleasure. After all, in New York amusements would be fewer, and their life, for a time, perhaps more quiet. Moreover, Ralph's dim glimpses of Mr. Spragg's past suggested that the latter was likely to be on his feet again at any moment, and atoning by redoubled prodigalities for his temporary straits; and beyond all these possibilities there was the book to be written—the book on which Ralph was sure he should get a real hold as soon as they settled down in New York.

Meanwhile the daily cost of living, and the bills that could not be deferred, were eating deep into Laura's subsidy. Ralph's anxieties returned, and his plight was brought home to him with a shock when, on going one day to engage passages, he learned that the prices were that of the "rush season," and one of the conditions immediate payment. At other times, he was told the rules were easier; but in September and October no exception could be made.

As he walked away with this fresh weight on his mind he caught sight of the strolling figure of Peter Van Degen—Peter lounging and luxuriating among the seductions of the boulevard with the disgusting ease of a man whose wants are all measured by money, and who always has enough to gratify them.

His present sense of these advantages revealed itself in the affability of his greeting to Ralph, and in his offhand request that the latter should "look up Clare," who had come over with him to get her winter finery.

"She's motoring to Italy next week with some of her long-haired friends —but I'm off for the other side; going back on the *Sorceress*. She's just been overhauled at Greenock, and we ought to have a good spin over. Better come along with me, old man."

The *Sorceress* was Van Degen's steam-yacht, most huge and complicated of her kind: it was his habit, after his semiannual flights to Paris and London, to take a joyous company back on her and let Clare return by steamer. The character of these parties made the invitation almost an offense to Ralph; but reflecting that it was probably a phrase distributed to every acquaintance when Van Degen was in a rosy mood, he merely answered: "Much obliged, my dear fellow; but Undine and I are sailing immediately."

Peter's glassy eye grew livelier. "Ah, to be sure—you're not over the honeymoon yet. How's the bride? Stunning as ever? My regards to her, please. I suppose she's too deep in dressmaking to be called on?—but don't you forget to look up Clare!" He hurried on in pursuit of a flitting petticoat and Ralph continued his walk home.

He prolonged it a little in order to put off telling Undine of his plight; for he could devise only one way of meeting the cost of the voyage, and that was to take it at once, and thus curtail their Parisian expenses. But he knew how unwelcome this plan would be, and he shrank the more from seeing Undine's face harden since, of late, he had so basked in its brightness.

When at last he entered the little salon she called "stuffy" he found her in conference with a blond-bearded gentleman who wore the red ribbon in his lapel, and who, on Ralph's appearance—and at a sign, as it appeared, from Mrs. Marvell—swept into his notecase some small objects that had lain on the table, and bowed himself out with a "Madame—Monsieur" worthy of the highest traditions.

Ralph looked after him with amusement. "Who's your friend—an ambassador or a tailor?"

Undine was rapidly slipping on her rings, which, as he now saw, had also been scattered over the table.

"Oh, it was only that jeweler I told you about—the one Bertha Shallum goes to."

"A jeweler? Good heavens, my poor girl! You're buying jewels?" The extravagance of the idea struck a laugh from him.

Undine's face did not harden: it took on, instead, an almost deprecating look. "Of course not—how silly you are! I only wanted a few old things reset. But I won't if you'd rather not."

She came to him and sat down at his side, laying her hand on his arm. He took the hand up and looked at the deep gleam of the sapphires in the old family ring he had given her.

"You won't have that reset?" he said, smiling and twisting the ring about on her finger; then he went on with his thankless explanation. "It's not that I don't want you to do this or that; it's simply that, for the moment, we're rather strapped. I've just been to see the steamer people, and our passages will cost a good deal more than I thought."

He mentioned the sum and the fact that he must give an answer the next day. Would she consent to sail that very Saturday? Or should they go a fortnight later, in a slow boat from Plymouth?

Undine frowned on both alternatives. She was an indifferent sailor and shrank from the possible "nastiness" of the cheaper boat. She wanted to get the voyage over as quickly and luxuriously as possible—Bertha Shallum had told her that in a "deck-suite" no one need be seasick—but she wanted still more to have another week or two of Paris; and it was always hard to make her see why circumstances could not be bent to her wishes.

"This week? But how on earth can I be ready? Besides, we're dining at Enghien with the Shallums on Saturday, and motoring to Chantilly with the Jim Driscolls on Sunday. I can't imagine how you thought we could go this week!"

But she still opposed the cheap steamer, and after they had carried the question on to Voisin's, and there unprofitably discussed it through a long luncheon, it seemed no nearer a solution.

"Well, think it over—let me know this evening," Ralph said, proportioning the waiter's fee to a bill burdened by Undine's reckless choice of *primeurs*.

His wife was to join the newly arrived Mrs. Shallum in a round of the rue de la Paix; and he had seized the opportunity of slipping off to a classical performance at the Français. On their arrival in Paris he had taken Undine to one of these entertainments, but it left her too weary and puzzled for him to renew the attempt, and he had not found time to go back without her. He was glad now to shed his cares in such an atmosphere. The play was of the greatest, the interpretation that of the vanishing grand manner which lived in his first memories of the Parisian stage, and his surrender to such influences as complete as in his early days. Caught up in the fiery chariot of art, he felt once more the tug of its coursers in his muscles, and the rush of their flight still throbbed in him when he walked back late to the hotel.

13

HE had expected to find Undine still out; but on the stairs he crossed Mrs. Shallum, who threw at him from under an immense hat-brim: "Yes, she's in, but you'd better come and have tea with me at the Luxe. I don't think husbands are wanted!"

Ralph laughingly rejoined that that was just the moment for them to appear; and Mrs. Shallum swept on, crying back: "All the same, I'll wait for you!"

In the sitting-room Ralph found Undine seated behind a tea-table on the other side of which, in an attitude of easy intimacy, Peter Van Degen stretched his lounging length.

He did not move on Ralph's appearance, no doubt thinking their kinship close enough to make his nod and "Hullo!" a sufficient greeting. Peter in intimacy was given to miscalculations of the sort, and Ralph's first movement was to glance at Undine and see how it affected her. But her eyes gave out the vivid rays that noise and banter always struck from them; her face, at such moments, was like a theater with all the lusters blazing. That the illumination should have been kindled by his cousin's husband was not precisely agreeable to Marvell, who thought Peter a bore in society and an insufferable nuisance on closer terms. But he was becoming blunted to Undine's lack of discrimination; and his own treatment of Van Degen was always tempered by his sympathy for Clare.

He therefore listened with apparent good-humor to Peter's suggestion of an evening at a *petit théâtre* with the Harvey Shallums, and joined in the laugh with which Undine declared: "Oh, Ralph won't go—he only likes the theaters where they walk around in bathtowels and talk poetry. Isn't that what you've just been seeing?" she added, with a turn of the neck that shed her brightness on him.

"What? One of those five-barrelled shows at the Français? Great Scott, Ralph—no wonder your wife's pining for the Folies Bergère!"

"She needn't, my dear fellow. We never interfere with each other's vices."

Peter, unsolicited, was comfortably lighting a cigarette. "Ah, there's the secret of domestic happiness. Marry somebody who likes all the things you don't, and make love to somebody who likes all the things you do."

Undine laughed appreciatively. "Only it dooms poor Ralph to such awful frumps. Can't you see the sort of woman who'd love his sort of play?"

"Oh, I can see her fast enough—my wife loves 'em," said their visitor, rising with a grin; while Ralph threw out: "So don't waste your pity on me!" and Undine's laugh had the slight note of asperity that the mention of Clare always elicited.

"Tomorrow night, then, at Paillard's," Van Degen concluded. "And about the other business—that's a go, too? I leave it to you to settle the date."

The nod and laugh they exchanged seemed to hint at depths of collusion from which Ralph was pointedly excluded; and he wondered how large a program of pleasure they had already had time to sketch out. He disliked the idea of Undine's being too frequently seen with Van Degen, whose Parisian reputation was not fortified by the connections that propped it up in New York; but he did not want to interfere with her pleasure, and he was still wondering what to say when, as the door closed, she turned to him gaily.

"I'm so glad you've come! I've got some news for you." She laid a light touch on his arm.

Touch and tone were enough to disperse his anxieties, and he answered that he was in luck to find her already in when he had supposed her engaged, over a Nouveau Luxe tea-table, in repairing the afternoon's ravages.

"Oh, I didn't shop much—I didn't stay out long." She raised a kindling face to him. "And what do you think I've been doing? While you were sitting in your stuffy old theater, worrying about the money I was spending (oh, you needn't fib—I know you were!) I was saving you hundreds and thousands. I've saved you the price of our passage!"

Ralph laughed in pure enjoyment of her beauty. When she shone on him like that what did it matter what nonsense she talked?

"You wonderful woman—how did you do it? By countermanding a tiara?"

"You know I'm not such a fool as you pretend!" She held him at arm's length with a nod of joyous mystery. "You'll simply never guess! I've made Peter Van Degen ask us to go home on the *Sorceress*. What do you say to that?"

She flashed it out on a laugh of triumph, without appearing to have a doubt of the effect the announcement would produce.

Ralph stared at her. "The *Sorceress*? You *made* him?"

"Well, I managed it, I worked him round to it! He's crazy about the idea now—but I don't think he'd thought of it before he came."

"I should say not!" Ralph ejaculated. "He never would have had the cheek to think of it."

"Well, I've made him, anyhow! Did you ever know such luck?"

"Such luck?" He groaned at her obstinate innocence. "Do you suppose I'll let you cross the ocean on the *Sorceress*?"

She shrugged impatiently. "You say that because your cousin doesn't go on her."

"If she doesn't, it's because it's no place for decent women."

"It's Clare's fault if it isn't. Everybody knows she's crazy about you, and she makes him feel it. That's why he takes up with other women."

Her anger reddened her cheeks and dropped her brows like a black bar above her glowing eyes. Even in his recoil from what she said Ralph felt the tempestuous heat of her beauty. But for the first time his latent resentments rose in him, and he gave her back wrath for wrath.

"Is that the precious stuff he tells you?"

"Do you suppose I had to wait for him to tell me? Everybody knows it—everybody in New York knew she was wild when you married. That's why she's always been so nasty to me. If you won't go on the *Sorceress* they'll all say it's because she was jealous of me and wouldn't let you."

Ralph's indignation had already flickered down to disgust. Undine was no longer beautiful—she seemed to have the face of her thoughts. He stood up with an impatient laugh.

"Is that another of his arguments? I don't wonder they're convincing —" But as quickly as it had come the sneer dropped, yielding to a wave of pity, the vague impulse to silence and protect her. How could he have given way to the provocation of her weakness, when his business was to defend her from it and lift her above it? He recalled his old dreams of saving her from Van Degenism—it was not thus that he had imagined the rescue.

"Don't let's pay Peter the compliment of squabbling over him," he said, turning away to pour himself a cup of tea.

When he had filled his cup he sat down beside Undine, with a smile. "No doubt he was joking—and thought you were; but if you really made him believe we might go with him you'd better drop him a line."

Undine's brow still gloomed. "You refuse, then?"

"Refuse? I don't need to! Do you want to succeed to half the chorus-world of New York?"

"They won't be on board with us, I suppose!"

"The echoes of their conversation will. It's the only language Peter knows."

"He told me he longed for the influence of a good woman —" She checked herself, reddening at Ralph's laugh.

"Well, tell him to apply again when he's been under it a month or two. Meanwhile we'll stick to the liners."

Ralph was beginning to learn that the only road to her reason lay through her vanity, and he fancied that if she could be made to see Van Degen as an object of ridicule she might give up the idea of the *Sorceress* of her own accord. But her will hardened slowly under his joking opposition, and she became no less formidable as she grew more calm. He was used to women who, in such cases, yielded as a matter of course to masculine judgments: if one pronounced a man "not decent" the question was closed. But it was Undine's habit to ascribe all interference with her plans to personal motives, and he could see that she attributed his opposition to the furtive machinations of poor Clare. It was odious to him to prolong the discussion, for the accent of recrimination was the one he most dreaded on her lips. But the moment came when he had to take the brunt of it, averting his thoughts as best he might from the glimpse it gave of a world of mean familiarities, of reprisals drawn from the vulgarist of vocabularies. Certain retorts sped through the air like the flight of household utensils, certain charges rang out like accusations of tampering with the groceries. He stiffened himself against such comparisons, but they stuck in his imagination and left him thankful when Undine's anger yielded to a burst of tears. He had held his own and gained his point. The trip on the *Sorceress* was given up, and a note of withdrawal dispatched to Van Degen; but at the same time Ralph cabled his sister to ask if she could increase her loan. For he had conquered only at the cost of a concession: Undine was to stay in Paris till October, and they were to sail on a fast steamer, in a deck-suite, like the Harvey Shallums.

Undine's ill-humor was soon dispelled by any new distraction, and she gave herself to the untroubled enjoyment of Paris. The Shallums were the center of a like-minded group, and in the hours the ladies could spare from their dressmakers the restaurants shook with their hilarity and the suburbs with the shriek of their motors. Van Degen, who had postponed his sailing, was a frequent sharer in these amusements; but Ralph counted on New York influences to detach him from Undine's train. He was learning to influence her through her social instincts where he had once tried to appeal to other sensibilities.

His worst moment came when he went to see Clare Van Degen, who, on the eve of departure, had begged him to come to her hotel. He found her less restless and rattling than usual, with a look in her eyes that reminded him of the days when she had haunted his thoughts. The visit passed off without vain returns to the past; but as he was leaving she surprised him by saying: "Don't let Peter make a goose of your wife."

Ralph reddened, but laughed.

"Oh, Undine's wonderfully able to defend herself, even against such seductions as Peter's."

Mrs. Van Degen looked down with a smile at the bracelets on her thin brown wrist. "His personal seductions—yes. But as an inventor of amusements he's inexhaustible; and Undine likes to be amused."

Ralph made no reply but showed no annoyance. He simply took her hand and kissed it as he said goodbye; and she turned from him without audible farewell.

As the day of departure approached, Undine's absorption in her dresses almost precluded the thought of amusement. Early and late she was closeted with fitters and packers—even the competent Céleste not being trusted to handle the treasures now pouring in—and Ralph cursed his weakness in not restraining her, and then fled for solace to museums and galleries.

He could not rouse in her any scruple about incurring fresh debts, yet he knew she was no longer unaware of the value of money. She had learned to bargain, pare down prices, evade fees, browbeat the small tradespeople and wheedle concessions from the great—not, as Ralph perceived, from any effort to restrain her expenses, but only to prolong and intensify the pleasure of spending. Pained by the trait, he tried to laugh her out of it. He told her once that she had a miserly hand—showing her, in proof, that, for all their softness, the fingers would not bend back, or the pink palm open. But she retorted a little sharply that it was no wonder, since she'd heard nothing talked of since their marriage but economy; and this left him without any answer. So the purveyors continued to mount to their apartment, and Ralph, in the course of his frequent flights from it, found himself always dodging the corners of black glazed boxes and swaying pyramids of pasteboard; always lifting his hat to sidling milliners' girls, or effacing himself before slender *vendeuses* floating by in a mist of opopanax. He felt incompetent to pronounce on the needs to which these visitors ministered; but the reappearance among them of the blond-bearded jeweller gave him ground for fresh fears. Undine had assured him that she had given up the idea of having her ornaments reset, and there had been ample time for their return; but on his questioning her she explained that there had been delays and "bothers" and put him in the wrong by asking ironically if he supposed she was buying things "for pleasure" when she knew as well as he that there wasn't any money to pay for them.

But his thoughts were not all dark. Undine's moods still infected him, and when she was happy he felt an answering lightness. Even when her amusements were too primitive to be shared he could enjoy their reflection in her face. Only, as he looked back, he was struck by the evanescence, the lack of substance, in their moments of sympathy, and by the permanent marks left by each breach between them. Yet he still fancied that someday the balance might be reversed, and that as she acquired a finer sense of values the depths in her would find a voice.

Something of this was in his mind when, the afternoon before their departure, he came home to help her with their last arrangements. She had begged him, for the day, to leave her alone in their cramped salon, into which belated bundles were still pouring; and it was nearly dark when he returned. The evening before she had seemed pale and nervous, and at the last moment had excused herself from dining with the Shallums at a suburban restaurant. It was so unlike her to miss any opportunity of the kind that Ralph had felt a little anxious. But with the arrival of the packers she was afoot and in command again, and he withdrew submissively, as Mr. Spragg, in the early Apex days, might have fled from the spring storm of "housecleaning."

When he entered the sitting-room, he found it still in disorder. Every chair was hidden under scattered dresses, tissue-paper surged from the yawning trunks and, prone among her heaped-up finery, Undine lay with closed eyes on the sofa.

She raised her head as he entered, and then turned listlessly away.

"My poor girl, what's the matter? Haven't they finished yet?"

Instead of answering she pressed her face into the cushion and began to sob. The violence of her weeping shook her hair down on her shoulders, and her hands, clenching the arm of the sofa, pressed it away from her as if any contact were insufferable.

Ralph bent over her in alarm. "Why, what's wrong, dear? What's happened?"

Her fatigue of the previous evening came back to him—a puzzled hunted look in her eyes; and with the memory a vague wonder revived. He had fancied himself fairly disencumbered of the stock formulas about the hallowing effects of motherhood, and there were many reasons for not welcoming the news he suspected she had to give; but the woman a man loves is always a special case, and everything was different that befell Undine. If this was what had befallen her it was wonderful and divine: for the moment that was all he felt.

"Dear, tell me what's the matter," he pleaded.

She sobbed on unheedingly and he waited for her agitation to subside. He shrank from the phrases considered appropriate to the situation, but he wanted to hold her close and give her the depth of his heart in a long kiss.

Suddenly she sat upright and turned a desperate face on him. "Why on earth are you staring at me like that? Anybody can see what's the matter!"

He winced at her tone, but managed to get one of her hands in his; and they stayed thus in silence, eye to eye.

"Are you as sorry as all that?" he began at length, conscious of the flatness of his voice.

"Sorry—sorry? I'm—I'm —" She snatched her hand away, and went on weeping.

"But, Undine—dearest—by and by you'll feel differently—I know you will!"

"Differently? Differently? When? In a year? It *takes* a year—a whole year out of life! What do I care how I shall feel in a year?"

The chill of her tone struck in. This was more than a revolt of the nerves: it was a settled, a reasoned resentment. Ralph found himself groping for extenuations, evasions—anything to put a little warmth into her!

"Who knows? Perhaps, after all, it's a mistake."

There was no answering light in her face. She turned her head from him wearily.

"Don't you think, dear, you may be mistaken?"

"Mistaken? How on earth can I be mistaken?"

Even in that moment of confusion he was struck by the cold competence of her tone, and wondered how she could be so sure.

"You mean you've asked—you've consulted —?"

The irony of it took him by the throat. They were the very words he might have spoken in some miserable secret colloquy—the words he was speaking to his wife!

She repeated dully: "I know I'm not mistaken."

There was another long silence. Undine lay still, her eyes shut, drumming on the arm of the sofa with a restless hand. The other lay cold in Ralph's clasp, and through it there gradually stole to him the benumbing

influence of the thoughts she was thinking: the sense of the approach of
illness, anxiety, and expense, and of the general unnecessary disorganization
of their lives.

"That's all you feel, then?" he asked at length a little bitterly, as if to
disguise from himself the hateful fact that he felt it, too. He stood up and
moved away. "That's all?" he repeated.

"Why, what else do you expect me to feel? I feel horribly ill, if that's
what you want." He saw the sobs trembling up through her again.

"Poor dear—poor girl. . . . I'm so sorry—so dreadfully sorry!"

The senseless reiteration seemed to exasperate her. He knew it by the
quiver that ran through her like the premonitory ripple on smooth water
before the coming of the wind. She turned about on him and jumped to her
feet.

"Sorry—you're sorry? *You're* sorry? Why, what earthly difference will it
make to *you?*" She drew back a few steps and lifted her slender arms from
her sides. "Look at me—see how I look—how I'm going to look! *You* won't
hate yourself more and more every morning when you get up and see yourself in the glass! *Your* life's going on just as usual! But what's mine going to
be for months and months? And just as I'd been to all this bother—fagging
myself to death about all these things —" her tragic gesture swept the disor-
dered room—"just as I thought I was going home to enjoy myself, and look
nice, and see people again, and have a little pleasure after all our worries —" She dropped back on the sofa with another burst of tears. "For all
the good this rubbish will do me now! I loathe the very sight of it!" she
sobbed with her face in her hands.

14

I T was one of the distinctions of Mr. Claud Walsingham Popple that his
studio was never too much encumbered with the attributes of his art to
permit the installing, in one of its cushioned corners, of an elaborately
furnished tea-table flanked by the most varied seductions in sandwiches and
pastry.

Mr. Popple, like all great men, had at first had his ups and downs; but
his reputation had been permanently established by the verdict of a wealthy
patron who, returning from an excursion into other fields of portraiture, had
given it as the final fruit of his experience that Popple was the only man
who could "do pearls." To sitters for whom this was of the first consequence
it was another of the artist's merits that he always subordinated art to

elegance, in life as well as in his portraits. The "messy" element of production was no more visible in his expensively screened and tapestried studio than its results were perceptible in his painting; and it was often said, in praise of his work, that he was the only artist who kept his studio tidy enough for a lady to sit to him in a new dress.

Mr. Popple, in fact, held that the personality of the artist should at all times be dissembled behind that of the man. It was his opinion that the essence of good-breeding lay in tossing off a picture as easily as you lit a cigarette. Ralph Marvell had once said of him that when he began a portrait he always turned back his cuffs and said: "Ladies and gentlemen, you can see there's absolutely nothing here"; and Mrs. Fairford supplemented the description by defining his painting as "chafing-dish" art.

On a certain late afternoon of December, some four years after Mr. Popple's first meeting with Miss Undine Spragg of Apex, even the symbolic chafing-dish was nowhere visible in his studio; the only evidence of its recent activity being the full-length portrait of Mrs. Ralph Marvell, who, from her lofty easel and her heavily garlanded frame, faced the doorway with the air of having been invited to "receive" for Mr. Popple.

The artist himself, becomingly clad in mouse-colored velveteen, had just turned away from the picture to hover above the teacups; but his place had been taken by the considerably broader bulk of Mr. Peter Van Degen, who, tightly molded into a coat of the latest cut, stood before the portrait in the attitude of a first arrival.

"Yes, it's good—it's damn good, Popp; you've hit the hair off ripplingly; but the pearls ain't big enough," he pronounced.

A slight laugh sounded from the raised dais behind the easel.

"Of course they're not! But it's not *his* fault, poor man; *he* didn't give them to me!" As she spoke Mrs. Ralph Marvell rose from a monumental gilt armchair of pseudo-Venetian design and swept her long draperies to Van Degen's side.

"He might, then—for the privilege of painting you!" the latter rejoined, transferring his bulging stare from the counterfeit to the original. His eyes rested on Mrs. Marvell's in what seemed a quick exchange of understanding; then they passed on to a critical inspection of her person. She was dressed for the sitting in something faint and shining, above which the long curves of her neck looked dead white in the cold light of the studio; and her hair, all a shadowless rosy gold, was starred with a hard glitter of diamonds.

"The privilege of painting me? Mercy, I have to pay for being painted! He'll tell you he's giving me the picture—but what do you suppose this cost?" She laid a fingertip on her shimmering dress.

Van Degen's eye rested on her with cold enjoyment. "Does the price come higher than the dress?"

She ignored the allusion. "Of course what they charge for is the cut —"

"What they cut away? That's what they ought to charge for, ain't it, Popp?"

Undine took this with cool disdain, but Mr. Popple's sensibilities were offended.

"My dear Peter—really—the artist, you understand, sees all this as a pure question of color, of pattern; and it's a point of honor with the *man* to steel himself against the personal seduction."

Mr. Van Degen received this protest with a sound of almost vulgar derision, but Undine thrilled agreeably under the glance which her portrayer cast on her. She was flattered by Van Degen's notice, and thought his impertinence witty; but she glowed inwardly at Mr. Popple's eloquence. After more than three years of social experience she still thought he "spoke beautifully," like the hero of a novel, and she ascribed to jealousy the lack of seriousness with which her husband's friends regarded him. His conversation struck her as intellectual, and his eagerness to have her share his thoughts was in flattering contrast to Ralph's growing tendency to keep his to himself. Popple's homage seemed the subtlest proof of what Ralph could have made of her if he had "really understood" her. It was but another step to ascribe all her past mistakes to the lack of such understanding; and the satisfaction derived from this thought had once impelled her to tell the artist that he alone knew how to rouse her "higher self." He had assured her that the memory of her words would thereafter hallow his life; and as he hinted that it had been stained by the darkest errors she was moved at the thought of the purifying influence she exerted.

Thus it was that a man should talk to a true woman—but how few whom she had known possessed the secret! Ralph, in the first months of their marriage, had been eloquent too, had even gone the length of quoting poetry; but he disconcerted her by his baffling twists and strange allusions (she always scented ridicule in the unknown), and the poets he quoted were esoteric and abstruse. Mr. Popple's rhetoric was drawn from more familiar sources, and abounded in favorite phrases and in moving reminiscences of the Fifth Reader. He was moreover as literary as he was artistic; possessing an unequalled acquaintance with contemporary fiction, and dipping even into the lighter type of memoirs, in which the old acquaintances of history are served up in the disguise of "A Royal Sorceress" or "Passion in a Palace." The mastery with which Mr. Popple discussed the novel of the day, especially in relation to the sensibilities of its hero and heroine, gave Undine a sense of intellectual activity which contrasted strikingly with Marvell's flippant estimate of such works. "Passion," the artist implied, would have been the dominant note of his life, had it not been held in check by a sentiment of exalted chivalry, and by the sense that a nature of such emotional intensity as his must always be "ridden on the curb."

Van Degen was helping himself from the tray of iced cocktails which stood near the tea-table, and Popple, turning to Undine, took up the thread of his discourse. But why, he asked, why allude before others to feelings so few could understand? The average man—lucky devil!—(with a compassionate glance at Van Degen's back) the average man knew nothing of the fierce conflict between the lower and higher natures; and even the woman whose eyes had kindled it—how much did *she* guess of its violence? Did she know—Popple recklessly asked—how often the artist was forgotten in the man—how often the man would take the bit between his teeth, were it not that the look in her eyes recalled some sacred memory, some lesson learned perhaps beside his mother's knee?

"I say, Popp—was that where you learned to mix this drink? Because it does the old lady credit," Van Degen called out, smacking his lips; while the artist, dashing a nervous hand through his hair, muttered: "Hang it, Peter—is *nothing* sacred to you?"

It pleased Undine to feel herself capable of inspiring such emotions. She would have been fatigued by the necessity of maintaining her own talk on Popple's level, but she liked to listen to him, and especially to have others overhear what he said to her.

Her feeling for Van Degen was different. There was more similarity of tastes between them, though his manner flattered her vanity less than Popple's. She felt the strength of Van Degen's contempt for everything he did not understand or could not buy: that was the only kind of "exclusiveness" that impressed her. And he was still to her, as in her inexperienced days, the master of the mundane science she had once imagined that Ralph Marvell possessed. During the three years since her marriage she had learned to make distinctions unknown to her girlish categories. She had found out that she had given herself to the exclusive and the dowdy when the future belonged to the showy and the promiscuous; that she was in the case of those who have cast in their lot with a fallen cause, or—to use an analogy more within her range—who have hired an opera-box on the wrong night. It was all confusing and exasperating. Apex ideals had been based on the myth of "old families" ruling New York from a throne of Revolutionary tradition, with the new millionaires paying them feudal allegiance. But experience had long since proved the delusiveness of the simile. Mrs. Marvell's classification of the world into the visited and the unvisited was as obsolete as a medieval cosmogony. Some of those whom Washington Square left unvisited were the center of social systems far outside its ken, and as indifferent to its opinions as the constellations to the reckonings of the astronomers; and all these systems joyously revolved about their central sun of gold.

There were moments after Undine's return to New York when she was tempted to class her marriage with the hateful early mistakes from the memories of which she had hoped it would free her. Since it was never her habit to accuse herself of such mistakes it was inevitable that she should gradually come to lay the blame on Ralph. She found a poignant pleasure, at this stage of her career, in the question: "What does a young girl know of life?" And the poignancy was deepened by the fact that each of the friends to whom she put the question seemed convinced that—had the privilege been his—he would have known how to spare her the disenchantment it implied.

The conviction of having blundered was never more present to her than when, on this particular afternoon, the guests invited by Mr. Popple to view her portrait began to assemble before it.

Some of the principal figures of Undine's group had rallied for the occasion, and almost all were in exasperating enjoyment of the privileges for which she pined. There was young Jim Driscoll, heir-apparent of the house, with his short, stout, mistrustful wife, who hated society, but went everywhere lest it might be thought she had been left out; the "beautiful Mrs. Beringer," a lovely, aimless being, who kept (as Laura Fairford said) a home for stray opinions, and could never quite tell them apart; little Dicky Bowles, whom everyone invited because he was understood to "say things" if one didn't; the Harvey Shallums, fresh from Paris, and dragging in their wake a bewildered nobleman vaguely designated as "the count," who offered cautious conversational openings, like an explorer trying beads on savages; and, behind these more salient types, the usual filling in of those who are seen everywhere because they have learned to catch the social eye. Such a company was one to flatter the artist as much as his sitter, so completely did it represent that unanimity of opinion which constitutes social strength. Not one of the number was troubled by any personal theory of art: all they asked of a portrait was that the costume should be sufficiently "lifelike," and the face not too much so; and a long experience in idealizing flesh and realizing dress fabrics had enabled Mr. Popple to meet both demands.

"Hang it," Peter Van Degen pronounced, standing before the easel in an attitude of inspired interpretation, "the great thing in a man's portrait is to catch the likeness—we all know that; but with a woman's it's different—a woman's picture has got to be pleasing. Who wants it about if it isn't? Those big chaps who blow about what they call realism—how do *their* portraits look in a drawing-room? Do you suppose they ever ask themselves that? *They* don't care—they're not going to live with the things! And what do they know of drawing-rooms, anyhow? Lots of them haven't even got a dress-suit. There's where old Popp has the pull over 'em—*he* knows how we live and what we want."

This was received by the artist with a deprecating murmur, and by his public with warm expressions of approval.

"Happily in this case," Popple began ("as in that of so many of my sitters," he hastily put in), "there has been no need to idealize—nature herself has outdone the artist's dream."

Undine, radiantly challenging comparison with her portrait, glanced up at it with a smile of conscious merit, which deepened as young Jim Driscoll declared: "By Jove, Mamie, you must be done exactly like that for the new music-room."

His wife turned a cautious eye upon the picture.

"How big is it? For our house it would have to be a good deal bigger," she objected; and Popple, fired by the thought of such a dimensional opportunity, rejoined that it would be the chance of all others to "work in" a marble portico and a court-train: he had just done Mrs. Lycurgus Ambler in a court-train and feathers, and as *that* was for Buffalo, of course, the pictures needn't clash.

"Well, it would have to be a good deal bigger than Mrs. Ambler's," Mrs. Driscoll insisted; and on Popple's suggestion that in that case he might "work in" Driscoll, in court-dress also—("You've been presented? Well, you *will* be—you'll *have* to, if I do the picture—which will make a lovely memento")—Van Degen turned aside to murmur to Undine: "Pure bluff, you know—Jim couldn't pay for a photograph. Old Driscoll's high and dry since the Ararat investigation."

She threw him a puzzled glance, having no time, in her crowded existence, to follow the perturbations of Wall Street save as they affected the hospitality of Fifth Avenue.

"You mean they've lost their money? Won't they give their fancy-ball, then?"

Van Degen shrugged. "Nobody knows how it's coming out. That queer chap Elmer Moffatt threatens to give old Driscoll a fancy-ball—says he's going to dress him in stripes! It seems he knows too much about the Apex street-railways."

Undine paled a little. Though she had already tried on her costume for the Driscoll ball her disappointment at Van Degen's announcement was effaced by the mention of Moffatt's name. She had not had the curiosity to follow the reports of the "Ararat Trust Investigation," but once or twice lately, in the snatches of smoking-room talk, she had been surprised by a vague allusion to Elmer Moffatt, as to an erratic financial influence, half ridiculed, yet already half redoubtable. Was it possible that the redoubtable element had prevailed? That the time had come when Elmer Moffatt—the Elmer Moffatt of Apex!—could, even for a moment, cause consternation in the Driscoll camp? He had always said he "saw things big"; but no one had ever believed he was destined to carry them out on the same scale. Yet apparently in those idle Apex days, while he seemed to be "loafing and fooling," as her father called it, he had really been sharpening his weapons of aggression; there had been something, after all, in the effect of loose-drifting power she had always felt in him. Her heart beat faster, and she longed to question Van Degen; but she was afraid of betraying herself, and turned back to the group about the picture.

Mrs. Driscoll was still presenting objections in a tone of small mild obstinacy. "Oh, it's a *likeness,* of course—I can see that; but there's one thing I must say, Mr. Popple. It looks like a last year's dress."

The attention of the ladies instantly rallied to the picture, and the artist paled at the challenge.

"It doesn't look like a last year's face, anyhow—that's what makes them all wild," Van Degen murmured.

Undine gave him back a quick smile. She had already forgotten about Moffatt. Any triumph in which she shared left a glow in her veins, and the success of the picture obscured all other impressions. She saw herself thronging in a central panel at the spring exhibition, with the crowd pushing about the picture, repeating her name; and she decided to stop on the way home and telephone her press agent to do a paragraph about Popple's tea.

But in the hall, as she drew on her cloak, her thoughts reverted to the Driscoll fancy-ball. What a blow if it were given up after she had taken so much trouble about her dress! She was to go as the Empress Josephine, after the Prudhon portrait in the Louvre. The dress was already fitted and partly embroidered, and she foresaw the difficulty of persuading the dressmaker to take it back.

"Why so pale and sad, fair cousin? What's up?" Van Degen asked, as they emerged from the lift in which they had descended alone from the studio.

"I don't know—I'm tired of posing. And it was so frightfully hot."

"Yes. Popple always keeps his place at low-neck temperature, as if the portraits might catch cold." Van Degen glanced at his watch. "Where are you off to?"

"West End Avenue, of course—if I can find a cab to take me there."

It was not the least of Undine's grievances that she was still living in the house which represented Mr. Spragg's first real-estate venture in New York. It had been understood, at the time of her marriage, that the young couple were to be established within the sacred precincts of fashion; but on their return from the honeymoon the still untenanted house in West End Avenue had been placed at their disposal, and in view of Mr. Spragg's financial embarrassment even Undine had seen the folly of refusing it. That first winter, moreover, she had not regretted her exile; while she awaited her boy's birth she was glad to be out of sight of Fifth Avenue, and to take her hateful compulsory exercise where no familiar eye could fall on her. And the next year, of course, her father would give them a better house.

But the next year rents had risen in the Fifth Avenue quarter, and meanwhile little Paul Marvell, from his beautiful pink cradle, was already interfering with his mother's plans. Ralph, alarmed by the fresh rush of expenses, sided with his father-in-law in urging Undine to resign herself to West End Avenue; and thus after three years she was still submitting to the incessant pinpricks inflicted by the incongruity between her social and geographical situation—the need of having to give a West Side address to her tradesmen, and the deeper irritation of hearing her friends say: "Do let me give you a lift home, dear—Oh, I'd forgotten! I'm afraid I haven't the time to go so far —"

It was bad enough to have no motor of her own, to be avowedly dependent on "lifts," openly and unconcealably in quest of them, and perpetually plotting to provoke their offer (she did so hate to be seen in a cab!); but to miss them, as often as not, because of the remoteness of her destination, emphasized the hateful sense of being "out of things."

Van Degen looked out at the long snow-piled street, down which the lamps were beginning to put their dreary yellow splashes.

"Of course, you won't get a cab on a night like this. If you don't mind the open car, you'd better jump in with me. I'll run you out to the High Bridge and give you a breath of air before dinner."

The offer was tempting, for Undine's triumph in the studio had left her tired and nervous—she was beginning to learn that success may be as fatiguing as failure. Moreover, she was going to a big dinner that evening, and the fresh air would give her the eyes and complexion she needed; but in the back of her mind there lingered the vague sense of a forgotten engagement. As she tried to recall it she felt Van Degen raising the fur collar about her chin.

"Got anything you can put over your head? Will that lace thing do? Come along, then." He pushed her through the swinging doors, and added with a laugh, as they reached the street: "You're not afraid of being seen with me, are you? It's all right at this hour—Ralph's still swinging on a strap in the elevated."

The winter twilight was deliciously cold, and as they swept through Central Park, and gathered impetus for their northward flight along the darkening boulevard, Undine felt the rush of physical joy that drowns scruples and silences memory. Her scruples, indeed, were not serious; but Ralph disliked her being too much with Van Degen, and it was her way to get what she wanted with as little "fuss" as possible. Moreover, she knew it was a mistake to make herself too accessible to a man of Peter's sort: her impatience to enjoy was curbed by an instinct for holding off and biding her time that resembled the patient skill with which her father had conducted the sale of his "bad" real estate in the Pure Water Move days. But now and then youth had its way—she could not always resist the present pleasure. And it was amusing, too, to be "talked about" with Peter Van Degen, who was noted for not caring for "nice women." She enjoyed the thought of triumphing over meretricious charms: it ennobled her in her own eyes to influence such a man for good.

Nevertheless, as the motor flew on through the icy twilight, her present cares flew with it. She could not shake off the thought of the useless fancy dress which symbolized the other crowding expenses she had not dared confess to Ralph. Van Degen heard her sigh, and bent down, lowering the speed of the motor.

"What's the matter? Isn't everything all right?"

His tone made her suddenly feel that she could confide in him, and though she began by murmuring that it was nothing she did so with the conscious purpose of being persuaded to confess. And his extraordinary "niceness" seemed to justify her and to prove that she had been right in trusting her instinct rather than in following the counsels of prudence. Heretofore, in their talks, she had never gone beyond the vaguest hint of material "bothers"—as to which dissimulation seemed vain while one lived in West End Avenue! But now that the avowal of a definite worry had been wrung from her she felt the injustice of the view generally taken of poor Peter. For he had been neither too enterprising nor too cautious (though people said of him that he "didn't care to part"); he had just laughed away, in bluff brotherly fashion, the gnawing thought of the fancy dress, had assured her he'd give a ball himself rather than miss seeing her wear it, and had added: "Oh, hang waiting for the bill—won't a couple of thou' make it all right?" in a tone that showed what a small matter money was to anyone who took the larger view of life.

The whole incident passed off so quickly and easily that within a few minutes she had settled down—with a nod for his "Everything jolly again now?"—to untroubled enjoyment of the hour. Peace of mind, she said to herself, was all she needed to make her happy—and that was just what Ralph had never given her! At the thought his face seemed to rise before her, with the sharp lines of care between the eyes: it was almost like a part of his "nagging" that he should thrust himself in at such a moment! She tried to shut her eyes to the face; but a moment later it was replaced by another, a small odd likeness of itself; and with a cry of compunction she started up from her furs.

"Mercy! It's the boy's birthday—I was to take him to his grandmother's. She was to have a cake for him, and Ralph was to come up town. I *knew* there was something I'd forgotten!"

15

I N the Dagonet drawing-room the lamps had long been lit, and Mrs. Fairford, after a last impatient turn, had put aside the curtains of worn damask to strain her eyes into the darkening square. She came back to the hearth, where Charles Bowen stood leaning between the prim caryatides of the white marble chimney-piece.

"No sign of her. She's simply forgotten."

Bowen looked at his watch, and turned to compare it with the high-waisted Empire clock.

"Six o'clock. Why not telephone again? There must be some mistake. Perhaps she knew Ralph would be late."

Laura laughed. "I haven't noticed that she follows Ralph's movements so closely. When I telephoned just now the servant said she'd been out since two. The nurse waited till half-past four, not liking to come without orders; and now it's too late for Paul to come."

She wandered away toward the farther end of the room, where, through half-open doors, a shining surface of mahogany reflected a flower-wreathed cake in which two candles dwindled.

"Put them out, please," she said to someone in the background; then she shut the doors and turned back to Bowen.

"It's all so unlucky—my grandfather giving up his drive, and mother backing out of her hospital meeting, and having all the committee down on her. And Henley: I'd even coaxed Henley away from his bridge! He escaped again just before you came. Undine promised she'd have the boy here at four. It's not as if it had never happened before. She's always breaking her engagements."

"She has so many that it's inevitable some should get broken."

"Ah, if she'd only choose! Now that Ralph has had to go into business, and is kept in his office so late, it's cruel of her to drag him out every night. He told us the other day they hadn't dined at home for a month. Undine doesn't seem to notice how hard he works."

Bowen gazed meditatively at the crumbling fire. "No—why should she?"

"Why *should* she? Really, Charles —!"

"Why should she, when she knows nothing about it?"

"She may know nothing about his business; but she must know it's her extravagance that's forced him into it." Mrs. Fairford looked at Bowen reproachfully. "You talk as if you were on her side!"

"Are there sides already? If so, I want to look down on them impartially from the heights of pure speculation. I want to get a general view of the whole problem of American marriages."

Mrs. Fairford dropped into her armchair with a sigh. "If that's what you want you must make haste! Most of them don't last long enough to be classified."

"I grant you it takes an active mind. But the weak point is so frequently the same that after a time one knows where to look for it."

"What do you call the weak point?"

He paused. "The fact that the average American looks down on his wife."

Mrs. Fairford was up with a spring. "If that's where paradox lands you!"

Bowen mildly stood his ground. "Well—doesn't he prove it? How much does he let her share in the real business of life? How much does he rely on her judgment and help in the conduct of serious affairs? Take Ralph, for instance—you say his wife's extravagance forces him to work too hard; but that's not what's wrong. It's normal for a man to work hard for a woman— what's abnormal is his not caring to tell her anything about it."

"To tell Undine? She'd be bored to death if he did!"

"Just so; she'd even feel aggrieved. But why? Because it's against the custom of the country. And whose fault is that? The man's again—I don't mean Ralph, I mean the genus he belongs to: homo sapiens, Americanus. Why haven't we taught our women to take an interest in our work? Simply because we don't take enough interest in *them*."

Mrs. Fairford, sinking back into her chair, sat gazing at the vertiginous depths above which his thought seemed to dangle her.

"*You* don't? The American man doesn't—the most slaving, self-effacing, self-sacrificing —?"

"Yes; and the most indifferent: there's the point. The 'slaving's' no argument against the indifference. To slave for women is part of the old American tradition; lots of people give their lives for dogmas they've ceased to believe in. Then again, in this country the passion for making money has preceded the knowing how to spend it, and the American man lavishes his fortune on his wife because he doesn't know what else to do with it."

"Then you call it a mere want of imagination for a man to spend his money on his wife?"

"Not necessarily—but it's a want of imagination to fancy it's all he owes her. Look about you and you'll see what I mean. Why does the European woman interest herself so much more in what the men are doing? Because she's so important to them that they make it worth her while! She's not a parenthesis, as she is here—she's in the very middle of the picture. I'm not implying that Ralph isn't interested in his wife—he's a passionate, a pathetic exception. But even he has to conform to an environment where all the romantic values are reversed. Where does the real life of most American men lie? In some woman's drawing-room or in their offices? The answer's obvious, isn't it? The emotional center of gravity's not the same in the two hemispheres. In the effete societies it's love, in our new one it's business. In America the real *crime passionnel* is a 'big steal'—there's more excitement in wrecking railways than homes."

Bowen paused to light another cigarette, and then took up his theme. "Isn't that the key to our easy divorces? If we cared for women in the old barbarous possessive way do you suppose we'd give them up as readily as we do? The real paradox is the fact that the men who make, materially, the biggest sacrifices for their women, should do least for them ideally and romantically. And what's the result—how do the women avenge themselves? All my sympathy's with them, poor deluded dears, when I see their fallacious little attempts to trick out the leavings tossed them by the preoccupied male—the money and the motors and the clothes—and pretend to themselves and each other that *that's* what really constitutes life! Oh, I know what you're going to say—it's less and less of a pretense with them, I grant you; they're more and more succumbing to the force of the suggestion; but here and there I fancy there's one who still sees through the humbug, and knows that money and motors and clothes are simply the big bribe she's paid for keeping out of some man's way!"

Mrs. Fairford presented an amazed silence to the rush of this tirade; but when she rallied it was to murmur: "And is Undine one of the exceptions?"

Her companion took the shot with a smile. "No—she's a monstrously perfect result of the system: the completest proof of its triumph. It's Ralph who's the victim and the exception."

"Ah, poor Ralph!" Mrs. Fairford raised her head quickly. "I hear him now. I suppose," she added in an undertone, "we can't give him your explanation for his wife's having forgotten to come?"

Bowen echoed her sigh, and then seemed to toss it from him with his cigarette-end; but he stood in silence while the door opened and Ralph Marvell entered.

"Well, Laura! Hallo, Charles—have you been celebrating too?" Ralph turned to his sister. "It's outrageous of me to be so late, and I daren't look my son in the face! But I stayed downtown to make provision for his future birthdays." He returned Mrs. Fairford's kiss. "Don't tell me the party's over, and the guest of honor gone to bed?"

As he stood before them, laughing and a little flushed, the strain of long fatigue sounding through his gaiety and looking out of his anxious eyes, Mrs. Fairford threw a glance at Bowen and then turned away to ring the bell.

"Sit down, Ralph—you look tired. I'll give you some tea."

He dropped into an armchair. "I did have rather a rush to get here—but hadn't I better join the revelers? Where are they?"

He walked to the end of the room and threw open the dining-room doors. "Hallo—where have they all gone to? What a jolly cake!" He went up to it. "Why, it's never even been cut!"

Mrs. Fairford called after him: "Come and have your tea first."

"No, no—tea afterward, thanks. Are they all upstairs with my grandfather? I must make my peace with Undine —"

His sister put her arm through his, and drew him back to the fire.

"Undine didn't come."

"Didn't come? Who brought the boy, then?"

"He didn't come either. That's why the cake's not cut."

Ralph frowned. "What's the mystery? Is he ill, or what's happened?"

"Nothing's happened—Paul's all right. Apparently Undine forgot. She never went home for him, and the nurse waited till it was too late to come."

She saw his eyes darken; but he merely gave a slight laugh and drew out his cigarette case. "Poor little Paul—poor chap!" He moved toward the fire. "Yes, please—some tea."

He dropped back into his chair with a look of weariness, as if some strong stimulant had suddenly ceased to take effect on him; but before the tea-table was brought back he had glanced at his watch and was on his feet again.

"But this won't do. I must rush home and see the poor chap before dinner. And my mother—and my grandfather? I want to say a word to them —I must make Paul's excuses!"

"Grandfather's taking his nap. And mother had to rush out for a post-poned committee meeting—she left as soon as we heard Paul wasn't com-ing."

"Ah, I see." He sat down again. "Yes, make the tea strong, please. I've had a beastly fagging sort of day."

He leaned back with half-closed eyes, his untouched cup in his hand. Bowen took leave, and Laura sat silent, watching her brother under lowered lids while she feigned to be busy with the kettle. Ralph presently emptied his cup and put it aside; then, sinking into his former attitude, he clasped his hands behind his head and lay staring apathetically into the fire. But suddenly he came to life and started up. A motor-horn had sounded outside, and there was a noise of wheels at the door.

"There's Undine! I wonder what could have kept her." He jumped up and walked to the door; but it was Clare Van Degen who came in.

At sight of him she gave a little murmur of pleasure. "What luck to find you! No, not luck—I came because I knew you'd be here. He never comes near me, Laura: I have to hunt him down to get a glimpse of him!"

Slender and shadowy in her long furs, she bent to kiss Mrs. Fairford and then turned back to Ralph. "Yes, I knew I'd catch you here. I knew it was the boy's birthday, and I've brought him a present: a vulgar expensive Van Degen offering. I've not enough imagination left to find the right thing, the thing it takes feeling and not money to buy. When I look for a present nowadays I never say to the shopman: 'I want this or that'—I simply say: 'Give me something that costs so much.' " She drew a parcel from her muff. "Where's the victim of my vulgarity? Let me crush him under the weight of my gold."

Mrs. Fairford sighed out "Clare—Clare!" and Ralph smiled at his cousin.

"I'm sorry; but you'll have to depute me to present it. The birthday's over; you're too late."

She looked surprised. "Why, I've just left Mamie Driscoll, and she told me Undine was still at Popple's studio a few minutes ago: Popple's giving a tea to show the picture."

"Popple's giving a tea?" Ralph struck an attitude of mock consternation.

"Ah, in that case —! In Popple's society who wouldn't forget the flight of time?"

He had recovered his usual easy tone, and Laura saw that Mrs. Van Degen's words had dispelled his preoccupation. He turned to his cousin. "Will you trust me with your present for the boy?"

Clare gave him the parcel. "I'm sorry not to give it myself. I said what I did because I knew what you and Laura were thinking—but it's really a battered old Dagonet bowl that came down to me from our revered great-grandmother."

"What—the heirloom you used to eat your porridge out of?" Ralph detained her hand to put a kiss on it. "That's dear of you!"

She threw him one of her strange glances. "Why not say: 'That's like you?' But you don't remember what I'm like." She turned away to glance at the clock. "It's late, and I must be off. I'm going to a big dinner at the Chauncey Ellings'—but you must be going there too, Ralph? You'd better let me drive you home."

In the motor Ralph leaned back in silence, while the rug was drawn over their knees, and Clare restlessly fingered the row of gold-topped objects in the rack at her elbow. It was restful to be swept through the crowded streets in this smooth fashion, and Clare's presence at his side gave him a vague sense of ease.

For a long time now feminine nearness had come to mean to him, not this relief from tension, but the ever-renewed dread of small daily deceptions, evasions, subterfuges. The change had come gradually, marked by one disillusionment after another; but there had been one moment that formed the point beyond which there was no returning. It was the moment, a month or two before his boy's birth, when, glancing over a batch of belated Paris bills, he had come on one from the jeweler he had once found in private conference with Undine. The bill was not large, but two of its items stood out sharply. "Resetting pearl and diamond pendant. Resetting sapphire and diamond ring." The pearl and diamond pendant was his mother's wedding present; the ring was the one he had given Undine on their engagement. That they were both family relics, kept unchanged through several generations, scarcely mattered to him at the time: he felt only the stab of his wife's deception. She had assured him in Paris that she had not had her jewels reset. He had noticed, soon after their return to New York, that she had left off her engagement ring; but the others were soon discarded also, and in answer to his question she had told him that, in her ailing state, rings "worried" her. Now he saw she had deceived him, and, forgetting everything else, he went to her, bill in hand. Her tears and distress filled him with immediate contrition. Was this a time to torment her about trifles? His anger seemed to cause her actual physical fear, and at the sight he abased himself in entreaties for forgiveness. When the scene ended she had pardoned him, and the reset ring was on her finger. . . .

Soon afterward, the birth of the boy seemed to wipe out these humiliating memories; yet Marvell found in time that they were not effaced, but only momentarily crowded out of sight. In reality, the incident had a meaning out of proportion to its apparent seriousness, for it put in his hand a clue to a new side of his wife's character. He no longer minded her having lied about the jeweller; what pained him was that she had been unconscious of the wound she inflicted in destroying the identity of the jewels. He saw that, even after their explanation, she still supposed he was angry only because she had deceived him; and the discovery that she was completely unconscious of states of feeling on which so much of his inner life depended marked a new stage in their relation.

He was not thinking of all this as he sat beside Clare Van Degen; but it was part of the chronic disquietude which made him more alive to his cousin's sympathy, her shy unspoken understanding. After all, he and she were of the same blood and had the same traditions. She was light and frivolous, without strength of will or depth of purpose; but she had the frankness of her foibles, and she would never have lied to him or traded on his tenderness.

Clare's nervousness gradually subsided, and she lapsed into a low-voiced mood which seemed like an answer to his secret thought. But she did not sound the personal note, and they chatted quietly of commonplace things: of the dinner-dance at which they were presently to meet, of the costume she had chosen for the Driscoll fancy-ball, the recurring rumors of old Driscoll's financial embarrassment, and the mysterious personality of Elmer Moffatt, on whose movements Wall Street was beginning to fix a fascinated eye. When Ralph, the year after his marriage, had renounced his profession to go into partnership with a firm of real-estate agents, he had come in contact for the first time with the drama of "business," and whenever he could turn his attention from his own tasks he found a certain interest in watching the fierce interplay of its forces. In the downtown world he had heard things of Moffatt that seemed to single him out from the common herd of money-makers: anecdotes of his coolness, his lazy good-temper, the humorous detachment he preserved in the heat of conflicting interests; and his figure was enlarged by the mystery that hung about it—the fact that no one seemed to know whence he came, or how he had acquired the information which, for the moment, was making him so formidable.

"I should like to see him," Ralph said; "he must be a good specimen of the one of the few picturesque types we've got."

"Yes—it might be amusing to fish him out; but the most picturesque types in Wall Street are generally the tamest in a drawing-room." Clare considered. "But doesn't Undine know him? I seem to remember seeing them together."

"Undine and Moffatt? Then *you* know him—you've met him?"

"Not actually met him—but he's been pointed out to me. It must have been some years ago. Yes—it was one night at the theater, just after you announced your engagement." He fancied her voice trembled slightly, as though she thought he might notice her way of dating her memories. "You came into our box," she went on, "and I asked you the name of the red-faced man who was sitting in the stall next to Undine. You didn't know, but someone told us it was Moffatt."

Marvell was more struck by her tone than by what she was saying. "If Undine knows him it's odd she's never mentioned it," he answered indifferently.

The motor stopped at his door and Clare, as she held out her hand, turned a first full look on him.

"Why do you never come to see me? I miss you more than ever," she said.

He pressed her hand without answering, but after the motor had rolled away he stood for a while on the pavement, looking after it.

When he entered the house the hall was still dark and the small over-furnished drawing-room empty. The parlor maid told him that Mrs. Marvell had not yet come in, and he went upstairs to the nursery. But on the threshold the nurse met him with the whispered request not to make a noise, as it had been hard to quiet the boy after the afternoon's disappointment, and she had just succeeded in putting him to sleep.

Ralph went down to his own room and threw himself in the old college armchair in which, four years previously, he had sat the night out, dreaming of Undine. He had no study of his own, and he had crowded into his narrow bedroom his prints and bookshelves, and the other relics of his youth. As he sat among them now the memory of that other night swept over him—the night when he had heard the "call"! Fool as he had been not to recognize its meaning then, he knew himself triply mocked in being, even now, at its mercy. The flame of love that had played about his passion for his wife had died down to its embers; all the transfiguring hopes and illusions were gone, but they had left an unquenchable ache for her nearness, her smile, her touch. His life had come to be nothing but a long effort to win these mercies by one concession after another: the sacrifice of his literary projects, the exchange of his profession for an uncongenial business, and the incessant struggle to make enough money to satisfy her increasing exactions. That was where the "call" had led him. . . .

The clock struck eight, but it was useless to begin to dress till Undine came in, and he stretched himself out in his chair, reached for a pipe and took up the evening paper. His passing annoyance had died out; he was usually too tired after his day's work for such feelings to keep their edge long. But he was curious—disinterestedly curious—to know what pretext Undine would invent for being so late, and what excuse she would have found for forgetting the little boy's birthday.

He read on till half-past eight; then he stood up and sauntered to the

window. The avenue below it was deserted; not a carriage or motor turned
the corner around which he expected Undine to appear, and he looked idly
in the opposite direction. There too the perspective was nearly empty, so
empty that he singled out, a dozen blocks away, the blazing lamps of a large
touring-car that was bearing furiously down the avenue from Morningside.
As it drew nearer its speed slackened, and he saw it hug the curb and stop at
his door. By the light of the street lamp he recognized his wife as she sprang
out and detected a familiar silhouette in her companion's fur-coated figure.
Then the motor flew on and Undine ran up the steps.

Ralph went out on the landing. He saw her coming up quickly, as if to
reach her room unperceived; but when she caught sight of him she stopped,
her head thrown back and the light falling on her blown hair and glowing
face.

"Well?" she said, smiling up at him.

"They waited for you all the afternoon in Washington Square—the boy
never had his birthday," he answered.

Her color deepened, but she instantly rejoined: "Why, what happened?
Why didn't the nurse take him?"

"You said you were coming to fetch him, so she waited."

"But I telephoned —"

He said to himself: "Is *that* the lie?" and answered: "Where from?"

"Why, the studio, of course —" She flung her cloak open, as if to attest
her veracity. "The sitting lasted longer than usual—there was something
about the dress he couldn't get —"

"But I thought he was giving a tea."

"He had tea afterward; he always does. And he asked some people in to
see my portrait. That detained me too. I didn't know they were coming, and
when they turned up I couldn't rush away. It would have looked as if I
didn't like the picture." She paused and they gave each other a searching
simultaneous glance. "Who told you it was a tea?" she asked.

"Clare Van Degen. I saw her at my mother's."

"So you weren't unconsoled after all —!"

"The nurse didn't get any message. My people were awfully disappointed; and the poor boy has cried his eyes out."

"Dear me! What a fuss! But I might have known my message wouldn't
be delivered. Everything always happens to put me in the wrong with your
family."

With a little air of injured pride she started to go to her room; but he put
out a hand to detain her.

"You've just come from the studio?"

"Yes. It is awfully late? I must go and dress. We're dining with the
Ellings, you know."

"I know. . . . How did you come? In a cab?"

She faced him limpidly. "No; I couldn't find one that would bring me—

so Peter gave me a lift, like an angel. I'm blown to bits. He had his open car."

Her color was still high, and Ralph noticed that her lower lip twitched a little. He had led her to the point they had reached solely to be able to say: "If you're straight from the studio, how was it that I saw you coming down from Morningside?"

Unless he asked her that there would be no point in his cross-questioning, and he would have sacrificed his pride without a purpose. But suddenly, as they stood there face to face, almost touching, she became something immeasurably alien and far off, and the question died on his lips.

"Is that all?" she asked with a slight smile.

"Yes; you'd better go and dress," he said, and turned back to his room.

16

THE turnings of life seldom show a signpost; or rather, though the sign is always there, it is usually placed some distance back, like the notices that give warning of a bad hill or a level railway crossing.

Ralph Marvell, pondering upon this, reflected that for him the sign had been set, more than three years earlier, in an Italian ilex grove. That day his life had brimmed over—so he had put it at the time. He saw now that it had brimmed over indeed: brimmed to the extent of leaving the cup empty, or at least of uncovering the dregs beneath the nectar. He knew now that he should never hereafter look at his wife's hand without remembering something he had read in it that day. Its surface-language had been sweet enough, but under the rosy lines he had seen the warning letters.

Since then he had been walking with a ghost: the miserable ghost of his illusion. Only he had somehow vivified, colored, substantiated it, by the force of his own great need—as a man might breathe a semblance of life into a dear drowned body that he cannot give up for dead. All this came to him with aching distinctness the morning after his talk with his wife on the stairs. He had accused himself, in midnight retrospect, of having failed to press home his conclusion because he dared not face the truth. But he knew this was not the case. It was not the truth he feared, it was another lie. If he had foreseen a chance of her saying: "Yes, I was with Peter Van Degen, and for the reason you think," he would have put it to the touch, stood up to the blow like a man; but he knew she would never say that. She would go on eluding and doubling, watching him as he watched her; and at that game she was sure to beat him in the end.

On their way home from the Elling dinner this certainty had become so insufferable that it nearly escaped him in the cry: "You needn't watch me—I shall never again watch you!" But he had held his peace, knowing she would not understand. How little, indeed, she ever understood, had been made clear to him when, the same night, he had followed her upstairs through the sleeping house. She had gone on ahead while he stayed below to lock doors and put out lights, and he had supposed her to be already in her room when he reached the upper landing; but she stood there waiting, in the spot where he had waited for her a few hours earlier. She had shone her vividest at dinner, with the revolving brilliancy that collective approval always struck from her; and the glow of it still hung on her as she paused there in the dimness, her shining cloak dropped from her white shoulders.

"Ralphie —" she began, a soft hand on his arm.

He stopped, and she pulled him about so that their faces were close, and he saw her lips curving for a kiss. Every line of her face sought him, from the sweep of the narrowed eyelids to the dimples that played away from her smile. His eye received the picture with distinctness; but for the first time it did not pass into his veins. It was as if he had been struck with a subtle blindness that permitted images to give their color to the eye but communicated nothing to the brain.

"Good night," he said, as he passed on.

When a man felt in that way about a woman he was surely in a position to deal with his case impartially. This came to Ralph as the joyless solace of the morning. At last the bandage was off and he could see. And what did he see? Only the uselessness of driving his wife to subterfuges that were no longer necessary. Was Van Degen her lover? Probably not—the suspicion died as it rose. She would not take more risks than she could help, and it was admiration, not love, that she wanted. She wanted to enjoy herself, and her conception of enjoyment was publicity, promiscuity—the band, the banners, the crowd, the close contact of covetous impulses, and the sense of walking among them in cool security. Any personal entanglement might mean "bother," and bother was the thing she most abhorred. Probably, as the queer formula went, his "honor" was safe: he could count on the letter of her fidelity. At the moment the conviction meant no more to him than if he had been assured of the honesty of the first stranger he met in the street. A stranger—that was what she had always been to him. So malleable outwardly, she had remained insensible to the touch of the heart.

These thoughts accompanied him on his way to business the next morning. Then, as the routine took him back, the feeling of strangeness diminished. There he was again at his daily task—nothing tangible was altered. He was there for the same purpose as yesterday: to make money for his wife and child. The woman he had turned from on the stairs a few hours earlier was still his wife and the mother of Paul Marvell. She was an inherent part of his life; the inner disruption had not resulted in any outward upheaval.

And with the sense of inevitableness there came a sudden wave of pity. Poor Undine! She was what the gods had made her—a creature of skin-deep reactions, a mote in the beam of pleasure. He had no desire to "preach down" such heart as she had—he felt only a stronger wish to reach it, teach it, move it to something of the pity that filled his own. They were fellow-victims in the *noyade* of marriage, but if they ceased to struggle perhaps the drowning would be easier for both. . . . Meanwhile the first of the month was at hand, with its usual batch of bills; and there was no time to think of any struggle less pressing than that connected with paying them. . . .

Undine had been surprised, and a little disconcerted, at her husband's acceptance of the birthday incident. Since the resetting of her bridal ornaments the relations between Washington Square and West End Avenue had been more and more strained; and the silent disapproval of the Marvell ladies was more irritating to her than open recrimination. She knew how keenly Ralph must feel her last slight to his family, and she had been frightened when she guessed that he had seen her returning with Van Degen. He must have been watching from the window, since, credulous as he always was, he evidently had a reason for not believing her when she told him she had come from the studio. There was therefore something both puzzling and disturbing in his silence; and she made up her mind that it must be either explained or cajoled away.

These thoughts were with her as she dressed; but at the Ellings' they fled like ghosts before light and laughter. She had never been more open to the suggestions of immediate enjoyment. At last she had reached the envied situation of the pretty woman with whom society must reckon, and if she had only had the means to live up to her opportunities she would have been perfectly content with life, with herself and her husband. She still thought Ralph "sweet" when she was not bored by his good advice or exasperated by his inability to pay her bills. The question of money was what chiefly stood between them; and now that this was momentarily disposed of by Van Degen's offer she looked at Ralph more kindly—she even felt a return of her first impersonal affection for him. Everybody could see that Clare Van Degen was "gone" on him, and Undine always liked to know that what belonged to her was coveted by others.

Her reassurance had been fortified by the news she had heard at the Elling dinner—the published fact of Harmon B. Driscoll's unexpected victory. The Ararat investigation had been mysteriously stopped—quashed, in the language of the law—and Elmer Moffatt "turned down," as Van Degen (who sat next to her) expressed it.

"I don't believe we'll ever hear of that gentleman again," he said contemptuously; and their eyes crossed gaily as she exclaimed: "Then they'll give the fancy-ball after all?"

"I should have given you one anyhow—shouldn't you have liked that as well?"

"Oh, you can give me one too!" she returned; and he bent closer to say: "By Jove, I will—and anything else you want."

But on the way home her fears revived. Ralph's indifference struck her as unnatural. He had not returned to the subject of Paul's disappointment, had not even asked her to write a word of excuse to his mother. Van Degen's way of looking at her at dinner—he was incapable of graduating his glances—had made it plain that the favor she had accepted would necessitate her being more conspicuously in his company (though she was still resolved that it should be on just such terms as she chose); and it would be extremely troublesome if, at this juncture, Ralph should suddenly turn suspicious and secretive.

Undine, hitherto, had found more benefits than drawbacks in her marriage; but now the tie began to gall. It was hard to be criticized for every grasp at opportunity by a man so avowedly unable to do the reaching for her! Ralph had gone into business to make more money for her; but it was plain that the "more" would never be much, and that he would not achieve the quick rise to affluence which was man's natural tribute to woman's merits. Undine felt herself trapped, deceived; and it was intolerable that the agent of her disillusionment should presume to be the critic of her conduct.

Her annoyance, however, died out with her fears. Ralph, the morning after the Elling dinner, went his way as usual, and after nerving herself for the explosion which did not come she set down his indifference to the dulling effect of "business." No wonder poor women whose husbands were always "downtown" had to look elsewhere for sympathy! Van Degen's check helped to calm her, and the weeks whirled on toward the Driscoll ball.

The ball was as brilliant as she had hoped, and her own part in it as thrilling as a page from one of the "society novels" with which she had cheated the monotony of Apex days. She had no time for reading now: every hour was packed with what she would have called life, and the intensity of her sensations culminated on that triumphant evening. What could be more delightful than to feel that, while all the women envied her dress, the men did not so much as look at it? Their admiration was all for herself, and her beauty deepened under it as flowers take a warmer color in the rays of sunset. Only Van Degen's glance weighed on her a little too heavily. Was it possible that he might become a "bother" less negligible than those he had relieved her of? Undine was not greatly alarmed—she still had full faith in her powers of self-defense; but she disliked to feel the least crease in the smooth surface of existence. She had always been what her parents called "sensitive."

As the winter passed, material cares once more assailed her. In the thrill of liberation produced by Van Degen's gift she had been imprudent—had launched into fresh expenses. Not that she accused herself of extravagance:

she had done nothing not really necessary. The drawing-room, for instance, cried out to be "done over," and Popple, who was an authority on decoration, had shown her, with a few strokes of his pencil, how easily it might be transformed into a French "period" room, all curves and cupids: just the setting for a pretty woman and his portrait of her. But Undine, still hopeful of leaving West End Avenue, had heroically resisted the suggestion, and contented herself with the renewal of the curtains and carpet, and the purchase of some fragile gilt chairs which, as she told Ralph, would be "so much to the good" when they moved—the explanation, as she made it, seemed an additional evidence of her thrift.

Partly as a result of these exertions she had a "nervous breakdown" toward the middle of the winter, and her physician having ordered massage and a daily drive it became necessary to secure Mrs. Heeny's attendance and to engage a motor by the month. Other unforeseen expenses—the bills, that, at such times, seem to run up without visible impulsion—were added to by a severe illness of little Paul's: a long costly illness, with three nurses and frequent consultations. During these days Ralph's anxiety drove him to what seemed to Undine foolish excesses of expenditure and when the boy began to get better the doctors advised country air. Ralph at once hired a small house at Tuxedo and Undine of course accompanied her son to the country; but she spent only the Sundays with him, running up to town during the week to be with her husband, as she explained. This necessitated the keeping up of two households, and even for so short a time the strain on Ralph's purse was severe. So it came about that the bill for the fancy-dress was still unpaid, and Undine left to wonder distractedly what had become of Van Degen's money. That Van Degen seemed also to wonder was becoming unpleasantly apparent: his check had evidently not brought in the return he expected, and he put his grievance to her frankly one day when he motored down to lunch at Tuxedo.

They were sitting, after luncheon, in the low-ceilinged drawing-room to which Undine had adapted her usual background of cushions, bric-a-brac and flowers—since one must make one's setting "homelike," however little one's habits happened to correspond with that particular effect. Undine, conscious of the intimate charm of her *mise-en-scène*, and of the recovered freshness and bloom which put her in harmony with it, had never been more sure of her power to keep her friend in the desired state of adoring submission. But Peter, as he grew more adoring, became less submissive; and there came a moment when she needed all her wits to save the situation. It was easy enough to rebuff him, the easier as his physical proximity always roused in her a vague instinct of resistance; but it was hard so to temper the rebuff with promise that the game of suspense should still delude him. He put it to her at last, standing squarely before her, his batrachian sallowness unpleasantly flushed, and primitive man looking out of the eyes from which a frock-coated gentleman usually pined at her.

"Look here—the installment plan's all right; but ain't you a bit behind even on that?" (She had brusquely eluded a nearer approach.) "Anyhow, I think I'd rather let the interest accumulate for a while. This is goodbye till I get back from Europe."

The announcement took her by surprise. "Europe? Why, when are you sailing?"

"On the first of April: good day for a fool to acknowledge his folly. I'm beaten, and I'm running away."

She sat looking down, her hand absently occupied with the twist of pearls he had given her. In a flash she saw the peril of this departure. Once off on the *Sorceress*, he was lost to her—the power of old associations would prevail. Yet if she were as "nice" to him as he asked—"nice" enough to keep him—the end might not be much more to her advantage. Hitherto she had let herself drift on the current of their adventure, but she now saw what port she had half-unconsciously been trying for. If she had striven so hard to hold him, had "played" him with such patience and such skill, it was for something more than her passing amusement and convenience: for a purpose the more tenaciously cherished that she had not dared name it to herself. In the light of this discovery she saw the need of feigning complete indifference.

"Ah, you happy man! It's goodbye indeed, then," she threw back at him, lifting a plaintive smile to his frown.

"Oh, you'll turn up in Paris later, I suppose—to get your things for Newport."

"Paris? Newport? They're not on my map! When Ralph can get away we shall go to the Adirondacks for the boy. I hope I shan't need Paris clothes there! It doesn't matter, at any rate," she ended, laughing, "because nobody I care about will see me."

Van Degen echoed her laugh. "Oh, come—that's rough on Ralph!"

She looked down with a slight increase of color. "I oughtn't to have said it, ought I? But the fact is I'm unhappy—and a little hurt —"

"Unhappy? Hurt?" He was at her side again. "Why, what's wrong?"

She lifted her eyes with a grave look. "I thought you'd be sorrier to leave me."

"Oh, it won't be for long—it needn't be, you know." He was perceptibly softening. "It's damnable, the way you're tied down. Fancy rotting all summer in the Adirondacks! Why do you stand it? You oughtn't to be bound for life by a girl's mistake."

The lashes trembled slightly on her cheek. "Aren't we all bound by our mistakes—we women? Don't let us talk of such things! Ralph would never let me go abroad without him." She paused, and then, with a quick upward sweep of the lids: "After all, it's better it should be goodbye—since I'm paying for another mistake in being so unhappy at your going."

"Another mistake? Why do you call it that?"

"Because I've misunderstood you—or you me." She continued to smile at him wistfully. "And some things are best mended by a break."

He met her smile with a loud sigh—she could feel him in the meshes again. "*Is* it to be a break between us?"

"Haven't you just said so? Anyhow, it might as well be, since we shan't be in the same place again for months."

The frock-coated gentleman once more languished from his eyes: she thought she trembled on the edge of victory. "Hang it," he broke out, "you ought to have a change—you're looking awfully pulled down. Why can't you coax your mother to run over to Paris with you? Ralph couldn't object to that."

She shook her head. "I don't believe she could afford it, even if I could persuade her to leave father. You know father hasn't done very well lately: I shouldn't like to ask him for the money."

"You're so confoundedly proud!" He was edging nearer. "It would all be so easy if you'd only be a little fond of me. . . ."

She froze to her sofa-end. "We women can't repair our mistakes. Don't make me more miserable by reminding me of mine."

"Oh, nonsense! There's nothing cash won't do. Why won't you let me straighten things out for you?"

Her color rose again, and she looked him quickly and consciously in the eye. It was time to play her last card. "You seem to forget that I am—married," she said.

Van Degen was silent—for a moment she thought he was swaying to her in the flush of surrender. But he remained doggedly seated, meeting her look with an odd clearing of his heated gaze, as if a shrewd businessman had suddenly replaced the pining gentleman at the window.

"Hang it—so am I!" he rejoined; and Undine saw that in the last issue he was still the stronger of the two.

17

NOTHING was bitterer to her than to confess to herself the failure of her power; but her last talk with Van Degen had taught her a lesson almost worth the abasement. She saw the mistake she had made in taking money from him, and understood that if she drifted into repeating that mistake her future would be irretrievably compromised. What she wanted was not a hand-to-mouth existence of precarious intrigue: to one with her gifts the privileges of life should come openly. Already in her short experience she had seen enough of the women who sacrifice future security for immediate success, and she meant to lay solid foundations before she began to build up the light superstructure of enjoyment.

Nevertheless it was galling to see Van Degen leave, and to know that for the time he had broken away from her. Over a nature so insensible to the spells of memory, the visible and tangible would always prevail. If she could have been with him again in Paris, where, in the shining spring days, every sight and sound ministered to such influences, she was sure she could have regained her hold. And the sense of frustration was intensified by the fact that everyone she knew was to be there: her potential rivals were crowding the eastbound steamers. New York was a desert, and Ralph's seeming unconsciousness of the fact increased her resentment. She had had but one chance at Europe since her marriage, and that had been wasted through her husband's unaccountable perversity. She knew now with what packed hours of Paris and London they had paid for their empty weeks in Italy.

Meanwhile the long months of the New York spring stretched out before her in all their social vacancy to the measureless blank of a summer in the Adirondacks. In her girlhood she had plumbed the dim depths of such summers; but then she had been sustained by the hope of bringing some capture to the surface. Now she knew better: there were no "finds" for her in that direction. The people she wanted would be at Newport or in Europe, and she was too resolutely bent on a definite object, too sternly animated by her father's business instinct, to turn aside in quest of casual distractions.

The chief difficulty in the way of her attaining any distant end had always been her reluctance to plod through the intervening stretches of dullness and privation. She had begun to see this, but she could not always master the weakness: never had she stood in greater need of Mrs. Heeny's "Go slow, Undine!" Her imagination was incapable of long flights. She could not cheat her impatience with the mirage of far-off satisfactions, and for the moment present and future seemed equally void. But her desire to go to Europe and to rejoin the little New York world that was reforming itself in London and Paris was fortified by reasons which seemed urgent enough to justify an appeal to her father.

She went down to his office to plead her case, fearing Mrs. Spragg's intervention. For some time past Mr. Spragg had been rather continuously overworked, and the strain was beginning to tell on him. He had never quite regained, in New York, the financial security of his Apex days. Since he had changed his base of operations his affairs had followed an uncertain course, and Undine suspected that his breach with his old political ally, the Representative Rolliver who had seen him through the muddiest reaches of the Pure Water Move, was not unconnected with his failure to get a footing in Wall Street. But all this was vague and shadowy to her. Even had "business" been less of a mystery, she was too much absorbed in her own affairs to project herself into her father's case; and she thought she was sacrificing enough to delicacy of feeling in sparing him the "bother" of Mrs. Spragg's opposition.

When she came to him with a grievance he always heard her out with the same mild patience; but the long habit of "managing" him had made her, in his own language, "discount" this tolerance, and when she ceased to speak her heart throbbed with suspense as he leaned back, twirling an invisible toothpick under his sallow moustache. Presently he raised a hand to stroke the limp beard in which the moustache was merged; then he groped for the Masonic emblem that had lost itself in one of the folds of his depleted waistcoat.

He seemed to fish his answer from the same rusty depths, for as his fingers closed about the trinket he said: "Yes, the heated term *is* trying in New York. That's why the Fresh Air Fund pulled my last dollar out of me last week."

Undine frowned: there was nothing more irritating, in these encounters with her father, than his habit of opening the discussion with a joke.

"I wish you'd understand that I'm serious, Father. I've never been strong since the baby was born, and I need a change. But it's not only that: there are other reasons for my wanting to go."

Mr. Spragg still held to his mild tone of banter. "I never knew you short on reasons, Undie. Trouble is you don't always know other people's when you see 'em."

His daughter's lips tightened. "I know your reasons when I see them, father: I've heard them often enough. But you can't know mine because I haven't told you—not the real ones."

"Jehoshaphat! I thought they were all real as long as you had a use for them."

Experience had taught her that such protracted trifling usually concealed an exceptional vigor of resistance, and the suspense strengthened her determination.

"My reasons are all real enough," she answered; "but there's one more serious than the others."

Mr. Spragg's brows began to jut. "More bills?"

"No." She stretched out her hand and began to finger the dusty objects on his desk. "I'm unhappy at home."

"Unhappy —!" His start overturned the gorged wastepaper basket and shot a shower of paper across the rug. He stooped to put the basket back; then he turned his slow fagged eyes on his daughter. "Why, he worships the ground you walk on, Undie."

"That's not always a reason, for a woman —" It was the answer she would have given to Popple or Van Degen, but she saw in an instant the mistake of thinking it would impress her father. In the atmosphere of sentimental casuistry to which she had become accustomed, she had forgotten that Mr. Spragg's private rule of conduct was as simple as his business morality was complicated.

He glowered at her under thrust-out brows. "It isn't a reason, isn't it? I can seem to remember the time when you used to think it was equal to a whole carload of whitewash."

She blushed a bright red, and her own brows were leveled at his above her stormy steel-gray eyes. The sense of her blunder made her angrier with him, and more ruthless.

"I can't expect you to understand—you never *have*, you or Mother, when it came to my feelings. I suppose some people are born sensitive—I can't imagine anybody'd *choose* to be so. Because I've been too proud to complain you've taken it for granted that I was perfectly happy. But my marriage was a mistake from the beginning; and Ralph feels just as I do about it. His people hate me, they've always hated me; and he looks at everything as they do. They've never forgiven me for his having had to go into business—with their aristocratic ideas they look down on a man who works for his living. Of course it's all right for *you* to do it, because you're not a Marvell or a Dagonet; but they think Ralph ought to just lie back and let you support the baby and me."

This time she had found the right note: she knew it by the tightening of her father's slack muscles and the sudden straightening of his back.

"By George, he pretty near does!" he exclaimed, bringing down his fist on the desk. "They haven't been taking it out of you about that, have they?"

"They don't fight fair enough to say so. They just egg him on to turn against me. They only consented to his marrying me because they thought you were so crazy about the match you'd give us everything, and he'd have nothing to do but sit at home and write books."

Mr. Spragg emitted a derisive groan. "From what I hear of the amount of business he's doing I guess he could keep the Poet's Corner going right along. I suppose the old man was right—he hasn't got it in him to make money."

"Of course not; he wasn't brought up to it, and in his heart of hearts he's ashamed of having to do it. He told me it was killing a little more of him every day."

"Do they back him up in that kind of talk?"

"They back him up in everything. Their ideas are all different from ours. They look down on us—can't you see that? Can't you guess how they treat me from the way they've acted to you and Mother?"

He met this with a puzzled stare. "The way they've acted to me and Mother? Why, we never so much as set eyes on them."

"That's just what I mean! I don't believe they've even called on mother this year, have they? Last year they just left their cards without asking. And why do you suppose they never invite you to dine? In their set lots of people older than you and Mother dine out every night of the winter—society's full of them. The Marvells are ashamed to have you meet their friends: that's the reason. They're ashamed to have it known that Ralph married an Apex girl, and that you and mother haven't always had your own servants and carriages; and Ralph's ashamed of it too, now he's got over being crazy about me. If he was free I believe he'd turn round tomorrow and marry that Ray girl his mother's saving up for him."

Mr. Spragg listened with a heavy brow and pushed-out lip. His daughter's outburst seemed at last to have roused him to a faint resentment. After she had ceased to speak he remained silent, twisting an inky penhandle between his fingers; then he said: "I guess Mother and I can worry along without having Ralph's relatives drop in; but I'd like to make it clear to them that if you came from Apex your income came from there too. I presume they'd be sorry if Ralph was left to support you on *his*."

She saw that she had scored in the first part of the argument, but every watchful nerve reminded her that the hardest stage was still ahead.

"Oh, they're willing enough he should take your money—that's only natural, they think."

A chuckle sounded deep down under Mr. Spragg's loose collar. "There seems to be practical unanimity on that point," he observed. "But I don't see," he continued, jerking round his bushy brows on her, "how going to Europe is going to help you out."

Undine leaned close enough for her lowered voice to reach him. "Can't you understand that, knowing how they all feel about me—and how Ralph feels—I'd give almost anything to get away?"

Her father looked at her compassionately. "I guess most of us feel that once in a way when we're young, Undine. Later on you'll see going away ain't much use when you've got to turn round and come back."

She nodded at him with close-pressed lips, like a child in possession of some solemn secret.

"That's just it—that's the reason I'm so wild to go; because it *might* mean I wouldn't ever have to come back."

"Not come back? What on earth are you talking about?"

"It might mean that I could get free—begin over again. . . ."

He had pushed his seat back with a sudden jerk and cut her short by striking his palm on the arm of the chair.

"For the Lord's sake, Undine—do you know what you're saying?"

"Oh, yes, I know." She gave him back a confident smile. "If I can get away soon—go straight over to Paris . . . there's someone there who'd do anything . . . who *could* do anything . . . if I was free. . . ."

Mr. Spragg's hands continued to grasp his chair-arms. "Good God, Undine Marvell—are you sitting there in your sane senses and talking to me of what you could do if you were *free*?"

Their glances met in an interval of speechless communion; but Undine did not shrink from her father's eyes and when she lowered her own it seemed to be only because there was nothing left for them to say.

"I know just what I could do if I were free. I could marry the right man," she answered boldly.

He met her with a murmur of helpless irony. "The right man? The right man? Haven't you had enough of trying for him yet?"

As he spoke the door behind them opened, and Mr. Spragg looked up abruptly.

The stenographer stood on the threshold, and above her shoulder Undine perceived the ingratiating grin of Elmer Moffatt.

" 'A little farther lend thy guiding hand'—but I guess I can go the rest of the way alone," he said, insinuating himself through the doorway with an airy gesture of dismissal; then he turned to Mr. Spragg and Undine.

"I agree entirely with Mrs. Marvell—and I'm happy to have the opportunity of telling her so," he proclaimed, holding his hand out gallantly.

Undine stood up with a laugh. "It sounded like old times, I suppose— you thought Father and I were quarreling? But we never quarrel any more: he always agrees with me." She smiled at Mr. Spragg and turned her shining eyes on Moffatt.

"I wish that treaty had been signed a few years sooner!" the latter rejoined in his usual tone of humorous familiarity.

Undine had not met him since her marriage, and of late the adverse turn of his fortunes had carried him quite beyond her thoughts. But his actual presence was always stimulating, and even through her self-absorption she was struck by his air of almost defiant prosperity. He did not look like a man who has been beaten; or rather he looked like a man who does not know when he is beaten; and his eye had the gleam of mocking confidence that had carried him unabashed through his lowest hours at Apex.

"I presume you're here to see me on business?" Mr. Spragg inquired, rising from his chair with a glance that seemed to ask his daughter's silence.

"Why, yes, Senator," rejoined Moffatt, who was given, in playful moments, to the bestowal of titles high-sounding. "At least I'm here to ask you a little question that may lead to business."

Mr. Spragg crossed the office and held open the door. "Step this way, please," he said, guiding Moffatt out before him, though the latter hung back to exclaim: "No family secrets, Mrs. Marvell—anybody can turn the fierce white light on *me!*"

With the closing of the door Undine's thoughts turned back to her own preoccupations. It had not struck her as incongruous that Moffatt should have business dealings with her father: she was even a little surprised that Mr. Spragg should still treat him so coldly. But she had no time to give to such considerations. Her own difficulties were too importunately present to her. She moved restlessly about the office, listening to the rise and fall of the two voices on the other side of the partition without once wondering what they were discussing.

What should she say to her father when he came back—what argument was most likely to prevail with him? If he really had no money to give her she was imprisoned fast—Van Degen was lost to her, and the old life must go on interminably. . . . In her nervous pacings she paused before the blotched looking-glass that hung in a corner of the office under a steel engraving of Daniel Webster. Even that defective surface could not disfigure her, and she drew fresh hope from the sight of her beauty. Her few weeks of ill-health had given her cheeks a subtler curve and deepened the shadows beneath her eyes, and she was handsomer than before her marriage. No, Van Degen was not lost to her even! From narrowed lids to parted lips her face was swept by a smile like refracted sunlight. He was not lost to her while she could smile like that! Besides, even if her father had no money, there were always mysterious ways of "raising" it—in the old Apex days he had often boasted of such feats. As the hope rose her eyes widened trustfully, and this time the smile that flowed up to them was as limpid as a child's. That was the way her father liked her to look at him. . . .

The door opened, and she heard Mr. Spragg say behind her: "No, sir, I won't—that's final."

He came in alone, with a brooding face, and lowered himself heavily into his chair. It was plain that the talk between the two men had had an abrupt ending. Undine looked at her father with a passing flicker of curiosity. Certainly it was an odd coincidence that Moffatt should have called while she was there. . . .

"What did he want?" she asked, glancing back toward the door.

Mr. Spragg mumbled his invisible toothpick. "Oh, just another of his wildcat schemes—some real-estate deal he's in."

"Why did he come to *you* about it?"

He looked away from her, fumbling among the letters on the desk. "Guess he'd tried everybody else first. He'd go and ring the devil's front-doorbell if he thought he could get anything out of him."

"I suppose he did himself a lot of harm by testifying in the Ararat investigation?"

"Yes, *sir*—he's down and out this time."

He uttered the words with a certain satisfaction. His daughter did not answer, and they sat silent, facing each other across the littered desk. Under their brief talk about Elmer Moffatt currents of rapid intelligence seemed to be flowing between them. Suddenly Undine leaned over the desk, her eyes widening trustfully, and the limpid smile flowing up to them.

"Father, I did what you wanted that one time, anyhow—won't you listen to me and help me out now?"

18

UNDINE stood alone on the landing outside her father's office.

Only once before had she failed to gain her end with him—and there was a peculiar irony in the fact that Moffatt's intrusion should have brought before her the providential result of her previous failure. Not that she confessed to any real resemblance between the two situations. In the present case she knew well enough what she wanted, and how to get it. But the analogy had served her father's purpose, and Moffatt's unlucky entrance had visibly strengthened his resistance.

The worst of it was that the obstacles in the way were real enough. Mr. Spragg had not put her off with vague asseverations—somewhat against her will he had forced his proofs on her, showing her how much above his promised allowance he had contributed in the last three years to the support of her household. Since she could not accuse herself of extravagance—having still full faith in her gift of "managing"—she could only conclude that it was impossible to live on what her father and Ralph could provide; and this seemed a practical reason for desiring her freedom. If she and Ralph parted he would, of course, return to his family, and Mr. Spragg would no longer be burdened with a helpless son-in-law. But even this argument did not move him. Undine, as soon as she had risked Van Degen's name, found herself face to face with a code of domestic conduct as rigid as its exponent's business principles were elastic. Mr. Spragg did not regard divorce as intrinsically wrong or even inexpedient; and of its social disadvantages he had never even heard. Lots of women did it, as Undine said; and if their reasons were adequate they were justified. If Ralph Marvell had been a drunkard or "unfaithful" Mr. Spragg would have approved Undine's desire to divorce him; but that it should be prompted by her inclination for another man— and a man with a wife of his own—was as shocking to him as it would have been to the most uncompromising of the Dagonets and Marvells. Such things happened, as Mr. Spragg knew, but they should not happen to any woman of his name while he had the power to prevent it; and Undine recognized that for the moment he had that power.

As she emerged from the elevator she was surprised to see Moffatt in the vestibule. His presence was an irritating reminder of her failure, and she walked past him with a rapid bow; but he overtook her.

"Mrs. Marvell—I've been waiting to say a word to you."

If it had been anyone else she would have passed on; but Moffatt's voice had always a detaining power. Even now that she knew him to be defeated and negligible the power asserted itself, and she paused to say: "I'm afraid I can't stop—I'm late for an engagement."

"I shan't make you much later; but if you'd rather have me call round at your house —"

"Oh, I'm so seldom in." She turned a wondering look on him. "What is it you wanted to say?"

"Just two words. I've got an office in this building and the shortest way would be to come up there for a minute." As her look grew distant he added: "I think what I've got to say is worth the trip."

His face was serious, without underlying irony: the face he wore when he wanted to be trusted.

"Very well," she said, turning back.

Undine, glancing at her watch as she came out of Moffatt's office, saw that he had been true to his promise of not keeping her more than ten minutes. The fact was characteristic. Under all his incalculableness there had always been a hard foundation of reliability: it seemed to be a matter of choice with him whether he let one feel that solid bottom or not. And in specific matters the same quality showed itself in an accuracy of statement, a precision of conduct, that contrasted curiously with his usual hyperbolic banter and his loose lounging manner. No one could be more elusive yet no one could be firmer to the touch.

Her face had cleared and she moved more lightly as she left the building. Moffatt's communication had not been completely clear to her, but she understood the outline of the plan he had laid before her, and was satisfied with the bargain they had struck. He had begun by reminding her of her promise to introduce him to any friend of hers who might be useful in the way of business. Over three years had passed since they had made the pact, and Moffatt had kept loyally to his side of it. With the lapse of time the whole matter had become less important to her, but she wanted to prove her good faith, and when he reminded her of her promise she at once admitted it.

"Well, then—I want you to introduce me to your husband."

Undine was surprised; but beneath her surprise she felt a quick sense of relief. Ralph was easier to manage than so many of her friends—and it was a mark of his present indifference to acquiesce in anything she suggested.

"My husband? Why, what can he do for you?"

Moffatt explained at once, in the fewest words, as his way was when it came to business. He was interested in a big "deal" which involved the purchase of a piece of real estate held by a number of wrangling heirs. The real-estate broker with whom Ralph Marvell was associated represented these heirs, but Moffatt had his reasons for not approaching him directly. And he didn't want to go to Marvell with a "business proposition"—it would be better to be thrown with him socially, as if by accident. It was with that object that Moffatt had just appealed to Mr. Spragg, but Mr. Spragg, as usual, had "turned him down," without even consenting to look into the case.

"He'd rather have you miss a good thing than have it come to you through me. I don't know what on earth he thinks it's in my power to do to you—or ever was, for that matter," he added. "Anyhow," he went on to explain, "the power's all on your side now; and I'll show you how little the doing will hurt you as soon as I can have a quiet chat with your husband." He branched off again into technicalities, nebulous projections of capital and interest, taxes and rents, from which she finally extracted, and clung to, the central fact that if the "deal went through" it would mean a commission of forty thousand dollars to Marvell's firm, of which something over a fourth would come to Ralph.

"By Jove, that's an amazing fellow!" Ralph Marvell exclaimed, turning back into the drawing-room, a few evenings later, at the conclusion of one of their little dinners.

Undine looked up from her seat by the fire. She had had the inspired thought of inviting Moffatt to meet Clare Van Degen, Mrs. Fairford and Charles Bowen. It had occurred to her that the simplest way of explaining Moffatt was to tell Ralph that she had unexpectedly discovered an old Apex acquaintance in the protagonist of the great Ararat Trust fight. Moffatt's defeat had not wholly divested him of interest. As a factor in affairs he no longer inspired apprehension, but as the man who had dared to defy Harmon B. Driscoll he was a conspicuous and, to some minds, almost an heroic figure.

Undine remembered that Clare and Mrs. Fairford had once expressed a wish to see this braver of the Olympians, and her suggestion that he should be asked to meet them gave Ralph evident pleasure. It was long since she had made any conciliatory sign to his family.

Moffatt's social gifts were hardly of a kind to please the two ladies: he would have shone more brightly in Peter Van Degen's set than in his wife's. But neither Clare nor Mrs. Fairford had expected a man of conventional cut, and Moffatt's loud easiness was obviously less disturbing to them than to their hostess. Undine felt only his crudeness, and the tacit criticism passed on it by the mere presence of such men as her husband and Bowen; but Mrs. Fairford seemed to enjoy provoking him to fresh excesses of slang and hyperbole. Gradually she drew him into talking of the Driscoll campaign, and he became recklessly explicit. He seemed to have nothing to hold back: all the details of the prodigious exploit poured from him with Homeric volume. Then he broke off abruptly, thrusting his hands into his trouser-pockets and shaping his red lips to a whistle which he checked as his glance met Undine's. To conceal his embarrassment he leaned back in his chair, looked about the table with complacency, and said "I don't mind if I do" to the servant who approached to refill his champagne glass.

The men sat long over their cigars; but after an interval Undine called Charles Bowen into the drawing-room to settle some question in dispute between Clare and Mrs. Fairford, and thus gave Moffatt a chance to be alone with her husband. Now that their guests had gone she was throbbing with anxiety to know what had passed between the two; but when Ralph rejoined her in the drawing-room she continued to keep her eyes on the fire and twirl her fan listlessly.

"That's an amazing chap," Ralph repeated, looking down at her. "Where was it you ran across him—out at Apex?"

As he leaned against the chimney-piece, lighting his cigarette, it struck Undine that he looked less fagged and lifeless than usual, and she felt more and more sure that something important had happened during the moment of isolation she had contrived.

She opened and shut her fan reflectively. "Yes—years ago; father had some business with him and brought him home to dinner one day."

"And you've never seen him since?"

She waited, as if trying to piece her recollections together. "I suppose I must have; but all that seems so long ago," she said sighing. She had been given, of late, to such plaintive glances toward her happy girlhood; but Ralph seemed not to notice the allusion.

"Do you know," he exclaimed after a moment, "I don't believe the fellow's beaten yet."

She looked up quickly. "Don't you?"

"No; and I could see that Bowen didn't either. He strikes me as the kind of man who develops slowly, needs a big field, and perhaps makes some big mistakes, but gets where he wants to in the end. Jove, I wish I could put him in a book! There's something epic about him—a kind of epic effrontery."

Undine's pulses beat faster as she listened. Was it not what Moffatt had always said of himself—that all he needed was time and elbowroom? How odd that Ralph, who seemed so dreamy and unobservant, should instantly have reached the same conclusion! But what she wanted to know was the practical result of their meeting.

"What did you and he talk about when you were smoking?"

"Oh, he got on the Driscoll fight again—gave us some extraordinary details. The man's a thundering brute, but he's full of observation and humor. Then, after Bowen joined you, he told me about a new deal he's gone into—rather a promising scheme, but on the same titanic scale. It's just possible, by the way, that we may be able to do something for him: part of the property he's after is held in our office." He paused, knowing Undine's indifference to business matters; but the face she turned to him was alive with interest.

"You mean you might sell the property to him?"

"Well, if the thing comes off. There would be a big commission if we did." He glanced down on her half ironically. "You'd like that, wouldn't you?"

She answered with a shade of reproach: "Why do you say that? I haven't complained."

"Oh, no; but I know I've been a disappointment as a money-maker."

She leaned back in her chair, closing her eyes as if in utter weariness and indifference, and in a moment she felt him bending over her. "What's the matter? Don't you feel well?"

"I'm a little tired. It's nothing." She pulled her hand away and burst into tears.

Ralph knelt down by her chair and put his arm about her. It was the first time he had touched her since the night of the boy's birthday, and the sense of her softness woke a momentary warmth in his veins.

"What is it, dear? What is it?"

Without turning her head she sobbed out: "You seem to think I'm too selfish and odious—that I'm just pretending to be ill."

"No, no," he assured her, smoothing back her hair. But she continued to sob on in a gradual crescendo of despair, till the vehemence of her weeping began to frighten him, and he drew her to her feet and tried to persuade her to let herself be led upstairs. She yielded to his arm, sobbing in short exhausted gasps, and leaning her whole weight on him as he guided her along the passage to her bedroom. On the lounge to which he lowered her she lay white and still, tears trickling through her lashes and her handkerchief pressed against her lips. He recognized the symptoms with a sinking heart: she was on the verge of a nervous attack such as she had had in the winter, and he foresaw with dismay the disastrous train of consequences, the doctors' and nurses' bills, and all the attendant confusion and expense. If only Moffatt's project might be realized—if for once he could feel a round sum in his pocket, and be freed from the perpetual daily strain!

The next morning Undine, though calmer, was too weak to leave her bed, and her doctor prescribed rest and absence of worry—later, perhaps, a change of scene. He explained to Ralph that nothing was so wearing to a high-strung nature as monotony, and that if Mrs. Marvell were contemplating a Newport season it was necessary that she should be fortified to meet it. In such cases he often recommended a dash to Paris or London, just to tone up the nervous system.

Undine regained her strength slowly, and as the days dragged on the suggestion of the European trip recurred with increasing frequency. But it came always from her medical adviser: she herself had grown strangely passive and indifferent. She continued to remain upstairs on her lounge, seeing no one but Mrs. Heeny, whose daily ministrations had once more been prescribed, and asking only that the noise of Paul's play should be kept from her. His scamperings overhead disturbed her sleep, and his bed was moved into the day nursery, above his father's room. The child's early romping did not trouble Ralph, since he himself was always awake before daylight. The days were not long enough to hold his cares, and they came and stood by him through the silent hours, when there was no other sound to drown their voices.

Ralph had not made a success of his business. The real-estate brokers who had taken him into partnership had done so only with the hope of profiting by his social connections; and in this respect the alliance had been a failure. It was in such directions that he most lacked facility, and so far he had been of use to his partners only as an office-drudge. He was resigned to the continuance of such drudgery, though all his powers cried out against it; but even for the routine of business his aptitude was small, and he began to feel that he was not considered an addition to the firm. The difficulty of finding another opening made him fear a break; and his thoughts turned hopefully to Elmer Moffatt's hint of a "deal." The success of the negotiation might bring advantages beyond the immediate pecuniary profit; and that, at the present juncture, was important enough in itself.

Moffatt reappeared two days after the dinner, presenting himself in West End Avenue in the late afternoon with the explanation that the business in hand necessitated discretion, and that he preferred not to be seen in Ralph's office. It was a question of negotiating with the utmost privacy for the purchase of a small strip of land between two large plots already acquired by purchasers cautiously designated by Moffatt as his "parties." How far he "stood in" with the parties he left it to Ralph to conjecture; but it was plain that he had a large stake in the transaction, and that it offered him his first chance of recovering himself since Driscoll had "thrown" him. The owners of the coveted plot did not seem anxious to sell, and there were personal reasons for Moffatt's not approaching them through Ralph's partners, who were the regular agents of the estate: so that Ralph's acquaintance with the conditions, combined with his detachments from the case, marked him out as a useful intermediary.

Their first talk left Ralph with a dazzled sense of Moffatt's strength and keenness, but with a vague doubt as to the "straightness" of the proposed transaction. Ralph had never seen his way clearly in that dim underworld of affairs where men of the Moffatt and Driscoll type moved like shadowy destructive monsters beneath the darting small fry of the surface. He knew that "business" has created its own special morality; and his musings on man's relation to his self-imposed laws had shown him how little human conduct is generally troubled about its own sanctions. He had a vivid sense of the things a man of his kind didn't do; but his inability to get a mental grasp on large financial problems made it hard to apply to them so simple a measure as this inherited standard. He only knew, as Moffatt's plan developed, that it seemed all right while he talked of it with its originator, but vaguely wrong when he thought it over afterward. It occurred to him to consult his grandfather; and if he renounced the idea for the obvious reason that Mr. Dagonet's ignorance of business was as fathomless as his own, this was not his sole motive. Finally it occurred to him to put the case hypothetically to Mr. Spragg. As far as Ralph knew, his father-in-law's business record was unblemished; yet one felt in him an elasticity of adjustment not allowed for in the Dagonet code.

Mr. Spragg listened thoughtfully to Ralph's statement of the case, growling out here and there a tentative correction, and turning his cigar between his lips as he seemed to turn the problem over in the loose grasp of his mind.

"Well, what's the trouble with it?" he asked at length, stretching his big square-toed shoes against the grate of his son-in-law's dining-room, where, in the after-dinner privacy of a family evening, Ralph had seized the occasion to consult him.

"The trouble?" Ralph considered. "Why, that's just what I should like you to explain to me."

Mr. Spragg threw back his head and stared at the garlanded French clock on the chimney-piece. Mrs. Spragg was sitting upstairs in her daughter's bedroom, and the silence of the house seemed to hang about the two men like a listening presence.

"Well, I dunno but what I agree with the doctor who said there warn't any diseases, but only sick people. Every case is different, I guess." Mr. Spragg, munching his cigar, turned a ruminating glance on Ralph. "Seems to me it all boils down to one thing. Was this fellow we're supposing about under any obligation to the other party—the one he was trying to buy the property from?"

Ralph hesitated. "Only the obligation recognized between decent men to deal with each other decently."

Mr. Spragg listened to this with the suffering air of a teacher compelled to simplify upon his simplest questions.

"Any personal obligation, I meant. Had the other fellow done him a good turn any time?"

"No—I don't imagine them to have had any previous relations at all."

His father-in-law stared. "Where's your trouble, then?" He sat for a moment frowning at the embers. "Even when it's the other way round it ain't always so easy to decide how far that kind of thing's binding . . . and they say shipwrecked fellows'll make a meal of a friend as quick as they would of a total stranger." He drew himself together with a shake of his shoulders and pulled back his feet from the grate. "But I don't see the conundrum in your case. I guess it's up to both parties to take care of their own skins."

He rose from his chair and wandered upstairs to Undine.

That was the Wall Street code: it all "boiled down" to the personal obligation, to the salt eaten in the enemy's tent. Ralph's fancy wandered off on a long trail of speculation from which he was pulled back with a jerk by the need of immediate action. Moffatt's "deal" could not wait: quick decisions were essential to effective action, and brooding over ethical shades of difference might work more ill than good in a world committed to swift adjustments. The arrival of several unforeseen bills confirmed this view, and once Ralph had adopted it he began to take a detached interest in the affair.

In Paris, in his younger days, he had once attended a lesson in acting given at the Conservatoire by one of the great lights of the theater, and had seen an apparently uncomplicated role of the classic repertory, familiar to him through repeated performances, taken to pieces before his eyes, dissolved into its component elements, and built up again with a minuteness of elucidation and a range of reference that made him feel as though he had been let into the secret of some age-long natural process. As he listened to Moffatt the remembrance of that lesson came back to him. At the outset the "deal," and his own share in it, had seemed simple enough: he would have put on his hat and gone out on the spot in the full assurance of being able to transact the affair. But as Moffatt talked he began to feel as blank and blundering as the class of dramatic students before whom the great actor had analyzed his part. The affair was in fact difficult and complex, and Moffatt saw at once just where the difficulties lay and how the personal idiosyncrasies of "the parties" affected them. Such insight fascinated Ralph, and he strayed off into wondering why it did not qualify every financier to be a novelist, and what intrinsic barrier divided the two arts.

Both men had strong incentives for hastening the affair; and within a fortnight after Moffatt's first advance Ralph was able to tell him that his offer was accepted. Over and above his personal satisfaction he felt the thrill of the agent whom some powerful negotiator has charged with a delicate mission: he might have been an eager young Jesuit carrying compromising papers to his superior. It had been stimulating to work with Moffatt, and to study at close range the large powerful instrument of his intelligence.

As he came out of Moffatt's office at the conclusion of this visit Ralph met Mr. Spragg descending from his eyrie. He stopped short with a backward glance at Moffatt's door.

"Hallo—what were you doing in there with those cutthroats?"

Ralph judged discretion to be essential. "Oh, just a little business for the firm."

Mr. Spragg said no more, but resorted to the soothing labial motion of revolving his phantom toothpick.

"How's Undie getting along?" he merely asked, as he and his son-in-law descended together in the elevator.

"She doesn't seem to feel much stronger. The doctor wants her to run over to Europe for a few weeks. She thinks of joining her friends the Shallums in Paris."

Mr. Spragg was again silent, but he left the building at Ralph's side, and the two walked along together toward Wall Street.

Presently the older man asked: "How did you get acquainted with Moffatt?"

"Why, by chance—Undine ran across him somewhere and asked him to dine the other night."

"Undine asked him to dine?"

"Yes: she told me you used to know him out at Apex."

Mr. Spragg appeared to search his memory for confirmation of the fact. "I believe he used to be round there at one time. I've never heard any good of him yet." He paused at a crossing and looked probingly at his son-in-law. "Is she terribly set on this trip to Europe?"

Ralph smiled. "You know how it is when she takes a fancy to do anything—"

Mr. Spragg, by a slight lift of his brooding brows, seemed to convey a deep if unspoken response.

"Well, I'd let her do it this time—I'd let her do it," he said as he turned down the steps of the subway.

Ralph was surprised, for he had gathered from some frightened references of Mrs. Spragg's that Undine's parents had wind of her European plan and were strongly opposed to it. He concluded that Mr. Spragg had long since measured the extent of profitable resistance, and knew just when it became vain to hold out against his daughter or advise others to do so.

Ralph, for his own part, had no inclination to resist. As he left Moffatt's office his inmost feeling was one of relief. He had reached the point of recognizing that it was best for both that his wife should go. When she returned perhaps their lives would readjust themselves—but for the moment he longed for some kind of benumbing influence, something that should give relief to the dull daily ache of feeling her so near and yet so inaccessible. Certainly there were more urgent uses for their brilliant windfall: heavy arrears of household debts had to be met, and the summer would bring its own burden. But perhaps another stroke of luck might befall him: he was getting to have the drifting dependence on "luck" of the man conscious of his inability to direct his life. And meanwhile it seemed easier to let Undine have what she wanted.

Undine, on the whole, behaved with discretion. She received the good news languidly and showed no unseemly haste to profit by it. But it was as hard to hide the light in her eyes as to dissemble the fact that she had not only thought out every detail of the trip in advance, but had decided exactly how her husband and son were to be disposed of in her absence. Her suggestion that Ralph should take Paul to his grandparents, and that the West End Avenue house should be let for the summer, was too practical not to be acted on; and Ralph found she had already put her hand on the Harry Lipscombs, who, after three years of neglect, were to be dragged back to favor and made to feel, as the first step in their reinstatement, the necessity of hiring for the summer months a cool airy house on the West Side. On her return from Europe, Undine explained, she would of course go straight to Ralph and the boy in the Adirondacks; and it seemed a foolish extravagance to let the house stand empty when the Lipscombs were so eager to take it.

As the day of departure approached it became harder for her to temper her beams; but her pleasure showed itself so amiably that Ralph began to think she might, after all, miss the boy and himself more than she imagined. She was tenderly preoccupied with Paul's welfare, and, to prepare for his translation to his grandparents' she gave the household in Washington Square more of her time than she had accorded it since her marriage. She explained that she wanted Paul to grow used to his new surroundings; and with that object she took him frequently to his grandmother's, and won her way into old Mr. Dagonet's sympathies by her devotion to the child and her pretty way of joining in his games.

Undine was not consciously acting a part: this new phase was as natural to her as the other. In the joy of her gratified desires she wanted to make everybody about her happy. If only everyone would do as she wished she would never be unreasonable. She much preferred to see smiling faces about her, and her dread of the reproachful and dissatisfied countenance gave the measure of what she would do to avoid it.

These thoughts were in her mind when, a day or two before sailing, she came out of the Washington Square house with her boy. It was a late spring afternoon, and she and Paul had lingered on till long past the hour sacred to his grandfather's nap. Now, as she came out into the square she saw that, however well Mr. Dagonet had borne their protracted romp, it had left his playmate flushed and sleepy; and she lifted Paul in her arms to carry him to the nearest cab-stand.

As she raised herself she saw a thick-set figure approaching her across the square; and a moment later she was shaking hands with Elmer Moffatt. In the bright spring air he looked seasonably glossy and prosperous; and she noticed that he wore a bunch of violets in his buttonhole. His small black eyes twinkled with approval as they rested on her, and Undine reflected that, with Paul's arms about her neck, and his little flushed face against her own, she must present a not unpleasing image of young motherhood.

"That the heir apparent?" Moffatt asked; adding "Happy to make your acquaintance, sir," as the boy, at Undine's bidding, held out a fist sticky with sugar-plums.

"He's been spending the afternoon with his grandfather, and they played so hard that he's sleepy," she explained. Little Paul, at that stage in his career, had a peculiar grace of wide-gazing deep-lashed eyes and arched cherubic lips, and Undine saw that Moffatt was not insensible to the picture she and her son composed. She did not dislike his admiration, for she no longer felt any shrinking from him—she would even have been glad to thank him for the service he had done her husband if she had known how to allude to it without awkwardness. Moffatt seemed equally pleased at the meeting, and they looked at each other almost intimately over Paul's tumbled curls.

"He's a mighty fine fellow and no mistake—but isn't he rather an armful for you?" Moffatt asked, his eyes lingering with real kindliness on the child's face.

"Oh, we haven't far to go. I'll pick up a cab at the corner."

"Well, let me carry him that far anyhow," said Moffatt.

Undine was glad to be relieved of her burden, for she was unused to the child's weight, and disliked to feel that her skirt was dragging on the pavement. "Go to the gentleman, Pauly—he'll carry you better than Mother," she said.

The little boy's first movement was one of recoil from the ruddy sharp-eyed countenance that was so unlike his father's delicate face; but he was an obedient child, and after a moment's hesitation he wound his arms trustfully about the red gentleman's neck.

"That's a good fellow—sit tight and I'll give you a ride," Moffatt cried, hoisting the boy to his shoulder.

Paul was not used to being perched at such a height, and his nature was hospitable to new impressions. "Oh, I like it up here—you're higher than Father!" he exclaimed; and Moffatt hugged him with a laugh.

"It must feel mighty good to come uptown to a fellow like you in the evenings," he said, addressing the child but looking at Undine, who also laughed a little.

"Oh, they're a dreadful nuisance, you know; but Paul's a very good boy."

"I wonder if he knows what a friend I've been to him lately," Moffatt went on, as they turned into Fifth Avenue.

Undine smiled: she was glad he should have given her an opening.

"He shall be told as soon as he's old enough to thank you. I'm so glad you came to Ralph about that business."

"Oh, I gave him a leg up, and I guess he's given me one too. Queer the way things come round—he's fairly put me in the way of a fresh start."

Their eyes met in a silence which Undine was the first to break. "It's been awfully nice of you to do what you've done—right along. And this last thing has made a lot of difference to us."

"Well, I'm glad you feel that way. I never wanted to be anything but 'nice,' as you call it." Moffatt paused a moment and then added: "If you're less scared of me than your father is I'd be glad to call round and see you once in a while."

The quick blood rushed to her cheeks. There was nothing challenging, demanding in his tone—she guessed at once that if he made the request it was simply for the pleasure of being with her, and she liked the magnanimity implied. Nevertheless she was not sorry to have to answer: "Of course, I'll always be glad to see you—only, as it happens, I'm just sailing for Europe."

"For Europe?" The word brought Moffatt to a stand so abruptly that little Paul lurched on his shoulder.

"For Europe?" he repeated. "Why, I thought you said the other evening you expected to stay on in town till July. Didn't you think of going to the Adirondacks?"

Flattered by his evident disappointment, she became high and careless in her triumph. "Oh, yes—but that's all changed. Ralph and the boy are going; but I sail on Saturday to join some friends in Paris—and later I may do some motoring in Switzerland and Italy."

She laughed a little in the mere enjoyment of putting her plans into words and Moffatt laughed too, but with an edge of sarcasm.

"I see—I see: everything's changed, as you say, and your husband can blow you off to the trip. Well, I hope you'll have a first-class time."

Their glances crossed again, and something in his cool scrutiny impelled Undine to say, with a burst of candor: "If I do, you know, I shall owe it all to you!"

"Well, I always told you I meant to act white by you," he answered.

They walked on in silence, and presently he began again in his usual joking strain: "See what one of the Apex girls has been up to?"

Apex was too remote for her to understand the reference, and he went on: "Why, Millard Binch's wife—Indiana Frusk that was. Didn't you see in the papers that Indiana'd fixed it up with James J. Rolliver to marry her? They say it was easy enough squaring Millard Binch—you'd know it *would* be—but it cost Rolliver near a million to mislay Mrs. R. and the children. Well, Indiana's pulled it off, anyhow; she always *was* a bright girl. But she never came up to you."

"Oh —" she stammered with a laugh, astonished and agitated by his news. Indiana Frusk and Rolliver! It showed how easily the thing could be done. If only her father had listened to her! If a girl like Indiana Frusk could gain her end so easily, what might not Undine have accomplished? She knew Moffatt was right in saying that Indiana had never come up to her. . . . She wondered how the marriage would strike Van Degen. . . .

She signalled to a cab and they walked toward it without speaking. Undine was recalling with intensity that one of Indiana's shoulders was higher than the other, and that people in Apex had thought her lucky to catch Millard Binch, the druggist's clerk, when Undine herself had cast him off after a lingering engagement. And now Indiana Frusk was to be Mrs. James J. Rolliver!

Undine got into the cab and bent forward to take little Paul.

Moffatt lowered his charge with exaggerated care, and a "Steady there, steady," that made the child laugh; then, stooping over, he put a kiss on Paul's lips before handing him over to his mother.

19

"THE Parisian Diamond Company—Anglo-American branch."
     Charles Bowen, seated, one rainy evening of the Paris season, in a corner of the great Nouveau Luxe restaurant, was lazily trying to resolve his impressions of the scene into the phrases of a letter to his old friend Mrs. Henley Fairford.

The long habit of unwritten communion with this lady—in no way conditioned by the short rare letters they actually exchanged—usually caused his notations, in absence, to fall into such terms when the subject was of a kind to strike an answering flash from her. And who but Mrs. Fairford would see, from his own precise angle, the fantastic improbability, the layers on layers of unsubstantialness, on which the seemingly solid scene before him rested?

The dining-room of the Nouveau Luxe was at its fullest, and, having contracted on the garden side through stress of weather, had even overflowed to the farther end of the long hall beyond: so that Bowen, from his corner, surveyed a seemingly endless perspective of plumed and jeweled heads, of shoulders bare or black-coated, encircling the close-packed tables. He had come half an hour before the time he had named to his expected guest, so that he might have the undisturbed amusement of watching the picture compose itself again before his eyes. During some forty years' perpetual exercise of his perceptions he had never come across anything that gave them the special titillation produced by the sight of the dinner-hour at the Nouveau Luxe: the same sense of putting his hand on human nature's passion for the factitious, its incorrigible habit of imitating the imitation.

As he sat watching the familiar faces swept toward him on the rising tide of arrival—for it was one of the joys of the scene that the type was always the same even when the individual was not—he hailed with renewed appreciation this costly expression of a social ideal. The dining-room at the Nouveau Luxe represented, on such a spring evening, what unbounded material power had devised for the delusion of its leisure: a phantom "society," with all the rules, smirks, gestures of its model, but evoked out of promiscuity and incoherence while the other had been the product of continuity and choice. And the instinct which had driven a new class of world-compellers to bind themselves to slavish imitation of the superseded, and their prompt and reverent faith in the reality of the sham they had created, seemed to Bowen the most satisfying proof of human permanence.

With this thought in his mind he looked up to greet his guest. The Comte Raymond de Chelles, straight, slim and gravely smiling, came toward him with frequent pauses of salutation at the crowded tables; saying, as he seated himself and turned his pleasant eyes on the scene: "*Il n'y a pas à dire*, my dear Bowen, it's charming and sympathetic and original—we owe America a debt of gratitude for inventing it!"

Bowen felt a last touch of satisfaction: they were the very words to complete his thought.

"My dear fellow, it's really you and your kind who are responsible. It's the direct creation of feudalism, like all the great social upheavals!"

Raymond de Chelles stroked his handsome brown moustache. "I should have said, on the contrary, that one enjoyed it for the contrast. It's such a refreshing change from our institutions—which are, nevertheless, the necessary foundations of society. But just as one may have an infinite admiration for one's wife, and yet occasionally —" he waved a light hand toward the spectacle. "This, in the social order, is the diversion, the permitted diversion, that your original race has devised: a kind of superior Bohemia, where one may be respectable without being bored."

Bowen laughed. "You've put it in a nutshell: the ideal of the American woman is to be respectable without being bored; and from that point of view this world they've invented has more originality than I gave it credit for."

Chelles thoughtfully unfolded his napkin. "My impression's a superficial one, of course—for as to what goes on underneath—!" He looked across the room. "If I married I shouldn't care to have my wife come here too often."

Bowen laughed again. "She'd be as safe as in a bank! Nothing ever goes on! Nothing that ever happens here is real."

"Ah, *quant à cela* —" the Frenchman murmured, inserting a fork into his melon.

Bowen looked at him with enjoyment—he was such a precious footnote to the page! The two men, accidentally thrown together some years previously during a trip up the Nile, always met again with pleasure when Bowen returned to France. Raymond de Chelles, who came of a family of moderate fortune, lived for the greater part of the year on his father's estates in Burgundy; but he came up every spring to the *entresol* of the old marquis's hotel for a two months' study of human nature, applying to the pursuit the discriminating taste and transient ardor that give the finest bloom to pleasure. Bowen liked him as a companion and admired him as a charming specimen of the Frenchman of his class, embodying in his lean, fatigued and finished person that happy mean of simplicity and intelligence of which no other race has found the secret. If Raymond de Chelles had been English he would have been a mere fox-hunting animal, with appetites but without tastes; but in his lighter Gallic clay the wholesome territorial savor, the inherited passion for sport and agriculture, were blended with an openness to finer sensations, a sense of the come-and-go of ideas, under which one felt the tight hold of two or three inherited notions, religious, political, and domestic, in total contradiction to his surface attitude. That the inherited notions would in the end prevail, everything in his appearance declared, from the distinguished slant of his nose to the narrow forehead under his thinning hair; he was the kind of man who would inevitably "revert" when he married. But meanwhile the surface he presented to the play of life was broad enough to take in the fantastic spectacle of the Nouveau Luxe; and to see its gestures reflected in a Latin consciousness was an endless entertainment to Bowen.

The tone of his guest's last words made him take them up. "But is the lady you allude to more than a hypothesis? Surely you're not thinking of getting married?"

Chelles raised his eyebrows ironically. "When hasn't one to think of it, in my situation? One hears of nothing else at home—one knows that, like death, it has to come." His glance, which was still mustering the room, came to a sudden pause and kindled.

"Who's the lady over there—fair-haired, in white—the one who's just come in with the red-faced man? They seem to be with a party of your compatriots."

Bowen followed his glance to a neighboring table, where, at the moment, Undine Marvell was seating herself at Peter Van Degen's side, in the company of the Harvey Shallums, the beautiful Mrs. Beringer and a dozen other New York figures.

She was so placed that as she took her seat she recognized Bowen and sent him a smile across the tables. She was more simply dressed than usual, and the pink lights, warming her cheeks and striking gleams from her hair, gave her face a dewy freshness that was new to Bowen. He had always thought her beauty too obvious, too bathed in the bright publicity of the American air; but tonight she seemed to have been brushed by the wing of poetry, and its shadow lingered in her eyes.

Chelles's gaze made it evident that he had received the same impression.

"One is sometimes inclined to deny your compatriots actual beauty—to charge them with producing the effect without having the features; but in this case—you say you know the lady?"

"Yes: she's the wife of an old friend."

"The wife? She's married? There, again, it's so puzzling! Your young girls look so experienced, and your married women sometimes so—unmarried."

"Well, they often are—in these days of divorce!"

The other's interest quickened. "Your friend's divorced?"

"Oh, no; heaven forbid! Mrs. Marvell hasn't been long married; and it was a love-match of the good old kind."

"Ah—and the husband? Which is he?"

"He's not here—he's in New York."

"Feverishly adding to a fortune already monstrous?"

"No; not precisely monstrous. The Marvells are not well off," said Bowen, amused by his friend's interrogations.

"And he allows an exquisite being like that to come to Paris without him—and in company with the red-faced gentleman who seems so alive to his advantages?"

"We don't 'allow' our women this or that; I don't think we set much store by the compulsory virtues."

His companion received this with amusement. "If you're as detached as that, why does the obsolete institution of marriage survive with you?"

"Oh, it still has its uses. One couldn't be divorced without it."

Chelles laughed again; but his straying eye still followed the same direction, and Bowen noticed that the fact was not unremarked by the object of his contemplation. Undine's party was one of the liveliest in the room: the American laugh rose above the din of the orchestra as the American toilets dominated the less daring effects at the other tables. Undine, on entering, had seemed to be in the same mood as her companions; but Bowen saw that, as she became conscious of his friend's observation, she isolated herself in a kind of soft abstraction; and he admired the adaptability which enabled her to draw from such surroundings the contrasting graces of reserve.

They had greeted each other with all the outer signs of cordiality, but Bowen fancied she would not care to have him speak to her. She was evidently dining with Van Degen, and Van Degen's proximity was the last fact she would wish to have transmitted to the critics in Washington Square. Bowen was therefore surprised when, as he rose to leave the restaurant, he heard himself hailed by Peter.

"Hallo—hold on! When did you come over? Mrs. Marvell's dying for the last news about the old homestead."

Undine's smile confirmed the appeal. She wanted to know how lately Bowen had left New York, and pressed him to tell her when he had last seen her boy, how he was looking, and whether Ralph had been persuaded to go down to Clare's on Saturdays and get a little riding and tennis? And dear Laura—was she well too, and was Paul with her, or still with his grandmother? They were all dreadfully bad correspondents, and so was she, Undine laughingly admitted; and when Ralph had last written her these questions had still been undecided.

As she smiled up at Bowen he saw her glance stray to the spot where his companion hovered; and when the diners rose to move toward the garden for coffee she said, with a sweet note and a detaining smile: "Do come with us—I haven't half finished."

Van Degen echoed the request, and Bowen, amused by Undine's arts, was presently introducing Chelles, and joining with him in the party's transit to the terrace.

The rain had ceased, and under the clear evening sky the restaurant garden opened green depths that skillfully hid its narrow boundaries. Van Degen's company was large enough to surround two of the tables on the terrace, and Bowen noted the skill with which Undine, leaving him to Mrs. Shallum's care, contrived to draw Raymond de Chelles to the other table. Still more noticeable was the effect of this stratagem on Van Degen, who also found himself relegated to Mrs. Shallum's group. Poor Peter's state was betrayed by the irascibility which wreaked itself on a jostling waiter, and found cause for loud remonstrance in the coldness of the coffee and the badness of the cigars; and Bowen, with something more than the curiosity of the looker-on, wondered whether this were the real clue to Undine's conduct. He had always smiled at Mrs. Fairford's fears for Ralph's domestic peace. He thought Undine too clear-headed to forfeit the advantages of her marriage; but it now struck him that she might have had a glimpse of larger opportunities. Bowen, at the thought, felt the pang of the sociologist over the individual havoc wrought by every social readjustment: it had so long been clear to him that poor Ralph was a survival, and destined, as such, to go down in any conflict with the rising forces.

20

SOME six weeks later, Undine Marvell stood at the window smiling down on her recovered Paris.

Her hotel sitting-room had, as usual, been flowered, cushioned and lamp-shaded into a delusive semblance of stability; and she had really felt, for the last few weeks, that the life she was leading there must be going to last—it seemed so perfect an answer to all her wants!

As she looked out at the thronged street, on which the summer light lay like a blush of pleasure, she felt herself naturally akin to all the bright and careless freedom of the scene. She had been away from Paris for two days, and the spectacle before her seemed more rich and suggestive after her brief absence from it. Her senses luxuriated in all its material details: the throng-ing motors, the brilliant shops, the novelty and daring of the women's dresses, the piled-up colors of the ambulant flowercarts, the appetizing expanse of the fruiterers' windows, even the chromatic effects of the *petits fours* behind the plate-glass of the pastry cooks: all the surface sparkle and variety of the inexhaustible streets of Paris.

The scene before her typified to Undine her first real taste of life. How meager and starved the past appeared in comparison with this abundant present! The noise, the crowd, the promiscuity beneath her eyes symbolized the glare and movement of her life. Every moment of her days was packed with excitement and exhilaration. Everything amused her: the long hours of bargaining and debate with dressmakers and jewelers, the crowded lunches at fashionable restaurants, the perfunctory dash through a picture-show or the lingering visit to the last new milliner; the afternoon motor-rush to some leafy suburb, where tea and music and sunset were hastily absorbed on a crowded terrace above the Seine; the whirl home through the Bois to dress for dinner and start again on the round of evening diversions; the dinner at the Nouveau Luxe or the Café de Paris, and the little play at the Capucines or the Variétés, followed, because the night was "too lovely," and it was a shame to waste it, by a breathless flight back to the Bois, with supper in one of its lamp-hung restaurants, or, if the weather forbade, a tumultuous progress through the midnight haunts where "ladies" were not supposed to show themselves, and might consequently taste the thrill of being occasionally taken for their opposites.

As the varied vision unrolled itself, Undine contrasted it with the pale monotony of her previous summers. The one she most resented was the first after her marriage, the European summer out of whose joys she had been cheated by her own ignorance and Ralph's perversity. They had been free then, there had been no child to hamper their movements, their money anxieties had hardly begun, the face of life had been fresh and radiant, and she had been doomed to waste such opportunities on a succession of ill-smelling Italian towns. She still felt it to be her deepest grievance against her husband; and now that, after four years of petty household worries, another chance of escape had come, he already wanted to drag her back to bondage!

This fit of retrospection had been provoked by two letters which had come that morning. One was from Ralph, who began by reminding her that he had not heard from her for weeks, and went on to point out, in his usual tone of good-humored remonstrance, that since her departure the drain on her letter of credit had been deep and constant. "I wanted you," he wrote, "to get all the fun you could out of the money I made last spring; but I didn't think you'd get through it quite so fast. Try to come home without leaving too many bills behind you. Your illness and Paul's cost more than I expected, and Lipscomb has had a bad knock in Wall Street, and hasn't yet paid his first quarter. . . ."

Always the same monotonous refrain! Was it her fault that she and the boy had been ill? Or that Harry Lipscomb had been "on the wrong side" of Wall Street? Ralph seemed to have money on the brain: his business life had certainly deteriorated him. And, since he hadn't made a success of it after all, why shouldn't he turn back to literature and try to write his novel? Undine, the previous winter, had been dazzled by the figures which a well-known magazine editor whom she had met at dinner had named as within reach of the successful novelist. She perceived for the first time that literature was becoming fashionable, and instantly decided that it would be amusing and original if she and Ralph should owe their prosperity to his talent. She already saw herself, as the wife of a celebrated author, wearing "artistic" dresses and doing the drawing-room over with Gothic tapestries and dim lights in altar candlesticks. But when she suggested Ralph's taking up his novel he answered with a laugh that his brains were sold to the firm—that when he came back at night the tank was empty. . . . And now he wanted her to sail for home in a week!

The other letter excited a deeper resentment. It was an appeal from Laura Fairford to return and look after Ralph. He was overworked and out of spirits, she wrote, and his mother and sister, reluctant as they were to interfere, felt they ought to urge Undine to come back to him. Details followed, unwelcome and officious. What right had Laura Fairford to preach to her of wifely obligations? No doubt Charles Bowen had sent home a highly colored report—and there was really a certain irony in Mrs. Fairford's criticizing her sister-in-law's conduct on information obtained from such a source!

Undine turned from the window and threw herself down on her deeply cushioned sofa. She was feeling the pleasant fatigue consequent on her trip to the country, whither she and Mrs. Shallum had gone with Raymond de Chelles to spend a night at the old marquis's château. When her traveling companions, an hour earlier, had left her at her door, she had half-promised to rejoin them for a late dinner in the Bois; and as she leaned back among the cushions disturbing thoughts were banished by the urgent necessity of deciding what dress she should wear.

These bright weeks of the Parisian spring had given her a first real glimpse into the art of living. From the experts who had taught her to subdue the curves of her figure and soften her bright free stare with dusky pencillings, to the skilled purveyors of countless forms of pleasure—the theaters and restaurants, the green and blossoming suburbs, the whole shining shifting spectacle of nights and days—every sight and sound and word had combined to charm her perceptions and refine her taste. And her growing friendship with Raymond de Chelles had been the most potent of these influences.

Chelles, at once immensely "taken," had not only shown his eagerness to share in the helter-skelter motions of Undine's party, but had given her glimpses of another, still more brilliant existence, that life of the inaccessible "Faubourg" of which the first tantalizing hints had but lately reached her. Hitherto she had assumed that Paris existed for the stranger, that its native life was merely an obscure foundation for the dazzling superstructure of hotels and restaurants in which her compatriots disported themselves. But lately she had begun to hear about other American women, the women who had married into the French aristocracy, and who led, in the high-walled houses beyond the Seine which she had once thought so dull and dingy, a life that made her own seem as undistinguished as the social existence of the Mealey House. Perhaps what most exasperated her was the discovery, in this impenetrable group, of the Miss Wincher who had poisoned her far-off summer at Potash Springs. To recognize her old enemy in the Marquise de Trézac who so frequently figured in the Parisian chronicle was the more irritating to Undine because her intervening social experiences had caused her to look back on Nettie Wincher as a frumpy girl who wouldn't have "had a show" in New York.

Once more all the accepted values were reversed, and it turned out that Miss Wincher had been in possession of some key to success on which Undine had not yet put her hand. To know that others were indifferent to what she had thought important was to cheapen all present pleasure and turn the whole force of her desires in a new direction. What she wanted for the moment was to linger on in Paris, prolonging her flirtation with Chelles, and profiting by it to detach herself from her compatriots and enter doors closed to their approach. And Chelles himself attracted her: she thought him as "sweet" as she had once thought Ralph, whose fastidiousness and refinement were blended in him with a delightful foreign vivacity. His chief value, however, lay in his power of exciting Van Degen's jealousy. She knew enough of French customs to be aware that such devotion as Chelles's was not likely to have much practical bearing on her future; but Peter had an alarming way of lapsing into security, and as a spur to his ardor she knew the value of other men's attentions.

It had become Undine's fixed purpose to bring Van Degen to a definite expression of his intentions. The case of Indiana Frusk, whose brilliant marriage the journals of two continents had recently chronicled with un-precedented richness of detail, had made less impression on him than she hoped. He treated it as a comic episode without special bearing on their case, and once, when Undine cited Rolliver's expensive fight for freedom as an instance of the power of love over the most invulnerable natures, had answered carelessly: "Oh, his first wife was a laundress, I believe."

But all about them couples were unpairing and pairing again with an ease and rapidity that encouraged Undine to bide her time. It was simply a question of making Van Degen want her enough, and of not being obliged to abandon the game before he wanted her as much as she meant he should. This was precisely what would happen if she were compelled to leave Paris now. Already the event had shown how right she had been to come abroad: the attention she attracted in Paris had reawakened Van Degen's fancy, and her hold over him was stronger than when they had parted in America. But the next step must be taken with coolness and circumspection; and she must not throw away what she had gained by going away at a stage when he was surer of her than she of him.

She was still intensely considering these questions when the door behind her opened and he came in.

She looked up with a frown and he gave a deprecating laugh. "Didn't I knock? Don't look so savage! They told me downstairs you'd got back, and I just bolted in without thinking."

He had widened and purpled since their first encounter, five years earlier, but his features had not matured. His face was still the face of a covetous bullying boy, with a large appetite for primitive satisfactions and a sturdy belief in his intrinsic right to them. It was all the more satisfying to Undine's vanity to see his look change at her tone from command to conciliation, and from conciliation to the entreaty of a capriciously treated animal.

"What a ridiculous hour for a visit!" she exclaimed, ignoring his excuse.

"Well, if you disappear like that, without a word —"

"I told my maid to telephone you I was going away."

"You couldn't make time to do it yourself, I suppose?"

"We rushed off suddenly; I'd hardly time to get to the station."

"You rushed off where, may I ask?" Van Degen still lowered down on her.

"Oh, didn't I tell you? I've been down staying at Chelles's château in Burgundy." Her face lit up and she raised herself eagerly on her elbow.

"It's the most wonderful old house you ever saw: a real castle, with towers, and water all round it, and a funny kind of bridge they pull up. Chelles said he wanted me to see just how they lived at home, and I did; I saw everything: the tapestries that Louis Quinze gave them, and the family portraits, and the chapel, where their own priest says mass, and they sit by themselves in a balcony with crowns all over it. The priest was a lovely old man—he said he'd give anything to convert me. Do you know, I think there's something very beautiful about the Roman Catholic religion? I've often felt I might have been happier if I'd had some religious influence in my life."

She sighed a little, and turned her head away. She flattered herself that she had learned to strike the right note with Van Degen. At this crucial stage he needed a taste of his own methods, a glimpse of the fact that there were women in the world who could get on without him.

He continued to gaze down at her sulkily. "Were the old people there? You never told me you knew his mother."

"I don't. They weren't there. But it didn't make a bit of difference, because Raymond sent down a cook from the Luxe."

"Oh, Lord," Van Degen groaned, dropping down on the end of the sofa. "Was the cook got down to chaperon you?"

Undine laughed. "You talk like Ralph! I had Bertha with me."

"*Bertha!*" His tone of contempt surprised her. She had supposed that Mrs. Shallum's presence had made the visit perfectly correct.

"You went without knowing his parents, and without their inviting you? Don't you know what that sort of thing means out here? Chelles did it to brag about you at his club. He wants to compromise you—that's his game!"

"Do you suppose he does?" A flicker of a smile crossed her lips. "I'm so unconventional: when I like a man I never stop to think about such things. But I ought to, of course—you're quite right." She looked at Van Degen thoughtfully. "At any rate, he's not a married man."

Van Degen had got to his feet again and was standing accusingly before her; but as she spoke the blood rose to his neck and ears.

"What difference does that make?"

"It might make a good deal. I see," she added, "how careful I ought to be about going round with you."

"With *me?*" His face fell at the retort; then he broke into a laugh. He adored Undine's "smartness," which was of precisely the same quality as his own. "Oh, that's another thing: you can always trust me to look after you!"

"With your reputation? Much obliged!"

Van Degen smiled. She knew he liked such allusions, and was pleased that she thought him compromising.

"Oh, I'm as good as gold. You've made a new man of me!"

"Have I?" She considered him in silence for a moment. "I wonder what you've done to me but make a discontented woman of me—discontented with everything I had before I knew you?"

The change of tone was thrilling to him. He forgot her mockery, forgot his rival, and sat down at her side, almost in possession of her waist. "Look here," he asked, "where are we going to dine tonight?"

His nearness was not agreeable to Undine, but she liked his free way, his contempt for verbal preliminaries. Ralph's reserves and delicacies, his perpetual desire that he and she should be attuned to the same key, had always vaguely bored her; whereas in Van Degen's manner she felt a hint of the masterful way that had once subdued her in Elmer Moffatt. But she drew back, releasing herself.

"Tonight? I can't—I'm engaged."

"I know you are: engaged to *me!* You promised last Sunday you'd dine with me out of town tonight."

"How can I remember what I promised last Sunday? Besides, after what you've said, I see I oughtn't to."

"What do you mean by what I've said?"

"Why, that I'm imprudent; that people are talking —"

He stood up with an angry laugh. "I suppose you're dining with Chelles. Is that it?"

"Is that the way you cross-examine Clare?"

"I don't care a hang what Clare does—I never have."

"That must—in some ways—be rather convenient for her!"

"Glad you think so. *Are* you dining with him?"

She slowly turned the wedding ring upon her finger. "You know I'm *not* married to you—yet!"

He took a random turn through the room; then he came back and planted himself wrathfully before her. "Can't you see the man's doing his best to make a fool of you?"

She kept her amused gaze on him. "Does it strike you that it's such an awfully easy thing to do?"

The edges of his ears were purple. "I sometimes think it's easier for these damned little dancing-masters than for one of us."

Undine was still smiling up at him; but suddenly her face grew grave. "What does it matter what I do or don't do, when Ralph has ordered me home next week?"

"Ordered you home?" His face changed. "Well, you're not going, are you?"

"What's the use of saying such things?" She gave a disenchanted laugh. "I'm a poor man's wife, and can't do the things my friends do. It's not because Ralph loves me that he wants me back—it's simply because he can't afford to let me stay!"

Van Degen's perturbation was increasing. "But you mustn't go—it's preposterous! Why should a woman like you be sacrificed when a lot of dreary frumps have everything they want? Besides, you can't chuck me like this! Why, we're all to motor down to Aix next week, and perhaps take a dip into Italy—"

"*Oh, Italy* —" she murmured on a note of yearning.

He was closer now, and had her hands. "You'd love that, wouldn't you? As far as Venice, anyhow; and then in August there's Trouville—you've never tried Trouville? There's an awfully jolly crowd there—and the motoring's ripping in Normandy. If you say so I'll take a villa there instead of going back to Newport. And I'll put the *Sorceress* in commission, and you can make up parties and run off whenever you like, to Scotland or Norway —" He hung above her. "Don't dine with Chelles tonight! Come with me, and we'll talk things over; and next week we'll run down to Trouville to choose the villa."

Undine's heart was beating fast, but she felt within her a strange lucid force of resistance. Because of that sense of security she left her hands in Van Degen's. So Mr. Spragg might have felt at the tensest hour of the Pure Water move. She leaned forward, holding her suitor off by the pressure of her bent-back palms.

"Kiss me goodbye, Peter; I sail on Wednesday," she said.

It was the first time she had permitted him a kiss, and as his face darkened down on her she felt a moment's recoil. But her physical reactions were never very acute: she always vaguely wondered why people made "such a fuss," were so violently for or against such demonstrations. A cool spirit within her seemed to watch over and regulate her sensations, and leave her capable of measuring the intensity of those she provoked.

She turned to look at the clock. "You must go now—I shall be hours late for dinner."

"Go—after that?" He held her fast. "Kiss me again," he commanded.

It was wonderful how cool she felt—how easily she could slip out of his grasp! Any man could be managed like a child if he were really in love with one. . . .

"Don't be a goose, Peter; do you suppose I'd have kissed you if —"

"If what—what—what?" he mimicked her ecstatically, not listening.

She saw that if she wished to make him hear her she must put more distance between them, and she rose and moved across the room. From the fireplace she turned to add—"if we hadn't been saying goodbye?"

"Goodbye—now? What's the use of talking like that?" He jumped up and followed her. "Look here, Undine—I'll do anything on earth you want; only don't talk of going! If you'll only stay I'll make it all as straight and square as you please. I'll get Bertha Shallum to stop over with you for the summer; I'll take a house at Trouville and make my wife come out there. Hang it, she *shall*, if you say so! Only be a little good to me!"

Still she stood before him without speaking, aware that her implacable brows and narrowed lips would hold him off as long as she chose.

"What's the matter, Undine? Why don't you answer? You know you can't go back to that deadly dry-rot!"

She swept about on him with indignant eyes. "I can't go on with my present life either. It's hateful—as hateful as the other. If I don't go home I've got to decide on something different."

"What do you mean by 'something different'?" She was silent, and he insisted: "Are you really thinking of marrying Chelles?"

She started as if he had surprised a secret. "I'll never forgive you if you speak of it —"

"Good Lord! Good Lord!" he groaned.

She remained motionless, with lowered lids, and he went up to her and pulled her about so that she faced him. "Undine, honor bright—do you think he'll marry you?"

She looked at him with a sudden hardness in her eyes. "I really can't discuss such things with you."

"Oh, for the Lord's sake don't take that tone! I don't half know what I'm saying . . . but you mustn't throw yourself away a second time. I'll do anything you want—I swear I will!"

A knock on the door sent them apart, and a servant entered with a telegram.

Undine turned away to the window with the narrow blue slip. She was glad of the interruption: the sense of what she had at stake made her want to pause a moment and to draw breath.

The message was a long cable signed with Laura Fairford's name. It told her that Ralph had been taken suddenly ill with pneumonia, that his condition was serious and that the doctors advised his wife's immediate return.

Undine had to read the words over two or three times to get them into her crowded mind; and even after she had done so she needed more time to see their bearing on her own situation. If the message had concerned her boy her brain would have acted more quickly. She had never troubled herself over the possibility of Paul's falling ill in her absence, but she understood now that if the cable had been about him she would have rushed to the earliest steamer. With Ralph it was different. Ralph was always perfectly well—she could not picture him as being suddenly at death's door and in need of her. Probably his mother and sister had had a panic: they were always full of sentimental terrors. The next moment an angry suspicion flashed across her: what if the cable were a device of the Marvell women to bring her back? Perhaps it had been sent with Ralph's connivance! No doubt Bowen had written home about her—Washington Square had received some monstrous report of her doings! . . . Yes, the cable was clearly an echo of Laura's letter—mother and daughter had cooked it up to spoil her pleasure. Once the thought had occurred to her it struck root in her mind and began to throw out giant branches.

Van Degen followed her to the window, his face still flushed and working. "What's the matter?" he asked, as she continued to stare silently at the telegram.

She crumpled the strip of paper in her hand. If only she had been alone, had had a chance to think out her answers!

"What on earth's the matter?" he repeated.

"Oh, nothing—nothing."

"Nothing? When you're as white as a sheet?"

"Am I?" She gave a slight laugh. "It's only a cable from home."

"Ralph?"

She hesitated. "No. Laura."

"What the devil is *she* cabling you about?"

"She says Ralph wants me."

"Now—at once?"

"At once."

Van Degen laughed impatiently. "Why don't he tell you so himself? What business is it of Laura Fairford's?"

Undine's gesture implied a "What indeed?"

"Is that all she says?"

She hesitated again. "Yes—that's all." As she spoke she tossed the telegram into the basket beneath the writing-table. "As if I didn't *have* to go anyhow?" she exclaimed.

With an aching clearness of vision she saw what lay before her—the hurried preparations, the long tedious voyage on a steamer chosen at haphazard, the arrival in the deadly July heat, and the relapse into all the insufferable daily fag of nursery and kitchen—she saw it and her imagination recoiled.

Van Degen's eyes still hung on her: she guessed that he was intensely engaged in trying to follow what was passing through her mind. Presently he came up to her again, no longer perilous and importunate, but awkwardly tender, ridiculously moved by her distress.

"Undine, listen: won't you let me make it all right for you to stay?"

Her heart began to beat more quickly, and she let him come close, meeting his eyes coldly but without anger.

"What do you call 'making it all right'? Paying my bills? Don't you see that's what I hate, and will never let myself be dragged into again?" She laid her hand on his arm. "The time has come when I must be sensible, Peter; that's why we must say goodbye."

"Do you mean to tell me you're going back to Ralph?"

She paused a moment; then she murmured between her lips: "I shall never go back to him."

"Then you *do* mean to marry Chelles?"

"I've told you we must say goodbye. I've got to look out for my future."

He stood before her, irresolute, tormented, his lazy mind and impatient senses laboring with a problem beyond their power. "Ain't I here to look out for your future?" he said at last.

"No one shall look out for it in the way you mean. I'd rather never see you again—"

He gave her a baffled stare. "Oh, damn it—if that's the way you feel!" He turned and flung away toward the door.

She stood motionless where he left her, every nerve strung to the highest pitch of watchfullness. As she stood there, the scene about her stamped itself on her brain with the sharpest precision. She was aware of the fading of the summer light outside, of the movements of her maid, who was laying out her dinner dress in the room beyond, and of the fact that the tea roses on her writing-table, shaken by Van Degen's tread, were dropping their petals over Ralph's letter, and down on the crumpled telegram which she could see through the trellised sides of the scrap-basket.

In another moment Van Degen would be gone. Worse yet, while he wavered in the doorway the Shallums and Chelles, after vainly awaiting her, might dash back from the Bois and break in on them. These and other chances rose before her, urging her to action; but she held fast, immovable, unwavering, a proud yet plaintive image of renunciation.

Van Degen's hand was on the door. He half-opened it and then turned back.

"That's all you've got to say, then?"

"That's all."

He jerked the door open and passed out. She saw him stop in the ante-room to pick up his hat and stick, his heavy figure silhouetted against the glare of the wall-lights. A ray of the same light fell on her where she stood in the unlit sitting-room, and her reflection bloomed out like a flower from the mirror that faced her. She looked at the image and waited.

Van Degen put his hat on his head and slowly opened the door into the outer hall. Then he turned abruptly, his bulk eclipsing her reflection as he plunged back into the room and came up to her.

"I'll do anything you say, Undine; I'll do anything in God's world to keep you!"

She turned her eyes from the mirror and let them rest on his face, which looked as small and withered as an old man's, with a lower lip that trembled queerly. . . .

Book Three

21

THE spring in New York proceeded through more than its usual extremes of temperature to the threshold of a sultry June.

Ralph Marvell, wearily bent to his task, felt the fantastic humors of the weather as only one more incoherence in the general chaos of his case. It was strange enough, after four years of marriage, to find himself again in his old brown room in Washington Square. It was hardly there that he had expected Pegasus to land him; and, like a man returning to the scenes of his childhood, he found everything on a much smaller scale than he had imagined. Had the Dagonet boundaries really narrowed, or had the breach in the walls of his own life let in a wider vision?

Certainly there had come to be other differences between his present and his former self than that embodied in the presence of his little boy in the next room. Paul, in fact, was now the chief link between Ralph and his past. Concerning his son he still felt and thought, in a general way, in the terms of the Dagonet tradition; he still wanted to implant in Paul some of the reserves and discriminations which divided that tradition from the new spirit of limitless concession. But for himself it was different. Since his transaction with Moffatt he had had the sense of living under a new dispensation. He was not sure that it was any worse than the other; but then he was no longer very sure about anything. Perhaps this growing indifference was merely the reaction from a long nervous strain: that his mother and sister thought it so was shown by the way in which they mutely watched and hovered. Their discretion was like the hushed tread about a sick-bed. They permitted themselves no criticism of Undine; he was asked no awkward questions, subjected to no ill-timed sympathy. They simply took him back, on his own terms, into the life he had left them to; and their silence had none of those subtle implications of disapproval which may be so much more wounding than speech.

For a while he received a weekly letter from Undine. Vague and disappointing though they were, these missives helped him through the days; but he looked forward to them rather as a pretext for replies than for their actual contents. Undine was never at a loss for the spoken word: Ralph had often wondered at her verbal range and her fluent use of terms outside the current vocabulary. She had certainly not picked these up in books, since she never opened one: they seemed rather like some odd transmission of her preaching grandparent's oratory. But in her brief and colorless letters she repeated the same bald statements in the same few terms. She was well, she had been "round" with Bertha Shallum, she had dined with the Jim Driscolls or May Beringer or Dicky Bowles, the weather was too lovely or too awful; such was the gist of her news. On the last page she hoped Paul was well and sent him a kiss; but she never made a suggestion concerning his care or asked a question about his pursuits. One could only infer that, knowing in what good hands he was, she judged such solicitude superfluous; and it was thus that Ralph put the matter to his mother.

"Of course she's not worrying about the boy—why should she? She knows that with you and Laura he's as happy as a king."

To which Mrs. Marvell would answer gravely: "When you write, be sure to say I shan't put on his thinner flannels as long as this east wind lasts."

As for her husband's welfare, Undine's sole allusion to it consisted in the invariable expression of the hope that he was getting along all right: the phrase was always the same, and Ralph learned to know just how far down the third page to look for it. In a postscript she sometimes asked him to tell her mother about a new way of doing hair or cutting a skirt; and this was usually the most eloquent passage of the letter.

What satisfaction he extracted from these communications he would have found it hard to say; yet when they did not come he missed them hardly less than if they had given him all he craved. Sometimes the mere act of holding the blue or mauve sheet and breathing its scent was like holding his wife's hand and being enveloped in her fresh young fragrance: the sentimental disappointment vanished in the penetrating physical sensation. In other moods it was enough to trace the letters of the first line and the last for the desert of perfunctory phrases between the two to vanish, leaving him only the vision of their interlaced names, as of a mystic bond which her own hand had tied. Or else he saw her, closely, palpably before him, as she sat at her writing-table, frowning and a little flushed, her bent nape showing the light on her hair, her short lip pulled up by the effort of composition; and this picture had the violent reality of dream-images on the verge of waking. At other times, as he read her letter, he felt simply that at least in the moment of writing it she had been with him. But in one of the last she had said (to excuse a bad blot and an incoherent sentence): "Everybody's talking to me at once, and I don't know what I'm writing." That letter he had thrown into the fire. . . .

After the first few weeks, the letters came less and less regularly: at the end of two months they ceased. Ralph had got into the habit of watching for them on the days when a foreign post was due, and as the weeks went by without a sign he began to invent excuses for leaving the office earlier and hurrying back to Washington Square to search the letter-box for a big tinted envelope with a straggling blotted superscription. Undine's departure had given him a momentary sense of liberation: at that stage in their relations any change would have brought relief. But now that she was gone he knew she could never really go. Though his feeling for her had changed, it still ruled his life. If he saw her in her weakness he felt her in her power: the power of youth and physical radiance that clung to his disenchanted memories as the scent she used clung to her letters. Looking back at their four years of marriage he began to ask himself if he had done all he could to draw her half-formed spirit from its sleep. Had he not expected too much at first, and grown too indifferent in the sequel? After all, she was still in the toy age; and perhaps the very extravagance of his love had retarded her growth, helped to imprison her in a little circle of frivolous illusions. But the last months had made a man of him, and when she came back he would know how to lift her to the height of his experience.

So he would reason, day by day, as he hastened back to Washington Square; but when he opened the door, and his first glance at the hall table showed him there was no letter there, his illusions shrivelled down to their weak roots. She had not written: she did not mean to write. He and the boy were no longer a part of her life. When she came back everything would be as it had been before, with the dreary difference that she had tasted new pleasures and that their absence would take the savor from all he had to give her. Then the coming of another foreign mail would lift his hopes, and as he hurried home he would imagine new reasons for expecting a letter. . . .

Week after week he swung between the extremes of hope and dejection, and at last, when the strain had become unbearable, he cabled her. The answer ran: "Very well best love writing"; but the promised letter never came. . . .

He went on steadily with his work: he even passed through a phase of exaggerated energy. But his baffled youth fought in him for air. Was this to be the end? Was he to wear his life out in useless drudgery? The plain prose of it, of course, was that the economic situation remained unchanged by the sentimental catastrophe and that he must go on working for his wife and child. But at any rate, as it was mainly for Paul that he would henceforth work, it should be on his own terms and according to his inherited notions of "straightness." He would never again engage in any transaction resembling his compact with Moffatt. Even now he was not sure there had been anything crooked in that; but the fact of his having instinctively referred the point to Mr. Spragg rather than to his grandfather implied a presumption against it.

His partners were quick to profit by his sudden spurt of energy, and his work grew no lighter. He was not only the youngest and most recent member of the firm, but the one who had so far added least to the volume of its business. His hours were the longest, his absences, as summer approached, the least frequent and the most grudgingly accorded. No doubt his associates knew that he was pressed for money and could not risk a break. They "worked" him, and he was aware of it, and submitted because he dared not lose his job. But the long hours of mechanical drudgery were telling on his active body and undisciplined nerves. He had begun too late to subject himself to the persistent mortification of spirit and flesh which is a condition of the average business life; and after the long dull days in the office the evenings at his grandfather's whist-table did not give him the counter-stimulus he needed.

Almost everyone had gone out of town; but now and then Miss Ray came to dine, and Ralph, seated beneath the family portraits and opposite the desiccated Harriet, who had already faded to the semblance of one of her own great-aunts, listened languidly to the kind of talk that the originals might have exchanged about the same table when New York gentility centerd in the Battery and the Bowling Green. Mr. Dagonet was always pleasant to see and hear, but his sarcasms were growing faint and recondite: they had as little bearing on life as the humors of a Restoration comedy. As for Mrs. Marvell and Miss Ray, they seemed to the young man even more spectrally remote: hardly anything that mattered to him existed for them, and their prejudices reminded him of signposts warning off trespassers who have long since ceased to intrude.

Now and then he dined at his club and went on to the theater with some young men of his own age; but he left them afterward, half vexed with himself for not being in the humor to prolong the adventure. There were moments when he would have liked to affirm his freedom in however commonplace a way: moments when the vulgarest way would have seemed the most satisfying. But he always ended by walking home alone and tip-toeing upstairs through the sleeping house lest he should wake his boy. . . .

On Saturday afternoons, when the business world was hurrying to the country for golf and tennis, he stayed in town and took Paul to see the Spraggs. Several times since his wife's departure he had tried to bring about closer relations between his own family and Undine's; and the ladies of Washington Square, in their eagerness to meet his wishes, had made various friendly advances to Mrs. Spragg. But they were met by a mute resistance which made Ralph suspect that Undine's strictures on his family had taken root in her mother's brooding mind; and he gave up the struggle to bring together what had been so effectually put asunder.

If he regretted his lack of success it was chiefly because he was so sorry for the Spraggs. Soon after Undine's marriage they had abandoned their polychrome suite at the Stentorian, and since then their peregrinations had carried them through half the hotels of the metropolis. Undine, who had early discovered her mistake in thinking hotel life fashionable, had tried to persuade her parents to take a house of their own; but though they refrained from taxing her with inconsistency they did not act on her suggestion. Mrs. Spragg seemed to shrink from the thought of "going back to housekeeping," and Ralph suspected that she depended on the transit from hotel to hotel as the one element of variety in her life. As for Mr. Spragg, it was impossible to imagine anyone in whom the domestic sentiments were more completely unlocalized and disconnected from any fixed habits; and he was probably aware of his changes of abode chiefly as they obliged him to ascend from the subway, or descend from the elevated, a few blocks higher up or lower down.

Neither husband nor wife complained to Ralph of their frequent displacements, or assigned to them any cause save the vague one of "guessing they could do better"; but Ralph noticed that the decreasing luxury of their life synchronized with Undine's growing demands for money. During the last few months they had transferred themselves to the Malibran, a tall narrow structure resembling a grain-elevator divided into cells, where linoleum and lincrusta simulated the stucco and marble of the Stentorian, and fagged businessmen and their families consumed the watery stews dispensed by "colored help" in the gray twilight of a basement dining-room.

Mrs. Spragg had no sitting-room, and Paul and his father had to be received in one of the long public parlors, between ladies seated at rickety desks in the throes of correspondence and groups of listlessly conversing residents and callers.

The Spraggs were intensely proud of their grandson, and Ralph perceived that they would have liked to see Paul charging uproariously from group to group and thrusting his bright curls and cherubic smile upon the general attention. The fact that the boy preferred to stand between his grandfather's knees and play with Mr. Spragg's Masonic emblem, or dangle his legs from the arm of Mrs. Spragg's chair, seemed to his grandparents evidence of ill-health or undue repression, and he was subjected by Mrs. Spragg to searching inquiries as to how his food set, and whether he didn't think his Popper was too strict with him. A more embarrassing problem was raised by the "surprise" (in the shape of peanut candy or chocolate creams) which he was invited to hunt for in Gran'ma's pockets, and which Ralph had to confiscate on the way home lest the dietary rules of Washington Square should be too visibly infringed.

Sometimes Ralph found Mrs. Heeny, ruddy and jovial, seated in the armchair opposite Mrs. Spragg, and regaling her with selections from a new batch of clippings. During Undine's illness of the previous winter Mrs. Heeny had become a familiar figure to Paul, who had learned to expect almost as much from her bag as from his grandmother's pockets; so that the intemperate Saturdays at the Malibran were usually followed by languid and abstemious Sundays in Washington Square.

Mrs. Heeny, being unaware of this sequel to her bounties, formed the habit of appearing regularly on Saturdays, and while she chatted with his grandmother the little boy was encouraged to scatter the grimy carpet with face-creams and bunches of clippings in his thrilling quest for the sweets at the bottom of her bag.

"I declare, if he ain't in just as much of a hurry f'r everything as his mother!" she exclaimed one day in her rich rolling voice; and stooping to pick up a long strip of newspaper which Paul had flung aside she added, as she smoothed it out: "I guess 'f he was a little mite older he'd be better pleased with this 'n with the candy. It's the very thing I was trying to find for you the other day, Mrs. Spragg," she went on, holding the bit of paper at arm's length; and she began to read out, with a loudness proportioned to the distance between her eyes and the text:

"With two such sprinters as 'Pete' Van Degen and Dicky Bowles to set the pace, it's no wonder the New York set in Paris has struck a livelier gait than ever this spring. It's a high-pressure season and no mistake, and no one lags behind less than the fascinating Mrs. Ralph Marvell, who is to be seen daily and nightly in all the smartest restaurants and naughtiest theaters, with so many devoted swains in attendance that the rival beauties of both worlds are said to be making catty comments. But then Mrs. Marvell's gowns are almost as good as her looks—and how can you expect the other women to stand for such a monopoly?"

To escape the strain of these visits, Ralph once or twice tried the experiment of leaving Paul with his grandparents and calling for him in the late afternoon; but one day, on reentering the Malibran, he was met by a small abashed figure clad in a kaleidoscopic tartan and a green velvet cap with a silver thistle. After this experience of the "surprises" of which Gran'ma was capable when she had a chance to take Paul shopping Ralph did not again venture to leave his son, and their subsequent Saturdays were passed together in the sultry gloom of the Malibran.

Conversation with the Spraggs was almost impossible. Ralph could talk with his father-in-law in his office, but in the hotel parlor Mr. Spragg sat in a ruminating silence broken only by the emission of an occasional "Well—well" addressed to his grandson. As for Mrs. Spragg, her son-in-law could not remember having had a sustained conversation with her since the distant day when he had first called at the Stentorian, and had been "entertained," in Undine's absence, by her astonished mother. The shock of that encounter had moved Mrs. Spragg to eloquence; but Ralph's entrance into the family, without making him seem less of a stranger, appeared once for all to have relieved her of the obligation of finding something to say to him.

The one question she invariably asked: "You heard from Undie?" had been relatively easy to answer while his wife's infrequent letters continued to arrive; but a Saturday came when he felt the blood rise to his temples as, for the fourth consecutive week, he stammered out, under the snapping eyes of Mrs. Heeny: "No, not by this post either—I begin to think I must have lost a letter"; and it was then that Mr. Spragg, who had sat silently looking up at the ceiling, cut short his wife's exclamation by an inquiry about real estate in the Bronx. After that, Ralph noticed, Mrs. Spragg never again renewed her question; and he understood that his father-in-law had guessed his embarrassment and wished to spare it.

Ralph had never thought of looking for any delicacy of feeling under Mr. Spragg's large lazy irony, and the incident drew the two men nearer together. Mrs. Spragg, for her part, was certainly not delicate; but she was simple and without malice, and Ralph liked her for her silent acceptance of her diminished state. Sometimes, as he sat between the lonely primitive old couple, he wondered from what source Undine's voracious ambitions had been drawn: all she cared for, and attached importance to, was as remote from her parents' conception of life as her impatient greed from their passive stoicism.

One hot afternoon toward the end of June Ralph suddenly wondered if Clare Van Degen were still in town. She had dined in Washington Square some ten days earlier, and he remembered her saying that she had sent the children down to Long Island, but that she herself meant to stay on in town till the heat grew unbearable. She hated her big showy place on Long Island, she was tired of the spring trip to London and Paris, where one met at every turn the faces one had grown sick of seeing all winter, and she declared that in the early summer New York was the only place in which one could escape from New Yorkers. . . . She put the case amusingly, and it was like her to take up any attitude that went against the habits of her set; but she lived at the mercy of her moods, and one could never tell how long anyone of them would rule her.

As he sat in his office, with the noise and glare of the endless afternoon rising up in hot waves from the street, there wandered into Ralph's mind a vision of her shady drawing-room. All day it hung before him like the mirage of a spring before a dusty traveler: he felt a positive thirst for her presence, for the sound of her voice, the wide spaces and luxurious silences surrounding her.

It was perhaps because, on that particular day, a spiral pain was twisting around in the back of his head, and digging in a little deeper with each twist, and because the figures on the balance sheet before him were hopping about like black imps in an infernal forward-and-back, that the picture hung there so persistently. It was a long time since he had wanted anything as much as, at that particular moment, he wanted to be with Clare and hear her voice; and as soon as he had ground out the day's measure of work he rang up the Van Degen palace and learned that she was still in town.

The lowered awnings of her inner drawing-room cast a luminous shadow on old cabinets and consoles, and on the pale flowers scattered here and there in vases of bronze and porcelain. Clare's taste was as capricious as her moods, and the rest of the house was not in harmony with this room. There was, in particular, another drawing-room, which she now described as

Peter's creation, but which Ralph knew to be partly hers: a heavily decorated apartment, where Popple's portrait of her throned over a waste of gilt
furniture. It was characteristic that today she had had Ralph shown in by
another way; and that, as she had spared him the polyphonic drawing-room,
so she had skillfully adapted her own appearance to her soberer background.
She sat near the window, reading, in a clear cool dress: and at his entrance
she merely slipped a finger between the pages and looked up at him.

Her way of receiving him made him feel that her restlessness and stridency were as unlike her genuine self as the gilded drawing-room, and that
this quiet creature was the only real Clare, the Clare who had once been so
nearly his, and who seemed to want him to know that she had never wholly
been anyone else's.

"Why didn't you let me know you were still in town?" he asked, as he
sat down in the sofa-corner near her chair.

Her dark smile deepened. "I hoped you'd come and see."

"One never knows, with you."

He was looking about the room with a kind of confused pleasure in its
pale shadows and spots of dark rich color. The old lacquer screen behind
Clare's head looked like a lusterless black pool with gold leaves floating on
it; and another piece, a little table at her elbow, had the brown bloom and
the pearlike curves of an old violin.

"I like to be here," Ralph said.

She did not make the mistake of asking: "Then why do you never
come?" Instead, she turned away, and drew an inner curtain across the
window to shut out the sunlight which was beginning to slant in under the
awning.

The mere fact of her not answering, and the final touch of well-being
which her gesture gave, reminded him of other summer days they had spent
together, long rambling boy-and-girl days in the hot woods and sunny fields,
when they had never thought of talking to each other unless there was
something they particularly wanted to say. His tired fancy strayed off for a
second to the thought of what it would have been like to come back, at the
end of the day, to such a sweet community of silence; but his mind was too
crowded with importunate facts for any lasting view of visionary distances.
The thought faded, and he merely felt how restful it was to have her
near. . . .

"I'm glad you stayed in town: you must let me come again," he said.

"I suppose you can't always get away," she answered; and she began to
listen, with grave intelligent eyes, to his description of his tedious days.

With her eyes on him he felt the exquisite relief of talking about himself
as he had not dared to talk to anyone since his marriage. He would not for
the world have confessed his discouragement, his consciousness of incapac-
ity; to Undine and in Washington Square any hint of failure would have
been taken as a criticism of what his wife demanded of him. Only to Clare

Van Degen could he cry out his present despondency and his loathing of the interminable task ahead.

"A man doesn't know till he tries it how killing uncongenial work is, and how it destroys the power of doing what one's fit for, even if there's time for both. But there's Paul to be looked out for, and I daren't chuck my job—I'm in mortal terror of its chucking me. . . ."

Little by little he slipped into a detailed recital of all his lesser worries, the most recent of which was his experience with the Lipscombs, who, after a two months' tenancy of the West End Avenue house, had decamped without paying their rent.

Clare laughed contemptuously. "Yes—I heard he'd come to grief and been suspended from the Stock Exchange, and I see in the papers that his wife's retort has been to sue for a divorce."

Ralph knew that, like all their clan, his cousin regarded a divorce suit as a vulgar and unnecessary way of taking the public into one's confidence. His mind flashed back to the family feast in Washington Square in celebration of his engagement. He recalled his grandfather's chance allusion to Mrs. Lipscomb, and Undine's answer, fluted out on her highest note: "Oh, I guess she'll get a divorce pretty soon. He's been a disappointment to her."

Ralph could still hear the horrified murmur with which his mother had rebuked his laugh. For he had laughed—had thought Undine's speech fresh and natural! Now he felt the ironic rebound of her words. Heaven knew he had been a disappointment to her; and what was there in her own feeling, or in her inherited prejudices, to prevent her seeking the same redress as Mabel Lipscomb? He wondered if the same thought were in his cousin's mind. . . .

They began to talk of other things: books, pictures, plays; and one by one the closed doors opened and light was let into dusty shuttered places. Clare's mind was neither keen nor deep: Ralph, in the past, had often smiled at her rash ardors and vague intensities. But she had his own range of allusions, and a great gift of momentary understanding; and he had so long beaten his thoughts out against a blank wall of incomprehension that her sympathy seemed full of insight.

She began by a question about his writing, but the subject was distasteful to him, and he turned the talk to a new book in which he had been interested. She knew enough of it to slip in the right word here and there; and thence they wandered on to kindred topics. Under the warmth of her attention his torpid ideas awoke again, and his eyes took their fill of pleasure as she leaned forward, her thin brown hands clasped on her knees and her eager face reflecting all his feelings.

There was a moment when the two currents of sensation were merged in one, and he began to feel confusedly that he was young and she was kind, and that there was nothing he would like better than to go on sitting there, not much caring what she said or how he answered, if only she would let him look at her and give him one of her thin brown hands to hold. Then the corkscrew in the back of his head dug into him again with a deeper thrust, and she seemed suddenly to recede to a great distance and be divided from him by a fog of pain. The fog lifted after a minute, but it left him queerly remote from her, from the cool room with its scents and shadows, and from all the objects which, a moment before, had so sharply impinged upon his senses. It was as though he looked at it all through a rain-blurred pane, against which his hand would strike if he held it out to her. . . .

That impression passed also, and he found himself thinking how tired he was and how little anything mattered. He recalled the unfinished piece of work on his desk, and for a moment had the odd illusion that it was there before him. . . .

She exclaimed: "But are you going?" and her exclamation made him aware that he had left his seat and was standing in front of her. . . . He fancied there was some kind of appeal in her brown eyes; but she was so dim and far off that he couldn't be sure of what she wanted, and the next moment he found himself shaking hands with her, and heard her saying something kind and cold about its having been so nice to see him. . . .

Halfway up the stairs little Paul, shining and rosy from supper, lurked in ambush for his evening game. Ralph was fond of stooping down to let the boy climb up his outstretched arms to his shoulders, but today, as he did so, Paul's hug seemed to crush him in a vice, and the shout of welcome that accompanied it racked his ears like an explosion of steam-whistles. The queer distance between himself and the rest of the world was annihilated again: everything stared and glared and clutched him. He tried to turn away his face from the child's hot kisses; and as he did so he caught sight of a mauve envelope among the hats and sticks on the hall table.

Instantly he passed Paul over to his nurse, stammered out a word about being tired, and sprang up the long flights to his study. The pain in his head had stopped, but his hands trembled as he tore open the envelope. Within it was a second letter bearing a French stamp and addressed to himself. It looked like a business communication and had apparently been sent to Undine's hotel in Paris and forwarded to him by her hand. "Another bill!" he reflected grimly, as he threw it aside and felt in the outer envelope for her letter. There was nothing there, and after a first sharp pang of disappointment he picked up the enclosure and opened it.

Inside was a lithographed circular, headed "Confidential" and bearing the Paris address of a firm of private detectives who undertook, in conditions of attested and inviolable discretion, to investigate "delicate" situations, look up doubtful antecedents, and furnish reliable evidence of misconduct—all on the most reasonable terms.

For a long time Ralph sat and stared at this document; then he began to laugh and tossed it into the scrap-basket. After that, with a groan, he dropped his head against the edge of his writing table.

22

WHEN he woke, the first thing he remembered was the fact of having cried.

He could not think how he had come to be such a fool. He hoped to heaven no one had seen him. He supposed he must have been worrying about the unfinished piece of work at the office: where was it, by the way, he wondered? Why—where he had left it the day before, of course! What a ridiculous thing to worry about—but it seemed to follow him about like a dog. . . .

He said to himself that he must get up presently and go down to the office. Presently—when he could open his eyes. Just now there was a dead weight on them; he tried one after another in vain. The effort set him weakly trembling, and he wanted to cry again. Nonsense! He must get out of bed.

He stretched his arms out, trying to reach something to pull himself up by; but everything slipped away and evaded him. It was like trying to catch at bright short waves. Then suddenly his fingers clasped themselves about something firm and warm. A hand: a hand that gave back his pressure! The relief was inexpressible. He lay still and let the hand hold him, while mentally he went through the motions of getting up and beginning to dress. So indistinct were the boundaries between thought and action that he really felt himself moving about the room, in a queer disembodied way, as one treads the air in sleep. Then he felt the bedclothes over him and the pillows under his head.

"I *must* get up," he said, and pulled at the hand.

It pressed him down again: down into a dim deep pool of sleep. He lay there for a long time, in a silent blackness far below light and sound; then he gradually floated to the surface with the buoyancy of a dead body. But his body had never been more alive. Jagged strokes of pain tore through it, hands dragged at it with nails that bit like teeth. They wound thongs about him, bound him, tied weights to him, tried to pull him down with them; but still he floated, floated, danced on the fiery waves of pain, with barbed light pouring down on him from an arrowy sky.

Charmed intervals of rest, blue sailings on melodious seas, alternated with the anguish. He became a leaf on the air, a feather on a current, a straw on the tide, the spray of the wave spinning itself to sunshine as the wave toppled over into gulfs of blue. . . .

He woke on a stony beach, his legs and arms still lashed to his sides and the thongs cutting into him; but the fierce sky was hidden, and hidden by his own languid lids. He felt the ecstasy of decreasing pain, and courage came to him to open his eyes and look about him. . . .

The beach was his own bed; the tempered light lay on familiar things, and someone was moving about in a shadowy way between bed and window. He was thirsty, and someone gave him a drink. His pillow burned, and someone turned the cool side out. His brain was clear enough now for him to understand that he was ill, and to want to talk about it; but his tongue hung in his throat like a clapper in a bell. He must wait till the rope was pulled. . . .

So time and life stole back on him, and his thoughts labored weakly with dim fears. Slowly he cleared a way through them, adjusted himself to his strange state, and found out that he was in his own room, in his grandfather's house, that alternating with the white-capped faces about him were those of his mother and sister, and that in a few days—if he took his beef-tea and didn't fret—Paul would be brought up from Long Island, whither, on account of the great heat, he had been carried off by Clare Van Degen.

No one named Undine to him, and he did not speak of her. But one day, as he lay in bed in the summer twilight, he had a vision of a moment, a long way behind him—at the beginning of his illness, it must have been—when he had called out for her in his anguish, and someone had said: "She's coming: she'll be here next week."

Could it be that next week was not yet here? He supposed that illness robbed one of all sense of time, and he lay still, as if in ambush, watching his scattered memories come out one by one and join themselves together. If he watched long enough he was sure he should recognize one that fitted into his picture of the day when he had asked for Undine. And at length a face came out of the twilight: a freckled face, benevolently bent over him under a starched cap. He had not seen the face for a long time, but suddenly it took shape and fitted itself into the picture. . . .

Laura Fairford sat nearby, a book on her knee. At the sound of his voice she looked up.

"What was the name of the first nurse?"

"The first —?"

"The one that went away."

"Oh—Miss Hicks, you mean?"

"How long is it since she went?"

"It must be three weeks. She had another case."

He thought this over carefully; then he spoke again. "Call Undine."

She made no answer, and he repeated irritably: "Why don't you call her? I want to speak to her."

Mrs. Fairford laid down her book and came to him.

"She's not here—just now."

He dealt with this also, laboriously. "You mean she's out—she's not in the house?"

"I mean she hasn't come yet."

As she spoke Ralph felt a sudden strength and hardness in his brain and body. Everything in him became as clear as noon.

"But it was before Miss Hicks left that you told me you'd sent for her, and that she'd be here the following week. And you say Miss Hicks has been gone three weeks."

This was what he had worked out in his head, and what he meant to say to his sister; but something seemed to snap shut in his throat, and he closed his eyes without speaking.

Even when Mr. Spragg came to see him he said nothing. They talked about his illness, about the hot weather, about the rumors that Harmon B. Driscoll was again threatened with indictment; and then Mr. Spragg pulled himself out of his chair and said: "I presume you'll call round at the office before you leave the city."

"Oh, yes: as soon as I'm up," Ralph answered. They understood each other.

Clare had urged him to come down to Long Island and complete his convalescence there, but he preferred to stay in Washington Square till he should be strong enough for the journey to the Adirondacks, whither Laura had already preceded him with Paul. He did not want to see anyone but his mother and grandfather till his legs could carry him to Mr. Spragg's office.

It was an oppressive day in mid-August, with a yellow mist of heat in the sky, when at last he entered the big office-building. Swirls of dust lay on the mosaic floor, and a stale smell of decayed fruit and salt air and steaming asphalt filled the place like a fog. As he shot up in the elevator someone slapped him on the back, and turning he saw Elmer Moffatt at his side, smooth and rubicund under a new straw hat.

Moffatt was loudly glad to see him. "I haven't laid eyes on you for months. At the old stand still?"

"So am I," he added, as Ralph assented. "Hope to see you there again someday. Don't forget it's *my* turn this time: glad if I can be any use to you. So long." Ralph's weak bones ached under his handshake.

"How's Mrs. Marvell?" he turned back from his landing to call out; and Ralph answered: "Thanks; she's very well."

Mr. Spragg sat alone in his murky inner office, the fly-blown engraving of Daniel Webster above his head and the congested scrap-basket beneath his feet. He looked fagged and sallow, like the day.

Ralph sat down on the other side of the desk. For a moment his throat contracted as it had when he had tried to question his sister; then he asked: "Where's Undine?"

Mr. Spragg glanced at the calendar that hung from a hat-peg on the door. Then he released the Masonic emblem from his grasp, drew out his watch and consulted it critically.

"If the train's on time I presume she's somewhere between Chicago and Omaha round about now."

Ralph stared at him, wondering if the heat had gone to his head.

"I don't understand."

"The Twentieth Century's generally considered the best route to Dakota," explained Mr. Spragg, who pronounced the word *rowt*.

"Do you mean to say Undine's in the United states?"

Mr. Spragg's lower lip groped for the phantom toothpick. "Why, let me see: hasn't Dakota been a state a year or two now?"

"Oh, God —" Ralph cried, pushing his chair back violently and striding across the narrow room.

As he turned, Mr. Spragg stood up and advanced a few steps. He had given up the quest for the toothpick, and his drawn-in lips were no more than a narrow depression in his beard. He stood before Ralph, absently shaking the loose change in his trouser-pockets.

Ralph felt the same hardness and lucidity that had come to him when he had heard his sister's answer.

"She's gone, you mean? Left me? With another man?"

Mr. Spragg drew himself up with a kind of slouching majesty. "My daughter is not that style. I understand Undine thinks there have been mistakes on both sides. She considers the tie was formed too hastily. I believe desertion is the usual plea in such cases."

Ralph stared about him, hardly listening. He did not resent his father-in-law's tone. In a dim way he guessed that Mr. Spragg was suffering hardly less than himself. But nothing was clear to him save the monstrous fact suddenly upheaved in his path. His wife had left him, and the plan for her evasion had been made and executed while he lay helpless: she had seized the opportunity of his illness to keep him in ignorance of her design. The humor of it suddenly struck him and he laughed.

"Do you mean to tell me that Undine's divorcing *me?*"

"I presume that's her plan," Mr. Spragg admitted.

"For desertion?" Ralph pursued, still laughing.

His father-in-law hesitated a moment; then he answered: "You've always done all you could for my daughter. There wasn't any other plea she could think of. She presumed this would be the most agreeable to your family."

"It was good of her to think of that!"

Mr. Spragg's only comment was a sigh.

"Does she imagine I won't fight it?" Ralph broke out with sudden passion.

His father-in-law looked at him thoughtfully. "I presume you realize it ain't easy to change Undine, once she's set on a thing."

"Perhaps not. But if she really means to apply for a divorce I can make it a little less easy for her to get."

"That's so," Mr. Spragg conceded. He turned back to his revolving chair, and seating himself in it began to drum on the desk with cigar-stained fingers.

"And by God, I will!" Ralph thundered. Anger was the only emotion in him now. He had been fooled, cheated, made a mock of; but the score was not settled yet. He turned back and stood before Mr. Spragg.

"I suppose she's gone with Van Degen?"

"My daughter's gone alone, sir. I saw her off at the station. I understood she was to join a lady friend."

At every point Ralph felt his hold slip off the surface of his father-in-law's impervious fatalism.

"Does she suppose Van Degen's going to marry her?"

"Undine didn't mention her future plans to me." After a moment Mr. Spragg appended: "If she had, I should have declined to discuss them with her."

Ralph looked at him curiously, perceiving that he intended in this negative way to imply his disapproval of his daughter's course.

"I shall fight it—I shall fight it!" the young man cried again. "You may tell her I shall fight it to the end!"

Mr. Spragg pressed the nib of his pen against the dust-coated inkstand. "I suppose you would have to engage a lawyer. She'll know it that way," he remarked.

"She'll know it—you may count on that!"

Ralph had begun to laugh again. Suddenly he heard his own laugh and it pulled him up. What was he laughing about? What was he talking about? The thing was to act—to hold his tongue and act. There was no use uttering windy threats to this broken-spirited old man. A fury of action burned in Ralph, pouring light into his mind and strength into his muscles. He caught up his hat and turned to the door.

As he opened it Mr. Spragg rose again and came forward with his slow shambling step. He laid his hand on Ralph's arm.

"I'd 'a' given anything—anything short of my girl herself—not to have this happen to you, Ralph Marvell."

"Thank you, sir," said Ralph.

They looked at each other for a moment; then Mr. Spragg added: "But it *has* happened, you know. Bear that in mind. Nothing you can do will change it. Time and again, I've found that a good thing to remember."

23

I N the Adirondacks Ralph Marvell sat day after day on the balcony of his little house above the lake, staring at the great white cloud-reflections in the water and at the dark line of trees that closed them in. Now and then he got into the canoe and paddled himself through a winding chain of ponds to some lonely clearing in the forest; and there he lay on his back in the pine-needles and watched the great clouds form and dissolve themselves above his head.

All his past life seemed to be symbolized by the building-up and break-ing-down of those fluctuating shapes, which incalculable wind-currents per-petually shifted and remodeled or swept from the zenith like a pinch of dust.

His sister told him that he looked well—better than he had in years; and there were moments when his listlessness, his stony insensibility to the small pricks and frictions of daily life, might have passed for the serenity of recovered health.

There was no one with whom he could speak of Undine. His family had thrown over the whole subject a pall of silence which even Laura Fairford shrank from raising. As for his mother, Ralph had seen at once that the idea of talking over the situation was positively frightening to her. There was no provision for such emergencies in the moral order of Washington Square. The affair was a "scandal," and it was not in the Dagonet tradition to acknowledge the existence of scandals. Ralph recalled a dim memory of his childhood, the tale of a misguided friend of his mother's who had left her husband for a more congenial companion, and who, years later, returning ill and friendless to New York, had appealed for sympathy to Mrs. Marvell. The latter had not refused to give it; but she had put on her black cashmere and two veils when she went to see her unhappy friend, and had never men-tioned these errands of mercy to her husband.

Ralph suspected that the constraint shown by his mother and sister was partly due to their having but a dim and confused view of what had hap-pened. In their vocabulary the word "divorce" was wrapped in such a dark veil of innuendo as no ladylike hand would care to lift. They had not reached the point of differentiating divorces, but classed them indistinc-tively as disgraceful incidents, in which the woman was always to blame, but the man, though her innocent victim, was yet inevitably contaminated. The time involved in the "proceedings" was viewed as a penitential season during which it behooved the family of the persons concerned to behave as if they were dead; yet any open allusion to the reason for adopting such an attitude would have been regarded as the height of indelicacy.

Mr. Dagonet's notion of the case was almost as remote from reality. All he asked was that his grandson should "thrash" somebody, and he could not be made to understand that the modern drama of divorce is sometimes cast without a Lovelace.

"You might as well tell me there was nobody but Adam in the garden when Eve picked the apple. You say your wife was discontented? No woman ever knows she's discontented till some man tells her so. My God! I've seen smashups before now; but I never yet saw a marriage dissolved like a business partnership. Divorce without a lover? Why, it's—it's as unnatural as getting drunk on lemonade."

After this first explosion Mr. Dagonet also became silent; and Ralph perceived that what annoyed him most was the fact of the "scandal's" not being one in any gentlemanly sense of the word. It was like some nasty business mess, about which Mr. Dagonet couldn't pretend to have an opinion, since such things didn't happen to men of his kind. That such a thing should have happened to his only grandson was probably the bitterest experience of his pleasantly uneventful life; and it added a touch of irony to Ralph's unhappiness to know how little, in the whole affair, he was cutting the figure Mr. Dagonet expected him to cut.

At first he had chafed under the taciturnity surrounding him: had passionately longed to cry out his humiliation, his rebellion, his despair. Then he began to feel the tonic effect of silence; and the next stage was reached when it became clear to him that there was nothing to say. There were thoughts and thoughts: they bubbled up perpetually from the black springs of his hidden misery, they stole on him in the darkness of night, they blotted out the light of day; but when it came to putting them into words and applying them to the external facts of the case, they seemed totally unrelated to it. One more white and sun-touched glory had gone from his sky; but there seemed no way of connecting that with such practical issues as his being called on to decide whether Paul was to be put in knickerbockers or trousers, and whether he should go back to Washington Square for the winter or hire a small house for himself and his son.

The latter question was ultimately decided by his remaining under his grandfather's roof. November found him back in the office again, in fairly good health, with an outer skin of indifference slowly forming over his lacerated soul. There had been a hard minute to live through when he came back to his old brown room in Washington Square. The walls and tables were covered with photographs of Undine: effigies of all shapes and sizes, expressing every possible sentiment dear to the photographic tradition. Ralph had gathered them all up when he had moved from West End Avenue after Undine's departure for Europe, and they throned over his other possessions as her image had throned over his future the night he had sat in that very room and dreamed of soaring up with her into the blue. . . .

It was impossible to go on living with her photographs about him; and one evening, going up to his room after dinner, he began to unhang them from the walls, and to gather them up from bookshelves and mantelpiece and tables. Then he looked about for some place in which to hide them. There were drawers under his bookcases; but they were full of old discarded things, and even if he emptied the drawers, the photographs, in their heavy frames, were almost all too large to fit into them. He turned next to the top shelf of his cupboard; but here the nurse had stored Paul's old toys, his sand-pails, shovels and croquet-box. Every corner was packed with the vain impedimenta of living, and the mere thought of clearing a space in the chaos was too great an effort.

He began to replace the pictures one by one; and the last was still in his hand when he heard his sister's voice outside. He hurriedly put the portrait back in its usual place on his writing-table, and Mrs. Fairford, who had been dining in Washington Square, and had come up to bid him good night, flung her arms about him in a quick embrace and went down to her carriage.

The next afternoon, when he came home from the office, he did not at first see any change in his room; but when he had lit his pipe and thrown himself into his armchair he noticed that the photograph of his wife's picture by Popple no longer faced him from the mantelpiece. He turned to his writing-table, but her image had vanished from there too; then his eye, making the circuit of the walls, perceived that they also had been stripped. Not a single photograph of Undine was left; yet so adroitly had the work of elimination been done, so ingeniously the remaining objects readjusted, that the change attracted no attention.

Ralph was angry, sore, ashamed. He felt as if Laura, whose hand he instantly detected, had taken a cruel pleasure in her work, and for an instant he hated her for it. Then a sense of relief stole over him. He was glad he could look about him without meeting Undine's eyes, and he understood that what had been done to his room he must do to his memory and his imagination: he must so readjust his mind that, whichever way he turned his thoughts, her face should no longer confront him. But that was a task that Laura could not perform for him, a task to be accomplished only by the hard continuous tension of his will.

With the setting in of the mood of silence all desire to fight his wife's suit died out. The idea of touching publicly on anything that had passed between himself and Undine had become unthinkable. Insensibly he had been subdued to the point of view about him, and the idea of calling on the law to repair his shattered happiness struck him as even more grotesque than it was degrading. Nevertheless, some contradictory impulse of his divided spirit made him resent, on the part of his mother and sister, a too-ready acceptance of his attitude. There were moments when their tacit assumption that his wife was banished and forgotten irritated him like the hushed tread of sympathizers about the bed of an invalid who will not admit that he suffers.

His irritation was aggravated by the discovery that Mrs. Marvell and Laura had already begun to treat Paul as if he were an orphan. One day, coming unnoticed into the nursery, Ralph heard the boy ask when his mother was coming back; and Mrs. Fairford, who was with him, answered: "She's not coming back, dearest; and you're not to speak of her to Father."

Ralph, when the boy was out of hearing, rebuked his sister for her answer. "I don't want you to talk of his mother as if she were dead. I don't want you to forbid Paul to speak of her."

Laura, though usually so yielding, defended herself. "What's the use of encouraging him to speak of her when he's never to see her? The sooner he forgets her the better."

Ralph pondered. "Later—if she asks to see him—I shan't refuse."

Mrs. Fairford pressed her lips together to check the answer: "She never will!"

Ralph heard it, nevertheless, and let it pass. Nothing gave him so profound a sense of estrangement from his former life as the conviction that his sister was probably right. He did not really believe that Undine would ever ask to see her boy; but if she did he was determined not to refuse her request.

Time wore on, the Christmas holidays came and went, and the winter continued to grind out the weary measure of its days. Toward the end of January Ralph received a registered letter, addressed to him at his office, and bearing in the corner of the envelope the names of a firm of Sioux Falls attorneys. He instantly divined that it contained the legal notification of his wife's application for divorce, and as he wrote his name in the postman's book he smiled grimly at the thought that the stroke of his pen was doubtless signing her release. He opened the letter, found it to be what he had expected, and locked it away in his desk without mentioning the matter to anyone.

He supposed that with the putting away of this document he was thrusting the whole subject out of sight; but not more than a fortnight later, as he sat in the subway on his way downtown, his eye was caught by his own name on the first page of the heavily headlined paper which the unshaved occupant of the next seat held between grimy fists. The blood rushed to Ralph's forehead as he looked over the man's arm and read: "Society Leader Gets Decree," and beneath it the subordinate clause: "Says Husband Too Absorbed in Business to Make Home Happy." For weeks afterward, wherever he went, he felt that blush upon his forehead. For the first time in his life the coarse fingering of public curiosity had touched the secret places of his soul, and nothing that had gone before seemed as humiliating as this trivial comment on his tragedy. The paragraph continued on its way through the press, and whenever he took up a newspaper he seemed to come upon it, slightly modified, variously developed, but always reverting with a kind of unctuous irony to his financial preoccupations and his wife's consequent loneliness. The phrase was even taken up by the paragraph writer, called forth excited letters from similarly situated victims, was commented on in humorous editorials and served as a text for pulpit denunciations of the growing craze for wealth; and finally, at his dentist's, Ralph came across it in a *Family Weekly*, as one of the "Heart Problems" propounded to subscribers, with a gramophone, a straight-front corset, and a vanity-box among the prizes offered for its solution.

24

"IF you'd only had the sense to come straight to me, Undine Spragg! There isn't a tip I couldn't have given you—not one!"

This speech, in which a faintly contemptuous compassion for her friend's case was blended with the frankest pride in her own, probably represented the nearest approach to "tact" that Mrs. James J. Rolliver had yet acquired. Undine was impartial enough to note in it a distinct advance on the youthful methods of Indiana Frusk; yet it required a good deal of self-control to take the words to herself with a smile, while they seemed to be laying a visible scarlet welt across the pale face she kept valiantly turned to her friend. The fact that she must permit herself to be pitied by Indiana Frusk gave her the uttermost measure of the depth to which her fortunes had fallen.

This abasement was inflicted on her in the staring gold apartment of the Hôtel Nouveau Luxe in which the Rollivers had established themselves on their recent arrival in Paris. The vast drawing-room, adorned only by two high-shouldered gilt baskets of orchids drooping on their wires, reminded Undine of the "Looey suite" in which the opening scenes of her own history had been enacted; and the resemblance and the difference were emphasized by the fact that the image of her past self was not inaccurately repeated in the triumphant presence of Indiana Rolliver.

"There isn't a tip I couldn't have given you—not one!" Mrs. Rolliver reproachfully repeated; and all Undine's superiorities and discriminations seemed to shrivel up in the crude blaze of the other's solid achievement.

There was little comfort in noting, for one's private delectation, that Indiana spoke of her husband as "Mr. Rolliver," that she twanged a piercing r, that one of her shoulders was still higher than the other, and that her striking dress was totally unsuited to the hour, the place and the occasion. She still did and was all that Undine had so sedulously learned not to be and to do; but to dwell on these obstacles to her success was but to be more deeply impressed by the fact that she had nevertheless succeeded.

Not much more than a year had elapsed since Undine Marvell, sitting in the drawing-room of another Parisian hotel, had heard the immense orchestral murmur of Paris rise through the open windows like the ascending movement of her own hopes. The immense murmur still sounded on, deafening and implacable as some elemental force; and the discord in her fate no more disturbed it than the motor wheels rolling by under the windows were disturbed by the particles of dust that they ground to finer powder as they passed.

"I could have told you one thing right off," Mrs. Rolliver went on with her ringing energy. "And that is, to get your divorce first thing. A divorce is always a good thing to have: you never can tell when you may want it. You ought to have attended to that before you even *began* with Peter Van Degen."

Undine listened, irresistibly impressed. "Did *you?*" she asked; but Mrs. Rolliver, at this, grew suddenly veiled and sibylline. She wound her big bejeweled hand through her pearls—there were ropes and ropes of them—and leaned back, modestly sinking her lids.

"I'm here, anyhow," she rejoined, with *"Circumspice!"* in look and tone.

Undine, obedient to the challenge, continued to gaze at the pearls. They were real; there was no doubt about that. And so was Indiana's marriage—if she kept out of certain states.

"Don't you see," Mrs. Rolliver continued, "that having to leave him when you did, and rush off to Dakota for six months, was—was giving him too much time to think; and giving it at the wrong time, too?"

"Oh, I see. But what could I do? I'm not an immoral woman."

"Of course not, dearest. You were merely thoughtless—that's what I meant by saying you ought to have had your divorce ready."

A flicker of self-esteem caused Undine to protest. "It wouldn't have made any difference. His wife would never have given him up."

"She's so crazy about him?"

"No, she hates him so. And she hates me, too, because she's in love with my husband."

Indiana bounced out of her lounging attitude and struck her hands together with a rattle of rings.

"In love with your husband? What's the matter, then? Why on earth didn't the four of you fix it up together?"

"You don't understand." (It was an undoubted relief to be able, at last, to say that to Indiana!) "Clare Van Degen thinks divorce wrong—or rather awfully vulgar."

"*Vulgar?*" Indiana flamed. "If that isn't just too much! A woman who's in love with another woman's husband? What does she think refined, I'd like to know? Having a lover, I suppose—like the women in these nasty French plays? I've told Mr. Rolliver I won't go to the theater with him again in Paris—it's too utterly low. And the swell society's just as bad: it's simply rotten. Thank goodness I was brought up in a place where there's some sense of decency left!" She looked compassionately at Undine. "It was New York that demoralized you—and I don't blame you for it. Out at Apex you'd have acted different. You never *never* would have given way to your feelings before you'd got your divorce."

A slow blush rose to Undine's forehead.

"He seemed so unhappy —" she murmured.

"Oh, I *know!*" said Indiana in a tone of cold competence. She gave Undine an impatient glance. "What was the understanding between you, when you left Europe last August to go out to Dakota?"

"Peter was to go to Reno in the autumn—so that it wouldn't look too much as if we were acting together. I was to come to Chicago to see him on his way out there."

"And he never came?"

"No."

"And he stopped writing?"

"Oh, he never writes."

Indiana heaved a deep sigh of intelligence. "There's one perfectly clear rule: never let out of your sight a man who doesn't write."

"I know. That's why I stayed with him—those few weeks last summer. . . ."

Indiana sat thinking, her fine shallow eyes fixed unblinkingly on her friend's embarrassed face.

"I suppose there isn't anybody else —?"

"Anybody —?"

"Well—now you've got your divorce: anybody else it would come in handy for?"

This was harder to bear than anything that had gone before: Undine could not have borne it if she had not had a purpose. "Mr. Van Degen owes it to me —" she began with an air of wounded dignity.

"Yes, yes, I know. But that's just talk. If there *is* anybody else —"

"I can't imagine what you think of me, Indiana!"

Indiana, without appearing to resent this challenge, again lost herself in meditation.

"Well, I'll tell him he's just *got* to see you," she finally emerged from it to say.

Undine gave a quick upward look: this was what she had been waiting for ever since she had read, a few days earlier, in the columns of her morning journal, that Mr. Peter Van Degen and Mr. and Mrs. James J. Rolliver

had been fellow passengers on board the *Semantic*. But she did not betray
her expectations by as much as the tremor of an eyelash. She knew her
friend well enough to pour out to her the expected tribute of surprise.

"Why, do you mean to say you know him, Indiana?"

"Mercy, yes! He's round here all the time. He crossed on the steamer
with us, and Mr. Rolliver's taken a fancy to him," Indiana explained, in the
tone of the absorbed bride to whom her husband's preferences are the sole
criterion.

Undine turned a tear-suffused gaze on her. "Oh, Indiana, if I could only
see him again I know it would be all right! He's awfully, awfully fond of me;
but his family have influenced him against me —"

"I know what *that* is!" Mrs. Rolliver interjected.

"But perhaps," Undine continued, "it would be better if I could meet
him first without his knowing beforehand—without your telling him. . . .
I love him too much to reproach him!" she added nobly.

Indiana pondered: it was clear that, though the nobility of the sentiment impressed her, she was disinclined to renounce the idea of taking a
more active part in her friend's rehabilitation. But Undine went on: "Of
course you've found out by this time that he's just a big spoiled baby.
Afterward—when I've seen him—if you'd talk to him; or if you'd only just
let him *be* with you, and see how perfectly happy you and Mr. Rolliver are!"

Indiana seized on this at once. "You mean that what he wants is the
influence of a home like ours? Yes, yes, I understand. I tell you what I'll do:
I'll just ask him round to dine, and let you know the day, without telling
him beforehand that you're coming."

"Oh, Indiana!" Undine held her in a close embrace, and then drew
away to say: "I'm so glad I found you. You must go round with me everywhere. There are lots of people here I want you to know."

Mrs. Rolliver's expression changed from vague sympathy to concentrated interest. "I suppose it's awfully gay here? Do you go round a great deal
with the American set?"

Undine hesitated for a fraction of a moment. "There are a few of them
who are rather jolly. But I particularly want you to meet my friend the
Marquis Roviano—he's from Rome; and a lovely Austrian woman, Baroness
Adelschein."

Her friend's face was brushed by a shade of distrust. "I don't know as I
care much about meeting foreigners," she said indifferently.

Undine smiled: it was agreeable at last to be able to give Indiana a
"point" as valuable as any of hers on divorce.

"Oh, some of them are awfully attractive; and *they'll* make you meet the
Americans."

Indiana caught this on the bound: one began to see why she had got on
in spite of everything.

"Of course I'd love to know your friends," she said, kissing Undine, who answered, giving back the kiss: "You know there's nothing on earth I wouldn't do for you."

Indiana drew back to look at her with a comic grimace under which a shade of anxiety was visible. "Well, that's a pretty large order. But there's just one thing you *can* do, dearest: please to let Mr. Rolliver alone!"

"Mr. Rolliver, my dear?" Undine's laugh showed that she took this for unmixed comedy. "That's a nice way to remind me that you're heaps and heaps better-looking than I am!"

Indiana gave her an acute glance. "Millard Binch didn't think so—not even at the very end."

"Oh, poor Millard!" The women's smiles mingled easily over the common reminiscence, and once again, on the threshold, Undine enfolded her friend.

In the light of the autumn afternoon she paused a moment at the door of the Nouveau Luxe, and looked aimlessly forth at the brave spectacle in which she seemed no longer to have a stake.

Many of her old friends had already returned to Paris: the Harvey Shallums, May Beringer, Dicky Bowles and other westward-bound nomads lingering on for a glimpse of the autumn theaters and fashions before hurrying back to inaugurate the New York season. A year ago Undine would have had no difficulty in introducing Indiana Rolliver to this group—a group above which her own aspirations already beat an impatient wing. Now her place in it had become too precarious for her to force an entrance for her protectress. Her New York friends were at no pains to conceal from her that in their opinion her divorce had been a blunder. Their logic was that of Apex reversed. Since she had not been "sure" of Van Degen, why in the world, they asked, had she thrown away a position she *was* sure of? Mrs. Harvey Shallum, in particular, had not scrupled to put the question squarely. "Chelles was awfully taken—he would have introduced you everywhere. I thought you were wild to know smart French people; I thought Harvey and I weren't good enough for you any longer. And now you've done your best to spoil everything! Of course I feel for you tremendously— that's the reason why I'm talking so frankly. You must be horribly depressed. Come and dine tonight—or no, if you don't mind I'd rather you chose another evening. I'd forgotten that I'd asked the Jim Driscolls, and it might be uncomfortable—for *you* . . ."

In another world she was still welcome, at first perhaps even more so than before: the world, namely, to which she had proposed to present Indiana Rolliver. Roviano, Madame Adelschein, and a few of the freer spirits of her old St. Moritz band, reappearing in Paris with the close of the watering-place season, had quickly discovered her and shown a keen interest in her liberation. It appeared in some mysterious way to make her more available for their purpose, and she found that, in the character of the last American divorcée, she was even regarded as eligible to the small and intimate inner circle of their loosely knit association. At first she could not make out what had entitled her to this privilege, and increasing enlightenment produced a revolt of the Apex puritanism which, despite some odd accommodations and compliances, still carried its head so high in her.

Undine had been perfectly sincere in telling Indiana Rolliver that she was not "an immoral woman." The pleasures for which her sex took such risks had never attracted her, and she did not even crave the excitement of having it thought that they did. She wanted, passionately and persistently, two things which she believed should subsist together in any well-ordered life: amusement and respectability; and despite her surface-sophistication her notion of amusement was hardly less innocent than when she had hung on the plumber's fence with Indiana Frusk.

It gave her, therefore, no satisfaction to find herself included among Madame Adelschein's intimates. It embarrassed her to feel that she was expected to be "queer" and "different," to respond to passwords and talk in innuendo, to associate with the equivocal and the subterranean and affect to despise the ingenuous daylight joys which really satisfied her soul. But the business shrewdness which was never quite dormant in her suggested that this was not the moment for such scruples. She must make the best of what she could get and wait her chance of getting something better; and meanwhile the most practical use to which she could put her shady friends was to flash their authentic nobility in the dazzled eyes of Mrs. Rolliver.

With this object in view she made haste, in a fashionable tea-room of the rue de Rivoli, to group about Indiana the most titled members of the band; and the felicity of the occasion would have been unmarred had she not suddenly caught sight of Raymond de Chelles sitting on the other side of the room.

She had not seen Chelles since her return to Paris. It had seemed preferable to leave their meeting to chance, and the present chance might have served as well as another but for the fact that among his companions were two or three of the most eminent ladies of the proud quarter beyond the Seine. It was what Undine, in moments of discouragement, characterized as "her luck" that one of these should be the hated Miss Wincher of Potash Springs, who had now become the Marquise de Trézac. Undine knew that Chelles and his compatriots, however scandalized at her European companions, would be completely indifferent to Mrs. Rolliver's appearance; but one gesture of Madame de Trézac's eyeglass would wave Indiana to her place and thus brand the whole party as "wrong."

All this passed through Undine's mind in the very moment of her noting the change of expression with which Chelles had signalled his recognition. If their encounter could have occurred in happier conditions it might have had far-reaching results. As it was, the crowded state of the tea-room, and the distance between their tables, sufficiently excused his restricting his greeting to an eager bow; and Undine went home heavy-hearted from this first attempt to reconstruct her past.

Her spirits were not lightened by the developments of the next few days. She kept herself well in the foreground of Indiana's life, and cultivated toward the rarely visible Rolliver a manner in which impersonal admiration for the statesman was tempered with the politest indifference to the man. Indiana seemed to do justice to her efforts and to be reassured by the result; but still there came no hint of a reward. For a time Undine restrained the question on her lips; but one afternoon, when she had inducted Indiana into the deepest mysteries of Parisian complexion-making, the importance of the service and the confidential mood it engendered seemed to warrant a discreet allusion to their bargain.

Indiana leaned back among her cushions with an embarrassed laugh.

"Oh, my dear, I've been meaning to tell you—it's off, I'm afraid. The dinner is, I mean. You see, Mr. Van Degen has seen you 'round with me, and the very minute I asked him to come and dine he guessed —"

"He guessed—and he wouldn't?"

"Well, no. He wouldn't. I hate to tell you."

"Oh —" Undine threw off a vague laugh. "Since you're intimate enough for him to tell you *that* he must have told you more—told you something to justify his behavior. He couldn't—even Peter Van Degen couldn't—just simply have said to you: 'I won't see her.' "

Mrs. Rolliver hesitated, visibly troubled to the point of regretting her intervention.

"He *did* say more?" Undine insisted. "He gave you a reason?"

"He said you'd know."

"Oh, how base—how base!" Undine was trembling with one of her little-girl rages, the storms of destructive fury before which Mr. and Mrs. Spragg had cowered when she was a charming golden-curled cherub. But life had administered some of the discipline which her parents had spared her, and she pulled herself together with a gasp of pain. "Of course he's been turned against me. His wife has the whole of New York behind her, and I've no one; but I know it would be all right if I could only see him."

Her friend made no answer, and Undine pursued, with an irrepressible outbreak of her old vehemence: "Indiana Rolliver, if you won't do it for me I'll go straight off to his hotel this very minute. I'll wait there in the hall till he sees me!"

Indiana lifted a protesting hand. "Don't, Undine—not that!"

"Why not?"

"Well—I wouldn't, that's all."

"You wouldn't? Why wouldn't you? You must have a reason." Undine faced her with leveled brows. "Without a reason you can't have changed so utterly since our last talk. You were positive enough then that I had a right to make him see me."

Somewhat to her surprise, Indiana made no effort to elude the challenge. "Yes, I did think so then. But I know now that it wouldn't do you the least bit of good."

"Have they turned him so completely against me? I don't care if they have! I know him—I can get him back."

"That's the trouble." Indiana shed on her a gaze of cold compassion. "It's not that anyone has turned him against you. It's worse than that —"

"What can be?"

"You'll hate me if I tell you."

"Then you'd better make him tell me himself!"

"I can't. I tried to. The trouble is that it was *you*—something you did, I mean. Something he found out about you —"

Undine, to restrain a spring of anger, had to clutch both arms of her chair. "About me? How fearfully false! Why, I've never even *looked* at anybody —!"

"It's nothing of that kind." Indiana's mournful headshake seemed to deplore, in Undine, an unsuspected moral obtuseness. "It's the way you acted to your own husband."

"I—my—to Ralph? *He* reproaches me for that? Peter Van Degen does?"

"Well, for one particular thing. He says that the very day you went off with him last year you got a cable from New York telling you to come back at once to Mr. Marvell, who was desperately ill."

"How on earth did he know?" The cry escaped Undine before she could repress it.

"It's true, then?" Indiana exclaimed. "Oh, Undine —"

Undine sat speechless and motionless, the anger frozen to terror on her lips.

Mrs. Rolliver turned on her the reproachful gaze of the deceived benefactress. "I didn't believe it when he told me; I'd never have thought it of you. Before you'd even applied for your divorce!"

Undine made no attempt to deny the charge or to defend herself. For a moment she was lost in the pursuit of an unseizable clue—the explanation of this monstrous last perversity of fate. Suddenly she rose to her feet with a set face.

"The Marvells must have told him—the beasts!" It relieved her to be able to cry it out.

"It was your husband's sister—what did you say her name was? When you didn't answer her cable, she cabled Mr. Van Degen to find out where you were and tell you to come straight back."

Undine stared. "He never did!"

"No."

"Doesn't that show you the story's all trumped up?"

Indiana shook her head. "He said nothing to you about it because he was with you when you received the first cable, and you told him it was from your sister-in-law, just worrying you as usual to go home; and when he asked if there was anything else in it you said there wasn't another thing."

Undine, intently following her, caught at this with a spring. "Then he knew it all along—he admits that? And it made no earthly difference to him at the time?" She turned almost victoriously on her friend. "Did he happen to explain *that*, I wonder?"

"Yes." Indiana's longanimity grew almost solemn. "It came over him gradually, he said. One day when he wasn't feeling very well he thought to himself: 'Would she act like that to *me* if I was dying?' And after that he never felt the same to you." Indiana lowered her empurpled lids. "Men have their feelings too—even when they're carried away by passion." After a pause she added: "I don't know as I can blame him, Undine. You see, you were his ideal."

25

U NDINE Marvell, for the next few months, tasted all the accumulated bitterness of failure.

After January the drifting hordes of her compatriots had scattered to the four quarters of the globe, leaving Paris to resume, under its low gray sky, its compacter winter personality. Noting, from her more and more deserted corner, each least sign of the social revival, Undine felt herself as stranded and baffled as after the ineffectual summers of her girlhood. She was not without possible alternatives; but the sense of what she had lost took the savor from all that was left. She might have attached herself to some migratory group winged for Italy or Egypt; but the prospect of travel did not in itself appeal to her, and she was doubtful of its social benefit. She lacked the adventurous curiosity which seeks its occasion in the unknown; and though she could work doggedly for a given object the obstacles to be overcome had to be as distinct as the prize.

Her one desire was to get back an equivalent of the precise value she had lost in ceasing to be Ralph Marvell's wife. Her new visiting card, bearing her Christian name in place of her husband's, was like the coin of a debased currency testifying to her diminished trading capacity. Her restricted means, her vacant days, all the minor irritations of her life, were as nothing compared to this sense of a lost advantage. Even in the narrowed field of a Parisian winter she might have made herself a place in some more or less extrasocial world; but her experiments in this line gave her no pleasure proportioned to the possible derogation. She feared to be associated

with "the wrong people," and scented a shade of disrespect in every amica-
ble advance. The more pressing attentions of one or two men she had
formerly known filled her with a glow of outraged pride, and for the first
time in her life she felt that even solitude might be preferable to certain
kinds of society.

Since ill health was the most plausible pretext for seclusion, it was
almost a relief to find that she was really growing "nervous" and sleeping
badly. The doctor she summoned advised her trying a small quiet place on
the Riviera, not too near the sea; and thither, in the early days of December, she transported herself with her maid and an omnibus-load of luggage.

The place disconcerted her by being really small and quiet, and for a few
days she struggled against the desire for flight. She had never before known
a world as colorless and negative as that of the large white hotel where
everybody went to bed at nine, and donkey rides over stony hills were the
only alternative to slow drives along dusty roads. Many of the dwellers in
this temple of repose found even these exercises too stimulating, and preferred to sit for hours under the palms in the garden, playing Patience,
embroidering, or reading odd volumes of Tauchnitz. Undine, driven by despair to an inspection of the hotel bookshelves, discovered that scarcely any
work they contained was complete; but this did not seem to trouble the
readers, who continued to feed their leisure with mutilated fiction, from
which they occasionally raised their eyes to glance mistrustfully at the new
arrival sweeping the garden gravel with her frivolous draperies. The inmates
of the hotel were of different nationalities, but their racial differences were
leveled by the stamp of a common mediocrity. All differences of tongue, of
custom, of physiognomy, disappeared in this deep community of insignificance, which was like some secret bond, with the manifold signs and passwords of its ignorances and its imperceptions. It was not the heterogeneous
mediocrity of the American summer hotel, where the lack of any standard is
the nearest approach to a tie, but an organized codified dullness, in conscious possession of its rights, and strong in the voluntary ignorance of any
others.

It took Undine a long time to accustom herself to such an atmosphere,
and meanwhile she fretted, fumed and flaunted, or abandoned herself to
long periods of fruitless brooding. Sometimes a flame of anger shot up in
her, dismally illuminating the path she had traveled and the blank wall to
which it led. At other moments past and present were enveloped in a dull
fog of rancor which distorted and faded even the image she presented to her
morning mirror. There were days when every young face she saw left in her
a taste of poison. But when she compared herself with the specimens of her
sex who plied their languid industries under the palms, or looked away as
she passed them in hall or staircase, her spirits rose, and she rang for her
maid and dressed herself in her newest and vividest. These were unprofitable triumphs, however. She never made one of her attacks on the orga-

nized disapproval of the community without feeling she had lost ground by it; and the next day she would lie in bed and send down capricious orders for food, which her maid would presently remove untouched, with instructions to transmit her complaints to the landlord.

Sometimes the events of the past year, ceaselessly revolving through her brain, became no longer a subject for criticism or justification but simply a series of pictures monotonously unrolled. Hour by hour, in such moods, she relived the incidents of her flight with Peter Van Degen: the part of her career that, since it had proved a failure, seemed least like herself and most difficult to justify. She had gone away with him, and had lived with him for two months: she, Undine Marvell, to whom respectability was the breath of life, to whom such follies had always been unintelligible and therefore inexcusable. She had done this incredible thing, and she had done it from a motive that seemed, at the time, as clear, as logical, as free from the distorting mists of sentimentality, as any of her father's financial enterprises. It had been a bold move, but it had been as carefully calculated as the happiest Wall Street "stroke." She had gone away with Peter because, after the decisive scene in which she had put her power to the test, to yield to him seemed the surest means of victory. Even to her practical intelligence it was clear that an immediate dash to Dakota might look too calculated; and she had preserved her self-respect by telling herself that she was really his wife, and in no way to blame if the law delayed to ratify the bond.

She was still persuaded of the justness of her reasoning; but she now saw that it had left certain risks out of account. Her life with Van Degen had taught her manythings. The two had wandered from place to place, spending a great deal of money, always more and more money; for the first time in her life she had been able to buy everything she wanted. For a while this had kept her amused and busy; but presently she began to perceive that her companion's view of their relation was not the same as hers. She saw that he had always meant it to be an unavowed tie, screened by Mrs. Shallum's companionship and Clare's careless tolerance; and that on those terms he would have been ready to shed on their adventure the brightest blaze of notoriety. But since Undine had insisted on being carried off like a sentimental schoolgirl he meant to shroud the affair in mystery, and was as zealous in concealing their relation as she was bent on proclaiming it. In the "powerful" novels which Popple was fond of lending her she had met with increasing frequency the type of heroine who scorns to love clandestinely, and proclaims the sanctity of passion and the moral duty of obeying its call. Undine had been struck by these arguments as justifying and even ennobling her course, and had let Peter understand that she had been actuated by the highest motives in openly associating her life with his; but he had opposed a placid insensibility to these allusions, and had persisted in treating her as though their journey were the kind of escapade that a man of the world is bound to hide. She had expected him to take her to all the showy

places where couples like themselves are relieved from a too sustained contemplation of nature by the distractions of the restaurant and the gaming-
table; but he had carried her from one obscure corner of Europe to another,
shunning fashionable hotels and crowded watering-places, and displaying an
ingenuity in the discovery of the unvisited and the out-of-season that gave
their journey an odd resemblance to her melancholy wedding-tour.

She had never for a moment ceased to remember that the Dakota di-
vorce-court was the objective point of this later honeymoon, and her allusions to the fact were as frequent as prudence permitted. Peter seemed in no
way disturbed by them. He responded with expressions of increasing tenderness, or the purchase of another piece of jewelry; and though Undine could
not remember his ever voluntarily bringing up the subject of their marriage
he did not shrink from her recurring mention of it. He seemed merely too
steeped in present well-being to think of the future; and she ascribed this to
the fact that his faculty of enjoyment could not project itself beyond the
moment. Her business was to make each of their days so agreeable that
when the last came he should be conscious of a void to be bridged over as
rapidly as possible; and when she thought this point had been reached she
packed her trunks and started for Dakota.

The next picture to follow was that of the dull months in the western
divorce-town, where, to escape loneliness and avoid comment, she had cast
in her lot with Mabel Lipscomb, who had lately arrived there on the same
errand.

Undine, at the outset, had been sorry for the friend whose new venture
seemed likely to result so much less brilliantly than her own; but compassion had been replaced by irritation as Mabel's unpruned vulgarities, her
enormous encroaching satisfaction with herself and her surroundings, began
to pervade every corner of their provisional household. Undine, during the
first months of her exile, had been sustained by the fullest confidence in her
future. When she had parted from Van Degen she had felt sure he meant to
marry her, and the fact that Mrs. Lipscomb was fortified by no similar hope
made her easier to bear with. Undine was almost ashamed that the unwooed
Mabel should be the witness of her own felicity, and planned to send her off
on a trip to Denver when Peter should announce his arrival; but the weeks
passed, and Peter did not come. Mabel, on the whole, behaved well in this
contingency. Undine, in her first exultation, had confided all her hopes and
plans to her friend, but Mabel took no undue advantage of the confidence.
She was even tactful in her loud fond clumsy way, with a tact that insistently boomed and buzzed about its victim's head. But one day she mentioned that she had asked to dinner a gentleman from Little Rock who had
come to Dakota with the same object as themselves, and whose acquaintance she had made through her lawyer.

The gentleman from Little Rock came to dine, and within a week Undine understood that Mabel's future was assured. If Van Degen had been at

hand Undine would have smiled with him at poor Mabel's infatuation and her suitor's crudeness. But Van Degen was not there. He made no sign, he sent no excuse; he simply continued to absent himself; and it was Undine who, in due course, had to make way for Mrs. Lipscomb's caller, and sit upstairs with a novel while the drawing-room below was given up to the enacting of an actual love story.

Even then, even to the end, Undine had to admit that Mabel had behaved "beautifully." But it is comparatively easy to behave beautifully when one is getting what one wants, and when someone else, who has not always been altogether kind, is not. The net result of Mrs. Lipscomb's magnanimity was that when, on the day of parting, she drew Undine to her bosom with the hand on which her new engagement ring blazed, Undine hated her as she hated everything else connected with her vain exile in the wilderness.

26

THE next phase in the unrolling vision was the episode of her return to New York. She had gone to the Malibran, to her parents—for it was a moment in her career when she clung passionately to the conformities, and when the fact of being able to say: "I'm here with my father and mother" was worth paying for even in the discomfort of that grim abode. Nevertheless, it was another thorn in her pride that her parents could not—for the meanest of material reasons—transfer themselves at her coming to one of the big Fifth Avenue hotels. When she had suggested it Mr. Spragg had briefly replied that, owing to the heavy expenses of her divorce suit, he couldn't for the moment afford anything better; and this announcement cast a deeper gloom over the future.

It was not an occasion for being "nervous," however; she had learned too many hard facts in the last few months to think of having recourse to her youthful methods. And something told her that if she made the attempt it would be useless. Her father and mother seemed much older, seemed tired and defeated, like herself.

Parents and daughter bore their common failure in a common silence, broken only by Mrs. Spragg's occasional tentative allusions to her grandson. But her anecdotes of Paul left a deeper silence behind them. Undine did not want to talk of her boy. She could forget him when, as she put it, things were "going her way," but in moments of discouragement the thought of him was an added bitterness, subtly different from her other bitter thoughts,

and harder to quiet. It had not occurred to her to try to gain possession of
the child. She was vaguely aware that the courts had given her his custody;
but she had never seriously thought of asserting this claim. Her parents'
diminished means and her own uncertain future made her regard the care of
Paul as an additional burden, and she quieted her scruples by thinking of
him as "better off" with Ralph's family, and of herself as rather touchingly
disinterested in putting his welfare before her own. Poor Mrs. Spragg was
pining for him, but Undine rejected her artless suggestion that Mrs. Heeny
should be sent to "bring him round." "I wouldn't ask them a favor for the
world—they're just waiting for a chance to be hateful to me," she scornfully
declared; but it pained her that her boy should be so near, yet inaccessible,
and for the first time she was visited by unwonted questionings as to her
share in the misfortunes that had befallen her. She had voluntarily stepped
out of her social frame, and the only person on whom she could with any
satisfaction have laid the blame was the person to whom her mind now
turned with a belated tenderness. It was thus, in fact, that she thought of
Ralph. His pride, his reserve, all the secret expressions of his devotion, the
tones of his voice, his quiet manner, even his disconcerting irony: these
seemed, in contrast to what she had since known, the qualities essential to
her happiness. She could console herself only by regarding it as part of her
sad lot that poverty, and the relentless animosity of his family, should have
put an end to so perfect a union: she gradually began to look on herself and
Ralph as the victims of dark machinations, and when she mentioned him
she spoke forgivingly, and implied that "everything might have been different" if "people" had not "come between" them.

She had arrived in New York in midseason, and the dread of seeing
familiar faces kept her shut up in her room at the Malibran, reading novels
and brooding over possibilities of escape. She tried to avoid the daily papers,
but they formed the staple diet of her parents, and now and then she could
not help taking one up and turning to the society column. Its perusal produced the impression that the season must be the gayest New York had ever
known. The Harmon B. Driscolls, young Jim and his wife, the Thurber Van
Degens, the Chauncey Ellings, and all the other Fifth Avenue potentates,
seemed to have their doors perpetually open to a stream of feasters among
whom the familiar presences of Grace Beringer, Bertha Shallum, Dicky
Bowles and Claud Walsingham Popple came and went with the irritating
sameness of the figures in a stage procession.

Among them also Peter Van Degen presently appeared. He had been on
a tour around the world, and Undine could not look at a newspaper without
seeing some allusion to his progress. After his return she noticed that his
name was usually coupled with his wife's: he and Clare seemed to be celebrating his homecoming in a series of festivities, and Undine guessed that
he had reasons for wishing to keep before the world the evidences of his
conjugal accord.

Mrs. Heeny's clippings supplied her with such items as her own reading missed; and one day the masseuse appeared with a long article from the leading journal of Little Rock, describing the brilliant nuptials of Mabel Lipscomb—now Mrs. Homer Branney—and her departure for "the Coast" in the bridegroom's private car. This put the last touch to Undine's irritation, and the next morning she got up earlier than usual, put on her most effective dress, went for a quick walk around the Park, and told her father when she came in that she wanted him to take her to the opera that evening.

Mr. Spragg stared and frowned. "You mean you want me to go round and hire a box for you?"

"Oh, no." Undine colored at the infelicitous allusion: besides, she knew now that the smart people who were "musical" went in stalls.

"I only want two good seats. I don't see why I should stay shut up. I want you to go with me," she added.

Her father received the latter part of the request without comment: he seemed to have gone beyond surprise. But he appeared that evening at dinner in a creased and loosely fitting dress-suit which he had probably not put on since the last time he had dined with his son-in-law, and he and Undine drove off together, leaving Mrs. Spragg to gaze after them with the pale stare of Hecuba.

Their stalls were in the middle of the house, and around them swept the great curve of boxes at which Undine had so often looked up in the remote Stentorian days. Then all had been one indistinguishable glitter, now the scene was full of familiar details: the house was thronged with people she knew, and every box seemed to contain a parcel of her past. At first she had shrunk from recognition; but gradually, as she perceived that no one noticed her, that she was merely part of the invisible crowd out of range of the exploring opera glasses, she felt a defiant desire to make herself seen. When the performance was over her father wanted to leave the house by the door at which they had entered, but she guided him toward the stockholders' entrance, and pressed her way among the furred and jeweled ladies waiting for their motors. "Oh, it's the wrong door—never mind, we'll walk to the corner and get a cab," she exclaimed, speaking loudly enough to be overheard. Two or three heads turned, and she met Dicky Bowles's glance, and returned his laughing bow. The woman talking to him looked around, colored slightly, and made a barely perceptible motion of her head. Just beyond her, Mrs. Chauncey Elling, plumed and purple, stared, parted her lips, and turned to say something important to young Jim Driscoll, who looked up involuntarily and then squared his shoulders and gazed fixedly at a distant point, as people do at a funeral. Behind them Undine caught sight of Clare Van Degen; she stood alone, and her face was pale and listless. "Shall I go up and speak to her?" Undine wondered. Some intuition told her that, alone of all the women present, Clare might have greeted her kindly; but she hung back, and Mrs. Harmon Driscoll surged by on Popple's arm. Popple crimsoned, coughed, and signaled despotically to Mrs. Driscoll's footman. Over his shoulder Undine received a bow from Charles Bowen, and behind Bowen she saw two or three other men she knew, and read in their faces surprise, curiosity, and the wish to show their pleasure at seeing her. But she grasped her father's arm and drew him out among the entangled motors and vociferating policemen.

Neither she nor Mr. Spragg spoke a word on the way home; but when they reached the Malibran her father followed her up to her room. She had dropped her cloak and stood before the wardrobe mirror studying her reflection when he came up behind her and she saw that he was looking at it too.

"Where did that necklace come from?"

Undine's neck grew pink under the shining circlet. It was the first time since her return to New York that she had put on a low dress and thus uncovered the string of pearls she always wore. She made no answer, and Mr. Spragg continued: "Did your husband give them to you?"

"Ralph!" She could not restrain a laugh.

"Who did, then?"

Undine remained silent. She really had not thought about the pearls, except in so far as she consciously enjoyed the pleasure of possessing them; and her father, habitually so unobservant, had seemed the last person likely to raise the awkward question of their origin.

"Why —" she began, without knowing what she meant to say.

"I guess you better send 'em back to the party they belong to," Mr. Spragg continued, in a voice she did not know.

"They belong to me!" she flamed up.

He looked at her as if she had grown suddenly small and insignificant. "You better send 'em back to Peter Van Degen the first thing tomorrow morning," he said as he went out of the room.

As far as Undine could remember, it was the first time in her life that he had ever ordered her to do anything; and when the door closed on him she had the distinct sense that the question had closed with it, and that she would have to obey. She took the pearls off and threw them from her angrily. The humiliation her father had inflicted on her was merged with the humiliation to which she had subjected herself in going to the opera, and she had never before hated her life as she hated it then.

All night she lay sleepless, wondering miserably what to do; and out of her hatred of her life, and her hatred of Peter Van Degen, there gradually grew a loathing of Van Degen's pearls. How could she have kept them, how have continued to wear them about her neck? Only her absorption in other cares could have kept her from feeling the humiliation of carrying about with her the price of her shame. Her novel-reading had filled her mind with the vocabulary of outraged virtue, and with pathetic allusions to woman's frailty, and while she pitied herself she thought her father heroic. She was proud to think that she had such a man to defend her, and rejoiced that it was in her power to express her scorn of Van Degen by sending back his jewels.

But her righteous ardor gradually cooled, and she was left once more to face the dreary problem of the future. Her evening at the opera had shown her the impossibility of remaining in New York. She had neither the skill nor the power to fight the forces of indifference leagued against her: she must get away at once, and try to make a fresh start. But, as usual, the lack of money hampered her. Mr. Spragg could no longer afford to make her the allowance she had intermittently received from him during the first years of her marriage, and since she was now without child or household she could hardly make it a grievance that he had reduced her income. But what he allowed her, even with the addition of her alimony, was absurdly insufficient. Not that she looked far ahead; she had always felt herself predestined to ease and luxury, and the possibility of a future adapted to her present budget did not occur to her. But she desperately wanted enough money to carry her without anxiety through the coming year.

When her breakfast tray was brought in she sent it away untouched and continued to lie in her darkened room. She knew that when she got up she must send back the pearls; but there was no longer any satisfaction in the thought, and she lay listlessly wondering how she could best transmit them to Van Degen.

As she lay there she heard Mrs. Heeny's voice in the passage. Hitherto she had avoided the masseuse, as she did everyone else associated with her past. Mrs. Heeny had behaved with extreme discretion, refraining from all direct allusions to Undine's misadventure; but her silence was obviously the criticism of a superior mind. Once again Undine had disregarded her injunction to "go slow," with results that justified the warning. Mrs. Heeny's very reserve, however, now marked her as a safe adviser; and Undine sprang up and called her in.

"My sakes, Undine! You look's if you'd been setting up all night with a remains!" the masseuse exclaimed in her round rich tones.

Undine, without answering, caught up the pearls and thrust them into Mrs. Heeny's hands.

"Good land alive!" The masseuse dropped into a chair and let the twist slip through her fat flexible fingers. "Well, you got a fortune right round your neck whenever you wear them, Undine Spragg."

Undine murmured something indistinguishable. "I want you to take them —" she began.

"Take 'em? Where to?"

"Why, to —" She was checked by the wondering simplicity of Mrs. Heeny's stare. The masseuse must know where the pearls had come from, yet it had evidently not occurred to her that Mrs. Marvell was about to ask her to return them to their donor. In the light of Mrs. Heeny's unclouded gaze the whole episode took on a different aspect, and Undine began to be vaguely astonished at her immediate submission to her father's will. The pearls were hers, after all!

"To be restrung?" Mrs. Heeny placidly suggested. "Why, you'd oughter to have it done right here before your eyes, with pearls that are worth what these are."

As Undine listened, a new thought shaped itself. She could not continue to wear the pearls: the idea had become intolerable. But for the first time she saw what they might be converted into, and what they might rescue her from; and suddenly she brought out: "Do you suppose I could get anything for them?"

"Get anything? Why, what—"

"Anything like what they're worth, I mean. They cost a lot of money: they came from the biggest place in Paris." Under Mrs. Heeny's simplifying eye it was comparatively easy to make these explanations. "I want you to try and sell them for me—I want you to do the best you can with them. I can't do it myself—but you must swear you'll never tell a soul," she pressed on breathlessly.

"Why, you poor child—it ain't the first time," said Mrs. Heeny, coiling the pearls in her big palm. "It's a pity, too: they're such beauties. But you'll get others," she added, as the necklace vanished into her bag.

A few days later there appeared from the same receptacle a bundle of bank notes considerable enough to quiet Undine's last scruples. She no longer understood why she had hesitated. Why should she have thought it necessary to give back the pearls to Van Degen? His obligation to her represented far more than the relatively small sum she had been able to realize on the necklace. She hid the money in her dress, and when Mrs. Heeny had gone on to Mrs. Spragg's room she drew the packet out, and counting the bills over, murmured to herself: "Now I can get away!"

Her one thought was to return to Europe; but she did not want to go alone. The vision of her solitary figure adrift in the spring mob of trans-Atlantic pleasure-seekers depressed and mortified her. She would be sure to run across acquaintances, and they would infer that she was in quest of a new opportunity, a fresh start, and would suspect her of trying to use them for the purpose. The thought was repugnant to her newly awakened pride, and she decided that if she went to Europe her father and mother must go with her. The project was a bold one, and when she broached it she had to run the whole gamut of Mr. Spragg's irony. He wanted to know what she expected to do with him when she got him there; whether she meant to introduce him to "all those old kings," how she thought he and her mother would look in court dress, and how she supposed he was going to get on without his New York paper. But Undine had been aware of having what he himself would have called "a pull" over her father since, the day after their visit to the opera, he had taken her aside to ask: "You sent back those pearls?" and she had answered coldly: "Mrs. Heeny's taken them."

After a moment of half-bewildered resistance her parents, perhaps secretly flattered by this first expression of her need for them, had yielded to her entreaty, packed their trunks, and stoically set out for the unknown. Neither Mr. Spragg nor his wife had ever before been out of their country; and Undine had not understood, till they stood beside her tongue-tied and helpless on the dock at Cherbourg, the task she had undertaken in uprooting them. Mr. Spragg had never been physically active, but on foreign shores he was seized by a strange restlessness, and a helpless dependence on his daughter. Mrs. Spragg's long habit of apathy was overcome by her dread of being left alone when her husband and Undine went out, and she delayed and impeded their expeditions by insisting on accompanying them; so that, much as Undine disliked sightseeing, there seemed no alternative between "going round" with her parents and shutting herself up with them in the crowded hotels to which she successively transported them.

The hotels were the only European institutions that really interested Mr. Spragg. He considered them manifestly inferior to those at home; but he was haunted by a statistical curiosity as to their size, their number, their cost and their capacity for housing and feeding the incalculable hordes of his countrymen. He went through galleries, churches and museums in a stolid silence like his daughter's; but in the hotels he never ceased to inquire and investigate, questioning everyone who could speak English, comparing bills, collecting prospectuses and computing the cost of construction and the probable return on the investment. He regarded the nonexistence of the cold-storage system as one more proof of European inferiority, and no longer wondered, in the absence of the room-to-room telephone, that foreigners hadn't yet mastered the first principles of time-saving.

After a few weeks it became evident to both parents and daughter that their unnatural association could not continue much longer. Mrs. Spragg's shrinking from everything new and unfamiliar had developed into a kind of settled terror, and Mr. Spragg had begun to be depressed by the incredible number of the hotels and their simply incalculable housing capacity.

"It ain't that they're any great shakes in themselves, any one of 'em; but there's such a darned lot of 'em: they're as thick as mosquitoes, every place you go." And he began to reckon up, on slips of paper, on the backs of bills and the margins of old newspapers, the number of travelers who could be simultaneously lodged, bathed and boarded on the continent of Europe. "Five hundred bedrooms—three hundred bathrooms—no; three hundred and fifty bathrooms, that one has: that makes, supposing two-thirds of 'em double up—do you s'pose as many as that do, Undie? That porter at Lucerne told me the Germans slept three in a room—well, call it eight hundred people; and three meals a day per head; no, four meals, with that afternoon tea they take; and the last place we were at—'way up on that mountain there—why, there were seventy-five hotels in that one spot alone, and all jam full—well, it beats me to know where all the people come from. . . ."

He had gone on in this fashion for what seemed to his daughter an endless length of days; and then suddenly he had roused himself to say: "See here, Undie, I got to go back and make the money to pay for all this."

There had been no question on the part of any of the three of Undine's returning with them; and after she had conveyed them to their steamer, and seen their vaguely relieved faces merged in the handkerchief-waving throng along the taffrail, she had returned alone to Paris and made her unsuccessful attempt to enlist the aid of Indiana Rolliver.

27

S HE was still brooding over this last failure when one afternoon, as she loitered on the hotel terrace, she was approached by a young woman whom she had seen sitting near the wheeled chair of an old lady wearing a crumpled black bonnet under a funny fringed parasol with a jointed handle.

The young woman, who was small, slight and brown, was dressed with a disregard of the fashion which contrasted oddly with the mauve powder on her face and the traces of artificial color in her dark untidy hair. She looked as if she might have several different personalities, and as if the one of the moment had been hanging up a long time in her wardrobe and been hurriedly taken down as probably good enough for the present occasion.

With her hands in her jacket pockets, and an agreeable smile on her boyish face, she strolled up to Undine and asked, in a pretty variety of Parisian English, if she had the pleasure of speaking to Mrs. Marvell.

On Undine's assenting, the smile grew more alert and the lady continued: "I think you know my friend Sacha Adelschein?"

No question could have been less welcome to Undine. If there was one point on which she was doggedly and puritanically resolved, it was that no extremes of social adversity should ever again draw her into the group of people among whom Madame Adelschein too conspicuously figured. Since her unsuccessful attempt to win over Indiana by introducing her to that group, Undine had been righteously resolved to remain aloof from it; and she was drawing herself up to her loftiest height of disapproval when the stranger, as if unconscious of it, went on: "Sacha speaks of you so often— she admires you so much.—I think you know also my cousin Chelles," she added, looking into Undine's eyes. "I am the Princess Estradina. I've come here with my mother for the air."

The murmur of negation died on Undine's lips. She found herself grappling with a new social riddle, and such surprises were always stimulating. The name of the untidy-looking young woman she had been about to repel was one of the most eminent in the impregnable quarter beyond the Seine. No one figured more largely in the Parisian chronicle than the Princess Estradina, and no name more impressively headed the list at every marriage, funeral and philanthropic entertainment of the Faubourg Saint Germain than that of her mother, the Duchesse de Dordogne, who must be no other than the old woman sitting in the bath-chair with the crumpled bonnet and the ridiculous sunshade.

But it was not the appearance of the two ladies that surprised Undine. She knew that social gold does not always glitter, and that the lady she had heard spoken of as Lili Estradina was notoriously careless of the conventions; but that she should boast of her intimacy with Madame Adelschein, and use it as a pretext for naming herself, overthrew all Undine's hierarchies.

"Yes—it's hideously dull here, and I'm dying of it. Do come over and speak to my mother. She's dying of it, too; but don't tell her so, because she hasn't found it out. There were so many things our mothers never found out," the princess rambled on, with her half-mocking half-intimate smile; and in another moment Undine, thrilled at having Mrs. Spragg thus coupled with a duchess, found herself seated between mother and daughter, and responding by a radiant blush to the elder lady's amiable opening: "You know my nephew Raymond—he's your great admirer."

How had it happened, whither would it lead, how long could it last? The questions raced through Undine's brain as she sat listening to her new friends—they seemed already too friendly to be called acquaintances!—replying to their inquiries, and trying to think far enough ahead to guess what they would expect her to say, and what tone it would be well to take. She was used to such feats of mental agility, and it was instinctive with her to become, for the moment, the person she thought her interlocutors expected her to be; but she had never had quite so new a part to play at such short notice. She took her cue, however, from the fact that the Princess Estradina, in her mother's presence, made no further allusion to her dear friend Sacha, and seemed somehow, though she continued to chat on in the same easy strain, to look differently and throw out different implications. All these shades of demeanor were immediately perceptible to Undine, who tried to adapt herself to them by combining in her manner a mixture of Apex dash and New York dignity; and the result was so successful that when she rose to go the princess, with a hand on her arm, said almost wistfully: "You're staying on too? Then do take pity on us! We might go on some trips together; and in the evenings we could make a bridge."

A new life began for Undine. The princess, chained to her mother's side, and frankly restive under her filial duty, clung to her new acquaintance

with a persistence too flattering to be analyzed. "My dear, I was on the brink
of suicide when I saw your name in the visitors' list," she explained; and
Undine felt like answering that she had nearly reached the same pass when
the princess's thin little hand had been held out to her. For the moment she
was dizzy with the effect of that random gesture. Here she was, at the lowest
ebb of her fortunes, miraculously rehabilitated, reinstated, and restored to
the old victorious sense of her youth and her power! Her sole graces, her
unaided personality, had worked the miracle; how should she not trust in
them hereafter?

Aside from her feeling of concrete attainment, Undine was deeply interested in her new friends. The princess and her mother, in their different
ways, were different from anyone else she had known. The princess, who
might have been of any age between twenty and forty, had a small triangular face with caressing impudent eyes, a smile like a silent whistle and the
gait of a baker's boy balancing his basket. She wore either baggy shabby
clothes like a man's, or rich draperies that looked as if they had been rained
on; and she seemed equally at ease in either style of dress, and carelessly
unconscious of both. She was extremely familiar and unblushingly inquisi-
tive, but she never gave Undine the time to ask her any questions or the
opportunity to venture on any freedom with her. Nevertheless she did not
scruple to talk of her sentimental experiences, and seemed surprised, and
rather disappointed, that Undine had so few to relate in return. She playfully accused her beautiful new friend of being *cachottière*, and at the sight of
Undine's blush cried out: "Ah, you funny Americans! Why do you all
behave as if love were a secret infirmity?"

The old duchess was even more impressive, because she fitted better into
Undine's preconceived picture of the Faubourg Saint Germain, and was
more like the people with whom she pictured the former Nettie Wincher as
living in privileged intimacy. The duchess was, indeed, more amiable and
accessible than Undine's conception of a duchess, and displayed a curiosity
as great as her daughter's, and much more puerile, concerning her new
friend's history and habits. But through her mild prattle, and in spite of her
limited perceptions, Undine felt in her the same clear impenetrable barrier
that she ran against occasionally in the princess; and she was beginning to
understand that this barrier represented a number of things about which she
herself had yet to learn. She would not have known this a few years earlier,
nor would she have seen in the duchess anything but the ruin of an ugly
woman, dressed in clothes that Mrs. Spragg wouldn't have touched. The
duchess certainly looked like a ruin; but Undine now saw that she looked
like the ruin of a castle.

The princess, who was unofficially separated from her husband, had with
her her two little girls. She seemed extremely attached to both—though
avowing for the younger a preference she frankly ascribed to the interesting
accident of its parentage—and she could not understand that Undine, as to

whose domestic difficulties she minutely informed herself, should have consented to leave her child to strangers. "For, to one's child, everyone but
one's self is a stranger; and whatever your *égarements*—" she began, breaking off with a stare when Undine interrupted her to explain that the courts
had ascribed all the wrongs in the case to her husband. "But then—but
then—" murmured the princess, turning away from the subject as if checked
by too deep an abyss of difference.

The incident had embarrassed Undine, and though she tried to justify
herself by allusions to her boy's dependence on his father's family, and to
the duty of not standing in his way, she saw that she made no impression.
"Whatever one's errors, one's child belongs to one," her hearer continued
to repeat; and Undine, who was frequently scandalized by the princess's
conversation, now found herself in the odd position of having to set a watch
upon her own in order not to scandalize the princess.

Each day, nevertheless, strengthened her hold on her new friends. After
her first flush of triumph she began indeed to suspect that she had been a
slight disappointment to the princess, had not completely justified the
hopes raised by the doubtful honor of being one of Sacha Adelschein's
intimates. Undine guessed that the princess had expected to find her more
amusing, "queerer," more startling in speech and conduct. Though by instinct she was none of these things, she was eager to go as far as was
expected; but she felt that her audacities were on lines too normal to be
interesting, and that the princess thought her rather schoolgirlish and old-
fashioned. Still, they had in common their youth, their boredom, their high
spirits and their hunger for amusement; and Undine was making the most of
these ties when one day, coming back from a trip to Monte Carlo with the
princess, she was brought up short by the sight of a lady—evidently a new
arrival—who was seated in an attitude of respectful intimacy beside the old
duchess's chair. Undine, advancing unheard over the fine gravel of the
garden path, recognized at a glance the Marquise de Trézac's drooping nose
and disdainful back, and at the same moment heard her say: "—and her
husband?"

"Her husband? But she's an American—she's divorced," the duchess
replied, as if she were merely stating the same fact in two different ways; and
Undine stopped short with a pang of apprehension.

The princess came up behind her. "Who's the solemn person with
Mamma? Ah, that old bore of a Trézac!" She dropped her long eyeglass with
a laugh. "Well, she'll be useful—she'll stick to Mamma like a leech, and we
shall get away oftener. Come, let's go and be charming to her."

She approached Madame de Trézac effusively, and after an interchange
of exclamations Undine heard her say: "You know my friend Mrs. Marvell?
No? How odd! Where do you manage to hide yourself, *chère Madame*?
Undine, here's a compatriot who hasn't the pleasure —"

"I'm such a hermit, dear Mrs. Marvell—the princess shows me what I miss," the Marquise de Trézac murmured, rising to give her hand to Undine, and speaking in a voice so different from that of the supercilious Miss Wincher that only her facial angle and the droop of her nose linked her to the hated vision of Potash Springs.

Undine felt herself dancing on a flood-tide of security. For the first time the memory of Potash Springs became a thing to smile at, and with the princess's arm through hers she shone back triumphantly on Madame de Trézac, who seemed to have grown suddenly obsequious and insignificant, as though the waving of the princess's wand had stripped her of all her false advantages.

But upstairs, in her own room, Undine's courage fell. Madame de Trézac had been civil, effusive even, because for the moment she had been taken off her guard by finding Mrs. Marvell on terms of intimacy with the Princess Estradina and her mother. But the force of facts would reassert itself. Far from continuing to see Undine through her French friends' eyes she would probably invite them to view her compatriot through the searching lens of her own ampler information. "The old hypocrite—she'll tell them everything," Undine murmured, wincing at the recollection of the dentist's assistant from Deposit, and staring miserably at her reflection in the dressing-table mirror. Of what use were youth and grace and good looks, if one drop of poison distilled from the envy of a narrow-minded woman was enough to paralyze them? Of course Madame de Trézac knew and remembered, and, secure in her own impregnable position, would never rest till she had driven out the intruder.

28

WHAT do you say to Nice tomorrow, dearest?" the princess suggested a few evenings later, as she followed Undine upstairs after a languid evening at bridge with the duchess and Madame de Trézac.

Halfway down the passage she stopped to open a door and, putting her finger to her lip, signed to Undine to enter. In the taper-lit dimness stood two small white beds, each surmounted by a crucifix and a palmbranch, and each containing a small brown sleeping child with a mop of hair and a curiously finished little face. As the princess stood gazing on their innocent slumbers she seemed for a moment like a third little girl, scarcely bigger and browner than the others; and the smile with which she watched them was as clear as theirs.

"*Ah, si seulement je pouvais choisir leurs amants!*" she sighed as she turned away.

"—Nice tomorrow," she repeated, as she and Undine walked on to their rooms with linked arms. "We may as well make hay while the Trézac shines. She bores Mamma frightfully, but Mamma won't admit it because they belong to the same *oeuvres*. Shall it be the eleven train, dear? We can lunch at the Royal and look in the shops—we may meet somebody amusing. Anyhow, it's better than staying here!"

Undine was sure the trip to Nice would be delightful. Their previous expeditions had shown her the princess's faculty for organizing such adventures. At Monte Carlo, a few days before, they had run across two or three amusing but unassorted people, and the princess, having fused them in a jolly lunch, had followed it up by a bout at baccarat, and, finally hunting down an eminent composer who had just arrived to rehearse a new production, had insisted on his asking the party to tea, and treating them to fragments of his opera.

A few days earlier, Undine's hope of renewing such pleasures would have been clouded by the dread of leaving Madame de Trézac alone with the duchess. But she had no longer any fear of Madame de Trézac. She had discovered that her old rival of Potash Springs was in actual dread of her disfavor, and nervously anxious to conciliate her, and the discovery gave her such a sense of the heights she had scaled, and the security of her footing, that all her troubled past began to seem like the result of some providential "design," and vague impulses of piety stirred in her as she and the princess whirled toward Nice through the blue and gold glitter of the morning.

They wandered about the lively streets, they gazed into the beguiling shops, the princess tried on hats and Undine bought them, and they lunched at the Royal on all sorts of succulent dishes prepared under the headwaiter's special supervision. But as they were savoring their "double" coffee and liqueurs, and Undine was wondering what her companion would devise for the afternoon, the princess clapped her hands together and cried out: "Dearest, I'd forgotten! I must desert you."

She explained that she'd promised the duchess to look up a friend who was ill—a poor wretch who'd been sent to Cimiez for her lungs—and that she must rush off at once, and would be back as soon as possible—well, if not in an hour, then in two at latest. She was full of compunction, but she knew Undine would forgive her, and find something amusing to fill up the time: she advised her to go back and buy the black hat with the osprey, and try on the crêpe de Chine they'd thought so smart: for anyone as good-looking as herself the woman would probably alter it for nothing; and they could meet again at the Palace Tea Rooms at four.

She whirled away in a cloud of explanations, and Undine, left alone, sat down on the Promenade des Anglais. She did not believe a word the princess had said. She had seen in a flash why she was being left, and why the plan had not been divulged to her beforehand; and she quivered with resentment and humiliation. "That's what she's wanted me for . . . that's why she made up to me. She's trying it today, and after this it'll happen regularly . . . she'll drag me over here every day or two . . . at least she thinks she will!"

A sincere disgust was Undine's uppermost sensation. She was as much ashamed as Mrs. Spragg might have been at finding herself used to screen a clandestine adventure.

"I'll let her see . . . I'll make her understand," she repeated angrily; and for a moment she was half-disposed to drive to the station and take the first train back. But the sense of her precarious situation withheld her; and presently, with bitterness in her heart, she got up and began to stroll toward the shops.

To show that she was not a dupe, she arrived at the designated meeting-place nearly an hour later than the time appointed; but when she entered the Tea Rooms the princess was nowhere to be seen. The rooms were crowded, and Undine was guided toward a small inner apartment where isolated couples were absorbing refreshments in an atmosphere of intimacy that made it seem incongruous to be alone. She glanced about for a face she knew, but none was visible, and she was just giving up the search when she beheld Elmer Moffatt shouldering his way through the crowd.

The sight was so surprising that she sat gazing with unconscious fixity at the round black head and glossy reddish face which kept appearing and disappearing through the intervening jungle of aigrettes. It was long since she had either heard of Moffatt or thought about him, and now, in her loneliness and exasperation, she took comfort in the sight of his confident capable face, and felt a longing to hear his voice and unbosom her woes to him. She had half risen to attract his attention when she saw him turn back and make way for a companion, who was cautiously steering her huge feathered hat between the tea-tables. The woman was of the vulgarest type; everything about her was cheap and gaudy. But Moffatt was obviously elated: he stood aside with a flourish to usher her in, and as he followed he shot out a pink shirt-cuff with jeweled links, and gave his moustache a gallant twist. Undine felt an unreasoning irritation: she was vexed with him both for not being alone and for being so vulgarly accompanied. As the couple seated themselves she caught Moffatt's glance and saw him redden to the edge of his white forehead; but he elaborately avoided her eye—he evidently wanted her to see him do it—and proceeded to minister to his companion's wants with an air of experienced gallantry.

The incident, trifling as it was, filled up the measure of Undine's bitterness. She thought Moffatt pitiably ridiculous, and she hated him for showing himself in such a light at that particular moment. Her mind turned back to her own grievance, and she was just saying to herself that nothing on earth should prevent her letting the princess know what she thought of her, when the lady in question at last appeared. She came hurriedly forward and behind her Undine perceived the figure of a slight quietly dressed man, as to whom her immediate impression was that he made everyone else in the room look as common as Moffatt. An instant later the color had flown to her face and her hand was in Raymond de Chelles's, while the princess, murmuring "Cimiez's such a long way off; but you *will* forgive me?" looked into her eyes with a smile that added: "See how I pay for what I get!"

Her first glance showed Undine how glad Raymond de Chelles was to see her. Since their last meeting his admiration for her seemed not only to have increased but to have acquired a different character. Undine, at an earlier stage in her career, might not have known exactly what the difference signified; but it was as clear to her now as if the princess had said—what her beaming eyes seemed, in fact, to convey—"I'm only too glad to do my cousin the same kind of turn you're doing me."

But Undine's increased experience, if it had made her more vigilant, had also given her a clearer measure of her power. She saw at once that Chelles, in seeking to meet her again, was not in quest of a mere passing adventure. He was evidently deeply drawn to her, and her present situation, if it made it natural to regard her as more accessible, had not altered the nature of his feeling. She saw and weighed all this in the first five minutes during which, over tea and muffins, the princess descanted on her luck in happening to run across her cousin, and Chelles, his enchanted eyes on Undine, expressed his sense of his good fortune. He was staying, it appeared, with friends at Beaulieu, and had run over to Nice that afternoon by the merest chance: he added that, having just learned of his aunt's presence in the neighborhood, he had already planned to present his homage to her.

"Oh, don't come to us—we're too dull!" the princess exclaimed. "Let us run over occasionally and call on you: we're dying for a pretext, aren't we?" she added, smiling at Undine.

The latter smiled back vaguely, and looked across the room. Moffatt, looking flushed and foolish, was just pushing back his chair. To carry off his embarrassment he put on an additional touch of importance; and as he swaggered out behind his companion, Undine said to herself, with a shiver: "If he'd been alone they would have found me taking tea with him."

Undine, during the ensuing weeks, returned several times to Nice with the princess; but, to the latter's surprise, she absolutely refused to have Raymond de Chelles included in their luncheon parties, or even apprised in advance of their expeditions.

The princess, always impatient of unnecessary dissimulation, had not attemptted to keep up the feint of the interesting invalid at Cimiez. She confessed to Undine that she was drawn to Nice by the presence there of the person without whom, for the moment, she found life intolerable, and whom she could not well receive under the same roof with her little girls and her mother. She appealed to Undine's sisterly heart to feel for her in her difficulty, and implied that—as her conduct had already proved—she would always be ready to render her friend a like service.

It was at this point that Undine checked her by a decided word. "I understand your position, and I'm very sorry for you, of course," she began (the princess stared at the "sorry"). "Your secret's perfectly safe with me, and I'll do anything I can for you . . . but if I go to Nice with you again you must promise not to ask your cousin to meet us."

The princess's face expressed the most genuine astonishment. "Oh, my dear, do forgive me if I've been stupid! He admires you so tremendously; and I thought —"

"You'll do as I ask, please—won't you?" Undine went on, ignoring the interruption and looking straight at her under level brows; and the princess, with a shrug, merely murmured: "What a pity! I fancied you liked him."

29

THE early spring found Undine once more in Paris. She had every reason to be satisfied with the result of the course she had pursued since she had pronounced her ultimatum on the subject of Raymond de Chelles. She had continued to remain on the best of terms with the princess, to rise in the estimation of the old duchess, and to measure the rapidity of her ascent in the upward gaze of Madame de Trézac; and she had given Chelles to understand that, if he wished to renew their acquaintance, he must do so in the shelter of his venerable aunt's protection.

To the princess she was careful to make her attitude equally clear. "I like your cousin very much—he's delightful, and if I'm in Paris this spring I hope I shall see a great deal of him. But I know how easy it is for a woman in my position to get talked about—and I have my little boy to consider."

Nevertheless, whenever Chelles came over from Beaulieu to spend a day with his aunt and cousin—an excursion he not infrequently repeated— Undine was at no pains to conceal her pleasure. Nor was there anything calculated in her attitude. Chelles seemed to her more charming than ever, and the warmth of his wooing was in flattering contrast to the cool reserve of his manners. At last she felt herself alive and young again, and it became a joy to look in her glass and to try on her new hats and dresses. . . .

The only menace ahead was the usual one of the want of money. While she had traveled with her parents she had been at relatively small expense, and since their return to America Mr. Spragg had sent her allowance regularly; yet almost all the money she had received for the pearls was already gone, and she knew her Paris season would be far more expensive than the quiet weeks on the Riviera.

Meanwhile the sense of reviving popularity, and the charm of Chelles's devotion, had almost effaced the ugly memories of failure, and refurbished that image of herself in other minds which was her only notion of self-seeing. Under the guidance of Madame de Trézac she had found a prettily furnished apartment in a not too inaccessible quarter, and in its light bright drawing-room she sat one June afternoon listening, with all the forbearance of which she was capable, to the counsels of her newly acquired guide.

"Everything but marriage—" Madame de Trézac was repeating, her long head slightly tilted, her features wearing the rapt look of an adept reciting a hallowed formula.

Raymond de Chelles had not been mentioned by either of the ladies, and the former Miss Wincher was merely imparting to her young friend one of the fundamental dogmas of her social creed; but Undine was conscious that the air between them vibrated with an unspoken name. She made no immediate answer, but her glance, passing by Madame de Trézac's dull countenance, sought her own reflection in the mirror behind her visitor's chair. A beam of spring sunlight touched the living masses of her hair and made the face beneath as radiant as a girl's. Undine smiled faintly at the promise her own eyes gave her, and then turned them back to her friend. "What can such women know about anything?" she thought compassionately.

"There's everything against it," Madame de Trézac continued in a tone of patient exposition. She seemed to be doing her best to make the matter clear. "In the first place, between people in society a religious marriage is necessary; and, since the Church doesn't recognize divorce, that's obviously out of the question. In France, a man of position who goes through the form of civil marriage with a divorced woman is simply ruining himself and her. They might much better—from her point of view as well as his—be 'friends,' as it's called over here: such arrangements are understood and allowed for. But when a Frenchman marries he wants to marry as his people always have. He knows there are traditions he can't fight against—and in his heart he's glad there are."

"Oh, I know: they've so much religious feeling. I admire that in them: their religion's so beautiful." Undine looked thoughtfully at her visitor. "I suppose even money—a great deal of money—wouldn't make the least bit of difference?"

"None whatever, except to make matters worse," Madame de Trézac decisively rejoined. She returned Undine's look with something of Miss Wincher's contemptuous authority. "But," she added, softening to a smile, "between ourselves—I can say it, since we're neither of us children—a woman with tact, who's not in a position to remarry, will find society extremely indulgent . . . provided, of course, she keeps up appearances. . . ."

Undine turned to her with the frown of a startled Diana. "We don't look at things that way out at Apex," she said coldly; and the blood rose in Madame de Trézac's sallow cheek.

"Oh, my dear, it's so refreshing to hear you talk like that! Personally, of course, I've never quite got used to the French view —"

"I hope no American woman ever does," said Undine.

She had been in Paris for about two months when this conversation took place, and in spite of her reviving self-confidence she was beginning to recognize the strength of the forces opposed to her. It had taken a long time to convince her that even money could not prevail against them; and, in the intervals of expressing her admiration for the Catholic creed, she now had violent reactions of militant Protestantism, during which she talked of the tyranny of Rome and recalled school stories of immoral Popes and persecuting Jesuits.

Meanwhile her demeanor to Chelles was that of the incorruptible but fearless American woman, who cannot even conceive of love outside of marriage, but is ready to give her devoted friendship to the man on whom, in happier circumstances, she might have bestowed her hand. This attitude was provocative of many scenes, during which her suitor's unfailing powers of expression—his gift of looking and saying all the desperate and devoted things a pretty woman likes to think she inspires—gave Undine the thrilling sense of breathing the very air of French fiction. But she was aware that too prolonged tension of these cords usually ends in their snapping, and that Chelles's patience was probably in inverse ratio to his ardor.

When Madame de Trézac had left her these thoughts remained in her mind. She understood exactly what each of her new friends wanted of her. The princess, who was fond of her cousin, and had the French sense of family solidarity, would have liked to see Chelles happy in what seemed to her the only imaginable way. Madame de Trézac would have liked to do what she could to second the princess's efforts in this or any other line; and even the old duchess—though piously desirous of seeing her favorite nephew married—would have thought it not only natural but inevitable that, while awaiting that happy event, he should try to induce an amiable young woman to mitigate the drawbacks of celibacy. Meanwhile, they might one and all weary of her if Chelles did; and a persistent rejection of his suit would probably imperil her scarcely gained footing among his friends. All this was clear to her, yet it did not shake her resolve. She was determined to give up Chelles unless he was willing to marry her; and the thought of her renunciation moved her to a kind of wistful melancholy.

In this mood her mind reverted to a letter she had just received from her mother. Mrs. Spragg wrote more fully than usual, and the unwonted flow of her pen had been occasioned by an event for which she had long yearned. For months she had pined for a sight of her grandson, had tried to screw up her courage to write and ask permission to visit him, and, finally breaking through her sedentary habits, had begun to haunt the neighborhood of Washington Square, with the result that one afternoon she had had the luck to meet the little boy coming out of the house with his nurse. She had spoken to him, and he had remembered her and called her "Granny"; and the next day she had received a note from Mrs. Fairford saying that Ralph would be glad to send Paul to see her. Mrs. Spragg enlarged on the delights of the visit and the growing beauty and cleverness of her grandson. She described to Undine exactly how Paul was dressed, how he looked and what he said, and told her how he had examined everything in the room, and, finally coming upon his mother's photograph, had asked who the lady was; and, on being told, had wanted to know if she was a very long way off, and when Granny thought she would come back.

As Undine reread her mother's pages, she felt an unusual tightness in her throat and two tears rose to her eyes. It was dreadful that her little boy should be growing up far away from her, perhaps dressed in clothes she would have hated; and wicked and unnatural that when he saw her picture he should have to be told who she was. "If I could only meet some good man who would give me a home and be a father to him," she thought—and the tears overflowed and ran down.

Even as they fell, the door was thrown open, to admit Raymond de Chelles, and the consciousness of the moisture still glistening on her cheeks perhaps strengthened her resolve to resist him, and thus made her more imperiously to be desired. Certain it is that on that day her suitor first alluded to a possibility which Madame de Trézac had prudently refrained from suggesting, and there fell upon Undine's attentive ears the magic phrase "annulment of marriage."

Her alert intelligence immediately set to work in this new direction; but almost at the same moment she became aware of a subtle change of tone in the princess and her mother, a change reflected in the corresponding decline of Madame de Trézac's cordiality. Undine, since her arrival in Paris, had necessarily been less in the princess's company, but when they met she had found her as friendly as ever. It was manifestly not a failing of the princess's to forget past favors, and though increasingly absorbed by the demands of town life she treated her new friend with the same affectionate frankness, and Undine was given frequent opportunities to enlarge her Parisian acquaintance, not only in the princess's intimate circle but in the majestic drawingrooms of the Hôtel de Dordogne. Now, however, there was a perceptible decline in these signs of hospitality, and Undine, on calling one day on the duchess, noticed that her appearance sent a visible flutter of discomfort through the circle about her hostess's chair. Two or three of the

ladies present looked away from the newcomer and at each other, and
several of them seemed spontaneously to encircle without approaching her,
while another—gray-haired, elderly and slightly frightened—with an
"Adieu, ma bonne tante" to the duchess, was hastily aided in her retreat
down the long line of old gilded rooms.

The incident was too mute and rapid to have been noticeable had it not
been followed by the duchess's resuming her conversation with the ladies
nearest her as though Undine had just gone out of the room instead of
entering it. The sense of having been thus rendered invisible filled Undine
with a vehement desire to make herself seen, and an equally strong sense
that all attempts to do so would be vain; and when, a few minutes later, she
issued from the portals of the Hôtel de Dordogne it was with the fixed
resolve not to enter them again till she had had an explanation with the
princess.

She was spared the trouble of seeking one by the arrival, early the next
morning, of Madame de Trézac, who, entering almost with the breakfast
tray, mysteriously asked to be allowed to communicate something of importance.

"You'll understand, I know, the princess's not coming herself —" Madame de Trézac began, sitting up very straight on the edge of the armchair
over which Undine's lace dressing-gown hung.

"If there's anything she wants to say to me, I don't," Undine answered,
leaning back among her rosy pillows, and reflecting compassionately that
the face opposite her was just the color of the *café au lait* she was pouring
out.

"There are things that are . . . that might seem too pointed . . . if
one said them one's self," Madame de Trézac continued. "Our dear Lili's so
good-natured . . . she so hates to do anything unfriendly; but she naturally
thinks first of her mother. . . ."

"Her mother? What's the matter with her mother?"

"I told her I knew you didn't understand. I was sure you'd take it in good
part. . . ."

Undine raised herself on her elbow. "What did Lili tell you to tell me?"

"Oh, not to *tell* you . . . simply to ask if, just for the present, you'd
mind avoiding the duchess's Thursdays . . . calling on any other day,
that is."

"Any other day? She's not at home on any other. Do you mean she
doesn't want me to call?"

"Well—not while the Marquise de Chelles is in Paris. She's the duchess's favorite niece—and of course they all hang together. That kind of
family feeling is something you naturally don't —"

Undine had a sudden glimpse of hidden intricacies.

"That was Raymond de Chelles's mother I saw there yesterday? The one
they hurried out when I came in?"

"It seems she was very much upset. She somehow heard your name."

"Why shouldn't she have heard my name? And why in the world should it upset her?"

Madame de Trézac heaved a hesitating sigh. "Isn't it better to be frank? She thinks she has reason to feel badly—they all do."

"To feel badly? Because her son wants to marry me?"

"Of course they know that's impossible." Madame de Trézac smiled compassionately. "But they're afraid of your spoiling his other chances."

Undine paused a moment before answering. "It won't be impossible when my marriage is annulled," she said.

The effect of this statement was less electrifying than she had hoped. Her visitor simply broke into a laugh. "My dear child! Your marriage annulled? Who can have put such a mad idea into your head?"

Undine's gaze followed the pattern she was tracing with a lustrous nail on her embroidered bedspread. "Raymond himself," she let fall.

This time there was no mistaking the effect she produced. Madame de Trézac, with a murmured "Oh," sat gazing before her as if she had lost the thread of her argument; and it was only after a considerable interval that she recovered it sufficiently to exclaim: "They'll never hear of it—absolutely never!"

"But they can't prevent it, can they?"

"They can prevent its being of any use to you."

"I see," Undine pensively assented.

She knew the tone she had taken was virtually a declaration of war; but she was in a mood when the act of defiance, apart from its strategic value, was a satisfaction in itself. Moreover, if she could not gain her end without a fight it was better that the battle should be engaged while Raymond's ardor was at its height. To provoke immediate hostilities she sent for him the same afternoon, and related, quietly and without comment, the incident of her visit to the duchess, and the mission with which Madame de Trézac had been charged. In the circumstances, she went on to explain, it was manifestly impossible that she should continue to receive his visits; and she met his wrathful comments on his relatives by the gently but firmly expressed resolve not to be the cause of any disagreement between himself and his family.

30

A FEW days after her decisive conversation with Raymond de Chelles, Undine, emerging from the doors of the Nouveau Luxe, where she had been to call on the newly arrived Mrs. Homer Branney, once more found herself face to face with Elmer Moffatt.

This time there was no mistaking his eagerness to be recognized. He stopped short as they met, and she read such pleasure in his eyes that she too stopped, holding out her hand.

"I'm glad you're going to speak to me," she said, and Moffatt reddened at the allusion.

"Well, I very nearly didn't. I didn't know you. You look about as old as you did when I first landed at Apex—remember?"

He turned back and began to walk at her side in the direction of the Champs Elysées.

"Say—this is all right!" he exclaimed; and she saw that his glance had left her and was ranging across the wide silvery square ahead of them to the congregated domes and spires beyond the river.

"Do you like Paris?" she asked, wondering what theaters he had been to.

"It beats everything." He seemed to be breathing in deeply the impression of fountains, sculpture, leafy avenues and long-drawn architectural distances fading into the afternoon haze.

"I suppose you've been to that old church over there?" he went on, his gold-topped stick pointing toward the towers of Notre Dame.

"Oh, of course; when I used to sightsee. Have you never been to Paris before?"

"No, this is my first look-round. I came across in March."

"In March?" she echoed inattentively. It never occurred to her that other people's lives went on when they were out of her range of vision, and she tried in vain to remember what she had last heard of Moffatt. "Wasn't that a bad time to leave Wall Street?"

"Well, so-so. Fact is, I was played out: needed a change." Nothing in his robust mien confirmed the statement, and he did not seem inclined to develop it. "I presume you're settled here now?" he went on. "I saw by the papers —"

"Yes," she interrupted; adding, after a moment: "It was all a mistake from the first."

"Well, I never thought he was your form," said Moffatt.

537

His eyes had come back to her, and the look in them struck her as something she might use to her advantage; but the next moment he had glanced away with a furrowed brow, and she felt she had not wholly fixed his attention.

"I live at the other end of Paris. Why not come back and have tea with me?" she suggested, half moved by a desire to know more of his affairs, and half by the thought that a talk with him might help to shed some light on hers.

In the open taxi-cab he seemed to recover his sense of well-being, and leaned back, his hands on the knob of his stick, with the air of a man pleasantly aware of his privileges. "This Paris is a thundering good place," he repeated once or twice as they rolled on through the crush and glitter of the afternoon; and when they had descended at Undine's door, and he stood in her drawing-room, and looked out on the horse-chestnut trees rounding their green domes under the balcony, his satisfaction culminated in the comment: "I guess this lays out West End Avenue!"

His eyes met Undine's with their old twinkle, and their expression encouraged her to murmur: "Of course, there are times when I'm very lonely."

She sat down behind the tea-table, and he stood at a little distance, watching her pull off her gloves with a queer comic twitch of his elastic mouth. "Well, I guess it's only when you want to be," he said, grasping a lyre-backed chair by its gilt cords, and sitting down astride of it, his light gray trousers stretching too tightly over his plump thighs. Undine was perfectly aware that he was a vulgar overdressed man, with a red crease of fat above his collar and an impudent swaggering eye; yet she liked to see him there, and was conscious that he stirred the fibers of a self she had forgotten but had not ceased to understand.

She had fancied her avowal of loneliness might call forth some sentimental phrase; but though Moffatt was clearly pleased to be with her she saw that she was not the center of his thoughts, and the discovery irritated her.

"I don't suppose *you've* known what it is to be lonely since you've been in Europe?" she continued as she held out his teacup.

"Oh," he said jocosely, "I don't always go round with a guide"; and she rejoined on the same note: "Then perhaps I shall see something of you."

"Why, there's nothing would suit me better; but the fact is, I'm probably sailing next week."

"Oh, are you? I'm sorry." There was nothing feigned in her regret.

"Anything I can do for you across the pond?"

She hesitated. "There's something you can do for me right off."

He looked at her more attentively, as if his practiced eye had passed through the surface of her beauty to what might be going on behind it. "Do you want my blessing again?" he asked with sudden irony.

Undine opened her eyes with a trustful look. "Yes—I do."

"Well—I'll be damned!" said Moffatt gaily.

"You've always been so awfully nice," she began; and he leaned back, grasping both sides of the chairback, and shaking it a little with his laugh.

He kept the same attitude while she proceeded to unfold her case, listening to her with the air of sober concentration that his frivolous face took on at any serious demand on his attention. When she had ended he kept the same look during an interval of silent pondering. "Is it the fellow who was over at Nice with you that day?"

She looked at him with surprise. "How did you know?"

"Why, I liked his looks," said Moffatt simply.

He got up and strolled toward the window. On the way he stopped before a table covered with showy trifles, and after looking at them for a moment singled out a dim old brown and golden book which Chelles had given her. He examined it lingeringly, as though it touched the spring of some choked-up sensibility for which he had no language. "Say —" he began: it was the usual prelude to his enthusiasms; but he laid the book down and turned back.

"Then you think if you had the cash you could fix it up all right with the Pope?"

Her heart began to beat. She remembered that he had once put a job in Ralph's way, and had let her understand that he had done it partly for her sake.

"Well," he continued, relapsing into hyperbole, "I wish I could send the old gentleman my check tomorrow morning: but the fact is I'm high and dry." He looked at her with a sudden odd intensity. "If I *wasn't*, I dunno but what —" The phrase was lost in his familiar whistle. "That's an awfully fetching way you do your hair," he said.

It was a disappointment to Undine to hear that his affairs were not prospering, for she knew that in his world "pull" and solvency were closely related, and that such support as she had hoped he might give her would be contingent on his own situation. But she had again a fleeting sense of his mysterious power of accomplishing things in the teeth of adversity; and she answered: "What I want is your advice."

He turned away and wandered across the room, his hands in his pockets. On her ornate writing desk he saw a photograph of Paul, bright-curled and sturdy-legged, in a manly reefer, and bent over it with a murmur of approval. "Say—what a fellow! Got him with you?"

Undine colored. "No —" she began; and seeing his look of surprise, she embarked on her usual explanation. "I can't tell you how I miss him," she ended, with a ring of truth that carried conviction to her own ears if not to Moffatt's.

"Why don't you get him back, then?"

"Why, I —"

Moffatt had picked up the frame and was looking at the photograph more closely. "Pants!" he chuckled. "I declare!"

He turned back to Undine. "Who *does* he belong to, anyhow?"

"Belong to?"

"Who got him when you were divorced? Did you?"

"Oh, I got everything," she said, her instinct of self-defense on the alert.

"So I thought." He stood before her, stoutly planted on his short legs, and speaking with an aggressive energy. "Well, I know what I'd do if he was mine."

"If he was yours?"

"And you tried to get him away from me. Fight you to a finish! If it cost me down to my last dollar I would."

The conversation seemed to be wandering from the point, and she answered, with a touch of impatience: "It wouldn't cost you anything like that. I haven't got a dollar to fight back with."

"Well, you ain't got to fight. Your decree gave him to you, didn't it? Why don't you send right over and get him? That's what I'd do if I was you."

Undine looked up. "But I'm awfully poor; I can't afford to have him here."

"You couldn't, up to now; but now you're going to get married. You're going to be able to give him a home and a father's care—and the foreign languages. That's what I'd say if I was you. . . . His father takes considerable stock in him, don't he?"

She colored, a denial on her lips; but she could not shape it. "We're both awfully fond of him, of course. . . . His father'd never give him up!"

"Just so." Moffatt's face had grown as sharp as glass. "You've got the Marvells running. All you've got to do's to sit tight and wait for their check." He dropped back to his equestrian seat on the lyre-backed chair.

Undine stood up and moved uneasily toward the window. She seemed to see her little boy as though he were in the room with her; she did not understand how she could have lived so long without him. . . . She stood for a long time without speaking, feeling behind her the concentrated irony of Moffatt's gaze.

"You couldn't lend me the money—manage to borrow it for me, I mean?" she finally turned back to ask.

He laughed. "If I could manage to borrow any money at this particular minute—well, I'd have to lend every dollar of it to Elmer Moffatt, Esquire. I'm stone-broke, if you want to know. And wanted for an investigation, too. That's why I'm over here improving my mind."

"Why, I thought you were going home next week?"

He grinned. "I am, because I've found out there's a party wants me to stay away worse than the courts want me back. Making the trip just for my private satisfaction—there won't be any money in it, I'm afraid."

Leaden disappointment descended on Undine. She had felt almost sure of Moffatt's helping her, and for an instant she wondered if some long-smoldering jealousy had flamed up under its cold cinders. But another look at his face denied her this solace; and his evident indifference was the last blow to her pride. The twinge it gave her prompted her to ask: "Don't you ever mean to get married?"

Moffatt gave her a quick look. "Why, I shouldn't wonder—one of these days. Millionaires always collect something; but I've got to collect my millions first."

He spoke coolly and half-humorously, and before he had ended she had lost all interest in his reply. He seemed aware of the fact, for he stood up and held out his hand.

"Well, so long, Mrs. Marvell. It's been uncommonly pleasant to see you; and you'd better think over what I've said."

She laid her hand sadly in his. "You've never had a child," she replied.

Book Four

31

N EARLY two years had passed since Ralph Marvell, waking from his long
sleep in the hot summer light of Washington Square, had found that
the face of life was changed for him.

In the interval he had gradually adapted himself to the new order of
things; but the months of adaptation had been a time of such darkness and
confusion that, from the vantage-ground of his recovered lucidity, he could
not yet distinguish the stages by which he had worked his way out; and even
now his footing was not secure.

His first effort had been to readjust his values—to take an inventory of
them, and reclassify them, so that one at least might be made to appear as
important as those he had lost; otherwise there could be no reason why he
should go on living. He applied himself doggedly to this attempt; but whenever he thought he had found a reason that his mind could rest in, it gave
way under him, and the old struggle for a foothold began again. His two
objects in life were his boy and his book. The boy was incomparably the
stronger argument, yet the less serviceable in filling the void. Ralph felt his
son all the while, and all through his other feelings; but he could not think
about him actively and continuously, could not forever exercise his eager
empty dissatisfied mind on the relatively simple problem of clothing, edu-
cating and amusing a little boy of six. Yet Paul's existence was the all-
sufficient reason for his own; and he turned again, with a kind of cold
fervor, to his abandoned literary dream. Material needs obliged him to go on
with his regular business; but, the day's work over, he was possessed of a
leisure as bare and as blank as an unfurnished house, yet that was at least his
own to furnish as he pleased.

Meanwhile he was beginning to show a presentable face to the world,
and to be once more treated like a man in whose case no one is particularly
interested. His men friends ceased to say: "Hallo, old chap, I never saw you
looking fitter!" and elderly ladies no longer told him they were sure he kept
too much to himself, and urged him to drop in any afternoon for a quiet
talk. People left him to his sorrow as a man is left to an incurable habit, an
unfortunate tie: they ignored it, or looked over its head if they happened to
catch a glimpse of it at his elbow.

These glimpses were given to them more and more rarely. The smothered springs of life were bubbling up in Ralph, and there were days when he was glad to wake and see the sun in his window, and when he began to plan his book, and to fancy that the planning really interested him. He could even maintain the delusion for several days—for intervals each time appreciably longer—before it shriveled up again in a scorching blast of disenchantment. The worst of it was that he could never tell when these hot gusts of anguish would overtake him. They came sometimes just when he felt most secure, when he was saying to himself: "After all, things are really worthwhile—" sometimes even when he was sitting with Clare Van Degen, listening to her voice, watching her hands, and turning over in his mind the opening chapters of his book.

"You ought to write"; they had one and all said it to him from the first; and he fancied he might have begun sooner if he had not been urged on by their watchful fondness. Everybody wanted him to write—everybody had decided that he ought to, that he would, that he must be persuaded to; and the incessant imperceptible pressure of encouragement—the assumption of those about him that because it would be good for him to write he must naturally be able to—acted on his restive nerves as a stronger deterrent than disapproval.

Even Clare had fallen into the same mistake; and one day, as he sat talking with her on the verandah of Laura Fairford's house on the Sound—where they now most frequently met—Ralph had half-impatiently rejoined: "Oh, if you think it's literature I need—!"

Instantly he had seen her face change, and the speaking hands tremble on her knee. But she achieved the feat of not answering him, or turning her steady eyes from the dancing midsummer water at the foot of Laura's lawn. Ralph leaned a little nearer, and for an instant his hand imagined the flutter of hers. But instead of clasping it he drew back, and rising from his chair wandered away to the other end of the verandah. . . . No, he didn't feel as Clare felt. If he loved her—as he sometimes thought he did—it was not in the same way. He had a great tenderness for her, he was more nearly happy with her than with anyone else; he liked to sit and talk with her, and watch her face and her hands, and he wished there were some way—some different way—of letting her know it; but he could not conceive that tenderness and desire could ever again be one for him: such a notion as that seemed part of the monstrous sentimental muddle on which his life had gone aground.

"I shall write—of course I shall write someday," he said, turning back to his seat. "I've had a novel in the back of my head for years; and now's the time to pull it out."

He hardly knew what he was saying; but before the end of the sentence he saw that Clare had understood what he meant to convey, and henceforth he felt committed to letting her talk to him as much as she pleased about his book. He himself, in consequence, took to thinking about it more consecutively; and just as his friends ceased to urge him to write, he sat down in earnest to begin.

The vision that had come to him had no likeness to any of his earlier imaginings. Two or three subjects had haunted him, pleading for expression, during the first years of his marriage; but these now seemed either too lyrical or too tragic. He no longer saw life on the heroic scale: he wanted to do something in which men should look no bigger than the insects they were. He contrived in the course of time to reduce one of his old subjects to these dimensions, and after nights of brooding he made a dash at it, and wrote an opening chapter that struck him as not too bad. In the exhilaration of this first attempt he spent some pleasant evenings revising and polishing his work; and gradually a feeling of authority and importance developed in him. In the morning, when he woke, instead of his habitual sense of lassitude, he felt an eagerness to be up and doing, and a conviction that his individual task was a necessary part of the world's machinery. He kept his secret with the beginner's deadly fear of losing his hold on his half-real creations if he let in any outer light on them; but he went about with a more assured step, shrank less from meeting his friends, and even began to dine out again, and to laugh at some of the jokes he heard.

Laura Fairford, to get Paul away from town, had gone early to the country; and Ralph, who went down to her every Saturday, usually found Clare Van Degen there. Since his divorce he had never entered his cousin's pinnacled palace; and Clare had never asked him why he stayed away. This mutual silence had been their sole allusion to Van Degen's share in the catastrophe, though Ralph had spoken frankly of its other aspects. They talked, however, most often of impersonal subjects—books, pictures, plays, or whatever the world that interested them was doing—and she showed no desire to draw him back to his own affairs. She was again staying late in town—to have a pretext, as he guessed, for coming down on Sundays to the Fairfords'—and they often made the trip together in her motor; but he had not yet spoken to her of having begun his book. One May evening, however, as they sat alone in the verandah, he suddenly told her that he was writing. As he spoke his heart beat like a boy's; but once the words were out they gave him a feeling of self-confidence, and he began to sketch his plan, and then to go into its details. Clare listened devoutly, her eyes burning on him through the dusk like the stars deepening above the garden; and when she got up to go in he followed her with a new sense of reassurance.

The dinner that evening was unusually pleasant. Charles Bowen, just back from his usual spring travels, had come straight down to his friends from the steamer; and the fund of impressions he brought with him gave Ralph a desire to be up and wandering. And why not—when the book was done? He smiled across the table at Clare.

"Next summer you'll have to charter a yacht, and take us all off to the

Aegean. We can't have Charles condescending to us about the out-of-the-way places he's been seeing."

Was it really he who was speaking, and his cousin who was sending him back her dusky smile? Well—why not, again? The seasons renewed themselves, and he too was putting out a new growth. "My book—my book—my book," kept repeating itself under all his thoughts, as Undine's name had once perpetually murmured there. That night as he went up to bed he said to himself that he was actually ceasing to think about his wife. . . .

As he passed Laura's door she called him in, and put her arms about him.

"You look so well, dear!"

"But why shouldn't I?" he answered gaily, as if ridiculing the fancy that he had ever looked otherwise. Paul was sleeping behind the next door, and the sense of the boy's nearness gave him a warmer glow. His little world was rounding itself out again, and once more he felt safe and at peace in its circle.

His sister looked as if she had something more to say; but she merely kissed him good night, and he went up whistling to his room.

The next morning he was to take a walk with Clare, and while he lounged about the drawing-room, waiting for her to come down, a servant came in with the Sunday papers. Ralph picked one up, and was absently unfolding it when his eye fell on his own name: a sight he had been spared since the last echoes of his divorce had subsided. His impulse was to fling the paper down, to hurl it as far from him as he could; but a grim fascination tightened his hold and drew his eyes back to the hated headline.

NEW YORK BEAUTY WEDS FRENCH NOBLEMAN
MRS. UNDINE MARVELL CONFIDENT POPE WILL
ANNUL PREVIOUS MARRIAGE
MRS. MARVELL TALKS ABOUT HER CASE

There it was before him in all its long-drawn horror—an "interview"—an "interview" of Undine's about her coming marriage! Ah, she talked about her case indeed! Her confidences filled the greater part of a column, and the only detail she seemed to have omitted was the name of her future husband, who was referred to by herself as "my fiancé" and by the interviewer as "the count" or "a prominent scion of the French nobility."

Ralph heard Laura's step behind him. He threw the paper aside and their eyes met.

"Is this what you wanted to tell me last night?"

"Last night?—Is it in the papers?"

"Who told you? Bowen? What else has he heard?"

"Oh, Ralph, what does it matter—what can it matter?"

"Who's the man? Did he tell you that?" Ralph insisted. He saw her growing agitation. "Why can't you answer? Is it anyone I know?"

"He was told in Paris it was his friend Raymond de Chelles."

Ralph laughed, and his laugh sounded in his own ears like an echo of the dreary mirth with which he had filled Mr. Spragg's office the day he had learned that Undine intended to divorce him. But now his wrath was seasoned with a wholesome irony. The fact of his wife's having reached another stage in her ascent fell into its place as a part of the huge human buffoonery.

"Besides," Laura went on, "it's all perfect nonsense, of course. How in the world can she have her marriage annulled?"

Ralph pondered: this put the matter in another light. "With a great deal of money I suppose she might."

"Well, she certainly won't get that from Chelles. He's far from rich, Charles tells me." Laura waited, watching him, before she risked: "That's what convinces me she wouldn't have him if she could."

Ralph shrugged. "There may be other inducements. But she won't be able to manage it." He heard himself speaking quite collectedly. Had Undine at last lost her power of wounding him?

Clare came in, dressed for their walk, and under Laura's anxious eyes he picked up the newspaper and held it out with a careless: "Look at this!"

His cousin's glance flew down the column, and he saw the tremor of her lashes as she read. Then she lifted her head. "But you'll be free!" Her face was as vivid as a flower.

"Free? I'm free now, as far as that goes!"

"Oh, but it will go so much further when she has another name—when she's a different person altogether! Then you'll really have Paul to yourself."

"Paul?" Laura intervened with a nervous laugh. "But there's never been the least doubt about his having Paul!"

They heard the boy's laughter on the lawn, and she went out to join him. Ralph was still looking at his cousin.

"You're glad, then?" came from him involuntarily; and she startled him by bursting into tears. He bent over and kissed her on the cheek.

32

RALPH, as the days passed, felt that Clare was right: if Undine married again he would possess himself more completely, be more definitely rid of his past. And he did not doubt that she would gain her end: he knew her violent desires and her cold tenacity. If she had failed to capture Van Degen it was probably because she lacked experience of that particular type of man, of his huge immediate wants and feeble vacillating purposes; most of all, because she had not yet measured the strength of the social consider-ations that restrained him. It was a mistake she was not likely to repeat, and her failure had probably been a useful preliminary to success. It was a long time since Ralph had allowed himself to think of her, and as he did so the overwhelming fact of her beauty became present to him again, no longer as an element of his being but as a power dispassionately estimated. He said to himself: "Any man who can feel at all will feel it as I did"; and the convic-tion grew in him that Raymond de Chelles, of whom he had formed an idea through Bowen's talk, was not the man to give her up, even if she failed to obtain the release his religion exacted.

Meanwhile Ralph was gradually beginning to feel himself freer and lighter. Undine's act, by cutting the last link between them, seemed to have given him back to himself; and the mere fact that he could consider his case in all its bearings, impartially and ironically, showed him the distance he had traveled, the extent to which he had renewed himself. He had been moved, too, by Clare's cry of joy at his release. Though the nature of his feeling for her had not changed he was aware of a new quality in their friendship. When he went back to his book again his sense of power had lost its asperity, and the spectacle of life seemed less like a witless dangling of limp dolls. He was well on in his second chapter now.

This lightness of mood was still on him when, returning one afternoon to Washington Square, full of projects for a long evening's work, he found his mother awaiting him with a strange face. He followed her into the drawing-room, and she explained that there had been a telephone message she didn't understand—something perfectly crazy about Paul—of course it was all a mistake. . . .

Ralph's first thought was of an accident, and his heart contracted. "Did Laura telephone?"

"No, no; not Laura. It seemed to be a message from Mrs. Spragg: some-thing about sending someone here to fetch him—a queer name like Heeny —to fetch him to a steamer on Saturday. I was to be sure to have his things packed . . . but of course it's a misunderstanding. . . ." She gave an un-certain laugh, and looked up at Ralph as though entreating him to return the reassurance she had given him.

"Of course, of course," he echoed.

He made his mother repeat her statement; but the unforeseen always flurried her, and she was confused and inaccurate. She didn't actually know who had telephoned: the voice hadn't sounded like Mrs. Spragg's. . . . A woman's voice; yes—oh, not a lady's! And there was certainly something about a steamer . . . but he knew how the telephone bewildered her . . . and she was sure she was getting a little deaf. Hadn't he better call up the

Malibran? Of course it was all a mistake—but . . . well, perhaps he *had* better go there himself. . . .

As he reached the front door a letter clinked in the box, and he saw his name on an ordinary looking business envelope. He turned the door-handle, paused again, and stopped to take out the letter. It bore the address of the firm of lawyers who had represented Undine in the divorce proceedings and as he tore open the envelope Paul's name started out at him.

Mrs. Marvell had followed him into the hall, and her cry broke the silence. "Ralph—Ralph—is it anything she's done?"

"Nothing—it's nothing." He stared at her. "What's the day of the week?"

"Wednesday. Why, what —?" She suddenly seemed to understand. "She's not going to take him away from us?"

Ralph dropped into a chair, crumpling the letter in his hand. He had been in a dream, poor fool that he was—a dream about his child! He sat gazing at the typewritten phrases that spun themselves out before him. "My client's circumstances now happily permitting . . . at last in a position to offer her son a home . . . long separation . . . a mother's feelings . . . every social and educational advantage" . . . and then, at the end, the poisoned dart that struck him speechless: "The courts having awarded her the sole custody. . . ."

The sole custody! But that meant that Paul was hers, hers only, hers for always: that his father had no more claim on him than any casual stranger in the street! And he, Ralph Marvell, a sane man, young, able-bodied, in full possession of his wits, had assisted at the perpetration of this abominable wrong, had passively forfeited his right to the flesh of his body, the blood of his being! But it couldn't be—of course, it couldn't be. The preposterousness of it proved that it wasn't true. There was a mistake somewhere; a mistake his own lawyer would instantly rectify. If a hammer hadn't been drumming in his head he could have recalled the terms of the decree—but for the moment all the details of the agonizing episode were lost in a blur of uncertainty.

To escape his mother's silent anguish of interrogation he stood up and said: "I'll see Mr. Spragg—of course, it's a mistake." But as he spoke he retraveled the hateful months during the divorce proceedings, remembering his incomprehensible lassitude, his acquiescence in his family's determination to ignore the whole episode, and his gradual lapse into the same state of apathy. He recalled all the old family catch-words, the full and elaborate vocabulary of evasion: "delicacy," "pride," "personal dignity," "preferring not to know about such things"; Mrs. Marvell's: "All I ask is that you won't mention the subject to your grandfather," Mr. Dagonet's: "Spare your mother, Ralph, whatever happens," and even Laura's terrified: "Of course, for Paul's sake, there must be no scandal."

For Paul's sake! And it was because, for Paul's sake, there must be no scandal, that he, Paul's father, had tamely abstained from defending his rights and contesting his wife's charges, and had thus handed the child over to her keeping!

As his cab whirled him up Fifth Avenue, Ralph's whole body throbbed with rage against the influences that had reduced him to such weakness. Then, gradually, he saw that the weakness was innate in him. He had been eloquent enough, in his free youth, against the conventions of his class; yet when the moment came to show his contempt for them they had mysteriously mastered him, deflecting his course like some hidden hereditary failing. As he looked back it seemed as though even his great disaster had been conventionalized and sentimentalized by this inherited attitude: that the thoughts he had thought about it were only those of generations of Dagonets, and that there had been nothing real and his own in his life but the foolish passion he had been trying so hard to think out of existence.

Halfway to the Malibran he changed his direction, and drove to the house of the lawyer he had consulted at the time of his divorce. The lawyer had not yet come uptown, and Ralph had a half hour of bitter meditation before the sound of a latch-key brought him to his feet. The visit did not last long. His host, after an affable greeting, listened without surprise to what he had to say, and when he had ended reminded him with somewhat ironic precision that, at the time of the divorce, he had asked for neither advice nor information—had simply declared that he wanted to "turn his back on the whole business" (Ralph recognized the phrase as one of his grandfather's), and, on hearing that in that case he had only to abstain from action, and was in no need of legal services, had gone away without further inquiries.

"You led me to infer you had your reasons —" the slighted counsellor concluded; and, in reply to Ralph's breathless question, he subjoined, "Why, you see, the case is closed, and I don't exactly know on what ground you can reopen it—unless, of course, you can bring evidence showing that the irregularity of the mother's life is such. . . ."

"She's going to marry again," Ralph threw in.

"Indeed? Well, that in itself can hardly be described as irregular. In fact, in certain circumstances, it might be construed as an advantage to the child."

"Then I'm powerless?"

"Why—unless there's an ulterior motive—through which pressure might be brought to bear."

"You mean that the first thing to do is to find out what she's up to?"

"Precisely. Of course, if it should prove to be a genuine case of maternal feeling, I won't conceal from you that the outlook's bad. At most, you could probably arrange to see your boy at stated intervals."

To see his boy at stated intervals! Ralph wondered how a sane man could sit there, looking responsible and efficient, and talk such rubbish. As he got up to go the lawyer detained him to add: "Of course there's no immediate cause for alarm. It will take time to enforce the provision of the Dakota decree in New York, and till it's done your son can't be taken from you. But there's sure to be a lot of nasty talk in the papers; and you're bound to lose in the end."

Ralph thanked him and left.

He sped northward to the Malibran, where he learned that Mr. and Mrs. Spragg were at dinner. He sent his name down to the subterranean restaurant, and Mr. Spragg presently appeared between the limp portières of the "Adam" writing-room. He had grown older and heavier, as if illness instead of health had put more flesh on his bones, and there were grayish tints in the hollows of his face.

"What's this about Paul?" Ralph exclaimed. "My mother's had a message we can't make out."

Mr. Spragg sat down, with the effect of immersing his spinal column in the depths of the armchair he selected. He crossed his legs, and swung one foot to and fro in its high wrinkled boot with elastic sides.

"Didn't you get a letter?" he asked.

"From my—from Undine's lawyers? Yes." Ralph held it out. "It's queer reading. She hasn't hitherto been very keen to have Paul with her."

Mr. Spragg, adjusting his glasses, read the letter slowly, restored it to the envelope and gave it back. "My daughter has intimated that she wishes these gentlemen to act for her. I haven't received any additional instructions from her," he said, with none of the curtness of tone that his stiff legal vocabulary implied.

"But the first communication I received was from you—at least from Mrs. Spragg."

Mr. Spragg drew his beard through his hand. "The ladies are apt to be a trifle hasty. I believe Mrs. Spragg had a letter yesterday instructing her to select a reliable escort for Paul; and I suppose she thought —"

"Oh, this is all too preposterous!" Ralph burst out, springing from his seat. "You don't for a moment imagine, do you—any of you—that I'm going to deliver up my son like a bale of goods in answer to any instructions in God's world?—Oh, yes, I know—I let him go—I abandoned my right to him . . . but I didn't know what I was doing. . . . I was sick with grief and misery. My people were awfully broken up over the whole business, and I wanted to spare them. I wanted, above all, to spare my boy when he grew up. If I'd contested the case you know what the result would have been. I let it go by default—I made no conditions—all I wanted was to keep Paul, and never to let him hear a word against his mother!"

Mr. Spragg received this passionate appeal in a silence that implied not so much disdain or indifference, as the total inability to deal verbally with emotional crises. At length, he said, a slight unsteadiness in his usually calm tones: "I presume at the time it was optional with you to demand Paul's custody."

"Oh, yes—it was optional," Ralph sneered.

Mr. Spragg looked at him compassionately. "I'm sorry you didn't do it," he said.

33

THE upshot of Ralph's visit was that Mr. Spragg, after considerable deliberation, agreed, pending farther negotiations between the opposing lawyers, to undertake that no attempt should be made to remove Paul from his father's custody. Nevertheless, he seemed to think it quite natural that Undine, on the point of making a marriage which would put it in her power to give her child a suitable home, should assert her claim on him. It was more disconcerting to Ralph to learn that Mrs. Spragg, for once departing from her attitude of passive impartiality, had eagerly abetted her daughter's move; he had somehow felt that Undine's desertion of the child had established a kind of mute understanding between himself and his mother-in-law.

"I thought Mrs. Spragg would know there's no earthly use trying to take Paul from me," he said with a desperate awkwardness of entreaty, and Mr. Spragg startled him by replying: "I presume his grandma thinks he'll belong to her more if we keep him in the family."

Ralph, abruptly awakened from his dream of recovered peace, found himself confronted on every side by indifference or hostility: it was as though the June fields in which his boy was playing had suddenly opened to engulf him. Mrs. Marvell's fears and tremors were almost harder to bear than the Spraggs' antagonism; and for the next few days Ralph wandered about miserably, dreading some fresh communication from Undine's lawyers, yet racked by the strain of hearing nothing more from them. Mr. Spragg had agreed to cable his daughter asking her to await a letter before enforcing her demands; but on the fourth day after Ralph's visit to the Malibran a telephone message summoned him to his father-in-law's office.

Half an hour later their talk was over and he stood once more on the landing outside Mr. Spragg's door. Undine's answer had come and Paul's fate was sealed. His mother refused to give him up, refused to await the arrival of her lawyer's letter, and reiterated, in more peremptory language, her demand that the child should be sent immediately to Paris in Mrs. Heeny's care.

Mr. Spragg, in face of Ralph's entreaties, remained pacific but remote. It was evident that, though he had no wish to quarrel with Ralph, he saw no reason for resisting Undine. "I guess she's got the law on her side," he said; and in response to Ralph's passionate remonstrances he added fatalistically: "I presume you'll have to leave the matter to my daughter."

Ralph had gone to the office resolved to control his temper and keep on the watch for any shred of information he might glean; but it soon became clear that Mr. Spragg knew as little as himself of Undine's projects, or of the stage her plans had reached. All she had apparently vouchsafed her parent was the statement that she intended to remarry, and the command to send Paul over; and Ralph reflected that his own betrothal to her had probably been announced to Mr. Spragg in the same curt fashion.

The thought brought back an overwhelming sense of the past. One by one the details of that incredible moment revived, and he felt in his veins the glow of rapture with which he had first approached the dingy threshold he was now leaving. There came back to him with peculiar vividness the memory of his rushing up to Mr. Spragg's office to consult him about a necklace for Undine. Ralph recalled the incident because his eager appeal for advice had been received by Mr. Spragg with the very phrase he had just used: "I presume you'll have to leave the matter to my daughter."

Ralph saw him slouching in his chair, swung sideways from the untidy desk, his legs stretched out, his hands in his pockets, his jaws engaged on the phantom toothpick; and, in a corner of the office, the figure of a middle-sized red-faced young man who seemed to have been interrupted in the act of saying something disagreeable.

"Why, it must have been then that I first saw Moffatt," Ralph reflected; and the thought suggested the memory of other, subsequent meetings in the same building, and of frequent ascents to Moffatt's office during the ardent weeks of their mysterious and remunerative "deal."

Ralph wondered if Moffatt's office were still in the Ararat; and on the way out he paused before the black tablet affixed to the wall of the vestibule and sought and found the name in its familiar place.

The next moment he was again absorbed in his own cares. Now that he had learned the imminence of Paul's danger, and the futility of pleading for delay, a thousand fantastic projects were contending in his head. To get the boy away—that seemed the first thing to do: to put him out of reach, and then invoke the law, get the case reopened, and carry the fight from court to court till his rights should be recognized. It would cost a lot of money—well, the money would have to be found. The first step was to secure the boy's temporary safety; after that, the question of ways and means would have to be considered. . . . Had there ever been a time, Ralph wondered, when that question hadn't been at the root of all the others?

He had promised to let Clare Van Degen know the result of his visit, and half an hour later he was in her drawing-room. It was the first time he had entered it since his divorce; but Van Degen was tarpon-fishing in California—and besides, he had to see Clare. His one relief was in talking to her, in feverishly turning over with her every possibility of delay and obstruction; and he marveled at the intelligence and energy she brought to the discussion of these questions. It was as if she had never before felt strongly enough about anything to put her heart or her brains into it; but now everything in her was at work for him.

She listened intently to what he told her; then she said: "You tell me it will cost a great deal; but why take it to the courts at all? Why not give the money to Undine instead of to your lawyers?"

Ralph looked at her in surprise, and she continued: "Why do you suppose she's suddenly made up her mind she must have Paul?"

"That's comprehensible enough to anyone who knows her. She wants him because he'll give her the appearance of respectability. Having him with her will prove, as no mere assertions can, that all the rights are on her side and the 'wrongs' on mine."

Clare considered. "Yes, that's the obvious answer. But shall I tell you what I think, my dear? You and I are both completely out-of-date. I don't believe Undine cares a straw for 'the appearance of respectability.' What she wants is the money for her annulment."

Ralph uttered an incredulous exclamation. "But don't you see?" she hurried on. "It's her only hope—her last chance. She's much too clever to burden herself with the child merely to annoy you. What she wants is to make you buy him back from her." She stood up and came to him with outstretched hands. "Perhaps I can be of use to you at last!"

"You?" He summoned up a haggard smile. "As if you weren't always—letting me load you with all my bothers!"

"Oh, if only I've hit on the way out of this one! Then there wouldn't be any others left!" Her eyes followed him intently as he turned away to the window and stood staring down at the sultry prospect of Fifth Avenue. As he turned over her conjecture its probability became more and more apparent. It put into logical relation all the incoherencies of Undine's recent conduct, completed and defined her anew as if a sharp line had been drawn about her fading image.

"If it's that, I shall soon know," he said, turning back into the room. His course had instantly become plain. He had only to resist and Undine would have to show her hand. Simultaneously with this thought there sprang up in his mind the remembrance of the autumn afternoon in Paris when he had come home and found her, among her half-packed finery, desperately bewailing her coming motherhood.

Clare's touch was on his arm. "If I'm right—you *will* let me help?"

He laid his hands on hers without speaking, and she went on:

"It will take a lot of money: all these lawsuits do. Besides, she'd be ashamed to sell him cheap. You must be ready to give her anything she wants. And I've got a lot saved up—money of my own, I mean. . . ."

"Your own?" As he looked at her the rare blush rose under her brown skin.

"My very own. Why shouldn't you believe me? I've been hoarding up my scrap of an income for years, thinking that someday I'd find I couldn't stand this any longer. . . ." Her gesture embraced their sumptuous setting. "But now I know I shall never budge. There are the children; and besides, things are easier for me since —" she paused, embarrassed.

"Yes, yes; I know." He felt like completing her phrase: "Since my wife has furnished you with the means of putting pressure on your husband —" but he simply repeated: "I know."

"And you *will* let me help?"

"Oh, we must get at the facts first." He caught her hands in his with sudden energy. "As you say, when Paul's safe there won't be another bother left!"

34

THE means of raising the requisite amount of money became, during the next few weeks, the anxious theme of all Ralph's thoughts. His lawyers' inquiries soon brought the confirmation of Clare's surmise, and it became clear that—for reasons swathed in all the ingenuities of legal verbiage—Undine might, in return for a substantial consideration, be prevailed on to admit that it was for her son's advantage to remain with his father.

The day this admission was communicated to Ralph his first impulse was to carry the news to his cousin. His mood was one of pure exaltation; he seemed to be hugging his boy to him as he walked. Paul and he were to belong to each other forever: no mysterious threat of separation could ever menace them again! He had the blissful sense of relief that the child himself might have had on waking out of a frightened dream and finding the jolly daylight in his room.

Clare at once renewed her entreaty to be allowed to aid in ransoming her little cousin, but Ralph tried to put her off by explaining that he meant to "look about."

"Look where? In the Dagonet coffers? Oh, Ralph, what's the use of pretending? Tell me what you've got to give her." It was amazing how his cousin suddenly dominated him. But as yet he couldn't go into the details of the bargain. That the reckoning between himself and Undine should be settled in dollars and cents seemed the last bitterest satire on his dreams: he felt himself miserably diminished by the smallness of what had filled his world.

Nevertheless, the looking about had to be done; and a day came when he found himself once more at the door of Elmer Moffatt's office. His thoughts had been drawn back to Moffatt by the insistence with which the latter's name had lately been put forward by the press in connection with a revival of the Ararat investigation. Moffatt, it appeared, had been regarded as one of the most valuable witnesses for the state; his return from Europe had been anxiously awaited, his unreadiness to testify caustically criticized; then at last he had arrived, had gone on to Washington—and had apparently had nothing to tell.

Ralph was too deep in his own troubles to waste any wonder over this anticlimax; but the frequent appearance of Moffatt's name in the morning papers acted as an unconscious suggestion. Besides, to whom else could he look for help? The sum his wife demanded could be acquired only by "a quick turn," and the fact that Ralph had once rendered the same kind of service to Moffatt made it natural to appeal to him now. The market, moreover, happened to be booming, and it seemed not unlikely that so experienced a speculator might have a "good thing" up his sleeve.

Moffatt's office had been transformed since Ralph's last visit. Paint, varnish and brass railings gave an air of opulence to the outer precincts, and the inner room, with its mahogany bookcases containing morocco-bound "sets" and its wide blue leather armchairs, lacked only a palm or two to resemble the lounge of a fashionable hotel. Moffatt himself, as he came forward, gave Ralph the impression of having been done over by the same hand: he was smoother, broader, more supremely tailored, and his whole person exhaled the faintest whiff of an expensive scent.

He installed his visitor in one of the blue armchairs, and sitting opposite, an elbow on his impressive "Washington" desk, listened attentively while Ralph made his request.

"You want to be put onto something good in a damned hurry?" Moffatt twisted his moustache between two plump square-tipped fingers with a little black growth on their lower joints. "I don't suppose," he remarked, "there's a sane man between here and San Francisco who isn't consumed by that yearning."

Having permitted himself this pleasantry he passed on to business. "Yes —it's a first-rate time to buy: no doubt of that. But you say you want to make a quick turnover? Heard of a soft thing that won't wait, I presume? That's apt to be the way with soft things—all kinds of 'em. There's always other fellows after them." Moffatt's smile was playful. "Well, I'd go considerably out of my way to do you a good turn, because you did me one when I needed it mighty bad. 'In youth you sheltered me.' Yes, sir, that's the kind I am." He stood up, sauntered to the other side of the room, and took a small object from the top of the bookcase.

"Fond of these pink crystals?" He held the oriental toy against the light. "Oh, I ain't a judge—but now and then I like to pick up a pretty thing." Ralph noticed that his eyes caressed it.

"Well—now let's talk. You say you've got to have the funds for your—your investment within three weeks. That's quick work. And you want a hundred thousand. Can you put up fifty?"

Ralph had been prepared for the question, but when it came he felt a moment's tremor. He knew he could count on half the amount from his grandfather; could possibly ask Fairford for a small additional loan—but what of the rest? Well, there was Clare. He had always known there would be no other way. And after all, the money was Clare's—it was Dagonet money. At least she said it was. All the misery of his predicament was distilled into the short silence that preceded his answer: "Yes—I think so."

"Well, I guess I can double it for you." Moffatt spoke with an air of Olympian modesty. "Anyhow, I'll try. Only don't tell the other girls!"

He proceeded to develop his plan to ears which Ralph tried to make alert and attentive, but in which perpetually, through the intricate concert of facts and figures, there broke the shout of a small boy racing across a suburban lawn. "When I pick him up tonight he'll be mine for good!" Ralph thought as Moffatt summed up: "There's the whole scheme in a nutshell; but you'd better think it over. I don't want to let you in for anything you ain't quite sure about."

"Oh, if you're sure—" Ralph was already calculating the time it would take to dash up to Clare Van Degen's on his way to catch the train for the Fairfords'.

His impatience made it hard to pay due regard to Moffatt's parting civilities. "Glad to have seen you," he heard the latter assuring him with a final hand-grasp. "Wish you'd dine with me some evening at my club"; and, as Ralph murmured a vague acceptance: "How's that boy of yours, by the way?" Moffatt continued. "He was a stunning chap last time I saw him. Excuse me if I've put my foot in it; but I understood you kept him with you . . . ? Yes, that's what I thought. . . . Well, so long."

Clare's inner sitting-room was empty; but the servant, presently returning, led Ralph into the gilded and tapestried wilderness where she occasionally chose to receive her visitors. There, under Popple's effigy of herself, she sat, small and alone, on a monumental sofa behind a tea-table laden with gold plate; while from his lofty frame on the opposite wall Van Degen, portrayed by a "powerful" artist, cast on her the satisfied eye of proprietorship.

Ralph, swept forward on the blast of his excitement, felt as in a dream the frivolous perversity of her receiving him in such a setting instead of in their usual quiet corner; but there was no room in his mind for anything but the cry that broke from him: "I believe I've done it!"

He sat down and explained to her by what means, trying, as best he could, to restate the particulars of Moffatt's deal; and her manifest ignorance of business methods had the effect of making his vagueness appear less vague.

"Anyhow, he seems to be sure it's a safe thing. I understand he's in with Rolliver now, and Rolliver practically controls Apex. This is some kind of a scheme to buy up all the works of public utility at Apex. They're practically sure of their charter, and Moffatt tells me I can count on doubling my investment within a few weeks. Of course I'll go into the details if you like—"

"Oh, no; you've made it all so clear to me!" She really made him feel he had. "And besides, what on earth does it matter? The great thing is that it's done." She lifted her sparkling eyes. "And now—my share—you haven't told me. . . ."

He explained that Mr. Dagonet, to whom he had already named the amount demanded, had at once promised him twenty-five thousand dollars, to be eventually deducted from his share of the estate. His mother had something put by that she insisted on contributing; and Henley Fairford, of his own accord, had come forward with ten thousand: it was awfully decent of Henley. . . .

"Even Henley!" Clare sighed. "Then I'm the only one left out?"

Ralph felt the color in his face. "Well, you see, I shall need as much as fifty —"

Her hands flew together joyfully. "But then you've got to let me help! Oh, I'm so glad—so glad! I've twenty thousand waiting."

He looked about the room, checked anew by all its oppressive implications. "You're a darling . . . but I couldn't take it."

"I've told you it's mine, every penny of it!"

"Yes, but supposing things went wrong?"

"Nothing *can*—if you'll only take it. . . ."

"I may lose it —"

"*I* sha'n't, if I've given it to you!" Her look followed his about the room and then came back to him. "Can't you imagine all it will make up for?"

The rapture of the cry caught him up with it. Ah, yes, he could imagine it all! He stooped his head above her hands. "I accept," he said; and they stood and looked at each other like radiant children.

She followed him to the door, and as he turned to leave he broke into a laugh. "It's queer, though, its happening in this room!"

She was close beside him, her hand on the heavy tapestry curtaining the door; and her glance shot past him to her husband's portrait. Ralph caught the look, and a flood of old tendernesses and hates welled up in him. He drew her under the portrait and kissed her vehemently.

35

WITHIN forty-eight hours Ralph's money was in Moffatt's hands, and the interval of suspense had begun.

The transaction over, he felt the deceptive buoyancy that follows on periods of painful indecision. It seemed to him that now at last life had freed him from all trammeling delusions, leaving him only the best thing in its gift—his boy.

The things he meant Paul to do and to be filled his fancy with happy pictures. The child was growing more and more interesting—throwing out countless tendrils of feeling and perception that delighted Ralph but preoccupied the watchful Laura.

"He's going to be exactly like you, Ralph —" she paused and then risked it: "For his own sake, I wish there were just a drop or two of Spragg in him."

Ralph laughed, understanding her. "Oh, the plodding citizen I've become will keep him from taking after the lyric idiot who begot him. Paul and I, between us, are going to turn out something first-rate."

His book too was spreading and throwing out tendrils, and he worked at it in the white heat of energy which his factitious exhilaration produced. For a few weeks everything he did and said seemed as easy and unconditioned as the actions in a dream.

Clare Van Degen, in the light of this mood, became again the comrade of his boyhood. He did not see her often, for she had gone down to the country with her children, but they communicated daily by letter or telephone, and now and then she came over to the Fairfords' for a night. There they renewed the long rambles of their youth, and once more the summer fields and woods seemed full of magic presences. Clare was no more intelligent, she followed him no farther in his flights; but some of the qualities that had become most precious to him were as native to her as its perfume to a flower. So, through the long June afternoons, they ranged together over many themes; and if her answers sometimes missed the mark it did not matter, because her silences never did.

Meanwhile Ralph, from various sources, continued to pick up a good deal of more or less contradictory information about Elmer Moffatt. It seemed to be generally understood that Moffatt had come back from Europe with the intention of testifying in the Ararat investigation, and that his former patron, the great Harmon B. Driscoll, had managed to silence him; and it was implied that the price of this silence, which was set at a considerable figure, had been turned to account in a series of speculations likely to lift Moffatt to permanent eminence among the rulers of Wall Street. The stories as to his latest achievement, and the theories as to the man himself, varied with the visual angle of each reporter: and whenever any attempt was made to focus his hard sharp personality some guardian divinity seemed to throw a veil of mystery over him. His detractors, however, were the first to own that there was "something about him"; it was felt that he had passed beyond the meteoric stage, and the business world was unanimous in recognizing that he had "come to stay." A dawning sense of his stability was even beginning to make itself felt in Fifth Avenue. It was said that he had bought a house in Seventy-second Street, then that he meant to build near the Park; one or two people (always "taken by a friend") had been to his flat in the Pactolus, to see his Chinese porcelains and Persian rugs; now and then he had a few important men to dine at a Fifth Avenue restaurant; his name began to appear in philanthropic reports and on municipal committees (there were even rumors of its having been put up at a well-known club); and the rector of a wealthy parish, who was raising funds for a chantry, was known to have met him at dinner and to have stated afterward that "the man was not wholly a materialist."

All these converging proofs of Moffatt's solidity strengthened Ralph's faith in his venture. He remembered with what astuteness and authority Moffatt had conducted their real estate transaction—how far off and unreal it all seemed!—and awaited events with the passive faith of a sufferer in the hands of a skillful surgeon.

The days moved on toward the end of June, and each morning Ralph opened his newspaper with a keener thrill of expectation. Any day now he might read of the granting of the Apex charter: Moffatt had assured him it would "go through" before the close of the month. But the announcement did not appear, and after what seemed to Ralph a decent lapse of time he telephoned to ask for news. Moffatt was away, and when he came back a few days later he answered Ralph's inquiries evasively, with an edge of irritation in his voice. The same day Ralph received a letter from his lawyer, who had been reminded by Mrs. Marvell's representatives that the latest date agreed on for the execution of the financial agreement was the end of the following week.

Ralph, alarmed, betook himself at once to the Ararat, and his first glimpse of Moffatt's round common face and fastidiously dressed person gave him an immediate sense of reassurance. He felt that under the circle of baldness on top of that carefully brushed head lay the solution of every monetary problem that could beset the soul of man. Moffatt's voice had recovered its usual cordial note, and the warmth of his welcome dispelled Ralph's last apprehension.

"Why, yes, everything's going along first-rate. They thought they'd hung us up last week—but they haven't. There may be another week's delay; but we ought to be opening a bottle of wine on it by the Fourth."

An office-boy came in with a name on a slip of paper, and Moffatt looked at his watch and held out a hearty hand. "Glad you came. Of course I'll keep you posted. . . . No, this way . . . look in again . . ." and he steered Ralph out by another door.

July came, and passed into its second week. Ralph's lawyer had obtained a postponement from the other side, but Undine's representatives had given him to understand that the transaction must be closed before the first of August. Ralph telephoned once or twice to Moffatt, receiving genially worded assurances that everything was "going their way"; but he felt a certain embarrassment in returning again to the office, and let himself drift through the days in a state of hungry apprehension. Finally one afternoon Henley Fairford, coming back from town (which Ralph had left in the morning to join his boy over Sunday), brought word that the Apex consolidation scheme had failed to get its charter. It was useless to attempt to reach Moffatt on Sunday, and Ralph wore on as he could through the succeeding twenty-four hours. Clare Van Degen had come down to stay with her youngest boy, and in the afternoon she and Ralph took the two children for a sail. A light breeze brightened the waters of the Sound, and they ran down the shore before it and then tacked out toward the sunset, coming back at last, under a failing breeze, as the summer sky passed from blue to a translucid green and then into the accumulating grays of twilight.

As they left the landing and walked up behind the children across the darkening lawn, a sense of security descended again on Ralph. He could not believe that such a scene and such a mood could be the disguise of any impending evil, and all his doubts and anxieties fell away from him.

The next morning, he and Clare traveled up to town together, and at the station he put her in the motor which was to take her to Long Island, and hastened down to Moffatt's office. When he arrived he was told that Moffatt was "engaged," and he had to wait for nearly half an hour in the outer office, where, to the steady click of the typewriter and the spasmodic buzzing of the telephone, his thoughts again began their restless circlings. Finally the inner door opened, and he found himself in the sanctuary. Moffatt was seated behind his desk, examining another little crystal vase somewhat like the one he had shown Ralph a few weeks earlier. As his visitor entered, he held it up against the light, revealing on its dewy sides an incised design as frail as the shadow of grass-blades on water.

"Ain't she a peach?" He put the toy down and reached across the desk to shake hands. "Well, well," he went on, leaning back in his chair, and pushing out his lower lip in a half-comic pout, "they've got us in the neck this time and no mistake. Seen this morning's *Radiator?* I don't know how the thing leaked out—but the reformers somehow got a smell of the scheme, and whenever they get swishing round something's bound to get spilt."

He talked gaily, genially, in his roundest tones and with his easiest gestures; never had he conveyed a completer sense of unhurried power; but Ralph noticed for the first time the crow's-feet about his eyes, and the sharpness of the contrast between the white of his forehead and the redness of the fold of neck above his collar.

"Do you mean to say it's not going through?"

"Not this time, anyhow. We're high and dry."

Something seemed to snap in Ralph's head, and he sat down in the nearest chair. "Has the common stock dropped a lot?"

"Well, you've got to lean over to see it." Moffatt pressed his fingertips together and added thoughtfully: "But it's *there* all right. We're bound to get our charter in the end."

"What do you call the end?"

"Oh, before the Day of Judgment, sure: next year, I guess."

"Next year?" Ralph flushed. "What earthly good will that do me?"

"I don't say it's as pleasant as driving your best girl home by moonlight. But that's how it is. And the stuff's safe enough any way—I've told you that right along."

"But you've told me all along I could count on a rise before August. You knew I had to have the money now."

"I knew you *wanted* to have the money now; and so did I, and several of my friends. I put you onto it because it was the only thing in sight likely to give you the return you wanted."

"You ought at least to have warned me of the risk!"

"Risk? I don't call it much of a risk to lie back in your chair and wait another few months for fifty thousand to drop into your lap. I tell you the thing's as safe as a bank."

"How do I know it is? You've misled me about it from the first."

Moffatt's face grew dark red to the forehead: for the first time in their acquaintance Ralph saw him on the verge of anger.

"Well, if you get stuck so do I. I'm in it a good deal deeper than you. That's about the best guarantee I can give; unless you won't take my word for that either." To control himself Moffatt spoke with extreme deliberation, separating his syllables like a machine cutting something into even lengths.

Ralph listened through a cloud of confusion; but he saw the madness of offending Moffatt, and tried to take a more conciliatory tone. "Of course I take your word for it. But I can't—I simply can't afford to lose. . . ."

"You ain't going to lose: I don't believe you'll even have to put up any margin. It's *there* safe enough, I tell you. . . ."

"Yes, yes, I understand. I'm sure you wouldn't have advised me —" Ralph's tongue seemed swollen, and he had difficulty in bringing out the words. "Only, you see—I can't wait; it's not possible; and I want to know if there isn't a way —"

Moffatt looked at him with a sort of resigned compassion, as a doctor looks at a despairing mother who will not understand what he has tried to imply without uttering the word she dreads. Ralph understood the look, but hurried on.

"You'll think I'm mad, or an ass, to talk like this; but the fact is, I must have the money." He waited and drew a hard breath. "I must have it: that's all. Perhaps I'd better tell you —"

Moffatt, who had risen, as if assuming that the interview was over, sat down again and turned an attentive look on him. "Go ahead," he said, more humanly than he had hitherto spoken.

"My boy . . . you spoke of him the other day . . . I'm awfully fond of him —" Ralph broke off, deterred by the impossibility of confiding his feeling for Paul to this coarse-grained man with whom he hadn't a sentiment in common.

Moffatt was still looking at him. "I should say you would be! He's as smart a little chap as I ever saw; and I guess he's the kind that gets better every day."

Ralph had collected himself, and went on with sudden resolution: "Well, you see—when my wife and I separated, I never dreamed she'd want the boy: the question never came up. If it had, of course—but she'd left him with me when she went away two years before, and at the time of the divorce I was a fool. . . . I didn't take the proper steps. . . ."

"You mean she's got sole custody?"

Ralph made a sign of assent, and Moffatt pondered. "That's bad—bad."

"And now I understand she's going to marry again—and of course I can't give up my son."

"She wants you to, eh?"

Ralph again assented.

Moffatt swung his chair about and leaned back in it, stretching out his plump legs and contemplating the tips of his varnished boots. He hummed a low tune behind inscrutable lips.

"That's what you want the money for?" he finally raised his head to ask.

The word came out of the depths of Ralph's anguish: "Yes."

"And why you want it in such a hurry. I see." Moffatt reverted to the study of his boots. "It's a lot of money."

"Yes. That's the difficulty. And I . . . she. . . ."

Ralph's tongue was again too thick for his mouth. "I'm afraid she won't wait . . . or take less. . . ."

Moffatt, abandoning the boots, was scrutinizing him through half-shut lids. "No," he said slowly, "I don't believe Undine Spragg'll take a single cent less."

Ralph felt himself whiten. Was it insolence or ignorance that had prompted Moffatt's speech? Nothing in his voice or face showed the sense of any shades of expression or of feeling: he seemed to apply to everything the measure of the same crude flippancy. But such considerations could not curb Ralph now. He said to himself "Keep your temper—keep your temper —" and his anger suddenly boiled over.

"Look here, Moffatt," he said, getting to his feet, "the fact that I've been divorced from Mrs. Marvell doesn't authorize anyone to take that tone to me in speaking of her."

Moffatt met the challenge with a calm stare under which there were dawning signs of surprise and interest. "That so? Well, if that's the case I presume I ought to feel the same way: I've been divorced from her myself."

For an instant the words conveyed no meaning to Ralph; then they surged up into his brain and flung him forward with half-raised arm. But he felt the grotesqueness of the gesture and his arm dropped back to his side. A series of unimportant and irrelevant things raced through his mind; then obscurity settled down on it. *"This* man . . . *this* man . . ." was the one fiery point in his darkened consciousness. . . ."What on earth are you talking about?" he brought out.

"Why, facts," said Moffatt, in a cool half-humorous voice. "You didn't know? I understood from Mrs. Marvell your folks had a prejudice against divorce, so I suppose she kept quiet about that early episode. The truth is," he continued amicably, "I wouldn't have alluded to it now if you hadn't taken rather a high tone with me about our little venture; but now it's out I guess you may as well hear the whole story. It's mighty wholesome for a man to have a round now and then with a few facts. Shall I go on?"

Ralph had stood listening without a sign, but as Moffatt ended he made a slight motion of acquiescence. He did not otherwise change his attitude, except to grasp with one hand the back of the chair that Moffatt pushed toward him.

"Rather stand . . . ?" Moffatt himself dropped back into his seat and took the pose of easy narrative. "Well, it was this way. Undine Spragg and I were made one at Opake, Nebraska, just nine years ago last month. My! She was a beauty then. Nothing much had happened to her before but being engaged for a year or two to a soft called Millard Binch; the same she passed on to Indiana Rolliver; and—well, I guess she liked the change. We didn't have what you'd called a society wedding: no best man or bridesmaids or Voice that Breathed o'er Eden. Fact is, Pa and Ma didn't know about it till it was over. But it was a marriage fast enough, as they found out when they tried to undo it. Trouble was, they caught on too soon; we only had a fortnight. Then they hauled Undine back to Apex, and—well, I hadn't the cash or the pull to fight 'em. Uncle Abner was a pretty big man out there then; and he had James J. Rolliver behind him. I always know when I'm licked; and I was licked that time. So we unlooped the loop, and they fixed it up for me to make a trip to Alaska. Let me see—that was the year before they moved over to New York. Next time I saw Undine I sat alongside of her at the theater the day your engagement was announced."

He still kept to his half-humorous minor key, as though he were in the first stages of an after-dinner speech; but as he went on his bodily presence, which hitherto had seemed to Ralph the mere average garment of vulgarity, began to loom, huge and portentous as some monster released from a magician's bottle. His redness, his glossiness, his baldness, and the carefully brushed ring of hair encircling it; the square line of his shoulders, the too careful fit of his clothes, the prominent luster of his scarf-pin, the growth of short black hair on his manicured hands, even the tiny cracks and crows'-feet beginning to show in the hard close surface of his complexion: all these solid witnesses to his reality and his proximity pressed on Ralph with the mounting pang of physical nausea.

"*This* man . . . *this* man . . ." he couldn't get beyond the thought: whichever way he turned his haggard thought, there was Moffatt bodily blocking the perspective. . . . Ralph's eyes roamed toward the crystal toy that stood on the desk beside Moffatt's hand. Faugh! That such a hand should have touched it!

Suddenly he heard himself speaking. "Before my marriage—did you know they hadn't told me?"

"Why, I understood as much. . . ."

Ralph pushed on: "You knew it the day I met you in Mr. Spragg's office?"

Moffatt considered a moment, as if the incident had escaped him. "Did we meet there?" He seemed benevolently ready for enlightenment. But Ralph had been assailed by another memory; he recalled that Moffatt had dined one night in his house, that he and the man who now faced him had sat at the same table, their wife between them. . . .

He was seized with another dumb gust of fury; but it died out and left him face to face with the uselessness, the irrelevance of all the old attitudes of appropriation and defiance. He seemed to be stumbling about in his inherited prejudices like a modern man in medieval armor. . . . Moffatt still sat at his desk, unmoved and apparently uncomprehending. "He doesn't even know what I'm feeling," flashed through Ralph; and the whole archaic structure of his rites and sanctions tumbled down about him.

Through the noise of the crash he heard Moffatt's voice going on without perceptible change of tone: "About that other matter now . . . you can't feel any meaner about it than I do, I can tell you that . . . but all we've got to do is to sit tight. . . ."

Ralph turned from the voice, and found himself outside on the landing, and then in the street below.

36

H E stood at the corner of Wall Street, looking up and down its hot summer perspective. He noticed the swirls of dust in the cracks of the pavement, the rubbish in the gutters, the ceaseless stream of perspiring faces that poured by under tilted hats.

He found himself, next, slipping northward between the glazed walls of the subway, another languid crowd in the seats about him and the nasal yelp of the stations ringing through the car like some repeated ritual wail. The blindness within him seemed to have intensified his physical perceptions, his sensitiveness to the heat, the noise, the smells of the disheveled mid-summer city; but combined with the acuter perception of these offenses was a complete indifference to them, as though he were some vivisected animal deprived of the power of discrimination.

Now he had turned into Waverly Place, and was walking westward toward Washington Square. At the corner he pulled himself up, saying half-aloud: "The office—I ought to be at the office." He drew out his watch and stared at it blankly. What the devil had he taken it out for? He had to go through a laborious process of readjustment to find out what it had to say. . . . Twelve o'clock. . . . Should he turn back to the office? It seemed easier to cross the square, go up the steps of the old house and slip his key into the door. . . .

The house was empty. His mother, a few days previously, had departed with Mr. Dagonet for their usual two months on the Maine coast, where Ralph was to join them with his boy. . . . The blinds were all drawn down, and the freshness and silence of the marble-paved hall laid soothing hands on him. . . . He said to himself: "I'll jump into a cab presently, and go and lunch at the club—" He laid down his hat and stick and climbed the carpetless stairs to his room. When he entered it he had the shock of feeling himself in a strange place: it did not seem like anything he had ever seen before. Then, one by one, all the old stale usual things in it confronted him, and he longed with a sick intensity to be in a place that was really strange.

"How on earth can I go on living here?" he wondered.

A careless servant had left the outer shutters open, and the sun was beating on the window-panes. Ralph pushed open the windows, shut the shutters, and wandered toward his armchair. Beads of perspiration stood on his forehead: the temperature of the room reminded him of the heat under the ilexes of the Sienese villa where he and Undine had sat through a long

July afternoon. He saw her before him, leaning against the tree trunk in her white dress, limpid and inscrutable. . . . "We were made one at Opake, Nebraska. . . ." Had she been thinking of it that afternoon at Siena, he wondered? Did she ever think of it at all? . . . It was she who had asked Moffatt to dine. She had said: "Father brought him home one day at Apex. . . . I don't remember ever having seen him since"—and the man she spoke of had had her in his arms . . . and perhaps it was really all she remembered!

She had lied to him—lied to him from the first . . . there hadn't been a moment when she hadn't lied to him, deliberately, ingeniously and inventively. As he thought of it, there came to him, for the first time in months, that overwhelming sense of her physical nearness which had once so haunted and tortured him. Her freshness, her fragrance, the luminous haze of her youth, filled the room with a mocking glory; and he dropped his head on his hands to shut it out. . . .

The vision was swept away by another wave of hurrying thoughts. He felt it was intensely important that he should keep the thread of every one of them, that they all represented things to be said or done, or guarded against; and his mind, with the unwondering versatility and tireless haste of the dreamer's brain, seemed to be pursuing them all simultaneously. Then they became as unreal and meaningless as the red specks dancing behind the lids against which he had pressed his fists clenched, and he had the feeling that if he opened his eyes they would vanish, and the familiar daylight look in on him. . . .

A knock disturbed him. The old parlor maid who was always left in charge of the house had come up to ask if he wasn't well, and if there was anything she could do for him. He told her no . . . he was perfectly well . . . or, rather, no, he wasn't . . . he supposed it must be the heat; and he began to scold her for having forgotten to close the shutters.

It wasn't her fault, it appeared, but Eliza's: her tone implied that he knew what one had to expect of Eliza . . . and wouldn't he go down to the nice cool shady dining-room, and let her make him an iced drink and a few sandwiches?

"I've always told Mrs. Marvell I couldn't turn my back for a second but what Eliza'd find a way to make trouble," the old woman continued, evidently glad of the chance to air a perennial grievance. "It's not only the things she *forgets* to do," she added significantly; and it dawned on Ralph that she was making an appeal to him, expecting him to take sides with her in the chronic conflict between herself and Eliza. He said to himself that perhaps she was right . . . that perhaps there was something he ought to do . . . that his mother was old, and didn't always see things; and for a while his mind revolved this problem with feverish intensity. . . .

"Then you'll come down, sir?"

"Yes."

The door closed, and he heard her heavy heels along the passage.

"But the money—where's the money to come from?" The question sprang out from some denser fold of the fog in his brain. The money—how on earth was he to pay it back? How could he have wasted his time in thinking of anything else while that central difficulty existed?

"But I can't . . . I can't . . . it's gone . . . and even if it weren't. . . ." He dropped back in his chair and took his head between his hands. He had forgotten what he wanted the money for. He made a great effort to regain hold of the idea, but all the whirring, shuttling, flying had abruptly ceased in his brain, and he sat with his eyes shut, staring straight into darkness. . . .

The clock struck, and he remembered that he had said he would go down to the dining-room. "If I don't she'll come up —" He raised his head and sat listening for the sound of the old woman's step: it seemed to him perfectly intolerable that anyone should cross the threshold of the room again.

"Why can't they leave me alone?" he groaned. . . . At length through the silence of the empty house, he fancied he heard a door opening and closing far below; and he said to himself: "She's coming."

He got to his feet and went to the door. He didn't feel anything now except the insane dread of hearing the woman's steps come nearer. He bolted the door and stood looking about the room. For a moment he was conscious of seeing it in every detail with a distinctness he had never before known; then everything in it vanished but the single narrow panel of a drawer under one of the bookcases. He went up to the drawer, knelt down and slipped his hand into it.

As he raised himself he listened again, and this time he distinctly heard the old servant's steps on the stairs. He passed his left hand over the side of his head, and down the curve of the skull behind the ear. He said to himself: "My wife . . . this will make it all right for her . . ." and a last flash of irony twitched through him. Then he felt again, more deliberately, for the spot he wanted, and put the muzzle of his revolver against it.

Book Five

37

I N a drawing-room hung with portraits of high-nosed personages in pe-
rukes and orders, a circle of ladies and gentlemen, looking not unlike
everyday versions of the official figures above their heads, sat examining
with friendly interest a little boy in mourning.

The boy was slim, fair and shy, and his small black figure, islanded in the
middle of the wide lustrous floor, looked curiously lonely and remote. This
effect of remoteness seemed to strike his mother as something intentional,
and almost naughty, for after having launched him from the door, and
waited to judge of the impression he produced, she came forward and, giving
him a slight push, said impatiently: "Paul! Why don't you go and kiss your
new granny?"

The boy, without turning to her, or moving, sent his blue glance gravely
about the circle. "Does she want me to?" he asked, in a tone of evident
apprehension; and on his mother's answering: "Of course, you silly!" he
added earnestly: "How many more do you think there'll be?"

Undine blushed to the ripples of her brilliant hair. "I never knew such a
child! They've turned him into a perfect little savage!"

Raymond de Chelles advanced from behind his mother's chair.

"He won't be a savage long with me," he said, stooping down so that his
fatigued finely drawn face was close to Paul's. Their eyes met and the boy
smiled. "Come along, old chap," Chelles continued in English, drawing the
little boy after him.

"Il est bien beau," the Marquise de Chelles observed, her eyes turning
from Paul's grave face to her daughter-in-law's vivid countenance.

"Do be nice, darling! Say, 'Bonjour, madame,' " Undine urged.

An odd mingling of emotions stirred in her while she stood watching
Paul make the round of the family group under her husband's guidance. It
was "lovely" to have the child back, and to find him, after their three years'
separation, grown into so endearing a figure: her first glimpse of him when,
in Mrs. Heeny's arms, he had emerged that morning from the steamer train,
had shown what an acquisition he would be. If she had had any lingering
doubts on the point, the impression produced on her husband would have
dispelled them. Chelles had been instantly charmed, and Paul, in a shy
confused way, was already responding to his advances. The Count and

Countess Raymond had returned but a few weeks before from their pro--
tracted wedding journey, and were staying—as they were apparently to do
whenever they came to Paris—with the old marquis, Raymond's father, who
had amicably proposed that little Paul Marvell should also share the hospitality of the Hôtel de Chelles. Undine, at first, was somewhat dismayed to
find that she was expected to fit the boy and his nurse into a corner of her
contracted *entresol*. But the possibility of a mother's not finding room for
her son, however cramped her own quarters, seemed not to have occurred to
her new relations, and the preparing of her dressing-room and boudoir for
Paul's occupancy was carried on by the household with a zeal which obliged
her to dissemble her lukewarmness.

Undine had supposed that on her marriage one of the great suites of the
Hôtel de Chelles would be emptied of its tenants and put at her husband's
disposal; but she had since learned that, even had such a plan occurred to
her parents-in-law, considerations of economy would have hindered it. The
old marquis and his wife, who were content, when they came up from
Burgundy in the spring, with a modest set of rooms looking out on the court
of their ancestral residence, expected their son and his wife to fit themselves
into the still smaller apartment which had served as Raymond's bachelor
lodging. The rest of the fine old moldering house—the tall-windowed *premier* on the garden, and the whole of the floor above—had been let for years
to old-fashioned tenants who would have been more surprised than their
landlord had he suddenly proposed to dispossess them. Undine, at first, had
regarded these arrangements as merely provisional. She was persuaded that,
under her influence, Raymond would soon convert his parents to more
modern ideas, and meanwhile she was still in the flush of a completer well-
being than she had ever known, and disposed, for the moment, to make
light of any inconveniences connected with it. The three months since her
marriage had been more nearly like what she had dreamed of than any of
her previous experiments in happiness. At last she had what she wanted,
and for the first time the glow of triumph was warmed by a deeper feeling.
Her husband was really charming (it was odd how he reminded her of
Ralph!), and after her bitter two years of loneliness and humiliation it was
delicious to find herself once more adored and protected.

The very fact that Raymond was more jealous of her than Ralph had
ever been—or at any rate less reluctant to show it—gave her a keener sense
of recovered power. None of the men who had been in love with her before
had been so frankly possessive, or so eager for reciprocal assurances of constancy. She knew that Ralph had suffered deeply from her intimacy with
Van Degen, but he had betrayed his feeling only by a more studied detachment; and Van Degen, from the first, had been contemptuously indifferent
to what she did or felt when she was out of his sight. As to her earlier
experiences, she had frankly forgotten them: her sentimental memories
went back no further than the beginning of her New York career.

Raymond seemed to attach more importance to love, in all its manifestations, than was usual or convenient in a husband; and she gradually began to be aware that her domination over him involved a corresponding loss of independence. Since their return to Paris she had found that she was expected to give a circumstantial report of every hour she spent away from him. She had nothing to hide, and no designs against his peace of mind except those connected with her frequent and costly sessions at the dressmakers'; but she had never before been called upon to account to anyone for the use of her time, and after the first amused surprise at Raymond's always wanting to know where she had been and whom she had seen she began to be oppressed by so exacting a devotion. Her parents, from her tenderest youth, had tacitly recognized her inalienable right to "go around," and Ralph—though from motives which she divined to be different—had shown the same respect for her freedom. It was therefore disconcerting to find that Raymond expected her to choose her friends, and even her acquaintances, in conformity not only with his personal tastes but with a definite and complicated code of family prejudices and traditions; and she was especially surprised to discover that he viewed with disapproval her intimacy with the princess Estradina.

"My cousin's extremely amusing, of course, but utterly mad and very *mal entourée*. Most of the people she has about her ought to be in prison or Bedlam: especially that unspeakable Madame Adelschein, who's a candidate for both. My aunt's an angel, but she's been weak enough to let Lili turn the Hôtel de Dordogne into an annex of Montmartre. Of course, you'll have to show yourself there now and then: in these days families like ours must hold together. But go to the *réunions de famille* rather than to Lili's intimate parties; go with me, or with my mother; don't let yourself be seen there alone. You're too young and good-looking to be mixed up with that crew. A woman's classed—or rather unclassed—by being known as one of Lili's set."

Agreeable as it was to Undine that an appeal to her discretion should be based on the ground of her youth and good looks, she was dismayed to find herself cut off from the very circle she had meant them to establish her in. Before she had become Raymond's wife there had been a moment of sharp tension in her relations with the princess Estradina and the old duchess. They had done their best to prevent her marrying their cousin, and had gone so far as openly to accuse her of being the cause of a breach between themselves and his parents. But Ralph Marvell's death had brought about a sudden change in her situation. She was now no longer a divorced woman struggling to obtain ecclesiastical sanction for her remarriage, but a widow whose conspicuous beauty and independent situation made her the object of lawful aspirations. The first person to seize on this distinction and make the most of it was her old enemy the Marquise de Trézac. The latter, who had been loudly charged by the house of Chelles with furthering her beautiful compatriot's designs, had instantly seen a chance of vindicating herself by taking the widowed Mrs. Marvell under her wing and favoring the attentions of other suitors. These were not lacking, and the expected result had followed. Raymond de Chelles, more than ever infatuated as attainment became less certain, had claimed a definite promise from Undine, and his family, discouraged by his persistent bachelorhood, and their failure to fix his attention on any of the amiable maidens obviously designed to continue the race, had ended by withdrawing their opposition and discovering in Mrs. Marvell the moral and financial merits necessary to justify their change of front.

"A good match? If she isn't, I should like to know what the Chelles call one!" Madame de Trézac went about indefatigably proclaiming. "Related to the best people in New York—well, by marriage, that is; and her husband left much more money than was expected. It goes to the boy, of course; but as the boy is with his mother she naturally enjoys the income. And her father's a rich man—much richer than is generally known; I mean what *we* call rich in America, you understand!"

Madame de Trézac had lately discovered that the proper attitude for the American married abroad was that of a militant patriotism; and she flaunted Undine Marvell in the face of the Faubourg like a particularly showy specimen of her national banner. The success of the experiment emboldened her to throw off the most sacred observances of her past. She took up Madame Adelschein, she entertained the James J. Rollivers, she resuscitated Creole dishes, she patronized Negro melodists, she abandoned her weekly teas for impromptu afternoon dances, and the prim drawing-room in which dowagers had droned echoed with a cosmopolitan hubbub.

Even when the period of tension was over, and Undine had been officially received into the family of her betrothed, Madame de Trézac did not at once surrender. She laughingly professed to have had enough of the proprieties, and declared herself bored by the social rites she had hitherto so piously performed. "You'll always find a corner of home here, dearest, when you get tired of their ceremonies and solemnities," she said as she embraced the bride after the wedding breakfast; and Undine hoped that the devoted Nettie would in fact provide a refuge from the extreme domesticity of her new state. But since her return to Paris, and her taking up her domicile in the Hôtel de Chelles, she had found Madame de Trézac less and less disposed to abet her in any assertion of independence.

"My dear, a woman must adopt her husband's nationality whether she wants to or not. It's the law, and it's the custom besides. If you wanted to amuse yourself with your Nouveau Luxe friends you oughtn't to have married Raymond—but of course I say that only in joke. As if any woman would have hesitated who'd had your chance! Take my advice—keep out of Lili's set just at first. Later . . . well, perhaps Raymond won't be so particular; but meanwhile you'd make a great mistake to go against his people —"

and Madame de Trézac, with a *"Chère Madame,"* swept forward from her tea-table to receive the first of the returning dowagers.

It was about this time that Mrs. Heeny arrived with Paul; and for a while Undine was pleasantly absorbed in her boy. She kept Mrs. Heeny in Paris for a fortnight, and between her more pressing occupations it amused her to listen to the masseuse's New York gossip and her comments on the social organization of the old world. It was Mrs. Heeny's first visit to Europe, and she confessed to Undine that she had always wanted to "see something of the aristocracy"—using the phrase as a naturalist might, with no hint of personal pretensions. Mrs. Heeny's democratic ease was combined with the strictest professional discretion, and it would never have occurred to her to regard herself, or to wish others to regard her, as anything but a manipulator of muscles; but in that character she felt herself entitled to admission to the highest circles.

"They certainly do things with style over here—but it's kinder one-horse after New York, ain't it? Is this what they call their season? Why, you dined home two nights last week. They ought to come over to New York and see!" And she poured into Undine's half-envious ear a list of the enter-tainments which had illuminated the last weeks of the New York winter. "I suppose you'll begin to give parties as soon as ever you get into a house of your own. You're not going to have one? Oh, well, then you'll give a lot of big weekends at your place down in the Shatter-country—that's where the swells all go to in the summer time, ain't it? But I dunno what your ma would say if she knew you were going to live on with *his* folks after you're done honeymooning. Why, we read in the papers you were going to live in some grand hotel or other—oh, they call their houses *hotels*, do they? That's funny: I suppose it's because they let out part of 'em. Well, you look hand-somer than ever, Undine; I'll take *that* back to your mother, anyhow. And he's dead in love, I can see that; reminds me of the way —" but she broke off suddenly, as if something in Undine's look had silenced her.

Even to herself, Undine did not like to call up the image of Ralph Marvell; and any mention of his name gave her a vague sense of distress. His death had released her, had given her what she wanted; yet she could honestly say to herself that she had not wanted him to die—at least not to die like that. . . . People said at the time that it was the hot weather—his own family had said so: he had never quite got over his attack of pneumo-nia, and the sudden rise of temperature—one of the fierce "heat-waves" that devastate New York in summer—had probably affected his brain: the doc-tors said such cases were not uncommon. . . . She had worn black for a few weeks—not quite mourning, but something decently regretful (the dressmakers were beginning to provide a special garb for such cases); and even since her remarriage, and the lapse of a year, she continued to wish that she could have got what she wanted without having had to pay that particular price for it.

This feeling was intensified by an incident—in itself far from unwelcome—which had occurred about three months after Ralph's death. Her lawyers had written to say that the sum of a hundred thousand dollars had been paid over to Marvell's estate by the Apex Consolidation Company; and as Marvell had left a will bequeathing everything he possessed to his son, this unexpected windfall handsomely increased Paul's patrimony. Undine had never relinquished her claim on her child; she had merely, by the advice of her lawyers, waived the assertion of her right for a few months after Marvell's death, with the express stipulation that her doing so was only a temporary concession to the feelings of her husband's family; and she had held out against all attempts to induce her to surrender Paul permanently. Before her marriage she had somewhat conspicuously adopted her husband's creed, and the Dagonets, picturing Paul as the prey of the Jesuits, had made the mistake of appealing to the courts for his custody. This had confirmed Undine's resistance, and her determination to keep the child. The case had been decided in her favor, and she had thereupon demanded, and obtained, an allowance of five thousand dollars, to be devoted to the bringing up and education of her son. This sum, added to what Mr. Spragg had agreed to give her, made up an income which had appreciably bettered her position, and justified Madame de Trézac's discreet allusions to her wealth. Nevertheless, it was one of the facts about which she least liked to think when any chance allusion evoked Ralph's image. The money was hers, of course; she had a right to it, and she was an ardent believer in "rights." But she wished she could have got it in some other way—she hated the thought of it as one more instance of the perverseness with which things she was entitled to always came to her as if they had been stolen.

The approach of summer, and the culmination of the Paris season, swept aside such thoughts. The Countess Raymond de Chelles, contrasting her situation with that of Mrs. Undine Marvell, and the fullness and animation of her new life with the vacant dissatisfied days which had followed on her return from Dakota, forgot the smallness of her apartment, the inconvenient proximity of Paul and his nurse, the interminable round of visits with her mother-in-law, and the long dinners in the solemn hotels of all the family connection. The world was radiant, the lights were lit, the music playing; she was still young, and better-looking than ever, with a countess's coronet, a famous château and a handsome and popular husband who adored her. And then suddenly the lights went out and the music stopped when one day Raymond, putting his arm about her, said in his tenderest tones: "And now, my dear, the world's had you long enough and it's my turn. What do you say to going down to Saint Désert?"

38

I N a window of the long gallery of the château de Saint Désert the new
Marquise de Chelles stood looking down the poplar avenue into the
November rain. It had been raining heavily and persistently for a longer
time than she could remember. Day after day the hills beyond the park had
been curtained by motionless clouds, the gutters of the long steep roofs had
gurgled with a perpetual overflow, the opaque surface of the moat been
peppered by a continuous pelting of big drops. The water lay in glassy
stretches under the trees and along the sodden edges of the garden-paths, it
rose in a white mist from the fields beyond, it exuded in a chill moisture
from the brick flooring of the passages and from the walls of the rooms on
the lower floor. Everything in the great empty house smelt of dampness: the
stuffing of the chairs, the threadbare folds of the faded curtains, the splendid
tapestries, that were fading, too, on the walls of the room in which Undine
stood, and the wide bands of crape which her husband had insisted on her
keeping on her black dresses till the last hour of her mourning for the old
marquis.

The summer had been more than usually inclement, and since her first
coming to the country Undine had lived through many periods of rainy
weather; but none which had gone before had so completely epitomized, so
summed up in one vast monotonous blur, the image of her long months at
Saint Désert.

When, the year before, she had reluctantly suffered herself to be torn
from the joys of Paris, she had been sustained by the belief that her exile
would not be of long duration. Once Paris was out of sight, she had even
found a certain lazy charm in the long warm days at Saint Désert. Her
parents-in-law had remained in town, and she enjoyed being alone with her
husband, exploring and appraising the treasures of the great half-abandoned
house, and watching her boy scamper over the June meadows or trot about
the gardens on the pony his stepfather had given him. Paul, after Mrs.
Heeny's departure, had grown fretful and restive, and Undine had found it
more and more difficult to fit his small exacting personality into her
cramped rooms and crowded life. He irritated her by pining for his Aunt
Laura, his Marvell granny, and old Mr. Dagonet's funny stories about gods
and fairies; and his wistful allusions to his games with Clare's children
sounded like a lesson he might have been drilled in to make her feel how
little he belonged to her. But once released from Paris, and blessed with

rabbits, a pony and the freedom of the fields, he became again all that a charming child should be, and for a time it amused her to share in his romps and rambles. Raymond seemed enchanted at the picture they made, and the quiet weeks of fresh air and outdoor activity gave her back a bloom that reflected itself in her tranquilized mood. She was the more resigned to this interlude because she was so sure of its not lasting. Before they left Paris a doctor had been found to say that Paul—who was certainly looking pale and pulled-down—was in urgent need of sea air, and Undine had nearly convinced her husband of the expediency of hiring a châlet at Deauville for July and August, when this plan, and with it every other prospect of escape, was dashed by the sudden death of the old marquis.

Undine, at first, had supposed that the resulting change could not be other than favorable. She had been on too formal terms with her father-in-law—a remote and ceremonious old gentleman to whom her own personality was evidently an insoluble enigma—to feel more than the merest conventional pang at his death; and it was certainly "more fun" to be a marchioness than a countess, and to know that one's husband was the head of the house. Besides, now they would have the château to themselves—or at least the old marquise, when she came, would be there as a guest and not a ruler—and visions of smart house-parties and big shoots lit up the first weeks of Undine's enforced seclusion. Then, by degrees, the inexorable conditions of French mourning closed in on her. Immediately after the long-drawn funeral observances the bereaved family—mother, daughters, sons and sons-in-law—came down to seclude themselves at Saint Désert; and Undine, through the slow, hot crape-smelling months, lived encircled by shrouded images of woe in which the only live points were the eyes constantly fixed on her least movements. The hope of escaping to the seaside with Paul vanished in the pained stare with which her mother-in-law received the suggestion. Undine learned the next day that it had cost the old marquise a sleepless night, and might have had more distressing results had it not been explained as a harmless instance of transatlantic oddness. Raymond entreated his wife to atone for her involuntary légèreté by submitting with a good grace to the usages of her adopted country; and he seemed to regard the remaining months of the summer as hardly long enough for this act of expiation. As Undine looked back on them, they appeared to have been composed of an interminable succession of identical days, in which attendance at early mass (in the coroneted gallery she had once so glowingly depicted to Van Degen) was followed by a great deal of conversational sitting about, a great deal of excellent eating, an occasional drive to the nearest town behind a pair of heavy draft horses, and long evenings in a lamp-heated drawing-room with all the windows shut, and the stout curé making an asthmatic fourth at the marquise's card-table.

Still, even these conditions were not permanent, and the discipline of the last years had trained Undine to wait and dissemble. The summer over, it was decided—after a protracted family conclave—that the state of the old marquise's health made it advisable for her to spend the winter with the married daughter who lived near Pau. The other members of the family returned to their respective estates, and Undine once more found herself alone with her husband. But she knew by this time that there was to be no thought of Paris that winter, or even the next spring. Worse still, she was presently to discover that Raymond's accession of rank brought with it no financial advantages. Having but the vaguest notion of French testamentary law, she was dismayed to learn that the compulsory division of property made it impossible for a father to benefit his eldest son at the expense of the others. Raymond was therefore little richer than before, and with the debts of honor of a troublesome younger brother to settle, and Saint Désert to keep up, his available income was actually reduced. He held out, indeed, the hope of eventual improvement, since the old marquis had managed his estates with a lofty contempt for modern methods, and the application of new principles of agriculture and forestry were certain to yield profitable results. But for a year or two, at any rate, this very change of treatment would necessitate the owner's continual supervision, and would not in the meanwhile produce any increase of income.

To *faire valoir* the family acres had always, it appeared, been Raymond's deepest-seated purpose, and all his frivolities dropped from him with the prospect of putting his hand to the plough. He was not, indeed, inhuman enough to condemn his wife to perpetual exile. He meant, he assured her, that she should have her annual spring visit to Paris—but he stared in dismay at her suggestion that they should take possession of the coveted *premier* of the Hôtel de Chelles. He was gallant enough to express the wish that it were in his power to house her on such a scale; but he could not conceal his surprise that she had ever seriously expected it. She was beginning to see that he felt her constitutional inability to understand anything about money as the deepest difference between them. It was a proficiency no one had ever expected her to acquire, and the lack of which she had even been encouraged to regard as a grace and to use as a pretext. During the interval between her divorce and her remarriage she had learned what things cost, but not how to do without them; and money still seemed to her like some mysterious and uncertain stream which occasionally vanished underground but was sure to bubble up again at one's feet. Now, however, she found herself in a world where it represented not the means of individual gratification but the substance binding together whole groups of interests, and where the uses to which it might be put in twenty years were considered before the reasons for spending it on the spot. At first she was sure she could laugh Raymond out of his prudence or coax him round to her point of view. She did not understand how a man so romantically in love could be so unpersuadable on certain points. Hitherto she had had to contend with personal moods, now she was arguing against a policy; and she

was gradually to learn that it was as natural to Raymond de Chelles to adore
her and resist her as it had been to Ralph Marvell to adore her and let her
have her way.

At first, indeed, he appealed to her good sense, using arguments evidently drawn from accumulations of hereditary experience. But his economic plea was as unintelligible to her as the silly problems about pen-
knives and apples in the "Mental Arithmetic" of her infancy; and when he
struck a tenderer note and spoke of the duty of providing for the son he
hoped for, she put her arms about him to whisper: "But then I oughtn't to
be worried. . . ."

After that, she noticed, though he was as charming as ever, he behaved
as if the case were closed. He had apparently decided that his arguments
were unintelligible to her, and under all his ardor she felt the difference
made by the discovery. It did not make him less kind, but it evidently made
her less important; and she had the half-frightened sense that the day she
ceased to please him she would cease to exist for him. That day was a long
way off, of course, but the chill of it had brushed her face; and she was no
longer heedless of such signs. She resolved to cultivate all the arts of patience and compliance, and habit might have helped them to take root if
they had not been nipped by a new cataclysm.

It was barely a week ago that her husband had been called to Paris to
straighten out a fresh tangle in the affairs of the troublesome brother whose
difficulties were apparently a part of the family tradition. Raymond's letters
had been hurried, his telegrams brief and contradictory, and now, as Undine
stood watching for the brougham that was to bring him from the station,
she had the sense that with his arrival all her vague fears would be confirmed. There would be more money to pay out, of course—since the funds
that could not be found for her just needs were apparently always forthcom-
ing to settle Hubert's scandalous prodigalities—and that meant a longer
perspective of solitude at Saint Désert, and a fresh pretext for postponing
the hospitalities that were to follow on their period of mourning.

The brougham—a vehicle as massive and lumbering as the pair that
drew it—presently rolled into the court, and Raymond's sable figure (she
had never before seen a man travel in such black clothes) sprang up the
steps to the door. Whenever Undine saw him after an absence she had a
curious sense of his coming back from unknown distances and not belonging to her or to any state of things she understood. Then habit reasserted
itself, and she began to think of him again with a querulous familiarity. But
she had learned to hide her feelings, and as he came in she put up her face
for a kiss.

"Yes—everything's settled —" his embrace expressed the satisfaction of
the man returning from an accomplished task to the joys of his fireside.

"Settled?" Her face kindled. "Without your having to pay?"

He looked at her with a shrug. "Of course, I've had to pay. Did you suppose Hubert's creditors would be put off with vanilla éclairs?"

"Oh, if *that's* what you mean—if Hubert has only to wire you at any time to be sure of his affairs being settled —!"

She saw his lips narrow and a line come out between his eyes. "Wouldn't it be a happy thought to tell them to bring tea?" he suggested.

"In the library, then. It's so cold here—and the tapestries smell so of rain."

He paused a moment to scrutinize the long walls, on which the fabulous blues and pinks of the great Boucher series looked as livid as withered roses. "I suppose they ought to be taken down and aired," he said.

She thought: "In *this* air—much good it would do them!" But she had already repented her outbreak about Hubert, and she followed her husband into the library with the resolve not to let him see her annoyance. Compared with the long gray gallery, the library, with its brown walls of books, looked warm and homelike, and Raymond seemed to feel the influence of the softer atmosphere. He turned to his wife and put his arm about her.

"I know it's been a trial to you, dearest; but this is the last time I shall have to pull the poor boy out."

In spite of herself she laughed incredulously: Hubert's "last times" were a household word.

But when tea had been brought, and they were alone over the fire, Raymond unfolded the amazing sequel. Hubert had found an heiress, Hubert was to be married, and henceforth the business of paying his debts (which might be counted on to recur as inevitably as the changes of the seasons) would devolve on his American bride—the charming Miss Looty Arlington, whom Raymond had remained over in Paris to meet.

"An American? He's marrying an American?" Undine wavered between wrath and satisfaction. She felt a flash of resentment at any other intruder's venturing upon her territory—("Looty Arlington? Who is she? What a name!")—but it was quickly superseded by the relief of knowing that henceforth, as Raymond said, Hubert's debts would be someone else's business. Then a third consideration prevailed. "But if he's engaged to a rich girl, why on earth do *we* have to pull him out?"

Her husband explained that no other course was possible. Though General Arlington was immensely wealthy ("her father's a general—a general manager, whatever that may be") he had exacted what he called "a clean slate" from his future son-in-law, and Hubert's creditors (the boy was such a donkey!) had in their possession certain papers that made it possible for them to press for immediate payment.

"Your compatriots' views on such matters are so rigid—and it's all to their credit—that the marriage would have fallen through at once if the least hint of Hubert's mess had got out—and then we should have had him on our hands for life."

Yes—from that point of view it was doubtless best to pay up; but Undine obscurely wished that their doing so had not incidentally helped an unknown compatriot to what the American papers were no doubt already announcing as "another brilliant foreign alliance."

"Where on earth did your brother pick up anybody respectable? Do you know where her people come from? I suppose she's perfectly awful," she broke out with a sudden escape of irritation.

"I believe Hubert made her acquaintance at a skating rink. They come from some new state—the general apologized for its not yet being on the map, but seemed surprised I hadn't heard of it. He said it was already known as one of 'the divorce states,' and the principal city had, in consequence, a very agreeable society. *La petite n'est vraiment pas trop mal.*"

"I daresay not! We're all good-looking. But she must be horribly common."

Raymond seemed sincerely unable to formulate a judgment. "My dear, you have your own customs. . . ."

"Oh, I know we're all alike to you!" It was one of her grievances that he never attempted to discriminate between Americans. "You see no difference between me and a girl one gets engaged to at a skating rink!"

He evaded the challenge by rejoining: "Miss Arlington's burning to know you. She says she's heard a great deal about you, and Hubert wants to bring her down next week. I think we'd better do what we can."

"Of course." But Undine was still absorbed in the economic aspect of the case. "If they're as rich as you say, I suppose Hubert means to pay you back by and by?"

"Naturally. It's all arranged. He's given me a paper." He drew her hands into his. "You see we've every reason to be kind to Miss Arlington."

"Oh, I'll be as kind as you like!" She brightened at the prospect of repayment. Yes, they would ask the girl down. . . . She leaned a little nearer to her husband. "But then after a while we shall be a good deal better off—especially, as you say, with no more of Hubert's debts to worry us." And leaning back far enough to give her upward smile, she renewed her plea for the *premier* in the Hôtel de Chelles: "Because, really, you know, as the head of the house you ought to —"

"Ah, my dear, as the head of the house I've so many obligations; and one of them is not to miss a good stroke of business when it comes my way."

Her hands slipped from his shoulders and she drew back. "What do you mean by a good stroke of business?"

"Why, an incredible piece of luck—it's what kept me on so long in Paris. Miss Arlington's father was looking for an apartment for the young couple, and I've let him the *premier* for twelve years on the understanding that he puts electric light and heating into the whole hotel. It's a wonderful chance, for of course we all benefit by it as much as Hubert."

"A wonderful chance . . . benefit by it as much as Hubert!" He

seemed to be speaking a strange language in which familiar-sounding syllables meant something totally unknown. Did he really think she was going to
coop herself up again in their cramped quarters while Hubert and his skat-
ing-rink bride luxuriated overhead in the coveted *premier?* All the resentments that had been accumulating in her during the long baffled months
since her marriage broke into speech. "It's extraordinary of you to do such a
thing without consulting me!"

"Without consulting you? But, my dear child, you've always professed
the most complete indifference to business matters—you've frequently
begged me not to bore you with them. You may be sure I've acted on the
best advice; and my mother, whose head is as good as a man's, thinks I've
made a remarkably good arrangement."

"I daresay—but I'm not always thinking about money, as you are."

As she spoke she had an ominous sense of impending peril; but she was
too angry to avoid even the risks she saw. To her surprise Raymond put his
arm about her with a smile. "There are many reasons why I have to think
about money. One is that *you* don't; and another is that I must look out for
the future of our son."

Undine flushed to the forehead. She had grown accustomed to such
allusions and the thought of having a child no longer filled her with the
resentful terror she had felt before Paul's birth. She had been insensibly
influenced by a different point of view, perhaps also by a difference in her
own feeling; and the vision of herself as the mother of the future Marquis de
Chelles was softened to happiness by the thought of giving Raymond a son.
But all these lightly rooted sentiments went down in the rush of her resentment, and she freed herself with a petulant movement. "Oh, my dear, you'd
better leave it to your brother to perpetuate the race. There'll be more room
for nurseries in their apartment!"

She waited a moment, quivering with the expectation of her husband's
answer; then, as none came except the silent darkening of his face, she
walked to the door and turned round to fling back: "Of course you can do
what you like with your own house, and make any arrangements that suit
your family, without consulting me; but you needn't think I'm ever going
back to live in that stuffy little hole, with Hubert and his wife splurging
round on top of our heads!"

"Ah—" said Raymond de Chelles in a low voice.

39

UNDINE did not fulfilll her threat. The month of May saw her back in the rooms she had declared she would never set foot in, and after her long sojourn among the echoing vistas of Saint Désert the exiguity of her Paris quarters seemed like cosiness.

In the interval manythings had happened. Hubert, permitted by his anxious relatives to anticipate the term of the family mourning, had been showily and expensively united to his heiress; the Hôtel de Chelles had been piped, heated and illuminated in accordance with the bride's requirements; and the young couple, not content with these utilitarian changes had moved doors, opened windows, torn down partitions, and given over the great trophied and pilastered dining-room to a decorative painter with a new theory of the human anatomy. Undine had silently assisted at this spectacle, and at the sight of the old marquise's abject acquiescence; she had seen the duchesse de Dordogne and the princesse Estradina go past her door to visit Hubert's *premier* and marvel at the American bathtubs and the Annamite bric-a-brac; and she had been present, with her husband, at the banquet at which Hubert had revealed to the astonished Faubourg the prehistoric episodes depicted on his dining-room walls. She had accepted all these necessities with the stoicism which the last months had developed in her; for more and more, as the days passed, she felt herself in the grasp of circumstances stronger than any effort she could oppose to them. The very absence of external pressure, of any tactless assertion of authority on her husband's part, intensified the sense of her helplessness. He simply left it to her to infer that, important as she might be to him in certain ways, there were others in which she did not weigh a feather.

Their outward relations had not changed since her outburst on the subject of Hubert's marriage. That incident had left her half-ashamed, half-frightened at her behavior, and she had tried to atone for it by the indirect arts that were her nearest approach to acknowledging herself in the wrong. Raymond met her advances with a good grace, and they lived through the rest of the winter on terms of apparent understanding. When the spring approached it was he who suggested that, since his mother had consented to Hubert's marrying before the year of mourning was over, there was really no reason why they should not go up to Paris as usual; and she was surprised at the readiness with which he prepared to accompany her.

A year earlier she would have regarded this as another proof of her

586

power; but she now drew her inferences less quickly. Raymond was as "lovely" to her as ever; but more than once, during their months in the country, she had had a startled sense of not giving him all he expected of her. She had admired him, before their marriage, as a model of social distinction; during the honeymoon he had been the most ardent of lovers; and with their settling down at Saint Désert she had prepared to resign herself to the society of a country gentleman absorbed in sport and agriculture. But Raymond, to her surprise, had again developed a disturbing resemblance to his predecessor. During the long winter afternoons, after he had gone over his accounts with the bailiff, or written his business letters, he took to dabbling with a paint-box, or picking out new scores at the piano; after dinner, when they went to the library, he seemed to expect to read aloud to her from the reviews and papers he was always receiving; and when he had discovered her inability to fix her attention he fell into the way of absorbing himself in one of the old brown books with which the room was lined. At first he tried—as Ralph had done—to tell her about what he was reading or what was happening in the world; but her sense of inadequacy made her slip away to other subjects, and little by little their talk died down to monosyllables.

Was it possible that, in spite of his books, the evenings seemed as long to Raymond as to her, and that he had suggested going back to Paris because he was bored at Saint Désert? Bored as she was herself, she resented his not finding her company all-sufficient, and was mortified by the discovery that there were regions of his life she could not enter.

But once back in Paris she had less time for introspection, and Raymond less for books. They resumed their dispersed and busy life, and in spite of Hubert's ostentatious vicinity, of the perpetual lack of money, and of Paul's innocent encroachments on her freedom, Undine, once more in her element, ceased to brood upon her grievances. She enjoyed going about with her husband, whose presence at her side was distinctly ornamental. He seemed to have grown suddenly younger and more animated, and when she saw other women looking at him she remembered how distinguished he was. It amused her to have him in her train, and driving about with him to dinners and dances, waiting for him on flower-decked landings, or pushing at his side through blazing theater lobbies, answered to her inmost ideal of domestic intimacy.

He seemed disposed to allow her more liberty than before, and it was only now and then that he let drop a brief reminder of the conditions on which it was accorded. She was to keep certain people at a distance, she was not to cheapen herself by being seen at vulgar restaurants and tea-rooms, she was to join with him in fulfillling certain family obligations (going to a good many dull dinners among the number); but in other respects she was free to fill her days as she pleased.

"Not that it leaves me much time," she admitted to Madame de Trézac;

"what with going to see his mother every day, and never missing one of his sisters' *jours*, and showing myself at the Hôtel de Dordogne whenever the duchess gives a pay-up party to the stuffy people Lili Estradina won't be bothered with, there are days when I never lay eyes on Paul, and barely have time to be waved and manicured; but, apart from that, Raymond's really much nicer and less fussy than he was."

Undine, as she grew older, had developed her mother's craving for a confidante, and Madame de Trézac had succeeded in that capacity to Mabel Lipscomb and Bertha Shallum.

"Less fussy?" Madame de Trézac's long nose lengthened thoughtfully. "H'm—are you sure that's a good sign?"

Undine stared and laughed. "Oh, my dear, you're so quaint! Why, nobody's jealous any more."

"No; that's the worst of it." Madame de Trézac pondered. "It's a thousand pities you haven't got a son."

"Yes; I wish we had." Undine stood up, impatient to end the conversation. Since she had learned that her continued childlessness was regarded by everyone about her as not only unfortunate but somehow vaguely derogatory to her, she had genuinely begun to regret it; and any allusion to the subject disturbed her.

"Especially," Madame de Trézac continued, "as Hubert's wife —"

"Oh, if *that's* all they want, it's a pity Raymond didn't marry Hubert's wife," Undine flung back; and on the stairs she murmured to herself: "Nettie has been talking to my mother-in-law."

But this explanation did not quiet her, and that evening, as she and Raymond drove back together from a party, she felt a sudden impulse to speak. Sitting close to him in the darkness of the carriage, it ought to have been easy for her to find the needed word; but the barrier of his indifference hung between them, and street after street slipped by, and the spangled blackness of the river unrolled itself beneath their wheels, before she leaned over to touch his hand.

"What is it, my dear?"

She had not yet found the word, and already his tone told her she was too late. A year ago, if she had slipped her hand in his, she would not have had that answer.

"Your mother blames me for our not having a child. Everybody thinks it's my fault."

He paused before answering, and she sat watching his shadowy profile against the passing lamps.

"My mother's ideas are old-fashioned; and I don't know that it's anybody's business but yours and mine."

"Yes, but —"

"Here we are." The brougham was turning under the archway of the hotel, and the light of Hubert's tall windows fell across the dusky court.

Raymond helped her out, and they mounted to their door by the stairs which Hubert had recarpeted in velvet, with a marble nymph lurking in the azaleas on the landing.

In the antechamber Raymond paused to take her cloak from her shoulders, and his eyes rested on her with a faint smile of approval.

"You never looked better; your dress is extremely becoming. Good night, my dear," he said, kissing her hand as he turned away.

Undine kept this incident to herself: her wounded pride made her shrink from confessing it even to Madame de Trézac. She was sure Raymond would "come back"; Ralph always had, to the last. During their remaining weeks in Paris she reassured herself with the thought that once they were back at Saint Désert she would easily regain her lost hold; and when Raymond suggested their leaving Paris she acquiesced without a protest. But at Saint Désert she seemed no nearer to him than in Paris. He continued to treat her with unvarying amiability, but he seemed wholly absorbed in the management of the estate, in his books, his sketching and his music. He had begun to interest himself in politics and had been urged to stand for his department. This necessitated frequent displacements: trips to Beaune or Dijon and occasional absences in Paris. Undine, when he was away, was not left alone, for the dowager marquise had established herself at Saint Désert for the summer, and relays of brothers and sisters-in-law, aunts, cousins and ecclesiastical friends and connections succeeded each other under its capacious roof. Only Hubert and his wife were absent. They had taken a villa at Deauville, and in the morning papers Undine followed the chronicle of Hubert's polo scores and of the Countess Hubert's racing toilets.

The days crawled on with a benumbing sameness. The old marquise and the other ladies of the party sat on the terrace with their needlework, the curé or one of the visiting uncles read aloud the *Journal des Débats* and prognosticated dark things of the Republic, Paul scoured the park and despoiled the kitchen-garden with the other children of the family, the inhabitants of the adjacent châteaux drove over to call, and occasionally the ponderous pair were harnessed to a landau as lumbering as the brougham, and the ladies of Saint Désert measured the dusty kilometers between themselves and their neighbors.

It was the first time that Undine had seriously paused to consider the conditions of her new life, and as the days passed she began to understand that so they would continue to succeed each other till the end. Everyone about her took it for granted that as long as she lived she would spend ten months of every year at Saint Désert and the remaining two in Paris. Of course, if health required it, she might go to *les eaux* with her husband; but the old marquise was very doubtful as to the benefit of a course of waters, and her uncle the duke and her cousin the canon shared her view. In the case of young married women, especially, the unwholesome excitement of

the modern watering-place was more than likely to do away with the possible benefit of the treatment. As to travel—had not Raymond and his wife
been to Egypt and Asia Minor on their wedding-journey? Such reckless
enterprise was unheard of in the annals of the house! Had they not spent
days and days in the saddle, and slept in tents among the Arabs? (Who
could tell, indeed, whether these imprudences were not the cause of the
disappointment which it had pleased heaven to inflict on the young couple?) No one in the family had ever taken so long a wedding-journey. One
bride had gone to England (even that was considered extreme), and another
—the artistic daughter—had spent a week in Venice; which certainly
showed that they were not behind the times, and had no old-fashioned
prejudices. Since wedding-journeys were the fashion, they had taken them;
but who had ever heard of traveling afterward? What could be the possible
object of leaving one's family, one's habits, one's friends? It was natural that
the Americans, who had no homes, who were born and died in hotels,
should have contracted nomadic habits; but the new marquise de Chelles
was no longer an American, and she had Saint Désert and the Hôtel de
Chelles to live in, as generations of ladies of her name had done before her.

Thus Undine beheld her future laid out for her, not directly and in blunt
words, but obliquely and affably, in the allusions, the assumptions, the insinuations of the amiable among whom her days were spent. Their
interminable conversations were carried on to the click of knitting-needles
and the rise and fall of industrious fingers above embroidery-frames; and as
Undine sat staring at the lustrous nails of her idle hands she felt that her
inability to occupy them was regarded as one of the chief causes of her
restlessness. The innumerable rooms of Saint Désert were furnished with
the embroidered hangings and tapestry chairs produced by generations of
diligent châtelaines, and the untiring needles of the old marquise, her
daughters and dependents were still steadily increasing the provision.

It struck Undine as curious that they should be willing to go on making
chair-coverings and bed-curtains for a house that didn't really belong to
them, and that she had a right to pull about and rearrange as she chose; but
then that was only a part of their whole incomprehensible way of regarding
themselves (in spite of their acute personal and parochial absorptions) as
minor members of a powerful and indivisible whole, the huge voracious
fetish they called The Family.

Notwithstanding their very definite theories as to what Americans were
and were not, they were evidently bewildered at finding no corresponding
sense of solidarity in Undine; and little Paul's rootlessness, his lack of all
local and linear ties, made them (for all the charm he exercised) regard him
with something of the shyness of pious Christians toward an elfin child. But
though mother and child gave them a sense of insuperable strangeness, it
plainly never occurred to them that both would not be gradually subdued to
the customs of Saint Désert. Dynasties had fallen, institutions changed,

manners and morals, alas, deplorably declined; but as far back as memory
went, the ladies of the line of Chelles had always sat at their needlework on
the terrace of Saint Désert, while the men of the house lamented the corruption of the government and the curé ascribed the unhappy state of the
country to the decline of religious feeling and the rise in the cost of living.
It was inevitable that, in the course of time, the new marquise should come
to understand the fundamental necessity of these things being as they were;
and meanwhile the forbearance of her husband's family exercised itself, with
the smiling discretion of their race, through the long succession of uneventful days.

Once, in September, this routine was broken in upon by the unannounced descent of a flock of motors bearing the Princess Estradina and a
chosen band from one watering-place to another. Raymond was away at the
time, but family loyalty constrained the old marquise to welcome her kins-
woman and the latter's friends; and Undine once more found herself immersed in the world from which her marriage had removed her.

The princess, at first, seemed totally to have forgotten their former intimacy, and Undine was made to feel that in a life so variously agitated the
episode could hardly have left a trace. But the night before her departure
the incalculable Lili, with one of her sudden changes of humor, drew her
former friend into her bedroom and plunged into an exchange of confidences. She naturally unfolded her own history first, and it was so packed
with incident that the courtyard clock had struck two before she turned her
attention to Undine.

"My dear, you're handsomer than ever; only perhaps a shade too stout.
Domestic bliss, I suppose? Take care! You need an emotion, a drama. . . .
You Americans are really extraordinary. You appear to live on change and
excitement; and then suddenly a man comes along and claps a ring on your
finger, and you never look through it to see what's going on outside. Aren't
you ever the least bit bored? Why do I never see anything of you anymore? I
suppose it's the fault of my venerable aunt—she's never forgiven me for
having a better time than her daughters. How can I help it if I don't look
like the curé's umbrella? I daresay she owes you the same grudge. But why
do you let her coop you up here? It's a thousand pities you haven't had a
child. They'd all treat you differently if you had."

It was the same perpetually reiterated condolence; and Undine flushed
with anger as she listened. Why indeed had she let herself be cooped up?
She could not have answered the princess's question: she merely felt the
impossibility of breaking through the mysterious web of traditions, conventions, prohibitions that enclosed her in their impenetrable network. But her
vanity suggested the obvious pretext, and she murmured with a laugh: "I
didn't know Raymond was going to be so jealous —"

The princess stared. "Is it Raymond who keeps you shut up here? And
what about his trips to Dijon? And what do you suppose he does with

himself when he runs up to Paris? Politics?" She shrugged ironically. "Politics don't occupy a man after midnight. Raymond jealous of you? *Ah, merci!* My dear, it's what I always say when people talk to me about fast Americans: you're the only innocent women left in the world. . . ."

40

AFTER the princess Estradina's departure, the days at Saint Désert succeeded each other indistinguishably; and more and more, as they passed, Undine felt herself drawn into the slow strong current already fed by so many tributary lives. Some spell she could not have named seemed to emanate from the old house which had so long been the custodian of an unbroken tradition: things had happened there in the same way for so many generations that to try to alter them seemed as vain as to contend with the elements.

Winter came and went, and once more the calendar marked the first days of spring; but though the horse-chestnuts of the Champs Elysées were budding snow still lingered in the grass drives of Saint Désert and along the ridges of the hills beyond the park. Sometimes, as Undine looked out of the windows of the Boucher gallery, she felt as if her eyes had never rested on any other scene. Even her occasional brief trips to Paris left no lasting trace: the life of the vivid streets faded to a shadow as soon as the black and white horizon of Saint Désert closed in on her again.

Though the afternoons were still cold she had lately taken to sitting in the gallery. The smiling scenes on its walls and the tall screens which broke its length made it more habitable than the drawing-rooms beyond; but her chief reason for preferring it was the satisfaction she found in having fires lit in both the monumental chimneys that faced each other down its long perspective. This satisfaction had its source in the old marquise's disapproval. Never before in the history of Saint Désert had the consumption of firewood exceeded a certain carefully calculated measure; but since Undine had been in authority this allowance had been doubled. If anyone had told her, a year earlier, that one of the chief distractions of her new life would be to invent ways of annoying her mother-in-law, she would have laughed at the idea of wasting her time on such trifles. But she found herself with a great deal of time to waste, and with a fierce desire to spend it in upsetting the immemorial customs of Saint Désert. Her husband had mastered her in essentials, but she had discovered innumerable small ways of irritating and hurting him, and one—and not the least effectual—was to do anything that went counter to his mother's prejudices. It was not that he always shared her views, or was a particularly subservient son; but it seemed to be one of his fundamental principles that a man should respect his mother's wishes, and see to it that his household respected them. All Frenchmen of his class appeared to share this view, and to regard it as beyond discussion: it was based on something so much more immutable than personal feeling that one might even hate one's mother and yet insist that her ideas as to the consumption of firewood should be regarded.

The old marquise, during the cold weather, always sat in her bedroom; and there, between the tapestried four-poster and the fireplace, the family grouped itself around the ground-glass of her single carcel lamp. In the evening, if there were visitors, a fire was lit in the library; otherwise the family again sat about the marquise's lamp till the footman came in at ten with tisane and biscuits de Reims; after which everyone bade the dowager good night and scattered down the corridors to chill distances marked by tapers floating in cups of oil.

Since Undine's coming the library fire had never been allowed to go out; and of late, after experimenting with the two drawing-rooms and the so-called "study" where Raymond kept his guns and saw the bailiff, she had selected the gallery as the most suitable place for the new and unfamiliar ceremony of afternoon tea. Afternoon refreshments had never before been served at Saint Désert except when company was expected; when they had invariably consisted in a decanter of sweet port and a plate of small dry cakes—the kind that kept. That the complicated rites of the tea-urn, with its offering-up of perishable delicacies, should be enacted for the sole enjoyment of the family, was a thing so unheard of that for a while Undine found sufficient amusement in elaborating the ceremonial, and in making the ancestral plate groan under more varied viands; and when this palled she devised the plan of performing the office in the gallery and lighting sacrificial fires in both chimneys.

She had said to Raymond, at first: "It's ridiculous that your mother should sit in her bedroom all day. She says she does it to save fires; but if we have a fire downstairs why can't she let hers go out, and come down? I don't see why I should spend my life in your mother's bedroom."

Raymond made no answer, and the marquise did, in fact, let her fire go out. But she did not come down—she simply continued to sit upstairs without a fire.

At first this also amused Undine; then the tacit criticism implied began to irritate her. She hoped Raymond would speak of his mother's attitude: she had her answer ready if he did! But he made no comment, he took no notice; her impulses of retaliation spent themselves against the blank surface of his indifference. He was as amiable, as considerate as ever; as ready, within reason, to accede to her wishes and gratify her whims. Once or twice, when she suggested running up to Paris to take Paul to the dentist, or to

look for a servant, he agreed to the necessity and went up with her. But
instead of going to an hotel they went to their apartment, where carpets
were up and curtains down, and a caretaker prepared primitive food at
uncertain hours; and Undine's first glimpse of Hubert's illuminated windows
deepened her rancor and her sense of helplessness.

As Madame de Trézac had predicted, Raymond's vigilance gradually
relaxed, and during their excursions to the capital Undine came and went
as she pleased. But her visits were too short to permit of her falling in with
the social pace, and when she showed herself among her friends she felt
countrified and out-of-place, as if even her clothes had come from Saint
Désert. Nevertheless her dresses were more than ever her chief preoccupation: in Paris she spent hours at the dressmaker's, and in the country the
arrival of a box of new gowns was the chief event of the vacant days. But
there was more bitterness than joy in the unpacking, and the dresses hung
in her wardrobe like so many unfulfilled promises of pleasure, reminding
her of the days at the Stentorian when she had reviewed other finery with
the same cheated eyes. In spite of this, she multiplied her orders, writing up
to the dressmakers for patterns, and to the milliners for boxes of hats which
she tried on, and kept for days, without being able to make a choice. Now
and then she even sent her maid up to Paris to bring back great assortments
of veils, gloves, flowers and laces; and after periods of painful indecision she
ended by keeping the greater number, lest those she sent back should turn
out to be the ones that were worn in Paris. She knew she was spending too
much money, and she had lost her youthful faith in providential solutions;
but she had always had the habit of going out to buy something when she
was bored, and never had she been in greater need of such solace.

The dullness of her life seemed to have passed into her blood: her
complexion was less animated, her hair less shining. The change in her
looks alarmed her, and she scanned the fashion-papers for new scents and
powders, and experimented in facial bandaging, electric massage and other
processes of renovation. Odd atavisms woke in her, and she began to pore
over patent medicine advertisements, to send stamped envelopes to beauty
doctors and professors of physical development, and to brood on the advantage of consulting faith-healers, mind-readers and their kindred adepts. She
even wrote to her mother for the receipts of some of her grandfather's
forgotten nostrums, and modified her daily life, and her hours of sleeping,
eating and exercise, in accordance with each new experiment.

Her constitutional restlessness lapsed into an apathy like Mrs. Spragg's,
and the least demand on her activity irritated her. But she was beset by
endless annoyances: bickerings with discontented maids, the difficulty of
finding a tutor for Paul, and the problem of keeping him amused and occupied without having him too much on her hands. A great liking had sprung
up between Raymond and the little boy, and during the summer Paul was
perpetually at his stepfather's side in the stables and the park. But with the

coming of winter Raymond was oftener away, and Paul developed a persistent cold that kept him frequently indoors. The confinement made him fretful and exacting, and the old marquise ascribed the change in his behavior to the deplorable influence of his tutor, a "laic" recommended by one of Raymond's old professors. Raymond himself would have preferred an abbé: it was in the tradition of the house, and though Paul was not of the house it seemed fitting that he should conform to its ways. Moreover, when the married sisters came to stay they objected to having their children exposed to the tutor's influence, and even implied that Paul's society might be contaminating. But Undine, though she had so readily embraced her husband's faith, stubbornly resisted the suggestion that she should hand over her son to the Church. The tutor therefore remained; but the friction caused by his presence was so irritating to Undine that she began to consider the alternative of sending Paul to school. He was still small and tender for the experiment; but she persuaded herself that what he needed was "hardening," and having heard of a school where fashionable infancy was subjected to this process, she entered into correspondence with the master. His first letter convinced her that his establishment was just the place for Paul; but the second contained the price-list, and after comparing it with the tutor's keep and salary she wrote to say that she feared her little boy was too young to be sent away from home.

Her husband, for some time past, had ceased to make any comment on her expenditure. She knew he thought her too extravagant, and felt sure he was minutely aware of what she spent; for Saint Désert projected on economic details a light as different as might be from the haze that veiled them in West End Avenue. She therefore concluded that Raymond's silence was intentional, and ascribed it to his having shortcomings of his own to conceal. The Princess Estradina's pleasantry had reached its mark. Undine did not believe that her husband was seriously in love with another woman— she could not conceive that anyone could tire of her of whom she had not first tired—but she was humiliated by his indifference, and it was easier to ascribe it to the arts of a rival than to any deficiency in herself. It exasperated her to think that he might have consolations for the outward monotony of his life, and she resolved that when they returned to Paris he should see that she was not without similar opportunities.

March, meanwhile, was verging on April, and still he did not speak of leaving. Undine had learned that he expected to have such decisions left to him, and she hid her impatience lest her showing it should incline him to delay. But one day, as she sat at tea in the gallery, he came in in his riding-clothes and said: "I've been over to the other side of the mountain. The February rains have weakened the dam of the Alette, and the vineyards will be in danger if we don't rebuild at once."

She suppressed a yawn, thinking, as she did so, how dull he always looked when he talked of agriculture. It made him seem years older, and she reflected with a shiver that listening to him probably gave her the same look.

He went on, as she handed him his tea: "I'm sorry it should happen just now. I'm afraid I shall have to ask you to give up your spring in Paris."

"Oh, no—no!" she broke out. A throng of half-subdued grievances choked in her: she wanted to burst into sobs like a child.

"I know it's a disappointment. But our expenses have been unusually heavy this year."

"It seems to me they always are. I don't see why we should give up Paris because you've got to make repairs to a dam. Isn't Hubert ever going to pay back that money?"

He looked at her with a mild surprise. "But surely you understood at the time that it won't be possible till his wife inherits?"

"Till General Arlington dies, you mean? He doesn't look much older than you!"

"You may remember that I showed you Hubert's note. He has paid the interest quite regularly."

"That's kind of him!" She stood up, flaming with rebellion. "You can do as you please; but I mean to go to Paris."

"My mother is not going. I didn't intend to open our apartment."

"I understand. But I shall open it—that's all!"

He had risen too, and she saw his face whiten. "I prefer that you shouldn't go without me."

"Then I shall go and stay at the Nouveau Luxe with my American friends."

"That never!"

"Why not?"

"I consider it unsuitable."

"Your considering it so doesn't prove it."

They stood facing each other, quivering with an equal anger; then he controlled himself and said in a more conciliatory tone: "You never seem to see that there are necessities —"

"Oh, neither do you—that's the trouble. You can't keep me shut up here all my life, and interfere with everything I want to do, just by saying it's unsuitable."

"I've never interfered with your spending your money as you please."

It was her turn to stare, sincerely wondering. "Mercy, I should hope not, when you've always grudged me every penny of yours!"

"You know it's not because I grudge it. I would gladly take you to Paris if I had the money."

"You can always find the money to spend on this place. Why don't you sell it if it's so fearfully expensive?"

"Sell it? Sell Saint Désert?"

The suggestion seemed to strike him as something monstrously, almost fiendishly significant: as if her random word had at last thrust into his hand the clue to their whole unhappy difference. Without understanding this, she guessed it from the change in his face: it was as if a deadly solvent had suddenly decomposed its familiar lines.

"Well, why not?" His horror spurred her on. "You might sell some of the things in it anyhow. In America we're not ashamed to sell what we can't afford to keep." Her eyes fell on the storied hangings at his back. "Why, there's a fortune in this one room: you could get anything you chose for those tapestries. And you stand here and tell me you're a pauper!"

His glance followed hers to the tapestries, and then returned to her face. "Ah, you don't understand," he said.

"I understand that you care for all this old stuff more than you do for me, and that you'd rather see me unhappy and miserable than touch one of your great-grandfather's armchairs."

The color came slowly back to his face, but it hardened into lines she had never seen. He looked at her as though the place where she stood were empty. "You don't understand," he said again.

41

THE incident left Undine with the baffled feeling of not being able to count on any of her old weapons of aggression. In all her struggles for authority her sense of the rightfullness of her cause had been measured by her power of making people do as she pleased. Raymond's firmness shook her faith in her own claims, and a blind desire to wound and destroy replaced her usual businesslike intentness on gaining her end. But her ironies were as ineffectual as her arguments, and his imperviousness was the more exasperating because she divined that some of the things she said would have hurt him if anyone else had said them: it was the fact of their coming from her that made them innocuous. Even when, at the close of their talk, she had burst out: "If you grudge me everything I care about we'd better separate," he had merely answered with a shrug: "It's one of the things we don't do —" and the answer had been like the slamming of an iron door in her face.

An interval of silent brooding had resulted in a reaction of rebellion. She dared not carry out her threat of joining her compatriots at the Nouveau Luxe: she had too clear a memory of the results of her former revolt. But neither could she submit to her present fate without attempting to make Raymond understand his selfish folly. She had failed to prove it by

argument, but she had an inherited faith in the value of practical demonstration. If he could be made to see how easily he could give her what she
wanted perhaps he might come round to her view.

With this idea in mind, she had gone up to Paris for twenty-four hours,
on the pretext of finding a new nurse for Paul; and the steps then taken had
enabled her, on the first occasion, to set her plan in motion. The occasion
was furnished by Raymond's next trip to Beaune. He went off early one
morning, leaving word that he should not be back till night; and on the
afternoon of the same day she stood at her usual post in the gallery, scanning the long perspective of the poplar avenue.

She had not stood there long before a black speck at the end of the
avenue expanded into a motor that was presently throbbing at the entrance.
Undine, at its approach, turned from the window, and as she moved down
the gallery her glance rested on the great tapestries, with their ineffable
minglings of blue and rose, as complacently as though they had been mirrors
reflecting her own image.

She was still looking at them when the door opened and a servant
ushered in a small swarthy man who, in spite of his conspicuously London-
made clothes, had an odd exotic air, as if he had worn rings in his ears or
left a bale of spices at the door.

He bowed to Undine, cast a rapid eye up and down the room, and then,
with his back to the windows, stood intensely contemplating the wall that
faced them.

Undine's heart was beating excitedly. She knew the old marquise was
taking her afternoon nap in her room, yet each sound in the silent house
seemed to be that of her heels on the stairs.

"Ah —" said the visitor.

He had begun to pace slowly down the gallery, keeping his face to the
tapestries, like an actor playing to the footlights.

"*Ah* —" he said again.

To ease the tension of her nerves Undine began: "They were given by
Louis the Fifteenth to the Marquis de Chelles who —"

"Their history has been published," the visitor briefly interposed; and
she colored at her blunder.

The swarthy stranger, fitting a pair of eyeglasses to a nose that was like
an instrument of precision, had begun a closer and more detailed inspection
of the tapestries. He seemed totally unmindful of her presence, and his air of
lofty indifference was beginning to make her wish she had not sent for him.
His manner in Paris had been so different!

Suddenly he turned and took off the glasses, which sprang back into a
fold of his clothing like retracted feelers.

"Yes." He stood and looked at her without seeing her. "Very well. I have
brought down a gentleman."

"A gentleman —?"

"The greatest American collector—he buys only the best. He will not be long in Paris, and it was his only chance of coming down."

Undine drew herself up. "I don't understand—I never said the tapestries were for sale."

"Precisely. But this gentleman buys only things that are not for sale."

It sounded dazzling and she wavered. "I don't know—you were only to put a price on them —"

"Let me see him look at them first; then I'll put a price on them," he chuckled; and without waiting for her answer he went to the door and opened it. The gesture revealed the fur-coated back of a gentleman who stood at the opposite end of the hall examining the bust of a seventeenth-century field-marshal.

The dealer addressed the back respectfully. "Mr. Moffatt!"

Moffatt, who appeared to be interested in the bust, glanced over his shoulder without moving. "See here —"

His glance took in Undine, widened to astonishment and passed into apostrophe. "Well, if this ain't the darnedest —!" He came forward and took her by both hands. "Why, what on earth are you doing down here?"

She laughed and blushed, in a tremor at the odd turn of the adventure. "I live here. Didn't you know?"

"Not a word—never thought of asking the party's name." He turned jovially to the bowing dealer. "Say—I told you those tapestries 'd have to be out and outers to make up for the trip; but now I see I was mistaken."

Undine looked at him curiously. His physical appearance was unchanged: he was as compact and ruddy as ever, with the same astute eyes under the same guileless brow; but his self-confidence had become less aggressive, and she had never seen him so gallantly at ease.

"I didn't know you'd become a great collector."

"The greatest! Didn't he tell you so? I thought that was why I was allowed to come."

She hesitated. "Of course, you know, the tapestries are not for sale —"

"That so? I thought that was only his dodge to get me down. Well, I'm glad they ain't: it'll give us more time to talk."

Watch in hand, the dealer intervened. "If, nevertheless, you would first take a glance. Our train —"

"It ain't mine!" Moffatt interrupted. "At least not if there's a later one."

Undine's presence of mind had returned. "Of course there is," she said gaily. She led the way back into the gallery, half hoping the dealer would allege a pressing reason for departure. She was excited and amused at Moffatt's unexpected appearance, but humiliated that he should suspect her of being in financial straits. She never wanted to see Moffatt except when she was happy and triumphant.

The dealer had followed the other two into the gallery, and there was a moment's pause while they all stood silently before the tapestries. "By George!" Moffatt finally brought out.

"They're historical, you know: the king gave them to Raymond's great-great-grandfather. The other day when I was in Paris," Undine hurried on, "I asked Mr. Fleischhauer to come down some time and tell us what they're worth . . . and he seems to have misunderstood . . . to have thought we meant to sell them." She addressed herself more pointedly to the dealer. "I'm sorry you've had the trip for nothing."

Mr. Fleischhauer inclined himself eloquently. "It is not nothing to have seen such beauty."

Moffatt gave him a humorous look. "I'd hate to see Mr. Fleischhauer miss his train —"

"I shall not miss it: I miss nothing," said Mr. Fleischhauer. He bowed to Undine and backed toward the door.

"See here," Moffatt called to him as he reached the threshold, "you let the motor take you to the station, and charge up this trip to me."

When the door closed he turned to Undine with a laugh. "Well, this beats the band. I thought of course you were living up in Paris."

Again she felt a twinge of embarrassment. "Oh, French people—I mean my husband's kind—always spend a part of the year on their estates."

"But not this part, do they? Why, everything's humming up there now. I was dining at the Nouveau Luxe last night with the Driscolls and Shallums and Mrs. Rolliver, and all your old crowd were there whooping things up."

The Driscolls and Shallums and Mrs. Rolliver! How carelessly he reeled off their names! One could see from his tone that he was one of them and wanted her to know it. And nothing could have given her a completer sense of his achievement—of the number of millions he must be worth. It must have come about very recently, yet he was already at ease in his new honors —he had the metropolitan tone. While she examined him with these thoughts in her mind she was aware of his giving her as close a scrutiny. "But I suppose you've got your own crowd now," he continued; "you always *were* a lap ahead of me." He sent his glance down the lordly length of the room. "It's sorter funny to see you in this kind of place; but you look it—you always *do* look it!"

She laughed. "So do you—I was just thinking it!" Their eyes met. "I suppose you must be awfully rich."

He laughed, too, holding her eyes. "Oh, out of sight! The Consolidation set me on my feet. I own pretty near the whole of Apex. I came down to buy these tapestries for my private car."

The familiar accent of hyperbole exhilarated her. "I don't suppose I could stop you if you really wanted them!"

"Nobody can stop me now if I want anything."

They were looking at each other with challenge and complicity in their eyes. His voice, his look, all the loud confident vigorous things he embodied and expressed, set her blood beating with curiosity. "I didn't know you and Rolliver were friends," she said.

"Oh *Jim*—" his accent verged on the protective. "Old Jim's all right. He's in Congress now. I've got to have somebody up in Washington." He had thrust his hands in his pockets, and with his head thrown back and his lips shaped to the familiar noiseless whistle, was looking slowly and discerningly about him.

Presently his eyes reverted to her face. "So this is what I helped you to get," he said. "I've always meant to run over someday and take a look. What is it they call you—a marquise?"

She paled a little, and then flushed again. "What made you do it?" she broke out abruptly. "I've often wondered."

He laughed. "What—lend you a hand? Why, my business instinct, I suppose. I saw you were in a tight place that time I ran across you in Paris— and I hadn't any grudge against you. Fact is, I've never had the time to nurse old scores, and if you neglect 'em they die off like goldfish." He was still composedly regarding her. "It's funny to think of your having settled down to this kind of life; I hope you've got what you wanted. This is a great place you live in."

"Yes; but I see a little too much of it. We live here most of the year." She had meant to give him the illusion of success, but some underlying community of instinct drew the confession from her lips.

"That so? Why on earth don't you cut it and come up to Paris?"

"Oh, Raymond's absorbed in the estates—and we haven't got the money. This place eats it all up."

"Well, that sounds aristocratic; but ain't it rather out of date? When the swells are hard-up nowadays they generally chip off an heirloom." He wheeled round again to the tapestries. "There are a good many Paris seasons hanging right here on this wall."

"Yes—I know." She tried to check herself, to summon up a glittering equivocation; but his face, his voice, the very words he used, were like so many hammer strokes demolishing the unrealities that imprisoned her. Here was someone who spoke her language, who knew her meanings, who understood instinctively all the deep-seated wants for which her acquired vocabulary had no terms; and as she talked she once more seemed to herself intelligent, eloquent and interesting.

"Of course it's frightfully lonely down here," she began; and through the opening made by the admission the whole flood of her grievances poured forth. She tried to let him see that she had not sacrificed herself for nothing; she touched on the superiorities of her situation, she gilded the circumstances of which she called herself the victim, and let titles, offices and attributes shed their utmost luster on her tale; but what she had to boast of seemed small and tinkling compared with the evidences of his power.

"Well, it's a downright shame you don't go round more," he kept saying; and she felt ashamed of her tame acceptance of her fate.

When she had told her story she asked for his; and for the first time she listened to it with interest. He had what he wanted at last. The Apex Consolidation scheme, after a long interval of suspense, had obtained its charter and shot out huge ramifications. Rolliver had "stood in" with him at the critical moment, and between them they had "chucked out" old Harmon B. Driscoll bag and baggage, and got the whole town in their control. Absorbed in his theme, and forgetting her inability to follow him, Moffatt launched out on an epic recital of plot and counterplot, and she hung, a new Desdemona, on his conflict with the new anthropophagi. It was of no consequence that the details and the technicalities escaped her: she knew their meaningless syllables stood for success, and what that meant was as clear as day to her. Every Wall Street term had its equivalent in the language of Fifth Avenue, and while he talked of building up railways she was building up palaces, and picturing all the multiple lives he would lead in them. To have things had always seemed to her the first essential of existence, and as she listened to him the vision of the things he could have unrolled itself before her like the long triumph of an Asiatic conqueror.

"And what are you going to do next?" she asked, almost breathlessly, when he had ended.

"Oh, there's always a lot to do next. Business never goes to sleep."

"Yes; but I mean besides business."

"Why—everything I can, I guess." He leaned back in his chair with an air of placid power, as if he were so sure of getting what he wanted that there was no longer any use in hurrying, huge as his vistas had become.

She continued to question him, and he began to talk of his growing passion for pictures and furniture, and of his desire to form a collection which should be a great representative assemblage of unmatched specimens. As he spoke she saw his expression change, and his eyes grow younger, almost boyish, with a concentrated look in them that reminded her of long-forgotten things.

"I mean to have the best, you know; not just to get ahead of the other fellows, but because I know it when I see it. I guess that's the only good reason," he concluded; and he added, looking at her with a smile: "It was what you were always after, wasn't it?"

42

UNDINE had gained her point, and the *entresol* of the Hôtel de Chelles reopened its doors for the season.

Hubert and his wife, in expectation of the birth of an heir, had withdrawn to the sumptuous château which General Arlington had hired for them near Compiègne, and Undine was at least spared the sight of their bright windows and animated stairway. But she had to take her share of the felicitations which the whole far-reaching circle of friends and relations distributed to every member of Hubert's family on the approach of the happy event. Nor was this the hardest of her trials. Raymond had done what she asked—he had stood out against his mother's protests, set aside considerations of prudence, and consented to go up to Paris for two months; but he had done so on the understanding that during their stay they should exercise the most unremitting economy. As dinner-giving put the heaviest strain on their budget, all hospitality was suspended; and when Undine attempted to invite a few friends informally she was warned that she could not do so without causing the gravest offense to the many others genealogically entitled to the same attention.

Raymond's insistence on this rule was simply part of an elaborate and inveterate system of "relations" (the whole of French social life seemed to depend on the exact interpretation of that word), and Undine felt the uselessness of struggling against such mysterious inhibitions. He reminded her, however, that their inability to receive would give them all the more opportunity for going out, and he showed himself more socially disposed than in the past. But his concession did not result as she had hoped. They were asked out as much as ever, but they were asked to big dinners, to impersonal crushes, to the kind of entertainment it is a slight to be omitted from but no compliment to be included in. Nothing could have been more galling to Undine, and she frankly bewailed the fact to Madame de Trézac.

"Of course it's what was sure to come of being mewed up for months and months in the country. We're out of everything, and the people who are having a good time are simply too busy to remember us. We're only asked to the things that are made up from visiting lists."

Madame de Trézac listened sympathetically, but did not suppress a candid answer.

"It's not altogether that, my dear; Raymond's not a man his friends

603

forget. It's rather more, if you'll excuse my saying so, the fact of your being —you personally—in the wrong set."

"The wrong set? Why, I'm in *his* set—the one that thinks itself too good for all the others. That's what you've always told me when I've said it bored me."

"Well, that's what I mean —" Madame de Trézac took the plunge. "It's not a question of *your* being bored."

Undine colored; but she could take the hardest thrusts where her personal interest was involved. "You mean that *I'm* the bore, then?"

"Well, you don't work hard enough—you don't keep up. It's not that they don't admire you—your looks, I mean; they think you beautiful; they're delighted to bring you out at their big dinners, with the Sèvres and the plate. But a woman has got to be something more than good-looking to have a chance to be intimate with them: she's got to know what's being said about things. I watched you the other night at the duchess's, and half the time you hadn't an idea what they were talking about. I haven't always, either; but then I have to put up with the big dinners."

Undine winced under the criticism; but she had never lacked insight into the cause of her own failures, and she had already had premonitions of what Madame de Trézac so bluntly phrased. When Raymond ceased to be interested in her conversation she had concluded it was the way of husbands; but since then it had been slowly dawning on her that she produced the same effect on others. Her entrances were always triumphs; but they had no sequel. As soon as people began to talk they ceased to see her. Any sense of insufficiency exasperated her, and she had vague thoughts of cultivating herself, and went so far as to spend a morning in the Louvre and go to one or two lectures by a fashionable philosopher. But though she returned from these expeditions charged with opinions, their expression did not excite the interest she had hoped. Her views, if abundant, were confused, and the more she said the more nebulous they seemed to grow. She was disconcerted, moreover, by finding that everybody appeared to know about the things she thought she had discovered, and her comments clearly produced more bewilderment than interest.

Remembering the attention she had attracted on her first appearance in Raymond's world she concluded that she had "gone off" or grown dowdy, and instead of wasting more time in museums and lecture-halls she prolonged her hours at the dressmaker's and gave up the rest of the day to the scientific cultivation of her beauty.

"I suppose I've turned into a perfect frump down there in that wilderness," she lamented to Madame de Trézac, who replied inexorably: "Oh, no, you're as handsome as ever; but people here don't go on looking at each other forever as they do in London."

Meanwhile financial cares became more pressing. A dunning letter from one of her tradesmen fell into Raymond's hands, and the talk it led to ended in his making it clear to her that she must settle her personal debts without his aid. All the "scenes" about money which had disturbed her past had ended in some mysterious solution of her difficulty. Disagreeable as they were, she had always, vulgarly speaking, found they paid; but now it was she who was expected to pay. Raymond took his stand without ill-temper or apology: he simply argued from inveterate precedent. But it was impossible for Undine to understand a social organization which did not regard the indulging of woman as its first purpose, or to believe that anyone taking another view was not moved by avarice or malice; and the discussion ended in mutual acrimony.

The morning afterward, Raymond came into her room with a letter in his hand.

"Is this your doing?" he asked. His look and voice expressed something she had never known before: the disciplined anger of a man trained to keep his emotions in fixed channels, but knowing how to fill them to the brim.

The letter was from Mr. Fleischhauer, who begged to transmit to the Marquis de Chelles an offer for his Boucher tapestries from a client prepared to pay the large sum named on condition that it was accepted before his approaching departure for America.

"What does it mean?" Raymond continued, as she did not speak.

"How should I know? It's a lot of money," she stammered, shaken out of her self-possession. She had not expected so prompt a sequel to the dealer's visit, and she was vexed with him for writing to Raymond without consulting her. But she recognized Moffatt's high-handed way, and her fears faded in the great blaze of the sum he offered.

Her husband was still looking at her. "It was Fleischhauer who brought a man down to see the tapestries one day when I was away at Beaune?"

He had known, then—everything was known at Saint Désert!

She wavered a moment and then gave him back his look.

"Yes—it was Fleischhauer; and I sent for him."

"You sent for him?"

He spoke in a voice so veiled and repressed that he seemed to be consciously saving it for some premeditated outbreak. Undine felt its menace, but the thought of Moffatt sent a flame through her, and the words he would have spoken seemed to fly to her lips.

"Why shouldn't I? Something had to be done. We can't go on as we are. I've tried my best to economize—I've scraped and scrimped, and gone without heaps of things I've always had. I've moped for months and months at Saint Désert, and given up sending Paul to school because it was too expensive, and asking my friends to dine because we couldn't afford it. And you expect me to go on living like this for the rest of my life, when all you've got to do is to hold out your hand and have two million francs drop into it!"

Her husband stood looking at her coldly and curiously, as though she were some alien apparition his eyes had never before beheld.

"Ah, that's your answer—that's all you feel when you lay hands on things that are sacred to us!" He stopped a moment, and then let his voice break out with the volume she had felt it to be gathering. "And you're all alike," he exclaimed, "every one of you. You come among us from a country we don't know, and can't imagine, a country you care for so little that before you've been a day in ours you've forgotten the very house you were born in—if it wasn't torn down before you knew it! You come among us speaking our language and not knowing what we mean; wanting the things we want, and not knowing why we want them; aping our weaknesses, exaggerating our follies, ignoring or ridiculing all we care about—you come from hotels as big as towns, and from towns as flimsy as paper, where the streets haven't had time to be named, and the buildings are demolished before they're dry, and the people are as proud of changing as we are of holding to what we have—and we're fools enough to imagine that because you copy our ways and pick up our slang you understand anything about the things that make life decent and honorable for us!"

He stopped again, his white face and drawn nostrils giving him so much the look of an extremely distinguished actor in a fine part that, in spite of the vehemence of his emotion, his silence might have been the deliberate pause for a *réplique*. Undine kept him waiting long enough to give the effect of having lost her cue—then she brought out, with a little soft stare of incredulity: "Do you mean to say you're going to refuse such an offer?"

"Ah —!" He turned back from the door, and picking up the letter that lay on the table between them, tore it in pieces and tossed the pieces on the floor. "That's how I refuse it!"

The violence of his tone and gesture made her feel as though the fluttering strips were so many lashes laid across her face, and a rage that was half fear possessed her.

"How dare you speak to me like that? Nobody's ever dared to before. Is talking to a woman in that way one of the things you call decent and honorable? Now that I know what you feel about me I don't want to stay in your house another day. And I don't mean to—I mean to walk out of it this very hour!"

For a moment they stood face to face, the depths of their mutual incomprehension at last bared to each other's angry eyes; then Raymond, his glance traveling past her, pointed to the fragments of paper on the floor.

"If you're capable of that you're capable of anything!" he said as he went out of the room.

43

S HE watched him go in a kind of stupor, knowing that when they next met he would be as courteous and self-possessed as if nothing had happened, but that everything would nevertheless go on in the same way—in *his* way—and that there was no more hope of shaking his resolve or altering his point of view than there would have been of transporting the deep-rooted masonry of Saint Désert by means of the wheeled supports on which Apex architecture performed its easy transits.

One of her childish rages possessed her, sweeping away every feeling save the primitive impulse to hurt and destroy; but search as she would she could not find a crack in the strong armor of her husband's habits and prejudices. For a long time she continued to sit where he had left her, staring at the portraits on the walls as though they had joined hands to imprison her. Hitherto she had almost always felt herself a match for circumstances, but now the very dead were leagued to defeat her: people she had never seen and whose names she couldn't even remember seemed to be plotting and contriving against her under the escutcheoned gravestones of Saint Désert.

Her eyes turned to the old warm-toned furniture beneath the pictures, and to her own idle image in the mirror above the mantelpiece. Even in that one small room there were enough things of price to buy a release from her most pressing cares; and the great house, in which the room was a mere cell, and the other greater house in Burgundy, held treasures to deplete even such a purse as Moffatt's. She liked to see such things about her—without any real sense of their meaning she felt them to be the appropriate setting of a pretty woman, to embody something of the rareness and distinction she had always considered she possessed; and she reflected that if she had still been Moffatt's wife he would have given her just such a setting, and the power to live in it as became her.

The thought sent her memory flying back to things she had turned it from for years. For the first time since their far-off weeks together she let herself relive the brief adventure. She had been drawn to Elmer Moffatt from the first—from the day when Ben Frusk, Indiana's brother, had brought him to a church picnic at Mulvey's Grove, and he had taken instant possession of Undine, sitting in the big "stage" beside her on the "ride" to the grove, supplanting Millard Binch (to whom she was still, though intermittently and incompletely, engaged), swinging her between the trees, rowing her on the lake, catching and kissing her in "forfeits," awarding her the first prize in the beauty show he hilariously organized and gallantly carried out, and finally (no one knew how) contriving to borrow a buggy and a fast colt from old Mulvey, and driving off with her at a two-forty gait while Millard and the others took their dust in the crawling stage.

No one in Apex knew where young Moffatt had come from, and he offered no information on the subject. He simply appeared one day behind the counter in Luckaback's Dollar Shoe Store, drifted thence to the office of Semple and Binch, the coal merchants, reappeared as the stenographer of the police court, and finally edged his way into the powerhouse of the Apex Waterworks. He boarded with old Mrs. Flynn, down in North Fifth Street, on the edge of the red-light slum, he never went to church or attended lectures, or showed any desire to improve or refine himself; but he managed to get himself invited to all the picnics and lodge sociables, and at a supper of the Phi Upsilon Society, to which he had contrived to affiliate himself, he made the best speech that had been heard there since young Jim Rolliver's first flights. The brothers of Undine's friends all pronounced him "great," though he had fits of uncouthness that made the young women slower in admitting him to favor. But at the Mulvey's Grove picnic he suddenly seemed to dominate them all, and Undine, as she drove away with him, tasted the public triumph which was necessary to her personal enjoyment.

After that he became a leading figure in the youthful world of Apex, and no one was surprised when the Sons of Jonadab (the local temperance Society) invited him to deliver their Fourth of July oration. The ceremony took place, as usual, in the Baptist church, and Undine, all in white, with a red rose in her breast, sat just beneath the platform, with Indiana jealously glaring at her from a less privileged seat, and poor Millard's long neck craning over the row of prominent citizens behind the orator.

Elmer Moffatt had been magnificent, rolling out his alternating effects of humor and pathos, stirring his audience by moving references to the Blue and the Gray, convulsing them by a new version of Washington and the Cherry Tree (in which the infant patriot was depicted as having cut down the tree to check the deleterious spread of cherry bounce), dazzling them by his erudite allusions and apt quotations (he confessed to Undine that he had sat up half the night over Bartlett), and winding up with a peroration that drew tears from the Grand Army pensioners in the front row and caused the minister's wife to say that many a sermon from that platform had been less uplifting.

An ice-cream supper always followed the "exercises," and as repairs were being made in the church basement, which was the usual scene of the festivity, the minister had offered the use of his house. The long table ran through the doorway between parlor and study, and another was set in the passage outside, with one end under the stairs. The stair-rail was wreathed in fire-weed and early goldenrod, and temperance texts in smilax decked the walls. When the first course had been dispatched the young ladies, gallantly seconded by the younger of the "Sons," helped to ladle out and carry in the ice cream, which stood in great pails on the larder floor, and to replenish the jugs of lemonade and coffee. Elmer Moffatt was indefatigable in performing these services, and when the minister's wife pressed him to sit down and take a mouthful himself he modestly declined the place reserved for him among the dignitaries of the evening, and withdrew with a few chosen spirits to the dim table-end beneath the stairs. Explosions of hilarity came from this corner with increasing frequency, and now and then tumultuous rappings and howls of "Song! Song!" followed by adjurations to "Cough it up" and "Let her go," drowned the conversational efforts at the other table.

At length the noise subsided, and the group was ceasing to attract attention when, toward the end of the evening, the upper table, drooping under the lengthy elucubrations of the minister and the president of the Temperance Society, called on the orator of the day for a few remarks. There was an interval of scuffling and laughter beneath the stairs, and then the minister's lifted hand enjoined silence and Elmer Moffatt got to his feet.

"Step out where the ladies can hear you better, Mr. Moffatt!" the minister called. Moffatt did so, steadying himself against the table and twisting his head about as if his collar had grown too tight. But if his bearing was vacillating his smile was unabashed, and there was no lack of confidence in the glance he threw at Undine Spragg as he began: "Ladies and gentlemen, if there's one thing I like better than another about getting drunk—and I like most everything about it except the next morning—it's the opportunity you've given me of doing it right here, in the presence of this Society, which, as I gather from its literature, knows more about the subject than anybody else. Ladies and gentlemen"—he straightened himself, and the tablecloth slid toward him—"ever since you honored me with an invitation to address you from the temperance platform I've been assiduously studying that literature; and I've gathered from your own evidence—what I'd strongly suspected before—that all your converted drunkards had a hell of a good time before you got at 'em, and that . . . and that a good many of 'em have gone on having it since. . . ."

At this point he broke off, swept the audience with his confident smile, and then, collapsing, tried to sit down on a chair that didn't happen to be there, and disappeared among his agitated supporters.

There was a nightmare moment during which Undine, through the doorway, saw Ben Frusk and the others close about the fallen orator to the crash of crockery and tumbling chairs; then someone jumped up and shut the parlor door, and a long-necked Sunday-school teacher, who had been nervously waiting his chance, and had almost given it up, rose from his feet and recited "High Tide at Gettysburg" amid hysterical applause.

The scandal was considerable, but Moffatt, though he vanished from the social horizon, managed to keep his place in the powerhouse till he went off for a week and turned up again without being able to give a satisfactory reason for his absence. After that he drifted from one job to another, now extolled for his "smartness" and business capacity, now dismissed in disgrace as an irresponsible loafer. His head was always full of immense nebulous schemes for the enlargement and development of any business he happened to be employed in. Sometimes his suggestions interested his employers, but proved unpractical and inapplicable; sometimes he wore out their patience or was thought to be a dangerous dreamer. Whenever he found there was no hope of his ideas being adopted he lost interest in his work, came late and left early, or disappeared for two or three days at a time without troubling himself to account for his absences. At last even those who had been cynical enough to smile over his disgrace at the temperance supper began to speak of him as a hopeless failure, and he lost the support of the feminine community when one Sunday morning, just as the Baptist and Methodist churches were releasing their congregations, he walked up Eubaw Avenue with a young woman less known to those sacred edifices than to the saloons of North Fifth Street.

Undine's estimate of people had always been based on their apparent power of getting what they wanted—provided it came under the category of things she understood wanting. Success was beauty and romance to her; yet it was at the moment when Elmer Moffatt's failure was most complete and flagrant that she suddenly felt the extent of his power. After the Eubaw Avenue scandal he had been asked not to return to the surveyor's office to which Ben Frusk had managed to get him admitted; and on the day of his dismissal he met Undine in Main Street, at the shopping hour, and, sauntering up cheerfully, invited her to take a walk with him. She was about to refuse when she saw Millard Binch's mother looking at her disapprovingly from the opposite street-corner.

"Oh, well, I will —" she said; and they walked the length of Main Street and out to the immature park in which it ended. She was in a mood of aimless discontent and unrest, tired of her engagement to Millard Binch, disappointed with Moffatt, half-ashamed of being seen with him, and yet not sorry to have it known that she was independent enough to choose her companions without regard to the Apex verdict.

"Well, I suppose you know I'm down and out," he began; and she responded virtuously: "You must have wanted to be, or you wouldn't have behaved the way you did last Sunday."

"Oh, shucks!" he sneered. "What do I care, in a one-horse place like this? If it hadn't been for you I'd have got a move on long ago."

She did not remember afterward what else he said: she recalled only the expression of a great sweeping scorn of Apex, into which her own disdain of it was absorbed like a drop in the sea, and the affirmation of a soaring self-confidence that seemed to lift her on wings. All her own attempts to get what she wanted had come to nothing; but she had always attributed her lack of success to the fact that she had had no one to second her. It was strange that Elmer Moffatt, a shiftless outcast from even the small world she despised, should give her, in the very moment of his downfall, the sense of being able to succeed where she had failed. It was a feeling she never had in his absence, but that his nearness always instantly revived; and he seemed nearer to her now than he had ever been. They wandered on to the edge of the vague park, and sat down on a bench behind the empty bandstand.

"I went with that girl on purpose, and you know it," he broke out abruptly. "It makes me too damned sick to see Millard Binch going around looking as if he'd patented you."

"You've got no right —" she interrupted; and suddenly she was in his arms, and feeling that no one had ever kissed her before. . . .

The week that followed was a big bright blur—the wildest vividest moment of her life. And it was only eight days later that they were in the train together, Apex and all her plans and promises behind them, and a bigger and brighter blur ahead, into which they were plunging as the "Limited" plunged into the sunset. . . .

Undine stood up, looking about her with vague eyes, as if she had come back from a long distance. Elmer Moffatt was still in Paris—he was in reach, within telephone call. She stood hesitating a moment; then she went into her dressing-room, and turning over the pages of the telephone book, looked out the number of the Nouveau Luxe. . . .

44

U NDINE had been right in supposing that her husband would expect their life to go on as before. There was no appreciable change in the situation save that he was more often absent—finding abundant reasons, agricultural and political, for frequent trips to Saint Désert—and that, when in Paris, he no longer showed any curiosity concerning her occupations and engagements. They lived as much apart as if their cramped domicile had been a palace; and when Undine—as she now frequently did—joined the Shallums or Rollivers for a dinner at the Nouveau Luxe, or a party at a *petit théâtre*, she was not put to the trouble of prevaricating.

Her first impulse, after her scene with Raymond, had been to ring up Indiana Rolliver and invite herself to dine. It chanced that Indiana (who was now in full social progress, and had "run over" for a few weeks to get her dresses for Newport) had organized for the same evening a showy cosmopolitan banquet in which she was enchanted to include the Marquise de Chelles; and Undine, as she had hoped, found Elmer Moffatt of the party. When she drove up to the Nouveau Luxe she had not fixed on any plan of action; but once she had crossed its magic threshold her energies revived like plants in water. At last she was in her native air again, among associations she shared and conventions she understood; and all her self-confidence returned as the familiar accents uttered the accustomed things.

Save for an occasional perfunctory call, she had hitherto made no effort to see her compatriots, and she noticed that Mrs. Jim Driscoll and Bertha Shallum received her with a touch of constraint; but it vanished when they remarked the cordiality of Moffatt's greeting. Her seat was at his side, and her old sense of triumph returned as she perceived the importance his notice conferred, not only in the eyes of her own party but of the other diners. Moffatt was evidently a notable figure in all the worlds represented about the crowded tables, and Undine saw that many people who seemed personally unacquainted with him were recognizing and pointing him out. She was conscious of receiving a large share of the attention he attracted, and, bathed again in the bright air of publicity, she remembered the evening when Raymond de Chelles's first admiring glance had given her the same sense of triumph.

This inopportune memory did not trouble her: she was almost grateful to Raymond for giving her the touch of superiority her compatriots clearly felt in her. It was not merely her title and her "situation," but the experiences she had gained through them, that gave her this advantage over the loud vague company. She had learned things they did not guess: shades of conduct, turns of speech, tricks of attitude—and easy and free and enviable as she thought them, she would not for the world have been back among them at the cost of knowing no more than they.

Moffatt made no allusion to his visit to Saint Désert; but when the party had regrouped itself about coffee and liqueurs on the terrace, he bent over to ask confidentially: "What about my tapestries?"

She replied in the same tone: "You oughtn't to have let Fleischhauer write that letter. My husband's furious."

He seemed honestly surprised. "Why? Didn't I offer him enough?"

"He's furious that anyone should offer anything. I thought when he found out what they were worth he might be tempted; but he'd rather see me starve than part with one of his grandfather's snuff-boxes."

"Well, he knows now what the tapestries are worth. I offered more than Fleischhauer advised."

"Yes, but you were in too much of a hurry."

"I've got to be; I'm going back next week."

She felt her eyes cloud with disappointment. "Oh, why do you? I hoped you might stay on."

They looked at each other uncertainly a moment; then he dropped his voice to say: "Even if I did, I probably shouldn't see anything of you."

"Why not? Why won't you come and see me? I've always wanted to be friends."

He came the next day and found in her drawing-room two ladies whom she introduced as her sisters-in-law. The ladies lingered on for a long time, sipping their tea stiffly and exchanging low-voiced remarks while Undine talked with Moffatt; and when they left, with small sidelong bows in his direction, Undine exclaimed: "Now you see how they all watch me!"

She began to go into the details of her married life, drawing on the experiences of the first months for instances that scarcely applied to her present liberated state. She could thus, without great exaggeration, picture herself as entrapped into a bondage hardly conceivable to Moffatt, and she saw him redden with excitement as he listened. "I call it darned low—darned low —" he broke in at intervals.

"Of course I go round more now," she concluded. "I mean to see my friends—I don't care what he says."

"What *can* he say?"

"Oh, he despises Americans—they all do."

"Well, I guess we can still sit up and take nourishment."

They laughed and slipped back to talking of earlier things. She urged him to put off his sailing—there were so manythings they might do together: sightseeing and excursions—and she could perhaps show him some of the private collections he hadn't seen, the ones it was hard to get admitted to. This instantly roused his attention, and after naming one or two collections he had already seen she hit on one he had found inaccessible and was particularly anxious to visit. "There's an Ingres there that's one of the things I came over to have a look at; but I was told there was no use trying."

"Oh, I can easily manage it: the duke's Raymond's uncle." It gave her a peculiar satisfaction to say it: she felt as though she were taking a surreptitious revenge on her husband. "But he's down in the country this week," she continued, "and no one—not even the family—is allowed to see the pictures when he's away. Of course his Ingres are the finest in France."

She ran it off glibly, though a year ago she had never heard of the painter, and did not, even now, remember whether he was an old master or one of the very new ones whose names one hadn't had time to learn.

Moffatt put off sailing, saw the duke's Ingres under her guidance, and accompanied her to various other private galleries inaccessible to strangers. She had lived in almost total ignorance of such opportunities, but now that she could use them to advantage she showed a surprising quickness in picking up "tips," ferreting out rare things and getting a sight of hidden treasures. She even acquired as much of the jargon as a pretty woman needs to produce the impression of being well-informed; and Moffatt's sailing was more than once postponed.

They saw each other almost daily, for she continued to come and go as she pleased, and Raymond showed neither surprise nor disapproval. When they were asked to family dinners she usually excused herself at the last moment on the plea of a headache and, calling up Indiana or Bertha Shallum, improvised a little party at the Nouveau Luxe; and on other occasions she accepted such invitations as she chose, without mentioning to her husband where she was going.

In this world of lavish pleasures she lost what little prudence the discipline of Saint Désert had inculcated. She could never be with people who had all the things she envied without being hypnotized into the belief that she had only to put her hand out to obtain them, and all the unassuaged rancors and hungers of her early days in West End Avenue came back with increased acuity. She knew her wants so much better now, and was so much more worthy of the things she wanted!

She had given up hoping that her father might make another hit in Wall Street. Mrs. Spragg's letters gave the impression that the days of big strokes were over for her husband, that he had gone down in the conflict with forces beyond his measure. If he had remained in Apex the tide of its new prosperity might have carried him to wealth; but New York's huge waves of success had submerged instead of floating him, and Rolliver's enmity was a hand perpetually stretched out to strike him lower. At most, Mr. Spragg's tenacity would keep him at the level he now held, and though he and his wife had still further simplified their way of living Undine understood that their self-denial would not increase her opportunities. She felt no compunction in continuing to accept an undiminished allowance: it was the hereditary habit of the parent animal to despoil himself for his progeny. But this conviction did not seem incompatible with a sentimental pity for her parents. Aside from all interested motives, she wished for their own sakes that they were better off. Their personal requirements were pathetically limited, but renewed prosperity would at least have procured them the happiness of giving her what she wanted.

Moffatt lingered on; but he began to speak more definitely of sailing, and Undine foresaw the day when, strong as her attraction was, stronger influences would snap it like a thread. She knew she interested and amused him, and that it flattered his vanity to be seen with her, and to hear that rumor coupled their names; but he gave her, more than anyone she had ever known, the sense of being detached from his life, in control of it, and able, without weakness or uncertainty, to choose which of its calls he should obey. If the call were that of business—of any of the great perilous affairs he handled like a snakecharmer spinning the deadly reptiles about his head— she knew she would drop from his life like a loosened leaf.

These anxieties sharpened the intensity of her enjoyment, and made the contrast keener between her crowded sparkling hours and the vacant months at Saint Désert. Little as she understood of the qualities that made Moffatt what he was, the results were of the kind most palpable to her. He used life exactly as she would have used it in his place. Some of his enjoyments were beyond her range, but even these appealed to her because of the money that was required to gratify them. When she took him to see some inaccessible picture, or went with him to inspect the treasures of a famous dealer, she saw that the things he looked at moved him in a way she could not understand, and that the actual touching of rare textures—bronze or marble, or velvets flushed with the bloom of age—gave him sensations like those her own beauty had once roused in him. But the next moment he was laughing over some commonplace joke, or absorbed in a long cipher cable handed to him as they reentered the Nouveau Luxe for tea, and his aesthetic emotions had been thrust back into their own compartment of the great steel strongbox of his mind.

Her new life went on without comment or interference from her husband, and she saw that he had accepted their altered relation, and intended merely to keep up an external semblance of harmony. To that semblance she knew he attached intense importance: it was an article of his complicated social creed that a man of his class should appear to live on good terms with his wife. For different reasons it was scarcely less important to Undine: she had no wish to affront again the social reprobation that had so nearly wrecked her. But she could not keep up the life she was leading without more money, a great deal more money; and the thought of contracting her expenditure was no longer tolerable.

One afternoon, several weeks later, she came in to find a tradesman's representative waiting with a bill. There was a noisy scene in the anteroom before the man threateningly withdrew—a scene witnessed by the servants, and overheard by her mother-in-law, whom she found seated in the drawing-room when she entered.

The old marquise's visits to her daughter-in-law were made at long intervals but with ritual regularity; she called every other Friday at five, and Undine had forgotten that she was due that day. This did not make for greater cordiality between them, and the altercation in the anteroom had been too loud for concealment. The marquise was on her feet when her daughter-in-law came in, and instantly said with lowered eyes: "It would perhaps be best for me to go."

"Oh, I don't care. You're welcome to tell Raymond you've heard me insulted because I'm too poor to pay my bills—he knows it well enough already!" The words broke from Undine unguardedly, but once spoken they nourished her defiance.

"I'm sure my son has frequently recommended greater prudence —" the marquise murmured.

"Yes! It's a pity he didn't recommend it to your other son instead! All the money I was entitled to has gone to pay Hubert's debts."

"Raymond has told me that there are certain things you fail to understand—I have no wish whatever to discuss them." The marquise had gone toward the door; with her hand on it she paused to add: "I shall say nothing whatever of what has happened."

Her icy magnanimity added the last touch to Undine's wrath. They knew her extremity, one and all, and it did not move them. At most, they would join in concealing it like a blot on their honor. And the menace grew and mounted, and not a hand was stretched to help her. . . .

Hardly a half-hour earlier Moffatt, with whom she had been visiting a "private view," had sent her home in his motor with the excuse that he must hurry back to the Nouveau Luxe to meet his stenographer and sign a batch of letters for the New York mail. It was therefore probable that he was still at home—that she should find him if she hastened there at once. An overwhelming desire to cry out her wrath and wretchedness brought her to her feet and sent her down to hail a passing cab. As it whirled her through the bright streets powdered with amber sunlight her brain throbbed with confused intentions. She did not think of Moffatt as a power she could use, but simply as someone who knew her and understood her grievance. It was essential to her at that moment to be told that she was right and that everyone opposed to her was wrong.

At the hotel she asked his number and was carried up in the lift. On the landing she paused a moment, disconcerted—it had occurred to her that he might not be alone. But she walked on quickly, found the number and knocked. . . . Moffatt opened the door, and she glanced beyond him and saw that the big bright sitting-room was empty.

"Hullo!" he exclaimed, surprised; and as he stood aside to let her enter she saw him draw out his watch and glance at it surreptitiously. He was expecting someone, or he had an engagement elsewhere—something claimed him from which she was excluded. The thought flushed her with sudden resolution. She knew now what she had come for—to keep him from everyone else, to keep him for herself alone.

"Don't send me away!" she said, and laid her hand on his beseechingly.

45

S HE advanced into the room and slowly looked about her. The big vulgar writing-table wreathed in bronze was heaped with letters and papers. Among them stood a lapis bowl in a Renaissance mounting of enamel and a vase of Phoenician glass that was like a bit of rainbow caught in cobwebs. On a table against the window a little Greek marble lifted its pure lines. On every side some rare and sensitive object seemed to be shrinking back from the false colors and crude contours of the hotel furniture. There were no books in the room, but the florid console under the mirror was stacked with old numbers of *Town Talk* and the New York *Radiator*. Undine recalled the dingy hall-room that Moffatt had lodged in at Mrs. Flynn's, over Hober's livery stable, and her heart beat at the signs of his altered state. When her eyes came back to him their lids were moist.

"Don't send me away," she repeated. He looked at her and smiled. "What is it? What's the matter?"

"I don't know—but I had to come. Today, when you spoke again of sailing, I felt as if I couldn't stand it." She lifted her eyes and looked in his profoundly.

He reddened a little under her gaze, but she could detect no softening or confusion in the shrewd steady glance he gave her back.

"Things going wrong again—is that the trouble?" he merely asked with a comforting inflexion.

"They always *are* wrong; it's all been an awful mistake. But I shouldn't care if you were here and I could see you sometimes. You're so *strong*: that's what I feel about you, Elmer. I was the only one to feel it that time they all turned against you out at Apex. . . . Do you remember the afternoon I met you down on Main Street, and we walked out together to the park? I knew then that you were stronger than any of them. . . ."

She had never spoken more sincerely. For the moment all thought of self-interest was in abeyance, and she felt again, as she had felt that day, the instinctive yearning of her nature to be one with his. Something in her voice must have attested it, for she saw a change in his face.

"You're not the beauty you were," he said irrelevantly; "but you're a lot more fetching."

The oddly qualified praise made her laugh with mingled pleasure and annoyance.

"I suppose I must be dreadfully changed —"

"You're all right!—But I've got to go back home," he broke off abruptly. "I've put it off too long."

She paled and looked away, helpless in her sudden disappointment. "I knew you'd say that. . . . And I shall just be left here. . . ." She sat down on the sofa near which they had been standing, and two tears formed on her lashes and fell.

Moffatt sat down beside her, and both were silent. She had never seen him at a loss before. She made no attempt to draw nearer, or to use any of the arts of cajolery; but presently she said, without rising: "I saw you look at your watch when I came in. I suppose somebody else is waiting for you."

"It don't matter."

"Some other woman?"

"It don't matter."

"I've wondered so often—but of course I've got no right to ask." She stood up slowly, understanding that he meant to let her go.

"Just tell me one thing—did you never miss me?"

"Oh, damnably!" he brought out with sudden bitterness.

She came nearer, sinking her voice to a low whisper. "It's the only time I ever really cared—all through!"

He had risen, too, and they stood intensely gazing at each other. Moffatt's face was fixed and grave, as she had seen it in hours she now found herself rapidly reliving.

"I believe you *did*," he said.

"Oh, Elmer—if I'd known—if I'd only known!"

He made no answer, and she turned away, touching with an unconscious hand the edge of the lapis bowl among his papers.

"Elmer, if you're going away it can't do any harm to tell me—is there anyone else?"

He gave a laugh that seemed to shake him free. "In that kind of way? Lord, no! Too busy!"

She came close again and laid a hand on his shoulder. "Then why not— why shouldn't we —?" She leaned her head back so that her gaze slanted up through her wet lashes. "I can do as I please—my husband does. They think so differently about marriage over here: it's just a business contract. As long as a woman doesn't make a show of herself no one cares." She put her other hand up, so that she held him facing her. "I've always felt, all through everything, that I belonged to you."

Moffatt left her hands on his shoulders, but did not lift his own to clasp them. For a moment she thought she had mistaken him, and a leaden sense of shame descended on her. Then he asked: "You say your husband goes with other women?"

Lili Estradina's taunt flashed through her and she seized on it. "People have told me so—his own relations have. I've never stooped to spy on him. . . ."

"And the women in your set—I suppose it's taken for granted they all do the same?"

She laughed.

"Everything fixed up for them, same as it is for the husbands, eh? Nobody meddles or makes trouble if you know the ropes?"

"No, nobody . . . it's all quite easy. . . ." She stopped, her faint smile checked, as his backward movement made her hands drop from his shoulders.

"And that's what you're proposing to me? That you and I should do like the rest of 'em?" His face had lost its comic roundness and grown harsh and dark, as it had when her father had taken her away from him at Opake. He turned on his heel, walked the length of the room and halted with his back to her in the embrasure of the window. There he paused a full minute, his hands in his pockets, staring out at the perpetual interweaving of motors in the luminous setting of the square. Then he turned and spoke from where he stood.

"Look here, Undine, if I'm to have you again I don't want to have you that way. That time out in Apex, when everybody in the place was against me, and I was down and out, you stood up to them and stuck by me. Remember that walk down Main Street? Don't I!—and the way the people glared and hurried by; and how you kept on alongside of me, talking and laughing, and looking your Sunday best. When Abner Spragg came out to Opake after us and pulled you back I was pretty sore at your deserting; but I came to see it was natural enough. You were only a spoiled girl, used to having everything you wanted; and I couldn't give you a thing then, and the folks you'd been taught to believe in all told you I never would. Well, I did look like a back number, and no blame to you for thinking so. I used to say it to myself over and over again, laying awake nights and totting up my mistakes . . . and then there were days when the wind set another way, and I knew I'd pull it off yet, and I thought you might have held on. . . ." He stopped, his head a little lowered, his concentrated gaze on her flushed face. "Well, anyhow," he broke out, "you were my wife once, and you were my wife first—and if you want to come back you've got to come that way: not slink through the back way when there's no one watching, but walk in by the front door, with your head up, and your Main Street look."

Since the days when he had poured out to her his great fortune-building projects she had never heard him make so long a speech; and her heart, as she listened, beat with a new joy and terror. It seemed to her that the great moment of her life had come at last—the moment all her minor failures and successes had been building up with blind indefatigable hands.

"Elmer—Elmer —" she sobbed out.

She expected to find herself in his arms, shut in and shielded from all her troubles; but he stood his ground across the room, immovable.

"Is it yes?"

She faltered the word after him: "Yes —?"

"Are you going to marry me?"

She stared, bewildered. "Why, Elmer—marry you? You forget!"

"Forget what? That you don't want to give up what you've got?"

"How can I? Such things are not done out here. Why, I'm a Catholic; and the Catholic Church —" She broke off, reading the end in his face. "But later, perhaps . . . things might change. Oh, Elmer, if only you'd stay over here and let me see you sometimes!"

"Yes—the way your friends see each other. We're differently made out in Apex. When I want that sort of thing I go down to North Fifth Street for it."

She paled under the retort, but her heart beat high with it. What he asked was impossible—and she gloried in his asking it. Feeling her power, she tried to temporize. "At least if you stayed we could be friends—I shouldn't feel so terribly alone."

He laughed impatiently. "Don't talk magazine stuff to me, Undine Spragg. I guess we want each other the same way. Only our ideas are different. You've got all muddled, living out here among a lot of loafers who call it a career to run round after every petticoat. I've got my job out at home, and I belong where my job is."

"Are you going to be tied to business all your life?" Her smile was faintly depreciatory.

"I guess business is tied to me: Wall Street acts as if it couldn't get along without me." He gave his shoulders a shake and moved a few steps nearer. "See here, Undine—you're the one that don't understand. If I was to sell out tomorrow, and spend the rest of my life reading art magazines in a pink villa, I wouldn't do what you're asking me. And I've about as much idea of dropping business as you have of taking to district nursing. There are things a man doesn't do. I understand why your husband won't sell those tapestries —till he's got to. His ancestors are *his* business: Wall Street's mine."

He paused, and they silently faced each other. Undine made no attempt to approach him: she understood that if he yielded it would be only to recover his advantage and deepen her feeling of defeat. She put out her hand and took up the sunshade she had dropped on entering. "I suppose it's goodbye then," she said.

"You haven't got the nerve?"

"The nerve for what?"

"To come where you belong: with me."

She laughed a little and then sighed. She wished he would come nearer, or look at her differently: she felt, under his cool eye, no more compelling than a woman of wax in a showcase.

"How could I get a divorce? With my religion —"

"Why, you were born a Baptist, weren't you? That's where you used to attend church when I waited round the corner, Sunday mornings, with one of old Hober's buggies." They both laughed, and he went on: "If you'll come along home with me I'll see you get your divorce all right. Who cares what they do over here? You're an American, ain't you? What you want is the homemade article."

She listened, discouraged yet fascinated by his sturdy inaccessibility to all her arguments and objections. He knew what he wanted, saw his road before him, and acknowledged no obstacles. Her defense was drawn from reasons he did not understand, or based on difficulties that did not exist for him; and gradually she felt herself yielding to the steady pressure of his will. Yet the reasons he brushed away came back with redoubled tenacity whenever he paused long enough for her to picture the consequences of what he exacted.

"You don't know—you don't understand —" she kept repeating; but she knew that his ignorance was part of his terrible power, and that it was hopeless to try to make him feel the value of what he was asking her to give up.

"See here, Undine," he said slowly, as if he measured her resistance though he couldn't fathom it, "I guess it had better be yes or no right here. It ain't going to do either of us any good to drag this thing out. If you want to come back to me, come—if you don't, we'll shake hands on it now. I'm due in Apex for a directors' meeting on the twentieth, and as it is I'll have to cable for a special to get me out there. No, no, don't cry—it ain't that kind of a story . . . but I'll have a deck suite for you on the *Semantic* if you'll sail with me the day after tomorrow."

46

I N the great high-ceilinged library of a private hotel overlooking one of the new quarters of Paris, Paul Marvell stood listlessly gazing out into the twilight.

The trees were budding symmetrically along the avenue below; and Paul, looking down, saw, between windows and treetops, a pair of tall iron gates with gilt ornaments, the marble curb of a semicircular drive, and bands of spring flowers set in turf. He was now a big boy of nearly nine, who went to a fashionable private school, and he had come home that day for the Easter holidays. He had not been back since Christmas, and it was the first time he had seen the new hotel which his stepfather had bought, and in which Mr. and Mrs. Moffatt had hastily established themselves, a few weeks earlier, on their return from a flying trip to America. They were always coming and going; during the two years since their marriage they had been perpetually dashing over to New York and back, or rushing down to Rome or up to the Engadine: Paul never knew where they were except when a telegram announced that they were going somewhere else. He did not even know that there was any method of communication between mothers and sons less laconic than that of the electric wire; and once, when a boy at school asked him if his mother often wrote, he had answered in all sincerity: "Oh yes—I got a telegram last week."

He had been almost sure—as sure as he ever was of anything—that he should find her at home when he arrived; but a message (for she hadn't had time to telegraph) apprised him that she and Mr. Moffatt had run down to Deauville to look at a house they thought of hiring for the summer; they were taking an early train back, and would be at home for dinner—were in fact having a lot of people to dine.

It was just what he ought to have expected, and had been used to ever since he could remember; and generally he didn't mind much, especially since his mother had become Mrs. Moffatt, and the father he had been most used to, and liked best, had abruptly disappeared from his life. But the new hotel was big and strange, and his own room, in which there was not a toy or a book, or one of his dear battered relics (none of the new servants—they were always new—could find his things, or think where they had been put), seemed the loneliest spot in the whole house. He had gone up there after his solitary luncheon, served in the immense marble dining-room by a foot-man on the same scale, and had tried to occupy himself with pasting post-cards into his album; but the newness and sumptuousness of the room em-barrassed him—the white fur rugs and brocade chairs seemed maliciously on the watch for smears and ink-spots—and after a while he pushed the album aside and began to roam through the house.

He went to all the rooms in turn: his mother's first, the wonderful lacy bedroom, all pale silks and velvets, artful mirrors and veiled lamps, and the boudoir as big as a drawing-room, with pictures he would have liked to know about, and tables and cabinets holding things he was afraid to touch. Mr. Moffatt's rooms came next. They were soberer and darker, but as big and splendid; and in the bedroom, on the brown wall, hung a single picture —the portrait of a boy in gray velvet—that interested Paul most of all. The boy's hand rested on the head of a big dog, and he looked infinitely noble and charming, and yet (in spite of the dog) so sad and lonely that he too might have come home that very day to a strange house in which none of his old things could be found.

From these rooms Paul wandered downstairs again. The library attracted him most: there were rows and rows of books, bound in dim browns and golds, and old faded reds as rich as velvet: they all looked as if they might have had stories in them as splendid as their bindings. But the bookcases were closed with gilt trellising, and when Paul reached up to open one, a

servant told him that Mr. Moffatt's secretary kept them locked because the
books were too valuable to be taken down. This seemed to make the library
as strange as the rest of the house, and he passed on to the ballroom at the
back. Through its closed doors he heard a sound of hammering, and when
he tried the door-handle a servant passing with a trayful of glasses told him
that "they" hadn't finished, and wouldn't let anybody in.

The mysterious pronoun somehow increased Paul's sense of isolation,
and he went on to the drawing-rooms, steering his way prudently between
the gold armchairs and shining tables, and wondering whether the wigged
and corseleted heroes on the walls represented Mr. Moffatt's ancestors, and
why, if they did, he looked so little like them. The dining-room beyond was
more amusing, because busy servants were already laying the long table. It
was too early for the florist, and the center of the table was empty, but down
the sides were gold baskets heaped with pulpy summer fruits—figs, strawber-
ries and big blushing nectarines. Between them stood crystal decanters with
red and yellow wine, and little dishes full of sweets; and against the walls
were sideboards with great pieces of gold and silver, ewers and urns and
branching candelabra, which sprinkled the green marble walls with starlike
reflections.

After a while he grew tired of watching the coming and going of white-
sleeved footmen, and of listening to the butler's vociferated orders, and
strayed back into the library. The habit of solitude had given him a passion
for the printed page, and if he could have found a book anywhere—any
kind of a book—he would have forgotten the long hours and the empty
house. But the tables in the library held only massive unused inkstands and
immense immaculate blotters: not a single volume had slipped its golden
prison.

His loneliness had grown overwhelming, and he suddenly thought of
Mrs. Heeny's clippings. His mother, alarmed by an insidious gain in weight,
had brought the masseuse back from New York with her, and Mrs. Heeny,
with her old black bag and waterproof, was established in one of the grand
bedrooms lined with mirrors. She had been loud in her joy at seeing her
little friend that morning, but four years had passed since their last parting,
and her personality had grown remote to him. He saw too many people, and
they too often disappeared and were replaced by others: his scattered affections had ended by concentrating themselves on the charming image of the
gentleman he called his French father; and since his French father had
vanished no one else seemed to matter much to him.

"Oh, well," Mrs. Heeny had said, discerning the reluctance under his
civil greeting, "I guess you're as strange here as I am, and we're both pretty
strange to each other. You just go and look around, and see what a lovely
home your ma's got to live in; and when you get tired of that, come up here
to me and I'll give you a look at my clippings."

The word woke a train of dormant associations, and Paul saw himself seated on a dingy carpet, between two familiar taciturn old presences, while he rummaged in the depths of a bag stuffed with strips of newspaper.

He found Mrs. Heeny sitting in a pink armchair, her bonnet perched on a pink-shaded electric lamp and her numerous implements spread out on an immense pink toilet-table. Vague as his recollection of her was, she gave him at once a sense of reassurance that nothing else in the house conveyed, and after he had examined all her scissors and pastes and nail-polishers he turned to the bag, which stood on the carpet at her feet as if she were waiting for a train.

"My, my!" she said, "do you want to get into that again? How you used to hunt in it for taffy, to be sure, when your pa brought you up to Grandma Spragg's o' Saturdays! Well, I'm afraid there ain't any taffy in it now; but there's piles and piles of lovely new clippings you ain't seen."

"My papa?" He paused, his hand among the strips of newspaper. "My papa never saw my Grandma Spragg. He never went to America."

"Never went to America? Your pa never—? Why, land alive!" Mrs. Heeny gasped, a blush empurpling her large warm face. "Why, Paul Marvell, don't you remember your own father, you that bear his name?" she exclaimed.

The boy blushed, also, conscious that it must have been wrong to forget, and yet not seeing how he was to blame.

"That one died a long long time ago, didn't he? I was thinking of my French father," he explained.

"Oh, mercy," ejaculated Mrs. Heeny; and as if to cut the conversation short she stooped over, creaking like a ship, and thrust her plump strong hand into the bag.

"Here, now, just you look at these clippings—I guess you'll find a lot in them about your ma. Where do they come from? Why, out of the papers, of course," she added, in response to Paul's inquiry. "You'd oughter start a scrapbook yourself—you're plenty old enough. You could make a beauty just about your ma, with her picture pasted in the front—and another about Mr. Moffatt and his collections. There's one I cut out the other day that says he's the greatest collector in America."

Paul listened, fascinated. He had the feeling that Mrs. Heeny's clippings, aside from their great intrinsic interest, might furnish him the clue to many things he didn't understand, and that nobody had ever had time to explain to him. His mother's marriages, for instance: he was sure there was a great deal to find out about them. But she always said: "I'll tell you all about it when I come back"—and when she came back it was invariably to rush off somewhere else. So he had remained without a key to her transitions, and had had to take for granted numberless things that seemed to have no parallel in the experience of the other boys he knew.

"Here—here it is," said Mrs. Heeny, adjusting the big tortoiseshell spectacles she had taken to wearing, and reading out in a slow chant that seemed to Paul to come out of some lost remoteness of his infancy.

" 'It is reported in London that the price paid by Mr. Elmer Moffatt for the celebrated *Gray Boy* is the largest sum ever given for a Vandyck. Since Mr. Moffatt began to buy extensively it is estimated in art circles that values have gone up at least seventy-five percent.' "

But the price of the *Gray Boy* did not interest Paul, and he said a little impatiently: "I'd rather hear about my mother."

"To be sure you would! You wait now." Mrs. Heeny made another dive, and again began to spread her clippings on her lap like cards on a big black table.

"Here's one about her last portrait—no, here's a better one about her pearl necklace, the one Mr. Moffatt gave her last Christmas. 'The necklace, which was formerly the property of an Austrian Archduchess, is composed of five hundred perfectly matched pearls that took thirty years to collect. It is estimated among dealers in precious stones that since Mr. Moffatt began to buy the price of pearls has gone up over fifty percent.' "

Even this did not fix Paul's attention. He wanted to hear about his mother and Mr. Moffatt, and not about their things; and he didn't quite know how to frame his question. But Mrs. Heeny looked kindly at him and he tried. "Why is mother married to Mr. Moffatt now?"

"Why, you must know that much, Paul." Mrs. Heeny again looked warm and worried. "She's married to him because she got a divorce—that's why." And suddenly she had another inspiration. "Didn't she ever send you over any of those splendid clippings that came out the time they were married? Why, I declare, that's a shame; but I must have some of 'em right here."

She dived again, shuffled, sorted, and pulled out a long discolored strip. "I've carried this round with me ever since, and so many's wanted to read it, it's all torn." She smoothed out the paper and began:

" 'Divorce and remarriage of Mrs. Undine Spragg–de Chelles. American marquise renounces ancient French title to wed railroad king. Quick work untying and tying. Boy and girl romance renewed.

" 'Reno, November 23d. The Marquise de Chelles, of Paris, France, formerly Mrs. Undine Spragg Marvell, of Apex City and New York, got a decree of divorce at a special session of the court last night, and was remarried fifteen minutes later to Mr. Elmer Moffatt, the billionaire railroad king, who was the marquise's first husband.

" 'No case has ever been railroaded through the divorce courts of this state at a higher rate of speed: as Mr. Moffatt said last night, before he and his bride jumped onto their east-bound special, every record has been broken. It was just six months ago yesterday that the present Mrs. Moffatt came to Reno to look for her divorce. Owing to a delayed train, her counsel was late yesterday in receiving some necessary papers, and it was feared the decision would have to be held over; but Judge Toomey, who is a personal friend of Mr. Moffatt's, held a night session and rushed it through so that the happy couple could have the knot tied and board their special in time for Mrs. Moffatt to spend Thanksgiving in New York with her aged parents. The hearing began at 7:10 P.M. and at eight o'clock the bridal couple were steaming out of the station.

"'At the trial Mrs. Spragg–de Chelles, who wore copper velvet and sables, gave evidence as to the brutality of her French husband, but she had to talk fast as time pressed, and Judge Toomey wrote the entry at top speed, and then jumped into a motor with the happy couple and drove to the Justice of the Peace, where he acted as best man to the bridegroom. The latter is said to be one of the six wealthiest men east of the Rockies. His gifts to the bride are a necklace and tiara of pigeon-blood rubies belonging to Queen Marie Antoinette, a million dollar check and a house in New York. The happy pair will pass the honeymoon in Mrs. Moffatt's new home, 5009 Fifth Avenue, which is an exact copy of the Pitti Palace, Florence. They plan to spend their springs in France.'"

Mrs. Heeny drew a long breath, folded the paper and took off her spectacles. "There," she said, with a benignant smile and a tap on Paul's cheek, "now you see how it all happened. . . ."

Paul was not sure he did; but he made no answer. His mind was too full of troubled thoughts. In the dazzling description of his mother's latest nuptials one fact alone stood out for him—that she had said things that weren't true of his French father. Something he had half-guessed in her, and averted his frightened thoughts from, took his little heart in an iron grasp. She said things that weren't true. . . . That was what he had always feared to find out. . . . She had got up and said before a lot of people things that were awfully false about his dear French father. . . .

The sound of a motor turning in at the gates made Mrs. Heeny exclaim "Here they are!" and a moment later Paul heard his mother calling to him. He got up reluctantly, and stood wavering till he felt Mrs. Heeny's astonished eye upon him. Then he heard Mr. Moffatt's jovial shout of "Paul Marvell, ahoy there!" and roused himself to run downstairs.

As he reached the landing he saw that the ballroom doors were open and all the lusters lit. His mother and Mr. Moffatt stood in the middle of the shining floor, looking up at the walls; and Paul's heart gave a wondering bound, for there, set in great gilt panels, were the tapestries that had always hung in the gallery at Saint Désert.

"Well, Senator, it feels good to shake your fist again!" his stepfather said, taking him in a friendly grasp; and his mother, who looked handsomer and taller and more splendidly dressed than ever, exclaimed: "Mercy! How they've cut his hair!" before she bent to kiss him.

"Oh, Mother, Mother!" he burst out, feeling, between his mother's face and the others, hardly less familiar, on the walls, that he was really at home again, and not in a strange house.

"Gracious, how you squeeze!" she protested, loosening his arms. "But you look splendidly—and how you've grown!" She turned away from him and began to inspect the tapestries critically. "Somehow they look smaller here," she said with a tinge of disappointment.

Mr. Moffatt gave a slight laugh and walked slowly down the room, as if to study its effect. As he turned back his wife said: "I didn't think you'd ever get them."

He laughed again, more complacently. "Well, I don't know as I ever should have, if General Arlington hadn't happened to bust up."

They both smiled, and Paul, seeing his mother's softened face, stole his hand in hers and began: "Mother, I took a prize in composition —"

"Did you? You must tell me about it tomorrow. No, I really must rush off now and dress—I haven't even placed the dinner-cards." She freed her hand, and as she turned to go Paul heard Mr. Moffatt say: "Can't you ever give him a minute's time, Undine?"

She made no answer, but sailed through the door with her head high, as she did when anything annoyed her; and Paul and his stepfather stood alone in the illuminated ballroom.

Mr. Moffatt smiled good-naturedly at the little boy and then turned back to the contemplation of the hangings.

"I guess you know where those come from, don't you?" he asked in a tone of satisfaction.

"Oh, yes," Paul answered eagerly, with a hope he dared not utter that, since the tapestries were there, his French father might be coming too.

"You're a smart boy to remember them. I don't suppose you ever thought you'd see them here?"

"I don't know," said Paul, embarrassed.

"Well, I guess you wouldn't have if their owner hadn't been in a pretty tight place. It was like drawing teeth for him to let them go."

Paul flushed up, and again the iron grasp was on his heart. He hadn't, hitherto, actually disliked Mr. Moffatt, who was always in a good humor, and seemed less busy and absent-minded than his mother; but at that instant he felt a rage of hate for him. He turned away and burst into tears.

"Why, hullo, old chap—why, what's up?" Mr. Moffatt was on his knees beside the boy, and the arms embracing him were firm and friendly. But Paul, for the life of him, couldn't answer: he could only sob and sob as the great surges of loneliness broke over him.

"Is it because your mother hadn't time for you? Well, she's like that, you know; and you and I have got to lump it," Mr. Moffatt continued, getting to his feet. He stood looking down at the boy with a queer smile. "If we two chaps stick together it won't be so bad—we can keep each other warm, don't you see? I like you first rate, you know; when you're big enough I mean to put you in my business. And it looks as if one of these days you'd be the richest boy in America. . . ."

*   *   *

The lamps were lit, the vases full of flowers, the footmen assembled on the landing and in the vestibule below, when Undine descended to the drawing-room. As she passed the ballroom door she glanced in approvingly at the tapestries. They really looked better than she had been willing to admit: they made her ballroom the handsomest in Paris. But something had put her out on the way up from Deauville, and the simplest way of easing her nerves had been to affect indifference to the tapestries. Now she had quite recovered her good humor, and as she glanced down the list of guests she was awaiting she said to herself, with a sigh of satisfaction, that she was glad she had put on her rubies.

For the first time since her marriage to Moffatt she was about to receive in her house the people she most wished to see there. The beginnings had been a little difficult; their first attempt in New York was so unpromising that she feared they might not be able to live down the sensational details of their reunion, and had insisted on her husband's taking her back to Paris. But her apprehensions were unfounded. It was only necessary to give people the time to pretend they had forgotten; and already they were all pretending beautifully. The French world had of course held out longest; it had strong-holds she might never capture. But already seceders were beginning to show themselves, and her dinner-list that evening was graced with the names of an authentic duke and a not too-damaged countess. In addition, of course, she had the Shallums, the Chauncey Ellings, May Beringer, Dicky Bowles, Walsingham Popple, and the rest of the New York frequenters of the Nouveau Luxe; she had even, at the last minute, had the amusement of adding Peter Van Degen to their number. In the evening there were to be Spanish dancing and Russian singing; and Dicky Bowles had promised her a grand duke for her next dinner, if she could secure the new tenor who always refused to sing in private houses.

Even now, however, she was not always happy. She had everything she wanted, but she still felt, at times, that there were other things she might want if she knew about them. And there had been moments lately when she had had to confess to herself that Moffatt did not fit into the picture. At first she had been dazzled by his success and subdued by his authority. He had given her all she had ever wished for, and more than she had ever dreamed of having: he had made up to her for all her failures and blunders, and there were hours when she still felt his dominion and exulted in it. But there were others when she saw his defects and was irritated by them: when his loudness and redness, his misplaced joviality, his familiarity with the servants, his alternating swagger and ceremony with her friends, jarred on perceptions that had developed in her unawares. Now and then she caught herself thinking that his two predecessors—who were gradually becoming merged in her memory—would have said this or that differently, behaved otherwise in such and such a case. And the comparison was almost always to Moffatt's disadvantage.

This evening, however, she thought of him indulgently. She was pleased with his clever stroke in capturing the Saint Désert tapestries, which General Arlington's sudden bankruptcy, and a fresh gambling scandal of Hubert's, had compelled their owner to part with. She knew that Raymond de Chelles had told the dealers he would sell his tapestries to anyone but Mr. Elmer Moffatt, or a buyer acting for him; and it amused her to think that, thanks to Elmer's astuteness, they were under her roof after all, and that Raymond and all his clan were by this time aware of it. These facts disposed her favorably toward her husband, and deepened the sense of well-being with which—according to her invariable habit—she walked up to the mirror above the mantelpiece and studied the image it reflected.

She was still lost in this pleasing contemplation when her husband entered, looking stouter and redder than ever, in evening clothes that were a little too tight. His shirt front was as glossy as his baldness, and in his buttonhole he wore the red ribbon bestowed on him for waiving his claim to a Velasquez that was wanted for the Louvre. He carried a newspaper in his hand, and stood looking about the room with a complacent eye.

"Well, I guess this is all right," he said, and she answered briefly: "Don't forget you're to take down Madame de Follerive; and for goodness' sake don't call her 'Countess.' "

"Why, she is one, ain't she?" he returned good-humoredly.

"I wish you'd put that newspaper away," she continued; his habit of leaving old newspapers about the drawing-room annoyed her.

"Oh, that reminds me —" instead of obeying her he unfolded the paper. "I brought it in to show you something. Jim Driscoll's been appointed ambassador to England."

"Jim Driscoll —!" She caught up the paper and stared at the paragraph he pointed to. Jim Driscoll—that pitiful nonentity, with his stout mistrustful commonplace wife! It seemed extraordinary that the government should have hunted up such insignificant people. And immediately she had a great vague vision of the splendors they were going to—all the banquets and ceremonies and precedences. . . .

"I shouldn't say she'd want to, with so few jewels —" She dropped the paper and turned to her husband. "If you had a spark of ambition, that's the kind of thing you'd try for. You could have got it just as easily as not!"

He laughed and thrust his thumbs in his waistcoat armholes with the gesture she disliked. "As it happens, it's about the one thing I couldn't."

"You couldn't? Why not?"

"Because you're divorced. They won't have divorced ambassadresses."

"They won't? Why not, I'd like to know?"

"Well, I guess the court ladies are afraid there'd be too many pretty women in the embassies," he answered jocularly.

She burst into an angry laugh, and the blood flamed up into her face. "I never heard of anything so insulting!" she cried, as if the rule had been invented to humiliate her.

There was a noise of motors backing and advancing in the court, and she heard the first voices on the stairs. She turned to give herself a last look in the glass, saw the blaze of her rubies, the glitter of her hair, and remembered the brilliant names on her list.

But under all the dazzle a tiny black cloud remained. She had learned that there was something she could never get, something that neither beauty nor influence nor millions could ever buy for her. She could never be an ambassador's wife; and as she advanced to welcome her first guests she said to herself that it was the one part she was really made for.